THE COMIC MARK TWAIN READER

The Most Humorous Selections from His Stories, Sketches, Novels, Travel Books and Speeches

OTHER BOOKS BY CHARLES NEIDER

Fiction

Naked Eye
The Authentic Death of Hendry Jones
The White Citadel

Nonfiction

Edge of the World: Ross Island, Antarctica
Susy: A Childhood
Mark Twain
The Frozen Sea: A Study of Franz Kafka

SOME BOOKS EDITED BY CHARLES NEIDER

The Autobiography of Mark Twain
Mark Twain: Life As I Find It
The Adventures of Colonel Sellers, by Mark Twain
The Complete Short Stories of Mark Twain
The Complete Humorous Sketches and Tales of Mark Twain
The Complete Essays of Mark Twain
The Travels of Mark Twain
The Complete Novels of Mark Twain
The Complete Travel Books of Mark Twain
George Washington: A Biography, by Washington Irving
The Complete Tales of Washington Irving
The Complete Stories of Robert Louis Stevenson
Short Novels of the Masters
Great Short Stories from the World's Literature
Antarctica
Man Against Nature

THE COMIC
MARK TWAIN
READER

THE MOST HUMOROUS SELECTIONS FROM HIS STORIES,
SKETCHES, NOVELS, TRAVEL BOOKS
AND SPEECHES

Edited with an Introduction and Notes by

CHARLES NEIDER

Doubleday & Company, Inc.
Garden City, New York
1977

Library of Congress Cataloging in Publication Data

Clemens, Samuel Langhorne, 1835-1910.
The comic Mark Twain reader.

Includes bibliographical references and index.
I. Title.
PS1302.N37 818'.4'09

ISBN: 0-385-11334-X
Library of Congress Catalog Card Number 76-23785

Printed in the United States of America
First Edition

To

Harold Kuebler

Contents

Introduction

We all know of Mark Twain's dark side, his pessimism regarding the human condition, his deterministic views of man's fate, his sarcasms on the deleterious effects of religion, his extreme sensitivity to man's mistreatment of man. Yet it is his genius as a humorist rather than as a thinker or artist that makes him so rare in any country or time and gives us such great pleasure, a sense of renewal, a profound solace; in short that nourishes us.

Vietnam, Watergate: the times have been rough, and laughter is a healing emotion. Therefore I have thought it worthwhile to make a sizable volume exclusively of Twain's comic writings, drawn from an examination of the whole corpus of his work. Oddly enough, this is the first time such a volume has been produced, as far as I know. It is not representative of his whole career but it brings us closer to the heartbeat of an extraordinary ability. He is no mere funny man, a professional comic. Rather, he has an innate perspective that sees with remarkable clarity, precision, depth and empathy that life, and not the least his own, is comical and barely rational at its very core.

His humor lasts because its basis is a large humanity, a representation of man's foibles, and because it rarely descends to cheap-shot single jokes, gags and one-liners. It also survives because its language is vernacular, idiomatic and rich in slang. Much of the slang is still viable. His language dates so much less than that of most of his English and American contemporaries. He is very vital in his idiom. And when he is at his best his invention is magnificent. Great humor, when blended with wonderful language, wisdom and humaneness, is an irresistible and priceless treasure. It seems to reside in the very center of the human drama and perhaps for this reason to surpass our understanding.

So much of Mark Twin's humor is indebted to the American yarn and the American vernacular that a few reflections on the yarn and the vernacular may illuminate for us his salient qualities as a vernacular stylist and remind us that, far from being the originator of a humorous vernacular style, he was its culminating point.

A number of differences have been noted between the style of President Lyndon Johnson's administration and that of President Kennedy. One of the significant differences lies in the approach of the two presidents to humor. Johnson, it has been observed, was an eager and apt yarn spinner, who liked to tell stories with a political point. His manner and speeches were casual, almost homespun. He enjoyed phrases like "I'm in tall cotton tonight" or "My old daddy used to say." Kennedy, on the other hand, was an intellectual, detached man who enjoyed wit more than comedy and a wry aphorism more than a yarn. He has been aptly called the first Irish Brahmin. On occasion his wit was aimed at himself, as when he introduced himself in France with, "I am the man who accompanied Jacqueline Kennedy to Paris."

Both Brahmin wit and yarn humor have had a long history in the United States and have suggested two aspects of the American mind and character, one related to urban life and formal learning, the other to rural life and homespun learning. The classic centers of these two somewhat antipodal styles were New England for wit and the Old Southwest for yarn humor, and the classic confrontation occurred in the 1828 campaign which saw the election of Andrew Jackson, himself no humorist, as the first President from the western lands. It is interesting to note that Kennedy, from Boston, represented the first style and Johnson, from the New Southwest, the second, despite the fact that they were of the same party and of the same political persuasion.

It was not until the Jackson administration that the printed yarn came into its own. Before then the yarn had flourished mostly in its oral form and was related by yarn spinners known for their skepticism and their droll and deadpan manner. Skepticism seemed to flourish naturally in the back country. The ideas and experiences of Europe were tested in the proving ground of the unsettled land and the result was a lasting skepticism regarding Europe, ideas and many other things, including Easterners and their ways. If the yarn spinners seemed to recognize no limits in their will to exaggerate, this was understandable, at least to some foreign observers, in view of the vastness and mystery of the new country. Anything seemed possible in a country so unknown and so full of surprises. Hyperbole was the stock in trade even of the early guidebooks, which presumed to offer factual knowledge. It was great to take in the suckers, whether you were a land speculator or a yarn spinner. The yarn spinners were the chief entertainers in a rural society that had a surplus of time and where much time was spent in gregariousness and travel: in the country store, the meeting house, the courthouse, in the stagecoach, on the river boat, at the campfire: heavy time if empty, delightful time when yarns could be swapped and could be heard from the mouths of local artists.

"Well," goes an anonymous Down East yarn, "Uncle Zeke and I took it into our heads on Saturday afternoon to go a gunning after ducks, in father's skiff. So in we got and sculled down the river. A proper sight of ducks flew backwards and forwards, I tell ye, and by'm-by a few on 'em lit down by the mash and went to feeding. I cotched up my powder-horn to prime, and it slipped right out of my hand and sunk to the bottom of the river. The water was so clear I could see the horn on the bottom. Now I couldn't swim a jot, so sez I to Uncle Zeke, 'You're a pretty clever fellow, just let me take your powder-horn to prime.' And don't you think, the stingy critter wouldn't. Well, says I, 'You're a pretty good diver, 'un if you'll dive and get it I'll give you primin'.' I thought he'd leave his powder-horn but he didn't, but stuck it in his pocket and down he went—and there he stayed. I looked down, and what do you think the critter was doing? There he was, setting right on the bottom of the river, pouring the powder out of my horn into hizen."

The rise of the penny press in the Jacksonian decade encouraged the change from the oral to the written form of the yarn. The penny press, unlike the old "blanket-sheet" newspaper, was interested in local color and welcomed the work of the regional humorists, the Down Easters like Seba Smith and Benjamin Shillaber, and the humorists of the Old Southwest like Augustus Baldwin Longstreet and George Washington Harris. It was the latter who wrote the famous stories which he collected under the title of *Sut Lovingood's Yarns*. Men like these early humorists carried on the tradition in print of the oral yarn spinners, in manner and matter alike.

One of the first yarn spinners in American politics, surpassed in fame only by Lincoln, was Davy Crockett, who used the yarn as he did the whisky treat, to obtain votes. Crockett was a great one for the tall tale, as well as invective used for political ends. Like Lincoln he was skeptical, quaint, unhurried as he told his yarns. Once, when he found himself running for Congress against an opponent with a very winning smile, he decided that the smile was costing him votes, so he made the following stump speech about it.

"Yes, gentlemen, he may get some votes by *grinning*, for he can out-*grin* me, and you know I ain't slow. And to prove to you that I am not I will tell you the following. You all know I love hunting. Well, I discovered a long time ago that a coon couldn't stand my grin. I could bring one tumbling down from the highest tree. I never wasted powder and lead when I wanted one of these creturs. Well, as I was walking out one night, a few hundred yards from my house, looking carelessly about me, I saw a coon on one of the highest limbs of an old tree. The night was very moony and clear and old Rattler was with me. But Rattler won't bark at a coon, he's a queer dog in that way. So I thought I'd bring the coon down in the usual way, by a grin.

"I set myself, and after grinning at the coon a reasonable time found that he didn't come down. I wondered what was the reason and I took another steady grin at him. Still he was up there. It made me a little mad. So I felt around and got an old limb about five feet long and, planting one end on the ground, I placed my chin on the other and took a *rest*. I then grinned my best for about five minutes but the coon hung on. So, finding I could not bring him down by grinning, I went over to the house, got my ax, returned to the tree and began to cut away. Down it come and I run forward, but damn if the coon was there. I found that what I had taken for one was a large knot on a branch of the tree and, upon looking at it closely, I saw that I had grinned all the bark off and left the knot perfectly smooth.

"Now, fellow-citizens, you must be convinced that in the grinning line I myself am not slow. Yet when I look upon my opponent's countenance I must admit that he is my superior. You must all admit it. Therefore be wide awake—look sharp—and do not let him grin you out of your votes."

There are several points of resemblance between Crockett and Lincoln. Both were backwoodsmen, both had charm and great physical strength, both were master folk storytellers, and both were politicians who used yarns and other forms of humor tellingly in electioneering and in debate. Lincoln was very fond of humor of a rather broad taste, and when he was President delighted in the work of such humorists, skeptics and satirists of the day as Artemus

Ward, Petroleum Vesuvius Nasby and Orpheus C. Kerr. The story is well known that he read a chapter from Ward to his cabinet before reading to them the final draft of the Emancipation Proclamation. William Herndon, Lincoln's law partner and after Lincoln's death his biographer, relates a typical Lincoln yarn, this one about an old-line Baptist preacher in a backwoods meeting house who had for his text on one occasion, "I am the Christ, whom I shall represent today." A little blue lizard ran up beneath the preacher's coarse linen pants and although the preacher slapped away at his legs while continuing the sermon the lizard went on about his business. The preacher, growing desperate, loosened the button which held his pants up, and suddenly he kicked his pants off.

"But meanwhile," Lincoln is supposed to have said, "Mr. Lizard had passed the equatorial line of the waist-band and was calmly exploring that part of the preacher's anatomy which lay underneath the back of his shirt. Things were now growing interesting but the sermon was still grinding on. The next movement on the preacher's part was for the collar button, and with one sweep of his arm off came the tow linen shirt. The congregation sat for an instant as if dazed. At length an old lady in the rear of the room rose up and, glancing at the excited object in the pulpit, shouted at the top of her voice, 'If you represent Christ then I'm done with the Bible!'"

Ward, Nasby and Kerr were members of a new breed of humorist, who had added something new to the old skepticism: theatrics. After the Civil War the country had more leisure, more easy money, and people wanted entertainment. The minstrel show, the lecture platform, the show boat and touring companies all came into their own although they had their origins before the war. The theatrical humorist was not slow to take the hint. More often than not he used a pseudonym, performed on the lecture circuit and had a bagful of theatrical tricks such as illiterate spelling and atrocious punning. Like an actor, he preferred to hold up a mask of ambiguity between his private self and his audience. The theatrical humorist's range was more national than regional and he did not specialize in creating local types.

Mark Twain benefited consciously and thoroughly from the work of his predecessors and from the fashions of his time. Among his several accomplishments, he brought the yarn to a state of near-perfection. His retelling in print of the jumping-frog yarn that he had heard in California gave him his first national fame. In his travel books he often stopped the narrative to insert a favorite yarn, such as "Buck Fanshaw's Funeral" in *Roughing It* and "Jim Baker's Bluejay Yarn" in *A Tramp Abroad.* He seemed to luxuriate in his power to make his yarns long but not tedious. The American yarn had important influences on him. It is well known that one of his triumphs in *Huckleberry Finn* was his introduction in breadth and depth of mock-oral language into the American novel and his mastering the American spoken idiom in print. In this accomplishment he was aided by an incomparable ear and a subtle memory. His particular triumph was dependent on his decision to tell the story from the point of view and in the language of its protagonist.

His stylistic achievement probably did not seem novel to contemporary American humorists, since for a generation or more American humorists of the yarn-spinning stripe had been busily writing in the vernacular for the popular press. Even an amateur like the anonymous author of *Sketches and Eccentricities of Col. David Crockett* was able to suggest the way, although unconsciously, when he wrote down four vivid hunting tales told him by Crockett, and set them down as nearly as he could in Crockett's own words. *Sketches* was published slightly more than half a century before *Huckleberry Finn,* yet the hunting stories sound almost contemporaneous with the novel. Mark Twain's singularity resided in the fact that he applied his training as a humorist to the medium of the novel. This seems now like an easy and fairly obvious transfer of energy. That it wasn't so even in the case of a writer as gifted as Twain may be judged by the fact that not many of his novels have the released, vernacular style of *Huckleberry Finn.*

In 1895 Twain published a brief essay, "How to Tell a Story," in which he contended that the humorous story is American, the comic story is English and the witty story is French. Although he did not mention the yarn as such, in the context it is clear that what he had to say about the humorous story could also be applied to the American yarn. His reflections on the humorous story revealed some distinctive aspects of American humor and the American yarn. They may be summarized as follows. The art of telling a humorous story (he meant by word of mouth, not in print) "was created in America, and has remained at home." The humorous story depends on the manner of the telling, the other two on the matter. The humorous story may be spun out to great length, it may wander as it pleases and it need not arrive anywhere in particular. The other two must be brief and end with a point. The humorous story is the only difficult one to tell, for it is a work of "high and delicate art" and can be properly told only by a master of timing, the pause, mimicry, suggestion and self-control. The other two can be told by a machine. The humorous story is told gravely and with a deadpan style. The other two are told with pathetically eager delight and sometimes with guffaws, which is enough to make one want "to renounce joking and lead a better life."

This patriotic view of humor, at least some of it offered with tongue in cheek, contains a surprising turnabout, for Mark Twain is accusing the British and the French stories of being obvious and left-handed, the very things which early travelers to the United States, especially British ones, charged American humor with being.

It is worth noting that in Mark Twain's explanation the humorous story is told in the guise of an imagined and droll character and not straight out in the manner of the comic and the witty stories. The creation of "distance" between audience and story, in which the teller pretends to be an unaware and innocent middleman, is typical of yarn humor. For Mark Twain the special charm of the humorous story is that it is projected, dramatized. The teller is an actor whose function it is to give the illusion of standing aside while the story unfolds itself. Mark Twain's complaint about the tellers of comic and witty stories is that they get in the way of the stories. This insistence on the teller's modesty harks back to an ambiguity of the backwoods. Although men like Crockett were admired for their individualism it was still required of them, for the democratic game, to be modest and retiring at times, as when Lincoln, asking a crowd of people to vote for him, said he would appreciate a victory but that if the people did not elect him it was no matter. There was ambiguity for Englishmen too. Visiting Englishmen in the early years of the American nation were displeased by the boasting, excessively individualistic behavior of the backwoodsmen. Yet the English had their own brand of rugged individualism, which was manifested in the many eccentrics who had affected a humour or an odd habit of mind.

Mark Twain kept telling yarns most of his life, down to the last pessimistic years, during which he dictated parts of his autobiography. In the autobiography he told yarns about bowling, pool, dueling, and he retold the old yarn from *Roughing It*, "His Grandfather's Old Ram," to show how he had handled it on the lecture platform. These yarns were dictated in the new century. Even before the closing of the previous one the yarn had begun to seem old-fashioned and no longer adequately representative of one American way of life: the non-urban way. It was no longer in the mainstream of American humor, which took a turn for subtlety, sophistication, urbanity and a measure of open narcissism. The poor if not pure fool of the regional and theatrical humorists and of Mark Twain became the pure if not poor neurotic of twentieth-century humorists like Thurber. Finley Peter Dunne and Will Rogers were carry-overs from the school of social critics like Ward and Nasby. By the time of Will Rogers homespun humor was reduced to pithy sentences or brief disconnected paragraphs. The drawl and the understated manner were still in evidence but the spinning rope that was Will Rogers's trademark seemed largely to have replaced the spinning yarn of the nineteenth century.

The tempo of American life which accompanied the increasing urbanization, mechanization and finally the suburbanization of the country gave a quietus to the old yarn, at least for general humorous consumption. The brisk comedy of vaudeville, radio and eventually television could better reflect the nation's urgent tempo. Perhaps, however, the yarn is more viable than one thinks. It is still, at any rate, alive in electioneering, in legislative debates, in liars' clubs and in its original activity in the mouths of locally famous yarn spinners here and there across the country.

Mark Twain's sketches never gained for themselves the illustrious reputation earned by his other kinds of writing but no one interested in American humor can long remain indifferent to them. They comprised a substantial share of his literary apprenticeship and developed so thoroughly his flair of genius that they made their way into his important books long after he had decided he had broken their spell. As with the short story he was long on hodgepodge in form and short on French neatness. It is often not easy to say which is a story and which a sketch, and sometimes it is not possible. In the long run it makes little difference, for fortunately his minor works carry the impress of his literary features so strongly that they possess an intrinsic value quite apart from any they might have gathered to themselves by being more akin to the usual genres.

Some of Mark Twain's well-wishers were embarrassed by his sketches and were ready to consign them to oblivion. Albert Bigelow Paine, his friend and official biographer, in discussing a collection of items titled *Sketches New and Old*, published in 1875, said, "Many of them are amusing, some of them delightful, but most of them seem ephemeral. If we except 'The Jumping Frog,' and possibly 'A True Story' (and the latter was altogether out of place in the collection), there is no reason to suppose that any of its contents will escape oblivion." Its contents included such tales as "My Watch," "Political Economy" and "The Experience of the McWilliamses with Membranous Croup," all published in my volume of Mark Twain's collected stories. The remainder are included in my collection of his humorous sketches. So much for Paine's gift of prophecy. William Dean Howells praised *Sketches* in the *Atlantic* on its publication. The sketches are a minor side of Mark Twain but it ought to be noted that they are a particularly brilliant and representative side.

He began writing them at an early age, before he left Hannibal, Missouri, his birthplace, and the newspapers of the day made their publication possible. The blights of bigness and sameness had not yet come to the papers. There were no press associations and no syndicates. Each paper had an intimate, personal, local tone rare today and reflected the personality of its editor and of the town or region in which it was read. Today a reader's slim hope of a hearing is in the Letters to the Editor section of the editorial pages. In those earlier times the papers welcomed contributions from its readers, particularly pithy paragraphs from bright men. If you were clever enough you could work your way up to whole sketches. The reward was a haven from anonymity.

It was not only a question of appearing in your local paper. Because papers did not jealously guard their copyright status, if you were good other papers would reprint your items, and your fame might spread over a whole region, as it did in the case of Mark Twain. Those paragraphs of comment, news, observation, hoax, skit and sketch were his apprenticeship on the American literary scene, although it is doubtful that he ever regarded them in so portentous a way. He used what was available to him in outlet and matter and the result is that his beginnings and his career were so different from those of the masters of the predominant New England school.

But release from anonymity was only the first part of the reward. Later there was payment in greenbacks and gold. And so he wrote sketches for the Hannibal *Journal*, the New Orleans *True Delta*, the

Territorial Enterprise of Virginia City, Nevada, the San Francisco *Morning Call* and the *Daily Alta California*, for the *Californian* and the *Golden Era* and the Buffalo *Express* and the New York *Galaxy*. Beginning in the Fifties, he continued writing sketches into the Seventies. He traveled a familiar road to fame, that of Artemus Ward, Josh Billings and Nasby, all humorists, all commentators—and all lecturers and showmen. For once one's fame was established in the paragraphic way the lecture circuit beckoned with its gold as it competed with other forms of entertainment: the minstrel show, music hall, variety show and the circus.

The humorous lecturer in those days was invariably a showman and "quaint" in style and matter. He availed himself of the appurtenances of showmanship: pseudonyms, advance agents, puff advertisements, colored lithographs, odd posters. The poster announcing Mark Twain's first lecture, held in San Francisco in 1866, contained the following information:

> Maguire's Academy of Music/ Pine Street, near Montgomery/ The Sandwich Islands/ Mark Twain/ (Honolulu Correspondent of the Sacramento Union)/ Will Deliver A/ Lecture on the Sandwich Islands/ at the Academy of Music/ On Tuesday Evening, Oct. 2d/ (1866)/ In which passing mention will be made of Harris, Bishop/ Staley, the American missionaries, etc., and the absurd/ customs and characteristics of the natives duly discussed/ and described. A Splendid Orchestra/ is in town, but *has not* been engaged/ Also/ A Den of Ferocious Wild Beasts/ will be on exhibition in the next block/ Magnificent Fire-works/ were in contemplation for this occa-/ sion, but the idea has been abandoned/ A Grand Torchlight Procession/ may be expected; in fact, the public are/ privileged to expect whatever they please./ Dress Circle, $1.00. Family Circle, 50¢./ Doors open at 7 o'clock. The Trouble to begin at 8 o'clock.

Lectures had a wide audience, for they were written up in the newspapers and often quoted at length. Just as Mark Twain the lecturer was aggrandized by Mark Twain the writer of sketches, so the writer of sketches was benefited by the lecturer through the creation of a greater market for his wares. And just as the lectures were influenced by the competing forms of entertainment, so they in turn influenced them. The sketches in particular established Mark Twain's fame as "the wild humorist of the Pacific slope" and "the moralist of the Main." In the sketches we find more than mere echoes of the variety shows he no doubt enjoyed during his years of piloting on the Mississippi (he did not pilot showboats but they flourished on the river in his time) and of the Negro minstrel shows he so enjoyed. The "nigger" show, as it was known, with its formalized dialogue between the middleman (the straight man) and the end man (Tambo for tambourine, also Banjo for banjo) and Bones (for castanets) made itself felt in his early writings and even in his later ones.

He was a man of strong opinions. Self-educated, he was surprisingly well read, especially in history. His journalistic apprenticeship often showed in his work. He was bold, direct, impatient, restless. He was a traveler who claimed to loathe travel, yet who endured a great deal of it and often gave the impression of enjoying it. Like Henry James, he was fascinated by the innocent and ignorant American among the tradition-encrusted Europeans. He was an optimist by physiology and a pessimist by sustained observation of "the damned human race." Like Voltaire, he was a self-appointed correction officer of the species. Some of Voltaire's *Philosophical Dictionary* sounds as if it had been written by Mark Twain, especially the section on "fatalism": determinism or a variant of it.

He was a haloed clown. A dogmatic, saddened, weary tragedian. A nightwatchman patrolling with his smoking torch the dark streets of sham, cant and oppression. A bloodhound sniffing out injustice. A Bessemer oven blasting at it. A knight-errant cantering to the aid of unfranchised holocausting damsels in distress. A linx-eyed observer of his own foibles and those of the race. A competent journalist who like every professional enjoyed the exercise of his skill. An amateur literary man in every sense, including love of the vocation. A dogged researcher into the Case of Adam and Eve. A stout defender of Satan on the ground that Satan was the original underdog. "I have no special regard for Satan; but I can at least claim that I have no prejudice against him. It may even be that I lean a little his way, on account of his not having a fair show. All religions issue bibles against him, and say the most injurious things about him, but we never hear *his* side."

The man with the unruly mop and the assassin's drawl telling the nations how to behave. The printer's apprentice from Hannibal sounding off to the globe and, like Ambrose Bierce, finding it, in the end, mostly rotten, inherited as it is by man. No ivory tower man, no Humor for Humor's sake man, not even a Cigar for Cigar's sake man. At times a deliberate censor of his work, withholding it from public view through paying too much homage to the power of public opinion. Sometimes, extending himself beyond the sphere of his competence, as in the Shakespeare essay, very human, which is to say very foolish.

A man of moods and whims. He detested the French, derided the Italians, adored the English and covertly respected the Germans and Austrians while overtly ridiculing their language and certain of their institutions, such as student dueling. A republican, he waxed warm through contact with the English nobility and the Viennese court, warm enough to neutralize some of the acid of his thoughts and prose and to set down statements, as in "The Memorable Assassination," which show his perspective to have blown away in the winds of monarchical excitement. In short, he was masculine, personal, sarcastic, tender, nostalgic—and very funny.

I have been flitting about in an effort to call his full figure to mind, not merely the image of a man writing at a desk but of one who, like Dickens, went out and met his large audience and enthralled them. His public did not simply read him, they saw him and felt they knew him as a friend. In few instances in modern literature has there been so little "distance" between an author and his audience. This fact profoundly influenced his writing. If one wishes to read him as his contemporaries did one ought to keep in mind the vitality of his public image. He was an extraordinary figure, impressive not only to his countrymen but to many people abroad, and not only as a novelist and sage but as a platform figure as well. The following contemporary account (signed "R. C. B.," it appeared in *The Critic* of April 25, 1896) affords a striking view of him on the Australian lecture circuit that time when he was circling the globe to pay off his many debts.

"As a lecturer—or rather, story-teller, for the author objects to be called a lecturer—Mark Twain is, and has proved himself to be, in his opening Australian 'At Homes,' a decided success. Like Charles Dickens, he relies entirely on his old books for the pabulum of his discourses, but, unlike the author of *Pickwick*, he does not read long extracts from the books. He takes some of his best stories—'The Jumping Frog,' *Huck Finn*, the difficulties of the German language, *par exemple*—and re-tells them, with many subtle additions of humor and some fresh observations, in the most irresistibly amusing manner. He is in no sense a disappointment as a humorist. He starts his audience laughing in the very first sentence he utters, and for two hours keeps them in a continual roar. The only serious moments occur when, with the unutterable pathos of which the true humorist alone is capable, he interpolates a few pathetic touches which almost make the tears mingle with the smiles. Every story he tells serves the purpose of illustrating a moral, and, although, for the most part, he talks in low, slow, conversational tones, at times he rises to real bursts of eloquence—not the polished grandiloquent eloquence of the average American speaker, but the eloquence conveyed in simple words and phrases, and prompted by some deep and sincerely felt sentiment. The author has the power of seeming to jest at his serious side, just as in his books; but there is no mistaking the seriousness with which, for example, he is moved by the remembrance of the iniquities perpetrated on liberty in the old slavery days amid which Huck Finn and Jim the slave lived. He makes the most unexpected anecdotes point the most unexpected morals, but it is the recital of the old, familiar stories without any moral attaching to them which pleases most, coming as they do warm from the brain of the man who invented them.

"Mark Twain steals unobtrusively on to the platform, dressed in the regulation evening-clothes, with the trouser-pockets cut high up, into which he occasionally dives both hands. He bows with a quiet dignity to the roaring cheers which greet him at every 'At Home.' Then, with natural, unaffected gesture, and with scarcely any prelude, he gets under weigh with his first story. He is a picturesque figure on the stage. His long, shaggy, white hair surmounts a face full of intellectual fire. The eyes, arched with bushy brows, and which seem to be closed most of the time while he is speaking, flash out now and then from their deep sockets with a genial, kindly, pathetic look, and the face is deeply drawn with the furrows accumulated during an existence of sixty years. He talks in short sentences, with a peculiar smack of the lips at the end of each. His language is just that of his books, full of the quaintest Americanisms, and showing an utter disregard for the polished diction of most lecturers. 'It was not' is always ''twarn't' with Mark Twain, and 'mighty fine' and 'my kingdom' and 'they done it' and 'catched,' and various other purely trans-atlantic words and phrases, crop up profusely during his talk. He speaks slowly, lazily, and wearily, as a man dropping off to sleep, rarely raising his voice above a conversational tone; but it has that characteristic nasal sound which penetrates to the back of the largest building. His figure is rather slight, not above middle height, and the whole man suggests an utter lack of physical energy. As a matter of fact, Mark Twain detests exercise, and the attraction must be very strong to induce him to go very far out of doors. With the exception of an occasional curious trot, as when recounting his buck-jumping experiences, Mark Twain stands perfectly still in one place during the whole of the time he is talking to the audience. He rarely moves his arms, unless it is to adjust his spectacles or to show by action how a certain thing was done. His characteristic attitude is to stand quite still, with the right arm across the abdomen and the left resting on it and supporting his chin. In this way he talks on for nearly two hours; and, while the audience is laughing uproariously, he never by any chance relapses into a smile. To have read Mark Twain is a delight, but to have seen and heard him is a joy not readily to be forgotten."

Long after the minstrel show gave way in popularity to the variety show, Mark Twain, an old man, wrote nostalgically, "Where now is Billy Rice? He was a joy to me and so were the other stars of the nigger show—Billy Birch, David Wambold, Backus and a delightful dozen of their brethren who made life a pleasure to me forty years ago and later. Birch, Wambold and Backus are gone years ago; and with them departed to return no more forever, I suppose, the real nigger show—the genuine nigger show, the extravagant nigger show —the show which to me had no peer and whose peer has not yet arrived, in my experience. We have the grand opera; and I have witnessed and greatly enjoyed the first act of everything which Wagner created, but the effect on me has always been so powerful that one act was quite sufficient; whenever I have witnessed two acts I have gone away physically exhausted; and whenever I have ventured an entire opera the result has been the next thing to suicide. But if I could have the nigger show back again in its pristine purity and perfection I should have but little further use for opera. It seems to me that to the elevated mind and the sensitive spirit the hand organ and the nigger show are a standard and a summit to whose rarefied altitude the other forms of musical art may not reach." And he continued in the same vein, recalling the color and the technique of the minstrel show.

Mark Twain's sketches contain his brand of humor in what is perhaps its purest form. In them more than elsewhere he indulged in fun for its own sake. It is true that in his autobiography he denied that he had ever been a humorist of the "mere" sort but his practice belied him. In a discussion of a pirated edition of *Mark Twain's Library of Humor* he said, "This book is a very interesting curiosity in one way. It reveals the surprising fact that within the compass of these forty years wherein I have been playing professional humorist before the public, I have had for company seventy-eight other American humorists. Each and every one of the seventy-eight rose in my time, became conspicuous and popular, and by and by vanished. A number of these names were as familiar in their day as are the names of George Ade and Dooley today—yet they have all so completely passed from sight now that there is probably not a youth of fifteen years of age in the country whose eye would light with recognition at the mention of any one of the seventy-eight names. . . . In this mortuary volume I find Nasby, Artemus Ward, Yawcob Strauss, Derby, Burdette, Eli Perkins, the 'Danbury News Man,' Orpheus C. Kerr, Smith O'Brien, Josh Billings and a score of others, maybe two score, whose writings and sayings were once in everybody's mouth but are now heard of no more and are no longer mentioned. . . . Why have they perished? Because they were merely humorists. Humorists of the 'mere' sort cannot survive. Humor is only a fragrance, a decoration. Often it is merely an odd trick of speech and of spelling, as in the case of Ward and Billings and Nasby and the 'Disbanded Volunteer,' and presently the fashion passes and the fame along with it. There are those who say a novel should be a work of art solely and you must not preach in it, you must not teach in it. That may be true as regards novels but it is not true as regards humor. Humor must not professedly teach and it must not professedly preach, but it must do both if it would live forever. By forever, I mean thirty years. . . . I have always preached. That is the reason that I have lasted thirty years. If the humor came of its own accord and uninvited I have allowed it a place in my sermon but I was not writing the sermon for the sake of the humor. I should have written the sermon just the same, whether any humor applied for admission or not."

The reader need only browse through the present volume to see that Mark Twain did not always consider it necessary to "preach." Nor did he always believe that humor is only a fragrance. Is laughter indeed only a fragrance, a decoration, and is frowning the substance of life? Some of his merely humorous things *have* survived forever—because of their play of fancy, their wit, their invention, their fresh and idiomatic prose. The vogue of coy illiteracy practiced by Ward and Billings was bound to die, if only because it represented not a way of seeing life but of exploiting tricks of style and manner. "If the humor came of its own accord and uninvited." Fortunately for us it came often in that way, the way of inspiration. "I should have written the sermon just the same." Yes, for he had much to say. His statement notwithstanding, he was graced with the power to enjoy the comic aspect of things for its own sake and to enjoy laughter as few have experienced it, with invective when he was aroused but for the most part with a kindliness which makes the use of his rare gift seem little short of miraculous and epic.

Princeton, New Jersey
July 1976

Tell the truth or trump—but get the trick.

Nothing so needs reforming as other people's habits.

—"Pudd'nhead Wilson's Calendar" in *Pudd'nhead Wilson*

It could probably be shown by facts and figures that there is no distinctly native American criminal class except Congress.

By trying we can easily learn to endure adversity. Another man's, I mean.

In the first place God made idiots. This was for practice. Then He made School Boards.

—"Pudd'nhead Wilson's New Calendar" in *Following the Equator*

THE COMIC MARK TWAIN READER

The Most Humorous Selections from His Stories, Sketches, Novels, Travel Books and Speeches

The Notorious Jumping Frog of Calaveras County

In compliance with the request of a friend of mine, who wrote me from the East, I called on good-natured, garrulous old Simon Wheeler, and inquired after my friend's friend, Leonidas W. Smiley, as requested to do, and I hereunto append the result. I have a lurking suspicion that *Leonidas W.* Smiley is a myth; that my friend never knew such a personage; and that he only conjectured that if I asked old Wheeler about him, it would remind him of his infamous *Jim* Smiley, and he would go to work and bore me to death with some exasperating reminiscence of him as long and as tedious as it should be useless to me. If that was the design, it succeeded.

I found Simon Wheeler dozing comfortably by the bar-room stove of the dilapidated tavern in the decayed mining camp of Angel's, and I noticed that he was fat and bald-headed, and had an expression of winning gentleness and simplicity upon his tranquil countenance. He roused up, and gave me good day. I told him that a friend of mine had commissioned me to make some inquiries about a cherished companion of his boyhood named *Leonidas W.* Smiley —*Rev. Leonidas W.* Smiley, a young minister of the Gospel, who he had heard was at one time a resident of Angel's Camp. I added that if Mr. Wheeler could tell me anything about this Rev. Leonidas W. Smiley, I would feel under many obligations to him.

Simon Wheeler backed me into a corner and blockaded me there with his chair, and then sat down and reeled off the monotonous narrative which follows this paragraph. He never smiled, he never frowned, he never changed his voice from the gentle-flowing key to which he tuned his initial sentence, he never betrayed the slightest suspicion of enthusiasm; but all through the interminable narrative there ran a vein of impressive earnestness and sincerity, which showed me plainly that, so far from his imagining that there was anything ridiculous or funny about his story, he regarded it as a really important matter, and admired its two heroes as men of transcendent genius in *finesse*. I let him go on in his own way, and never interrupted him once.

"Rev. Leonidas W. H'm, Reverend Le—well, there was a feller here once by the name of *Jim* Smiley, in the winter of '49—or maybe it was the spring of '50—I don't recollect exactly, somehow, though what makes me think it was one or the other is because I remember the big flume warn't finished when he first come to the camp; but anyway, he was the curiousest man about always betting on anything that turned up you ever see, if he could get anybody to bet on the other side; and if he couldn't he'd change sides. Any way that suited the other man would suit *him*—any way just so's he got a bet, *he* was satisfied. But still he was lucky, uncommon lucky; he most always come out winner. He was always ready and laying for a chance; there couldn't be no solit'ry thing mentioned but that feller'd offer to bet on it, and take ary side you please, as I was just telling you. If there was a horse-race, you'd find him flush or you'd find him busted at the end of it; if there was a dog-fight, he'd bet on it; if there was a cat-fight, he'd bet on it; if there was a chicken-fight, he'd bet on it; why, if there was two birds setting on a fence, he would bet you which one would fly first; or if there was a camp-meeting, he would be there reg'lar to bet on Parson Walker, which he judged to be the best exhorter about here, and so he was too, and a good man. If he even see a straddle-bug start to go anywheres, he would bet you how long it would take him to get to—to wherever he was going to, and if you took him up, he would foller that straddle-bug to Mexico but what he would find out where he was bound for and how long he was on the road. Lots of the boys here has seen that Smiley, and can tell you about him. Why, it never made no difference to *him*—he'd bet on *any* thing—the dangdest feller. Parson Walker's wife laid very sick once, for a good while, and it seemed as if they warn't going to save her; but one morning he come in, and Smiley up and asked him how she was, and he said she was considerable better—thank the Lord for his inf'nite mercy—and coming on so smart that with the blessing of Prov'dence she'd get well yet; and Smiley, before he thought, says, 'Well, I'll resk two-and-a-half she don't anyway.'

"Thish-yer Smiley had a mare—the boys called her the fifteen-minute nag, but that was only in fun, you know, because of course she was faster than that—and he used to win money on that horse, for all she was so slow and always had the asthma, or the distemper, or the consumption, or something of that kind. They used to give her two or three hundred yards' start, and then pass her under way; but always at the fag end of the race she'd get excited and desperate like, and come cavorting and straddling up, and scattering her legs around limber, sometimes in the air, and sometimes out to one side among the fences, and kicking up m-o-r-e dust and raising m-o-r-e racket with her coughing and sneezing and blowing her nose—and *always* fetch up at the stand just about a neck ahead, as near as you could cipher it down.

"And he had a little small bull-pup, that to look at him you'd think he warn't worth a cent but to set around and look ornery and lay for a chance to steal something. But as soon as money was up on him he was a different dog; his under-jaw'd begin to stick out like the fo'castle of a steamboat, and his teeth would uncover and shine like the furnaces. And a dog might tackle him and bully-rag him, and bite him, and throw him over his shoulder two or three times, and Andrew Jackson—which was the name of the pup—Andrew Jackson would never let on but what *he* was satisfied, and hadn't expected nothing else—and the bets being doubled and doubled on the other side all the time, till the money was all up; and then all of a sudden he would grab that other dog jest by the j'int of his hind leg and freeze to it—not chaw, you understand, but only just grip and hang on till they throwed up the sponge, if it was a year. Smiley always come out winner on that pup, till he harnessed a dog once that didn't have no hind legs, because they'd been sawed off in a circular saw, and when the thing had gone along far enough, and the money was all up, and he come to make a snatch for his pet holt, he see in a minute how he'd been imposed on, and how the other dog had him in the door, so to speak, and he 'peared surprised, and then he looked sorter discouraged-like, and didn't try no more to win the fight, and so he got shucked out bad. He give Smiley a look, as much as to say his heart was broke, and it was *his* fault, for putting up a dog that hadn't no hind legs for him to take holt of, which was his main dependence in a fight, and then he limped off a piece and laid down and died. It was a good pup, was that Andrew Jackson, and would have made a name for hisself if he'd lived, for the stuff was in him and he had genius—I know it, because he hadn't no opportunities to speak of, and it don't stand to reason that a dog could make such a fight as he could under them circumstances if he hadn't no talent. It always makes me feel sorry when I think of that last fight of his'n, and the way it turned out.

"Well, thish-yer Smiley had rat-tarriers, and chicken cocks, and tomcats and all them kind of things, till you couldn't rest, and you couldn't fetch nothing for him to bet on but he'd match you. He ketched a frog one day, and took him home, and said he cal'lated to educate him; and so he never done nothing for three months but set in his back yard and learn that frog to jump. And you bet you he *did* learn him, too. He'd give him a little punch behind, and the next minute you'd see that frog whirling in the air like a doughnut—see him turn one summerset, or maybe a couple, if he got a good start, and come down flat-footed and all right, like a cat. He got him up so in the matter of ketching flies, and kep' him in practice so constant, that he'd nail a fly every time as fur as he could see him. Smiley said all a frog wanted was education, and he could do 'most anything—and I believe him. Why, I've seen him set Dan'l Webster down here on this floor—Dan'l Webster was the name of the frog—and sing out, 'Flies, Dan'l, flies!' and quicker'n you could wink he'd spring straight up and snake a fly off'n the counter there, and flop down on the floor ag'in as solid as a gob of mud, and fall to scratching the side of his head with his hind foot as indifferent as if he hadn't no idea he'd been doin' any more'n any frog might do. You never see a frog so modest and straightfor'ard as he was, for all he was so gifted. And when it come to fair and square jumping on a dead level, he could get over more ground at one straddle than any animal of his breed you ever see. Jumping on a dead level was his strong suit, you understand; and when it come to that, Smiley would ante up money on him as long as he had a red. Smiley was monstrous proud of his frog, and well he might be, for fellers that had traveled and been everywheres all said he laid over any frog that ever *they* see.

"Well, Smiley kep' the beast in a little lattice box, and he used to fetch him down-town sometimes and lay for a bet. One day a feller —a stranger in the camp, he was—come acrost him with his box, and says:

"'What might it be that you've got in the box?'

"And Smiley says, sorter indifferent-like, 'It might be a parrot, or it might be a canary, maybe, but it ain't—it's only just a frog.'

"And the feller took it, and looked at it careful, and turned it round this way and that, and says, 'H'm—so 'tis. Well, what's *he* good for?'

"'Well,' Smiley says, easy and careless, 'he's good enough for *one* thing, I should judge—he can outjump any frog in Calaveras County.'

"The feller took the box again, and took another long, particular look, and give it back to Smiley, and says, very deliberate, 'Well,' he says, 'I don't see no p'ints about that frog that's any better'n any other frog.'

"'Maybe you don't,' Smiley says. 'Maybe you understand frogs and maybe you don't understand 'em; maybe you've had experience, and maybe you ain't only a amature, as it were. Anyways, I've got *my* opinion, and I'll resk forty dollars that he can outjump any frog in Calaveras County.'

"And the feller studied a minute, and then says, kinder sad-like, 'Well, I'm only a stranger here, and I ain't got no frog; but if I had a frog, I'd bet you.'

"And then Smiley says, 'That's all right—that's all right—if you'll hold my box a minute, I'll go and get you a frog.' And so the feller took the box, and put up his forty dollars along with Smiley's, and set down to wait.

"So he set there a good while thinking and thinking to himself, and then he got the frog out and prized his mouth open and took a teaspoon and filled him full of quail-shot—filled him pretty near up to his chin—and set him on the floor. Smiley he went to the swamp and slopped around in the mud for a long time, and finally he ketched a frog, and fetched him in, and give him to this feller, and says:

"'Now, if you're ready, set him alongside of Dan'l, with his fore paws just even with Dan'l's, and I'll give the word.' Then he says, 'One—two—three—*git!*' and him and the feller touched up the frogs from behind, and the new frog hopped off lively, but Dan'l give a heave, and hysted up his shoulders—so—like a Frenchman, but it warn't no use—he couldn't budge; he was planted as solid as a church, and he couldn't no more stir than if he was anchored out. Smiley was a good deal surprised, and he was disgusted too, but he didn't have no idea what the matter was, of course.

"The feller took the money and started away; and when he was going out at the door, he sorter jerked his thumb over his shoulder—so—at Dan'l, and says again, very deliberate, 'Well,' he says, '*I* don't see no p'ints about that frog that's any better'n any other frog.'

"Smiley he stood scratching his head and looking down at Dan'l a long time, and at last he says, 'I do wonder what in the nation that frog throw'd off for—I wonder if there ain't something the matter with him—he 'pears to look mighty baggy, somehow.' And he ketched Dan'l by the nap of the neck, and hefted him, and says, 'Why blame my cats if he don't weigh five pound!' and turned him upside down and he belched out a double handful of shot. And then he see how it was, and he was the maddest man—he set the frog down and took out after that feller, but he never ketched him. And—"

[Here Simon Wheeler heard his name called from the front yard, and got up to see what was wanted.] And turning to me as he moved away, he said: "Just set where you are, stranger, and rest easy—I ain't going to be gone a second."

But, by your leave, I did not think that a continuation of the history of the enterprising vagabond *Jim* Smiley would be likely to afford me much information concerning the Rev. *Leonidas W.* Smiley, and so I started away.

At the door I met the sociable Wheeler returning, and he buttonholed me and recommenced:

"Well, thish-yer Smiley had a yaller one-eyed cow that didn't have no tail, only just a short stump like a bannanner, and—"

However, lacking both time and inclination, I did not wait to hear about the afflicted cow, but took my leave.

1865

Journalism in Tennessee

The editor of the Memphis *Avalanche* swoops thus mildly down upon a correspondent who posted him as a Radical:—"While he was writing the first word, the middle, dotting his i's, crossing his t's, and punching his period, he knew he was concocting a sentence that was saturated with infamy and reeking with falsehood." *Exchange*

I was told by the physician that a Southern climate would improve my health, and so I went down to Tennessee, and got a berth on the *Morning Glory and Johnson County War-Whoop* as associate editor. When I went on duty I found the chief editor sitting tilted back in a three-legged chair with his feet on a pine table. There was another pine table in the room and another afflicted chair, and both were half buried under newspapers and scraps and sheets of manuscript. There was a wooden box of sand, sprinkled with cigar stubs and "old soldiers," and a stove with a door hanging by its upper hinge. The chief editor had a long-tailed black cloth frock-coat on, and white linen pants. His boots were small and neatly blacked. He wore a ruffled shirt, a large seal-ring, a standing collar of obsolete pattern, and a checkered neckerchief with the ends hanging down. Date of costume about 1848. He was smoking a cigar, and trying to think of a word, and in pawing his hair he had rumpled his locks a good deal. He was scowling fearfully, and I judged that he was concocting a particularly knotty editorial. He told me to take the exchanges and skim through them and write up the "Spirit of the Tennessee Press," condensing into the article all of their contents that seemed of interest.

I wrote as follows:

SPIRIT OF THE TENNESSEE PRESS

The editors of the Semi-Weekly Earthquake *evidently labor under a misapprehension with regard to the Ballyhack railroad. It is not the ob-*

ject of the company to leave Buzzardville off to one side. On the contrary, they consider it one of the most important points along the line, and consequently can have no desire to slight it. The gentlemen of the Earthquake *will, of course, take pleasure in making the correction.*

John W. Blossom, Esq., the able editor of the Higginsville Thunderbolt and Battle Cry of Freedom, *arrived in the city yesterday. He is stopping at the Van Buren House.*

We observe that our contemporary of the Mud Springs Morning Howl *has fallen into the error of supposing that the election of Van Werter is not an established fact, but he will have discovered his mistake before this reminder reaches him, no doubt. He was doubtless misled by incomplete election returns.*

It is pleasant to note that the city of Blathersville is endeavoring to contract with some New York gentlemen to pave its well-nigh impassable streets with the Nicholson pavement. The Daily Hurrah *urges the measure with ability, and seems confident of ultimate success.*

I passed my manuscript over to the chief editor for acceptance, alteration, or destruction. He glanced at it and his face clouded. He ran his eye down the pages, and his countenance grew portentous. It was easy to see that something was wrong. Presently he sprang up and said:

"Thunder and lighting! Do you suppose I am going to speak of those cattle that way? Do you suppose my subscribers are going to stand such gruel as that? Give me the pen!"

I never saw a pen scrape and scratch its way so viciously, or plow through another man's verbs and adjectives so relentlessly. While he was in the midst of his work, somebody shot at him through the open window, and marred the symmetry of my ear.

"Ah," said he, "that is that scoundrel Smith, of the *Moral Volcano*—he was due yesterday." And he snatched a navy revolver from his belt and fired. Smith dropped, shot in the thigh. The shot spoiled Smith's aim, who was just taking a second chance, and he crippled a stranger. It was me. Merely a finger shot off.

Then the chief editor went on with his erasures and interlineations. Just as he finished them a hand-grenade came down the stove-pipe, and the explosion shivered the stove into a thousand fragments. However, it did no further damage, except that a vagrant piece knocked a couple of my teeth out.

"That stove is utterly ruined," said the chief editor.

I said I believed it was.

"Well, no matter—don't want it this kind of weather. I know the man that did it. I'll get him. Now, *here* is the way this stuff ought to be written."

I took the manuscript. It was scarred with erasures and interlineations till its mother wouldn't have known it if it had had one. It now read as follows:

SPIRIT OF THE TENNESSEE PRESS

The inveterate liars of the Semi-Weekly Earthquake *are evidently endeavoring to palm off upon a noble and chivalrous people another of their vile and brutal falsehoods with regard to that most glorious conception of the nineteenth century, the Ballyhack railroad. The idea that Buzzardville was to be left off at one side originated in their own fulsome brains—or rather in the settlings which* they *regard as brains. They had better swallow this lie if they want to save their abandoned reptile carcasses the cowhiding they so richly deserve.*

That ass, Blossom, of the Higginsville Thunderbolt and Battle Cry of Freedom, *is down here again sponging at the Van Buren.*

We observe that the besotted blackguard of the Mud Springs Morning Howl *is giving out, with his usual propensity for lying, that Van Werter is not elected. The heaven-born mission of journalism is to disseminate truth; to eradicate error; to educate, refine, and elevate the tone of public morals and manners, and make all men more gentle, more virtuous, more charitable, and in all ways better, and holier, and happier; and yet this black-hearted scoundrel degrades his great office persistently to the dissemination of falsehood, calumny, vituperation, and vulgarity.*

Blathersville wants a Nicholson pavement—it wants a jail and a poorhouse more. The idea of a pavement in a one-horse town composed of two gin-mills, a blacksmith shop, and that mustard-plaster of a newspaper, the Daily Hurrah! *The crawling insect, Buckner, who edits the* Hurrah, *is braying about his business with his customary imbecility, and imagining that he is talking sense.*

"Now *that* is the way to write—peppery and to the point. Mush-and-milk journalism gives me the fan-tods."

About this time a brick came through the window with a splintering crash, and gave me a considerable of a jolt in the back. I moved out of range—I began to feel in the way.

The chief said, "That was the Colonel, likely. I've been expecting him for two days. He will be up now right away."

He was correct. The Colonel appeared in the door a moment afterward with a dragoon revolver in his hand.

He said, "Sir, have I the honor of addressing the poltroon who edits this mangy sheet?"

"You have. Be seated, sir. Be careful of the chair, one of its legs is gone. I believe I have the honor of addressing the putrid liar, Colonel Blatherskite Tecumseh?"

"Right, sir. I have a little account to settle with you. If you are at leisure we will begin."

"I have an article on the 'Encouraging Progress of Moral and Intellectual Development in America' to finish, but there is no hurry. Begin."

Both pistols rang out their fierce clamor at the same instant. The chief lost a lock of his hair, and the Colonel's bullet ended its career in the fleshy part of my thigh. The Colonel's left shoulder was clipped a little. They fired again. Both missed their men this time, but I got my share, a shot in the arm. At the third fire both gentlemen were wounded slightly, and I had a knuckle chipped. I then said, I believed I would go out and take a walk, as this was a private matter, and I had a delicacy about participating in it further. But both gentlemen begged me to keep my seat, and assured me that I was not in the way.

They then talked about the elections and the crops while they reloaded, and I fell to tying up my wounds. But presently they opened fire again with animation, and every shot took effect—but it is proper to remark that five out of the six fell to my share. The sixth one mortally wounded the Colonel, who remarked, with fine humor, that he would have to say good morning now, as he had business uptown. He then inquired the way to the undertaker's and left.

The chief turned to me and said, "I am expecting company to dinner, and shall have to get ready. It will be a favor to me if you will read proof and attend to the customers."

I winced a little at the idea of attending to the customers, but I was too bewildered by the fusillade that was still ringing in my ears to think of anything to say.

He continued, "Jones will be here at three—cowhide him. Gillespie will call earlier, perhaps—throw him out of the window. Ferguson will be along about four—kill him. That is all for to-day, I believe. If you have any odd time, you may write a blistering article on the police—give the chief inspector rats. The cowhides are under the table; weapons in the drawer—ammunition there in the corner—

lint and bandages up there in the pigeonholes. In case of accident, go to Lancet, the surgeon, down-stairs. He advertises—we take it out in trade."

He was gone. I shuddered. At the end of the next three hours I had been through perils so awful that all peace of mind and all cheerfulness were gone from me. Gillespie had called and thrown *me* out of the window. Jones arrived promptly, and when I got ready to do the cowhiding he took the job off my hands. In an encounter with a stranger, not in the bill of fare, I had lost my scalp. Another stranger, by the name of Thompson, left me a mere wreck and ruin of chaotic rags. And at last, at bay in the corner, and beset by an infuriated mob of editors, blacklegs, politicians, and desperadoes, who raved and swore and flourished their weapons about my head till the air shimmered with glancing flashes of steel, I was in the act of resigning my berth on the paper when the chief arrived, and with him a rabble of charmed and enthusiastic friends. Then ensued a scene of riot and carnage such as no human pen, or steel one either, could describe. People were shot, probed, dismembered, blown up, thrown out of the window. There was a brief tornado of murky blasphemy, with a confused and frantic war-dance glimmering through it, and then all was over. In five minutes there was silence, and the gory chief and I sat alone and surveyed the sanguinary ruin that strewed the floor around us.

He said, "You'll like this place when you get used to it."

I said, "I'll have to get you to excuse me; I think maybe I might write to suit you after a while; as soon as I had had some practice and learned the language I am confident I could. But, to speak the plain truth, that sort of energy of expression has its inconveniences, and a man is liable to interruption. You see that yourself. Vigorous writing is calculated to elevate the public, no doubt, but then I do not like to attract so much attention as it calls forth. I can't write with comfort when I am interrupted so much as I have been to-day. I like this berth well enough, but I don't like to be left here to wait on the customers. The experiences are novel, I grant you, and entertaining, too, after a fashion, but they are not judiciously distributed. A gentleman shoots at you through the window and cripples *me;* a bombshell comes down the stove-pipe for your gratification and sends the stove door down *my* throat; a friend drops in to swap compliments with you, and freckles *me* with bullet-holes till my skin won't hold my principles; you go to dinner, and Jones comes with his cowhide, Gillespie throws me out of the window, Thompson tears all my clothes off, and an entire stranger takes my scalp with the easy freedom of an old acquaintance; and in less than five minutes all the blackguards in the country arrive in their warpaint, and proceed to scare the rest of me to death with their tomahawks. Take it altogether, I never had such a spirited time in all my life as I have had to-day. No; I like you, and I like your calm unruffled way of explaining things to the customers, but you see I am not used to it. The Southern heart is too impulsive; Southern hospitality is too lavish with the stranger. The paragraphs which I have written to-day, and into whose cold sentences your masterly hand has infused the fervent spirit of Tennesseean journalism, will wake up another nest of hornets. All that mob of editors will come—and they will come hungry, too, and want somebody for breakfast. I shall have to bid you adieu. I decline to be present at these festivities. I came South for my health, I will go back on the same errand, and suddenly. Tennesseean journalism is too stirring for me."

After which we parted with mutual regret, and I took apartments at the hospital.

1869

The Facts in the Great Beef Contract

In as few words as possible I wish to lay before the nation what share, howsoever small, I have had in this matter—this matter which has so exercised the public mind, engendered so much ill-feeling, and so filled the newspapers of both continents with distorted statements and extravagant comments.

The origin of this distressful thing was this—and I assert here that every fact in the following résumé can be amply proved by the official records of the General Government:

John Wilson Mackenzie, of Rotterdam, Chemung County, New Jersey, deceased, contracted with the General Government, on or about the 10th day of October, 1861, to furnish to General Sherman the sum total of thirty barrels of beef.

Very well.

He started after Sherman with the beef, but when he got to Washington, Sherman had gone to Manassas; so he took the beef and followed him there, but arrived too late; he followed him to Nashville, and from Nashville to Chattanooga, and from Chattanooga to Atlanta—but he never could overtake him. At Atlanta he took a fresh start and followed him clear through his march to the sea. He arrived too late again by a few days; but hearing that Sherman was going out in the *Quaker City* excursion to the Holy Land, he took shipping for Beirut, calculating to head off the other vessel. When he arrived in Jerusalem with his beef, he learned that Sherman had not sailed in the *Quaker City,* but had gone to the Plains to fight the Indians. He returned to America and started for the Rocky Mountains. After sixty-eight days of arduous travel on the Plains, and when he had got within four miles of Sherman's headquarters, he was tomahawked and scalped, and the Indians got the beef. They got all of it but one barrel. Sherman's army captured that, and so, even in death, the bold navigator partly fulfilled his contract. In his will, which he had kept like a journal, he bequeathed the contract to his son Bartholomew W. Bartholomew W. made out the following bill, and then died:

THE UNITED STATES
In account with JOHN WILSON MACKENZIE, of
New Jersey, deceased

		Dr.
To thirty barrels of beef for General Sherman, at $100,		$3,000
To traveling expenses and transportation		14,000
	Total	$17,000
	Rec'd Pay't.	

He died then; but he left the contract to Wm. J. Martin, who tried to collect it, but died before he got through. *He* left it to Barker J. Allen, and he tried to collect it also. He did not survive. Barker J. Allen left it to Anson G. Rogers, who attempted to collect it, and got along as far as the Ninth Auditor's Office, when Death, the great Leveler, came all unsummoned, and foreclosed on *him* also. He left the bill to a relative of his in Connecticut, Vengeance Hopkins by name, who lasted four weeks and two days, and made the best time on record, coming within one of reaching the Twelfth Auditor. In his will he gave the contract bill to his uncle, by the name of O-be-joyful Johnson. It was too undermining for Joyful. His last words were: "Weep not for me—*I* am willing to go." And so he was, poor soul. Seven people inherited the contract after that; but they all died. So it came into my hands at last. It fell to me through a relative by the name of Hubbard—Bethlehem Hubbard, of Indiana. He had had a grudge against me for a long time; but in his last moments he sent for me, and forgave me everything, and, weeping, gave me the beef contract.

This ends the history of it up to the time that I succeeded to the property. I will now endeavor to set myself straight before the nation in everything that concerns my share in the matter. I took this beef contract, and the bill for mileage and transportation, to the President of the United States.

He said, "Well, sir, what can I do for you?"

I said, "Sire, on or about the 10th day of October, 1861, John Wilson Mackenzie, of Rotterdam, Chemung County, New Jersey, deceased, contracted with the General Government to furnish to General Sherman the sum total of thirty barrels of beef—"

He stopped me there, and dismissed me from his presence—kindly, but firmly. The next day I called on the Secretary of State.

He said, "Well, sir?"

I said, "Your Royal Highness: on or about the 10th day of October, 1861, John Wilson Mackenzie, of Rotterdam, Chemung County, New Jersey, deceased, contracted with the General Government to furnish to General Sherman the sum total of thirty barrels of beef—"

"That will do, sir—that will do; this office has nothing to do with contracts for beef."

I was bowed out. I thought the matter all over, and finally, the following day, I visited the Secretary of the Navy, who said, "Speak quickly, sir; do not keep me waiting."

I said, "Your Royal Highness, on or about the 10th day of October, 1861, John Wilson Mackenzie, of Rotterdam, Chemung County, New Jersey, deceased, contracted with the General Government to General Sherman the sum total of thirty barrels of beef—"

Well, it was as far as I could get. *He* had nothing to do with beef contracts for General Sherman, either. I began to think it was a curious kind of a government. It looked somewhat as if they wanted to get out of paying for that beef. The following day I went to the Secretary of the Interior.

I said, "Your Imperial Highness, on or about the 10th day of October—"

"That is sufficient, sir. I have heard of you before. Go, take your infamous beef contract out of this establishment. The Interior Department has nothing whatever to do with subsistence for the army."

I went away. But I was exasperated now. I said I would haunt them; I would infest every department of this iniquitous government till that contract business was settled. I would collect that bill, or fall, as fell my predecessors, trying. I assailed the Postmaster-General; I besieged the Agricultural Department; I waylaid the Speaker of the House of Representatives. *They* had nothing to do with army contracts for beef. I moved upon the Commissioner of the Patent Office.

I said, "Your August Excellency, on or about—"

"Perdition! have you got *here* with your incendiary beef contract, at last? We have *nothing* to do with beef contracts for the army, my dear sir."

"Oh, that is all very well—but *somebody* has got to pay for that beef. It has got to be paid *now,* too, or I'll confiscate this old Patent Office and everything in it."

"But, my dear sir—"

"It don't make any difference, sir. The Patent Office is liable for that beef, I reckon; and, liable or not liable, the Patent Office has got to pay for it."

Never mind the details. It ended in a fight. The Patent Office won. But I found out something to my advantage. I was told that the Treasury Department was the proper place for me to go to. I went there. I waited two hours and a half, and then I was admitted to the First Lord of the Treasury.

I said, "Most noble, grave, and reverend Signor, on or about the 10th day of October, 1861, John Wilson Macken—"

"That is sufficient, sir. I have heard of you. Go to the First Auditor of the Treasury."

I did so. He sent me to the Second Auditor. The Second Auditor sent me to the Third, and the Third sent me to the First Comptroller of the Corn-Beef Division. This began to look like business. He examined his books and all his loose papers, but found no minute of the beef contract. I went to the Second Comptroller of the Corn-Beef Division. He examined his books and his loose papers, but with no success. I was encouraged. During that week I got as far as the Sixth Comptroller in that division; the next week I got through the Claims Department; the third week I began and completed the Mislaid Contracts Department, and got a foothold in the Dead Reckoning Department. I finished that in three days. There was only one place left for it now. I laid siege to the Commissioner of Odds and Ends. To his clerk, rather—he was not there himself. There were sixteen beautiful young ladies in the room, writing in books, and there were seven well-favored young clerks showing them how. The young women smiled up over their shoulders, and the clerks smiled back at them, and all went merry as a marriage bell. Two or three clerks that were reading the newspapers looked at me rather hard, but went on reading, and nobody said anything. However, I had been used to this kind of alacrity from Fourth Assistant Junior Clerks all through my eventful career, from the very day I entered the first office of the Corn-Beef Bureau clear till I passed out of the last one in the Dead Reckoning Division. I had got so accomplished by this time that I could stand on one foot from the moment I entered an office till a clerk spoke to me, without changing more than two, or maybe three, times.

So I stood there till I had changed four different times. Then I said to one of the clerks who was reading:

"Illustrious Vagrant, where is the Grand Turk?"

"What do you mean, sir? whom do you mean? If you mean the Chief of the Bureau, he is out."

"Will he visit the harem to-day?"

The young man glared upon me awhile, and then went on reading his paper. But I knew the ways of those clerks. I knew I was safe if he got through before another New York mail arrived. He only had two more papers left. After a while he finished them, and then he yawned and asked me what I wanted.

"Renowned and honored Imbecile: on or about—"

"You are the beef-contract man. Give me your papers."

He took them, and for a long time he ransacked his odds and ends. Finally he found the Northwest Passage, as *I* regarded it—he found the long-lost record of that beef contract—he found the rock upon which so many of my ancestors had split before they ever got to it. I was deeply moved. And yet I rejoiced—for I had survived. I said with emotion, "Give it me. The government will settle now." He waved me back, and said there was something yet to be done first.

"Where is this John Wilson Mackenzie?" said he.

"Dead."

"When did he die?"

"He didn't die at all—he was killed."

"How?"

"Tomahawked."

"Who tomahawked him?"

"Why, an Indian, of course. You didn't suppose it was the superintendent of a Sunday-school, did you?"

"No. An Indian, was it?"

"The same."

"Name of the Indian?"

"His name? *I* don't know his name."

"*Must* have his name. Who saw the tomahawking done?"

"I don't know."

"You were not present yourself, then?"

"Which you can see by my hair. I was absent."

"Then how do you know that Mackenzie is dead?"

"Because he certainly died at that time, and I have every reason to believe that he has been dead ever since. I *know* he has, in fact."

"We must have proofs. Have you got the Indian?"

"Of course not."

"Well, you must get him. Have you got the tomahawk?"

"I never thought of such a thing."

"You must get the tomahawk. You must produce the Indian and the tomahawk. If Mackenzie's death can be proven by these, you can then go before the commission appointed to audit claims with some show of getting your bill under such headway that your children may possibly live to receive the money and enjoy it. But that man's death *must* be proven. However, I may as well tell you that the government will never pay that transportation and those traveling expenses of the lamented Mackenzie. It *may* possibly pay for the barrel of beef that Sherman's soldiers captured, if you can get a relief bill through Congress making an appropriation for that purpose; but it will not pay for the twenty-nine barrels the Indians ate."

"Then there is only a hundred dollars due me, and *that* isn't certain! After all Mackenzie's travels in Europe, Asia, and America with that beef; after all his trials and tribulations and transportation; after the slaughter of all those innocents that tried to collect that bill! Young man, why didn't the First Comptroller of the Corn-Beef Division tell me this?"

"He didn't know anything about the genuineness of your claim."

"Why didn't the Second tell me? why didn't the Third? why didn't all those divisions and departments tell me?"

"None of them knew. We do things by routine here. You have followed the routine and found out what you wanted to know. It is the best way. It is the only way. It is very regular, and very slow, but it is very certain."

"Yes, certain death. It has been, to the most of our tribe. I begin to feel that I, too, am called. Young man, you love the bright creature yonder with the gentle blue eyes and the steel pens behind her ears—I see it in your soft glances; you wish to marry her—but you are poor. Here, hold out your hand—here is the beef contract; go, take her and be happy! Heaven bless you, my children!"

This is all I know about the great beef contract that has created so much talk in the community. The clerk to whom I bequeathed it died. I know nothing further about the contract, or any one connected with it. I only know that if a man lives long enough he can trace a thing through the Circumlocution Office of Washington and find out, after much labor and trouble and delay, that which he could have found out on the first day if the business of the Circumlocution Office were as ingeniously systematized as it would be if it were a great private mercantile institution.

1870

How I Edited an Agricultural Paper

I did not take temporary editorship of an agricultural paper without misgivings. Neither would a landsman take command of a ship without misgivings. But I was in circumstances that made the salary an object. The regular editor of the paper was going off for a holiday, and I accepted the terms he offered, and took his place.

The sensation of being at work again was luxurious, and I wrought all the week with unflagging pleasure. We went to press, and I waited a day with some solicitude to see whether my effort was going to attract any notice. As I left the office, toward sundown, a group of men and boys at the foot of the stairs dispersed with one impulse, and gave me passageway, and I heard one or two of them say: "That's him!" I was naturally pleased by this incident. The next morning I found a similar group at the foot of the stairs, and scattering couples and individuals standing here and there in the street and over the way, watching me with interest. The group separated and fell back as I approached, and I heard a man say, "Look at his eye!" I pretended not to observe the notice I was attracting, but secretly I was pleased with it, and was purposing to write an account of it to my aunt. I went up the short flight of stairs, and heard cheery voices and a ringing laugh as I drew near the door, which I opened, and caught a glimpse of two young rural-looking men, whose faces blanched and lengthened when they saw me, and then they both plunged through the window with a great crash. I was surprised.

In about half an hour an old gentleman, with a flowing beard and a fine but rather austere face, entered, and sat down at my invitation. He seemed to have something on his mind. He took off his hat and set it on the floor, and got out of it a red silk handkerchief and a copy of our paper.

He put the paper on his lap, and while he polished his spectacles with his handkerchief he said, "Are you the new editor?"

I said I was.

"Have you ever edited an agricultural paper before?"

"No," I said; "this is my first attempt."

"Very likely. Have you had any experience in agriculture practically?"

"No; I believe I have not."

"Some instinct told me so," said the old gentleman, putting on his spectacles, and looking over them at me with asperity, while he folded his paper into a convenient shape. "I wish to read you what must have made me have that instinct. It was this editorial. Listen, and see if it was you that wrote it:

"*'Turnips should never be pulled, it injures them. It is much better to send a boy up and let him shake the tree.'*

"Now, what do you think of that?—for I really suppose you wrote it?"

"Think of it? Why, I think it is good. I think it is sense. I have no doubt that every year millions and millions of bushels of turnips are spoiled in this township alone by being pulled in a half-ripe condition, when, if they had sent a boy up to shake the tree—"

"Shake your grandmother! Turnips don't grow on trees!"

"Oh, they don't, don't they? Well, who said they did? The language was intended to be figurative, wholly figurative. Anybody that knows anything will know that I meant that the boy should shake the vine."

Then this old person got up and tore his paper all into small shreds, and stamped on them, and broke several things with his cane, and said I did not know as much as a cow; and then went out and banged the door after him, and, in short, acted in such a way that I fancied he was displeased about something. But not knowing what the trouble was, I could not be any help to him.

Pretty soon after this a long, cadaverous creature, with lanky locks hanging down to his shoulders, and a week's stubble bristling from the hills and valleys of his face, darted within the door, and halted, motionless, with finger on lip, and head and body bent in listening attitude. No sound was heard. Still he listened. No sound. Then he turned the key in the door, and came elaborately tiptoeing toward me till he was within long reaching distance of me, when he stopped and, after scanning my face with intense interest for a while, drew a folded copy of our paper from his bosom, and said:

"There, you wrote that. Read it to me—quick! Relieve me. I suffer."

I read as follows; and as the sentences fell from my lips I could see the relief come, I could see the drawn muscles relax, and the anxiety go out of the face, and rest and peace steal over the features like the merciful moonlight over a desolate landscape:

The guano is a fine bird, but great care is necessary in rearing it. It should not be imported earlier than June or later than September. In the winter it should be kept in a warm place, where it can hatch out its young.

It is evident that we are to have a backward season for grain. Therefore it will be well for the farmer to begin setting out his corn-stalks and planting his buckwheat cakes in July instead of August.

Concerning the pumpkin. This berry is a favorite with the natives of the interior of New England, who prefer it to the gooseberry for the making of fruit-cake, and who likewise give it the preference over the raspberry for feeding cows, as being more filling and fully as satisfying. The pumpkin is the only esculent of the orange family that will thrive in the North, except the gourd and one or two varieties of the squash. But the custom of planting it in the front yard with the shrubbery is fast going out of vogue, for it is now generally conceded that the pumpkin as a shade tree is a failure.

Now, as the warm weather approaches, and the ganders begin to spawn—

The excited listener sprang toward me to shake hands, and said:

"There, there—that will do. I know I am all right now, because you have read it just as I did, word for word. But, stranger, when I first read it this morning, I said to myself, I never, never believed it before, notwithstanding my friends kept me under watch so strict, but now I believe I *am* crazy; and with that I fetched a howl that you might have heard two miles, and started out to kill somebody—because, you know, I knew it would come to that sooner or later, and so I might as well begin. I read one of them paragraphs over again, so as to be certain, and then I burned my house down and started. I have crippled several people, and have got one fellow up a tree, where I can get him if I want him. But I thought I would call in here as I passed along and make the thing perfectly certain; and now it *is* certain, and I tell you it is lucky for the chap that is in the tree. I should have killed him sure, as I went back. Good-by, sir, good-by; you have taken a great load off my mind. My reason has stood the strain of one of your agricultural articles, and I know that nothing can ever unseat it now. *Good*-by, sir."

I felt a little uncomfortable about the cripplings and arsons this person had been entertaining himself with, for I could not help feeling remotely accessory to them. But these thoughts were quickly banished, for the regular editor walked in! [I thought to myself, Now if you had gone to Egypt as I recommended you to, I might have had a chance to get my hand in; but you wouldn't do it, and here you are. I sort of expected you.]

The editor was looking sad and perplexed and dejected.

He surveyed the wreck which that old rioter and those two young farmers had made, and then said: "This is a sad business—a very sad business. There is the mucilage-bottle broken, and six panes of glass, and a spittoon, and two candlesticks. But that is not the worst. The reputation of the paper is injured—and permanently, I fear. True, there never was such a call for the paper before, and it never sold such a large edition or soared to such celebrity;—but does one want to be famous for lunacy, and prosper upon the infirmities of his mind? My friend, as I am an honest man, the street out here is full of people, and others are roosting on the fences, waiting to get a glimpse of you, because they think you are crazy. And well they might after reading your editorials. They are a disgrace to journalism. Why, what put it into your head that you could edit a paper of this nature? You do not seem to know the first rudiments of agriculture. You speak of a furrow and a harrow as being the same thing; you talk of the moulting season for cows; and you recommend the domestication of the pole-cat on account of its playfulness and its excellence as a ratter! Your remark that clams will lie quiet if music be played to them was superfluous—entirely superfluous. Nothing disturbs clams. Clams *always* lie quiet. Clams care nothing whatever about music. Ah, heavens and earth, friend! if you had made the acquiring of ignorance the study of your life, you could not have graduated with higher honor than you could today. I never saw anything like it. Your observation that the horse-chestnut as an article of commerce is steadily gaining in favor is simply calculated to destroy this journal. I want you to throw up your situation and go. I want no more holiday—I could not enjoy it if I had it. Certainly not with you in my chair. I would always stand in dread of what you might be going to recommend next. It makes me lose all patience every time I think of your discussing oyster-beds under the head of 'Landscape Gardening.' I want you to go. Nothing on earth could persuade me to take another holiday. Oh! why didn't you *tell* me you didn't know anything about agriculture?"

"*Tell* you, you corn-stalk, you cabbage, you son of a cauliflower? It's the first time I ever heard such an unfeeling remark. I tell you I have been in the editorial business going on fourteen years, and it is the first time I ever heard of a man's having to know anything in order to edit a newspaper. You turnip! Who write the dramatic critiques for the second-rate papers? Why, a parcel of promoted shoemakers and apprentice apothecaries, who know just as much about good acting as I do about good farming and no more. Who review the books? People who never wrote one. Who do up the heavy leaders on finance? Parties who have had the largest opportunities for knowing nothing about it. Who criticize the Indian campaigns? Gentlemen who do not know a war-whoop from a wigwam, and who never have had to run a foot-race with a tomahawk, or pluck arrows out of the several members of their families to build the evening camp-fire with. Who write the temperance appeals, and clamor about the flowing bowl? Folks who will never draw another sober breath till they do it in the grave. Who edit the agricultural papers, you—yam? Men, as a general thing, who fail in the poetry line, yellow-colored novel line, sensation-drama line, city-editor line, and finally fall back on agriculture as a temporary reprieve from the poorhouse. *You* try to tell *me* anything about the newspaper business! Sir, I have been through it from Alpha to Omaha, and I tell you that the less a man knows the bigger the noise he makes and the higher the salary he commands. Heaven knows if I had but been ignorant instead of cultivated, and impudent instead of diffident, I could have made a name for myself in this cold, selfish world. I take my leave, sir. Since I have been treated as you have treated me, I am perfectly willing to go. But I have done my duty. I have fulfilled my contract as far as I was permitted to do it. I said I could make your paper of interest to all classes—and I have. I said I could run your circulation up to twenty thousand copies, and if I had had two more weeks I'd have done it. And I'd have given you the best class of readers that ever an agricultural paper had—not a farmer in it, nor a solitary individual who could tell a watermelon-tree from a peach-vine to save his life. *You* are the loser by this rupture, not me, Pie-plant. *Adios*."

I then left.

1870

Experience of the McWilliamses with Membranous Croup

As related to the author of this book by Mr. McWilliams, a pleasant New York gentleman whom the said author met by chance on a journey.

Well, to go back to where I was before I digressed to explain to you how that frightful and incurable disease, membranous croup, was ravaging the town and driving all mothers mad with terror, I called Mrs. McWilliams's attention to little Penelope, and said:

"Darling, I wouldn't let that child be chewing that pine stick if I were you."

"Precious, where is the harm in it?" said she, but at the same time preparing to take away the stick—for women cannot receive even the most palpably judicious suggestion without arguing it; that is, married women.

I replied:

"Love, it is notorious that pine is the least nutritious wood that a child can eat."

My wife's hand paused, in the act of taking the stick, and returned itself to her lap. She bridled perceptibly, and said:

"Hubby, you know better than that. You know you do. Doctors *all* say that the turpentine in pine wood is good for weak back and the kidneys."

"Ah—I was under a misapprehension. I did not know that the child's kidneys and spine were affected, and that the family physician had recommended—"

"Who said the child's spine and kidneys were affected?"

"My love, you intimated it."

"The idea! I never intimated anything of the kind."

"Why, my dear, it hasn't been two minutes since you said—"

"Bother what I said! I don't care what I did say. There isn't any harm in the child's chewing a bit of pine stick if she wants to, and you know it perfectly well. And she *shall* chew it, too. So there, now!"

"Say no more, my dear. I now see the force of your reasoning, and I will go and order two or three cords of the best pine wood to-day. No child of mine shall want while I—"

"Oh, *please* go along to your office and let me have some peace. A body can never make the simplest remark but you must take it up and go to arguing and arguing and arguing till you don't know what you are talking about, and you *never* do."

"Very well, it shall be as you say. But there is a want of logic in your last remark which—"

However, she was gone with a flourish before I could finish, and had taken the child with her. That night at dinner she confronted me with a face as white as a sheet:

"Oh, Mortimer, there's another! Little Georgie Gordon is taken."

"Membranous croup?"

"Membranous croup."

"Is there any hope for him?"

"None in the wide world. Oh, what is to become of us!"

By and by a nurse brought in our Penelope to say good night and offer the customary prayer at the mother's knee. In the midst of "Now I lay me down to sleep," she gave a slight cough! My wife fell back like one stricken with death. But the next moment she was up and brimming with the activities which terror inspires.

She commanded that the child's crib be removed from the nursery to our bedroom; and she went along to see the order executed. She took me with her, of course. We got matters arranged with speed. A cot-bed was put up in my wife's dressing-room for the nurse. But now Mrs. McWilliams said we were too far away from the other baby, and what if *he* were to have the symptoms in the night—and she blanched again, poor thing.

We then restored the crib and the nurse to the nursery and put up a bed for ourselves in a room adjoining.

Presently, however, Mrs. McWilliams said suppose the baby should catch it from Penelope? This thought struck a new panic to her heart, and the tribe of us could not get the crib out of the nursery again fast enough to satisfy my wife, though she assisted in her own person and well-nigh pulled the crib to pieces in her frantic hurry.

We moved down-stairs; but there was no place there to stow the nurse, and Mrs. McWilliams said the nurse's experience would be an inestimable help. So we returned, bag and baggage, to our own bedroom once more, and felt a great gladness, like storm-buffeted birds that have found their nest again.

Mrs. McWilliams sped to the nursery to see how things were going on there. She was back in a moment with a new dread. She said:

"What *can* make Baby sleep so?"

I said:

"Why, my darling, Baby *always* sleeps like a graven image."

"I know. I know; but there's something peculiar about his sleep now. He seems to—to—he seems to breathe so *regularly*. Oh, this is dreadful."

"But, my dear, he always breathes regularly."

"Oh, I know it, but there's something frightful about it now. His nurse is too young and inexperienced. Maria shall stay there with her, and be on hand if anything happens."

"That is a good idea, but who will help *you*?"

"You can help me all I want. I wouldn't allow anybody to do anything but myself, anyhow, at such a time as this."

I said I would feel mean to lie abed and sleep, and leave her to watch and toil over our little patient all the weary night. But she reconciled me to it. So old Maria departed and took up her ancient quarters in the nursery.

Penelope coughed twice in her sleep.

"Oh, why *don't* that doctor come! Mortimer, this room is too warm. This room is certainly too warm. Turn off the register—quick!"

I shut it off, glancing at the thermometer at the same time, and wondering to myself if 70 *was* too warm for a sick child.

The coachman arrived from down-town now with the news that our physician was ill and confined to his bed. Mrs. McWilliams turned a dead eye upon me, and said in a dead voice:

"There is a Providence in it. It is foreordained. He never was sick before. Never. We have not been living as we ought to live, Mortimer. Time and time again I have told you so. Now you see the result. Our child will never get well. Be thankful if you can forgive yourself; I never can forgive *my*self."

I said, without intent to hurt, but with heedless choice of words, that I could not see that we had been living such an abandoned life.

"*Mortimer!* Do you want to bring the judgment upon Baby, too!"

Then she began to cry, but suddenly exclaimed:

"The doctor must have sent medicines!"

I said:

"Certainly. They are here. I was only waiting for you to give me a chance."

"Well do give them to me! Don't you know that every moment is precious now? But what was the use in sending medicines, when he *knows* that the disease is incurable?"

I said that while there was life there was hope.

"Hope! Mortimer, you know no more what you are talking about than the child unborn. If you would– As I live, the directions say give one teaspoonful once an hour! Once an hour!—as if we had a whole year before us to save the child in! Mortimer, please hurry. Give the poor perishing thing a tablespoonful, and *try* to be quick!"

"Why, my dear, a tablespoonful might–"

"*Don't* drive me frantic! . . . There, there, there, my precious, my own; it's nasty bitter stuff, but it's good for Nelly—good for mother's precious darling; and it will make her well. There, there, there, put the little head on mamma's breast and go to sleep, and pretty soon—oh, I know she can't live till morning! Mortimer, a tablespoonful every half-hour will– Oh, the child needs belladonna, too; I know she does—and aconite. Get them, Mortimer. Now do let me have my way. You know nothing about these things."

We now went to bed, placing the crib close to my wife's pillow. All this turmoil had worn upon me, and within two minutes I was something more than half asleep. Mrs. McWilliams roused me:

"Darling, is that register turned on?"

"No."

"I thought as much. Please turn it on at once. This room is cold."

I turned it on, and presently fell asleep again. I was aroused once more:

"Dearie, would you mind moving the crib to your side of the bed? It is nearer the register."

I moved it, but had a collision with the rug and woke up the child. I dozed off once more, while my wife quieted the sufferer. But in a little while these words came murmuring remotely through the fog of my drowsiness:

"Mortimer, if we only had some goose grease—will you ring?"

I climbed dreamily out, and stepped on a cat, which responded with a protest and would have got a convincing kick for it if a chair had not got it instead.

"Now, Mortimer, why do you want to turn up the gas and wake up the child again?"

"Because I want to see how much I am hurt, Caroline."

"Well, look at the chair, too—I have no doubt it is ruined. Poor cat, suppose you had—"

"Now I am not going to suppose anything about the cat. It never would have occurred if Maria had been allowed to remain here and attend to these duties, which are in her line and are not in mine."

"Now, Mortimer, I should think you would be ashamed to make a remark like that. It is a pity if you cannot do the few little things I ask of you at such an awful time as this when our child—"

"There, there, I will do anything you want. But I can't raise anybody with this bell. They're all gone to bed. Where is the goose grease?"

"On the mantelpiece in the nursery. If you'll step there and speak to Maria—"

I fetched the goose grease and went to sleep again. Once more I was called:

"Mortimer, I so hate to disturb you, but the room is still too cold for me to try to apply this stuff. Would you mind lighting the fire? It is all ready to touch a match to."

I dragged myself out and lit the fire, and then sat down disconsolate.

"Mortimer, don't sit there and catch your death of cold. Come to bed."

As I was stepping in she said:

"But wait a moment. Please give the child some more of the medicine."

Which I did. It was a medicine which made a child more or less lively; so my wife made use of its waking interval to strip it and grease it all over with the goose oil. I was soon asleep once more, but once more I had to get up.

"Mortimer, I feel a draft. I feel it distinctly. There is nothing so bad for this disease as a draft. Please move the crib in front of the fire."

I did it; and collided with the rug again, which I threw in the fire. Mrs. McWilliams sprang out of bed and rescued it and we had some words. I had another trifling interval of sleep, and then got up, by request, and constructed a flax-seed poultice. This was placed upon the child's breast and left there to do its healing work.

A wood-fire is not a permanent thing. I got up every twenty minutes and renewed ours, and this gave Mrs. McWilliams the opportunity to shorten the times of giving the medicines by ten minutes, which was a great satisfaction to her. Now and then, between times, I reorganized the flax-seed poultices, and applied sinapisms and other sorts of blisters where unoccupied places could be found upon the child. Well, toward morning the wood gave out and my wife wanted me to go down cellar and get some more. I said:

"My dear, it is a laborious job, and the child must be nearly warm enough, with her extra clothing. Now mightn't we put on another layer of poultices and–"

I did not finish, because I was interrupted. I lugged wood up from below for some little time, and then turned in and fell to snoring as only a man can whose strength is all gone and whose soul is worn out. Just at broad daylight I felt a grip on my shoulder that brought me to my senses suddenly. My wife was glaring down upon me and gasping. As soon as she could command her tongue she said:

"It is all over! All over! The child's perspiring! What *shall* we do?"

"Mercy, how you terrify me! *I* don't know what we ought to do. Maybe if we scraped her and put her in the draft again–"

"Oh, idiot! There is not a moment to lose! Go for the doctor. Go yourself. Tell him he *must* come, dead or alive."

I dragged that poor sick man from his bed and brought him. He looked at the child and said she was not dying. This was joy unspeakable to me, but it made my wife as mad as if he had offered her a personal affront. Then he said the child's cough was only caused by some trifling irritation or other in the throat. At this I thought my wife had a mind to show him the door. Now the doctor said he would make the child cough harder and dislodge the trouble. So he gave her something that sent her into a spasm of coughing, and presently up came a little wood splinter or so.

"This child has no membranous croup," said he. "She has been chewing a bit of pine shingle or something of the kind, and got some little slivers in her throat. They won't do her any hurt."

"No," said I, "I can well believe that. Indeed, the turpentine that is in them is very good for certain sorts of diseases that are peculiar to children. My wife will tell you so."

But she did not. She turned away in disdain and left the room; and since that time there is one episode in our life which we never refer to. Hence the tide of our days flows by in deep and untroubled serenity.

Very few married men have such an experience as McWilliams's, and so the author of this book thought that maybe the novelty of it would give it a passing interest to the reader.

1875

The Invalid's Story

I seem sixty and married, but these effects are due to my condition and sufferings, for I am a bachelor, and only forty-one. It will be hard for you to believe that I, who am now but a shadow, was a hale, hearty man two short years ago—a man of iron, a very athlete! —yet such is the simple truth. But stranger still than this fact is the way in which I lost my health. I lost it through helping to take care of a box of guns on a two-hundred-mile railway journey one winter's night. It is the actual truth, and I will tell you about it.

I belong in Cleveland, Ohio. One winter's night, two years ago, I reached home just after dark, in a driving snow-storm, and the first thing I heard when I entered the house was that my dearest boyhood friend and schoolmate, John B. Hackett, had died the day before, and that his last utterance had been a desire that I would take his remains home to his poor old father and mother in Wisconsin. I was greatly shocked and grieved, but there was no time to waste in emotions; I must start at once. I took the card, marked "Deacon Levi Hackett, Bethlehem, Wisconsin," and hurried off through the whistling storm to the railway-station. Arrived there I found the long white-pine box which had been described to me; I fastened the card to it with some tacks, saw it put safely aboard the express-car, and then ran into the eating-room to provide myself with a sandwich and some cigars. When I returned, presently, there was my coffin-box *back again,* apparently, and a young fellow examining around it, with a card in his hands, and some tacks and a hammer! I was astonished and puzzled. He began to nail on his card, and I rushed out to the express-car, in a good deal of a state of mind, to ask for an explanation. But no—there was my box, all right, in the express-car; it hadn't been disturbed. [The fact is that without my suspecting it a prodigious mistake had been made. I was carrying off a box of *guns* which that young fellow had come to the station to ship to a rifle company in Peoria, Illinois, and *he* had got my corpse!] Just then the conductor sang out "All aboard," and I jumped into the express-car and got a comfortable seat on a bale of buckets. The expressman was there, hard at work—a plain man of fifty, with a simple, honest, good-natured face, and a breezy, practical heartiness in his general style. As the train moved off a stranger skipped into the car and set a package of peculiarly mature and capable Limburger cheese on one end of my coffin-box—I mean my box of guns. That is to say, I know *now* that it was Limburger cheese, but at that time I never had heard of the article in my life, and of course was wholly ignorant of its character. Well, we sped through the wild night, the bitter storm raged on, a cheerless misery stole over me, my heart went down, down, down! The old expressman made a brisk remark or two about the tempest and the arctic weather, slammed his sliding doors to, and bolted them, closed his window down tight, and then went bustling around, here and there and yonder, setting things to rights, and all the time contentedly humming "Sweet By and By," in a low tone, and flatting a good deal. Presently I began to detect a most evil and searching odor stealing about on the frozen air. This depressed my spirits still more, because of course I attributed it to my poor departed friend. There was something infinitely saddening about his calling himself to my remembrance in this dumb, pathetic way, so it was hard to keep the tears back. Moreover, it distressed me on account of the old expressman, who, I was afraid, might notice it. However, he went humming tranquilly on, and gave no sign; and for this I was grateful. Grateful, yes, but still uneasy; and soon I began to feel more and more uneasy every minute, for every minute that went by that odor thickened up the more, and got to be more and more gamy and hard to stand. Presently, having got things arranged to his satisfaction, the expressman got some wood and made up a tremendous fire in his stove. This distressed me more than I can tell, for I could not but feel that it was a mistake. I was sure that the effect would be deleterious upon my poor departed friend. Thompson—the expressman's name was Thompson, as I found out in the course of the night—now went poking around his car, stopping up whatever stray cracks he could find, remarking that it didn't make any difference what kind of a night it was outside, he calculated to make *us* comfortable, anyway. I said nothing, but I believed he was not choosing the right way. Meantime he was humming to himself just as before; and meantime, too, the stove was getting hotter and hotter, and the place closer and closer. I felt myself growing pale and qualmish, but grieved in silence and said nothing. Soon I noticed that the "Sweet By and By" was gradually fading out; next it ceased altogether, and there was an ominous stillness. After a few moments Thompson said—

"Pfew! I reckon it ain't no cinnamon 't I've loaded up thish-yer stove with!"

He gasped once or twice, then moved toward the cof—gun-box, stood over that Limburger cheese part of a moment, then came back and sat down near me, looking a good deal impressed. After a contemplative pause, he said, indicating the box with a gesture—

"Friend of yourn?"

"Yes," I said with a sigh.

"He's pretty ripe, *ain't* he!"

Nothing further was said for perhaps a couple of minutes, each being busy with his own thoughts; then Thompson said, in a low, awed voice—

"Sometimes it's uncertain whether they're really gone or not—*seem* gone, you know—body warm, joints limber—and so, although you *think* they're gone, you don't really know. I've had cases in my car. It's perfectly awful, becuz *you* don't know what minute they'll rise up and look at you!" Then, after a pause, and slightly lifting his elbow toward the box,—"But *he* ain't in no trance! No, sir, I go bail for *him!*"

We sat some time, in meditative silence, listening to the wind and the roar of the train; then Thompson said, with a good deal of feeling:

"Well-a-well, we've all got to go, they ain't no getting around it. Man that is born of woman is of few days and far between, as Scriptur' says. Yes, you look at it any way you want to, it's awful solemn and cur'us: they ain't *nobody* can get around it; *all's* got to go—just *everybody,* as you may say. One day you're hearty and strong"—here he scrambled to his feet and broke a pane and stretched his nose out at it a moment or two, then sat down again while I struggled up and thrust my nose out at the same place, and this we kept on doing every now and then—"and next day he's cut down like the grass, and the places which knowed him then knows him no more forever, as Scriptur' says. Yes'ndeedy, it's awful solemn and cur'us; but we've all got to go, one time or another; they ain't no getting around it."

There was another long pause; then—

"What did he die of?"

I said I didn't know.

"How long has he ben dead?"

It seemed judicious to enlarge the facts to fit the probabilities; so I said:

"Two or three days."

But it did no good; for Thompson received it with an injured look which plainly said, "Two or three *years*, you mean." Then he went right along, placidly ignoring my statement, and gave his views at considerable length upon the unwisdom of putting off burials too long. Then he lounged off toward the box, stood a moment, then came back on a sharp trot and visited the broken pane, observing:

"'Twould 'a' ben a dum sight better, all around, if they'd started him along last summer."

Thompson sat down and buried his face in his red silk handkerchief, and began to slowly sway and rock his body like one who is doing his best to endure the almost unendurable. By this time the fragrance—if you may call it fragrance—was just about suffocating, as near as you can come at it. Thompson's face was turning gray; I knew mine hadn't any color left in it. By and by Thompson rested his forehead in his left hand, with his elbow on his knee, and sort of waved his red handkerchief toward the box with his other hand, and said:

"I've carried a many a one of 'em—some of 'em considerable overdue, too—but, lordy, he just lays over 'em all!—and does it *easy*. Cap, they was heliotrope to *him!*"

This recognition of my poor friend gratified me, in spite of the sad circumstances, because it had so much the sound of a compliment.

Pretty soon it was plain that something had got to be done. I suggested cigars. Thompson thought it was a good idea. He said: "Likely it'll modify him some."

We puffed gingerly along for a while, and tried hard to imagine that things were improved. But it wasn't any use. Before very long, and without any consultation, both cigars were quietly dropped from our nerveless fingers at the same moment. Thompson said, with a sigh:

"No, Cap, it don't modify him worth a cent. Fact is, it makes him worse, becuz it appears to stir up his ambition. What do you reckon we better do, now?"

I was not able to suggest anything; indeed, I had to be swallowing and swallowing all the time, and did not like to trust myself to speak. Thompson fell to maundering, in a desultory and low-spirited way, about the miserable experiences of this night; and he got to referring to my poor friend by various titles—sometimes military ones, sometimes civil ones; and I noticed that as fast as my poor friend's effectiveness grew, Thompson promoted him accordingly—gave him a bigger title. Finally he said:

"I've got an idea. Suppos'n' we buckle down to it and give the Colonel a bit of a shove toward t'other end of the car?—about ten foot, say. He wouldn't have so much influence, then, don't you reckon?"

I said it was a good scheme. So we took in a good fresh breath at the broken pane, calculating to hold it till we got through; then we went there and bent over that deadly cheese and took a grip on the box. Thompson nodded "All ready," and then we threw ourselves forward with all our might; but Thompson slipped, and slumped down with his nose on the cheese, and his breath got loose. He gagged and gasped, and floundered up and made a break for the door, pawing the air and saying hoarsely, "Don't hender me!—gimme the road! I'm a-dying; gimme the road!" Out on the cold platform I sat down and held his head awhile, and he revived. Presently he said:

"Do you reckon we started the Gen'rul any?"

I said no; we hadn't budged him.

"Well, then, *that* idea's up the flume. We got to think up something else. He's suited wher' he is, I reckon; and if that's the way he feels about it, and has made up his mind that he don't wish to be disturbed, you bet he's a-going to have his own way in the business. Yes, better leave him right wher' he is, long as he wants it so; becuz he holds all the trumps, don't you know, and so it stands to reason that the man that lays out to alter his plans for him is going to get left."

But we couldn't stay out there in that mad storm; we should have frozen to death. So we went in again and shut the door, and began to suffer once more and take turns at the break in the window. By and by, as we were starting away from a station where we had stopped a moment Thompson pranced in cheerily, and exclaimed:

"We're all right, now! I reckon we've got the Commodore this time. I judge I've got the stuff here that'll take the tuck out of him."

It was carbolic acid. He had a carboy of it. He sprinkled it all around everywhere; in fact he drenched everything with it, rifle-box, cheese and all. Then we sat down, feeling pretty hopeful. But it wasn't for long. You see the two perfumes began to mix, and then —well, pretty soon we made a break for the door; and out there Thompson swabbed his face with his bandanna and said in a kind of disheartened way:

"It ain't no use. We can't buck agin *him*. He just utilizes everything we put up to modify him with, and gives it his own flavor and plays it back on us. Why, Cap, don't you know, it's as much as a hundred times worse in there now than it was when he first got a-going. I never *did* see one of 'em warm up to his work so, and take such a dumnation interest in it. No, sir, I never did, as long as I've ben on the road; and I've carried a many a one of 'em, as I was telling you."

We went in again after we were frozen pretty stiff; but my, we couldn't *stay* in, now. So we just waltzed back and forth, freezing, and thawing, and stifling, by turns. In about an hour we stopped at another station; and as we left it Thompson came in with a bag, and said—

"Cap, I'm a-going to chance him once more—just this once; and if we don't fetch him this time, the thing for us to do, is to just throw up the sponge and withdraw from the canvass. That's the way *I* put it up."

He had brought a lot of chicken feathers, and dried apples, and leaf tobacco, and rags, and old shoes, and sulphur, and asafetida, and one thing or another; and he piled them on a breadth of sheet iron in the middle of the floor, and set fire to them.

When they got well started, I couldn't see, myself, how even the corpse could stand it. All that went before was just simply poetry to that smell—but mind you, the original smell stood up out of it just as sublime as ever—fact is, these other smells just seemed to give it a better hold; and my, how rich it was! I didn't make these reflections there—there wasn't time—made them on the platform. And breaking for the platform, Thompson got suffocated and fell; and before I got him dragged out, which I did by the collar, I was mighty near gone myself. When we revived, Thompson said dejectedly:

"We got to stay out here, Cap. We got to do it. They ain't no other way. The Governor wants to travel alone, and he's fixed so he can outvote us."

And presently he added:

"And don't you know, we're *pisoned.* It's *our* last trip, you can make up your mind to it. Typhoid fever is what's going to come of this. I feel it a-coming right now. Yes, sir, we're elected, just as sure as you're born."

We were taken from the platform an hour later, frozen and insensible, at the next station, and I went straight off into a virulent fever, and never knew anything again for three weeks. I found out, then, that I had spent that awful night with a harmless box of rifles and a lot of innocent cheese; but the news was too late to save *me;* imagination had done its work, and my health was permanently shattered; neither Bermuda nor any other land can ever bring it back to me. This is my last trip; I am on my way home to die.

1882

The McWilliamses and the Burglar Alarm

The conversation drifted smoothly and pleasantly along from weather to crops, from crops to literature, from literature to scandal, from scandal to religion; then took a random jump, and landed on the subject of burglar alarms. And now for the first time Mr. McWilliams showed feeling. Whenever I perceive this sign on this man's dial, I comprehend it, and lapse into silence, and give him opportunity to unload his heart. Said he, with but ill-controlled emotion:

I do not go one single cent on burglar alarms, Mr. Twain—not a single cent—and I will tell you why. When we were finishing our house, we found we had a little cash left over, on account of the plumber not knowing it. I was for enlightening the heathen with it, for I was always unaccountably down on the heathen somehow; but Mrs. McWilliams said no, let's have a burglar alarm. I agreed to this compromise. I will explain that whenever I want a thing, and Mrs. McWilliams wants another thing, and we decide upon the thing that Mrs. McWilliams wants—as we always do—she calls that a compromise. Very well: the man came up from New York and put in the alarm, and charged three hundred and twenty-five dollars for it, and said we could sleep without uneasiness now. So we did for awhile—say a month. Then one night we smelled smoke, and I was advised to get up and see what the matter was. I lit a candle, and started toward the stairs, and met a burglar coming out of a room with a basket of tinware, which he had mistaken for solid silver in the dark. He was smoking a pipe. I said, "My friend, we do not allow smoking in this room." He said he was a stranger, and could not be expected to know the rules of the house: said he had been in many houses just as good as this one, and it had never been objected to before. He added that as far as his experience went, such rules had never been considered to apply to burglars, anyway.

I said: "Smoke along, then, if it is the custom, though I think that the conceding of a privilege to a burglar which is denied to a bishop is a conspicuous sign of the looseness of the times. But waiving all that, what business have you to be entering this house in this furtive and clandestine way, without ringing the burglar alarm?"

He looked confused and ashamed, and said, with embarrassment: "I beg a thousand pardons. I did not know you had a burglar alarm, else I would have rung it. I beg you will not mention it where my parents may hear of it, for they are old and feeble, and such a seemingly wanton breach of the hallowed conventionalities of our Christian civilization might all too rudely sunder the frail bridge which hangs darkling between the pale and evanescent present and the solemn great deeps of the eternities. May I trouble you for a match?"

I said: "Your sentiments do you honor, but if you will allow me to say it, metaphor is not your best hold. Spare your thigh; this kind light only on the box, and seldom there, in fact, if my experience may be trusted. But to return to business: how did you get in here?"

"Through a second-story window."

It was even so. I redeemed the tinware at pawnbroker's rates, less cost of advertising, bade the burglar good-night, closed the window after him, and retired to headquarters to report. Next morning we sent for the burglar-alarm man, and he came up and explained that the reason the alarm did not "go off" was that no part of the house but the first floor was attached to the alarm. This was simply idiotic; one might as well have no armor on at all in battle as to have it only on his legs. The expert now put the whole second story on the alarm, charged three hundred dollars for it, and went his way. By and by, one night, I found a burglar in the third story, about to start down a ladder with a lot of miscellaneous property. My first impulse was to crack his head with a billiard cue; but my second was to refrain from this attention, because he was between me and the cue rack. The second impulse was plainly the soundest, so I refrained, and proceeded to compromise. I redeemed the property at former rates, after deducting ten per cent, for use of ladder, it being my ladder, and next day we sent down for the expert once more, and had the third story attached to the alarm, for three hundred dollars.

By this time the "annunciator" had grown to formidable dimensions. It had forty-seven tags on it, marked with the names of the various rooms and chimneys, and it occupied the space of an ordinary wardrobe. The gong was the size of a wash-bowl, and was placed above the head of our bed. There was a wire from the house to the coachman's quarters in the stable, and a noble gong alongside his pillow.

We should have been comfortable now but for one defect. Every morning at five the cook opened the kitchen door, in the way of business, and rip went that gong! The first time this happened I thought the last day was come sure. I didn't think it *in* bed—no, but out of it—for the first effect of that frightful gong is to hurl you across the house, and slam you against the wall, and then curl you up, and squirm you like a spider on a stove lid, till somebody shuts the kitchen door. In solid fact, there is no clamor that is even remotely comparable to the dire clamor which that gong makes. Well, this catastrophe happened every morning regularly at five o'clock, and lost us three hours sleep; for, mind you, when that thing wakes you, it doesn't merely wake you in spots; it wakes you all over, conscience and all, and you are good for eighteen hours of wide-awakeness subsequently—eighteen hours of the very most inconceivable wide-awakeness that you ever experienced in your life. A stranger died on our hands one time, and we vacated and left him in our room overnight. Did that stranger wait for the general judgment? *No,* sir; he got up at five the next morning in the most prompt and unostentatious way. I knew he would; I knew it mighty well. He collected his life-insurance, and lived happy ever after, for there was plenty of proof as to the perfect squareness of his death.

Well, we were gradually fading toward a better land, on account of the daily loss of sleep; so we finally had the expert up again, and he ran a wire to the outside of the door, and placed a switch there, whereby Thomas, the butler, always made one little mistake—he switched the alarm off at night when he went to bed, and switched it on again at daybreak in the morning, just in time for the cook to open the kitchen door, and enable that gong to slam us across the house, sometimes breaking a window with one or the other of us. At the end of a week we recognized that this switch business was a delusion and a snare. We also discovered that a band of burglars had been lodging in the house the whole time—not exactly to steal, for there wasn't much left now, but to hide from the police, for they were hot pressed, and they shrewdly judged that the detectives would never think of a tribe of burglars taking sanctuary in a house notoriously protected by the most imposing and elaborate burglar alarm in America.

Sent down for the expert again, and this time he struck a most dazzling idea—he fixed the thing so that opening the kitchen door would take off the alarm. It was a noble idea, and he charged accordingly. But you already foresee the result. I switched on the alarm every night at bed-time, no longer trusting on Thomas's frail memory; and as soon as the lights were out the burglars walked in at the kitchen door, thus taking the alarm off without waiting for the cook to do it in the morning. You see how aggravatingly we were situated. For months we couldn't have any company. Not a spare bed in the house; all occupied by burglars.

Finally, I got up a cure of my own. The expert answered the call, and ran another ground wire to the stable, and established a switch there, so that the coachman could put on and take off the alarm. That worked first rate, and a season of peace ensued, during which we got to inviting company once more and enjoying life.

But by and by the irrepressible alarm invented a new kink. One winter's night we were flung out of bed by the sudden music of that awful gong, and when we hobbled to the annunciator, turned up the gas, and saw the word "Nursery" exposed, Mrs. McWilliams fainted dead away, and I came precious near doing the same thing myself. I seized my shotgun, and stood timing the coachman whilst that appalling buzzing went on. I knew that his gong had flung him out, too, and that he would be along with his gun as soon as he could jump into his clothes. When I judged that the time was ripe, I crept to the room next the nursery, glanced through the window, and saw the dim outline of the coachman in the yard below, standing at present-arms and waiting for a chance. Then I hopped into the nursery and fired, and in the same instant the coachman fired at the red flash of my gun. Both of us were successful; I crippled a nurse, and he shot off all my back hair. We turned up the gas, and telephoned for a surgeon. There was not a sign of a burglar, and no window had been raised. One glass was absent, but that was where the coachman's charge had come through. Here was a fine mystery—a burglar alarm "going off" at midnight of its own accord, and not a burglar in the neighborhood!

The expert answered the usual call, and explained that it was a

"False alarm." Said it was easily fixed. So he overhauled the nursery window, charged a remunerative figure for it, and departed.

What we suffered from false alarms for the next three years no stylographic pen can describe. During the next three months I always flew with my gun to the room indicated, and the coachman always sallied forth with his battery to support me. But there was never anything to shoot at—windows all tight and secure. We always sent down for the expert next day, and he fixed those particular windows so they would keep quiet a week or so, and always remembered to send us a bill about like this:

Wire	$2.15
Nipple	.75
Two hours' labor	1.50
Wax	.47
Tape	.34
Screws	.15
Recharging battery	.98
Three hours' labor	2.25
String	.02
Lard	.66
Pond's Extract	1.25
Springs at 50	2.00
Railroad fares	7.25
	$19.77

At length a perfectly natural thing came about—after we had answered three or four hundred false alarms—to wit, we stopped answering them. Yes, I simply rose up calmly, when slammed across the house by the alarm, calmly inspected the annunciator, took note of the room indicated, and then calmly disconnected that room from the alarm, and went back to bed as if nothing had happened. Moreover, I left that room off permanently, and did not send for the expert. Well, it goes without saying that in the course of time *all* the rooms were taken off, and the entire machine was out of service.

It was at this unprotected time that the heaviest calamity of all happened. The burglars walked in one night and carried off the burglar alarm! yes, sir, every hide and hair of it: ripped it out, tooth and nail; springs, bells, gongs, battery, and all; they took a hundred and fifty miles of copper wire; they just cleaned her out, bag and baggage, and never left us a vestige of her to swear at—swear by, I mean.

We had a time of it to get her back; but we accomplished it finally, for money. The alarm firm said that what we needed now was to have her put in right—with their new patent springs in the windows to make false alarms impossible, and their new patent clock attached to take off and put on the alarm morning and night without human assistance. That seemed a good scheme. They promised to have the whole thing finished in ten days. They began work, and we left for the summer. They worked a couple of days; then *they* left for the summer. After which the burglars moved in, and began *their* summer vacation. When we returned in the fall, the house was as empty as a beer closet in premises where painters have been at work. We refurnished, and then sent down to hurry up the expert. He came up and finished the job, and said: "Now this clock is set to put on the alarm every night at 10, and take it off every morning at 5:45. All you've got to do is to wind her up every week, and then leave her alone—she will take care of the alarm herself."

After that we had a most tranquil season during three months. The bill was prodigious, of course, and I had said I would not pay it until the new machinery had proved itself to be flawless. The time stipulated was three months. So I paid the bill, and the very next day the alarm went to buzzing like ten thousand bee swarms at ten o'clock in the morning. I turned the hands around twelve hours, according to instructions, and this took off the alarm; but there was another hitch at night, and I had to set her ahead twelve hours once more to get her to put the alarm on again. That sort of nonsense went on a week or two, then the expert came up and put in a new clock. He came up every three months during the next three years, and put in a new clock. But it was always a failure. His clocks all had the same perverse defect: they would put the alarm on in the daytime, and they would *not* put it on at night; and if you forced it on yourself, they *would* take it off again the minute your back was turned.

Now there is the history of that burglar alarm—everything just as it happened; nothing extenuated, and naught set down in malice. Yes, sir,—and when I had slept nine years with burglars, and maintained an expensive burglar alarm the whole time, for their protection, not mine, and at my sole cost—for not a d——d cent could I ever get *them* to contribute—I just said to Mrs. McWilliams that I had had enough of that kind of pie; so with her full consent I took the whole thing out and traded it off for a dog, and shot the dog. I don't know what *you* think about it, Mr. Twain; but *I* think those things are made solely in the interest of the burglars. Yes, sir, a burglar alarm combines in its person all that is objectionable about a fire, a riot, and a harem, and at the same time had none of the compensating advantages, of one sort or another, that customarily belong with that combination. Good-by: I get off here.

1882

Playing Courier

A time would come when we must go from Aix-les-Bains to Geneva, and from thence, by a series of day-long and tangled journeys, to Bayreuth in Bavaria. I should have to have a courier, of course, to take care of so considerable a party as mine.

But I procrastinated. The time slipped along, and at last I woke up one day to the fact that we were ready to move and had no courier. I then resolved upon what I felt was a foolhardy thing, but I was in the humor of it. I said I would make the first stage without help—I did it.

I brought the party from Aix to Geneva by myself—four people. The distance was two hours and more, and there was one change of cars. There was not an accident of any kind, except leaving a valise and some other matters on the platform—a thing which can hardly be called an accident, it is so common. So I offered to conduct the party all the way to Bayreuth.

This was a blunder, though it did not seem so at the time. There was more detail than I thought there would be: 1, two persons whom we had left in a Genevan pension some weeks before must be collected and brought to the hotel; 2, I must notify the people on the Grand Quay who store trunks to bring seven of our stored trunks to the hotel and carry back seven which they would find piled in the lobby; 3, I must find out what part of Europe Bayreuth was in and buy seven railway tickets for that point; 4, I must send a telegram to a friend in the Netherlands; 5, it was now two in the afternoon, and we must look sharp and be ready for the first night train and make sure of sleeping-car tickets; 6, I must draw money at the bank.

It seemed to me that the sleeping-car tickets must be the most important thing, so I went to the station myself to make sure; hotel messengers are not always brisk people. It was a hot day, and I ought to have driven, but it seemed better economy to walk. It did not turn out so, because I lost my way and trebled the distance. I applied for the tickets, and they asked me which route I wanted to go by, and that embarrassed me and made me lose my head, there were so many people standing around, and I not knowing anything about the routes and not supposing there were going to be two; so I judged it best to go back and map out the road and come again.

I took a cab this time, but on my way up-stairs at the hotel I remembered that I was out of cigars, so I thought it would be well to get some while the matter was in my mind. It was only round the corner, and I didn't need the cab. I asked the cabman to wait where he was. Thinking of the telegram and trying to word it in my head, I forgot the cigars and the cab, and walked on indefinitely. I was going to have the hotel people send the telegram, but as I could not be far from the post-office by this time, I thought I would do it myself. But it was further than I had supposed. I found the place at last and wrote the telegram and handed it in. The clerk was a severe-looking, fidgety man, and he began to fire French questions at me in such a liquid form that I could not detect the joints between his words, and this made me lose my head again. But an Englishman stepped up and said the clerk wanted to know where he was to send the telegram. I could not tell him, because it was not my telegram, and I explained that I was merely sending it for a member of my party. But nothing would pacify the clerk but the address; so I said that if he was so particular I would go back and get it.

However, I thought I would go and collect those lacking two persons first, for it would be best to do everything systematically and in order, and one detail at a time. Then I remembered the cab was eating up my substance down at the hotel yonder; so I called another cab and told the man to go down and fetch it to the post-office and wait till I came.

I had a long, hot walk to collect those people, and when I got there they couldn't come with me because they had heavy satchels and must have a cab. I went away to find one, but before I ran across any I noticed that I had reached the neighborhood of the Grand Quay—at least I thought I had—so I judged I could save time by stepping around and arranging about the trunks. I stepped around about a mile, and although I did not find the Grand Quay, I found a cigar shop, and remembered about the cigars. I said I was going to Bayreuth, and wanted enough for the journey. The man asked me which route I was going to take. I said I did not know. He said he would recommend me to go by Zurich and various other places which he named, and offered to sell me seven second-class through tickets for twenty-two dollars apiece, which would be throwing off the discount which the railroads allowed him. I was already tired of riding second-class on first-class tickets, so I took him up.

By and by I found Natural & Co.'s storage office, and told them to send seven of our trunks to the hotel and pile them up in the lobby. It seemed to me that I was not delivering the whole of the message, still it was all I could find in my head.

Next I found the bank and asked for some money, but I had left my letter of credit somewhere and was not able to draw. I remembered now that I must have left it lying on the table where I wrote my telegram; so I got a cab and drove to the post-office and went up-stairs, and they said that a letter of credit had indeed been left on the table, but that it was now in the hands of the police authorities, and it would be necessary for me to go there and prove property. They sent a boy with me, and we went out the back way and walked a couple of miles and found the place; and then I remembered about my cabs, and asked the boy to send them to me when he got back to the post-office. It was nightfall now, and the Mayor had gone to dinner. I thought I would go to dinner myself, but the officer on duty thought differently, and I stayed. The Mayor dropped in at half past ten, but said it was too late to do anything to-night—come at 9.30 in the morning. The officer wanted to keep me all night, and said I was a suspicious-looking person, and probably did not own the letter of credit, and didn't know what a letter of credit was, but merely saw the real owner leave it lying on the table, and wanted to get it because I was probably a person that would want anything he could get, whether it was valuable or not. But the Mayor said he saw nothing suspicious about me, and that I seemed a harmless person and nothing the matter with me but a wandering mind, and not much of that. So I thanked him and he set me free, and I went home in my three cabs.

As I was dog-tired and in no condition to answer questions with discretion, I thought I would not disturb the Expedition at that time of night, as there was a vacant room I knew of at the other end of the hall; but I did not quite arrive there, as a watch had been set, the Expedition being anxious about me. I was placed in a galling situation. The Expedition sat stiff and forbidding on four chairs in a row, with shawls and things all on, satchels and guide-books in lap. They had been sitting like that for four hours, and the glass going down all the time. Yes, and they were waiting—waiting for me. It seemed to me that nothing but a sudden, happily contrived, and brilliant *tour de force* could break this iron front and make a diversion in my favor; so I shied my hat into the arena and followed it with a skip and a jump, shouting blithely:

"Ha, ha, here we all are, Mr. Merryman!"

Nothing could be deeper or stiller than the absence of applause which followed. But I kept on; there seemed no other way, though my confidence, poor enough before, had got a deadly check and was in effect gone.

I tried to be jocund out of a heavy heart, I tried to touch the other hearts there and soften the bitter resentment in those faces by throwing off bright and airy fun and making of the whole ghastly thing a joyously humorous incident, but this idea was not well conceived. It was not the right atmosphere for it. I got not one smile; not one line in those offended faces relaxed; I thawed nothing of the winter that looked out of those frosty eyes. I started one more breezy, poor effort, but the head of the Expedition cut into the center of it and said:

"Where have you been?"

I saw by the manner of this that the idea was to get down to cold business now. So I began my travels, but was cut short again.

"Where are the two others? We have been in frightful anxiety about them."

"Oh, they're all right. I was to fetch a cab. I will go straight off, and—"

"Sit down! Don't you know it is eleven o'clock? Where did you leave them?"

"At the pension."

"Why didn't you bring them?"

"Because we couldn't carry the satchels. And so I thought—"

"Thought! You should not try to think. One cannot think without the proper machinery. It is two miles to that pension. Did you go there without a cab?"

"I—well, I didn't intend to; it only happened so."

"How did it happen so?"

"Because I was at the post-office and I remembered that I had left a cab waiting here, and so, to stop that expense, I sent another cab to—to—"

"To what?"

"Well, I don't remember now, but I think the new cab was to have the hotel pay the old cab, and send it away."

"What good would that do?"

"What good would it do? It would stop the expense, wouldn't it?"

"By putting the new cab in its place to continue the expense?"

I didn't say anything.

"Why didn't you have the new cab come back for you?"

"Oh, that is what I did. I remember now. Yes, that is what I did. Because I recollect that when I—"

"Well, then, why didn't it come back for you?"

"To the post-office? Why, it did."

"Very well, then, how did you come to walk to the pension?"

"I—I don't quite remember how that happened. Oh, yes, I do remember now. I wrote the despatch to send to the Netherlands, and—"

"Oh, thank goodness, you did accomplish something! I wouldn't have had you fail to send—what makes you look like that! You are trying to avoid my eye. That despatch is the most important thing that— You haven't sent that despatch!"

"I haven't said I didn't send it."

"You don't need to. Oh, dear, I wouldn't have had that telegram fail for anything. Why didn't you send it?"

"Well, you see, with so many things to do and think of, I—they're very particular there, and after I had written the telegram—"

"Oh, never mind, let it go, explanations can't help the matter now—what will he think of us?"

"Oh, that's all right, that's all right, he'll think we gave the telegram to the hotel people, and that they—"

"Why, certainly! Why didn't you do that? There was no other rational way."

"Yes, I know, but then I had it on my mind that I must be sure and get to the bank and draw some money—"

"Well, you are entitled to some credit, after all, for thinking of that, and I don't wish to be too hard on you, though you must acknowledge yourself that you have cost us all a good deal of trouble, and some of it not necessary. How much did you draw?"

"Well, I–I had an idea that–that–"

"That what?"

"That–well, it seems to me that in the circumstances–so many of us, you know, and–and–"

"What are you mooning about? Do turn your face this way and let me–why, you haven't drawn any money!"

"Well, the banker said–"

"Never mind what the banker said. You must have had a reason of your own. Not a reason, exactly, but something which–"

"Well, then, the simple fact was that I hadn't my letter of credit."

"Hadn't your letter of credit?"

"Hadn't my letter of credit."

"Don't repeat me like that. Where was it?"

"At the post-office."

"What was it doing there?"

"Well, I forgot it and left it there."

"Upon my word, I've seen a good many couriers, but of all the couriers that ever I–"

"I've done the best I could."

"Well, so you have, poor thing, and I'm wrong to abuse you so when you've been working yourself to death while we've been sitting here only thinking of our vexations instead of feeling grateful for what you were trying to do for us. It will all come out right. We can take the 7.30 train in the morning just as well. You've bought the tickets?"

"I have–and it's a bargain, too. Second class."

"I'm glad of it. Everybody else travels second class, and we might just as well save that ruinous extra charge. What did you pay?"

"Twenty-two dollars apiece–through to Bayreuth."

"Why, I didn't know you could buy through tickets anywhere but in London and Paris."

"Some people can't, maybe; but some people can–of whom I am one of which, it appears."

"It seems a rather high price."

"On the contrary, the dealer knocked off his commission."

"Dealer?"

"Yes–I bought them at a cigar shop."

"That reminds me. We shall have to get up pretty early, and so there should be no packing to do. Your umbrella, your rubbers, your cigars—what is the matter?"

"Hang it, I've left the cigars at the bank."

"Just think of it! Well, your umbrella?"

"I'll have that all right. There's no hurry."

"What do you mean by that?"

"Oh, that's all right; I'll take care of—"

"Where is that umbrella?"

"It's just the merest step—it won't take me—"

"Where is it?"

"Well, I think I left it at the cigar shop; but anyway—"

"Take your feet out from under that thing. It's just as I expected! Where are your rubbers?"

"They—well—"

"Where are your rubbers?"

"It's got so dry now—well, everybody says there's not going to be another drop of—"

"Where—are—your—rubbers?"

"Well, you see—well, it was this way. First, the officer said—"

"What officer?"

"Police officer; but the Mayor, he—"

"What Mayor?"

"Mayor of Geneva; but I said—"

"Wait. What is the matter with you?"

"Who, me? Nothing. They both tried to persuade me to stay, and—"

"Stay where?"

"Well, the fact is—"

"Where have you been? What's kept you out till half past ten at night?"

"Oh, you see, after I lost my letter of credit, I—"

"You are beating around the bush a good deal. Now, answer the question in just one straightforward word. Where are those rubbers?"

"They—well, they're in the county jail."

I started a placating smile, but it petrified. The climate was unsuitable. Spending three or four hours in jail did not seem to the Expedition humorous. Neither did it to me, at bottom.

I had to explain the whole thing, and, of course, it came out then that we couldn't take the early train, because that would leave my letter of credit in hock still. It did look as if we had all got to go to bed estranged and unhappy, but by good luck that was prevented. There happened to be mention of the trunks, and I was able to say I had attended to that feature.

"There, you are just as good and thoughtful and painstaking and intelligent as you can be, and it's a shame to find so much fault with you, and there sha'n't be another word of it. You've done beautifully, admirably, and I'm sorry I ever said one ungrateful word to you."

This hit deeper than some of the other things and made me uncomfortable, because I wasn't feeling as solid about that trunk errand as I wanted to. There seemed somehow to be a defect about it somewhere, though I couldn't put my finger on it, and didn't like to stir the matter just now, it being late and maybe well enough to let well enough alone.

Of course there was music in the morning, when it was found that we couldn't leave by the early train. But I had no time to wait; I got only the opening bars of the overture, and then started out to get my letter of credit.

It seemed a good time to look into the trunk business and rectify it if it needed it, and I had a suspicion that it did. I was too late. The concierge said he had shipped the trunks to Zurich the evening before. I asked him how he could do that without exhibiting passage tickets.

"Not necessary in Switzerland. You pay for your trunks and send them where you please. Nothing goes free but your hand-baggage."

"How much did you pay on them?"

"A hundred and forty francs."

"Twenty-eight dollars. There's something wrong about that trunk business, sure."

Next I met the porter. He said:

"You have not slept well, is it not? You have the worn look. If you would like a courier, a good one has arrived last night, and is not engaged for five days already, by the name of Ludi. We recommend him; *das heisst,* the Grand Hôtel Beau Rivage recommends him."

I declined with coldness. My spirit was not broken yet. And I did not like having my condition taken notice of in this way. I was at the county jail by nine o'clock, hoping that the Mayor might chance to come before his regular hour; but he didn't. It was dull there. Every time I offered to touch anything, or look at anything, or do anything, or refrain from doing anything, the policeman said it was "*défendu*." I thought I would practise my French on him, but he wouldn't have that either. It seemed to make him particularly bitter to hear his own tongue.

The Mayor came at last, and then there was no trouble; for the minute he had convened the Supreme Court—they always do whenever there is valuable property in dispute—and got everything shipshape and sentries posted, and had prayer by the chaplain, my unsealed letter was brought and opened, and there wasn't anything in it but some photographs; because, as I remembered now, I had taken out the letter of credit so as to make room for the photographs, and had put the letter in my other pocket, which I proved to everybody's satisfaction by fetching it out and showing it with a good deal of exultation. So then the court looked at each other in a vacant kind of way, and then at me, and then at each other again, and finally let me go, but said it was imprudent for me to be at large, and asked me what my profession was. I said I was a courier. They lifted up their eyes in a kind of reverent way and said, "*Du lieber Gott!*" and I said a word of courteous thanks for their apparent admiration and hurried off to the bank.

However, being a courier was already making me a great stickler for order and system and one thing at a time and each thing in its own proper turn; so I passed by the bank and branched off and started for the two lacking members of the Expedition. A cab lazied by, and I took it upon persuasion. I gained no speed by this, but it was a reposeful turnout and I liked reposefulness. The week-long jubilations over the six hundredth anniversary of the birth of Swiss liberty and the Signing of the Compact was at flood-tide, and all the streets were clothed in fluttering flags.

The horse and the driver had been drunk three days and nights, and had known no stall nor bed meantime. They looked as I felt—dreamy and seedy. But we arrived in course of time. I went in and rang, and asked a housemaid to rush out the lacking members. She said something which I did not understand, and I returned to the chariot. The girl had probably told me that those people did not belong on her floor, and that it would be judicious for me to go higher, and ring from floor to floor till I found them; for in those Swiss flats there does not seem to be any way to find the right family but to be patient and guess your way along up. I calculated that I must wait fifteen minutes, there being three details inseparable from an occasion of this sort: 1, put on hats and come down and climb in; 2, return of one to get "my other glove"; 3, presently, return of the other one to fetch "my *French Verbs at a Glance*." I would muse during the fifteen minutes and take it easy.

A very still and blank interval ensued, and then I felt a hand on my shoulder and started. The intruder was a policeman. I glanced up and perceived that there was new scenery. There was a good deal of a crowd, and they had that pleased and interested look which such a crowd wears when they see that somebody is out of luck. The horse was asleep, and so was the driver, and some boys had hung them and me full of gaudy decorations stolen from the innumerable banner-poles. It was a scandalous spectacle. The officer said:

"I'm sorry, but we can't have you sleeping here all day."

I was wounded, and said with dignity:

"I beg your pardon, I was not sleeping; I was thinking."

"Well, you can think if you want to, but you've got to think to yourself; you disturb the whole neighborhood."

It was a poor joke, and it made the crowd laugh. I snore at night sometimes, but it is not likely that I would do such a thing in the daytime and in such a place. The officer undecorated us, and seemed sorry for our friendlessness, and really tried to be humane, but he said we mustn't stop there any longer or he would have to charge us rent—it was the law, he said, and he went on to say in a sociable way that I was looking pretty moldy, and he wished he knew—

I shut him off pretty austerely, and said I hoped one might celebrate a little these days, especially when one was personally concerned.

"Personally?" he asked. "How?"

"Because six hundred years ago an ancestor of mine signed the compact."

He reflected a moment, then looked me over and said:

"Ancestor! It's my opinion you signed it yourself. For of all the old ancient relics that ever I—but never mind about that. What is it you are waiting here for so long?"

I said:

"I'm not waiting here so long at all. I'm waiting fifteen minutes till they forget a glove and a book and go back and get them." Then I told him who they were that I had come for.

He was very obliging, and began to shout inquiries to the tiers of heads and shoulders projecting from the windows above us. Then a woman away up there sang out:

"Oh, they? Why, I got them a cab and they left here long ago—half past eight, I should say."

It was annoying. I glanced at my watch, but didn't say anything. The officer said:

"It is a quarter of twelve, you see. You should have inquired better. You have been asleep three-quarters of an hour, and in such a sun as this. You are baked—baked black. It is wonderful. And you will miss your train, perhaps. You interest me greatly. What is your occupation?"

I said I was a courier. It seemed to stun him, and before he could come to we were gone.

When I arrived in the third story of the hotel I found our quarters vacant. I was not surprised. The moment a courier takes his eye off his tribe they go shopping. The nearer it is to train-time the surer they are to go. I sat down to try and think out what I had best do next, but presently the hall-boy found me there, and said the Expedition had gone to the station half an hour before. It was the first time I had known them to do a rational thing, and it was very confusing. This is one of the things that make a courier's life so difficult and uncertain. Just as matters are going the smoothest, his people will strike a lucid interval, and down go all his arrangements to wreck and ruin.

The train was to leave at twelve noon sharp. It was now ten minutes after twelve. I could be at the station in ten minutes. I saw I had no great amount of leeway, for this was the lightning express, and on the Continent the lightning expresses are pretty fastidious about getting away some time during the advertised day. My people were the only ones remaining in the waiting-room; everybody else had passed through and "mounted the train," as they say in those regions. They were exhausted with nervousness and fret, but I comforted them and heartened them up, and we made our rush.

But no; we were out of luck again. The doorkeeper was not satisfied with the tickets. He examined them cautiously, deliberately, suspiciously; then glared at me awhile, and after that he called another official. The two examined the tickets and called another official. These called others, and the convention discussed and discussed, and gesticulated and carried on, until I begged that they would consider how time was flying, and just pass a few resolutions and let us go. Then they said very courteously that there was a defect in the tickets, and asked me where I got them.

I judged I saw what the trouble was now. You see, I had bought the tickets in a cigar shop, and, of course, the tobacco smell was on them; without doubt, the thing they were up to was to work the tickets through the Custom House and to collect duty on that smell. So I resolved to be perfectly frank; it is sometimes the best way. I said:

"Gentlemen, I will not deceive you. These railway tickets—"

"Ah, pardon, monsieur! These are not railway tickets."

"Oh," I said, "is that the defect?"

"Ah, truly yes, monsieur. These are lottery tickets, yes; and it is a lottery which has been drawn two years ago."

I affected to be greatly amused; it is all one can do in such circumstances; it is all one can do, and yet there is no value in it; it deceives nobody, and you can see that everybody around pities you and is ashamed of you. One of the hardest situations in life, I think, is to be full of grief and a sense of defeat and shabbiness that way, and yet have to put on an outside of archness and gaiety, while all the time you know that your own Expedition, the treasures of your heart, and whose love and reverence you are by the custom of our civilization entitled to, are being consumed with humiliation before strangers to see you earning and getting a compassion which is a stigma, a brand—a brand which certifies you to be—oh, anything and everything which is fatal to human respect.

I said, cheerily, it was all right, just one of those little accidents that was likely to happen to anybody—I would have the right tickets in two minutes, and we would catch the train yet, and, moreover, have something to laugh about all through the journey. I did get the tickets in time, all stamped and complete, but then it turned out that I couldn't take them, because in taking so much pains about the two missing members I had skipped the bank and hadn't the money. So then the train left, and there didn't seem to be anything to do but go back to the hotel, which we did; but it was kind of melancholy and not much said. I tried to start a few subjects, like scenery and transubstantiation, and those sorts of things, but they didn't seem to hit the weather right.

We had lost our good rooms, but we got some others which were pretty scattering, but would answer. I judged things would brighten now, but the Head of the Expedition said, "Send up the trunks." It made me feel pretty cold. There was a doubtful something about that trunk business. I was almost sure of it. I was going to suggest—

But a wave of the hand sufficiently restrained me, and I was informed that we would now camp for three days and see if we could rest up.

I said all right, never mind ringing; I would go down and attend to the trunks myself. I got a cab and went straight to Mr. Charles Natural's place, and asked what order it was I had left there.

"To send seven trunks to the hotel."

"And were you to bring any back?"

"No."

"You are sure I didn't tell you to bring back seven that would be found piled in the lobby?"

"Absolutely sure you didn't."

"Then the whole fourteen are gone to Zurich or Jericho or somewhere, and there is going to be more debris around that hotel when the Expedition—"

I didn't finish, because my mind was getting to be in a good deal of a whirl, and when you are that way you think you have finished a sentence when you haven't, and you go mooning and dreaming away, and the first thing you know you get run over by a dray or a cow or something.

I left the cab there—I forgot it—and on my way back I thought it all out and concluded to resign, because otherwise I should be nearly sure to be discharged. But I didn't believe it would be a good idea to resign in person; I could do it by message. So I sent for Mr. Ludi and explained that there was a courier going to resign on account of incompatibility or fatigue or something, and as he had four or five vacant days, I would like to insert him into that vacancy if he thought he could fill it. When everything was arranged I got him to go up and say to the Expedition that, owing to an error made by Mr. Natural's people, we were out of trunks here, but would have plenty in Zurich, and we'd better take the first train, freight, gravel, or construction, and move right along.

He attended to that and came down with an invitation for me to go up—yes, certainly; and, while we walked along over to the bank to get money, and collect my cigars and tobacco, and to the cigar shop to trade back the lottery tickets and get my umbrella, and to Mr. Natural's to pay that cab and send it away, and to the county jail to get my rubbers and leave p. p. c. cards for the Mayor and Supreme Court, he described the weather to me that was prevailing on the upper levels there with the Expedition, and I saw that I was doing very well where I was.

I stayed out in the woods till 4 P.M., to let the weather moderate, and then turned up at the station just in time to take the three-o'clock express for Zurich along with the Expedition, now in the hands of Ludi, who conducted its complex affairs with little apparent effort or inconvenience.

Well, I had worked like a slave while I was in office, and done the very best I knew how; yet all that these people dwelt upon or seemed to care to remember were the defects of my administration, not its creditable features. They would skip over a thousand creditable features to remark upon and reiterate and fuss about just one fact, till it seemed to me they would wear it out; and not much of a fact, either, taken by itself—the fact that I elected myself courier in Geneva, and put in work enough to carry a circus to Jerusalem, and yet never even got my gang out of the town. I finally said I didn't wish to hear any more about the subject, it made me tired. And I told them to their faces that I would never be a courier again to save anybody's life. And if I live long enough I'll prove it. I think it's a difficult, brain-racking, overworked, and thoroughly ungrateful office, and the main bulk of its wages is a sore heart and a bruised spirit.

1891

The Fourth of July

[An after-dinner speech at a Fourth of July gathering, in London, of Americans]

MR. CHAIRMAN AND LADIES AND GENTLEMEN: I thank you for the compliment which has just been tendered me, and to show my appreciation of it I will not afflict you with many words. It is pleasant to celebrate in this peaceful way, upon this old mother soil, the anniversary of an experiment which was born of war with this same land so long ago, and wrought out to a successful issue by the devotion of our ancestors. It has taken nearly a hundred years to bring the English and Americans into kindly and mutually appreciative relations, but I believe it has been accomplished at last. It was a great step when the two last misunderstandings were settled by arbitration instead of cannon. It is another great step when England adopts our sewing-machines without claiming the invention—as usual. It was another when they imported one of our sleeping-cars the other day. And it warmed my heart more than I can tell, yesterday, when I witnessed the spectacle of an Englishman ordering an American sherry cobbler of his own free will and accord—and not only that but with a great brain and a level head reminding the barkeeper not to forget the strawberries. With a common origin, a common language, a common literature, a common religion and—common drinks, what is longer needful to the cementing of the two nations together in a permanent bond of brotherhood?

This is an age of progress, and ours is a progressive land. A great and glorious land, too—a land which has developed a Washington, a Franklin, a William M. Tweed, a Longfellow, a Motley, a Jay Gould, a Samuel C. Pomeroy, a recent Congress which has never had its equal (in some respects), and a United States Army which conquered sixty Indians in eight months by tiring them out—which is much better than uncivilized slaughter, God knows. We have a criminal jury system which is superior to any in the world; and its efficiency is only marred by the difficulty of finding twelve men every day who don't know anything and can't read. And I may observe that we have an insanity plea that would have saved Cain. I think I can say, and say with pride, that we have some legislatures that bring higher prices than any in the world.

I refer with effusion to our railway system, which consents to let us live, though it might do the opposite, being our owners. It only destroyed three thousand and seventy lives last year by collisions, and twenty-seven thousand two hundred and sixty by running over heedless and unnecessary people at crossings. The companies seriously regretted the killing of these thirty thousand people, and went so far as to pay for some of them—voluntarily, of course, for the meanest of us would not claim that we possess a court treacherous enough to enforce a law against a railway company. But, thank Heaven, the railway companies are generally disposed to do the right and kindly thing without compulsion. I know of an instance which greatly touched me at the time. After an accident the company sent home the remains of a dear distant old relative of mine in a basket, with the remark, "Please state what figure you hold him at—and return the basket." Now there couldn't be anything friendlier than that.

But I must not stand here and brag all night. However, you won't mind a body bragging a little about his country on the Fourth of July. It is a fair and legitimate time to fly the eagle. I will say only one more word of brag—and a hopeful one. It is this. We have a form of government which gives each man a fair chance and no favor. With us no individual is born with a right to look down upon his neighbor and hold him in contempt. Let such of us as are not dukes find our consolation in that. And we may find hope for the future in the fact that as unhappy as is the condition of our political morality to-day, England has risen up out of a far fouler since the days when Charles I. ennobled courtesans and all political place was a matter of bargain and sale. There is hope for us yet.*

1875

* At least the above is the speech which I was going to make, but our minister, General Schenck, presided, and after the blessing, got up and made a great long inconceivably dull harangue, and wound up by saying that inasmuch as speech-making did not seem to exhilarate the guests much, all further oratory would be dispensed with during the evening, and we could just sit and talk privately to our elbow-neighbors and have a good sociable time. It is known that in consequence of that remark forty-four perfected speeches died in the womb. The depression, the gloom, the solemnity that reigned over the banquet from that time forth will be a lasting memory with many that were there. By that one thoughtless remark General Schenck lost forty-four of the best friends he had in England. More than one said that night, "And this is the sort of person that is sent to represent us in a great sister empire!"

Plymouth Rock and the Pilgrims

Address at the First Annual Dinner, N. E. Society, Philadelphia, December 22, 1881

On calling upon Mr. Clemens to make response, President Rollins said:

"This sentiment has been assigned to one who was never *exactly* born in New England, nor, perhaps, were any of his ancestors. He is not *technically*, therefore, of New England descent. Under the painful circumstances in which he has found himself, however, he has done the best he could—he has had all his children born there,* and has made of *himself* a New England *ancestor*. He is a self-made man. More than this, and better even, in cheerful, hopeful, helpful literature he is of New England *ascent*. To *ascend* there in anything that's reasonable is difficult, for—confidentially, with the door shut—we all know that they are the brightest, ablest sons of that goodly land who never leave it, and it is among and above *them* that Mr. Twain has made his brilliant and permanent ascent—become a man of mark."

I rise to protest. I have kept still for years, but really I think there is no sufficient justification for this sort of thing. What do you want to celebrate those people for?—those ancestors of yours of 1620—the *Mayflower* tribe, I mean. What do you want to celebrate *them* for? Your pardon: the gentleman at my left assures me that you are not celebrating the Pilgrims themselves, but the landing of the Pilgrims at Plymouth Rock on the 22d of December. So you are celebrating their landing. Why, the other pretext was thin enough, but this is thinner than ever; the other was tissue, tinfoil, fish-bladder, but this is gold-leaf. Celebrating their landing! What was there remarkable about it, I would like to know? What can you be thinking of? Why, those Pilgrims had been at sea three or four months. It was the very

* A slight mistake: Mark Twain's children were born in Elmira, in the state of New York.

middle of winter: it was as cold as death off Cape Cod there. Why shouldn't they come ashore? If they *hadn't* landed there would be some reason for celebrating the fact. It would have been a case of monumental leatherheadedness which the world would not willingly let die. If it had been *you*, gentlemen, you probably wouldn't have landed, but you have no shadow of right to be celebrating, in your ancestors, gifts which they did not exercise, but only transmitted. Why, to be celebrating the mere landing of the Pilgrims—to be trying to make out that this most natural and simple and customary procedure was an extraordinary circumstance—a circumstance to be amazed at, and admired, aggrandized and glorified, at orgies like this for two hundred and sixty years—hang it, a horse would have known enough to land; a horse— Pardon again; the gentleman on my right assures me that it was not merely the landing of the Pilgrims that we are celebrating, but the Pilgrims themselves. So we have struck an inconsistency here—one says it was the landing, the other says it was the Pilgrims. It is an inconsistency characteristic of your intractable and disputatious tribe, for you never agree about anything but Boston. Well, then, what do you want to celebrate those Pilgrims for? They were a mighty hard lot—you know it. I grant you, without the slightest unwillingness, that they were a deal more gentle and merciful and just than were the people of Europe of that day; I grant you that they are better than their predecessors. But what of that?—that is nothing. People always progress. You are better than your fathers and grandfathers were (this is the first time I have ever aimed a measureless slander at the departed, for I consider such things improper). Yes, those among you who have not been in the penitentiary, if such there be, are better than your fathers and grandfathers were; but is that any sufficient reason for getting up annual dinners and celebrating you? No, by no means—by no means. Well, I repeat, those Pilgrims were a hard lot. They took good care of themselves, but they abolished everybody else's ancestors. I am a border-ruffian from the State of Missouri. I am a Connecticut Yankee by adoption. In me, you have Missouri morals, Connecticut culture; this, gentlemen, is the combination which makes the perfect man. But where are my ancestors? Whom shall I celebrate? Where shall I find the raw material?

My first American ancestor, gentlemen, was an Indian—an early Indian. Your ancestors skinned him alive, and I am an orphan. Later ancestors of mine were the Quakers William Robinson, Marmaduke Stevenson, *et al.* Your tribe chased them out of the country for their religion's sake; promised them death if they came back; for your ancestors had forsaken the homes they loved, and braved the perils of the sea, the implacable climate, and the savage wilderness, to acquire that highest and most precious of boons, freedom for every man on this broad continent to worship according to the dictates of his own conscience—and they were not going to allow a lot of pestiferous Quakers to interfere with it. Your ancestors broke forever the chains of political slavery, and gave the vote to every man in this wide land, excluding none!—none except those who did not belong to the orthodox church. Your ancestors—yes, they were a hard lot; but, nevertheless, they gave us religious liberty to worship as they required us to worship, and political liberty to vote as the church required; and so I the bereft one, I the forlorn one, am here to do my best to help you celebrate them right.

The Quaker woman Elizabeth Hooton was an ancestress of mine. Your people were pretty severe with her—you will confess that. But, poor thing! I believe they changed her opinions before she died, and took her into their fold; and so we have every reason to presume that when she died she went to the same place which your ancestors went to. It is a great pity, for she was a good woman. Roger Williams was an ancestor of mine. I don't really remember what your people did with him. But they banished him to Rhode Island, anyway. And then, I believe, recognizing that this was really carrying harshness to an unjustifiable extreme, they took pity on him and burned him. They were a hard lot! All those Salem witches were ancestors of mine! Your people made it tropical for them. Yes, they did; by pressure and the gallows they made such a clean deal with them that there hasn't been a witch and hardly a halter in our family from that day to this, and that is one hundred and eighty-nine years. The first slave brought into New England out of Africa by your progenitors was an ancestor of mine—for I am of a mixed breed, an infinitely shaded and exquisite Mongrel. I'm not one of your sham meerschaums that you can color in a week. No, my complexion is the patient art of eight generations. Well, in my own time, I had acquired a lot of my kin—by purchase, and swapping around, and one way and another—and was getting along very well. Then, with the inborn perversity of your lineage, you got up a war, and took them all away from me. And so, again am I bereft, again am I forlorn; no drop of my blood flows in the veins of any living being who is marketable.

O my friends, hear me and reform! I seek your good, not mine. You have heard the speeches. Disband these New England societies—nurseries of a system of steadily augmenting laudation and hosannaing, which, if persisted in uncurbed, may some day in the remote future beguile you into prevaricating and bragging. Oh, stop, stop, while you are still temperate in your appreciation of your ancestors! Hear me, I beseech you; get up an auction and sell Plymouth Rock! The Pilgrims were a simple and ignorant race. They never had seen any good rocks before, or at least any that were not watched, and so they were excusable for hopping ashore in frantic delight and clapping an iron fence around this one. But you, gentlemen, are educated; you are enlightened; you know that in the rich land of your nativity, opulent New England, overflowing with rocks, this one isn't worth, at the outside, more than thirty-five cents. Therefore, sell it, before it is injured by exposure, or at least throw it open to the patent-medicine advertisements, and let it earn its taxes.

Yes, hear your true friend—your only true friend—list to his voice. Disband these societies, hotbeds of vice, of moral decay—perpetuators of ancestral superstition. Here on this board I see water, I see milk, I see the wild and deadly lemonade. These are but steps upon the downward path. Next we shall see tea, then chocolate, then coffee—hotel coffee. A few more years—all too few, I fear—mark my words, we shall have cider! Gentlemen, pause ere it be too late. You are on the broad road which leads to dissipation, physical ruin, moral decay, gory crime, and the gallows! I beseech you, I implore you, in the name of your anxious friends, in the name of your impending widows and orphans, stop ere it be too late. Disband these New England societies, renounce these soul-blistering saturnalia, cease from varnishing the rusty reputations of your long-vanished ancestors—the super-high-moral old iron-clads of Cape Cod, the pious buccaneers of Plymouth Rock—go home, and try to learn to behave!

However, chaff and nonsense aside, I think I honor and appreciate your Pilgrim stock as much as you do yourselves, perhaps; and I indorse and adopt a sentiment uttered by a grandfather of mine once—a man of sturdy opinions, of sincere make of mind, and not given to flattery. He said: "People may talk as they like about that Pilgrim stock, but, after all's said and done, it would be pretty hard to improve on those people; and, as for me, I don't mind coming out flatfooted and saying there ain't any way to improve on them—except having them born in Missouri!"

1881

Woman, God Bless Her!*

The toast includes the sex, universally; it is to Woman comprehensively, wheresoever she may be found. Let us consider her ways. First comes the matter of dress. This is a most important consideration, and must be disposed of before we can intelligently proceed to examine the profounder depths of the theme. For text let us take the dress of two antipodal types—the savage woman of Central Africa and the cultivated daughter of our high modern civilization. Among the Fans, a great negro tribe, a woman when dressed for home, or to go out shopping or calling, doesn't wear anything at all but just her complexion. That is all; it is her entire outfit. It is the lightest costume in the world, but is made of the darkest material. It has often been mistaken for mourning. It is the trimmest, and neatest, and gracefulest costume that is now in fashion; it wears well, is fast colors, doesn't show dirt, you don't have to send it down-town to wash, and have some of it come back scorched with the flat-iron, and some of it with the buttons ironed off, and some of it petrified with starch, and some of it chewed by the calf, and some of it rotted with acids, and some of it exchanged for other customers' things that haven't any virtue but holiness, and ten-twelfths of the pieces overcharged for and the rest of the dozen "mislaid." And it always fits; it is the perfection of a fit. And it is the handiest dress in the whole realm of fashion. It is always ready, always "done up." When you call on a Fan lady and send up your card, the hired girl never says, "Please take a seat, madame is dressing; she'll be down in three-quarters of an hour." No, madame is always dressed, always ready to receive; and before you can get the door-mat before your eyes she is in your midst. Then, again, the

* A speech delivered before the New England Society in the City of New York, December 22, 1882.

Fan ladies don't go to church to see what each other has got on; and they don't go back home and describe it and slander it.

Such is the dark child of savagery, as to every-day toilet; and thus, curiously enough, she finds a point of contact with the fair daughter of civilization and high fashion—who often has "nothing to wear"; and thus these widely-separated types of the sex meet upon common ground. Yes, such is the Fan woman as she appears in her simple, unostentatious, every-day toilet; but on state occasions she is more dressy. At a banquet she wears bracelets; at a lecture she wears earrings and a belt; at a ball she wears stockings—and, with true feminine fondness for display, she wears them on her arms; at a funeral she wears a jacket of tar and ashes; at a wedding the bride who can afford it puts on pantaloons. Thus the dark child of savagery and the fair daughter of civilization meet once more upon common ground, and these two touches of nature make their whole world kin.

Now we will consider the dress of our other type. A large part of the daughter of civilization is her dress—as it should be. Some civilized women would lose half their charm without dress; and some would lose all of it. The daughter of modern civilization dressed at her utmost best, is a marvel of exquisite and beautiful art and expense. All the lands, all the climes, and all the arts are laid under tribute to furnish her forth. Her linen is from Belfast, her robe is from Paris, her lace is from Venice, or Spain, or France; her feathers are from the remote regions of Southern Africa, her furs from the remoter home of the iceberg and the aurora, her fan from Japan, her diamonds from Brazil, her bracelets from California, her pearls from Ceylon, her cameos from Rome; she has gems and trinkets from buried Pompeii, and others that graced comely Egyptian forms that have been dust and ashes now for forty centuries; her watch is from Geneva, her card-case is from China, her hair is from —from—I don't know where her hair is from; I never could find out. That is, her other hair—her public hair, her Sunday hair; I don't mean the hair she goes to bed with. Why, you ought to know the hair I mean; it's that thing which she calls a switch, and which resembles a switch as much as it resembles a brickbat or a shotgun, or any other thing which you correct people with. It's that thing which she twists and then coils round and round her head, beehive fashion, and then tucks the end in under the hive and harpoons it with a hairpin. And that reminds me of a trifle: any time you want to, you can glance around the carpet of a Pullman car, and go and pick up a hairpin; but not to save your life can you get any woman in that car to acknowledge that hairpin. Now, isn't that strange? But it's true. The woman who has never swerved from cast-iron veracity and fidelity in her whole life will, when confronted with this crucial test, deny her hairpin. She will deny that hairpin before a hundred witnesses. I have stupidly got into more trouble and more hot water trying to hunt up the owner of a hairpin in a Pullman car than by any other indiscretion of my life.

Well, you see what the daughter of civilization is when she is dressed, and you have seen what the daughter of savagery is when she isn't. Such is woman, as to costume. I come now to consider her in her higher and nobler aspects—as mother, wife, widow, grass-widow, mother-in-law, hired girl, telegraph operator, telephone helloer, queen, book-agent, wet-nurse, stepmother, boss, professional fat woman, professional double-headed woman, professional beauty, and so forth and so on.

We will simply discuss these few—let the rest of the sex tarry in Jericho till we come again. First in the list of right, and first in our gratitude, comes a woman who—why, dear me, I've been talking three-quarters of an hour! I beg a thousand pardons. But you see, yourselves, that I had a large contract. I have accomplished something, anyway. I have introduced my subject. And if I had till next Forefathers' Day, I am satisfied that I could discuss it as adequately and appreciatively as so gracious and noble a theme deserves. But as the matter stands now, let us finish as we began—and say, without jesting, but with all sincerity, "Woman—God bless her!"

1882

Glove Purchase in Gibraltar

[Early in June 1867 Clemens sailed on the *Quaker City*, a side-wheel steamship, on what had been advertised as a Holy Land excursion. Unlike most of his shipmates, he was a professional correspondent, chiefly for the San Francisco *Daily Alta California* but also for the New York *Tribune* and the New York *Herald*. After a stop at the Azores the ship visited Gibraltar.]

Every now and then, my glove purchase in Gibraltar last night intrudes itself upon me. Dan and the ship's surgeon and I had been up to the great square, listening to the music of the fine military bands, and contemplating English and Spanish female loveliness and fashion, and, at 9 o'clock, were on our way to the theatre, when we met the General, the Judge, the Commodore, the Colonel, and the Commissioner of the United States of America to Europe, Asia, and Africa, who had been to the Club House, to register their several titles and impoverish the bill of fare; and they told us to go over to the little variety store, near the Hall of Justice, and buy some kid gloves. They said they were elegant, and very moderate in price. It seemed a stylish thing to go to the theatre in kid gloves, and we acted upon the hint. A very handsome young lady in the store offered me a pair of blue gloves. I did not want blue, but she said they would look very pretty on a hand like mine. The remark touched me tenderly. I glanced furtively at my hand, and somehow it did seem rather a comely member. I tried a glove on my left, and blushed a little. Manifestly the size was too small for me. But I felt gratified when she said:

"Oh, it is just right!"—yet I knew it was no such thing.

I tugged at it diligently, but it was discouraging work. She said:

"Ah! I see *you* are accustomed to wearing kid gloves—but some gentlemen are *so* awkward about putting them on."

It was the last compliment I had expected. I only understand putting on the buckskin article perfectly. I made another effort, and tore the glove from the base of the thumb into the palm of the hand—and tried to hide the rent. She kept up her compliments, and I kept up my determination to deserve them or die:

"Ah, you have had experience!" [A rip down the back of the hand.] "They are just right for you—your hand is very small—if they tear you need not pay for them." [A rent across the middle.] "I can always tell when a gentleman understands putting on kid gloves. There is a grace about it that only comes with long practice." [The whole afterguard of the glove "fetched away," as the sailors say, the fabric parted across the knuckles, and nothing was left but a melancholy ruin.]

I was too much flattered to make an exposure, and throw the merchandise on the angel's hands. I was hot, vexed, confused, but still happy; but I hated the other boys for taking such an absorbing interest in the proceedings. I wished they were in Jericho. I felt exquisitely mean when I said cheerfully,—

"This one does very well; it fits elegantly. I like a glove that fits. No, never mind, ma'am, never mind; I'll put the other on in the street. It is warm here."

It *was* warm. It was the warmest place I ever was in. I paid the bill, and as I passed out with a fascinating bow, I thought I detected a light in the woman's eye that was gently ironical; and when I looked back from the street, and she was laughing all to herself about something or other, I said to myself, with withering sarcasm, "Oh, certainly; *you* know how to put on kid gloves, don't you?—a self-complacent ass, ready to be flattered out of your senses by every petticoat that chooses to take the trouble to do it!"

The silence of the boys annoyed me. Finally, Dan said, musingly:

"Some gentlemen don't know how to put on kid gloves at all; but some do."

And the doctor said (to the moon, I thought,)

"But it is always easy to tell when a gentleman is used to putting on kid gloves."

Dan soliloquized, after a pause:

"Ah, yes; there is a grace about it that only comes with long, very long practice."

"Yes, indeed, I've noticed that when a man hauls on a kid glove like he was dragging a cat out of an ash-hole by the tail, *he* understands putting on kid gloves; *he's* had ex—"

"Boys, enough of a thing's enough! You think you are very smart, I suppose, but I don't. And if you go and tell any of those old gossips in the ship about this thing, I'll never forgive you for it; that's all."

They let me alone then, for the time being. We always let each other alone in time to prevent ill feeling from spoiling a joke. But they had bought gloves, too, as I did. We threw all the purchases away together this morning. They were coarse, unsubstantial, freckled all over with broad yellow splotches, and could neither stand wear nor public exhibition. We had entertained an angel unawares, but we did not take her in. She did that for us.

From *The Innocents Abroad,* 1869

Parisian Shave

[From Marseilles, Clemens and some companions went by rail to Paris.]

Then we hunted for a barber-shop. From earliest infancy it had been a cherished ambition of mine to be shaved some day in a palatial barber-shop of Paris. I wished to recline at full length in a cushioned invalid chair, with pictures about me, and sumptuous furniture; with frescoed walls and gilded arches above me, and vistas of Corinthian columns stretching far before me; with perfumes of Araby to intoxicate my senses, and the slumbrous drone of distant noises to soothe me to sleep. At the end of an hour I would wake up regretfully and find my face as smooth and as soft as an infant's. Departing, I would lift my hands above that barber's head and say, "Heaven bless you, my son!"

So we searched high and low, for a matter of two hours, but never a barber-shop could we see. We saw only wig-making establishments, with shocks of dead and repulsive hair bound upon the heads of painted waxen brigands who stared out from glass boxes upon the passer-by, with their stony eyes, and scared him with the ghostly white of their countenances. We shunned these signs for a time, but finally we concluded that the wig-makers must of necessity be the barbers as well, since we could find no single legitimate representative of the fraternity. We entered and asked, and found that it was even so.

I said I wanted to be shaved. The barber inquired where my room was. I said, never mind where my room was, I wanted to be shaved—there, on the spot. The doctor said he would be shaved also. Then there was an excitement among those two barbers! There was a wild consultation, and afterwards a hurrying to and fro and a feverish gathering up of razors from obscure places and a ransacking for soap. Next they took us into a little mean, shabby back room; they got two ordinary sitting-room chairs and placed us in them, with our coats on. My old, old dream of bliss vanished into thin air!

I sat bolt upright, silent, sad, and solemn. One of the wig-making villains lathered my face for ten terrible minutes and finished by plastering a mass of suds into my mouth. I expelled the nasty stuff with a strong English expletive and said, "Foreigner, beware!" Then this outlaw strapped his razor on his boot, hovered over me ominously for six fearful seconds, and then swooped down upon me like the genius of destruction. The first rake of his razor loosened the very hide from my face and lifted me out of the chair. I stormed and raved, and the other boys enjoyed it. Their beards are not strong and thick. Let us draw the curtain over this harrowing scene. Suffice it that I submitted, and went through with the cruel infliction of a shave by a French barber; tears of exquisite agony coursed down my cheeks, now and then, but I survived. Then the incipient assassin held a basin of water under my chin and slopped its contents over my face, and into my bosom, and down the back of my neck, with a mean pretense of washing away the soap and blood. He dried my features with a towel, and was going to comb my hair; but I asked to be excused. I said, with withering irony, that it was sufficient to be skinned—I declined to be scalped.

I went away from there with my handkerchief about my face, and never, never, never desired to dream of palatial Parisian barber-shops any more. The truth is, as I believe I have since found out, that they have no barber-shops worthy of the name, in Paris—and no barbers, either, for that matter. The imposter who does duty as a barber, brings his pans and napkins and implements of torture to your residence and deliberately skins you in your private apartments. Ah, I have suffered, suffered, suffered, here in Paris, but never mind—the time is coming when I shall have a dark and bloody revenge. Some day a Parisian barber will come to my room to skin me, and from that day forth, that barber will never be heard of more.

From *The Innocents Abroad*, 1869

Billfinger

The next morning we were up and dressed at ten o'clock. We went to the *commissionaire* of the hotel—I don't know what a *commissionaire* is, but that is the man we went to—and told him we wanted a guide. He said the great International Exposition had drawn such multitudes of Englishmen and Americans to Paris that it would be next to impossible to find a good guide unemployed. He said he usually kept a dozen or two on hand, but he only had three now. He called them. One looked so like a very pirate that we let him go at once. The next one spoke with a simpering precision of pronunciation that was irritating, and said:

"If ze zhentlemans will to me make ze grande honneur to me rattain in hees serveece, I shall show to him every sing zat is magnifique to look upon in ze beautiful Parree. I speaky ze Angleesh pairfaitemaw."

He would have done well to have stopped there, because he had that much by heart and said it right off without making a mistake. But his self-complacency seduced him into attempting a flight into regions of unexplored English, and the reckless experiment was his ruin. Within ten seconds he was so tangled up in a maze of mutilated verbs and torn and bleeding forms of speech that no human ingenuity could ever have gotten him out of it with credit. It was plain enough that he could not "speaky" the English quite as "pairfaitemaw" as he had pretended he could.

The third man captured us. He was plainly dressed, but he had a noticeable air of neatness about him. He wore a high silk hat which was a little old, but had been carefully brushed. He wore second-hand kid gloves, in good repair, and carried a small rattan cane with a curved handle—a female leg, of ivory. He stepped as gently and as daintily as a cat crossing a muddy street; and oh, he was urbanity; he was quiet, unobtrusive self-possession; he was deference itself! He spoke softly and guardedly; and when he was about to make a statement on his sole responsibility, or offer a suggestion, he weighed it by drachms and scruples first, with the crook of his little stick placed meditatively to his teeth. His opening speech was perfect. It was perfect in construction, in phraseology, in grammar, in emphasis, in pronunciation—every thing. He spoke little and guardedly, after that. We were charmed. We were more than charmed—we were overjoyed. We hired him at once. We never even asked him his price. This man—our lackey, our servant, our unquestioning slave though he was, was still a gentleman—we could see that—while of the other two one was coarse and awkward, and the other was a born pirate. We asked our man Friday's name. He drew from his pocket-book a snowy little card, and passed it to us with a profound bow:

A. BILLFINGER,
Guide to Paris, France, Germany,
Spain, &c., &c.,
Grande Hotel du Louvre.

"Billfinger! Oh, carry me home to die!"

That was an "aside" from Dan. The atrocious name grated harshly on my ear, too. The most of us can learn to forgive, and even to like, a countenance that strikes us unpleasantly at first, but few of us, I fancy, become reconciled to a jarring name so easily. I was almost sorry we had hired this man, his name was so unbearable. However, no matter. We were impatient to start. Billfinger stepped to the door to call a carriage, and then the doctor said:

"Well, the guide goes with the barber-shop, with the billiard-table, with the gasless room, and may be with many another pretty romance of Paris. I expected to have a guide named Henri de Montmorency, or Armand de la Chartreuse, or something that would sound grand in letters to the villagers at home; but to think of a Frenchman by the name of Billfinger! Oh! this is absurd, you know. This will never do. We can't say Billfinger; it is nauseating. Name him over again: what had we better call him? Alexis du Caulaincourt?"

"Alphonse Henri Gustave de Hauteville," I suggested.

"Call him Ferguson," said Dan.

That was practical, unromantic good sense. Without debate, we expunged Billfinger *as* Billfinger, and called him Ferguson.

The carriage—an open barouche—was ready. Ferguson mounted beside the driver, and we whirled away to breakfast. As was proper, Mr. Ferguson stood by to transmit our orders and answer questions. Bye and bye, he mentioned casually—the artful adventurer—that he would go and get his breakfast as soon as we had finished ours. He knew we could not get along without him, and that we would not want to loiter about and wait for him. We asked him to sit down and eat with us. He begged, with many a bow, to be excused. It was not proper, he said; he would sit at another table. We ordered him peremptorily to sit down with us.

Here endeth the first lesson. It was a mistake.

As long as we had that fellow after that, he was always hungry; he was always thirsty. He came early; he stayed late; he could not pass a restaurant; he looked with a lecherous eye upon every wine shop. Suggestions to stop, excuses to eat and to drink were forever on his lips. We tried all we could to fill him so full that he would have no room to spare for a fortnight; but it was a failure. He did not hold enough to smother the cravings of his superhuman appetite.

He had another "discrepancy" about him. He was always wanting us to buy things. On the shallowest pretenses, he would inveigle us into shirt stores, boot stores, tailor shops, glove shops—any where under the broad sweep of the heavens that there seemed a chance of our buying any thing. Any one could have guessed that the shopkeepers paid him a per centage on the sales; but in our blessed innocence we didn't, until this feature of his conduct grew unbearably prominent. One day, Dan happened to mention that he thought of buying three or four silk dress patterns for presents. Ferguson's hungry eye was upon him in an instant. In the course of twenty minutes, the carriage stopped.

"What's this?"

"Zis is ze finest silk magazin in Paris—ze most celebrate."

"What did you come here for? We told you to take us to the palace of the Louvre."

"I suppose ze gentleman say he wish to buy some silk."

"You are not required to 'suppose' things for the party, Ferguson. We do not wish to tax your energies too much. We will bear some of the burden and heat of the day ourselves. We will endeavor to do such 'supposing' as is really necessary to be done. Drive on." So spake the doctor.

Within fifteen minutes the carriage halted again, and before another silk store. The doctor said:

"Ah, the palace of the Louvre: beautiful, beautiful edifice! Does the Emperor Napoleon live here now, Ferguson?"

"Ah, doctor! you do jest; zis is not ze palace; we come there directly. But since we pass right by zis store, where is such beautiful silk—"

"Ah! I see, I see. I meant to have told you that we did not wish to purchase any silks to-day; but in my absent-mindedness I forgot it. I also meant to tell you we wished to go directly to the Louvre; but I forgot that also. However, we will go there now. Pardon my seeming carelessness, Ferguson. Drive on."

Within the half hour, we stopped again—in front of another silk store. We were angry; but the doctor was always serene, always smooth-voiced. He said:

"At last! How imposing the Louvre is, and yet how small! how exquisitely fashioned! how charmingly situated!—Venerable, venerable pile—"

"Pairdon, doctor, zis is not ze Louvre—it is—"

"*What* is it?"

"I have ze idea—it come to me in a moment—zat ze silk in zis magazin—"

"Ferguson, how heedless I am. I fully intended to tell you that we did not wish to buy any silks to-day, and I also intended to tell you that we yearned to go immediately to the palace of the Louvre, but enjoying the happiness of seeing you devour four breakfasts this morning has so filled me with pleasurable emotions that I neglect the commonest interests of the time. However, we will proceed now to the Louvre, Ferguson."

"But doctor," (excitedly,) "it will take not a minute—not but one small minute! Ze gentleman need not to buy if he not wish to—but only *look* at ze silk—*look* at ze beautiful fabric." [Then pleadingly.] "*Sair*—just only one *leetle* moment!"

Dan said, "Confound the idiot! I don't want to see any silks to-day, and I *won't* look at them. Drive on."

And the doctor: "We need no silks now, Ferguson. Our hearts yearn for the Louvre. Let us journey on—let us journey on."

"But *doctor!* it is only one moment—one leetle moment. And ze time will be save—entirely save! Because zere is nothing to see, now —it is too late. It want ten minute to four and ze Louvre close at four—*only* one leetle moment, doctor!"

The treacherous miscreant! After four breakfasts and a gallon of champagne, to serve us such a scurvy trick. We got no sight of the countless treasures of art in the Louvre galleries that day, and our only poor little satisfaction was in the reflection that Ferguson sold not a solitary silk dress pattern.

I am writing this chapter partly for the satisfaction of abusing that accomplished knave, Billfinger, and partly to show whosoever shall read this how Americans fare at the hands of the Paris guides, and what sort of people Paris guides are. It need not be supposed that we were a stupider or an easier prey than our countrymen generally are, for we were not. The guides deceive and defraud every American who goes to Paris for the first time and sees its sights alone or in company with others as little experienced as himself. I shall visit Paris again some day, and then let the guides beware! I shall go in my war-paint—I shall carry my tomahawk along.

From *The Innocents Abroad,* 1869

Guide-English

[After spending some time in Genoa, Clemens and a few friends went to Milan.]

"Do you wis zo haut can be?"

That was what the guide asked, when we were looking up at the bronze horses on the Arch of Peace. It meant, do you wish to go up there? I give it as a specimen of guide-English. These are the people that make life a burthen to the tourist. Their tongues are never still. They talk forever and forever, and that is the kind of billingsgate they use. Inspiration itself could hardly comprehend them. If they would only show you a masterpiece of art, or a venerable tomb, or a prison-house, or a battle-field, hallowed by touching memories or historical reminiscences, or grand traditions, and then step aside and hold still for ten minutes and let you think, it would not be so bad. But they interrupt every dream, every pleasant train of thought, with their tiresome cackling. Sometimes when I have been standing before some cherished old idol of mine that I remembered years and years ago in pictures in the geography at school, I have thought I would give a whole world if the human parrot at my side would suddenly perish where he stood and leave me to gaze, and ponder, and worship.

No, we did not "wis zo haut can be." We wished to go to La Scala, the largest theatre in the world, I think they call it. We did so. It was a large place. Seven separate and distinct masses of humanity—six great circles and a monster parquette.

We wished to go the Ambrosian Library, and we did that also. We saw a manuscript of Virgil, with annotations in the handwriting of Petrarch, the gentleman who loved another man's Laura, and lavished upon her all through life a love which was a clear waste of the raw material. It was sound sentiment, but bad judgment. It brought both parties fame, and created a fountain of commiseration for them in sentimental breasts that is running yet. But who says a word in behalf of poor Mr. Laura? (I do not know his other name.) Who glorifies him? Who bedews him with tears? Who writes poetry about him? Nobody. How do you suppose *he* liked the state of things that has given the world so much pleasure? How did he enjoy having another man following his wife every where and making her name a familiar word in every garlic-exterminating mouth in Italy with his sonnets to her pre-empted eyebrows? *They* got fame and sympathy—he got neither. This is a peculiarly felicitous instance of what is called poetical justice. It is all very fine; but it does not chime with my notions of right. It is too one-sided—too ungenerous. Let the world go on fretting about Laura and Petrarch if it will; but as for me, my tears and my lamentations shall be lavished upon the unsung defendant.

We saw also an autograph letter of Lucrezia Borgia, a lady for whom I have always entertained the highest respect, on account of her rare histrionic capabilities, her opulence in solid gold goblets made of gilded wood, her high distinction as an operatic screamer, and the facility with which she could order a sextuple funeral and get the corpses ready for it. We saw one single coarse yellow hair from Lucrezia's head, likewise. It awoke emotions, but we still live. In this same library we saw some drawings by Michael Angelo (these Italians call him Mickel Angelo,) and Leonardo da Vinci. (They spell it Vinci and pronounce it Vinchy; foreigners always spell better than they pronounce.) We reserve our opinion of these sketches.

In another building they showed us a fresco representing some lions and other beasts drawing chariots; and they seemed to project so far from the wall that we took them to be sculptures. The artist had shrewdly heightened the delusion by painting dust on the creatures' backs, as if it had fallen there naturally and properly. Smart fellow—if it be smart to deceive strangers.

Elsewhere we saw a huge Roman amphitheatre, with its stone seats still in good preservation. Modernized, it is now the scene of more peaceful recreations than the exhibition of a party of wild beasts with Christians for dinner. Part of the time, the Milanese use it for a race track, and at other seasons they flood it with water and have spirited yachting regattas there. The guide told us these things, and he would hardly try so hazardous an experiment as the telling of a falsehood, when it is all he can do to speak the truth in English without getting the lock-jaw.

From *The Innocents Abroad,* 1869

Shortage of Soap

We have had a bath in Milan, in a public bath-house. They were going to put all three of us in one bath-tub, but we objected. Each of us had an Italian farm on his back. We could have felt affluent if we had been officially surveyed and fenced in. We chose to have three bath-tubs, and large ones—tubs suited to the dignity of aristocrats who had real estate, and brought it with them. After we were stripped and had taken the first chilly dash, we discovered that haunting atrocity that has embittered our lives in so many cities and villages of Italy and France—there was no soap. I called. A woman answered, and I barely had time to throw myself against the door—she would have been in, in another second. I said:

"Beware, woman! Go away from here—go away, now, or it will be the worse for you. I am an unprotected male, but I will preserve my honor at the peril of my life!"

These words must have frightened her, for she skurried away very fast.

Dan's voice rose on the air:

"Oh, bring some soap, why don't you!"

The reply was Italian. Dan resumed:

"Soap, you know—soap. That is what I want—soap. S-o-a-p, soap; s-o-p-e, soap; s-o-u-p, soap. Hurry up! I don't know how you Irish spell it, but I want it. Spell it to suit yourself, but fetch it. I'm freezing."

I heard the doctor say, impressively:

"Dan, how often have we told you that these foreigners can not understand English? Why will you not depend upon us? Why will you not tell *us* what you want, and let us ask for it in the language of the country? It would save us a great deal of the humiliation your reprehensible ignorance causes us. I will address this person in his mother tongue: 'Here, cospetto! corpo di Bacco! Sacramento!

Solferino!—Soap, you son of a gun!' Dan, if you would let *us* talk for you, you would never expose your ignorant vulgarity."

Even this fluent discharge of Italian did not bring the soap at once, but there was a good reason for it. There was not such an article about the establishment. It is my belief that there never had been. They had to send far up town, and to several different places before they finally got it, so they said. We had to wait twenty or thirty minutes. The same thing had occurred the evening before, at the hotel. I think I have divined the reason for this state of things at last. The English know how to travel comfortably, and they carry soap with them; other foreigners do not use the article.

At every hotel we stop at we always have to send out for soap, at the last moment, when we are grooming ourselves for dinner, and they put it in the bill along with the candles and other nonsense. In Marseilles they make half the fancy toilet soap we consume in America, but the Marseillaise only have a vague theoretical idea of its use, which they have obtained from books of travel, just as they have acquired an uncertain notion of clean shirts, and the peculiarities of the gorilla, and other curious matters. This reminds me of poor Blucher's note to the landlord in Paris:

"Paris, le 7 Juillet.

"Monsieur le Landlord—Sir: *Pourquoi* don't you *mettez* some *savon* in your bedchambers? *Est-ce que vous pensez* I will steal it? *La nuit passée* you charged me *pour deux chandelles* when I only had one; *hier vous avez* charged me *avec glace* when I had none at all; *tout les jours* you are coming some fresh game or other on me, *mais vous ne pouvez pas* play this *savon* dodge on me twice. *Savon* is a necessary *de la vie* to any body but a Frenchman, *et je l'aurai hors de cet hôtel* or make trouble. You hear *me*. *Allons*.

BLUCHER."

I remonstrated against the sending of this note, because it was so mixed up that the landlord would never be able to make head or tail of it; but Blucher said he guessed the old man could read the French of it and average the rest.

Blucher's French is bad enough, but it is not much worse than the English one finds in advertisements all over Italy every day. For instance, observe the printed card of the hotel we shall probably stop at on the shores of Lake Como:

> "NOTISH."
>
> "This hotel which the best it is in Italy and most superb, is handsome locate on the best situation of the lake, with the most splendid view near the Villas Melzy, to the King of Belgian, and Serbelloni. This hotel have recently enlarge, do offer all commodities on moderate price, at the strangers gentlemen who whish spend the seasons on the Lake Come."

How is that, for a specimen? In the hotel is a handsome little chapel where an English clergyman is employed to preach to such of the guests of the house as hail from England and America, and this fact is also set forth in barbarous English in the same advertisement. Wouldn't you have supposed that the adventurous linguist who framed the card would have known enough to submit it to that clergyman before he sent it to the printer?

From *The Innocents Abroad,* 1869

A Sort of People

[Clemens proceeded to Venice after a brief visit to Bellagio.]

Let me remark that there are Americans abroad in Italy who have actually forgotten their mother tongue in three months—forgot it in France. They can not even write their address in English in a hotel register. I append these evidences, which I copied *verbatim* from the register of a hotel in a certain Italian city:

"John P. Whitcomb, *Etats Unis.*

"Wm. L. Ainsworth, *travailleur* (he meant traveler, I suppose,) *Etats Unis.*

"George P. Morton *et fils, d'Amerique.*

"Lloyd B. Williams, *et trois amis, ville de* Boston, *Amerique.*

"J. Ellsworth Baker, *tout de suite de France, place de naissance Amerique, destination la Grand Bretagne.*"

I love this sort of people. A lady passenger of ours tells of a fellow-citizen of hers who spent eight weeks in Paris and then returned home and addressed his dearest old bosom friend Herbert as Mr. "Er-bare!" He apologized, though, and said, "'Pon my soul it is aggravating, but I cahn't help it—I have got so used to speaking nothing but French, my dear Erbare—damme there it goes again!—got so used to French pronunciation that I cahn't get rid of it—it is positively annoying, I assure you." This entertaining idiot, whose name was Gordon, allowed himself to be hailed three times in the street before he paid any attention, and then begged a thousand pardons and said he had grown so accustomed to hearing himself addressed as M'sieu Gor-r-*dong*," with a roll to the r, that he had forgotten the legitimate sound of his name! He wore a rose in his button-hole; he gave the French salutation—two flips of the hand in front of the face; he called Paris *Pairree* in ordinary English conversation; he carried envelopes bearing foreign postmarks protruding from his breast-pocket; he cultivated a moustache and imperial, and did what else he could to suggest to the beholder his pet fancy that he resembled Louis Napoleon—and in a spirit of thankfulness which is entirely unaccountable, considering the slim foundation there was for it, he praised his Maker that he was *as* he was, and went on enjoying his little life just the same as if he really *had* been deliberately designed and erected by the great Architect of the Universe.

Think of our Whitcombs, and our Ainsworths and our Williamses writing themselves down in dilapidated French in foreign hotel registers! We laugh at Englishmen, when we are at home, for sticking so sturdily to their national ways and customs, but we look back upon it from abroad very forgivingly. It is not pleasant to see an American thrusting his nationality forward *obtrusively* in a foreign land, but Oh, it is pitiable to see him making of himself a thing that is neither male nor female, neither fish, flesh, nor fowl—a poor, miserable, hermaphrodite Frenchman!

From *The Innocents Abroad,* 1869

A Skinning

We have seen famous pictures until our eyes are weary with looking at them and refuse to find interest in them any longer. And what wonder, when there are twelve hundred pictures by Palma the Younger in Venice and fifteen hundred by Tintoretto? And behold there are Titians and the works of other artists in proportion. We have seen Titian's celebrated Cain and Abel, his David and Goliath, his Abraham's Sacrifice. We have seen Tintoretto's monster picture, which is seventy-four feet long and I do not know how many feet high, and thought it a very commodious picture. We have seen pictures of martyrs enough, and saints enough, to regenerate the world. I ought not to confess it, but still, since one has no opportunity in America to acquire a critical judgment in art, and since I could not hope to become educated in it in Europe in a few short weeks, I may therefore as well acknowledge with such apologies as may be due, that to me it seemed that when I had seen one of these martyrs I had seen them all. They all have a marked family resemblance to each other, they dress alike, in coarse monkish robes and sandals, they are all bald headed, they all stand in about the same attitude, and without exception they are gazing heavenward with countenances which the Ainsworths, the Mortons and the Williamses, *et fils,* inform me are full of "expression." To me there is nothing tangible about these imaginary portraits, nothing that I can grasp and take a living interest in. If great Titian had only been gifted with prophecy, and had skipped a martyr, and gone over to England and painted a portrait of Shakespeare, even as a youth, which we could all have confidence in now, the world down to the latest generations would have forgiven him the lost martyr in the rescued seer. I think posterity could have spared one more martyr for the sake of a great historical picture of Titian's time and painted by his brush—such as Columbus returning in chains from the discovery of a world, for instance. The old masters did paint some Venetian historical pictures, and these we did not tire of looking at, notwithstanding representations of the formal introduction of defunct doges to the Virgin Mary in regions beyond the clouds clashed rather harshly with the proprieties, it seemed to us.

But humble as we are, and unpretending, in the matter of art, our researches among the painted monks and martyrs have not been wholly in vain. We have striven hard to learn. We have had some success. We have mastered some things, possibly of trifling import in the eyes of the learned, but to us they give pleasure, and we take as much pride in our little acquirements as do others who have learned far more, and we love to display them full as well. When we see a monk going about with a lion and looking tranquilly up to heaven, we know that that is St. Mark. When we see a monk with a book and a pen, looking tranquilly up to heaven, trying to think of a word, we know that that is St. Matthew. When we see a monk sitting on a rock, looking tranquilly up to heaven, with a human skull beside him, and without other baggage, we know that that is St. Jerome. Because we know that he always went flying light in the matter of baggage. When we see a party looking tranquilly up to heaven, unconscious that his body is shot through and through with arrows, we know that that is St. Sebastian. When we see other monks looking tranquilly up to heaven, but having no trade-mark, we always ask who those parties are. We do this because we humbly wish to learn. We have seen thirteen thousand St. Jeromes, and twenty-two thousand St. Marks, and sixteen thousand St. Matthews, and sixty thousand St. Sebastians, and four millions of assorted monks, undesignated, and we feel encouraged to believe that when we have seen some more of these various pictures, and had a larger experience, we shall begin to take an absorbing interest in them like our cultivated countrymen from *Amerique.*

Now it does give me real pain to speak in this almost unappreciative way of the old masters and their martyrs, because good friends of mine in the ship—friends who do thoroughly and conscientiously appreciate them and are in every way competent to discriminate between good pictures and inferior ones—have urged me for my own sake not to make public the fact that I lack this appreciation and this critical discrimination myself. I believe that what I have written and may still write about pictures will give them pain, and

I am honestly sorry for it. I even promised that I would hide my uncouth sentiments in my own breast. But alas! I never could keep a promise. I do not blame myself for this weakness, because the fault must lie in my physical organization. It is likely that such a very liberal amount of space was given to the organ which enables me to *make* promises, that the organ which should enable me to keep them was crowded out. But I grieve not. I like no halfway things. I had rather have one faculty nobly developed than two faculties of mere ordinary capacity. I certainly meant to keep that promise, but I find I can not do it. It is impossible to travel through Italy without speaking of pictures, and can I see them through others' eyes?

If I did not so delight in the grand pictures that are spread before me every day of my life by that monarch of all the old masters, Nature, I should come to believe, sometimes, that I had in me no appreciation of the beautiful, whatsoever.

It seems to me that whenever I glory to think that for once I have discovered an ancient painting that is beautiful and worthy of all praise, the pleasure it gives me is an infallible proof that it is *not* a beautiful picture and not in any wise worthy of commendation. This very thing has occurred more times than I can mention, in Venice. In every single instance the guide has crushed out my swelling enthusiasm with the remark:

"It is nothing—it is of the *Renaissance*."

I did not know what in the mischief the Renaissance was, and so always I had to simply say,

"Ah! so it is—I had not observed it before."

I could not bear to be ignorant before a cultivated negro, the offspring of a South Carolina slave. But it occurred too often for even my self-complacency, did that exasperating "It is nothing—it is of the *Renaissance*." I said at last:

"*Who* is this Renaissance? Where did he come from? Who gave him permission to cram the Republic with his execrable daubs?"

We learned, then, that Renaissance was not a man; that *renaissance* was a term used to signify what was at best but an imperfect rejuvenation of art. The guide said that after Titian's time and the time of the other great names we had grown so familiar with, high art declined; then it partially rose again—an inferior sort of painters sprang up, and these shabby pictures were the work of their hands. Then I said, in my heat, that I "wished to goodness high art had declined five hundred years sooner." The Renaissance pictures suit me very well, though sooth to say its school were too much given to painting real men and did not indulge enough in martyrs.

The guide I have spoken of is the only one we have had yet who knew any thing. He was born in South Carolina, of slave parents. They came to Venice while he was an infant. He has grown up here. He is well educated. He reads, writes, and speaks English, Italian, Spanish, and French, with perfect facility; is a worshipper of art and thoroughly conversant with it; knows the history of Venice by heart and never tires of talking of her illustrious career. He dresses better than any of us, I think, and is daintily polite. Negroes are deemed as good as white people, in Venice, and so this man feels no desire to go back to his native land. His judgment is correct.

I have had another shave. I was writing in our front room this afternoon and trying hard to keep my attention on my work and refrain from looking out upon the canal. I was resisting the soft influences of the climate as well as I could, and endeavoring to overcome the desire to be indolent and happy. The boys sent for a barber. They asked me if I would be shaved. I reminded them of my tortures in Genoa, Milan, Como; of my declaration that I would suffer no more on Italian soil. I said "Not any for me, if you please."

I wrote on. The barber began on the doctor. I heard him say:

"Dan, this is the easiest shave I have had since we left the ship."

He said again, presently:

"Why Dan, a man could go to sleep with this man shaving him."

Dan took the chair. Then he said:

"Why this is Titian. This is one of the old masters."

I wrote on. Directly Dan said:

"Doctor, it is perfect luxury. The ship's barber isn't any thing to him."

My rough beard was distressing me beyond measure. The barber was rolling up his apparatus. The temptation was too strong. I said:

"Hold on, please. Shave me also."

I sat down in the chair and closed my eyes. The barber soaped my face, and then took his razor and gave me a rake that well nigh threw me into convulsions. I jumped out of the chair: Dan and the doctor were both wiping blood off their faces and laughing.

I said it was a mean, disgraceful fraud.

They said that the misery of this shave had gone so far beyond any thing they had ever experienced before, that they could not bear the idea of losing such a chance of hearing a cordial opinion from me on the subject.

It was shameful. But there was no help for it. The skinning was begun and had to be finished. The tears flowed with every rake, and so did the fervent execrations. The barber grew confused, and brought blood every time. I think the boys enjoyed it better than anything they have seen or heard since they left home.

From *The Innocents Abroad*, 1869

An Ancient Playbill

[Clemens saw Florence and Pisa, then went to Rome.]

For me was reserved the high honor of discovering among the rubbish of the ruined Coliseum the only playbill of that establishment now extant. There is a suggestive smell of mint-drops about it still, a corner of it had evidently been chewed, and on the margin, in choice Latin, these words were written in a delicate female hand:

"Meet me on the Tarpeian Rock to-morrow evening, dear, at sharp seven. Mother will be absent on a visit to her friends in the Sabine Hills.

CLAUDIA."

Ah, where is that lucky youth to-day, and where the little hand that wrote those dainty lines? Dust and ashes these seventeen hundred years!

Thus reads the bill:

ROMAN COLISEUM

UNPARALLELED ATTRACTION!

NEW PROPERTIES! NEW LIONS! NEW GLADIATORS!

Engagement of the renowned
MARCUS MARCELLUS VALERIAN!

FOR SIX NIGHTS ONLY!

The management beg leave to offer to the public an entertainment surpassing in magnificence any thing that has heretofore been attempted on any stage. No expense has been spared to make the opening season one which shall be worthy the generous patronage which the management feel sure will crown their efforts. The management beg leave to state that they have succeeded in securing the services of a

GALAXY OF TALENT!

such as has not been beheld in Rome before.

The performance will commence this evening with a

GRAND BROADSWORD COMBAT!

between two young and promising amateurs and a celebrated Parthian gladiator who has just arrived a prisoner from the Camp of Verus.

This will be followed by a grand moral

BATTLE-AX ENGAGEMENT!

between the renowned Valerian (with one hand tied behind him,) and two gigantic savages from Britain.

After which the renowned Valerian (if he survive,) will fight with the broadsword,

LEFT-HANDED!

against six Sophomores and a Freshman from the Gladiatorial College!

A long series of brilliant engagements will follow, in which the finest talent of the Empire will take part.

After which the celebrated Infant Prodigy known as

"THE YOUNG ACHILLES,"

will engage four tiger whelps in combat, armed with no other weapon than his little spear!

The whole to conclude with a chaste and elegant

GENERAL SLAUGHTER!

In which thirteen African Lions and twenty-two Barbarian Prisoners will war with each other until all are exterminated.

BOX OFFICE NOW OPEN.

Dress Circle One Dollar; Children and Servants half price.

An efficient police force will be on hand to preserve order and keep the wild beasts from leaping the railings and discommoding the audience.

Doors open at 7; performance begins at 8.

POSITIVELY NO FREE LIST.

Diodorus Job Press.

It was as singular as it was gratifying that I was also so fortunate as to find among the rubbish of the arena, a stained and mutilated copy of the *Roman Daily Battle-Ax*, containing a critique upon this very performance. It comes to hand too late by many centuries to rank as news, and therefore I translate and publish it simply to show how very little the general style and phraseology of dramatic criticism has altered in the ages that have dragged their slow length along since the carriers laid this one damp and fresh before their Roman patrons:

"THE OPENING SEASON.—COLISEUM.—Notwithstanding the inclemency of the weather, quite a respectable number of the rank and fashion of the city assembled last night to witness the debut upon metropolitan boards of the young tragedian who has of late been winning such golden opinions in the amphitheatres of the provinces. Some sixty thousand persons were present, and but for the fact that the streets were almost impassable, it is fair to presume that the house would have been full. His august Majesty, the Emperor Aurelius, occupied the imperial box, and was the cynosure of all eyes. Many illustrious nobles and generals of the Empire graced the occasion with their presence, and not the least among them was the young patrician lieutenant whose laurels, won in the ranks of the "Thundering Legion," are still so green upon his brow. The cheer which greeted his entrance was heard beyond the Tiber!

"The late repairs and decorations add both to the comeliness and the comfort of the Coliseum. The new cushions are a great improvement upon the hard marble seats we have been so long accustomed to. The present management deserve well of the public. They have restored to the Coliseum the gilding, the rich upholstery and the uniform magnificence which old Coliseum frequenters tell us Rome was so proud of fifty years ago.

"The opening scene last night—the broadsword combat between two young amateurs and a famous Parthian gladiator who was sent here a prisoner—was very fine. The elder of the two young gentlemen handled his weapon with a grace that marked the possession of extraordinary talent. His feint of thrusting, followed instantly by a happily delivered blow which unhelmeted the Parthian, was received with hearty applause. He was not thoroughly up in the backhanded stroke, but it was very gratifying to his numerous friends to know that, in time, practice would have overcome this defect. However, he was killed. His sisters, who were present, expressed considerable regret. His mother left the Coliseum. The other youth maintained the contest with such spirit as to call forth enthusiastic bursts of applause. When at last he fell a corpse, his aged mother ran screaming, with hair disheveled and tears streaming from her eyes, and swooned away just as her hands were clutching at the railings of the arena. She was promptly removed by the police. Under the circumstances the woman's conduct was pardonable, perhaps, but we suggest that such exhibitions interfere with the decorum which should be preserved during the performances, and are highly improper in the presence of the Emperor. The Parthian prisoner fought bravely and well; and well he might, for he was fighting for both life and liberty. His wife and children were there to nerve his arm with their love, and to remind him of the old home he should see again if he conquered. When his second assailant fell, the woman clasped her children to her breast and wept for joy. But it was only a transient happiness. The captive staggered toward her and she saw that the liberty he had earned was earned too late. He was wounded unto death. Thus the first act closed in a manner which was entirely satisfactory. The manager was called before the curtain and returned his thanks for the honor done him, in a speech which was replete with wit and humor, and closed by hoping that his humble efforts to afford cheerful and instructive entertainment would continue to meet with the approbation of the Roman public.

"The star now appeared, and was received with vociferous applause and the simultaneous waving of sixty thousand handkerchiefs. Marcus Marcellus Valerian (stage name—his real name is Smith,) is a splendid specimen of physical development, and an artist of rare merit. His management of the battle-ax is wonderful. His gayety and his playfulness are irresistible, in his comic parts, and yet they are inferior to his sublime conceptions in the grave realm of tragedy. When his ax was describing fiery circles about the heads of the bewildered barbarians, in exact time with his springing body and his prancing legs, the audience gave way to uncontrollable bursts of laughter; but when the back of his weapon broke the skull of one and almost in the same instant its edge clove the other's body in twain, the howl of enthusiastic applause that shook the building, was the acknowledgment of a critical assemblage that he was a master of the noblest department of his profession. If he has a fault, (and we are sorry to even intimate that he has,) it is that of glancing at the audience, in the midst of the most exciting moments of the performance, as if seeking admiration. The pausing in a fight to bow when bouquets are thrown to him is also in bad taste. In the great left-handed combat he appeared to be looking at the audience half the time, instead of carving his adversaries; and when he had slain all the sophomores and was dallying with the freshman, he stooped and snatched a bouquet as it fell, and offered it to his adversary at a time when a blow was descending which promised favorably to be his death-warrant. Such levity is proper enough in the provinces, we make no doubt, but it ill suits the dignity of the metropolis. We trust our young friend will take these remarks in good part, for we mean them solely for his benefit. All who know us are aware that although we are at times justly severe upon tigers and martyrs, we never intentionally offend gladiators.

"The Infant Prodigy performed wonders. He overcame his four tiger whelps with ease, and with no other hurt than the loss of a portion of his scalp. The General Slaughter was rendered with a faithfulness to details which reflects the highest credit upon the late participants in it.

"Upon the whole, last night's performances shed honor not only upon the management but upon the city that encourages and sustains such wholesome and instructive entertainments. We would simply suggest that the practice of vulgar young boys in the gallery of shying peanuts and paper pellets at the tigers, and saying "Hi-yi!" and manifesting approbation or dissatisfaction by such observations as "Bully for the lion!" "Go it, Gladdy!" "Boots!" "Speech!" "Take a walk round the block!" and so on, are extremely reprehensible, when the Emperor is present, and ought to be stopped by the police. Several times last night, when the supernumeraries entered the arena to drag out the bodies, the young ruffians in the gallery shouted, "Supe! supe!" and also, "Oh, what a coat!" and "Why don't you pad them shanks?" and made use of various other remarks expressive of derision. These things are very annoying to the audience.

"A matinee for the little folks is promised for this afternoon, on which occasion several martyrs will be eaten by the tigers. The regular performance will continue every night till further notice. Material change of programme every evening. Benefit of Valerian, Tuesday, 29th, if he lives."

I have been a dramatic critic myself, in my time, and I was often surprised to notice how much more I knew about Hamlet than Forrest did; and it gratifies me to observe, now, how much better my brethren of ancient times knew how a broad sword battle ought to be fought than the gladiators.

From *The Innocents Abroad,* 1869

Guying the Guides

I wish to say one word about Michael Angelo Buonarotti. I used to worship the mighty genius of Michael Angelo—that man who was great in poetry, painting, sculpture, architecture—great in every thing he undertook. But I do not want Michael Angelo for breakfast—for luncheon—for dinner—for tea—for supper—for between meals. I like a change, occasionally. In Genoa, he designed every thing; in Milan he or his pupils designed every thing; he designed the Lake of Como; in Padua, Verona, Venice, Bologna, who did we ever hear of, from guides, but Michael Angelo? In Florence, he painted every thing, designed every thing, nearly, and what he did not design he used to sit on a favorite stone and look at, and they showed us the stone. In Pisa he designed every thing but the old shot-tower, and they would have attributed that to him if it had not been so awfully out of the perpendicular. He designed the piers of Leghorn and the custom house regulations of Civita Vecchia. But, here—here it is frightful. He designed St. Peter's; he designed the Pope; he designed the Pantheon, the uniform of the Pope's soldiers, the Tiber, the Vatican, the Coliseum, the Capitol, the Tarpeian Rock, the Barberini Palace, St. John Lateran, the Campagna, the Appian Way, the Seven Hills, the Baths of Caracalla, the Claudian Aqueduct, the Cloaca Maxima—the eternal bore designed the Eternal City, and unless all men and books do lie, he painted every thing in it! Dan said the other day to the guide, "Enough, enough, enough! Say no more! Lump the whole thing! say that the Creator made Italy from designs by Michael Angelo!"

I never felt so fervently thankful, so soothed, so tranquil, so filled with a blessed peace, as I did yesterday when I learned that Michael Angelo was dead.

But we have taken it out of this guide. He has marched us through miles of pictures and sculpture in the vast corridors of the

Vatican; and through miles of pictures and sculpture in twenty other palaces; he has shown us the great picture in the Sistine Chapel, and frescoes enough to frescoe the heavens—pretty much all done by Michael Angelo. So with him we have played that game which has vanquished so many guides for us—imbecility and idiotic questions. These creatures never suspect—they have no idea of a sarcasm.

He shows us a figure and says: "Statoo brunzo." (Bronze statue.)

We look at it indifferently and the doctor asks: "By Michael Angelo?"

"No—not know who."

Then he shows us the ancient Roman Forum. The doctor asks: "Michael Angelo?"

A stare from the guide. "No—thousan' year before he is born."

Then an Egyptian obelisk. Again: "Michael Angelo?"

"Oh, *mon dieu*, genteelmen! Zis is *two* thousan' year before he is born!"

He grows so tired of that unceasing question sometimes, that he dreads to show us any thing at all. The wretch has tried all the ways he can think of to make us comprehend that Michael Angelo is only responsible for the creation of a *part* of the world, but somehow he has not succeeded yet. Relief for overtasked eyes and brain from study and sightseeing is necessary, or we shall become idiotic sure enough. Therefore this guide must continue to suffer. If he does not enjoy it, so much the worse for him. We do.

In this place I may as well jot down a chapter concerning those necessary nuisances, European guides. Many a man has wished in his heart he could do without his guide; but knowing he could not, has wished he could get some amusement out of him as a remuneration for the affliction of his society. We accomplished this latter matter, and if our experience can be made useful to others they are welcome to it.

Guides know about enough English to tangle every thing up so that a man can make neither head or tail of it. They know their story by heart—the history of every statue, painting, cathedral or other wonder they show you. They know it and tell it as a parrot would—and if you interrupt, and throw them off the track, they have to go back and begin over again. All their lives long, they are employed in showing strange things to foreigners and listening to their bursts of admiration. It is human nature to take delight in exciting admiration. It is what prompts children to say "smart" things, and do absurd ones, and in other ways "show off" when company is present. It is what makes gossips turn out in rain and storm to go and be the first to tell a startling bit of news. Think, then, what a passion it becomes with a guide, whose privilege it is, every day, to show to strangers wonders that throw them into perfect ecstasies of admiration! He gets so that he could not by any possibility live in a soberer atmosphere. After we discovered this, we *never* went into ecstasies any more—we never admired any thing—we never showed any but impassible faces and stupid indifference in the presence of the sublimest wonders a guide had to display. We had found their weak point. We have made good use of it ever since. We have made some of those people savage, at times, but we have never lost our own serenity.

The doctor asks the questions, generally, because he can keep his countenance, and look more like an inspired idiot, and throw more imbecility into the tone of his voice than any man that lives. It comes natural to him.

The guides in Genoa are delighted to secure an American party, because Americans so much wonder, and deal so much in sentiment and emotion before any relic of Columbus. Our guide there fidgeted about as if he had swallowed a spring mattress. He was full of animation—full of impatience. He said:

"Come wis me, genteelmen!—come! I show you ze letter writing by Christopher Colombo!—write it himself!—write it wis his own hand!—come!"

He took us to the municipal palace. After much impressive fumbling of keys and opening of locks, the stained and aged document was spread before us. The guide's eyes sparkled. He danced about us and tapped the parchment with his finger:

"What I tell you, genteelmen! Is it not so? See! hand-writing Christopher Colombo!—write it himself!"

We looked indifferent—unconcerned. The doctor examined the document very deliberately, during a painful pause.—Then he said, without any show of interest:

"Ah—Ferguson—what—what did you say was the name of the party who wrote this?"

"Christopher Colombo! ze great Christopher Colombo!"

Another deliberate examination.

"Ah—did he write it himself, or—or how?"

"He write it himself!—Christopher Colombo! he's own hand-writing, write by himself!"

Then the doctor laid the document down and said:

"Why, I have seen boys in America only fourteen years old that could write better than that."

"But zis is ze great Christo—"

"I don't care who it is! It's the worst writing I ever saw. Now you mustn't think you can impose on us because we are strangers. We are not fools, by a good deal. If you have got any specimens of penmanship of real merit, trot them out!—and if you haven't, drive on!"

We drove on. The guide was considerably shaken up, but he made one more venture. He had something which he thought would overcome us. He said:

"Ah, genteelmen, you come wis me! I show you beautiful, O, magnificent bust Christopher Colombo!—splendid, grand, magnificent!"

He brought us before the beautiful bust—for it *was* beautiful—and sprang back and struck an attitude:

"Ah, look, genteelmen!—beautiful, grand,—bust Christopher Colombo!—beautiful bust, beautiful pedestal!"

The doctor put up his eye-glass—procured for such occasions:

"Ah—what did you say this gentleman's name was?"

"Christopher Colombo!—ze great Christopher Colombo!"

"Christopher Colombo—the great Christopher Colombo. Well, what did *he* do?"

"Discover America!—discover America, Oh, ze devil!"

"Discover America. No—that statement will hardly wash. We are just from America ourselves. We heard nothing about it. Christopher Colombo—pleasant name—is—is he dead?"

"Oh, corpo di Baccho!—three hundred year!"

"What did he die of?"

"I do not know!—I can not tell."

"Small-pox, think?"

"I do not know, genteelmen!—I do not know *what* he die of!"

"Measles, likely?"

"May be—may be—I do *not* know—I think he die of somethings."

"Parents living?"

"Im-posseeble!"

"Ah—which is the bust and which is the pedestal?"

"Santa Maria!—*zis* ze bust!—*zis* ze pedestal!"

"Ah, I see, I see—happy combination—very happy combination, indeed. Is—is this the first time this gentleman was ever on a bust?"

That joke was lost on the foreigner—guides can not master the subtleties of the American joke.

We have made it interesting for this Roman guide. Yesterday we spent three or four hours in the Vatican, again, that wonderful world of curiosities. We came very near expressing interest, sometimes—even admiration—it was very hard to keep from it. We succeeded though. Nobody else ever did, in the Vatican museums. The guide was bewildered—non-plussed. He walked his legs off, nearly, hunting up extraordinary things, and exhausted all his ingenuity on us, but it was a failure; we never showed any interest in any thing. He had reserved what he considered to be his greatest wonder till the last—a royal Egyptian mummy, the best preserved in the world, perhaps. He took us there. He felt so sure, this time, that some of his old enthusiasm came back to him:

"See, genteelmen!—Mummy! Mummy!"

The eye-glass came up as calmly, as deliberately as ever.

"Ah,—Ferguson—what did I understand you to say the gentleman's name was?"

"Name?—he got no name!—Mummy!—'Gyptian mummy!"

"Yes, yes. Born here?"

"No! *'Gyptian* mummy!"

"Ah, just so. Frenchman, I presume?"

"No!—*not* Frenchman, not Roman!—born in Egypta!"

"Born in Egypta. Never heard of Egypta before. Foreign locality, likely. Mummy—mummy. How calm he is—how self-possessed. Is, ah—is he dead?"

"Oh, *sacre bleu,* been dead three thousan' year!"

The doctor turned on him savagely:

"Here, now, what do you mean by such conduct as this! Playing us for Chinamen because we are strangers and trying to learn! Trying to impose your vile second-hand carcasses on *us!*—thunder and lightning, I've a notion to—to—if you've got a nice *fresh* corpse, fetch him out!—or by George we'll brain you!"

We make it exceedingly interesting for this Frenchman. However, he has paid us back, partly, without knowing it. He came to the hotel this morning to ask if we were up, and he endeavored as well as he could to describe us, so that the landlord would know which persons he meant. He finished with the casual remark that we were lunatics. The observation was so innocent and so honest that it amounted to a very good thing for a guide to say.

There is one remark (already mentioned,) which never yet has failed to disgust these guides. We use it always, when we can think of nothing else to say. After they have exhausted their enthusiasm pointing out to us and praising the beauties of some ancient bronze image or broken-legged statue, we look at it stupidly and in silence for five, ten, fifteen minutes—as long as we can hold out, in fact—and then ask:

"Is—is he dead?"

That conquers the serenest of them. It is not what they are looking for—especially a new guide. Our Roman Ferguson is the most patient, unsuspecting, long-suffering subject we have had yet. We shall be sorry to part with him. We have enjoyed his society very much. We trust he has enjoyed ours, but we are harassed with doubts.

From *The Innocents Abroad,* 1869

Turkish Bath

[Clemens visited Naples and Pompeii, then sailed for Turkey, where he wandered around Constantinople.]

When I think how I have been swindled by books of Oriental travel, I want a tourist for breakfast. For years and years I have dreamed of the wonders of the Turkish bath; for years and years I have promised myself that I would yet enjoy one. Many and many a time, in fancy, I have lain in the marble bath, and breathed the slumbrous fragrance of Eastern spices that filled the air; then passed through a weird and complicated system of pulling and hauling, and drenching and scrubbing, by a gang of naked savages who loomed vast and vaguely through the steaming mists, like demons; then rested for a while on a divan fit for a king; then passed through another complex ordeal, and one more fearful than the first; and, finally, swathed in soft fabrics, been conveyed to a princely saloon and laid on a bed of eider down, where eunuchs, gorgeous of costume, fanned me while I drowsed and dreamed, or contentedly gazed at the rich hangings of the apartment, the soft carpets, the sumptuous furniture, the pictures, and drank delicious coffee, smoked the soothing narghili, and dropped, at the last, into tranquil repose, lulled by sensuous odors from unseen censers, by the gentle influence of the narghili's Persian tobacco, and by the music of fountains that counterfeited the pattering of summer rain.

That was the picture, just as I got it from incendiary books of travel. It was a poor, miserable imposture. The reality is no more like it than the Five Points are like the Garden of Eden. They received me in a great court, paved with marble slabs; around it were broad galleries, one above another, carpeted with seedy matting, railed with unpainted balustrades, and furnished with huge rickety chairs, cushioned with rusty old mattresses, indented with impressions left by the forms of nine successive generations of men who had reposed upon them. The place was vast, naked, dreary; its court a barn, its galleries stalls for human horses. The cadaverous, half nude varlets that served in the establishment had nothing of poetry in their appearance, nothing of romance, nothing of Oriental splendor. They shed no entrancing odors—just the contrary. Their hungry eyes and their lank forms continually suggested one glaring, unsentimental fact—they wanted what they term in California "a square meal."

I went into one of the racks and undressed. An unclean starveling wrapped a gaudy table-cloth about his loins, and hung a white rag over my shoulders. If I had had a tub then, it would have come natural to me to take in washing. I was then conducted down stairs into the wet, slippery court, and the first things that attracted my attention were my heels. My fall excited no comment. They expected it, no doubt. It belonged in the list of softening, sensuous influences peculiar to this home of Eastern luxury. It was softening enough, certainly, but its application was not happy. They now gave me a pair of wooden clogs—benches in miniature, with leather straps over them to confine my feet (which they would have done, only I do not wear No. 13s.) These things dangled uncomfortably by the straps when I lifted up my feet, and came down in awkward and unexpected places when I put them on the floor again, and sometimes turned sideways and wrenched my ankles out of joint. However, it was all Oriental luxury, and I did what I could to enjoy it.

They put me in another part of the barn and laid me on a stuffy sort of pallet, which was not made of cloth of gold, or Persian shawls, but was merely the unpretending sort of thing I have seen in the negro quarters of Arkansas. There was nothing whatever in this dim marble prison but five more of these biers. It was a very solemn place. I expected that the spiced odors of Araby were going to steal over my senses now, but they did not. A copper-colored skeleton, with a rag around him, brought me a glass decanter of water, with a lighted tobacco pipe in the top of it, and a pliant stem a yard long, with a brass mouth-piece to it.

It was the famous "narghili" of the East—the thing the Grand Turk smokes in the pictures. This began to look like luxury. I took one blast at it, and it was sufficient; the smoke went in a great volume down into my stomach, my lungs, even into the uttermost parts of my frame. I exploded one mighty cough, and it was as if Vesuvius had let go. For the next five minutes I smoked at every pore, like a frame house that is on fire on the inside. Not any more narghili for me. The smoke had a vile taste, and the taste of a thousand infidel tongues that remained on that brass mouthpiece was viler still. I was getting discouraged. Whenever, hereafter, I see the cross-legged Grand Turk smoking his narghili, in pretended bliss, on the outside of a paper of Connecticut tobacco, I shall know him for the shameless humbug he is.

This prison was filled with hot air. When I had got warmed up sufficiently to prepare me for a still warmer temperature, they took me where it was—into a marble room, wet, slippery and steamy, and laid me out on a raised platform in the centre. It was very warm. Presently my man sat me down by a tank of hot water, drenched me well, gloved his hand with a coarse mitten, and began to polish me all over with it. I began to smell disagreeably. The more he polished the worse I smelt. It was alarming. I said to him:

"I perceive that I am pretty far gone. It is plain that I ought to be buried without any unnecessary delay. Perhaps you had better go after my friends at once, because the weather is warm, and I can not 'keep' long."

He went on scrubbing, and paid no attention. I soon saw that he was reducing my size. He bore hard on his mitten, and from under it rolled little cylinders, like maccaroni. It could not be dirt, for it was too white. He pared me down in this way for a long time. Finally I said:

"It is a tedious process. It will take hours to trim me to the size you want me; I will wait; go and borrow a jack-plane."

He paid no attention at all.

After a while he brought a basin, some soap, and something that seemed to be the tail of a horse. He made up a prodigious quantity of soap-suds, deluged me with them from head to foot, without warning me to shut my eyes, and then swabbed me viciously with the horse-tail. Then he left me there, a snowy statue of lather, and went away. When I got tired of waiting I went and hunted him up. He was propped against the wall, in another room, asleep. I woke him. He was not disconcerted. He took me back and flooded me with hot water, then turbaned my head, swathed me with dry table-cloths, and conducted me to a latticed chicken-coop in one of the galleries, and pointed to one of those Arkansas beds. I mounted it, and vaguely expected the odors of Araby again. They did not come.

The blank, unornamented coop had nothing about it of that oriental voluptuousness one reads of so much. It was more suggestive of the county hospital than any thing else. The skinny servitor brought a narghili, and I got him to take it out again without wasting any time about it. Then he brought the world-renowned Turkish coffee that poets have sung so rapturously for many generations, and I seized upon it as the last hope that was left of my old dreams of Eastern luxury. It was another fraud. Of all the unchristian beverages that ever passed my lips, Turkish coffee is the worst. The cup is small, it is smeared with grounds; the coffee is black, thick, unsavory of smell, and execrable in taste. The bottom of the cup has a muddy sediment in it half an inch deep. This goes down your throat, and portions of it lodge by the way, and produce a tickling aggravation that keeps you barking and coughing for an hour.

Here endeth my experience of the celebrated Turkish bath, and here also endeth my dream of the bliss the mortal revels in who passes through it. It is a malignant swindle. The man who enjoys it is qualified to enjoy any thing that is repulsive to sight or sense, and he that can invest it with a charm of poetry is able to do the same with any thing else in the world that is tedious, and wretched, and dismal, and nasty.

From *The Innocents Abroad,* 1869

That Girl in Yalta

[Clemens was a tourist in Sebastopol, Odessa and Yalta in Russia. Then he visited Smyrna (now Izmir) in Turkey.]

A portion of the city is pretty exclusively Turkish; the Jews have a quarter to themselves; the Franks another quarter; so, also, with the Armenians. The Armenians, of course, are Christians. Their houses are large, clean, airy, handsomely paved with black and white squares of marble, and in the centre of many of them is a square court, which has in it a luxuriant flower-garden and a sparkling fountain; the doors of all the rooms open on this. A very wide hall leads to the street door, and in this the women sit, the most of the day. In the cool of the evening they dress up in their best raiment and show themselves at the door. They are all comely of countenance, and exceedingly neat and cleanly; they look as if they were just out of a band-box. Some of the young ladies—many of them, I may say—are even very beautiful; they average a shade better than American girls—which treasonable words I pray may be forgiven me. They are very sociable, and will smile back when a stranger smiles at them, bow back when he bows, and talk back if he speaks to them. No introduction is required. An hour's chat at the door with a pretty girl one never saw before, is easily obtained, and is very pleasant. I have tried it. I could not talk any thing but English, and the girl knew nothing but Greek, or Armenian, or some such barbarous tongue, but we got along very well. I find that in cases like these, the fact that you can not comprehend each other isn't much of a drawback. In that Russian town of Yalta I danced an astonishing sort of dance an hour long, and one I had not heard of before, with a very pretty girl, and we talked incessantly, and laughed exhaustingly, and neither one ever knew what the other was driving at. But it was splendid. There were twenty people in the set, and the dance was very lively and complicated. It was complicated enough without me—with me it was more so. I threw in a figure now and then that surprised those Russians. But I have never ceased to think of that girl. I have written to her, but I can not direct the epistle because her name is one of those nine-jointed Russian affairs, and there are not letters enough in our alphabet to hold out. I am not reckless enough to try to pronounce it when I am awake, but I make a stagger at it in my dreams, and get up with the lockjaw in the morning. I am fading. I do not take my meals now, with any sort of regularity. Her dear name haunts me still in my dreams. It is awful on teeth. It never comes out of my mouth but it fetches an old snag along with it. And then the lockjaw closes down and nips off a couple of the last syllables—but they taste good.

From *The Innocents Abroad*, 1869

"Jericho"

[Clemens saw Beirut, then with seven other shipmates began an inland trip, heading for Baalbek, Damascus, Jerusalem and Jaffa. "We had nineteen serving-men and twenty-six pack-mules! It was a perfect caravan."]

By half-past six we were under way, and all the Syrian world seemed to be under way also. The road was filled with mule trains and long processions of camels. This reminds me that we have been trying for some time to think what a camel looks like, and now we have made it out. When he is down on all his knees, flat on his breast to receive his load, he looks something like a goose swimming; and when he is upright he looks like an ostrich with an extra set of legs. Camels are not beautiful, and their long under lip gives them an exceedingly "gallus"* expression. They have immense, flat, forked cushions of feet, that make a track in the dust like a pie with a slice cut out of it. They are not particular about their diet. They would eat a tombstone if they could bite it. A thistle grows about here which has needles on it that would pierce through leather, I think; if one touches you, you can find relief in nothing but profanity. The camels eat these. They show by their actions that they enjoy them. I suppose it would be a real treat to a camel to have a keg of nails for supper.

While I am speaking of animals, I will mention that I have a horse now by the name of "Jericho." He is a mare. I have seen remarkable horses before, but none so remarkable as this. I wanted a horse that could shy, and this one fills the bill. I had an idea that shying indicated spirit. If I was correct, I have got the most spirited horse on earth. He shies at every thing he comes across, with the utmost impartiality. He appears to have a mortal dread of telegraph

* Excuse the slang—no other word will describe it.—M. T.

poles, especially; and it is fortunate that these are on both sides of the road, because as it is now, I never fall off twice in succession on the same side. If I fell on the same side always, it would get to be monotonous after a while. This creature has scared at every thing he has seen to-day, except a haystack. He walked up to that with an intrepidity and a recklessness that were astonishing. And it would fill any one with admiration to see how he preserves his self-possession in the presence of a barley sack. This dare-devil bravery will be the death of this horse some day.

He is not particularly fast, but I think he will get me through the Holy Land. He has only one fault. His tail has been chopped off or else he has sat down on it too hard, some time or other, and he has to fight the flies with his heels. This is all very well, but when he tries to kick a fly off the top of his head with his hind foot, it is too much variety. He is going to get himself into trouble that way some day. He reaches around and bites my legs too. I do not care particularly about that, only I do not like to see a horse too sociable.

I think the owner of this prize had a wrong opinion about him. He had an idea that he was one of those fiery, untamed steeds, but he is not of that character. I know the Arab had this idea, because when he brought the horse out for inspection in Beirut, he kept jerking at the bridle and shouting in Arabic, "Ho! will you? Do you want to run away, you ferocious beast, and break your neck?" when all the time the horse was not doing any thing in the world, and only looked like he wanted to lean up against something and think. Whenever he is not shying at things, or reaching after a fly, he wants to do that yet. How it would surprise his owner to know this.

From *The Innocents Abroad,* 1869

A Party of Eight

We left Damascus at noon and rode across the plain a couple of hours, and then the party stopped a while in the shade of some fig-trees to give me a chance to rest. It was the hottest day we had seen yet—the sun-flames shot down like the shafts of fire that stream out before a blow-pipe; the rays seemed to fall in a steady deluge on the head and pass downward like rain from a roof. I imagined I could distinguish between the floods of rays—I thought I could tell when each flood struck my head, when it reached my shoulders, and when the next one came. It was terrible. All the desert glared so fiercely that my eyes were swimming in tears all the time. The boys had white umbrellas heavily lined with dark green. They were a priceless blessing. I thanked fortune that I had one, too, notwithstanding it was packed up with the baggage and was ten miles ahead. It is madness to travel in Syria without an umbrella. They told me in Beirut (these people who always gorge you with advice) that it was madness to travel in Syria without an umbrella. It was on this account that I got one.

But, honestly, I think an umbrella is a nuisance any where when its business is to keep the sun off. No Arab wears a brim to his fez, or uses an umbrella, or any thing to shade his eyes or his face, and he always looks comfortable and proper in the sun. But of all the ridiculous sights I ever have seen, our party of eight is the most so—they do cut such an outlandish figure. They travel single file; they all wear the endless white rag of Constantinople wrapped round and round their hats and dangling down their backs; they all wear thick green spectacles, with side-glasses to them; they all hold white umbrellas, lined with green, over their heads; without exception their stirrups are too short—they are the very worst gang of horsemen on earth; their animals to a horse trot fearfully hard—and when they get strung out one after the other; glaring straight ahead and breathless; bouncing high and out of turn, all along the line; knees well up and stiff, elbows flapping like a rooster's that is going to crow, and the long file of umbrellas popping convulsively up and down—when one sees this outrageous picture exposed to the light of day, he is amazed that the gods don't get out their thunderbolts and destroy them off the face of the earth! I do—I wonder at it. I wouldn't let any such caravan go through a country of mine.

And when the sun drops below the horizon and the boys close their umbrellas and put them under their arms, it is only a variation of the picture, not a modification of its absurdity.

But may be you can not see the wild extravagance of my panorama. You could if you were here. Here, you feel all the time just as if you were living about the year 1200 before Christ—or back to the patriarchs—or forward to the New Era. The scenery of the Bible is about you—the customs of the patriarchs are around you—the same people, in the same flowing robes, and in sandals, cross your path—the same long trains of stately camels go and come—the same impressive religious solemnity and silence rest upon the desert and the mountains that were upon them in the remote ages of antiquity, and behold, intruding upon a scene like this, comes this fantastic mob of green-spectacled Yanks, with their flapping elbows and bobbing umbrellas! It is Daniel in the lion's den with a green cotton umbrella under his arm, all over again.

My umbrella is with the baggage, and so are my green spectacles —and there they shall stay. I will not use them. I will show some respect for the eternal fitness of things. It will be bad enough to get sun-struck, without looking ridiculous into the bargain. If I fall, let me fall bearing about me the semblance of a Christian, at least.

From *The Innocents Abroad,* 1869

King Solomon-in-all-his-glory

[From Tiberias on the Sea of Galilee the party of eight proceeded southward.]

We took another swim in the Sea of Galilee at twilight yesterday, and another at sunrise this morning. We have not sailed, but three swims are equal to a sail, are they not? There were plenty of fish visible in the water, but we have no outside aids in this pilgrimage but "Tent Life in the Holy Land," "The Land and the Book," and other literature of like description—no fishing-tackle. There were no fish to be had in the village of Tiberias. True, we saw two or three vagabonds mending their nets, but never trying to catch any thing with them.

We did not go to the ancient warm baths two miles below Tiberias. I had no desire in the world to go there. This seemed a little strange, and prompted me to try to discover what the cause of this unreasonable indifference was. It turned out to be simply because Pliny mentions them. I have conceived a sort of unwarrantable unfriendliness toward Pliny and St. Paul, because it seems as if I can never ferret out a place that I can have to myself. It always and eternally transpires that St. Paul has been to that place, and Pliny has "mentioned" it.

In the early morning we mounted and started. And then a weird apparition marched forth at the head of the procession—a pirate, I thought, if ever a pirate dwelt upon land. It was a tall Arab, as swarthy as an Indian; young—say thirty years of age. On his head he had closely bound a gorgeous yellow and red striped silk scarf, whose ends, lavishly fringed with tassels, hung down between his shoulders and dallied with the wind. From his neck to his knees, in ample folds, a robe swept down that was a very star-spangled banner of curved and sinuous bars of black and white. Out of his back, somewhere, apparently, the long stem of a chibouk projected, and reached far above his right shoulder. Athwart his back, diagonally, and extending high above his left shoulder, was an Arab gun of Saladin's time, that was splendid with silver plating from stock clear up to the end of its measureless stretch of barrel. About his waist was bound many and many a yard of elaborately figured but sadly tarnished stuff that came from sumptuous Persia, and among the baggy folds in front the sunbeams glinted from a formidable battery of old brass-mounted horse-pistols and the gilded hilts of blood-thirsty knives. There were holsters for more pistols appended to the wonderful stack of long-haired goat-skins and Persian carpets, which the man had been taught to regard in the light of a saddle; and down among the pendulous rank of vast tassels that swung from that saddle, and clanging against the iron shovel of a stirrup that propped the warrior's knees up toward his chin, was a crooked, silver-clad scimetar of such awful dimensions and such implacable expression that no man might hope to look upon it and not shudder. The fringed and bedizened prince whose privilege it is to ride the pony and lead the elephant into a country village is poor and naked compared to this chaos of paraphernalia, and the happy vanity of the one is the very poverty of satisfaction compared to the majestic serenity, the overwhelming complacency of the other.

"*Who* is this? *What* is this?" That was the trembling inquiry all down the line.

"Our guard! From Galilee to the birthplace of the Saviour, the country is infested with fierce Bedouins, whose sole happiness it is, in this life, to cut and stab and mangle and murder unoffending Christians. Allah be with us!"

"Then hire a regiment! Would you send us out among these desperate hordes, with no salvation in our utmost need but this old turret?"

The dragoman laughed—not at the facetiousness of the simile, for verily, that guide or that courier or that dragoman never yet lived upon earth who had in him the faintest appreciation of a joke, even though that joke were so broad and so ponderous that if it fell on him it would flatten him out like a postage stamp—the dragoman laughed, and then, emboldened by some thought that was in his brain, no doubt, proceeded to extremities and winked.

In straits like these, when a man laughs, it is encouraging; when he winks, it is positively reassuring. He finally intimated that one guard would be sufficient to protect us, but that that one was an absolute necessity. It was because of the moral weight his awful panoply would have with the Bedouins. Then I said we didn't want any guard at all. If one fantastic vagabond could protect eight armed Christians and a pack of Arab servants from all harm, surely that detachment could protect themselves. He shook his head doubtfully. Then I said, just think of how it looks—think of how it would read, to self-reliant Americans, that we went sneaking through this deserted wilderness under the protection of this masquerading Arab, who would break his neck getting out of the country if a man that *was* a man ever started after him. It was a mean, low, degrading position. Why were we ever told to bring navy revolvers with us if we had to be protected at last by this infamous star-spangled scum of the desert? These appeals were vain—the dragoman only smiled and shook his head.

I rode to the front and struck up an acquaintance with King Solomon-in-all-his-glory, and got him to show me his lingering eternity of a gun. It had a rusty flint lock; it was ringed and barred and plated with silver from end to end, but it was as desperately out of the perpendicular as are the billiard cues of '49 that one finds yet in service in the ancient mining camps of California. The muzzle was eaten by the rust of centuries into a ragged filagree-work, like the end of a burnt-out stove-pipe. I shut one eye and peered within—it was flaked with iron rust like an old steamboat boiler. I borrowed the ponderous pistols and snapped them. They were rusty inside, too—had not been loaded for a generation. I went back, full of encouragement, and reported to the guide, and asked him to discharge this dismantled fortress. It came out, then. This fellow was a retainer of the Sheik of Tiberias. He was a source of Government revenue. He was to the Empire of Tiberias what the customs are to America. The Sheik imposed guards upon travelers and charged them for it. It is a lucrative source of emolument, and sometimes brings into the national treasury as much as thirty-five or forty dollars a year.

I knew the warrior's secret now; I knew the hollow vanity of his rusty trumpery, and despised his asinine complacency. I told on him, and with reckless daring the cavalcade rode straight ahead into the perilous solitudes of the desert, and scorned his frantic warnings of the mutilation and death that hovered about them on every side.

From *The Innocents Abroad,* 1869

A Fearless Man

The Nazarene girls are homely. Some of them have large, lustrous eyes, but none of them have pretty faces. These girls wear a single garment, usually, and it is loose, shapeless, of undecided color; it is generally out of repair, too. They wear, from crown to jaw, curious strings of old coins, after the manner of the belles of Tiberias, and brass jewelry upon their wrists and in their ears. They wear no shoes and stockings. They are the most human girls we have found in the country yet, and the best natured. But there is no question that these picturesque maidens sadly lack comeliness.

A pilgrim—the "Enthusiast"—said: "See that tall, graceful girl! look at the Madonna-like beauty of her countenance!"

Another pilgrim came along presently and said: "Observe that tall, graceful girl; what queenly Madonna-like gracefulness of beauty is in her countenance."

I said: "She is not tall, she is short; she is not beautiful, she is homely; she is graceful enough, I grant, but she is rather boisterous."

The third and last pilgrim moved by, before long, and he said: "Ah, what a tall, graceful girl! what Madonna-like gracefulness of queenly beauty!"

The verdicts were all in. It was time now, to look up the authorities for all these opinions. I found this paragraph, which follows. Written by whom? Wm. C. Grimes:

"After we were in the saddle, we rode down to the spring to have a last look at the women of Nazareth, who were, as a class, much the prettiest that we had seen in the East. As we approached the crowd a tall girl of nineteen advanced toward Miriam and offered her a cup of water. Her movement was graceful and queenly. We exclaimed on the spot at the Madonna-like beauty of her countenance. Whitely was suddenly thirsty, and begged for water, and drank it slowly, with his eyes over the top of the cup, fixed on her large black eyes, which gazed on him quite as curiously as he on her. Then Moreright wanted water. She gave it to him and he managed to spill it so as to ask for another cup, and by the time she came to me she saw through the operation; her eyes were full of fun as she looked at me. I laughed outright, and she joined me in as gay a shout as ever country maiden in old Orange county. I wished for a picture of her. A Madonna, whose face was a portrait of that beautiful Nazareth girl, would be a 'thing of beauty' and 'a joy forever.'"

That is the kind of gruel which has been served out from Palestine for ages. Commend me to Fennimore Cooper to find beauty in the Indians, and to Grimes to find it in the Arabs. Arab men are often fine looking, but Arab women are not. We can all believe that the Virgin Mary was beautiful; it is not natural to think otherwise; but does it follow that it is our duty to find beauty in these present women of Nazareth?

I love to quote from Grimes, because he is so dramatic. And because he is so romantic. And because he seems to care but little whether he tells the truth or not, so he scares the reader or excites his envy or his admiration.

He went through this peaceful land with one hand forever on his revolver, and the other on his pocket-handkerchief. Always, when he was not on the point of crying over a holy place, he was on the point of killing an Arab. More surprising things happened to him in Palestine than ever happened to any traveler here or elsewhere since Munchausen died.

At Beit Jin, where nobody had interfered with him, he crept out of his tent at dead of night and shot at what he took to be an Arab lying on a rock, some distance away, planning evil. The ball killed a wolf. Just before he fired, he makes a dramatic picture of himself—as usual, to scare the reader:

"Was it imagination, or did I see a moving object on the surface of the rock? If it were a man, why did he not now drop me? He had a beautiful shot as I stood out in my black boornoose against the white tent. I had the sensation of an entering bullet in my throat, breast, brain."

Reckless creature!

Riding toward Genessaret, they saw two Bedouins, and "we

looked to our pistols and loosened them quietly in our shawls," etc. Always cool.

In Samaria, he charged up a hill, in the face of a volley of stones; he fired into the crowd of men who threw them. He says:

"*I never lost an opportunity* of impressing the Arabs with the perfection of American and English weapons, and the danger of attacking any one of the armed Franks. I think the lesson of that ball not lost."

At Beitin he gave his whole band of Arab muleteers a piece of his mind, and then—

"I contented myself with a solemn assurance that if there occurred another instance of disobedience to orders, I would thrash the responsible party as he never dreamed of being thrashed, and if I could not find who was responsible, I would whip them all, from first to last, whether there was a governor at hand to do it or I had to do it myself."

Perfectly fearless, this man.

He rode down the perpendicular path in the rocks, from the Castle of Banias to the oak grove, at a flying gallop, his horse striding "thirty feet" at every bound. I stand prepared to bring thirty reliable witnesses to prove that Putnam's famous feat at Horseneck was insignificant compared to this.

Behold him—always theatrical—looking at Jerusalem—this time, by an oversight, with his hand off his pistol for once.

"I stood in the road, my hand on my horse's neck, and with my dim eyes sought to trace the outlines of the holy places which I had long before fixed in my mind, but the fast-flowing tears forbade my succeeding. There were our Mohammedan servants, a Latin monk, two Armenians and a Jew in our cortege, and all alike gazed with overflowing eyes."

If Latin monks and Arabs cried, I know to a moral certainty that the horses cried also, and so the picture is complete.

But when necessity demanded, he could be firm as adamant. In the Lebanon Valley an Arab youth—a Christian; he is particular to explain that Mohammedans do not steal—robbed him of a paltry ten dollars' worth of powder and shot. He convicted him before a sheik and looked on while he was punished by the terrible bastinado. Hear him:

"He (Mousa) was on his back in a twinkling, howling, shouting, screaming, but he was carried out to the piazza before the door, where we could see the operation, and laid face down. One man sat on his back and one on his legs, the latter holding up his feet, while a third laid on the bare soles a rhinoceros-hide koorbash* that whizzed through the air at every stroke. Poor Moreright was in agony, and Nama and Nama the Second (mother and sister of Mousa,) were on their faces begging and wailing, now embracing my knees and now Whitely's, while the brother, outside, made the air ring with cries louder than Mousa's. Even Yusef came and asked me on his knees to relent, and last of all, Betuni—the rascal had lost a feedbag in their house and had been loudest in his denunciations that morning—besought the Howajji to have mercy on the fellow."

But not he! The punishment was "suspended," at the *fifteenth blow,* to hear the confession. Then Grimes and his party rode away, and left the entire Christian family to be fined and as severely punished as the *Mohammedan sheik* should deem proper.

"As I mounted, Yusef once more begged me to interfere and have mercy on them, but I looked around at the dark faces of the crowd, and I couldn't find one drop of pity in my heart for them."

He closes his picture with a rollicking burst of humor which contrasts finely with the grief of the mother and her children.

One more paragraph:

"Then once more I bowed my head. It is no shame to have wept in Palestine. I wept, when I saw Jerusalem, I wept when I lay in the starlight at Bethlehem, I wept on the blessed shores of Galilee. My hand was no less firm on the rein, my finger did not tremble on the trigger of my pistol when I rode with it in my right hand along the shore of the blue sea" (weeping.) "My eye was not dimmed by those tears nor my heart in aught weakened. Let him who would

* "A Koorbash is Arabic for cowhide, the cow being a rhinoceros. It is the most cruel whip known to fame. Heavy as lead, and flexible as India rubber, usually about forty inches long and tapering gradually from an inch in diameter to a point, it administers a blow which *leaves its mark for time."—Scow Life in Egypt,* by the same author.—M. T.

sneer at my emotion close this volume here, for he will find little to his taste in my journeyings through Holy Land."

He never bored but he struck water.

I am aware that this is a pretty voluminous notice of Mr. Grimes' book. However, it is proper and legitimate to speak of it, for "Nomadic Life in Palestine" is a representative book—the representative of a *class* of Palestine books—and a criticism upon it will serve for a criticism upon them all. And since I am treating it in the comprehensive capacity of a representative book, I have taken the liberty of giving to both book and author fictitious names. Perhaps it is in better taste, any how, to do this. . . .

Some of us will be shot before we finish this pilgrimage. The pilgrims read "Nomadic Life" and keep themselves in a constant state of Quixotic heroism. They have their hands on their pistols all the time, and every now and then, when you least expect it, they snatch them out and take aim at Bedouins who are not visible, and draw their knives and make savage passes at other Bedouins who do not exist. I am in deadly peril always, for these spasms are sudden and irregular, and of course I can not tell when to be getting out of the way. If I am accidentally murdered, some time, during one of these romantic frenzies of the pilgrims, Mr. Grimes must be rigidly held to answer as an accessory before the fact. If the pilgrims would take deliberate aim and shoot at a man, it would be all right and proper—because that man would not be in any danger; but these random assaults are what I object to. I do not wish to see any more places like Esdraelon, where the ground is level and people can gallop. It puts melodramatic nonsense into the pilgrims' heads. All at once, when one is jogging along stupidly in the sun, and thinking about something ever so far away, here they come, at a stormy gallop, spurring and whooping at those ridgy old sore-backed plugs till their heels fly higher than their heads, and as they whiz by, out comes a little potato-gun of a revolver, there is a startling little pop, and a small pellet goes singing through the air. Now that I have begun this pilgrimage, I intend to go through with it, though sooth to say, nothing but the most desperate valor has kept me to my purpose up to the present time. I do not mind Bedouins,—I am not afraid of them; because neither Bedouins nor ordinary Arabs have shown any disposition to harm us, but I *do* feel afraid of my own comrades.

From *The Innocents Abroad*, 1869

The Benton House

[Rejoining the *Quaker City* at Jaffa, Clemens sailed to Alexandria, Egypt.]

Alexandria was too much like a European city to be novel, and we soon tired of it. We took the cars and came up here to ancient Cairo, which *is* an Oriental city and of the completest pattern. There is little about it to disabuse one's mind of the error if he should take it into his head that he was in the heart of Arabia. Stately camels and dromedaries, swarthy Egyptians, and likewise Turks and black Ethiopians, turbaned, sashed, and blazing in a rich variety of Oriental costumes of all shades of flashy colors, are what one sees on every hand crowding the narrow streets and the honey-combed bazaars. We are stopping at Shepherd's Hotel, which is the worst on earth except the one I stopped at once in a small town in the United States. It is pleasant to read this sketch in my note-book, now, and know that I can stand Shepherd's Hotel, sure, because I have been in one just like it in America and survived:

I stopped at the Benton House. It used to be a good hotel, but that proves nothing—I used to be a good boy, for that matter. Both of us have lost character of late years. The Benton is not a good hotel. The Benton lacks a very great deal of being a good hotel. Perdition is full of better hotels than the Benton.

It was late at night when I got there, and I told the clerk I would like plenty of lights, because I wanted to read an hour or two. When I reached No. 15 with the porter (we came along a dim hall that was clad in ancient carpeting, faded, worn out in many places, and patched with old scraps of oil cloth—a hall that sank under one's feet, and creaked dismally to every footstep,) he struck a light—two inches of sallow, sorrowful, consumptive tallow candle, that burned blue, and sputtered, and got discouraged and went out.

The porter lit it again, and I asked if that was all the light the clerk sent. He said, "Oh no, I've got another one here," and he produced another couple of inches of tallow candle. I said, "Light them both —I'll have to have one to see the other by." He did it, but the result was drearier than darkness itself. He was a cheery, accommodating rascal. He said he would go "somewheres" and steal a lamp. I abetted and encouraged him in his criminal design. I heard the landlord get after him in the hall ten minutes afterward.

"Where are you going with that lamp?"

"Fifteen wants it, sir."

"Fifteen! why he's got a double lot of candles—does the man want to illuminate the house?—does he want to get up a torch-light procession?—what *is* he up to, any how?"

"He don't like them candles—says he wants a lamp."

"Why what in the nation does—why I never heard of such a thing? What on earth can he want with that lamp?"

"Well, he only wants to read—that's what he says."

"Wants to read, does he?—ain't satisfied with a thousand candles, but has to have a lamp!—I do wonder what the devil that fellow wants that lamp for? Take him another candle, and then if——"

"But he wants the lamp—says he'll burn the d—d old house down if he don't get a lamp!" (a remark which I never made.)

"I'd like to see him at it once. Well, you take it along—but I swear it beats *my* time, though—and see if you can't find out what in the very nation he *wants* with that lamp."

And he went off growling to himself and still wondering and wondering over the unaccountable conduct of No. 15. The lamp was a good one, but it revealed some disagreeable things—a bed in the suburbs of a desert of room—a bed that had hills and valleys in it, and you'd have to accommodate your body to the impression left in it by the man that slept there last, before you could lie comfortably; a carpet that had seen better days; a melancholy washstand in a remote corner, and a dejected pitcher on it sorrowing over a broken nose; a looking-glass split across the centre, which chopped your head off at the chin and made you look like some dreadful unfinished monster or other; the paper peeling in shreds from the walls.

I sighed and said: "This is charming; and now don't you think you could get me something to read?"

The porter said, "Oh, certainly; the old man's got dead loads of books;" and he was gone before I could tell him what sort of literature I would rather have. And yet his countenance expressed the utmost confidence in his ability to execute the commission with credit to himself. The old man made a descent on him.

"What are you going to do with that pile of books?"

"Fifteen wants 'em, sir."

"Fifteen, is it? He'll want a warming-pan, next—he'll want a nurse! Take him every thing there is in the house—take him the bar-keeper—take him the baggage-wagon—take him a chambermaid! Confound me, I never saw any thing like it. What did he say he wants with those books?"

"Wants to read 'em, like enough; it ain't likely he wants to eat 'em, I don't reckon."

"Wants to read 'em—wants to read 'em this time of night, the infernal lunatic! Well, he can't have them."

"But he says he's mor'ly bound to have 'em; he says he'll just go a-rairin' and a-chargin' through this house and raise more——well, there's no tellin' what he won't do if he don't get 'em; because he's drunk and crazy and desperate, and nothing'll soothe him down but them cussed books." [I had not made any threats, and was not in the condition ascribed to me by the porter.]

"Well, go on; but I will be around when he goes to rairing and charging, and the first rair he makes I'll make him rair out of the window." And then the old gentleman went off, growling as before.

The genius of that porter was something wonderful. He put an armful of books on the bed and said "Good night" as confidently as if he knew perfectly well that those books were exactly my style of reading matter. And well he might. His selection covered the whole range of legitimate literature. It comprised "The Great Consummation," by Rev. Dr. Cummings—theology; "Revised Statutes of the State of Missouri"—law; "The Complete Horse-Doctor"—medicine; "The Toilers of the Sea," by Victor Hugo—romance; "The works of William Shakespeare"—poetry. I shall never cease to admire the tact and the intelligence of that gifted porter.

From *The Innocents Abroad,* 1869

The Great Pyramid of Cheops

[From Alexandria, Clemens and his companions went by rail to Cairo and then by donkey to Giza and the pyramids.]

A laborious walk in the flaming sun brought us to the foot of the great Pyramid of Cheops. It was a fairy vision no longer. It was a corrugated, unsightly mountain of stone. Each of its monstrous sides was a wide stairway which rose upward, step above step, narrowing as it went, till it tapered to a point far aloft in the air. Insect men and women—pilgrims from the *Quaker City*—were creeping about its dizzy perches, and one little black swarm were waving postage stamps from the airy summit—handkerchiefs will be understood.

Of course we were besieged by a rabble of muscular Egyptians and Arabs who wanted the contract of dragging us to the top—all tourists are. Of course you could not hear your own voice for the din that was around you. Of course the Sheiks said *they* were the only responsible parties; that all contracts must be made with them, all moneys paid over to them, and none exacted from us by any but themselves alone. Of course they contracted that the varlets who dragged us up should not mention buckshees once. For such is the usual routine. Of course we contracted with them, paid them, were delivered into the hands of the draggers, dragged up the Pyramids, and harried and be-deviled for buckshees from the foundation clear to the summit. We paid it, too, for we were purposely spread very far apart over the vast side of the Pyramid. There was no help near if we called, and the Herculeses who dragged us had a way of asking sweetly and flatteringly for buckshees, which was seductive, and of looking fierce and threatening to throw us down the precipice, which was persuasive and convincing.

Each step being full as high as a dinner-table; there being very,

very many of the steps; an Arab having hold of each of our arms and springing upward from step to step and snatching us with them, forcing us to lift our feet as high as our breasts every time, and do it rapidly and keep it up till we were ready to faint, who shall say it is not lively, exhilarating, lacerating, muscle-straining, bone-wrenching and perfectly excruciating and exhausting pastime, climbing the Pyramids? I beseeched the varlets not to twist *all* my joints asunder; I iterated, reiterated, even *swore* to them that I did not wish to beat any body to the top; did all I could to convince them that if I got there the last of all I would feel blessed above men and grateful to them forever; I begged them, prayed them, pleaded with them to let me stop and rest a moment—only one little moment: and they only answered with some more frightful springs, and an unenlisted volunteer behind opened a bombardment of determined boosts with his head which threatened to batter my whole political economy to wreck and ruin.

Twice, for one minute, they let me rest while they extorted bucksheesh, and then continued their maniac flight up the Pyramid. They wished to beat the other parties. It was nothing to them that I, a stranger, must be sacrificed upon the altar of their unholy ambition. But in the midst of sorrow, joy blooms. Even in this dark hour I had a sweet consolation. For I knew that except these Mohammedans repented they would go straight to perdition some day. And *they* never repent—they never forsake their paganism. This thought calmed me, cheered me, and I sank down, limp and exhausted, upon the summit, but happy, *so* happy and serene within.

On the one hand, a mighty sea of yellow sand stretched away toward the ends of the earth, solemn, silent, shorn of vegetation, its solitude uncheered by any forms of creature life; on the other, the Eden of Egypt was spread below us—a broad green floor, cloven by the sinuous river, dotted with villages, its vast distances measured and marked by the diminishing stature of receding clusters of palms. It lay asleep in an enchanted atmosphere. There was no sound, no motion. Above the date-plumes in the middle distance, swelled a domed and pinnacled mass, glimmering through a tinted, exquisite mist; away toward the horizon a dozen shapely pyramids watched over ruined Memphis: and at our feet the bland impassible Sphynx looked out upon the picture from her throne in the sands as placidly and pensively as she had looked upon its like full fifty lagging centuries ago.

We suffered torture no pen can describe from the hungry appeals for bucksheesh that gleamed from Arab eyes and poured incessantly from Arab lips. Why try to call up the traditions of vanished Egyptian grandeur; why try to fancy Egypt following dead Rameses to his tomb in the Pyramid, or the long multitude of Israel departing over the desert yonder? Why try to think at all? The thing was impossible. One must bring his meditations cut and dried, or else cut and dry them afterward.

The traditional Arab proposed, in the traditional way, to run down Cheops, cross the eighth of a mile of sand intervening between it and the tall pyramid of Cephron, ascend to Cephron's summit and return to us on the top of Cheops—all in nine minutes by the watch, and the whole service to be rendered for a single dollar. In the first flush of irritation, I said let the Arab and his exploits go to the mischief. But stay. The upper third of Cephron was coated with dressed marble, smooth as glass. A blessed thought entered my brain. He must infallibly break his neck. Close the contract with dispatch, I said, and let him go. He started. We watched. He went bounding down the vast broadside, spring after spring, like an ibex. He grew small and smaller till he became a bobbing pigmy, away down toward the bottom—then disappeared. We turned and peered over the other side—forty seconds—eighty seconds—a hundred—happiness, he is dead already!—two minutes—and a quarter—"There he goes!" Too true—it was too true. He was very small, now. Gradually, but surely, he overcame the level ground. He began to spring and climb again. Up, up, up—at last he reached the smooth coating—now for it. But he clung to it with toes and fingers, like a fly. He crawled this way and that—away to the right, slanting upward—away to the left, still slanting upward—and stood at last, a black peg on the summit, and waved his pigmy scarf! Then he crept downward to the raw steps again, then picked up his agile heels and flew. We lost him presently. But presently again we saw him under us, mounting with undiminished energy. Shortly he bounded into our midst with a gallant war-whoop. Time, eight minutes, forty-one seconds. He had won. His bones were intact. It was a failure. I reflected. I said to myself, he is tired, and must grow dizzy. I will risk another dollar on him.

He started again. Made the trip again. Slipped on the smooth coating—I almost had him. But an infamous crevice saved him. He was with us once more—perfectly sound. Time, eight minutes, forty-six seconds.

I said to Dan, "Lend me a dollar—I can beat this game, yet."

Worse and worse. He won again. Time, eight minutes, forty-eight seconds. I was out of all patience, now. I was desperate.—Money was no longer of any consequence. I said, "Sirrah, I will give you a hundred dollars to jump off this pyramid head first. If you do not like the terms, name your bet. I scorn to stand on expenses now. I will stay right here and risk money on you as long as Dan has got a cent."

I was in a fair way to win, now, for it was a dazzling opportunity for an Arab. He pondered a moment, and would have done it, I think, but his mother arrived, then, and interfered. Her tears moved me—I never can look upon the tears of woman with indifference—and I said I would give her a hundred to jump off, too.

But it was a failure. The Arabs are too high-priced in Egypt. They put on airs unbecoming to such savages.

We descended, hot and out of humor. The dragoman lit candles, and we all entered a hole near the base of the pyramid, attended by a crazy rabble of Arabs who thrust their services upon us uninvited. They dragged us up a long inclined chute, and dripped candle-grease all over us. This chute was not more than twice as wide and high as a Saratoga trunk, and was walled, roofed and floored with solid blocks of Egyptian granite as wide as a wardrobe, twice as thick and three times as long. We kept on climbing, through the oppressive gloom, till I thought we ought to be nearing the top of the pyramid again, and then came to the "Queen's Chamber," and shortly to the Chamber of the King. These large apartments were tombs. The walls were built of monstrous masses of smoothed granite, neatly joined together. Some of them were nearly as large square as an ordinary parlor. A great stone sarcophagus like a bathtub stood in the centre of the King's Chamber. Around it were gathered a picturesque group of Arab savages and soiled and tattered pilgrims, who held their candles aloft in the gloom while they chattered, and the winking blurs of light shed a dim glory down upon one of the irrepressible memento-seekers who was pecking at the venerable sarcophagus with his sacrilegious hammer.

We struggled out to the open air and the bright sunshine, and for the space of thirty minutes received ragged Arabs by couples, dozens and platoons, and paid them bucksheesh for services they swore and proved by each other that they had rendered, but which we had not been aware of before—and as each party was paid, they dropped into the rear of the procession and in due time arrived again with a newly-invented delinquent list for liquidation.

We lunched in the shade of the pyramid, and in the midst of this encroaching and unwelcome company, and then Dan and Jack and I started away for a walk. A howling swarm of beggars followed us—surrounded us—almost headed us off. A sheik, in flowing white bournous and gaudy head-gear, was with them. He wanted more bucksheesh. But we had adopted a new code—it was millions for defense, but not a cent for bucksheesh. I asked him if he could persuade the others to depart if we paid him. He said yes—for ten francs. We accepted the contract, and said—

"Now persuade your vassals to fall back."

He swung his long staff round his head and three Arabs bit the dust. He capered among the mob like a very maniac. His blows fell like hail, and wherever one fell a subject went down. We had to hurry to the rescue and tell him it was only necessary to damage them a little, he need not kill them.—In two minutes we were alone with the sheik, and remained so. The persuasive powers of this illiterate savage were remarkable.

From *The Innocents Abroad*, 1869

Cookery Complaints

It had long ago been decided in a noisy public meeting in the main cabin that we could not go to Lisbon, because we must surely be quarantined there. We did every thing by mass-meeting, in the good old national way, from swapping off one empire for another on the programme of the voyage down to complaining of the cookery and the scarcity of napkins. I am reminded, now, of one of these complaints of the cookery made by a passenger. The coffee had been steadily growing more and more execrable for the space of three weeks, till at last it had ceased to be coffee altogether and had assumed the nature of mere discolored water—so this person said. He said it was so weak that it was transparent an inch in depth around the edge of the cup. As he approached the table one morning he saw the transparent edge—by means of his extraordinary vision—long before he got to his seat. He went back and complained in a high-handed way to Capt. Duncan. He said the coffee was disgraceful. The Captain showed his. It seemed tolerably good. The incipient mutineer was more outraged than ever, then, at what he denounced as the partiality shown the captain's table over the other tables in the ship. He flourished back and got his cup and set it down triumphantly, and said:

"Just try that mixture once, Captain Duncan."

He smelt it—tasted it—smiled benignantly—then said:

"It *is* inferior—for *coffee*—but it is pretty fair *tea*."

The humbled mutineer smelt it, tasted it, and returned to his seat. He had made an egregious ass of himself before the whole ship. He did it no more. After that he took things as they came. That was me.

From *The Innocents Abroad,* 1869

A Newspaper Valedictory

In this place I will print an article which I wrote for the New York *Herald* the night we arrived. I do it partly because my contract with my publishers makes it compulsory; partly because it is a proper, tolerably accurate, and exhaustive summing up of the cruise of the ship and the performances of the pilgrims in foreign lands; and partly because some of the passengers have abused me for writing it, and I wish the public to see how thankless a task it is to put one's self to trouble to glorify unappreciative people. I was charged with "rushing into print" with these compliments. I did not rush. I had written news letters to the *Herald* sometimes, but yet when I visited the office that day I did not say any thing about writing a valedictory. I did go to the *Tribune* office to see if such an article was wanted, because I belonged on the regular staff of that paper and it was simply a duty to do it. The managing editor was absent, and so I thought no more about it. At night when the *Herald's* request came for an article, I did not "rush." In fact, I demured for a while, because I did not feel like writing compliments then, and therefore was afraid to speak of the cruise lest I might be betrayed into using other than complimentary language. However, I reflected that it would be a just and righteous thing to go down and write a kind word for the Hadjis—Hadjis are people who have made the pilgrimage—because parties not interested could not do it so feelingly as I, a fellow-Hadji, and so I penned the valedictory. I have read it, and read it again; and if there is a sentence in it that is not fulsomely complimentary to captain, ship and passengers, *I* can not find it. If it is not a chapter that any company might be proud to have a body write about them, my judgment is fit for nothing. With these remarks I confidently submit it to the unprejudiced judgment of the reader:

RETURN OF THE HOLY LAND EXCURSIONISTS—THE STORY OF THE CRUISE.

To the Editor of the Herald:

The steamer Quaker City has accomplished at last her extraordinary voyage and returned to her old pier at the foot of Wall street. The expedition was a success in some respects, in some it was not. Originally it was advertised as a "pleasure excursion." Well, perhaps, it was a pleasure excursion, but certainly it did not look like one; certainly it did not act like one. Any body's and every body's notion of a pleasure excursion is that the parties to it will of a necessity be young and giddy and somewhat boisterous. They will dance a good deal, sing a good deal, make love, but sermonize very little. Any body's and every body's notion of a well conducted funeral is that there must be a hearse and a corpse, and chief mourners and mourners by courtesy, many old people, much solemnity, no levity, and a prayer and a sermon withal. Three-fourths of the Quaker City's passengers were between forty and seventy years of age! There was a picnic crowd for you! It may be supposed that the other fourth was composed of young girls. But it was not. It was chiefly composed of rusty old bachelors and a child of six years. Let us average the ages of the Quaker City's pilgrims and set the figure down as fifty years. Is any man insane enough to imagine that this picnic of patriarchs sang, made love, danced, laughed, told anecdotes, dealt in ungodly levity? In my experience they sinned little in these matters. No doubt it was presumed here at home that these frolicsome veterans laughed and sang and romped all day, and day after day, and kept up a noisy excitement from one end of the ship to the other; and that they played blind-man's buff or danced quadrilles and waltzes on moonlight evenings on the quarterdeck; and that at odd moments of unoccupied time they jotted a laconic item or two in the journals they opened on such an elaborate plan when they left home, and then skurried off to their whist and euchre labors under the cabin lamps. If these things were presumed, the presumption was at fault. The venerable excursionists were not gay and frisky. They played no blind-man's buff; they dealt not in whist; they shirked not the irksome journal, for alas! most of them were even writing books. They never romped, they talked but little, they never sang, save in the nightly prayer-meeting.

The pleasure ship was a synagogue, and the pleasure trip was a funeral excursion without a corpse. (There is nothing exhilarating about a funeral excursion without a corpse.) A free, hearty laugh was a sound that was not heard oftener than once in seven days about those decks or in those cabins, and when it was heard it met with precious little sympathy. The excursionists danced, on three separate evenings, long, long ago, (it seems an age,) quadrilles, of a single set, made up of three ladies and five gentlemen, (the latter with handkerchiefs around their arms to signify their sex,) who timed their feet to the solemn wheezing of a melodeon; but even this melancholy orgie was voted to be sinful, and dancing was discontinued.

The pilgrims played dominoes when too much Josephus or Robinson's Holy Land Researches, or book-writing, made recreation necessary—for dominoes is about as mild and sinless a game as any in the world, perhaps, excepting always the ineffably insipid diversion they call croquet, which is a game where you don't pocket any balls and don't carom on any thing of any consequence, and when you are done nobody has to pay, and there are no refreshments to saw off, and, consequently, there isn't any satisfaction whatever about it—they played dominoes till they were rested, and then they blackguarded each other privately till prayer-time. When they were not seasick they were uncommonly prompt when the dinner-gong sounded. Such was our daily life on board the ship—solemnity, decorum, dinner, dominoes, devotions, slander. It was not lively enough for a pleasure trip; but if we had only had a corpse it would have made a noble funeral excursion. It is all over now; but when I look back the idea of these venerable fossils skipping forth on a six months' picnic, seems exquisitely refreshing. The advertised title of the expedition—"The Grand Holy Land Pleasure Excursion"—was a misnomer. "The Grand Holy Land Funeral Procession" would have been better—much better.

Wherever we went, in Europe, Asia, or Africa, we made a sensation, and, I suppose I may add, created a famine. None of us had ever been any where before; we all hailed from the interior; travel was a wild novelty to us, and we conducted ourselves in accordance with the natural instincts that were in us, and trammeled ourselves with no ceremonies, no conventionalities. We always took care to make it understood that we were Americans—Americans! When we found that a good many foreigners had hardly ever heard of America, and that a good many more knew it only as a barbarous province away off somewhere, that had lately been at war with somebody, we pitied the ignorance of the Old World, but abated no jot of our importance. Many and many a simple community in the Eastern hemisphere will remember for years the incursion of the strange horde in the year of our Lord 1867, that called themselves Americans, and seemed to imagine in some unaccountable way that they had a right to be proud of it. We generally created a famine, partly because the coffee on the Quaker City was unendurable, and sometimes the more substantial fare was not strictly first class; and partly because one naturally tires of sitting long at the same board and eating from the same dishes.

The people of those foreign countries are very, very ignorant. They looked curiously at the costumes we had brought from the wilds of America. They observed that we talked loudly at table sometimes. They noticed that we looked out for expenses, and got what we conveniently could out of a franc, and wondered where in the mischief we came from. In Paris they just simply opened their eyes and stared when we spoke to them in French! We never did succeed in making those idiots understand their own language. One of our passengers said to a shopkeeper, in reference to a proposed return to buy a pair of gloves, "*Allong restay trankeel—may be ve coom Moonday;*" and would you believe it, that shopkeeper, a born Frenchman, had to ask what it was that had been said. Sometimes it seems to me, somehow, that there must be a difference between Parisian French and Quaker City French.

The people stared at us every where, and we stared at them. We generally made them feel rather small, too, before we got done with them, because we bore down on them with America's greatness until we crushed them. And yet we took kindly to the manners and customs, and especially to the fashions of the various people we visited. When we left the Azores, we wore awful capotes and used fine tooth combs—successfully. When we came back from Tangier, in Africa, we were topped with fezzes of the bloodiest hue, hung with tassels like an Indian's scalp-lock. In France and Spain we attracted some attention in these costumes. In Italy they naturally took us for distempered Garibaldians, and set a gunboat to look for any thing significant in our changes of uniform. We made Rome howl. We could have made any place howl when we had all our clothes on. We got no fresh raiment in Greece—they had but little there of any kind. But at Constantinople, how we turned out! Turbans, scimetars, fezzes, horse-pistols, tunics, sashes, baggy trowsers, yellow slippers—Oh, we were gorgeous! The illustrious dogs of Constantinople barked their under jaws off, and even then failed to do us justice. They are all dead by this time. They could not go through such a run of business as we gave them and survive.

And then we went to see the Emperor of Russia. We just called on him as comfortably as if we had known him a century or so, and when we had finished our visit we variegated ourselves with selections from Russian costumes and sailed away again more picturesque than ever. In Smyrna we picked up camel's hair shawls and other dressy things from Persia; but in Palestine—ah, in Palestine—our splendid career ended. They didn't wear any clothes there to speak of. We were satisfied, and stopped. We made no experiments. We did not try their costume. But we astonished the natives of that country. We astonished them with such eccentricities of dress as we could muster. We prowled through the Holy Land, from Cesarea Philippi to Jerusalem and the Dead Sea, a weird procession of pilgrims, gotten up regardless of expense, solemn, gorgeous, green-spectacled, drowsing under blue umbrellas, and astride of a sorrier lot of horses, camels and asses than those that came out of Noah's ark, after eleven months of seasickness and short rations. If ever those children of Israel in Palestine forget when Gideon's Band went through there from America, they ought to be cursed once more and finished. It was the rarest spectacle that ever astounded mortal eyes, perhaps.

Well, we were at home in Palestine. It was easy to see that that was the grand feature of the expedition. We had cared nothing much about Europe. We galloped through the Louvre, the Pitti, the Ufizzi, the Vatican—all the galleries—and through the pictured and frescoed churches of Venice, Naples, and the cathedrals of Spain; some of us said that certain of the great works of the old masters were glorious creations of genius, (we found it out in the guide-book, though we got hold of the wrong picture sometimes,) and the others said they were disgraceful old daubs. We examined modern and ancient statuary with a critical eye in Florence, Rome, or any where we found it, and praised it if we saw fit, and if we didn't we said we preferred the wooden Indians in front of the cigar stores of America. But the Holy Land brought out all our enthusiasm. We fell into raptures by the barren shores of Galilee; we pondered at

Tabor and at Nazareth; we exploded into poetry over the questionable loveliness of Esdraelon; we meditated at Jezreel and Samaria over the missionary zeal of Jehu; we rioted—fairly rioted among the holy places of Jerusalem; we bathed in Jordan and the Dead Sea, reckless whether our accident-insurance policies were extra-hazardous or not, and brought away so many jugs of precious water from both places that all the country from Jericho to the mountains of Moab will suffer from drouth this year, I think. Yet, the pilgrimage part of the excursion was its pet feature—there is no question about that. After dismal, smileless Palestine, beautiful Egypt had few charms for us. We merely glanced at it and were ready for home.

They wouldn't let us land at Malta—quarantine; they would not let us land in Sardinia; nor at Algiers, Africa; nor at Malaga, Spain, nor Cadiz, nor at the Madeira islands. So we got offended at all foreigners and turned our backs upon them and came home. I suppose we only stopped at the Bermudas because they were in the programme. We did not care any thing about any place at all. We wanted to go home. Homesickness was abroad in the ship—it was epidemic. If the authorities of New York had known how badly we had it, they would have quarantined us here.

The grand pilgrimage is over. Good-bye to it, and a pleasant memory to it, I am able to say in all kindness. I bear no malice, no ill-will toward any individual that was connected with it, either as passenger or officer. Things I did not like at all yesterday I like very well to-day, now that I am at home, and always hereafter I shall be able to poke fun at the whole gang if the spirit so moves me to do, without ever saying a malicious word. The expedition accomplished all that its programme promised that it should accomplish, and we ought all to be satisfied with the management of the matter, certainly. Bye-bye!

MARK TWAIN.

I call that complimentary. It *is* complimentary; and yet I never have received a word of thanks for it from the Hadjis; on the contrary I speak nothing but the serious truth when I say that many of them even took exception to the article. In endeavoring to please them I slaved over that sketch for two hours, and had my labor for my pains. I never will do a generous deed again.

From *The Innocents Abroad,* 1869

The Cayote

[When Clemens's older brother, Orion, was appointed Secretary of Nevada Territory and offered Sam "the sublime position of private secretary under him," the latter, never having traveled away from home, eagerly accepted. The brothers boarded ship at St. Louis, sailed to "St. Joe" and there took the overland stage coach for Carson City, Nevada. Orion, Sam and a man named George Bemis were the passengers. They reached the Great Plains.]

Another night of alternate tranquillity and turmoil. But morning came, by and by. It was another glad awakening to fresh breezes, vast expanses of level greensward, bright sunlight, an impressive solitude utterly without visible human beings or human habitations, and an atmosphere of such amazing magnifying properties that trees that seemed close at hand were more than three miles away. We resumed undress uniform, climbed a-top of the flying coach, dangled our legs over the side, shouted occasionally at our frantic mules, merely to see them lay their ears back and scamper faster, tied our hats on to keep our hair from blowing away, and leveled an outlook over the world-wide carpet about us for things new and strange to gaze at. Even at this day it thrills me through and through to think of the life, the gladness and the wild sense of freedom that used to make the blood dance in my veins on those fine overland mornings!

Along about an hour after breakfast we saw the first prairie-dog villages, the first antelope, and the first wolf. If I remember rightly, this latter was the regular *cayote* (pronounced ky-*o*-te) of the farther deserts. And if it *was,* he was not a pretty creature or respectable either, for I got well acquainted with his race afterward, and can speak with confidence. The cayote is a long, slim, sick and sorry-looking skeleton, with a gray wolf-skin stretched over it, a tolerably bushy tail that forever sags down with a despairing expression of forsakenness and misery, a furtive and evil eye, and a long, sharp face, with slightly lifted lip and exposed teeth. He has a general slinking expression all over. The cayote is a living, breathing allegory of Want. He is *always* hungry. He is always poor, out of luck and friendless. The meanest creatures despise him, and even the fleas would desert him for a velocipede. He is so spiritless and cowardly that even while his exposed teeth are pretending a threat, the rest of his face is apologizing for it. And he is *so* homely!—so scrawny, and ribby, and coarse-haired, and pitiful. When he sees you he lifts his lip and lets a flash of his teeth out, and then turns a little out of the course he was pursuing, depresses his head a bit, and strikes a long, soft-footed trot through the sagebrush, glancing over his shoulder at you, from time to time, till he is about out of easy pistol range, and then he stops and takes a deliberate survey of you; he will trot fifty yards and stop again—another fifty and stop again; and finally the gray of his gliding body blends with the gray of the sage-brush, and he disappears. All this is when you make no demonstration against him; but if you do, he develops a livelier interest in his journey, and instantly electrifies his heels and puts such a deal of real estate between himself and your weapon, that by the time you have raised the hammer you see that you need a minie rifle, and by the time you have got him in line you need a rifled cannon, and by the time you have "drawn a bead" on him you see well enough that nothing but an unusually long-winded streak of lightning could reach him where he is now. But if you start a swift-footed dog after him, you will enjoy it ever so much—especially if it is a dog that has a good opinion of himself, and has been brought up to think he knows something about speed. The cayote will go swinging gently off on that deceitful trot of his, and every little while he will smile a fraudful smile over his shoulder that will fill that dog entirely full of encouragement and worldly ambition, and make him lay his head still lower to the ground, and stretch his neck further to the front, and pant more fiercely, and stick his tail out straighter behind, and move his furious legs with a yet wilder frenzy, and leave a broader and broader, and higher and denser cloud of desert sand smoking behind, and marking his long wake across the level plain! And all this time the dog is only a short twenty feet behind the cayote, and to save the soul of him he cannot understand why it is that he cannot get perceptibly closer; and he begins to get aggravated, and it makes him madder and madder to see how gently the cayote glides along and never pants or sweats or ceases to smile; and he grows still more and more incensed to see how shamefully he has been taken in by an entire stranger, and what an ignoble swindle that long, calm, soft-footed trot is; and next he notices that he is getting fagged, and that the cayote actually has to slacken speed a little to keep from running away from him—and *then* that town-dog is mad in earnest, and he begins to strain and weep and swear, and paw the sand higher than ever, and reach for the cayote with concentrated and desperate energy. This "spurt" finds him six feet behind the gliding enemy, and two miles from his friends. And then, in the instant that a wild new hope is lighting up his face, the cayote turns and smiles blandly upon him once more, and with a something about it which seems to say: "Well, I shall have to tear myself away from you, bub—business is business, and it will not do for me to be fooling along this way all day"—and forthwith there is a rushing sound, and the sudden splitting of a long crack through the atmosphere, and behold that dog is solitary and alone in the midst of a vast solitude!

It makes his head swim. He stops, and looks all around; climbs the nearest sand-mound, and gazes into the distance; shakes his head reflectively, and then, without a word, he turns and jogs along back to his train, and takes up a humble position under the hindmost wagon, and feels unspeakably mean, and looks ashamed, and hangs his tail at half-mast for a week. And for as much as a year after that, whenever there is a great hue and cry after a cayote, that dog will merely glance in that direction without emotion, and apparently observe to himself, "I believe I do not wish any of the pie."

From *Roughing It,* 1872

When the Buffalo Climbed a Tree

["At noon on the fifth day out" the brothers arrived at the crossing of the South Platte, a town called Overland City.]

It did seem strange enough to see a town again after what appeared to us such a long acquaintance with deep, still, almost lifeless and houseless solitude! We tumbled out into the busy street feeling like meteoric people crumbled off the corner of some other world, and wakened up suddenly in this. For an hour we took as much interest in Overland City as if we had never seen a town before. The reason we had an hour to spare was because we had to change our stage (for a less sumptuous affair, called a "mud-wagon") and transfer our freight of mails.

Presently we got under way again. We came to the shallow, yellow, muddy South Platte, with its low banks and its scattering flat sandbars and pigmy islands—a melancholy stream straggling through the centre of the enormous flat plain, and only saved from being impossible to find with the naked eye by its sentinel rank of scattering trees standing on either bank. The Platte was "up," they said—which made me wish I could see it when it was down, if it could look any sicker and sorrier. They said it was a dangerous stream to cross, now, because its quicksands were liable to swallow up horses, coach and passengers if an attempt was made to ford it. But the mails had to go, and we made the attempt. Once or twice in midstream the wheels sunk into the yielding sands so threateningly that we half believed we had dreaded and avoided the sea all our lives to be shipwrecked in a "mud-wagon" in the middle of a desert at last. But we dragged through and sped away toward the setting sun.

Next morning, just before dawn, when about five hundred and fifty miles from St. Joseph, our mud-wagon broke down. We were to be delayed five or six hours, and therefore we took horses, by invitation, and joined a party who were just starting on a buffalo hunt. It was noble sport galloping over the plain in the dewy freshness of the morning, but our part of the hunt ended in disaster and disgrace, for a wounded buffalo bull chased the passenger Bemis nearly two miles, and then he forsook his horse and took to a lone tree. He was very sullen about the matter for some twenty-four hours, but at last he began to soften little by little, and finally he said:

"Well, it was not funny, and there was no sense in those gawks making themselves so facetious over it. I tell you I was angry in earnest for awhile. I should have shot that long gangly lubber they called Hank, if I could have done it without crippling six or seven other people—but of course I couldn't, the old 'Allen's' so confounded comprehensive. I wish those loafers had been up in the tree; they wouldn't have wanted to laugh so. If I had had a horse worth a cent—but no, the minute he saw that buffalo bull wheel on him and give a bellow, he raised straight up in the air and stood on his heels. The saddle began to slip, and I took him round the neck and laid close to him, and began to pray. Then he came down and stood up on the other end awhile, and the bull actually stopped pawing sand and bellowing to contemplate the inhuman spectacle. Then the bull made a pass at him and uttered a bellow that sounded perfectly frightful, it was so close to me, and that seemed to literally prostrate my horse's reason, and make a raving distracted maniac of him, and I wish I may die if he didn't stand on his head for a quarter of a minute and shed tears. He was absolutely out of his mind—he was, as sure as truth itself, and he really didn't know what he was doing. Then the bull came charging at us, and my horse dropped down on all fours and took a fresh start—and then for the next ten minutes he would actually throw one handspring after another so fast that the bull began to get unsettled, too, and didn't know where to start in—and so he stood there sneezing, and shovelling dust over his back, and bellowing every now and then, and thinking he had got a fifteen-hundred dollar circus horse for breakfast, certain. Well, I was first out on his neck—the horse's, not the bull's—and then underneath, and next on his rump, and sometimes head up, and sometimes heels—but I tell you it seemed solemn and awful to be ripping and tearing and carrying on so in the presence of death, as you might say. Pretty soon the bull made a snatch for us and brought away some of my horse's tail (I suppose, but do not know, being pretty busy at the time), but *something* made him hungry for solitude and suggested to him to get up and hunt for it. And then you ought to have seen that spider-legged old skeleton go! and you ought to have seen the bull put out after him, too—head down, tongue out, tail up, bellowing like everything, and actually mowing down the weeds, and tearing up the earth, and boosting up the sand like a whirlwind! By George, it was a hot race! I and the saddle were back on the rump, and I had the bridle in my teeth and holding on to the pommel with both hands. First we left the dogs behind; then we passed a jackass rabbit; then we overtook a cayote, and were gaining on an antelope when the rotten girth let go and threw me about thirty yards off to the left, and as the saddle went down over the horse's rump he gave it a lift with his heels that sent it more than four hundred yards up in the air, I wish I may die in a minute if he didn't. I fell at the foot of the only solitary tree there was in nine counties adjacent (as any creature could see with the naked eye), and the next second I had hold of the bark with four sets of nails and my teeth, and the next second after that I was astraddle of the main limb and blaspheming my luck in a way that made my breath smell of brimstone. I *had* the bull, now, if he did not think of *one* thing. But that one thing I dreaded. I dreaded it very seriously. There was a possibility that the bull might not think of it, but there were greater chances that he would. I made up my mind what I would do in case he did. It was a little over forty feet to the ground from where I sat. I cautiously unwound the lariat from the pommel of my saddle—"

"Your *saddle*? Did you take your saddle up in the tree with you?"

"Take it up in the tree with me? Why, how you talk. Of course I didn't. No man could do that. It *fell* in the tree when it came down."

"Oh—exactly."

"Certainly. I unwound the lariat, and fastened one end of it to the limb. It was the very best green raw-hide, and capable of sustaining tons. I made a slip-noose in the other end, and then hung it down to see the length. It reached down twenty-two feet—half way to the ground. I then loaded every barrel of the Allen with a double charge. I felt satisfied. I said to myself, if he never thinks of that one thing that I dread, all right—but if he does, all right anyhow—I am fixed for him. But don't you know that the very thing a man dreads is the thing that always happens? Indeed it is so. I watched the bull, now, with anxiety—anxiety which no one can conceive of who has not been in such a situation and felt that at any moment death might come. Presently a thought came into the bull's eye. I knew it! said I—if my nerve fails now, I am lost. Sure enough, it was just as I had dreaded, he started in to climb the tree—"

"What, the bull?"

"Of course—who else?"

"But a bull can't climb a tree."

"He can't, can't he? Since you know so much about it, did you ever see a bull try?"

"No! I never dreamt of such a thing."

"Well, then, what is the use of your talking that way, then? Because you never saw a thing done, is that any reason why it can't be done?"

"Well, all right—go on. What did you do?"

"The bull started up, and got along well for about ten feet, then slipped and slid back. I breathed easier. He tried it again—got up a little higher—slipped again. But he came at it once more, and this time he was careful. He got gradually higher and higher, and my spirits went down more and more. Up he came—an inch at a time—with his eyes hot, and his tongue hanging out. Higher and higher—hitched his foot over the stump of a limb, and looked up, as much as to say, 'You are my meat, friend.' Up again—higher and higher, and getting more excited the closer he got. He was within ten feet of me! I took a long breath,—and then said I, 'It is now or never.' I had the coil of the lariat all ready; I paid it out slowly, till it hung right over his head; all of a sudden I let go of the slack, and the slip-noose fell fairly round his neck! Quicker than lightning I out with the Allen and let him have it in the face. It was an awful roar, and must have scared the bull out of his senses. When the smoke cleared away, there he was, dangling in the air, twenty foot from the ground, and going out of one convulsion into another faster than you could count! I didn't stop to count, anyhow—I shinned down the tree and shot for home."

"Bemis, is all that true, just as you have stated it?"

"I wish I may rot in my tracks and die the death of a dog if it isn't."

"Well, we can't refuse to believe it, and we don't. But if there were some proofs—"

"Proofs! Did I bring back my lariat?"

"No."

"Did I bring back my horse?"

"No."

"Did you ever see the bull again?"

"No."

"Well, then, what more do you want? I never saw anybody as particular as you are about a little thing like that."

I made up my mind that if this man was not a liar he only missed it by the skin of his teeth.

From *Roughing It,* 1872

A Hundred and Ten Tin Whistles

[At Salt Lake City the brothers put up at the Salt Lake House and unpacked their baggage. They stayed in the city two days.]

It is a luscious country for thrilling evening stories about assassinations of intractable Gentiles. I cannot easily conceive of anything more cosy than the night in Salt Lake which we spent in a Gentile den, smoking pipes and listening to tales of how Burton galloped in among the pleading and defenseless "Morisites" and shot them down, men and women, like so many dogs. And how Bill Hickman, a Destroying Angel, shot Drown and Arnold dead for bringing suit against him for a debt. And how Porter Rockwell did this and that dreadful thing. And how heedless people often come to Utah and make remarks about Brigham, or polygamy, or some other sacred matter, and the very next morning at daylight such parties are sure to be found lying up some back alley, contentedly waiting for the hearse.

And the next most interesting thing is to sit and listen to these Gentiles talk about polygamy; and how some portly old frog of an elder, or a bishop, marries a girl—likes her, marries her sister—likes her, marries another sister—likes her, takes another—likes her, marries her mother—likes her, marries her father, grandfather, great grandfather, and then comes back hungry and asks for more. And how the pert young thing of eleven will chance to be the favorite wife and her own venerable grandmother have to rank away down toward D 4 in their mutual husband's esteem, and have to sleep in the kitchen, as like as not. And how this dreadful sort of thing, this hiving together in one foul nest of mother and daughters, and the making a young daughter superior to her own mother in rank and authority, are things which Mormon women submit to because their religion teaches them that the more wives a man has on earth, and the more children he rears, the higher the place they will all have in the world to come—and the warmer, maybe, though they do not seem to say anything about that.

According to these Gentile friends of ours, Brigham Young's harem contains twenty or thirty wives. They said that some of them had grown old and gone out of active service, but were comfortably housed and cared for in the hennery—or the Lion House, as it is strangely named. Along with each wife were her children—fifty altogether. The house was perfectly quiet and orderly, when the children were still. They all took their meals in one room, and a happy and homelike sight it was pronounced to be. None of our party got an opportunity to take dinner with Mr. Young, but a Gentile by the name of Johnson professed to have enjoyed a sociable breakfast in the Lion House. He gave a preposterous account of the "calling of the roll," and other preliminaries, and the carnage that ensued when the buckwheat cakes came in. But he embellished rather too much. He said that Mr. Young told him several smart sayings of certain of his "two-year-olds," observing with some pride that for many years he had been the heaviest contributor in that line to one of the Eastern magazines; and then he wanted to show Mr. Johnson one of the pets that had said the last good thing, but he could not find the child. He searched the faces of the children in detail, but could not decide which one it was. Finally he gave it up with a sigh and said:

"I thought I would know the little cub again but I don't." Mr. Johnson said further, that Mr. Young observed that life was a sad, sad thing—"because the joy of every new marriage a man contracted was so apt to be blighted by the inopportune funeral of a less recent bride." And Mr. Johnson said that while he and Mr. Young were pleasantly conversing in private, one of the Mrs. Youngs came in and demanded a breast-pin, remarking that she had found out that he had been giving a breast-pin to No. 6, and *she*, for one, did not propose to let this partiality go on without making a satisfactory amount of trouble about it. Mr. Young reminded her that there was a stranger present. Mrs. Young said that if the state of things inside the house was not agreeable to the stranger, he could find room outside. Mr. Young promised the breast-pin, and she went away. But in a minute or two another Mrs. Young came in and demanded a breast-pin. Mr. Young began a remonstrance, but Mrs. Young cut him short. She said No. 6 had got one, and No. 11 was promised one, and it was "no use for him to try to impose on her—she hoped she knew her rights." He gave his promise, and she went. And presently three Mrs. Youngs entered in a body and opened on their husband a tempest of tears, abuse, and entreaty. They had heard all about No. 6, No. 11, and No. 14. Three more breast-pins were promised. They were hardly gone when nine more Mrs. Youngs filed into the presence, and a new tempest burst forth and raged round about the prophet and his guest. Nine breast-pins were promised, and the weird sisters filed out again. And in came eleven more, weeping and wailing and gnashing their teeth. Eleven promised breast-pins purchased peace once more.

"That is a specimen," said Mr. Young. "You see how it is. You see what a life I lead. A man *can't* be wise all the time. In a heedless moment I gave my darling No. 6—excuse my calling her thus, as her other name has escaped me for the moment—a breast-pin. It was only worth twenty-five dollars—that is, *apparently* that was its whole cost—but its ultimate cost was inevitably bound to be a good deal more. You yourself have seen it climb up to six hundred and fifty dollars—and alas, even that is not the end! For I have wives all over this Territory of Utah. I have dozens of wives whose *numbers,* even, I do not know without looking in the family Bible. They are scattered far and wide among the mountains and valleys of my realm. And mark you, every solitary one of them will hear of this wretched breast-pin, and every last one of them will have one or die. No 6's breast-pin will cost me twenty-five hundred dollars before I see the end of it. And these creatures will compare these pins together, and if one is a shade finer than the rest, they will all be thrown on my hands, and I will have to order a new lot to keep peace in the family. Sir, you probably did not know it, but all the time you were present with my children your every movement was watched by vigilant servitors of mine. If you had offered to give a child a dime, or a stick of candy, or any trifle of the kind, you would have been snatched out of the house instantly, provided it could be done before your gift left your hand. Otherwise it would be absolutely necessary for you to make an exactly similar gift to all my children—and knowing by experience the importance of the thing, I would have stood by and seen to it myself that you did it, and did it thoroughly. Once a gentleman gave one of my children a tin whistle—a veritable invention of Satan, sir, and one which I have an unspeakable horror of, and so would you if you had eighty or ninety children in your house. But the deed was done—the man escaped. I knew what the result was going to be, and I thirsted for vengeance. I ordered out a flock of Destroying Angels, and they hunted the man far into the fastnesses of the Nevada mountains. But they never caught him. I am not cruel, sir—I am not vindictive except when sorely outraged—but if I had caught him, sir, so help me Joseph Smith, I would have locked him into the nursery till the brats whistled him to death. By the slaughtered body of St. Parley Pratt (whom God assoil!) there was never anything on this earth like it! *I* knew who gave the whistle to the child, but I could not make those jealous mothers believe me. They believed *I* did it, and the result was just what any man of reflection could have foreseen: I had to order a hundred and ten whistles—I think we had a hundred and ten children in the house then, but some of them are off at college now—I had to order a hundred and ten of those shrieking things, and I wish I may never speak another word if we didn't have to talk on our fingers entirely, from that time forth until the children got tired of the whistles. And if ever another man gives a whistle to a child of mine and I get my hands on him, I will hang him higher than Haman! That is the word with the bark on it! Shade of Nephi! *You* don't know anything about married life. I am rich, and everybody knows it. I am benevolent, and everybody takes advantage of it. I have a strong fatherly instinct and all the foundlings are foisted on me. Every time a woman wants to do well by her darling, she puzzles her brain to cipher out some scheme for getting it into my hands. Why, sir, a woman came here once with a child of a curious lifeless sort of complexion (and so had the woman), and swore that the child was mine and she my wife—that I had married her at such-and-such a time in such-and-such a place, but she had forgotten her number, and of course I could not remember her name. Well, sir, she called my attention to the fact that the child looked like me, and really it did seem to resemble me—a common thing in the Territory—and, to cut the story short, I put it in my nursery, and she left. And by the ghost of Orson Hyde, when they came to wash the paint off that child it was an Injun! Bless my soul, you don't know anything about married life. It is a perfect dog's life, sir—a perfect dog's life. You can't economize. It isn't possible. I have tried keeping one set of bridal attire for all occasions. But it is of no use. First you'll marry a combination of calico and consumption that's as thin as a rail, and next you'll get a creature that's nothing more than the dropsy in disguise, and then you've got to eke out that bridal dress with an old balloon. That is the way it goes. And think of the wash-bill—(excuse these tears)—nine hundred and eighty-four pieces a week! No, sir, there is no such a thing as economy in a family like mine. Why, just the one item of cradles—think of it! And vermifuge! Soothing syrup! Teething rings! And 'papa's watches' for the babies to play with! And things to scratch the furniture with! And lucifer matches for them to eat, and pieces of glass to cut themselves with! The item of glass alone would support *your* family, I venture to say, sir. Let me scrimp and squeeze all I can, I still can't get ahead as fast as I feel I ought to, with my opportunities. Bless you, sir, at a time when I had seventy-two wives in this house, I groaned under the pressure of keeping thousands of dollars tied up in seventy-two bedsteads when the money ought to have been out at interest; and I just sold out the whole stock, sir, at a sacrifice, and built a bedstead seven feet long and ninety-six feet wide. But it was a failure, sir. I could *not* sleep. It appeared to me that the whole seventy-two women snored at once. The roar was deafening. And then the danger of it! That was what I was looking at. They would all draw in their breath at once, and you could actually see the walls of the house suck in—and then they would all exhale their breath at once, and you could see the walls swell out, and strain, and hear the rafters crack, and the shingles grind together. My friend, take an old man's advice, and *don't* encumber yourself with a large family—mind, I tell you, don't do it. In a small family, and in a small family only, you will find that comfort and that peace of mind which are the best at last of the blessings this world is able to afford us, and for the lack of which no accumulation of wealth, and no acquisition of fame, power, and greatness can ever compensate us. Take my word for it, ten or eleven wives is all you need—never go over it."

Some instinct or other made me set this Johnson down as being unreliable. And yet he was a very entertaining person, and I doubt if some of the information he gave us could have been acquired from any other source. He was a pleasant contrast to those reticent Mormons.

From *Roughing It,* 1872

A Genuine Mexican Plug

[At about noon of the twentieth day out from "St. Joe" the brothers reached Carson City, the capital of Nevada Territory. Sam Clemens's original idea had been to visit the Nevada Territory only briefly, then return home to Hannibal, Missouri. But he became "wonderfully fascinated with the new country" and decided to put off his return to "the States" for a while.]

I resolved to have a horse to ride. I had never seen such wild, free, magnificent horsemanship outside of a circus as these picturesquely-clad Mexicans, Californians and Mexicanized Americans displayed in Carson streets every day. How they rode! Leaning just gently forward out of the perpendicular, easy and nonchalant, with broad slouch-hat brim blown square up in front, and long *riata* swinging above the head, they swept through the town like the wind! The next minute they were only a sailing puff of dust on the far desert. If they trotted, they sat up gallantly and gracefully, and seemed part of the horse; did not go jiggering up and down after the silly Miss-Nancy fashion of the riding-schools. I had quickly learned to tell a horse from a cow, and was full of anxiety to learn more. I was resolved to buy a horse.

While the thought was rankling in my mind, the auctioneer came skurrying through the plaza on a black beast that had as many humps and corners on him as a dromedary, and was necessarily uncomely; but he was "going, going, at twenty-two!—horse, saddle and bridle at twenty-two dollars, gentlemen!" and I could hardly resist.

A man whom I did not know (he turned out to be the auctioneer's brother) noticed the wistful look in my eye, and observed that that was a very remarkable horse to be going at such a price; and added that the saddle alone was worth the money. It was a Spanish saddle, with ponderous *tapidaros,* and furnished with the ungainly sole-leather covering with the unspellable name. I said I had half a notion to bid. Then this keen-eyed person appeared to me to be "taking my measure"; but I dismissed the suspicion when he spoke, for his manner was full of guileless candor and truthfulness. Said he:

"I know that horse—know him well. You are a stranger, I take it, and so you might think he was an American horse, maybe, but I assure you he is not. He is nothing of the kind; but—excuse my speaking in a low voice, other people being near—he is, without the shadow of a doubt, a Genuine Mexican Plug!"

I did not know what a Genuine Mexican Plug was, but there was something about this man's way of saying it, that made me swear inwardly that I would own a Genuine Mexican Plug, or die.

"Has he any other—er—advantages?" I inquired, suppressing what eagerness I could.

He hooked his forefinger in the pocket of my army-shirt, led me to one side, and breathed in my ear impressively these words:

"He can out-buck anything in America!"

"Going, going, going—at *twent—ty*-four dollars and a half, gen—"

"Twenty-seven!" I shouted, in a frenzy.

"And sold!" said the auctioneer, and passed over the Genuine Mexican Plug to me.

I could scarcely contain my exultation. I paid the money, and put the animal in a neighboring livery-stable to dine and rest himself.

In the afternoon I brought the creature into the plaza, and certain citizens held him by the head, and others by the tail, while I mounted him. As soon as they let go, he placed all his feet in a bunch together, lowered his back, and then suddenly arched it upward, and shot me straight into the air a matter of three or four feet! I came as straight down again, lit in the saddle, went instantly up again, came down almost on the high pommel, shot up again, and came down on the horse's neck—all in the space of three or four seconds. Then he rose and stood almost straight up on his hind feet, and I, clasping his lean neck desperately, slid back into the saddle, and held on. He came down, and immediately hoisted his heels into the air, delivering a vicious kick at the sky, and stood on his forefeet. And then down he came once more, and began the original exercise of shooting me straight up again. The third time I went up I heard a stranger say:

"Oh, *don't* he buck, though!"

While I was up, somebody struck the horse a sounding thwack with a leathern strap, and when I arrived again the Genuine Mexican

Plug was not there. A Californian youth chased him up and caught him, and asked if he might have a ride. I granted him that luxury. He mounted the Genuine, got lifted into the air once, but sent his spurs home as he descended, and the horse darted away like a telegram. He soared over three fences like a bird, and disappeared down the road toward the Washoe Valley.

I sat down on a stone, with a sigh, and by a natural impulse one of my hands sought my forehead, and the other the base of my stomach. I believe I never appreciated, till then, the poverty of the human machinery—for I still needed a hand or two to place elsewhere. Pen cannot describe how I was jolted up. Imagination cannot conceive how disjointed I was—how internally, externally and universally I was unsettled, mixed up and ruptured. There was a sympathetic crowd around me, though.

One elderly-looking comforter said:

"Stranger, you've been taken in. Everybody in this camp knows that horse. Any child, any Injun, could have told you that he'd buck; he is the very worst devil to buck on the continent of America. You hear *me*. I'm Curry. *Old* Curry. Old *Abe* Curry. And moreover, he is a simon-pure, out-and-out, genuine d—d Mexican plug, and an uncommon mean one at that, too. Why, you turnip, if you had laid low and kept dark, there's chances to buy an *American* horse for mighty little more than you paid for that bloody old foreign relic."

I gave no sign; but I made up my mind that if the auctioneer's brother's funeral took place while I was in the Territory I would postpone all other recreations and attend it.

After a gallop of sixteen miles the Californian youth and the Genuine Mexican Plug came tearing into town again, shedding foam-flakes like the spume-spray that drives before a typhoon, and, with one final skip over a wheelbarrow and a Chinaman, cast anchor in front of the "ranch."

Such panting and blowing! Such spreading and contracting of the red equine nostrils, and glaring of the wild equine eye! But was the imperial beast subjugated? Indeed he was not. His lordship the Speaker of the House thought he was, and mounted him to go down to the Capitol; but the first dash the creature made was over a pile of telegraph poles half as high as a church; and his time to the Capitol—one mile and three quarters—remains unbeaten to this day. But then he took an advantage—he left out the mile, and only did the three quarters. That is to say, he made a straight cut across lots, preferring fences and ditches to a crooked road; and when the Speaker got to the Capitol he said he had been in the air so much he felt as if he had made the trip on a comet.

In the evening the Speaker came home afoot for exercise, and got the Genuine towed back behind a quartz wagon. The next day I loaned the animal to the Clerk of the House to go down to the Dana silver mine, six miles, and *he* walked back for exercise, and got the horse towed. Everybody I loaned him to always walked back; they never could get enough exercise any other way. Still, I continued to loan him to anybody who was willing to borrow him, my idea being to get him crippled, and throw him on the borrower's hands, or killed, and make the borrower pay for him. But somehow nothing ever happened to him. He took chances that no other horse ever took and survived, but he always came out safe. It was his daily habit to try experiments that had always before been considered impossible, but he always got through. Sometimes he miscalculated a little, and did not get his rider through intact, but *he* always got through himself. Of course I had tried to sell him; but that was a stretch of simplicity which met with little sympathy. The auctioneer stormed up and down the streets on him for four days, dispersing the populace, interrupting business, and destroying children, and never got a bid—at least never any but the eighteen-dollar one he hired a notoriously substanceless bummer to make. The people only smiled pleasantly, and restrained their desire to buy, if they had any. Then the auctioneer brought in his bill, and I withdrew the horse from the market. We tried to trade him off at private vendue next, offering him at a sacrifice for second-hand tombstones, old iron, temperance tracts—any kind of property. But holders were stiff, and we retired from the market again. I never tried to ride the horse any more. Walking was good enough exercise for a man like me, that had nothing the matter with him except ruptures, internal injuries, and such things. Finally I tried to *give* him away. But it was a failure. Parties said earthquakes were handy enough on the Pacific coast—they did not wish to own one. As a last resort I offered him to the Governor for the use of the "Brigade." His face lit up eagerly at first, but toned down again, and he said the thing would be too palpable.

Just then the livery stable man brought in his bill for six weeks keeping—stall-room for the horse, fifteen dollars; hay for the horse, two hundred and fifty! The Genuine Mexican Plug had eaten a ton of the article, and the man said he would have eaten a hundred if he had let him.

I will remark here, in all seriousness, that the regular price of hay during that year and a part of the next was really two hundred and fifty dollars a ton. During a part of the previous year it had sold at five hundred a ton, in gold, and during the winter before that there was such scarcity of the article that in several instances small quantities had brought eight hundred dollars a ton in coin! The consequence might be guessed without my telling it: people turned their stock loose to starve, and before the spring arrived Carson and Eagle valleys were almost literally carpeted with their carcases! Any old settler there will verify these statements.

I managed to pay the livery bill, and that same day I gave the Genuine Mexican Plug to a passing Arkansas emigrant whom fortune delivered into my hand. If this ever meets his eye, he will doubtless remember the donation.

Now whoever has the luck to ride a real Mexican plug will recognize the animal depicted in this chapter, and hardly consider him exaggerated—but the uninitiated will feel justified in regarding his portrait as a fancy sketch, perhaps.

From *Roughing It,* 1872

Mr. Arkansas

["By and by I was smitten with the silver fever." Clemens joined a prospecting party, the other members of which were a blacksmith and two lawyers. Eventually they came upon Honey Lake Smith's, "a sort of isolated inn on the Carson River," where they were marooned eight days and nights by a sudden flood.]

There were two men in the company who caused me particular discomfort. One was a little Swede, about twenty-five years old, who knew only one song, and he was forever singing it. By day we were all crowded into one small, stifling bar-room, and so there was no escaping this person's music. Through all the profanity, whisky-guzzling, "old sledge" and quarreling, his monotonous song meandered with never a variation in its tiresome sameness, and it seemed to me, at last, that I would be content to die, in order to be rid of the torture. The other man was a stalwart ruffian called "Arkansas," who carried two revolvers in his belt and a bowie knife projecting from his boot, and who was always drunk and always suffering for a fight. But he was so feared, that nobody would accommodate him. He would try all manner of little wary ruses to entrap somebody into an offensive remark, and his face would light up now and then when he fancied he was fairly on the scent of a fight, but invariably his victim would elude his toils and then he would show a disappointment that was almost pathetic. The landlord, Johnson, was a meek, well-meaning fellow, and Arkansas fastened on him early, as a promising subject, and gave him no rest day or night, for awhile. On the fourth morning, Arkansas got drunk and sat himself down to wait for an opportunity. Presently Johnson came in, just comfortably sociable with whisky, and said:

"I reckon the Pennsylvania 'lection—"

Arkansas raised his finger impressively and Johnson stopped. Arkansas rose unsteadily and confronted him. Said he:

"Wha-what do you know a-about Pennsylvania? Answer me that. Wha-what do you know 'bout Pennsylvania?"

"I was only goin' to say—"

"You was only goin' to *say*. *You* was! You was only goin' to say—*what* was you goin' to say? That's it! That's what *I* want to know. *I* want to know wha-what you (*'ic*) what you know about Pennsylvania, since you're makin' yourself so d—d free. Answer me that!"

"Mr. Arkansas, if you'd only let me—"

"Who's a henderin' you? Don't you insinuate nothing agin me!—don't you do it. Don't you come in here bullyin' around, and cussin' and goin' on like a lunatic—don't you do it. 'Coz *I* won't *stand* it. If fight's what you want, out with it! I'm your man! Out with it!"

Said Johnson, backing into a corner, Arkansas following, menacingly:

"Why, *I* never said nothing, Mr. Arkansas. You don't give a man no chance. I was only goin' to say that Pennsylvania was goin' to have an election next week—that was all—that was everything I was goin' to say—I wish I may never stir if it wasn't."

"Well then why d'n't you say it? What did you come swellin' around that way for, and tryin' to raise trouble?"

"Why *I* didn't come swellin' around, Mr. Arkansas—I just—"

"I'm a liar am I! Ger-reat Cæsar's ghost—"

"Oh, please, Mr. Arkansas, I never meant such a thing as that, I wish I may die if I did. All the boys will tell you that I've always spoke well of you, and respected you more'n any man in the house. Ask Smith. Ain't it so, Smith? Didn't I say, no longer ago than last night, that for a man that was a gentleman *all* the time and every way you took him, give me Arkansas? I'll leave it to any gentleman here if them warn't the very words I used. Come, now, Mr. Arkansas, le's take a drink—le's shake hands and take a drink. Come up—everybody! It's my treat. Come up, Bill, Tom, Bob, Scotty—come up. I want you all to take a drink with me and Arkansas—*old* Arkansas, I call him—bully old Arkansas. Gimme your hand agin. Look at him, boys—just take a *look* at him. Thar stands the whitest man in America!—and the man that denies it has got to fight *me*, that's all. Gimme that old flipper agin!"

They embraced, with drunken affection on the landlord's part and unresponsive toleration on the part of Arkansas, who, bribed by a drink, was disappointed of his prey once more. But the foolish landlord was so happy to have escaped butchery, that he went on talking when he ought to have marched himself out of danger. The consequence was that Arkansas shortly began to glower upon him dangerously, and presently said:

"Lan'lord, will you p-please make that remark over agin if you please?"

"I was a-sayin' to Scotty that my father was up'ards of eighty year old when he died."

"Was that *all* that you said?"

"Yes, that was all."

"Didn't say nothing but that?"

"No—nothing."

Then an uncomfortable silence.

Arkansas played with his glass a moment, lolling on his elbows on the counter. Then he meditatively scratched his left shin with his right boot, while the awkward silence continued. But presently he loafed away toward the stove, looking dissatisfied; roughly shouldered two or three men out of a comfortable position; occupied it himself, gave a sleeping dog a kick that sent him howling under a bench, then spread his long legs and his blanket-coat tails apart and proceeded to warm his back. In a little while he fell to grumbling to himself, and soon he slouched back to the bar and said:

"Lan'lord, what's your idea for rakin' up old personalities and blowin' about your father? Ain't this company agreeable to you? Ain't it? If this company ain't agreeable to you, p'r'aps we'd better leave. Is that your idea? Is that what you're coming at?"

"Why bless your soul, Arkansas, I warn't thinking of such a thing. My father and my mother—"

"Lan'lord, *don't* crowd a man! Don't do it. If nothing'll do you but a disturbance, out with it like a man (*'ic*)—but *don't* rake up old bygones and fling 'em in the teeth of a passel of people that wants to be peaceable if they could git a chance. What's the matter with you this mornin', anyway? I never see a man carry on so."

"Arkansas, I reely didn't mean no harm, and I won't go on with it if it's onpleasant to you. I reckon my licker's got into my head, and what with the flood, and havin' so many to feed and look out for—"

"So *that's* what's a-ranklin' in your heart, is it? You want us to leave do you? There's too many on us. You want us to pack up and swim. Is that it? Come!"

"Please be reasonable, Arkansas. Now *you* know that I ain't the man to—"

"Are you a threatenin' me? Are you? By George, the man don't live that can skeer me! Don't you try to come that game, my chicken—'cuz I can stand a good deal, but I won't stand that. Come out from behind that bar till I clean you! You want to drive us out, do you, you sneakin' underhanded hound! Come out from behind that bar! *I'll* learn you to bully and badger and browbeat a gentleman that's forever trying to befriend you and keep you out of trouble!"

"Please, Arkansas, please don't shoot! If there's got to be bloodshed—"

"Do you hear that, gentlemen? Do you hear him talk about bloodshed? So it's blood you want, is it, you ravin' desperado! You'd made up your mind to murder somebody this mornin'—I knowed it perfectly well. I'm the man, am I? It's me you're goin' to murder, is it? But you can't do it 'thout I get one chance first, you thievin' black-hearted, white-livered son of a nigger! Draw your weepon!"

With that, Arkansas began to shoot, and the landlord to clamber over benches, men and every sort of obstacle in a frantic desire to escape. In the midst of the wild hubbub the landlord crashed through a glass door, and as Arkansas charged after him the landlord's wife suddenly appeared in the door-way and confronted the desperado with a pair of scissors! Her fury was magnificent. With head erect and flashing eye she stood a moment and then advanced, with her weapon raised. The astonished ruffian hesitated, and then fell back a step. She followed. She backed him step by step into the middle of the bar-room, and then, while the wondering crowd closed up and gazed, she gave him such another tongue-lashing as never a cowed and shamefaced braggart got before, perhaps! As she finished and retired victorious, a roar of applause shook the house, and every man ordered "drinks for the crowd" in one and the same breath.

The lesson was entirely sufficient. The reign of terror was over, and the Arkansas domination broken for good. During the rest of the season of island captivity, there was one man who sat apart in a state of permanent humiliation, never mixing in any quarrel or uttering a boast, and never resenting the insults the once cringing crew now constantly leveled at him, and that man was "Arkansas."

From *Roughing It,* 1872

The Great Landslide Case

[Clemens returned to Carson City and to more prospecting. When he tired of failure at the latter he accepted an offer to go up to Virginia City and become city editor of the *Daily Territorial Enterprise,* for which he had written some amusing letters. At first he was paid a salary of $25 a week, then $40. Meanwhile, the times being very flush, he was speculating in various mine holdings.]

The mountains are very high and steep about Carson, Eagle and Washoe Valleys—very high and very steep, and so when the snow gets to melting off fast in the Spring and the warm surface-earth begins to moisten and soften, the disastrous land-slides commence. The reader cannot know what a land-slide is, unless he has lived in that country and seen the whole side of a mountain taken off some fine morning and deposited down in the valley, leaving a vast, treeless, unsightly scar upon the mountain's front to keep the circumstance fresh in his memory all the years that he may go on living within seventy miles of that place.

General Buncombe was shipped out to Nevada in the invoice of Territorial officers, to be United States Attorney. He considered himself a lawyer of parts, and he very much wanted an opportunity to manifest it—partly for the pure gratification of it and partly because his salary was Territorially meagre (which is a strong expression). Now the older citizens of a new territory look down upon the rest of the world with a calm, benevolent compassion, as long as it keeps out of the way—when it gets in the way they snub it. Sometimes this latter takes the shape of a practical joke.

One morning Dick Hyde rode furiously up to General Buncombe's door in Carson city and rushed into his presence without stopping to tie his horse. He seemed much excited. He told the General that he wanted him to conduct a suit for him and would pay him five hundred dollars if he achieved a victory. And then, with violent gestures and a world of profanity, he poured out his griefs. He said it was pretty well known that for some years he had been farming (or ranching as the more customary term is) in Washoe District, and making a successful thing of it, and furthermore it was known that his ranch was situated just in the edge of the valley, and that Tom Morgan owned a ranch immediately above it on the mountain side. And now the trouble was, that one of those hated and dreaded landslides had come and slid Morgan's ranch, fences, cabins, cattle, barns and everything down on top of *his* ranch and exactly covered up every single vestige of his property, to a depth of about thirty-eight feet. Morgan was in possession and refused to vacate the premises—said was occupying own cabin and not interfering with anybody else's—and said the cabin was standing on the same dirt and same ranch it had always stood on, and he would like to see anybody make him vacate.

"And when I reminded him," said Hyde, weeping, "that it was on top of my ranch and that he was trespassing, he had the infernal meanness to ask me why didn't I *stay* on my ranch and hold possession when I see him a-coming! Why didn't I *stay* on it, the blathering lunatic—by George, when I heard that racket and looked up that hill it was just like the whole world was a-ripping and a-tearing down that mountain side—splinters, and cord-wood, thunder and lightning, hail and snow, odds and ends of hay stacks, and awful clouds of dust! —trees going end over end in the air, rocks as big as a house jumping 'bout a thousand feet high and busting into ten million pieces, cattle turned inside out and a-coming head on with their tails hanging out between their teeth!—and in the midst of all that wrack and destruction sot that cussed Morgan on his gate-post, a-wondering why I didn't *stay and hold possession!* Laws bless me, I just took one glimpse, General, and lit out'n the county in three jumps exactly.

"But what grinds me is that that Morgan hangs on there and won't move off'n that ranch—says it's his'n and he's going to keep it—likes it better'n he did when it was higher up the hill. Mad! Well, I've been so mad for two days I couldn't find my way to town—been wandering around in the brush in a starving condition—got anything here to drink, General? But I'm here *now,* and I'm a-going to law. You hear *me!*"

Never in all the world, perhaps, were a man's feelings so outraged as were the General's. He said he had never heard of such high-handed conduct in all his life as this Morgan's. And he said there was no use in going to law—Morgan had no shadow of right to remain where he was—nobody in the wide world would uphold him in it, and no lawyer would take his case and no judge listen to it. Hyde said that right there was where he was mistaken—everybody in town sustained Morgan; Hal Brayton, a very smart lawyer, had taken his case; the courts being in vacation, it was to be tried before a referee, and ex-Governor Roop had already been appointed to that office and would open his court in a large public hall near the hotel at two that afternoon.

The General was amazed. He said he had suspected before that the people of that Territory were fools, and now he knew it. But he said rest easy, rest easy and collect the witnesses, for the victory was just as certain as if the conflict were already over. Hyde wiped away his tears and left.

At two in the afternoon referee Roop's Court opened, and Roop appeared throned among his sheriffs, the witnesses, and spectators, and wearing upon his face a solemnity so awe-inspiring that some of his fellow-conspirators had misgivings that maybe he had not comprehended, after all, that this was merely a joke. An unearthly stillness prevailed, for at the slightest noise the judge uttered sternly the command:

"Order in the Court!"

And the sheriffs promptly echoed it. Presently the General elbowed his way through the crowd of spectators, with his arms full of law-books, and on his ears fell an order from the judge which was the first respectful recognition of his high official dignity that had ever saluted them, and it trickled pleasantly through his whole system:

"Way for the United States Attorney!"

The witnesses were called—legislators, high government officers, ranchmen, miners, Indians, Chinamen, negroes. Three fourths of them were called by the defendant Morgan, but no matter, their testimony invariably went in favor of the plaintiff Hyde. Each new witness only added new testimony to the absurdity of a man's claiming to own another man's property because his farm had slid down on top of it. Then the Morgan lawyers made their speeches, and seemed to make singularly weak ones—they did really nothing to help the Morgan cause. And now the General, with exultation in his face, got up and made an impassioned effort; he pounded the table, he banged the law-books, he shouted, and roared, and howled, he quoted from everything and everybody, poetry, sarcasm, statistics, history, pathos, bathos, blasphemy, and wound up with a grand war-whoop for free speech, freedom of the press, free schools, the Glorious Bird of America and the principles of eternal justice! [Applause.]

When the General sat down, he did it with the conviction that if there was anything in good strong testimony, a great speech and believing and admiring countenances all around, Mr. Morgan's case was killed. Ex-Governor Roop leant his head upon his hand for some minutes, thinking, and the still audience waited for his decision. Then he got up and stood erect, with bended head, and thought again. Then he walked the floor with long, deliberate strides, his chin in his hand, and still the audience waited. At last he returned to his throne, seated himself, and began, impressively:

"Gentlemen, I feel the great responsibility that rests upon me this day. This is no ordinary case. On the contrary it is plain that it is the most solemn and awful that ever man was called upon to decide. Gentlemen, I have listened attentively to the evidence, and have perceived that the weight of it, the overwhelming weight of it, is in favor of the plaintiff Hyde. I have listened also to the remarks of counsel, with high interest—and especially will I commend the masterly and irrefutable logic of the distinguished gentleman who represents the plaintiff. But gentlemen, let us beware how we allow mere human testimony, human ingenuity in argument and human ideas of equity, to influence us at a moment so solemn as this. Gentlemen, it ill becomes us, worms as we are, to meddle with the decrees of Heaven. It is plain to me that Heaven, in its inscrutable wisdom, has seen fit to move this defendant's ranch for a purpose. We are but creatures, and we must submit. If Heaven has chosen to favor the defendant Morgan in this marked and wonderful manner; and if Heaven, dissatisfied with the position of the Morgan ranch upon the mountain side, has chosen to remove it to a position more eligible and more advantageous for its owner, it ill becomes us, insects as we are, to question the legality of the act or inquire into the reasons that prompted it. No—Heaven created the ranches and it is Heaven's prerogative to rearrange them, to experiment with them, to shift them around at its pleasure. It is for us to submit, without repining. I warn you that this thing which has happened is a thing with which the sacrilegious hands and brains and tongues of men must not meddle. Gentlemen, it is the verdict of this court that the plaintiff, Richard Hyde, has been deprived of his ranch by the visitation of God! And from this decision there is no appeal."

Buncombe seized his cargo of law-books and plunged out of the court-room frantic with indignation. He pronounced Roop to be a miraculous fool, an inspired idiot. In all good faith he returned at night and remonstrated with Roop upon his extravagant decision, and implored him to walk the floor and think for half an hour, and see if he could not figure out some sort of modification of the verdict. Roop yielded at last and got up to walk. He walked two hours and a half, and at last his face lit up happily and he told Buncombe it had occurred to him that the ranch underneath the new Morgan ranch still belonged to Hyde, that his title to the ground was just as good as it had ever been, and therefore he was of opinion that Hyde had a right to dig it out from under there and—

The General never waited to hear the end of it. He was always an impatient and irascible man, that way. At the end of two months the fact that he had been played upon with a joke had managed to bore itself, like another Hoosac Tunnel, through the solid adamant of his understanding.

From *Roughing It,* 1872

Buck Fanshaw's Funeral

Somebody has said that in order to know a community, one must observe the style of its funerals and know what manner of men they bury with most ceremony. I cannot say which class we buried with most eclat in our "flush times," the distinguished public benefactor or the distinguished rough—possibly the two chief grades or grand divisions of society honored their illustrious dead about equally; and hence, no doubt the philosopher I have quoted from would have needed to see two representative funerals in Virginia [City] before forming his estimate of the people.

There was a grand time over Buck Fanshaw when he died. He was a representative citizen. He had "killed his man"—not in his own quarrel, it is true, but in defence of a stranger unfairly beset by numbers. He had kept a sumptuous saloon. He had been the proprietor of a dashing helpmeet whom he could have discarded without the formality of a divorce. He had held a high position in the fire department and been a very Warwick in politics. When he died there was great lamentation throughout the town, but especially in the vast bottom-stratum of society.

On the inquest it was shown that Buck Fanshaw, in the delirium of a wasting typhoid fever, had taken arsenic, shot himself through the body, cut his throat, and jumped out of a four-story window and broken his neck—and after due deliberation, the jury, sad and tearful, but with intelligence unblinded by its sorrow, brought in a verdict of death "by the visitation of God." What could the world do without juries?

Prodigious preparations were made for the funeral. All the vehicles in town were hired, all the saloons put in mourning, all the municipal and fire-company flags hung at half-mast, and all the firemen ordered to muster in uniform and bring their machines duly draped in black. Now—let us remark in parenthesis—as all the peoples of the earth had representative adventurers in the Silverland, and as each adventurer had brought the slang of his nation or his locality with him, the combination made the slang of Nevada the richest and the most infinitely varied and copious that had ever existed anywhere in the world, perhaps, except in the mines of California in the "early days." Slang was the language of Nevada. It was hard to preach a sermon without it, and be understood. Such phrases as "You bet!" "Oh, no, I reckon not!" "No Irish need apply," and a hundred others, became so common as to fall from the lips of a speaker unconsciously—and very often when they did not touch the subject under discussion and consequently failed to mean anything.

After Buck Fanshaw's inquest, a meeting of the short-haired brotherhood was held, for nothing can be done on the Pacific coast without a public meeting and an expression of sentiment. Regretful resolutions were passed and various committees appointed; among others, a committee of one was deputed to call on the minister, a fragile, gentle, spirituel new fledgling from an Eastern theological seminary, and as yet unacquainted with the ways of the mines. The committeeman, "Scotty" Briggs, made his visit; and in after days it was worth something to hear the minister tell about it. Scotty was a stalwart rough, whose customary suit, when on weighty official business, like committee work, was a fire helmet, flaming red flannel shirt, patent leather belt with spanner and revolver attached, coat hung over arm, and pants stuffed into boot tops. He formed something of a contrast to the pale theological student. It is fair to say of Scotty, however, in passing, that he had a warm heart, and a strong love for his friends, and never entered into a quarrel when he could reasonably keep out of it. Indeed, it was commonly said that whenever one of Scotty's fights was investigated, it always turned out that it had originally been no affair of his, but that out of native goodheartedness he had dropped in of his own accord to help the man who was getting the worst of it. He and Buck Fanshaw were bosom friends, for years, and had often taken adventurous "pot-luck" together. On one occasion, they had thrown off their coats and taken the weaker side in a fight among strangers, and after gaining a hard-earned victory, turned and found that the men they were helping had deserted early, and not only that, but had stolen their coats and made off with them! But to return to Scotty's visit to the minister. He was on a sorrowful mission, now, and his face was the picture of woe. Being admitted to the presence he sat down before the clergyman, placed his fire-hat on an unfinished manuscript sermon under the minister's nose, took from it a red silk handkerchief, wiped his brow and heaved a sigh of dismal impressiveness, explanatory of his business. He choked, and even shed tears; but with an effort he mastered his voice and said in lugubrious tones:

"Are you the duck that runs the gospel-mill next door?"

"Am I the—pardon me, I believe I do not understand?"

With another sigh and a half-sob, Scotty rejoined:

"Why you see we are in a bit of trouble, and the boys thought maybe you would give us a lift, if we'd tackle you—that is, if I've got the rights of it and you are the head clerk of the doxology-works next door."

"I am the shepherd in charge of the flock whose fold is next door."

"The which?"

"The spiritual adviser of the little company of believers whose sanctuary adjoins these premises."

Scotty scratched his head, reflected a moment, and then said:

"You ruther hold over me, pard. I reckon I can't call that hand. Ante and pass the buck."

"How? I beg pardon. What did I understand you to say?"

"Well, you've ruther got the bulge on me. Or maybe we've both got the bulge, somehow. You don't smoke me and I don't smoke you. You see, one of the boys has passed in his checks and we want to give him a good send-off, and so the thing I'm on now is to roust out somebody to jerk a little chin-music for us and waltz him through handsome."

"My friend, I seem to grow more and more bewildered. Your observations are wholly incomprehensible to me. Cannot you simplify them in some way? At first I thought perhaps I understood you, but I grope now. Would it not expedite matters if you restricted yourself to categorical statements of fact unencumbered with obstructing accumulations of metaphor and allegory?"

Another pause, and more reflection. Then, said Scotty:

"I'll have to pass, I judge."

"How?"

"You've raised me out, pard."

"I still fail to catch your meaning."

"Why, that last lead of yourn is too many for me—that's the idea. I can't neither trump nor follow suit."

The clergyman sank back in his chair perplexed. Scotty leaned his head on his hand and gave himself up to thought. Presently his face came up, sorrowful but confident.

"I've got it now, so's you can savvy," he said. "What we want is a gospel-sharp. See?"

"A what?"

"Gospel-sharp. Parson."

"Oh! Why did you not say so before? I am a clergyman—a parson."

"Now you talk! You see my blind and straddle it like a man. Put it there!"—extending a brawny paw, which closed over the minister's small hand and gave it a shake indicative of fraternal sympathy and fervent gratification.

"Now we're all right, pard. Let's start fresh. Don't you mind my snuffling a little—becuz we're in a power of trouble. You see, one of the boys has gone up the flume—"

"Gone where?"

"Up the flume—throwed up the sponge, you understand."

"Thrown up the sponge?"

"Yes—kicked the bucket—"

"Ah—has departed to that mysterious country from whose bourne no traveler returns."

"Return! I reckon not. Why pard, he's *dead!*"

"Yes, I understand."

"Oh, you do? Well I thought maybe you might be getting tangled some more. Yes, you see he's dead again—"

"*Again?* Why, has he ever been dead before?"

"Dead before? No! Do you reckon a man has got as many lives as a cat? But you bet you he's awful dead now, poor old boy, and I wish I'd never seen this day. I don't want no better friend than Buck Fanshaw. I knowed him by the back; and when I know a man and like him, I freeze to him—you hear *me*. Take him all round, pard, there never was a bullier man in the mines. No man ever knowed Buck Fanshaw to go back on a friend. But it's all up, you know, it's all up. It ain't no use. They've scooped him."

"Scooped him?"

"Yes—death has. Well, well, well, we've got to give him up. Yes indeed. It's a kind of a hard world, after all, *ain't* it? But pard, he was a rustler! You ought to seen him get started once. He was a bully boy with a glass eye! Just spit in his face and give him room according to his strength, and it was just beautiful to see him peel and go in. He was the worst son of a thief that ever drawed breath. Pard, he was *on* it! He was on it bigger than an Injun!"

"On it? On what?"

"On the shoot. On the shoulder. On the fight, you understand. *He* didn't give a continental for *any*body. *Beg* your pardon, friend, for coming so near a cuss-word—but you see I'm on an awful strain, in this palaver, on account of having to cramp down and draw everything so mild. But we've got to give him up. There ain't any getting around that, I don't reckon. Now if we can get you to help plant him—"

"Preach the funeral discourse? Assist at the obsequies?"

"Obs'quies is good. Yes. That's it—that's our little game. We are going to get the thing up regardless, you know. He was always nifty himself, and so you bet you his funeral ain't going to be no slouch—solid silver door-plate on his coffin, six plumes on the hearse, and a nigger on the box in a biled shirt and a plug hat—how's that for high? And we'll take care of *you,* pard. We'll fix you all right. There'll be a kerridge for you; and whatever you want, you just 'scape out and we'll 'tend to it. We've got a shebang fixed up for you to stand behind, in No. 1's house, and don't you be afraid. Just go in and toot your horn, if you don't sell a clam. Put Buck through as bully as you can, pard, for anybody that knowed him will tell you that he was one of the whitest men that was ever in the mines. You can't draw it too strong. He never could stand it to see things going wrong. He's done more to make this town quiet and peaceable than any man in it. I've seen him lick four Greasers in eleven minutes, myself. If a thing wanted regulating, *he* warn't a man to go browsing around after somebody to do it, but he would prance in and regulate it himself. He warn't a Catholic. Scasely. He was down on 'em. His word was, 'No Irish need apply!' But it didn't make no difference about that when it came down to what a man's rights was—and so, when some roughs jumped the Catholic bone-yard and started in to stake out town-lots in it he *went* for 'em! And he *cleaned* 'em, too! I was there, pard, and I seen it myself."

"That was very well indeed—at least the impulse was—whether the act was strictly defensible or not. Had deceased any religious convictions? That is to say, did he feel a dependence upon, or acknowledge allegiance to a higher power?"

More reflection.

"I reckon you've stumped me again, pard. Could you say it over once more, and say it slow?"

"Well, to simplify it somewhat, was he, or rather had he ever been connected with any organization sequestered from secular concerns and devoted to self-sacrifice in the interests of morality?"

"All down but nine—set 'em up on the other alley, pard."

"What did I understand you to say?"

"Why, you're most too many for me, you know. When you get in with your left I hunt grass every time. Every time you draw, you fill; but I don't seem to have any luck. Lets have a new deal."

"How? Begin again?"

"That's it."

"Very well. Was he a good man, and—"

"There—I see that; don't put up another chip till I look at my hand. A good man, says you? Pard, it ain't no name for it. He was the best man that ever—pard, you would have doted on that man. He could lam any galoot of his inches in America. It was him that put down the riot last election before it got a start; and everybody said he was the only man that could have done it. He waltzed in with a spanner in one hand and a trumpet in the other, and sent fourteen men home on a shutter in less than three minutes. He had that riot all broke up and prevented nice before anybody ever got a chance to strike a blow. He was always for peace, and he would *have* peace—he could not stand disturbances. Pard, he was a great loss to this town. It would please the boys if you could chip in something like that and do him justice. Here once when the Micks got to throwing stones through the Methodis' Sunday school windows, Buck Fanshaw, all of his own notion, shut up his saloon and took a couple of six-shooters and mounted guard over the Sunday school. Says he, 'No Irish need apply!' And they didn't. He was the bulliest man in the mountains, pard! He could run faster, jump higher, hit harder, and hold more tangle-foot whisky without spilling it than any man in seventeen counties. Put that in, pard—it'll please the boys more than anything you could say. And you can say, pard, that he never shook his mother."

"Never shook his mother?"

"That's it—any of the boys will tell you so."

"Well, but why *should* he shake her?"

"That's what *I* say—but some people does."

"Not people of any repute?"

"Well, some that averages pretty so-so."

"In my opinion the man that would offer personal violence to his own mother, ought to—"

"Cheese it, pard; you've banked your ball clean outside the string. What I was a drivin' at, was, that he never *throwed off* on his mother—don't you see? No indeedy. He give her a house to live in, and town lots, and plenty of money; and he looked after her and took care of her all the time; and when she was down with the small-pox I'm d—d if he didn't set up nights and nuss her himself! *Beg* your pardon for saying it, but it hopped out too quick for yours truly. You've treated me like a gentleman, pard, and I ain't the man to hurt your feelings intentional. I think you're white. I think you're a square man, pard. I like you, and I'll lick any man that don't. I'll lick him till he can't tell himself from a last year's corpse! Put it *there!*" [Another fraternal handshake—and exit.]

The obsequies were all that "the boys" could desire. Such a marvel of funeral pomp had never been seen in Virginia. The plumed hearse, the dirge-breathing brass bands, the closed marts of business, the flags drooping at half mast, the long, plodding procession of uniformed secret societies, military battalions and fire companies, draped engines, carriages of officials, and citizens in vehicles and on foot, attracted multitudes of spectators to the sidewalks, roofs and windows; and for years afterward, the degree of grandeur attained by any civic display in Virginia was determined by comparison with Buck Fanshaw's funeral.

Scotty Briggs, as a pall-bearer and a mourner, occupied a prominent place at the funeral, and when the sermon was finished and the last sentence of the prayer for the dead man's soul ascended, he responded, in a low voice, but with feeling:

"AMEN. No Irish need apply."

As the bulk of the response was without apparent relevancy, it was probably nothing more than a humble tribute to the memory of the friend that was gone; for, as Scotty had once said, it was "his word."

Scotty Briggs, in after days, achieved the distinction of becoming the only convert to religion that was ever gathered from the Virginia roughs; and it transpired that the man who had it in him to espouse the quarrel of the weak out of inborn nobility of spirit was no mean timber whereof to construct a Christian. The making him one did not warp his generosity or diminish his courage; on the contrary it gave intelligent direction to the one and a broader field to the other. If his

Sunday-school class progressed faster than the other classes, was it matter for wonder? I think not. He talked to his pioneer small-fry in a language they understood! It was my large privilege, a month before he died, to hear him tell the beautiful story of Joseph and his brethren to his class "without looking at the book." I leave it to the reader to fancy what it was like, as it fell, riddled with slang, from the lips of that grave, earnest teacher, and was listened to by his little learners with a consuming interest that showed that they were as unconscious as he was that any violence was being done to the sacred proprieties!

From *Roughing It,* 1872

The Story of the Old Ram

[Becoming restless, Clemens took the stage coach to California.]

Every now and then, in these days, the boys used to tell me I ought to get one Jim Blaine to tell me the stirring story of his grandfather's old ram—but they always added that I must not mention the matter unless Jim was drunk at the time—just comfortably and sociably drunk. They kept this up until my curiosity was on the rack to hear the story. I got to haunting Blaine; but it was of no use, the boys always found fault with his condition; he was often moderately but never satisfactorily drunk. I never watched a man's condition with such absorbing interest, such anxious solicitude; I never so pined to see a man uncompromisingly drunk before. At last, one evening I hurried to his cabin, for I learned that this time his situation was such that even the most fastidious could find no fault with it—he was tranquilly, serenely, symmetrically drunk—not a hiccup to mar his voice, not a cloud upon his brain thick enough to obscure his memory. As I entered, he was sitting upon an empty powder-keg, with a clay pipe in one hand and the other raised to command silence. His face was round, red, and very serious; his throat was bare and his hair tumbled; in general appearance and costume he was a stalwart miner of the period. On the pine table stood a candle, and its dim light revealed "the boys" sitting here and there on bunks, candle-boxes, powder-kegs, etc. They said:

"Sh—! Don't speak—he's going to commence."

THE STORY OF THE OLD RAM.

I found a seat at once, and Blaine said:

"I don't reckon them times will ever come again. There never was a more bullier old ram than what he was. Grandfather fetched him from Illinois—got him of a man by the name of Yates—Bill Yates—maybe you might have heard of him; his father was a deacon—Baptist—and he was a rustler, too; a man had to get up ruther early to get the start of old Thankful Yates; it was him that put the Greens up to jining teams with my grandfather when he moved west. Seth Green was prob'ly the pick of the flock; he married a Wilkerson—Sarah Wilkerson—good cretur, she was—one of the likeliest heifers that was ever raised in old Stoddard, everybody said that knowed her. She could heft a bar'l of flour as easy as I can flirt a flapjack. And spin? Don't mention it! Independent? Humph! When Sile Hawkins come a browsing around her, she let him know that for all his tin he couldn't trot in harness alongside of *her*. You see, Sile Hawkins was—no, it warn't Sile Hawkins, after all—it was a galoot by the name of Filkins—I disremember his first name; but he *was* a stump—come into pra'r meeting drunk, one night, hooraying for Nixon, becuz he thought it was a primary; and old deacon Ferguson up and scooted him through the window and he lit on old Miss Jefferson's head, poor old filly. She was a good soul—had a glass eye and used to lend it to old Miss Wagner, that hadn't any, to receive company in; it warn't big enough, and when Miss Wagner warn't noticing, it would get twisted around in the socket, and look up, maybe, or out to one side, and every which way, while t' other one was looking as straight ahead as a spy-glass. Grown people didn't mind it, but it most always made the children cry, it was so sort of scary. She tried packing it in raw cotton, but it wouldn't work, somehow—the cotton would get loose and stick out and look so kind of awful that the children couldn't stand it no way. She was always dropping it out, and turning up her old dead-light on the company empty, and making them oncomfortable, becuz *she* never could tell when it hopped out, being blind on that side, you see. So somebody would have to hunch her and say, "Your game eye has fetched loose, Miss Wagner dear"—and then all of them would have to sit and wait till she jammed it in again—wrong side before, as a general thing, and green as a bird's egg, being a bashful cretur and easy sot back before company. But being wrong side before warn't much difference, anyway, becuz her own eye was sky-blue and the glass one was yaller on the front side, so whichever way she turned it it didn't match nohow. Old Miss Wagner was considerable on the borrow, she was. When she had a quilting, or Dorcas S'iety at her house she gen'ally borrowed Miss Higgins's wooden leg to stump around on; it was considerable shorter than her other pin, but much *she* minded that. She said she couldn't abide crutches when she had company, becuz they were so slow; said when she had company and things had to be done, she wanted to get up and hump herself. She was as bald as a jug, and so she used to borrow Miss Jacops's wig—Miss Jacops was the coffin-peddler's wife—a ratty old buzzard, he was, that used to go roosting around where people was sick, waiting for 'em; and there that old rip would sit all day, in the shade, on a coffin that he judged would fit the can'idate; and if it was a slow customer and kind of uncertain, he'd fetch his rations and a blanket along and sleep in the coffin nights. He was anchored out that way, in frosty weather, for about three weeks, once, before old Robbins's place, waiting for him; and after that, for as much as two years, Jacops was not on speaking terms with the old man, on account of his disapp'inting him. He got one of his feet froze, and lost money, too, becuz old Robbins took a favorable turn and got well. The next time Robbins got sick, Jacops tried to make up with him, and varnished up the same old coffin and fetched it along; but old Robbins was too many for him; he had him in, and 'peared to be powerful weak; he bought the coffin for ten dollars and Jacops was to pay it back and twenty-five more besides if Robbins didn't like the coffin after he'd tried it. And then Robbins died, and at the funeral he bursted off the lid and riz up in his shroud and told the parson to let up on the performances, becuz he could *not* stand such a coffin as that. You see he had been in a trance once before, when he was young, and he took the chances on another, cal'lating that if he made the trip it was money in his pocket, and if he missed fire he couldn't lose a cent. And by George he sued Jacops for the rhino and got jedgment; and he set up the coffin in his back parlor and said he 'lowed to take his time, now. It was always an aggravation to Jacops, the way that miserable old thing acted. He moved back to Indiany pretty soon—went to Wellsville—Wellsville was the place the Hogadorns was from. Mighty fine family. Old Maryland stock. Old Squire Hogadorn could carry around more mixed licker, and cuss better than most any man I ever see. His second wife was the widder Billings—she that was Becky Martin; her dam was deacon Dunlap's first wife. Her oldest child, Maria, married a missionary and died in grace—et up by the savages. They et *him*, too, poor feller—biled him. It warn't the custom, so they say, but they explained to friends of his'n that went down there to bring away his things, that they'd tried missionaries every other way and never could get any good out of 'em

—and so it annoyed all his relations to find out that that man's life was fooled away just out of a dern'd experiment, so to speak. But mind you, there ain't anything ever reely lost; everything that people can't understand and don't see the reason of does good if you only hold on and give it a fair shake; Prov'dence don't fire no blank ca'tridges, boys. That there missionary's substance, unbeknowns to himself, actu'ly converted every last one of them heathens that took a chance at the barbecue. Nothing ever fetched them but that. Don't tell *me* it was an accident that he was biled. There ain't no such a thing as an accident. When my uncle Lem was leaning up agin a scaffolding once, sick, or drunk, or suthin, an Irishman with a hod full of bricks fell on him out of the third story and broke the old man's back in two places. People said it was an accident. Much accident there was about that. He didn't know what he was there for, but he was there for a good object. If he hadn't been there the Irishman would have been killed. Nobody can ever make me believe anything different from that. Uncle Lem's dog was there. Why didn't the Irishman fall on the dog? Becuz the dog would a seen him a coming and stood from under. That's the reason the dog warn't appinted. A dog can't be depended on to carry out a special providence. Mark my words it was a put-up thing. Accidents don't happen, boys. Uncle Lem's dog—I wish you could a seen that dog. He was a reglar shepherd—or ruther he was part bull and part shepherd—splendid animal; belonged to parson Hagar before Uncle Lem got him. Parson Hagar belonged to the Western Reserve Hagars; prime family; his mother was a Watson; one of his sisters married a Wheeler; they settled in Morgan county, and he got nipped by the machinery in a carpet factory and went through in less than a quarter of a minute; his widder bought the piece of carpet that had his remains wove in, and people come a hundred mile to 'tend the funeral. There was fourteen yards in the piece. She wouldn't let them roll him up, but planted him just so—full length. The church was middling small where they preached the funeral, and they had to let one end of the coffin stick out of the window. They didn't bury him—they planted one end, and let him stand up, same as a monument. And they nailed a sign on it and put—put on—put on it—sacred to—the m-e-m-o-r-y —of fourteen y-a-r-d-s—of three-ply—car --- pet—containing all that was—m-o-r-t-a-l—of—of—W-i-l-l-i-a-m—W-h-e—"

Jim Blaine had been growing gradually drowsy and drowsier—his head nodded, once, twice, three times—dropped peacefully upon his breast, and he fell tranquilly asleep. The tears were running down the boys' cheeks—they were suffocating with suppressed laughter—and had been from the start, though I had never noticed it. I perceived that I was "sold." I learned then that Jim Blaine's peculiarity was that whenever he reached a certain stage of intoxication, no human power could keep him from setting out, with impressive unction, to tell about a wonderful adventure which he had once had with his grandfather's old ram—and the mention of the ram in the first sentence was as far as any man had ever heard him get, concerning it. He always maundered off, interminably, from one thing to another, till his whisky got the best of him and he fell asleep. What the thing was that happened to him and his grandfather's old ram is a dark mystery to this day, for nobody has ever yet found out.

From *Roughing It,* 1872

Fetch Her Out!

[Clemens spent some time in San Francisco, where he learned from Nevada that he had not struck it rich in silver-mine speculation after all. He was down on his luck now. "By and by, an old friend of mine, a miner, came down from one of the decayed mining-camps of Tuolumne, California, and I went back with him."]

In those days miners would flock in crowds to catch a glimpse of that rare and blessed spectacle, a woman! Old inhabitants tell how, in a certain camp, the news went abroad early in the morning that a woman was come! They had seen a calico dress hanging out of a wagon down at the camping-ground—sign of emigrants from over the great plains. Everybody went down there, and a shout went up when an actual, bonafide dress was discovered fluttering in the wind! The male emigrant was visible. The miners said:

"Fetch her out!"

He said: "It is my wife, gentlemen—she is sick—we have been robbed of money, provisions, everything, by the Indians—we want to rest."

"Fetch her out! We've got to see her!"

"But, gentlemen, the poor thing, she—"

"FETCH HER OUT!"

He "fetched her out," and they swung their hats and sent up three rousing cheers and a tiger; and they crowded around and gazed at her, and touched her dress, and listened to her voice with the look of men who listened to a *memory* rather than a present reality—and then they collected twenty-five hundred dollars in gold and gave it to the man, and swung their hats again and gave three more cheers, and went home satisfied.

Once I dined in San Francisco with the family of a pioneer, and talked with his daughter, a young lady whose first experience in San Francisco was an adventure, though she herself did not remember it, as she was only two or three years old at the time. Her father said that, after landing from the ship, they were walking up the street, a servant leading the party with the little girl in her arms. And presently a huge miner, bearded, belted, spurred, and bristling with deadly weapons—just down from a long campaign in the mountains, evidently—barred the way, stopped the servant, and stood gazing, with a face all alive with gratification and astonishment. Then he said, reverently:

"Well, if it ain't a child!" And then he snatched a little leather sack out of his pocket and said to the servant:

"There's a hundred and fifty dollars in dust, there, and I'll give it to you to let me kiss the child!"

That anecdote is *true*.

But see how things change. Sitting at that dinner-table, listening to that anecdote, if I had offered double the money for the privilege of kissing the same child, I would have been refused. Seventeen added years have far more than doubled the price.

And while upon this subject I will remark that once in Star City, in the Humboldt Mountains, I took my place in a sort of long, post-office single file of miners, to patiently await my chance to peep through a crack in the cabin and get a sight of the splendid new sensation—a genuine, live Woman! And at the end of half of an hour my turn came, and I put my eye to the crack, and there she was, with one arm akimbo, and tossing flap-jacks in a frying-pan with the other. And she was one hundred and sixty-five* years old, and hadn't a tooth in her head.

From *Roughing It,* 1872

* Being in calmer mood, now, I voluntarily knock off a hundred from that.—M. T.

Tom Quartz

One of my comrades there—another of those victims of eighteen years of unrequited toil and blighted hopes—was one of the gentlest spirits that ever bore its patient cross in a weary exile: grave and simple Dick Baker, pocket-miner of Dead-Horse Gulch.—He was forty-six, gray as a rat, earnest, thoughtful, slenderly educated, slouchily dressed and clay-soiled, but his heart was finer metal than any gold his shovel ever brought to light—than any, indeed, that ever was mined or minted.

Whenever he was out of luck and a little down-hearted, he would fall to mourning over the loss of a wonderful cat he used to own (for where women and children are not, men of kindly impulses take up with pets, for they must love something). And he always spoke of the strange sagacity of that cat with the air of a man who believed in his secret heart that there was something human about it—may be even supernatural.

I heard him talking about this animal once. He said:

"Gentlemen, I used to have a cat here, by the name of Tom Quartz, which you'd a took an interest in I reckon—most any body would. I had him here eight year—and he was the remarkablest cat *I* ever see. He was a large gray one of the Tom specie, an' he had more hard, natchral sense than any man in this camp—'n' a *power* of dignity—he wouldn't let the Gov'ner of Californy be familiar with him. He never ketched a rat in his life—'peared to be above it. He never cared for nothing but mining. He knowed more about mining, that cat did, than any man *I* ever, ever see. You couldn't tell *him* noth'n' 'bout placer diggin's—'n' as for pocket mining, why he was just born for it. He would dig out after me an' Jim when we went over the hills prospect'n', and he would trot along behind us for as much as five mile, if we went so fur. An' he had the best judgment, about mining ground—why you never see anything like it. When we went to work, he'd scatter a glance around, 'n' if he didn't think much of the indications, he would give a look as much as to say, 'Well, I'll have to get you to excuse *me*,' 'n' without another word he'd hyste his nose into the air 'n' shove for home. But if the ground suited him, he would lay low 'n' keep dark till the first pan was washed, 'n' then he would sidle up 'n' take a look, an' if there was about six or seven grains of gold *he* was satisfied—he didn't want no better prospect 'n' that—'n' then he would lay down on our coats and snore like a steamboat till we'd struck the pocket, an' then get up 'n' superintend. He was nearly lightnin' on superintending.

"Well, bye an' bye, up comes this yer quartz excitement. Every body was into it—every body was pick'n' 'n' blast'n' instead of shovelin' dirt on the hill side—every body was put'n' down a shaft instead of scrapin' the surface. Noth'n' would do Jim, but *we* must tackle the ledges, too, 'n' so we did. We commenced put'n' down a shaft, 'n' Tom Quartz he begin to wonder what in the Dickens it was all about. *He* hadn't ever seen any mining like that before, 'n' he was all upset, as you may say—he couldn't come to a right understanding of it no way—it was too many for *him*. He was down on it, too, you bet you—he was down on it powerful—'n' always appeared to consider it the cussedest foolishness out. But that cat, you know, was *always* agin new fangled arrangements—somehow he never could abide 'em. *You* know how it is with old habits. But by an' by Tom Quartz begin to git sort of reconciled a little, though he never *could* altogether understand that eternal sinkin' of a shaft an' never pannin' out any thing. At last he got to comin' down in the shaft, hisself, to try to cipher it out. An' when he'd git the blues, 'n' feel kind o' scruffy, 'n' aggravated 'n' disgusted—knowin' as he did, that the bills was runnin' up all the time an' we warn't makin' a cent—he would curl up on a gunny sack in the corner an' go to sleep. Well, one day when the shaft was down about eight foot, the rock got so hard that we had to put in a blast—the first blast'n' we'd ever done since Tom Quartz was born. An' then we lit the fuse 'n' clumb out 'n' got off 'bout fifty yards—'n' forgot 'n' left Tom Quartz sound asleep on the gunny sack. In 'bout a minute we seen a puff of smoke bust up out of the hole, 'n' then everything let go with an awful crash, 'n' about four million ton of rocks 'n' dirt 'n' smoke 'n' splinters shot up 'bout a mile an' a half into the air, an' by George, right in the dead centre of it was old Tom Quartz a goin' end over end, an' a snortin' an' a sneez'n', an' a clawin' an' a reachin' for things like all possessed. But it warn't no use, you know, it warn't no use. An' that was the last we see of *him* for about two minutes 'n' a half, an' then all of a sudden it begin to rain rocks and rubbage, an' directly he come down ker-whop about ten foot off f'm where we stood. Well, I reckon he was p'raps the orneriest lookin' beast you ever see. One ear was sot back on his neck, 'n' his tail was stove up, 'n' his eye-winkers were swinged off, 'n' he was all blacked up with powder an' smoke, an' all sloppy with mud 'n' slush f'm one end to the other. Well sir, it warn't no use to try to apologize—we couldn't say a word. He took a sort of a disgusted look at hisself, 'n' then he looked at us—an' it was just exactly the same as if he had said—'Gents, may be *you* think it's smart to take advantage of a cat that 'ain't had no experience of quartz minin', but *I* think *different*'—'an then he turned on his heel 'n' marched off home without ever saying another word.

"That was jest his style. An' may be you won't believe it, but after that you never see a cat so prejudiced agin quartz mining as what he was. An' by an' bye when he *did* get to goin' down in the shaft agin, you'd a been astonished at his sagacity. The minute we'd tetch off a blast 'n' the fuse'd begin to sizzle, he'd give a look as much as to say: 'Well, I'll have to git you to excuse *me,*' an' it was surpris'n' the way he'd shin out of that hole 'n' go f'r a tree. Sagacity? It ain't no name for it. 'Twas *inspiration!*"

I said, "Well, Mr. Baker, his prejudice against quartz-mining *was* remarkable, considering how he came by it. Couldn't you ever cure him of it?"

"*Cure him!* No! When Tom Quartz was sot once, he was *always* sot—and you might a blowed him up as much as three million times 'n' you'd never a broken him of his cussed prejudice agin quartz mining."

The affection and the pride that lit up Baker's face when he delivered this tribute to the firmness of his humble friend of other days, will always be a vivid memory with me.

From *Roughing It,* 1872

"Blanketing" the Admiral

After a three months' absence, I found myself in San Francisco again, without a cent. When my credit was about exhausted, (for I had become too mean and lazy, now, to work on a morning paper, and there were no vacancies on the evening journals,) I was created San Francisco correspondent of the *Enterprise*, and at the end of five months I was out of debt, but my interest in my work was gone; for my correspondence being a daily one, without rest or respite, I got unspeakably tired of it. I wanted another change. The vagabond instinct was strong upon me. Fortune favored and I got a new berth and a delightful one. It was to go down to the Sandwich Islands and write some letters for the Sacramento *Union*, an excellent journal and liberal with employees.

We sailed in the propeller *Ajax*, in the middle of winter. The almanac called it winter, distinctly enough, but the weather was a compromise between spring and summer. Six days out of port, it became summer altogether. We had some thirty passengers; among them a cheerful soul by the name of Williams, and three sea-worn old whaleship captains going down to join their vessels. These latter played euchre in the smoking room day and night, drank astonishing quantities of raw whisky without being in the least affected by it, and were the happiest people I think I ever saw. And then there was "the old Admiral—" a retired whaleman. He was a roaring, terrific combination of wind and lightning and thunder, and earnest, whole-souled profanity. But nevertheless he was tender-hearted as a girl. He was a raving, deafening, devastating typhoon, laying waste the cowering seas but with an unvexed refuge in the centre where all comers were safe and at rest. Nobody could know the "Admiral" without liking him; and in a sudden and dire emergency I think no friend of his would know which to choose—to be cursed by him or prayed for by a less efficient person.

His title of "Admiral" was more strictly "official" than any ever worn by a naval officer before or since, perhaps—for it was the voluntary offering of a whole nation, and came direct from the *people* themselves without any intermediate red tape—the people of the Sandwich Islands. It was a title that came to him freighted with affection, and honor, and appreciation of his unpretending merit. And in testimony of the genuineness of the title it was publicly ordained that an exclusive flag should be devised for him and used solely to welcome his coming and wave him God-speed in his going. From that time forth, whenever his ship was signaled in the offing, or he catted his anchor and stood out to sea, that ensign streamed from the royal halliards on the parliament house and the nation lifted their hats to it with spontaneous accord.

Yet he had never fired a gun or fought a battle in his life. When I knew him on board the *Ajax*, he was seventy-two years old and had plowed the salt water sixty-one of them. For sixteen years he had gone in and out of the harbor of Honolulu in command of a whaleship, and for sixteen more had been captain of a San Francisco and Sandwich Island passenger packet and had never had an accident or lost a vessel. The simple natives knew him for a friend who never failed them, and regarded him as children regard a father. It was a dangerous thing to oppress them when the roaring Admiral was around.

Two years before I knew the Admiral, he had retired from the sea on a competence, and had sworn a colossal nine-jointed oath that he would "never go within *smelling* distance of the salt water again as long as he lived." And he had conscientiously kept it. That is to say, *he* considered he had kept it, and it would have been more than dangerous to suggest to him, even in the gentlest way, that making eleven long sea voyages, as a passenger, during the two years that had transpired since he "retired," was only keeping the general spirit of it and not the strict letter.

The Admiral knew only one narrow line of conduct to pursue in any and all cases where there was a fight, and that was to shoulder his way straight in without an inquiry as to the rights or the merits of it, and take the part of the weaker side.—And this was the reason why he was always sure to be present at the trial of any universally execrated criminal to oppress and intimidate the jury with a vindictive pantomime of what he would do to them if he ever caught them out of the box. And this was why harried cats and outlawed dogs that knew him confidently took sanctuary under his chair in time of trouble. In the beginning he was the most frantic and bloodthirsty Union man that drew breath in the shadow of the Flag; but the instant the Southerners began to go down before the sweep of the Northern armies, he ran up the Confederate colors and from that time till the end was a rampant and inexorable secessionist.

He hated intemperance with a more uncompromising animosity than any individual I have ever met, of either sex, and he was never tired of storming against it and beseeching friends and strangers alike to be wary and drink with moderation. And yet if any creature had been guileless enough to intimate that his absorbing nine gallons of "straight" whisky during our voyage was any fraction short of rigid or inflexible abstemiousness, in that self-same moment the old man would have spun him to the uttermost parts of the earth in the whirlwind of his wrath. Mind, I am not saying his whisky ever affected his head or his legs, for it did not, in even the slightest degree. He was a capacious container, but he did not hold enough for that. He took a level tumblerful of whisky every morning before he put his clothes on —"to sweeten his bilgewater," he said.—He took another after he got the most of his clothes on, "to settle his mind and give him his bearings." He then shaved, and put on a clean shirt; after which he recited the Lord's Prayer in a fervent, thundering bass that shook the ship to her kelson and suspended all conversation in the main cabin. Then, at this stage, being invariably "by the head," or "by the stern," or "listed to port or starboard," he took one more to "put him on an even keel so that he would mind his hellum and not miss stays and go about, every time he came up in the wind."—And now, his state-room door swung open and the sun of his benignant face beamed redly out upon men and women and children, and he roared his "shipmets a'hoy!" in a way that was calculated to wake the dead and precipitate the final resurrection; and forth he strode, a picture to look at and a presence to enforce attention. Stalwart and portly; not a gray hair; broad-brimmed slouch hat; semi-sailor toggery of blue navy flannel—roomy and ample; a stately expanse of shirt-front and a liberal amount of black silk neck-cloth tied with a sailor knot; large chain and imposing seals impending from his fob; awe-inspring feet, and "a hand like the hand of Providence," as his whaling brethren expressed it; wrist-bands and sleeves pushed back half way to the elbow, out of respect for the warm weather, and exposing hairy arms, gaudy with red and blue anchors, ships, and goddesses of liberty tattooed in

India ink. But these details were only secondary matters—his face was the lodestone that chained the eye. It was a sultry disk, glowing determinedly out through a weather beaten mask of mahogany, and studded with warts, seamed with scars, "blazed" all over with unfailing fresh slips of the razor; and with cheery eyes, under shaggy brows, contemplating the world from over the back of a gnarled crag of a nose that loomed vast and lonely out of the undulating immensity that spread away from its foundations. At his heels frisked the darling of his bachelor estate, his terrier "Fan," a creature no larger than a squirrel. The main part of his daily life was occupied in looking after "Fan," in a motherly way, and doctoring her for a hundred ailments which existed only in his imagination.

The Admiral seldom read newspapers; and when he did he never believed anything they said. He read nothing, and believed in nothing, but "The Old Guard," a secession periodical published in New York. He carried a dozen copies of it with him, always, and referred to them for all required information. If it was not there, he supplied it himself, out of a bountiful fancy, inventing history, names, dates, and every thing else necessary to make his point good in an argument. Consequently he was a formidable antagonist in a dispute. Whenever he swung clear of the record and began to create history, the enemy was helpless and had to surrender. Indeed, the enemy could not keep from betraying some little spark of indignation at his manufactured history—and when it came to indignation, that was the Admiral's very "best hold." He was always ready for a political argument, and if nobody started one he would do it himself. With his third retort his temper would begin to rise, and within five minutes he would be blowing a gale, and within fifteen his smoking-room audience would be utterly stormed away and the old man left solitary and alone, banging the table with his fist, kicking the chairs, and roaring a hurricane of profanity. It got so, after a while, that whenever the Admiral approached, with politics in his eye, the passengers would drop out with quiet accord, afraid to meet him; and he would camp on a deserted field.

But he found his match at last, and before a full company. At one time or another, everybody had entered the lists against him and been routed, except the quiet passenger Williams. He had never been able to get an expression of opinion out of him on politics. But now, just as the Admiral drew near the door and the company were about to slip out, Williams said:

"Admiral, are you *certain* about that circumstance concerning the clergymen you mentioned the other day?"—referring to a piece of the Admiral's manufactured history.

Every one was amazed at the man's rashness. The idea of deliberately inviting annihilation was a thing incomprehensible. The retreat came to a halt; then everybody sat down again wondering, to await the upshot of it. The Admiral himself was as surprised as any one. He paused in the door, with his red handkerchief half raised to his sweating face, and contemplated the daring reptile in the corner.

"*Certain* of it? Am I *certain* of it? Do you think I've been lying about it? What do you take me for? Anybody that don't know that circumstance, don't know anything; a child ought to know it. Read your history! Read it up ———, and don't come asking a man if he's *certain* about a bit of A B C stuff that the very southern niggers know all about."

Here the Admiral's fires began to wax hot, the atmosphere thickened, the coming earthquake rumbled, he began to thunder and lighten. Within three minutes his volcano was in full irruption and he was discharging flames and ashes of indignation, belching black volumes of foul history aloft, and vomiting red-hot torrents of profanity from his crater. Meantime Williams sat silent, and apparently deeply and earnestly interested in what the old man was saying. By and by, when the lull came, he said in the most deferential way, and with the gratified air of a man who has had the mystery cleared up which had been puzzling him uncomfortably:

"*Now* I understand it. I always thought I knew that piece of history well enough, but was still afraid to trust it, because there was not that convincing particularity about it that one likes to have in history; but when you mentioned every name, the other day, and every date, and every little circumstance, in their just order and sequence, I said to myself, *this* sounds something like—*this* is history—*this* is putting it in a shape that gives a man confidence; and I said to myself afterward, I will just ask the Admiral if he is perfectly certain about the details, and if he is I will come out and thank him for clearing this matter up for me. And that is what I want to do now—for until you set that matter right it was nothing but just a confusion in my mind, without head or tail to it."

Nobody ever saw the Admiral look so mollified before, and so pleased. Nobody had ever received his bogus history as gospel before; its genuineness had always been called in question either by words or looks; but here was a man that not only swallowed it all down, but was grateful for the dose. He was taken a back; he hardly knew what to say; even his profanity failed him. Now, Williams continued, modestly and earnestly:

"But Admiral, in saying that this was the first stone thrown, and that this precipitated the war, you have overlooked a circumstance which you are perfectly familiar with, but which has escaped your memory. Now I grant you that what you have stated is correct in every detail—to wit: that on the 16th of October, 1860, two Massachusetts clergymen, named Waite and Granger, went in disguise to the house of John Moody, in Rockport, at dead of night, and dragged forth two southern women and their two little children, and after tarring and feathering them conveyed them to Boston and burned them alive in the State House square; and I also grant your proposition that this deed is what led to the secession of South Carolina on the 20th of December following. Very well." [Here the company were pleasantly surprised to hear Williams proceed to come back to the Admiral with his own invincible weapon—clean, pure, *manufactured history*, without a word of truth in it.] "Very well, I say. But Admiral, why overlook the Willis and Morgan case in South Carolina? You are too well informed a man not to know all about that circumstance. Your arguments and your conversations have shown you to be intimately conversant with every detail of this national quarrel. You develop matters of history every day that show plainly that you are no smatterer in it, content to nibble about the surface, but a man who has searched the depths and possessed yourself of everything that has a bearing upon the great question. Therefore, let me just recall to your mind that Willis and Morgan case—though I see by your face that the whole thing is already passing through your memory at this moment. On the 12th of August, 1860, *two months* before the Waite and Granger affair, two South Carolina clergymen, named John H. Morgan and Winthrop L. Willis, one a Methodist and the other an Old School Baptist, disguised themselves, and went at midnight to the house of a planter named Thompson—Archibald F. Thompson, Vice President under Thomas Jefferson,—and took thence, at midnight, his widowed aunt, (a Northern woman,) and her adopted child, an orphan named Mortimer Highie, afflicted with epilepsy and suffering at the time from white swelling on one of his legs, and compelled to walk on crutches in consequence; and the two ministers, in spite of the pleadings of the victims, dragged them to the bush, tarred and feathered them, and afterward burned them at the stake in the city of Charleston. You remember perfectly well what a stir it made; you remember perfectly well that even the Charleston *Courier* stigmatized the act as being unpleasant, of questionable propriety, and scarcely justifiable, and likewise that it would not be matter of surprise if retaliation ensued. And you remember also, that this thing was the *cause* of the Massachusetts outrage. Who, indeed, were the two Massachusetts ministers? and who were the two Southern women they burned? I do not need to remind *you*, Admiral, with your intimate knowledge of history, that Waite was the nephew of the woman burned in Charleston; that Granger was her cousin in the second degree, and that the woman they burned in Boston was the wife of John H. Morgan, and the still loved but divorced wife of Winthrop L. Willis. Now, Admiral, it is only fair that you should acknowledge that the first provocation came from the Southern preachers and that the Northern ones were justified in retaliating. In your arguments you never yet have shown the least disposition to withhold a just verdict or be in anywise unfair, when authoritative history condemned your position, and therefore I have no hesitation in asking you to take the original blame from the Massachusetts ministers, in this matter, and transfer it to the South Carolina clergymen where it justly belongs."

The Admiral was conquered. This sweet spoken creature who swallowed his fraudulent history as if it were the bread of life; basked in his furious blasphemy as if it were generous sunshine; found only calm, even-handed justice in his rampart partisanship; and flooded him with invented history so sugar-coated with flattery and deference that there was no rejecting it, was "too many" for him. He stammered some awkward, profane sentences about the ——— Willis and Morgan business having escaped his memory, but that he "remembered it now," and then, under pretence of giving Fan some medicine for an imaginary cough, drew out of the battle and went away, a vanquished man. Then cheers and laughter went up, and Williams, the ship's benefactor, was a hero. The news went about the vessel, champagne was ordered, an enthusiastic reception instituted in the smoking room, and everybody flocked thither to shake hands with the conqueror. The wheelsman said afterward, that the Admiral stood up behind the pilot house and "ripped and cursed all to himself" till he loosened the smokestack guys and becalmed the mainsail.

The Admiral's power was broken. After that, if he began an argument, somebody would bring Williams, and the old man would grow weak and begin to quiet down at once. And as soon as he was done, Williams in his dulcet, insinuating way, would invent some history (referring for proof, to the old man's own excellent memory and to copies of "The Old Guard" known not to be in his possession) that would turn the tables completely and leave the Admiral all abroad and helpless. By and by he came to so dread Williams and his gilded tongue that he would stop talking when he saw him approach, and finally ceased to mention politics altogether, and from that time forward there was entire peace and serenity in the ship.

From *Roughing It,* 1872

The Greeley Correspondence with Erickson

[Clemens visited the island of Hawaii.]

We stopped some time at one of the plantations, to rest ourselves and refresh the horses. We had a chatty conversation with several gentlemen present; but there was one person, a middle aged man, with an absent look in his face, who simply glanced up, gave us good-day and lapsed again into the meditations which our coming had interrupted. The planters whispered us not to mind him—crazy. They said he was in the Islands for his health; was a preacher; his home, Michigan. They said that if he woke up presently and fell to talking about a correspondence which he had some time held with Mr. Greeley about a trifle of some kind, we must humor him and listen with interest; and we must humor his fancy that this correspondence was the talk of the world.

It was easy to see that he was a gentle creature and that his madness had nothing vicious in it. He looked pale, and a little worn, as if with perplexing thought and anxiety of mind. He sat a long time, looking at the floor, and at intervals muttering to himself and nodding his head acquiescingly or shaking it in mild protest. He was lost in his thought, or in his memories. We continued our talk with the planters, branching from subject to subject. But at last the word "circumstance," casually dropped, in the course of conversation, attracted his attention and brought an eager look into his countenance. He faced about in his chair and said:

"Circumstance? What circumstance? Ah, I know—I know too well. So you have heard of it too." [With a sigh.] "Well, no matter—all the world has heard of it. All the world. The whole world. It is a large world, too, for a thing to travel so far in—now isn't it? Yes, yes—the Greeley correspondence with Erickson has created the saddest and bitterest controversy on both sides of the ocean—and still they keep it up! It makes us famous, but at what a sorrowful sacrifice! I was so sorry when I heard that it had caused that bloody and distressful war over there in Italy. It was little comfort to me, after so much bloodshed, to know that the victors sided with me, and the vanquished with Greeley.—It is little comfort to know that Horace Greeley is responsible for the battle of Sadowa, and not me. Queen Victoria wrote me that she felt just as I did about it—she said that as much as she was opposed to Greeley and the spirit he showed in the correspondence with me, she would not have had Sadowa happen for hundreds of dollars. I can show you her letter, if you would like to see it. But gentlemen, much as you may think you know about that unhappy correspondence, you cannot know the *straight* of it till you hear it from my lips. It has always been garbled in the journals, and even in history. Yes, even in history—think of it! Let me—*please* let me, give you the matter, exactly as it occurred. I truly will not abuse your confidence."

Then he leaned forward, all interest, all earnestness, and told his story—and told it appealingly, too, and yet in the simplest and most unpretentious way; indeed, in such a way as to suggest to one, all the time, that this was a faithful, honorable witness, giving evidence in the sacred interest of justice, and under oath. He said:

"Mrs. Beazeley—Mrs. Jackson Beazeley, widow, of the village of Campbellton, Kansas,—wrote me about a matter which was near her heart—a matter which many might think trivial, but to her it was a thing of deep concern. I was living in Michigan, then—serving in the ministry. She was, and is, an estimable woman—a woman to whom poverty and hardship have proven incentives to industry, in place of discouragements. Her only treasure was her son William, a youth just verging upon manhood; religious, amiable, and sincerely attached to agriculture. He was the widow's comfort and her pride. And so, moved by her love for him, she wrote me about a matter, as I have said before, which lay near her heart—because it lay near her boy's. She desired me to confer with Mr. Greeley about turnips. Turnips were the dream of her child's young ambition. While other youths were frittering away in frivolous amusements the precious years of budding vigor which God had given them for useful preparation, this boy was patiently enriching his mind with information concerning turnips. The sentiment which he felt toward the turnip was akin to adoration. He could not think of the turnip without emotion; he could not speak of it calmly; he could not contemplate it without exaltation. He could not eat it without shedding tears. All the poetry in his sensitive nature was in sympathy with the gracious vegetable. With the earliest pipe of dawn he sought his patch, and when the curtaining night drove him from it he shut himself up with his books and garnered statistics till sleep overcame him. On rainy days he sat and talked hours together with his mother about turnips. When company came, he made it his loving duty to put aside everything else and converse with them all the day long of his great joy in the turnip. And yet, was this joy rounded and complete? Was there no secret alloy of unhappiness in it? Alas, there was. There was a canker gnawing at his heart; the noblest inspiration of his soul eluded his endeavor—viz: he could not make of the turnip a climbing vine. Months went by; the bloom forsook his cheek, the fire faded out of his eye; sighings and abstraction usurped the place of smiles and cheerful converse. But a watchful eye noted these things and in time a motherly sympathy unsealed the secret. Hence the letter to me. She pleaded for attention—she said her boy was dying by inches.

"I was a stranger to Mr. Greeley, but what of that? The matter was urgent. I wrote and begged him to solve the difficult problem if possible and save the student's life. My interest grew, until it partook of the anxiety of the mother. I waited in much suspense.—At last the answer came.

"I found that I could not read it readily, the handwriting being unfamiliar and my emotions somewhat wrought up. It seemed to refer in part to the boy's case, but chiefly to other and irrelevant matters—such as paving-stones, electricity, oysters, and something which I took to be 'absolution' or 'agrarianism,' I could not be certain which; still, these appeared to be simply casual mentions, nothing more; friendly in spirit, without doubt, but lacking the connection or coherence necessary to make them useful.—I judged that my understanding was affected by my feelings, and so laid the letter away till morning.

"In the morning I read it again, but with difficulty and uncertainty still, for I had lost some little rest and my mental vision seemed clouded. The note was more connected, now, but did not meet the emergency it was expected to meet. It was too discursive. It appeared to read as follows, though I was not certain of some of the words:

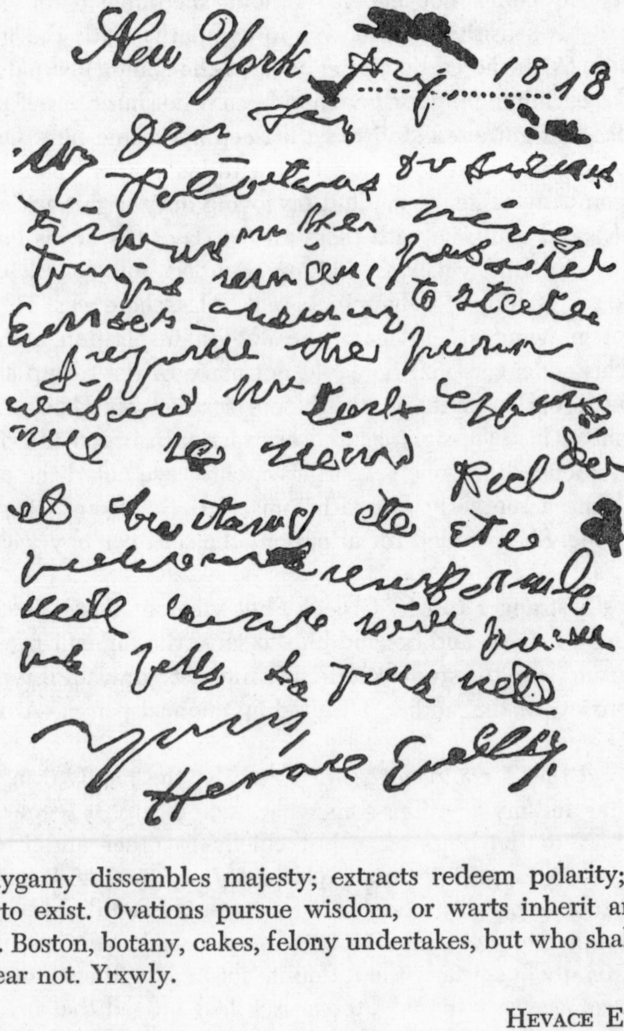
New York 1818

'Polygamy dissembles majesty; extracts redeem polarity; causes hitherto exist. Ovations pursue wisdom, or warts inherit and condemn. Boston, botany, cakes, felony undertakes, but who shall allay? We fear not. Yrxwly.

HEVACE EVEELOJ.'

"But there did not seem to be a word about turnips. There seemed to be no suggestion as to how they might be made to grow like vines. There was not even a reference to the Beazeleys. I slept upon the matter; I ate no supper, neither any breakfast next morning. So I resumed my work with a brain refreshed, and was very hopeful. *Now* the letter took a different aspect—all save the signature, which latter I judged to be only a harmless affectation of Hebrew. The epistle was necessarily from Mr. Greeley, for it bore the printed heading of *The Tribune*, and I had written to no one else there. The letter, I say, had taken a different aspect, but still its language was eccentric and avoided the issue. It now appeared to say:

'Bolivia extemporizes mackerel; borax esteems polygamy; sausages wither in the east. Creation perdu, is done; for woes inherent one can damn. Buttons, buttons, corks, geology underrates but we shall allay. My beer's out. Yrxwly,

HEVACE EVEELOJ.'

"I was evidently overworked. My comprehension was impaired. Therefore I gave two days to recreation, and then returned to my task greatly refreshed. The letter now took this form:

'Poultices do sometimes choke swine; tulips reduce posterity; causes leather to resist. Our notions empower wisdom, her let's afford while we can. Butter but any cakes, fill any undertaker, we'll wean him from his filly. We feel hot.

Yrxwly, HEVACE EVEELOJ.'

"I was still not satisfied. These generalities did not meet the question. They were crisp, and vigorous, and delivered with a confidence that almost compelled conviction; but at such a time as this, with a human life at stake, they seemed inappropriate, worldly, and in bad taste. At any other time I would have been not only glad, but proud, to receive from a man like Mr. Greeley a letter of this kind, and would have studied it earnestly and tried to improve myself all I could; but now, with that poor boy in his far home languishing for relief, I had no heart for learning.

"Three days passed by, and I read the note again. Again its tenor had changed. It now appeared to say:

'Potations do sometimes wake wines; turnips restrain passion; causes necessary to state. Infest the poor widow; her lord's effects will be void. But dirt, bathing, etc., etc., followed unfairly, will worm him from his folly—so swear not.

Yrxwly, HEVACE EVEELOJ.'

"This was more like it. But I was unable to proceed. I was too much worn. The word 'turnips' brought temporary joy and encouragement, but my strength was so much impaired, and the delay might be so perilous for the boy, that I relinquished the idea of pursuing the translation further, and resolved to do what I ought to have done at first. I sat down and wrote Mr. Greeley as follows:

"DEAR SIR: I fear I do not entirely comprehend your kind note. It cannot be possible, Sir, that 'turnips restrain passion'—at least the study or contemplation of turnips cannot—for it is this very employment that has scorched our poor friend's mind and sapped his bodily strength.—But if they *do* restrain it, will you bear with us a little further and explain how they should be prepared? I observe that you say 'causes necessary to state,' but you have omitted to state them.

"Under a misapprehension, you seem to attribute to me interested motives in this matter—to call it by no harsher term. But I assure you, dear sir, that if I seem to be 'infesting the widow,' it is all *seeming*, and void of reality. It is from no seeking of mine that I am in this position. She asked me, herself, to write you. I never have infested her—indeed I scarcely know her. I do not infest anybody. I try to go along, in my humble way, doing as near right as I can, never harming anybody, and never *throwing out insinuations*. As for 'her lord and his effects,' they are of no interest to me. I trust I have effects enough of my own—shall endeavor to get along with them, at any rate, and not go mousing around to get hold of somebody's that are 'void.' But do you not see?—this woman is a *widow*—she has no 'lord.' He is dead—or pretended to be, when they buried him. Therefore, no amount of 'dirt, bathing,' etc., etc., howsoever 'unfairly followed' will be likely to 'worm him from his folly'—if being dead and a ghost is 'folly.' Your closing remark is as unkind as it was uncalled for; and if report says true you might have applied it to yourself, sir, with more point and less impropriety.

Very Truly Yours, SIMON ERICKSON.

"In the course of a few days, Mr. Greeley did what would have saved a world of trouble, and much mental and bodily suffering and misunderstanding, if he had done it sooner. To-wit, he sent an intelligible rescript or translation of his original note, made in a plain hand by his clerk. Then the mystery cleared, and I saw that his heart had been right, all the time. I will recite the note in its clarified form:

"[Translation.]

'Potatoes do sometimes make vines; turnips remain passive: cause unnecessary to state. Inform the poor widow her lad's efforts will be vain. But diet, bathing, etc. etc., followed uniformly, will wean him from his folly—so fear not.

Yours, HORACE GREELEY.'

"But alas, it was too late, gentlemen—too late. The criminal delay had done its work—young Beazeley was no more. His spirit had taken its flight to a land where all anxieties shall be charmed away, all desires gratified, all ambitions realized. Poor lad, they laid him to his rest with a turnip in each hand."

So ended Erickson, and lapsed again into nodding, mumbling, and abstraction. The company broke up, and left him so. . . . But they did not say what drove him crazy. In the momentary confusion, I forgot to ask.

From *Roughing It*, 1872

Markiss, King of Liars

I stumbled upon one curious character in the Island of Maui. He became a sore annoyance to me in the course of time. My first glimpse of him was in a sort of public room in the town of Lahaina. He occupied a chair at the opposite side of the apartment, and sat eyeing our party with interest for some minutes, and listening as critically to what we were saying as if he fancied we were talking to him and expecting him to reply. I thought it very sociable in a stranger. Presently, in the course of conversation, I made a statement bearing upon the subject under discussion—and I made it with due modesty, for there was nothing extraordinary about it, and it was only put forth in illustration of a point at issue. I had barely finished when this person spoke out with rapid utterance and feverish anxiety:

"Oh, that was certainly remarkable, after a fashion, but you ought to have seen *my* chimney—you ought to have seen *my* chimney, sir! Smoke! I wish I may hang if—Mr. Jones, *you* remember that chimney—you *must* remember that chimney! No, no—I recollect, now, you warn't living on this side of the island then. But I am telling you nothing but the truth, and I wish I may never draw another breath if that chimney didn't smoke so that the smoke actually got *caked* in it and I had to dig it out with a pickaxe! You may smile, gentlemen, but the High Sheriff's got a hunk of it which I dug out before his eyes, and so it's perfectly easy for you to go and examine for yourselves."

The interruption broke up the conversation, which had already begun to lag, and we presently hired some natives and an out-rigger canoe or two, and went out to overlook a grand surf-bathing contest.

Two weeks after this, while talking in a company, I looked up and detected this same man boring through and through me with his intense eye, and noted again his twitching muscles and his feverish anxiety to speak. The moment I paused, he said:

"*Beg* your pardon, sir, beg your pardon, but it can only be considered remarkable when brought into strong outline by isolation. Sir, contrasted with a circumstance which occurred in my own experience, it instantly becomes commonplace. No, not that—for I will not speak so discourteously of any experience in the career of a stranger and a gentleman—but I am *obliged* to say that you could not, and you *would* not ever again refer to this tree as a *large* one, if you could behold, as I have, the great Yakmarack tree, in the island of Ounaska, sea of Kamtchatka—a tree, sir, not one inch less than four hundred and fifteen feet in solid diameter!—and I wish I may die in a minute if it isn't so! Oh, you needn't look so questioning, gentlemen; here's old Cap Saltmarsh can say whether I know what I'm talking about or not. I showed him the tree."

CAPTAIN SALTMARSH.—"Come, now, cat your anchor, lad—you're heaving too taut. You *promised* to show me that stunner, and I walked more than eleven mile with you through the cussedest jungle I ever see, a hunting for it; but the tree you showed me finally warn't as big around as a beer cask, and *you* know that your own self, Markiss."

"Hear the man talk! Of *course* the tree was reduced that way, but didn't I *explain* it? Answer me, didn't I? Didn't I say I wished you could have seen it when *I* first saw it? When you got up on your ear and called me names, and said I had brought you eleven miles to look at a sapling, didn't I *explain* to you that all the whale-ships in the North Seas had been wooding off of it for more than twenty-seven years? And did you s'pose the tree could last for-*ever*, con*found* it? I don't see why you want to keep back things that way, and try to injure a person that's never done *you* any harm."

Somehow this man's presence made me uncomfortable, and I was glad when a native arrived at that moment to say that Muckawow, the most companionable and luxurious among the rude war-chiefs of the Islands, desired us to come over and help him enjoy a missionary whom he had found trespassing on his grounds.

I think it was about ten days afterward that, as I finished a statement I was making for the instruction of a group of friends and acquaintances, and which made no pretence of being extraordinary, a familiar voice chimed instantly in on the heels of my last word, and said:

"But, my dear sir, there was *nothing* remarkable about that horse, or the circumstance either—nothing in the world! I mean no sort of offence when I say it, sir, but you really do not know anything whatever about speed. Bless your heart, if you could only have seen my mare Margaretta; *there* was a beast!—*there* was lightning for you! Trot! Trot is no name for it—she flew! How she *could* whirl a buggy along! I started her out once, sir—Colonel Bilgewater, *you* recollect that animal perfectly well—I started her out about thirty or thirty-five yards ahead of the awfullest storm I ever saw in my life, and it chased us upwards of eighteen miles! It did, by the everlasting hills! And I'm telling you nothing but the unvarnished truth when I say that not one single drop of rain fell on me—not a single *drop*, sir! And I swear to it! But my dog was a-swimming behind the wagon all the way!"

For a week or two I stayed mostly within doors, for I seemed to meet this person everywhere, and he had become utterly hateful to me. But one evening I dropped in on Captain Perkins and his friends, and we had a sociable time. About ten o'clock I chanced to be talking about a merchant friend of mine, and without really intending it, the remark slipped out that he was a little mean and parsimonious about paying his workmen. Instantly, through the steam of a hot whiskey punch on the opposite side of the room, a remembered voice shot—and for a moment I trembled on the imminent verge of profanity:

"Oh, my dear sir, really you expose yourself when you parade *that* as a surprising circumstance. Bless your heart and hide, you are ignorant of the very A B C of meanness! ignorant as the unborn babe! ignorant as unborn *twins!* You don't know *any thing* about it! It is pitiable to see you, sir, a well-spoken and prepossessing stranger, making such an enormous pow-wow here about a subject concerning which your ignorance is perfectly humiliating! Look me in the eye, if you please; look me in the eye. John James Godfrey was the son of poor but honest parents in the State of Mississippi—boyhood friend of mine—bosom comrade in later years. Heaven rest his noble spirit, he is gone from us now. John James Godfrey was hired by the Hayblossom Mining Company in California to do some blasting for them—the "Incorporated Company of Mean Men," the boys used to call it. Well, one day he drilled a hole about four feet deep and put in an awful blast of powder, and was standing over it ramming it down with an iron crowbar about nine foot long, when the cussed thing struck a spark and fired the powder, and scat! away John Godfrey whizzed like a skyrocket, him and his crowbar! Well, sir, he kept on going up in the air higher and higher, till he didn't look any bigger than a boy—and he kept going on up higher and higher, till he didn't look any bigger than a doll—and he kept on going up higher and higher, till he didn't look any bigger than a little small bee—and then he went out of sight! Presently he came in sight again, looking like a little small bee—and he came along down further and further, till he looked as big as a doll again—and down further and further, till he was as big as a boy again—and further and further, till he was a full-sized man once more; and then him and his crowbar came a wh-izz-ing down and lit right exactly in the same old tracks and went to r-ramming down, and r-ramming down, and r-ramming down again, just the same as if nothing had happened! Now do you know, that poor cuss warn't gone only sixteen minutes, and yet that Incorporated Company of Mean Men DOCKED HIM FOR THE LOST TIME!"

I said I had the headache, and so excused myself and went home. And on my diary I entered "another night spoiled" by this offensive loafer. And a fervent curse was set down with it to keep the item company. And the very next day I packed up, out of all patience, and left the Island.

Almost from the very beginning, I regarded that man as a liar.

. . . .

The line of points represents an interval of years. At the end of which time the opinion hazarded in that last sentence came to be gratifyingly and remarkably endorsed, and by wholly disinterested persons. The man Markiss was found one morning hanging to a beam of his own bedroom (the doors and windows securely fastened on the inside), dead; and on his breast was pinned a paper in his own handwriting begging his friends to suspect no innocent person of having anything to do with his death, for that it was the work of his own hands entirely. Yet the jury brought in the astounding verdict that deceased came to his death "by the hands of some person or persons unknown!" They explained that the perfectly undeviating consistency of Markiss's character for thirty years towered aloft as colossal and indestructible testimony, that whatever statement he chose to make was entitled to instant and unquestioning acceptance as a *lie*. And they furthermore stated their belief that he was not dead, and instanced the strong circumstantial evidence of his own word that he *was* dead—and beseeched the coroner to delay the funeral as long as possible, which was done. And so in the tropical climate of Lahaina the coffin stood open for seven days, and then even the loyal jury gave him up. But they sat on him again, and changed their verdict to "suicide induced by mental aberration"—because, said they, with penetration, "he said he was dead, and he *was* dead; and would he have told the truth if he had been in his right mind? *No*, sir."

From *Roughing It*, 1872

A Practical Joke

[After six months of "luxurious vagrancy" in the Hawaiian Islands, Clemens returned to San Francisco, where he gave a successful lecture, greatly to his surprise.]

I launched out as a lecturer, now, with great boldness. I had the field all to myself, for public lectures were almost an unknown commodity in the Pacific market. They are not so rare, now, I suppose. I took an old personal friend along to play agent for me, and for two or three weeks we roamed through Nevada and California and had a very cheerful time of it. Two days before I lectured in Virginia City, two stagecoaches were robbed within two miles of the town. The daring act was committed just at dawn, by six masked men, who sprang up alongside the coaches, presented revolvers at the heads of the drivers and passengers, and commanded a general dismount. Everybody climbed down, and the robbers took their watches and every cent they had. Then they took gunpowder and blew up the express specie boxes and got their contents. The leader of the robbers was a small, quick-spoken man, and the fame of his vigorous manner and his intrepidity was in everybody's mouth when we arrived.

The night after instructing Virginia, I walked over the desolate "divide" and down to Gold Hill, and lectured there. The lecture done, I stopped to talk with a friend, and did not start back till eleven. The "divide" was high, unoccupied ground, between the towns, the scene of twenty midnight murders and a hundred robberies. As we climbed up and stepped out on this eminence, the Gold Hill lights dropped out of sight at our backs, and the night closed down gloomy and dismal. A sharp wind swept the place, too, and chilled our perspiring bodies through.

"I tell you I don't like this place at night," said Mike the agent.

"Well, don't speak so loud," I said. "You needn't remind anybody that we are here."

Just then a dim figure approached me from the direction of Virginia—a man, evidently. He came straight at me, and I stepped aside to let him pass; he stepped in the way and confronted me again. Then I saw that he had a mask on and was holding something in my face—I heard a click-click and recognized a revolver in dim outline. I pushed the barrel aside with my hand and said:

"Don't!"

He ejaculated sharply:

"Your watch! Your money!"

I said:

"You can have them with pleasure—but take the pistol away from my face, please. It makes me shiver."

"No remarks! Hand out your money!"

"Certainly—I—"

"Put up your hands! Don't you go for a weapon! Put 'em up! Higher!"

I held them above my head.

A pause. Then:

"Are you going to hand out your money or not?"

I dropped my hands to my pockets and said:

"Certainly! I—"

"Put up your *hands!* Do you want your head blown off? Higher!"

I put them above my head again.

Another pause.

"*Are* you going to hand out your money or *not*? Ah-ah—again? Put up your hands! By George, you want the head shot off you awful bad!"

"Well, friend, I'm trying my best to please you. You tell me to give up my money, and when I reach for it you tell me to put up my hands. If you would only—. Oh, now—don't! All six of you at me! That other man will get away while.— Now please take some of those revolvers out of my face—*do,* if you *please!* Every time one of them clicks, my liver comes up into my throat! If you have a mother—any of you—or if any of you have ever *had* a mother—or a—grandmother—or a—"

"Cheese it! *Will* you give up your money, or have we got to—. There-there—none of that! Put up your *hands!*"

"Gentlemen—I know you are gentlemen by your—"

"Silence! If you want to be facetious, young man, there are times and places more fitting. *This* is a serious business."

"You prick the marrow of my opinion. The funerals I have attended in my time were comedies compared to it. Now *I* think—"

"Curse your palaver! Your money!—your money!—your money! Hold!—put up your hands!"

"Gentlemen, listen to reason. You *see* how I am situated—now *don't* put those pistols so close—I smell the powder. You see how I am situated. If I had four hands—so that I could hold up two and—"

"Throttle him! Gag him! Kill him!"

"Gentlemen, *don't!* Nobody's watching the other fellow. Why don't some of you—. Ouch! Take it away, please! Gentlemen, you see that I've got to hold up my hands; and so I can't take out my money—but if you'll be so kind as to take it out for me, I will do as much for you some—"

"Search him Beauregard—and stop his jaw with a bullet, quick, if he wags it again. Help Beauregard, Stonewall."

Then three of them, with the small, spry leader, adjourned to Mike and fell to searching him. I was so excited that my lawless fancy tortured me to ask my two men all manner of facetious questions about their rebel brother-generals of the South, but, considering the order they had received, it was but common prudence to keep still. When everything had been taken from me,—watch, money, and a multitude of trifles of small value,—I supposed I was free, and forthwith put my cold hands into my empty pockets and began an inoffensive jig to warm my feet and stir up some latent courage—but instantly all pistols were at my head, and the order came again:

"Be still! Put up your hands! And *keep* them up!"

They stood Mike up alongside of me, with strict orders to keep his hands above his head, too, and then the chief highwayman said:

"Beauregard, hide behind that boulder; Phil Sheridan, you hide behind that other one; Stonewall Jackson, put yourself behind that sagebush there. Keep your pistols bearing on these fellows, and if they take down their hands within ten minutes, or move a single peg, let them have it!"

Then three disappeared in the gloom toward the several ambushes, and the other three disappeared down the road toward Virginia.

It was depressingly still, and miserably cold. Now this whole thing was a practical joke, and the robbers were personal friends of ours in disguise, and twenty more lay hidden within ten feet of us during the whole operation, listening. Mike knew all this, and was in the joke, but I suspected nothing of it. To me it was most uncomfortably genuine.

When we had stood there in the middle of the road five minutes, like a couple of idiots, with our hands aloft, freezing to death by inches, Mike's interest in the joke began to wane. He said:

"The time's up, now, ain't it?"

"No, you keep still. Do you want to take any chances with those bloody savages?"

Presently Mike said:

"*Now* the time's up, anyway. I'm freezing."

"Well freeze. Better freeze than carry your brains home in a basket. Maybe the time *is* up, but how do *we* know?—got no watch to tell by. I mean to give them good measure. I calculate to stand here fifteen minutes or die. Don't you move."

So, without knowing it, I was making one joker very sick of his contract. When we took our arms down at last, they were aching with cold and fatigue, and when we went sneaking off, the dread I was in that the time might not yet be up and that we would feel bullets in a moment, was not sufficient to draw all my attention from the misery that racked my stiffened body.

The joke of these highwayman friends of ours was mainly a joke upon themselves; for they had waited for me on the cold hill-top two full hours before I came, and there was very little fun in that; they were so chilled that it took them a couple of weeks to get warm again. Moreover, I never had a thought that they would kill me to get money which it was so perfectly easy to get without any such folly, and so they did not really frighten me bad enough to make their enjoyment worth the trouble they had taken. I was only afraid that their weapons would go off accidentally. Their very numbers inspired me with confidence that no blood would be intentionally spilled. They were not smart; they ought to have sent only *one* highwayman, with a double-barrelled shot gun, if they desired to see the author of this volume climb a tree.

However, I suppose that in the long run I got the largest share of the joke at last; and in a shape not foreseen by the highwaymen; for the chilly exposure on the "divide" while I was in a perspiration gave me a cold which developed itself into a troublesome disease and kept my hands idle some three months, besides costing me quite a sum in doctor's bills. Since then I play no practical jokes on people and generally lose my temper when one is played upon me.

From *Roughing It*, 1872

Jim Baker's Bluejay Yarn

Animals talk to each other, of course. There can be no question about that; but I suppose there are very few people who can understand them. I never knew but one man who could. I knew he could, however, because he told me so himself. He was a middle-aged, simple-hearted miner who had lived in a lonely corner of California, among the woods and mountains, a good many years, and had studied the ways of his only neighbors, the beasts and the birds, until he believed he could accurately translate any remark which they made. This was Jim Baker. According to Jim Baker, some animals have only a limited education, and use only very simple words, and scarcely ever a comparison or a flowery figure; whereas, certain other animals have a large vocabulary, a fine command of language and a ready and fluent delivery; consequently these latter talk a great deal; they like it; they are conscious of their talent, and they enjoy "showing off." Baker said, that after long and careful observation, he had come to the conclusion that the blue-jays were the best talkers he had found among birds and beasts. Said he:—

"There's more *to* a blue-jay than any other creature. He has got more moods, and more different kinds of feelings than other creatures; and mind you, whatever a blue-jay feels, he can put into language. And no mere commonplace language, either, but rattling, out-and-out book-talk—and bristling with metaphor, too—just bristling! And as for command of language—why *you* never see a blue-jay get stuck for a word. No man ever did. They just boil out of him! And another thing: I've noticed a good deal, and there's no bird, or cow, or anything that uses as good grammar as a blue-jay. You may say a cat uses good grammar. Well, a cat does—but you let a cat get excited, once; you let a cat get to pulling fur with another cat on a shed, nights, and you'll hear grammar that will give you the lockjaw. Ignorant people think it's the *noise* which fighting cats make that is so aggravating, but it ain't so; it's the sickening grammar they use. Now I've never heard a jay use bad grammar but very seldom; and when they do, they are as ashamed as a human; they shut right down and leave.

"You may call a jay a bird. Well, so he is, in a measure—because he's got feathers on him, and don't belong to no church, perhaps; but otherwise he is just as much a human as you be. And I'll tell you for why. A jay's gifts, and instincts, and feelings, and interests, cover the whole ground. A jay hasn't got any more principle than a Congressman. A jay will lie, a jay will steal, a jay will deceive, a jay will betray; and four times out of five, a jay will go back on his solemnest promise. The sacredness of an obligation is a thing which you can't cram into no blue-jay's head. Now on top of all this, there's another thing: a jay can out-swear any gentleman in the mines. You think a cat can swear. Well, a cat can; but you give a blue-jay a subject that calls for his reserve-powers, and where is your cat? Don't talk to *me* —I know too much about this thing. And there's yet another thing: in the one little particular of scolding—just good, clean, out-and-out scolding—a blue-jay can lay over anything, human or divine. Yes, sir, a jay is everything that a man is. A jay can cry, a jay can laugh, a jay can feel shame, a jay can reason and plan and discuss, a jay likes gossip and scandal, a jay has got a sense of humor, a jay knows when he is an ass just as well as you do—maybe better. If a jay ain't human, he better take in his sign, that's all. Now I'm going to tell you a perfectly true fact about some blue-jays.

"When I first begun to understand jay language correctly, there was a little incident happened here. Seven years ago, the last man in this region but me, moved away. There stands his house,—been empty ever since; a log house, with a plank roof—just one big room, and no more; no ceiling—nothing between the rafters and the floor. Well, one Sunday morning I was sitting out here in front of my cabin, with my cat, taking the sun, and looking at the blue hills, and listening to the leaves rustling so lonely in the trees, and thinking of the home away yonder in the States, that I hadn't heard from in thirteen years, when a blue jay lit on that house, with an acorn in his mouth, and says, 'Hello, I reckon I've struck something.' When he spoke, the acorn dropped out of his mouth and rolled down the roof, of course, but he didn't care; his mind was all on the thing he had struck. It was a knot-hole in the roof. He cocked his head to one side, shut one eye and put the other one to the hole, like a 'possum looking down a jug;

then he glanced up with his bright eyes, gave a wink or two with his wings—which signifies gratification, you understand,—and says, 'It looks like a hole, it's located like a hole,—blamed if I don't believe it *is* a hole!'

"Then he cocked his head down and took another look; he glances up perfectly joyful, this time; winks his wings and his tail both, and says, 'O, no, this ain't no fat thing, I reckon! If I ain't in luck!—why it's a perfectly elegant hole!' So he flew down and got that acorn, and fetched it up and dropped it in, and was just tilting his head back, with the heavenliest smile on his face, when all of a sudden he was paralyzed into a listening attitude and that smile faded gradually out of his countenance like breath off'n a razor, and the queerest look of surprise took its place. Then he says, 'Why I didn't hear it fall!' He cocked his eye at the hole again, and took a long look; raised up and shook his head; stepped around to the other side of the hole and took another look from that side; shook his head again. He studied a while, then he just went into the *de*tails—walked round and round the hole and spied into it from every point of the compass. No use. Now he took a thinking attitude on the comb of the roof and scratched the back of his head with his right foot a minute, and finally says, 'Well, it's too many for *me*, that's certain; must be a mighty long hole; however, I ain't got no time to fool around here, I got to 'tend to business; I reckon it's all right—chance it, anyway.'

"So he flew off and fetched another acorn and dropped it in, and tried to flirt his eye to the hole quick enough to see what become of it, but he was too late. He held his eye there as much as a minute; then he raised up and sighed, and says, 'Consound it, I don't seem to understand this thing, no way; however, I'll tackle her again.' He fetched another acorn, and done his level best to see what become of it, but he couldn't. He says, 'Well, *I* never struck no such a hole as this, before; I'm of the opinion it's a totally new kind of a hole.' Then he begun to get mad. He held in for a spell, walking up and down the comb of the roof and shaking his head and muttering to himself; but his feelings got the upper hand of him, presently, and he broke loose and cussed himself black in the face. I never see a bird take on so about a little thing. When he got through he walks to the hole and looks in again for half a minute; then he says, 'Well, you're a long hole, and a deep hole, and a mighty singular hole altogether—but I've started in to fill you, and I'm d—d if I *don't* fill you, if it takes a hundred years!'

"And with that, away he went. You never see a bird work so since you was born. He laid into his work like a nigger, and the way he hove acorns into that hole for about two hours and a half was one of the most exciting and astonishing spectacles I ever struck. He never stopped to take a look any more—he just hove 'em in and went for more. Well at last he could hardly flop his wings, he was so tuckered out. He comes a-drooping down, once more, sweating like an ice-pitcher, drops his acorn in and says, '*Now* I guess I've got the bulge on you by this time!' So he bent down for a look. If you'll believe me, when his head come up again he was just pale with rage. He says, 'I've shoveled acorns enough in there to keep the family thirty years, and if I can see a sign of one of 'em I wish I may land in a museum with a belly full of sawdust in two minutes!'

"He just had strength enough to crawl up on to the comb and lean his back agin the chimbly, and then he collected his impressions and begun to free his mind. I see in a second that what I had mistook for profanity in the mines was only just the rudiments, as you may say.

"Another jay was going by, and heard him doing his devotions, and stops to inquire what was up. The sufferer told him the whole circumstance, and says, 'Now yonder's the hole, and if you don't believe me, go and look for yourself.' So this fellow went and looked, and comes back and says, 'How many did you say you put in there?' 'Not any less than two tons,' says the sufferer. The other jay went and looked again. He couldn't seem to make it out, so he raised a yell, and three more jays come. They all examined the hole, they all made the sufferer tell it over again, then they all discussed it, and got off as many leather-headed opinions about it as an average crowd of humans could have done.

"They called in more jays; then more and more, till pretty soon this whole region 'peared to have a blue flush about it. There must have been five thousand of them; and such another jawing and disputing and ripping and cussing, you never heard. Every jay in the whole lot put his eye to the hole and delivered a more chuckle-headed opinion about the mystery than the jay that went there before him. They examined the house all over, too. The door was standing half open, and at last one old jay happened to go and light on it and look in. Of course that knocked the mystery galley-west in a second. There lay the acorns, scattered all over the floor. He flopped his wings and raised a whoop. 'Come here!' he says, 'Come here, everybody; hang'd if this fool hasn't been trying to fill up a house with acorns!' They all came a-swooping down like a blue cloud, and as each fellow lit on the door and took a glance, the whole absurdity of the contract that that first jay had tackled hit him home and he fell over backwards suffocating with laughter, and the next jay took his place and done the same.

"Well, sir, they roosted around here on the house-top and the trees for an hour, and guffawed over that thing like human beings. It ain't any use to tell me a blue-jay hasn't got a sense of humor, because I know better. And memory, too. They brought jays here from all over the United States to look down that hole, every summer for three years. Other birds too. And they could all see the point, except an owl that come from Nova Scotia to visit the Yo Semite, and he took this thing in on his way back. He said he couldn't see anything funny in it. But then he was a good deal disappointed about Yo Semite, too."

From *A Tramp Abroad,* 1880

The Great French Duel

Much as the modern French duel is ridiculed by certain smart people, it is in reality one of the most dangerous institutions of our day. Since it is always fought in the open air the combatants are nearly sure to catch cold. M. Paul de Cassagnac, the most inveterate of the French duelists, has suffered so often in this way that he is at last a confirmed invalid; and the best physician in Paris has expressed the opinion that if he goes on dueling for fifteen or twenty years more,—unless he forms the habit of fighting in a comfortable room where damps and draughts cannot intrude,—he will eventually endanger his life. This ought to moderate the talk of those people who are so stubborn in maintaining that the French duel is the most health-giving of recreations because of the open-air exercise it affords. And it ought also to moderate that foolish talk about French duelists and socialist-hated monarchs being the only people who are immortal.

But it is time to get at my subject. As soon as I heard of the late fiery outbreak between M. Gambetta and M. Fourtou in the French Assembly, I knew that trouble must follow. I knew it because a long personal friendship with M. Gambetta had revealed to me the desperate and implacable nature of the man. Vast as are his physical proportions, I knew that the thirst for revenge would penetrate to the remotest frontiers of his person.

I did not wait for him to call on me, but went at once to him. As I expected, I found the brave fellow steeped in a profound French calm. I say French calm, because French calmness and English calmness have points of difference. He was moving swiftly back and forth among the *débris* of his furniture, now and then staving chance fragments of it across the room with his foot; grinding a constant grist of curses through his set teeth; and halting every little while to deposit another handful of his hair on the pile which he had been building of it on the table.

He threw his arms around my neck, bent me over his stomach to his breast, kissed me on both cheeks, hugged me four or five times, and then placed me in his own arm-chair. As soon as I had got well again, we began business at once.

I said I supposed he would wish me to act as his second, and he said, "Of course." I said I must be allowed to act under a French name, so that I might be shielded from obloquy in my country, in case of fatal results. He winced here, probably at the suggestion that dueling was not regarded with respect in America. However, he agreed to my requirement. This accounts for the fact that in all the newspaper reports M. Gambetta's second was apparently a Frenchman.

First, we drew up my principal's will. I insisted upon this, and stuck to my point. I said I had never heard of a man in his right mind going out to fight a duel without first making his will. He said he had never heard of a man in his right mind doing anything of the kind. When he had finished the will, he wished to proceed to a choice of his "last words." He wanted to know how the following words, as a dying exclamation, struck me:—

"I die for my God, for my country, for freedom of speech, for progress, and the universal brotherhood of man!"

I objected that this would require too lingering a death; it was a good speech for a consumptive, but not suited to the exigencies of the field of honor. We wrangled over a good many ante-mortem outbursts, but I finally got him to cut his obituary down to this, which he copied into his memorandum book, purposing to get it by heart:—

"I DIE THAT FRANCE MAY LIVE"

I said that this remark seemed to lack relevancy; but he said relevancy was a matter of no consequence in last words, what you wanted was thrill.

The next thing in order was the choice of weapons. My principal said he was not feeling well, and would leave that and the other details of the proposed meeting to me. Therefore I wrote the following note and carried it to M. Fourtou's friend:—

"SIR: M. Gambetta accepts M. Fourtou's challenge, and authorizes me to propose Plessis-Piquet as the place of meeting; to-morrow morning at daybreak as the time; and axes as the weapons. I am, sir, with great respect,

MARK TWAIN."

M. Fourtou's friend read this note, and shuddered. Then he turned to me, and said, with a suggestion of severity in his tone:—

"Have you considered, sir, what would be the inevitable result of such a meeting as this?"

"Well, for instance, what *would* it be?"

"Bloodshed!"

"That's about the size of it," I said. "Now, if it is a fair question, what was your side proposing to shed?"

I had him, there. He saw he had made a blunder, so he hastened to explain it away. He said he had spoken jestingly. Then he added that he and his principal would enjoy axes, and indeed prefer them, but such weapons were barred by the French code, and so I must change my proposal.

I walked the floor, turning the thing over in my mind, and finally it occurred to me that Gatling guns at fifteen paces would be a likely way to get a verdict on the field of honor. So I framed this idea into a proposition.

But it was not accepted. The code was in the way again. I proposed rifles; then double-barreled shot-guns; then, Colt's navy revolvers. These being all rejected, I reflected a while, and sarcastically suggested brick-bats at three quarters of a mile. I always hate to fool away a humorous thing on a person who has no perception of humor; and it filled me with bitterness when this man went soberly away to submit the last proposition to his principal.

He came back presently and said his principal was charmed with the idea of brick-bats at three quarters of a mile, but must decline on account of the danger to disinterested parties passing between. Then I said:—

"Well, I am at the end of my string, now. Perhaps *you* would be good enough to suggest a weapon? Perhaps you have even had one in your mind all the time?"

His countenance brightened, and he said with alacrity,—

"Oh, without doubt, monsieur!"

So he fell to hunting in his pockets,—pocket after pocket, and he had plenty of them,—muttering all the while, "Now, what could I have done with them?"

At last he was successful. He fished out of his vest pocket a couple of little things which I carried to the light and ascertained to be pistols. They were single-barreled and silver-mounted, and very dainty and pretty. I was not able to speak for emotion. I silently hung one of them on my watch chain, and returned the other. My companion in crime now unrolled a postage-stamp containing several cartridges, and gave me one of them. I asked if he meant to signify by this that our men were to be allowed but one shot apiece. He replied that the French code permitted no more. I then begged him to go on and suggest a distance, for my mind was growing weak and confused under the strain which had been put upon it. He named sixty-five yards. I nearly lost my patience. I said,—

"Sixty-five yards, with these instruments? Squirt-guns would be deadlier at fifty. Consider, my friend, you and I are banded together to destroy life, not make it eternal."

But with all my persuasions, all my arguments, I was only able to get him to reduce the distance to thirty-five yards; and even this concession he made with reluctance, and said with a sigh,—

"I wash my hands of this slaughter; on your head be it."

There was nothing for me but to go home to my old lion-heart and tell my humiliating story. When I entered, M. Gambetta was laying his last lock of hair upon the altar. He sprang toward me, exclaiming,

"You have made the fatal arrangements,—I see it in your eye!"

"I have."

His face paled a trifle, and he leaned upon the table for support. He breathed thick and heavily for a moment or two, so tumultuous were his feelings; then he hoarsely whispered,—

"The weapon, the weapon! Quick! what is the weapon?"

"This!" and I displayed that silver-mounted thing. He cast but one glance at it, then swooned ponderously to the floor.

When he came to, he said mournfully,—

"The unnatural calm to which I have subjected myself has told upon my nerves. But away with weakness! I will confront my fate like a man and a Frenchman."

He rose to his feet, and assumed an attitude which for sublimity has never been approached by man, and has seldom been surpassed by statues. Then he said, in his deep bass tones,—

"Behold, I am calm, I am ready; reveal to me the distance."

"Thirty-five yards." . . . .

I could not lift him up, of course; but I rolled him over, and poured water down his back. He presently came to, and said,—

"Thirty-five yards,—without a rest? But why ask? Since murder was that man's intention, why should he palter with small details? But mark you one thing: in my fall the world shall see how the chivalry of France meets death."

After a long silence he asked,—

"Was nothing said about that man's family standing up with him, as an offset to my bulk? But no matter; I would not stoop to make such a suggestion; if he is not noble enough to suggest it himself, he is welcome to this advantage, which no honorable man would take."

He now sank into a sort of stupor of reflection, which lasted some minutes; after which he broke silence with,—

"The hour,—what is the hour fixed for the collision?"

"Dawn, to-morrow."

He seemed greatly surprised, and immediately said,—

"Insanity! I never heard of such a thing. Nobody is abroad at such an hour."

"That is the reason I named it. Do you mean to say you want an audience?"

"It is no time to bandy words. I am astonished that M. Fourtou should ever have agreed to so strange an innovation. Go at once and require a later hour."

I ran down stairs, threw open the front door, and almost plunged into the arms of M. Fourtou's second. He said,—

"I have the honor to say that my principal strenuously objects to the hour chosen, and begs you will consent to change it to half past nine."

"Any courtesy, sir, which it is in our power to extend is at the service of your excellent principal. We agree to the proposed change of time."

"I beg you to accept the thanks of my client." Then he turned to a person behind him, and said, "You hear M. Noir, the hour is altered to half past nine." Whereupon M. Noir bowed, expressed his thanks, and went away. My accomplice continued:—

"If agreeable to you, your chief surgeons and ours shall proceed to the field in the same carriage, as is customary."

"It is entirely agreeable to me, and I am obliged to you for mentioning the surgeons, for I am afraid I should not have thought of them. How many shall I want? I suppose two or three will be enough?"

"Two is the customary number for each party. I refer to 'chief' surgeons; but considering the exalted positions occupied by our clients, it will be well and decorous that each of us appoint several consulting surgeons, from among the highest in the profession. These will come in their own private carriages. Have you engaged a hearse?"

"Bless my stupidity, I never thought of it! I will attend to it right away. I must seem very ignorant to you; but you must try to overlook that, because I have never had any experience of such a swell duel as this before. I have had a good deal to do with duels on the Pacific coast, but I see now that they were crude affairs. A hearse,—sho! we used to leave the elected lying around loose, and let anybody cord them up and cart them off that wanted to. Have you anything further to suggest?"

"Nothing, except that the head undertakers shall ride together, as is usual. The subordinates and mutes will go on foot, as is also usual. I will see you at eight o'clock in the morning, and we will then arrange the order of the procession. I have the honor to bid you a good day."

I returned to my client, who said, "Very well; at what hour is the engagement to begin?"

"Half past nine."

"Very good indeed. Have you sent the fact to the newspapers?"

"*Sir!* If after our long and intimate friendship you can for a moment deem me capable of so base a treachery"—

"Tut, tut! What words are these, my dear friend? Have I wounded you? Ah, forgive me; I am overloading you with labor. Therefore go on with the other details, and drop this one from your list. The bloody-minded Fourtou will be sure to attend to it. Or I myself—yes, to make certain, I will drop a note to my journalistic friend, M. Noir"—

"Oh, come to think, you may save yourself the trouble; that other second has informed M. Noir."

"H'm! I might have known it. It is just like that Fourtou, who always wants to make a display."

At half past nine in the morning the procession approached the field of Plessis-Piquet in the following order: first came our carriage, —nobody in it but M. Gambetta and myself; then a carriage containing M. Fourtou and his second; then a carriage containing two poet-orators who did not believe in God, and these had MS. funeral orations projecting from their breast pockets; then a carriage containing the head surgeons and their cases of instruments; then eight private carriages containing consulting surgeons; then a hack containing a coroner; then the two hearses; then a carriage containing the head undertakers; then a train of assistants and mutes on foot; and after these came plodding through the fog a long procession of camp followers, police, and citizens generally. It was a noble turn-out, and would have made a fine display if we had had thinner weather.

There was no conversation. I spoke several times to my principal, but I judge he was not aware of it, for he always referred to his note-book and muttered absently, "I die that France may live."

Arrived on the field, my fellow-second and I paced off the thirty-five yards, and then drew lots for choice of position. This latter was but an ornamental ceremony, for all choices were alike in such weather. These preliminaries being ended, I went to my principal and asked him if he was ready. He spread himself out to his full width, and said in a stern voice, "Ready! Let the batteries be charged."

The loading was done in the presence of duly constituted witnesses. We considered it best to perform this delicate service with the assistance of a lantern, on account of the state of the weather. We now placed our men.

At this point the police noticed that the public had massed themselves together on the right and left of the field; they therefore begged a delay, while they should put these poor people in a place of safety. The request was granted.

The police having ordered the two multitudes to take positions behind the duelists, we were once more ready. The weather growing still more opaque, it was agreed between myself and the other second that before giving the fatal signal we should each deliver a loud whoop to enable the combatants to ascertain each other's whereabouts.

I now returned to my principal, and was distressed to observe that he had lost a good deal of his spirit. I tried my best to hearten him. I said, "Indeed, sir, things are not as bad as they seem. Considering the character of the weapons, the limited number of shots allowed, the generous distance, the impenetrable solidity of the fog, and the added fact that one of the combatants is one-eyed and the other cross-eyed and near-sighted, it seems to me that this conflict need not necessarily be fatal. There are chances that both of you may survive. Therefore, cheer up; do not be downhearted."

This speech had so good an effect that my principal immediately stretched forth his hand and said, "I am myself again; give me the weapon."

I laid it, all lonely and forlorn, in the centre of the vast solitude of his palm. He gazed at it and shuddered. And still mournfully contemplating it, he murmured, in a broken voice,—

"Alas, it is not death I dread but mutilation."

I heartened him once more, and with such success that he presently said, "Let the tragedy begin. Stand at my back; do not desert me in this solemn hour, my friend."

I gave him my promise. I now assisted him to point his pistol toward the spot where I judged his adversary to be standing, and cautioned him to listen well and further guide himself by my fellow second's whoop. Then I propped myself against M. Gambetta's back, and raised a rousing "Whoop-ee!" This was answered from out the far distances of the fog, and I immediately shouted,—

"One,—two,—three,—*fire!*"

Two little sounds like *spit! spit!* broke upon my ear, and in the same instant I was crushed to the earth under a mountain of flesh. Bruised as I was, I was still able to catch a faint accent from above, to this effect,—

"I die for . . . for . . . perdition take it, what *is* it I die for? . . . oh, yes,—FRANCE! I die that France may live!"

The surgeons swarmed around with their probes in their hands, and applied their microscopes to the whole area of M. Gambetta's person, with the happy result of finding nothing in the nature of a wound. Then a scene ensued which was in every way gratifying and inspiriting.

The two gladiators fell upon each other's necks, with floods of proud and happy tears; that other second embraced me; the surgeons, the orators, the undertakers, the police, everybody embraced, everybody congratulated, everybody cried, and the whole atmosphere was filled with praise and with joy unspeakable.

It seemed to me then that I would rather be a hero of a French duel than a crowned and sceptred monarch.

When the commotion had somewhat subsided, the body of surgeons held a consultation, and after a good deal of debate decided that with proper care and nursing there was reason to believe that I would survive my injuries. My internal hurts were deemed the most serious, since it was apparent that a broken rib had penetrated my left lung, and that many of my organs had been pressed out so far to one side or the other of where they belonged, that it was doubtful if they would ever learn to perform their functions in such remote and unaccustomed localities. They then set my left arm in two places, pulled my right hip into its socket again, and re-elevated my nose. I was an object of great interest, and even admiration; and many sincere and warm-hearted persons had themselves introduced to me, and said they were proud to know the only man who had been hurt in a French duel in forty years.

I was placed in an ambulance at the very head of the procession; and thus with gratifying *éclat* I was marched into Paris, the most conspicuous figure in that great spectacle, and deposited at the hospital.

The cross of the Legion of Honor has been conferred upon me. However, few escape that distinction.

Such is the true version of the most memorable private conflict of the age.

I have no complaints to make against any one. I acted for myself, and I can stand the consequences. Without boasting, I think I may say I am not afraid to stand before a modern French duelist, but as long as I keep in my right mind I will never consent to stand behind one again.

From *A Tramp Abroad*, 1880

Cholley Adams

One of the first persons we encountered, as we walked up the street, was the Rev. Mr. ——, an old friend from America,—a lucky encounter, indeed, for his is a most gentle, refined and sensitive nature, and his company and companionship are a genuine refreshment. We knew he had been in Europe sometime, but were not at all expecting to run across him. Both parties burst forth into loving enthusiasms, and Rev. Mr. —— said,—

"I have got a brim-full reservoir of talk to pour out on you, and an empty one ready and thirsting to receive what you have got; we will sit up till midnight and have a good satisfying interchange, for I leave here early in the morning." We agreed to that, of course.

I had been vaguely conscious, for a while, of a person who was walking in the street abreast of us; I had glanced furtively at him once or twice, and noticed that he was a fine, large, vigorous young fellow, with an open, independent countenance, faintly shaded with a pale and even almost imperceptible crop of early down, and that he was clothed from head to heel in cool and enviable snow-white linen. I thought I had also noticed, that his head had a sort of listening tilt to it. Now about this time the Rev. Mr. —— said,—

"The side-walk is hardly wide enough for three, so I will walk behind; but keep the talk going, keep the talk going, there's no time to lose, and you may be sure I will do my share." He ranged himself behind us, and straightway that stately snow-white young fellow closed up to the side-walk alongside him, fetched him a cordial slap on the shoulder with his broad palm, and sung out with a hearty cheeriness,—

"*Americans,* for two-and-a-half and the money up! *Hey?*"

The Reverend winced, but said mildly,—

"Yes,—we are Americans."

"Lord love you, you can just bet that's what *I* am, every time! Put it there!"

He held out his Sahara of a palm, and the Reverend laid his diminutive hand in it, and got so cordial a shake that we heard his glove burst under it.

"Say, didn't I put you up right?"

"O, yes."

"Sho! I spotted you for *my* kind the minute I heard your clack. You been over here long?"

"About four months. Have you been over long?"

"*Long?* Well I should say so! Going on two *years,* by geeminy! Say, are you homesick?"

"No, I can't say that I am. Are you?"

"O, *hell* yes!" This with immense enthusiasm.

The Reverend shrunk a little, in his clothes, and we were aware, rather by instinct than otherwise, that he was throwing out signals of distress to us; but we did not interfere or try to succor him, for we were quite happy.

The young fellow hooked his arm into the Reverend's, now, with the confiding and grateful air of a waif who has been longing for a friend, and a sympathetic ear, and a chance to lisp once more the sweet accents of the mother tongue,—and then he limbered up the muscles of his mouth and turned himself loose,—and with such a relish! Some of his words were not Sunday school words, so I am obliged to put blanks where they occur.

"Yes indeedy! If *I* ain't an American there *ain't* any Americans, that's all. And when I heard you fellows gassing away in the good old American language, I'm ——— if it wasn't all I could do to keep from hugging you! My tongue's all warped with trying to curl it around these ——————— forsaken wind-galled nine-jointed German words here; now I *tell* you it's awful good to lay it over a Christian word once more and kind of let the old taste soak in. I'm from western New York. My name is Cholley Adams. I'm a student, you know. Been here going on two years. I'm learning to be a horse-doctor. I *like* that part of it, you know, but —————— these people, they won't learn a fellow in his own language, they make him learn in German; so before I could tackle the horse-doctoring I had to tackle this miserable language.

"First-off, I thought it would certainly give me the botts, but I don't mind it now. I've got it where the hair's short, I think; and dontchuknow, they made me learn Latin, too. Now between you and me, I wouldn't give a —— for all the Latin that was ever jabbered; and the first thing *I* calculate to do when I get through, is to just sit down and forget it. 'Twont take me long, and I don't mind the time, anyway. And I tell you what! the difference between school-teaching over yonder and school-teaching over here,—sho! *We* don't know anything about it! Here you've got to peg and peg and peg and there just ain't any let-up,—and what you learn here, you've got to *know,* dontchuknow,—or else you'll have one of these ——— spavined, spectacled, ring-boned, knock-kneed old professors in your hair. I've been here long *enough,* and I'm getting blessed tired of it, mind I *tell* you. The old man wrote me that he was coming over in June, and said he'd take me home in August, whether I was done with my education or not, but durn him, he didn't come; never said why; just sent me a hamper of Sunday school books, and told me to be good, and hold on a while. I don't take to Sunday school books, dontchuknow, —I don't hanker after them when I can get pie,—but I *read* them, anyway, because whatever the old man tells me to do, that's the thing that I'm a-going to *do,* or tear something you know. I buckled in and read all of those books, because he wanted me to; but that kind of thing don't excite *me,* I like something *hearty.* But I'm awful homesick. I'm homesick from ear-socket to crupper, and from crupper to hock joint; but it ain't any use, I've got to stay here, till the old man drops the rag and gives the word,—yes, *sir,* right here in this ——— country I've got to linger till the old man says *Come!*—and you bet your bottom dollar, Johnny, it *ain't* just as easy as it is for a cat to have twins!"

At the end of this profane and cordial explosion he fetched a prodigious "*Whoosh!*" to relieve his lungs and make recognition of the heat, and then he straightway dived into his narrative again for "Johnny's" benefit, beginning, "Well, ——— it ain't any use talking, some of those old American words *do* have a kind of a bully swing to them; a man can *express* himself with 'em,—a man can get at what he wants to *say,* dontchuknow."

When we reached our hotel and it seemed that he was about to lose the Reverend, he showed so much sorrow, and begged so hard and so earnestly that the Reverend's heart was not hard enough to hold out against the pleadings,—so he went away with the parent-honoring student, like a right Christian, and took supper with him in his lodgings and sat in the surf-beat of his slang and profanity till near midnight, and then left him,—left him pretty well talked out, but grateful "clear down to his frogs," as he expressed it. The Reverend said it had transpired during the interview that "Cholley" Adams's father was an extensive dealer in horses in western New York; this accounted for Cholley's choice of a profession. The Reverend brought away a pretty high opinion of Cholley as a manly young fellow, with stuff in him for a useful citizen; he considered him rather a rough gem, but a gem, nevertheless.

From *A Tramp Abroad*, 1880

The Laborious Ant

We followed the carriage road, and had our usual luck: we traveled under a beating sun, and always saw the shade leave the shady places before we could get to them. In all our wanderings we seldom managed to strike a piece of road at its time for being shady. We had a particularly hot time of it on that particular afternoon, and with no comfort but what we could get out of the fact that the peasants at work away up on the steep mountain sides above our heads were even worse off than we were. By and by it became impossible to endure the intolerable glare and heat any longer; so we struck across the ravine and entered the deep cool twilight of the forest, to hunt for what the guidebook called the "old road."

We found an old road, and it proved eventually to be the right one, though we followed it at the time with the conviction that it was the wrong one. If it was the wrong one there could be no use in hurrying, therefore we did not hurry, but sat down frequently on the soft moss and enjoyed the restful quiet and shade of the forest solitudes. There had been distractions in the carriage road,—school children, peasants, wagons, troops of pedestrianizing students from all over Germany,—but we had the old road all to ourselves.

Now and then, while we rested, we watched the laborious ant at his work. I found nothing new in him,—certainly nothing to change my opinion of him. It seems to me that in the matter of intellect the ant must be a strangely overrated bird. During many summers, now, I have watched him, when I ought to have been in better business, and I have not yet come across a living ant that seemed to have any more sense than a dead one. I refer to the ordinary ant, of course; I have had no experience of those wonderful Swiss and African ones which vote, keep drilled armies, hold slaves, and dispute about religion. Those particular ants may be all that the naturalist paints them, but I am persuaded that the average ant is a sham. I admit his industry, of course; he is the hardest working creature in the world,—when anybody is looking,—but his leather-headedness is the point I make against him. He goes out foraging, he makes a capture, and then what does he do? Go home? No,—he goes anywhere but home. He doesn't know where home is. His home may be only three feet away,—no matter, he can't find it. He makes his capture, as I have said; it is generally something which can be of no sort of use to himself or anybody else; it is usually seven times bigger than it ought to be; he hunts out the awkwardest place to take hold of it; he lifts it bodily up in the air by main force, and starts: not toward home, but in the opposite direction; not calmly and wisely, but with a frantic haste which is wasteful of his strength; he fetches up against a pebble, and instead of going around it, he climbs over it backwards dragging his booty after him, tumbles down on the other side, jumps up in a passion, kicks the dust off his clothes, moistens his hands, grabs his property viciously, yanks it this way then that, shoves it ahead of him a moment, turns tail and lugs it after him another moment, gets madder and madder, then presently hoists it into the air and goes tearing away in an entirely new direction; comes to a weed; it never occurs to him to go around it; no, he must climb it; and he does climb it, dragging his worthless property to the top—which is as bright a thing to do as it would be for me to carry a sack of flour from Heidelberg to Paris by way of Strasburg steeple; when he gets up there he finds that that is not the place; takes a cursory glance at the scenery and either climbs down again or tumbles down, and starts off once more—as usual, in a new direction. At the end of half an hour, he fetches up within six inches of the place he started from and lays his burden down; meantime he has been over all the ground for two yards around, and climbed all the weeds and pebbles he came across. Now he wipes the sweat from his brow, strokes his limbs, and then marches aimlessly off, in as violent a hurry as ever. He traverses a good deal of zig-zag country, and by and by stumbles on his same booty again. He does not remember to have ever seen it before; he looks around to see which is not the way home, grabs his bundle and starts; he goes through the same adventures he had before; finally stops to rest, and a friend comes along. Evidently the friend remarks that a last year's grasshopper leg is a very noble acquisition, and inquires where he got it. Evidently the proprietor does not remember exactly where he did get it, but thinks he got it "around here somewhere." Evidently the friend contracts to help him freight it home.

Then, with a judgment peculiarly antic, (pun not intentional,) they take hold of opposite ends of that grasshopper leg and begin to tug with all their might in opposite directions. Presently they take a rest and confer together. They decide that something is wrong, they can't make out what. Then they go at it again, just as before. Same result. Mutual recriminations follow. Evidently each accuses the other of being an obstructionist. They warm up, and the dispute ends in a fight. They lock themselves together and chew each other's jaws for a while; then they roll and tumble on the ground till one loses a horn or a leg and has to haul off for repairs. They make up and go to work again in the same old insane way, but the crippled ant is at a disadvantage; tug as he may, the other one drags off the booty and him at the end of it. Instead of giving up, he hangs on, and gets his shins bruised against every obstruction that comes in the way. By and by, when that grasshopper leg has been dragged all over the same old ground once more, it is finally dumped at about the spot where it originally lay, the two perspiring ants inspect it thoughtfully and decide that dried grasshopper legs are a poor sort of property after all, and then each starts off in a different direction to see if he can't find an old nail or something else that is heavy enough to afford entertainment and at the same time valueless enough to make an ant want to own it.

There in the Black Forest, on the mountain side, I saw an ant go through with such a performance as this with a dead spider of fully ten times his own weight. The spider was not quite dead, but too far gone to resist. He had a round body the size of a pea. The little ant—observing that I was noticing—turned him on his back, sunk his fangs into his throat, lifted him into the air and started vigorously off with him, stumbling over little pebbles, stepping on the spider's legs and tripping himself up, dragging him backwards, shoving him bodily ahead, dragging him up stones six inches high instead of going around them, climbing weeds twenty times his own height and jumping from their summits,—and finally leaving him in the middle of the road to be confiscated by any other fool of an ant that wanted him. I measured the ground which this ass traversed, and arrived at the conclusion that what he had accomplished inside of twenty minutes would constitute some such job as this,—relatively speaking,—for a man; to-wit: to strap two eight-hundred pound horses together, carry them eighteen hundred feet, mainly over (not around) bowlders averaging six feet high, and in the course of the journey climb up and jump from the top of one precipice like Niagara, and three steeples, each a hundred and twenty feet high; and then put the horses down, in an exposed place, without anybody to watch them, and go off to indulge in some other idiotic miracle for vanity's sake.

Science has recently discovered that the ant does not lay up anything for winter use. This will knock him out of literature, to some extent. He does not work, except when people are looking, and only then when the observer has a green, naturalistic look, and seems to be taking notes. This amounts to deception, and will injure him for the Sunday schools. He has not judgment enough to know what is good to eat from what isn't. This amounts to ignorance, and will impair the world's respect for him. He cannot stroll around a stump and find his way home again. This amounts to idiocy, and once the damaging fact is established, thoughtful people will cease to look up to him, the sentimental will cease to fondle him. His vaunted industry is but a vanity and of no effect, since he never gets home with anything he starts with. This disposes of the last remnant of his reputation and wholly destroys his main usefulness as a moral agent, since it will make the sluggard hesitate to go to him any more. It is strange beyond comprehension, that so manifest a humbug as the ant has been able to fool so many nations and keep it up so many ages without being found out.

From *A Tramp Abroad,* 1880

Nicodemus Dodge

Dental surgeons suggested doctors, doctors suggested death, death suggested skeletons,—and so, by a logical process the conversation melted out of one of these subjects and into the next, until the topic of skeletons raised up Nicodemus Dodge out of the deep grave in my memory where he had lain buried and forgotten for twenty-five years. When I was a boy in a printing office in Missouri, a loose-jointed, long-legged, tow-headed, jeans-clad, countrified cub of about sixteen lounged in one day, and without removing his hands from the depths of his trowsers pockets or taking off his faded ruin of a slouch hat, whose broken brim hung limp and ragged about his eyes and ears like a bug-eaten cabbage leaf, stared indifferently around, then leaned his hip against the editor's table, crossed his mighty brogans, aimed at a distant fly from a crevice in his upper teeth, laid him low, and said with composure,

"Whar's the boss?"

"I am the boss," said the editor, following this curious bit of architecture wonderingly along up to its clock-face with his eye.

"Don't want anybody fur to learn the business, 't ain't likely?"

"Well, I don't know. Would you like to learn it?"

"Pap's so po' he cain't run me no mo', so I want to git a show somers if I kin, 'tain't no diffunce what,—I'm strong and hearty, and I don't turn my back on no kind of work, hard nur soft."

"Do you think you would like to learn the printing business?"

"Well, I don't re'ly k'yer a durn what I *do* learn, so's I git a chance fur to make my way. I'd jist as soon learn print'n 's anything."

"Can you read?"

"Yes,—middlin'."

"Write?"

"Well, I've seed people could lay over me thar."

"Cipher?"

"Not good enough to keep store, I don't reckon, but up as fur as twelve-times-twelve I ain't no slouch. 'Tother side of that is what gits me."

"Where is your home?"

"I'm f'm old Shelby."

"What's your father's religious denomination?"

"Him? O, he's a blacksmith."

"No, no,—I don't mean his trade. What's his *religious* denomination?"

"*O,*—I didn't understand you befo'. He's a Freemason."

"No-no, you don't get my meaning yet. What I mean is, does he belong to any *church?*"

"*Now* you're talkin'! Couldn't make out what you was a tryin' to git through yo' head no way. B'long to a *church!* Why boss he's ben the pizenest kind of a Free-will Babtis' for forty year. They ain't no pizener ones 'n' what *he* is. Mighty good man, pap is. Everybody says that. If they said any diffrunt they wouldn't say it whar *I* wuz,—not *much* they wouldn't."

"What is your own religion?"

"Well, boss, you've kind o' got me, thar,—and yit you hain't got me so mighty much, nuther. I think 't if a feller he'ps another feller when he's in trouble, and don't cuss, and don't do no mean things, nur noth'n' he ain' no business to do, and don't spell the Savior's name with a little g, he ain't runnin' no resks,—he's about as saift as if he b'longed to a church."

"But suppose he did spell it with a little g,—what then?"

"Well, if he done it a-purpose, I reckon he wouldn't stand no chance,—he *oughtn't* to have no chance, anyway, I'm most rotten certain 'bout that."

"What is your name?"

"Nicodemus Dodge."

"I think maybe you'll do, Nicodemus. We'll give you a trial, anyway."

"All right."

"When would you like to begin?"

"Now."

So, within ten minutes after we had first glimpsed this nondescript he was one of us, and with his coat off and hard at it.

Beyond that end of our establishment which was furthest from the street, was a deserted garden, pathless, and thickly grown with the bloomy and villainous "jimpson" weed and its common friend the stately sunflower. In the midst of this mournful spot was a decayed and aged little "frame" house with but one room, one window, and no ceiling,—it had been a smoke-house a generation before. Nicodemus was given this lonely and ghostly den as a bed chamber.

The village smarties recognized a treasure in Nicodemus, right away,—a butt to play jokes on. It was easy to see that he was inconceivably green and confiding. George Jones had the glory of perpetrating the first joke on him; he gave him a cigar with a fire-cracker in it and winked to the crowd to come; the thing exploded presently and swept away the bulk of Nicodemus's eyebrows and eyelashes. He simply said,—

"I consider them kind of seeg'yars dangersome,"—and seemed to suspect nothing. The next evening Nicodemus waylaid George and poured a bucket of ice-water over him.

One day, while Nicodemus was in swimming, Tom McElroy "tied" his clothes. Nicodemus made a bonfire of Tom's, by way of retaliation.

A third joke was played upon Nicodemus, a day or two later,—he walked up the middle aisle of the village church, Sunday night, with a staring hand-bill pinned between his shoulders. The joker spent the remainder of the night, after church, in the cellar of a deserted house, and Nicodemus sat on the cellar door till toward breakfast time to make sure that the prisoner remembered that if any noise was made, some rough treatment would be the consequence. The cellar had two feet of stagnant water in it, and was bottomed with six inches of soft mud.

But I wander from the point. It was the subject of skeletons that brought this boy back to my recollection. Before a very long time had elapsed, the village smarties began to feel an uncomfortable consciousness of not having made a very shining success out of their attempts on the simpleton from "old Shelby." Experimenters grew scarce and chary. Now the young doctor came to the rescue. There was delight and applause when he proposed to scare Nicodemus to death, and explained how he was going to do it. He had a noble new skeleton,—the skeleton of the late and only local celebrity, Jimmy Finn, the village drunkard,—a grisly piece of property which he had bought of Jimmy Finn himself, at auction, for fifty dollars, under great competition, when Jimmy lay very sick in the tan-yard a fortnight before his death. The fifty dollars had gone promptly for whisky and had considerably hurried up the change of ownership in the skeleton. The doctor would put Jimmy Finn's skeleton in Nicodemus's bed!

This was done,—about half past ten in the evening. About Nicodemus's usual bedtime,—midnight,—the village jokers came creeping stealthily through the jimpson weeds and sunflowers toward the lonely frame den. They reached the window and peeped in. There sat the long-legged pauper, on his bed, in a very short shirt, and nothing more; he was dangling his legs contentedly back and forth, and wheezing the music of "Camptown Races" out of a paper-overlaid comb which he was pressing against his mouth; by him lay a new jewsharp, a new top, a solid india-rubber ball, a handful of painted marbles, five pounds of "store" candy, and a well-gnawed slab of gingerbread as big and as thick as a volume of sheet music. He had sold the skeleton to a traveling quack for three dollars and was enjoying the result!

From *A Tramp Abroad*, 1880

An American Party

The 7.30 table d'hôte at the great Schweitzerhof furnished a mighty array and variety of nationalities, but it offered a better opportunity to observe costumes than people, for the multitude sat at immensely long tables, and therefore the faces were mainly seen in perspective; but the breakfasts were served at small round tables, and then if one had the fortune to get a table in the midst of the assemblage he could have as many faces to study as he could desire. We used to try to guess out the nationalities, and generally succeeded tolerably well. Sometimes we tried to guess people's names; but that was a failure; that is a thing which probably requires a good deal of practice. We presently dropped it and gave our efforts to less difficult particulars. One morning I said,—

"There is an American party."

Harris said,—

"Yes,—but name the State."

I named one State, Harris named another. We agreed upon one thing, however,—that the young girl with the party was very beautiful, and very tastefully dressed. But we disagreed as to her age. I said she was eighteen. Harris said she was twenty. The dispute between us waxed warm and I finally said, with a pretense of being in earnest,—

"Well, there is one way to settle the matter,—I will go and ask her."

Harris said, sarcastically, "Certainly, that is the thing to do. All you need to do is to use the common formula over here: go and say, 'I'm an American!' Of course she will be glad to see you."

Then he hinted that perhaps there was no great danger of my venturing to speak to her.

I said, "I was only talking,—I didn't intend to approach her, but I see that you do not know what an intrepid person I am. I am not afraid of any woman that walks. I will go and speak to this young girl."

The thing I had in my mind was not difficult. I meant to address her in the most respectful way and ask her to pardon me if her strong resemblance to a former acquaintance of mine was deceiving me; and when she should reply that the name I mentioned was not the name she bore, I meant to beg pardon again, most respectfully, and retire. There would be no harm done. I walked to her table, bowed to the gentleman, then turned to her and was about to begin my little speech when she exclaimed,—

"I *knew* I wasn't mistaken,—I told John it was you! John said it probably wasn't, but I knew I was right. I said you would recognize me presently and come over; and I'm glad you did, for I shouldn't have felt much flattered if you had gone out of this room without recognizing me. Sit down, sit down,—how odd it is,—you are the last person I was ever expecting to see again."

This was a stupefying surprise. It took my wits clear away, for an instant. However, we shook hands cordially all around, and I sat down. But truly this was the tightest place I ever was in. I seemed to vaguely remember the girl's face, now, but I had no idea where I had seen it before, or what name belonged with it. I immediately tried to get up a diversion about Swiss scenery, to keep her from launching into topics that might betray that I did not know her, but it was of no use, she went right along upon matters which interested her more:

"O dear, what a night that was, when the sea washed the forward boats away,—do you remember it?"

"O, *don't* I!" said I,—but I didn't. I wished the sea had washed the rudder and the smoke-stack and the captain away,—then I could have located this questioner.

"And don't you remember how frightened poor Mary was, and how she cried?"

"Indeed I do!" said I. "Dear me, how it all comes back!"

I fervently wished it *would* come back,—but my memory was a blank. The wise way would have been to frankly own up; but I could not bring myself to do that, after the young girl had praised me so for recognizing her; so I went on, deeper and deeper into the mire, hoping for a chance clue but never getting one. The Unrecognizable continued, with vivacity,—

"Do you know, George married Mary, after all?"

"Why, no! Did he?"

"Indeed he did. He said he did not believe she was half as much to blame as her father was, and I thought he was right. Didn't you?"

"Of course he was. It was a perfectly plain case. I always said so."

"Why no you didn't!—at least that summer."

"Oh, no, not that summer. No, you are perfectly right about that. It was the following winter that I said it."

"Well, as it turned out, Mary was not in the least to blame,—it was all her father's fault,—at least his and old Darley's."

It was necessary to say something,—so I said,—

"I always regarded Darley as a troublesome old thing."

"So he was, but then they always had a great affection for him, although he had so many eccentricities. You remember that when the weather was the least cold, he would try to come into the house."

I was rather afraid to proceed. Evidently Darley was not a man,—he must be some other kind of animal,—possibly a dog, maybe an elephant. However, tails are common to all animals, so I ventured to say,—

"And what a tail he had!"

"*One!* He had a thousand!"

This was bewildering. I did not quite know what to say, so I only said,—

"Yes, he *was* rather well fixed in the matter of tails."

"For a negro, and a crazy one at that, I should say he was," said she.

It was getting pretty sultry for me. I said to myself, "Is it possible she is going to stop there, and wait for me to speak? If she does, the conversation is blocked. A negro with a thousand tails is a topic which a person cannot talk upon fluently and instructively without more or less preparation. As to diving rashly into such a vast subject,—"

But here, to my gratitude, she interrupted my thought by saying,—

"Yes, when it came to tales of his crazy woes, there was simply no end to them if anybody would listen. His own quarters were comfortable enough, but when the weather was cold, the family were sure to have his company,—nothing could keep him out of the house. But they always bore it kindly because he had saved Tom's life, years before. You remember Tom?"

"O, perfectly. Fine fellow he was, too."

"Yes he was. And what a pretty little thing his child was!"

"You may well say that. I never saw a prettier child."

"I used to delight to pet it and dandle it and play with it."

"So did I."

"You named it. What *was* that name? I can't call it to mind."

It appeared to me that the ice was getting pretty thin, here. I would have given something to know what the child's sex was. However, I had the good luck to think of a name that would fit either sex, —so I brought it out,—

"I named it Frances."

"From a relative, I suppose? But you named the one that died, too,—one that I never saw. What did you call that one?"

I was out of neutral names, but as the child was dead and she had never seen it, I thought I might risk a name for it and trust to luck. Therefore I said,—

"I called that one Thomas Henry."

She said, musingly,—

"That is very singular ...... very singular."

I sat still and let the cold sweat run down. I was in a good deal of trouble, but I believed I could worry through if she wouldn't ask me to name any more children. I wondered where the lightning was going to strike next. She was still ruminating over that last child's title, but presently she said,—

"I have always been sorry you were away at the time,—I would have had you name my child."

"*Your* child! Are you married?"

"I have been married thirteen years."

"Christened, you mean."

"No, married. The youth by your side is my son."

"It seems incredible,—even impossible. I do not mean any harm by it, but would you mind telling me if you are any over eighteen?—that is to say, will you tell me how old you are?"

"I was just nineteen the day of the storm we were talking about. That was my birth-day."

That did not help matters much, as I did not know the date of the storm. I tried to think of some non-committal thing to say, to keep up my end of the talk and render my poverty in the matter of reminiscences as little noticeable as possible, but I seemed to be about out of non-committal things. I was about to say, "You haven't changed a bit since then,"—but that was risky. I thought of saying "you have improved ever so much since then,"—but that wouldn't answer, of course. I was about to try a shy at the weather, for a saving change, when the girl slipped in ahead of me and said,—

"How I have enjoyed this talk over those happy old times,—haven't you?"

"I never have spent such a half hour in all my life before!" said I, with emotion; and I could have added, with a near approach to truth, "and I would rather be scalped than spend another one like it." I was holily grateful to be through with the ordeal, and was about to make my good-byes and get out, when the girl said,—

"But there is one thing that is ever so puzzling to me."

"Why what is that?"

"That dead child's name. What did you say it was?"

Here was another balmy place to be in: I had forgotten the child's name; I hadn't imagined it would be needed again. However, I had to pretend to know, anyway, so I said,—

"Joseph William."

The youth at my side corrected me, and said,—

"No,—Thomas Henry."

I thanked him,—in words,—and said, with trepidation,—

"O yes,—I was thinking of another child that I named,—I have named a great many, and I get them confused,—this one *was* named Henry Thompson,—"

"Thomas Henry," calmly interposed the boy.

I thanked him again,—strictly in words,—and stammered out,—

"Thomas Henry,—yes, Thomas Henry was the poor child's name. I named him for Thomas,—er,—Thomas Carlyle, the great author, you know,—and Henry—er,—er,—Henry the Eighth. The parents were very grateful to have a child named Thomas Henry."

"That makes it more singular than ever," murmured my beautiful friend.

"Does it? Why?"

"Because when the parents speak of that child now, they always call it Susan Amelia."

That spiked my gun. I could not say anything. I was entirely out of verbal obliquities; to go further would be to lie, and that I would not do; so I simply sat still and suffered,—sat mutely and resignedly there, and sizzled,—for I was being slowly fried to death in my own blushes. Presently the enemy laughed a happy laugh and said,—

"I *have* enjoyed this talk over old times, but you have not. I saw very soon that you were only pretending to know me, and so as I had wasted a compliment on you in the beginning, I made up my mind to punish you. And I have succeeded pretty well. I was glad to see that you knew George and Tom and Darley, for I had never heard of them before and therefore could not be sure that you had; and I was glad to learn the names of those imaginary children, too. One can get quite a fund of information out of you if one goes at it cleverly. Mary and the storm, and the sweeping away of the forward boats, were facts—all the rest was fiction. Mary was my sister; her full name was Mary ——. *Now* do you remember me?"

"Yes," I said, "I do remember you now; and you are as hard-hearted as you were thirteen years ago in that ship, else you wouldn't have punished me so. You haven't changed your nature nor your person, in any way at all; you look just as young as you did then, you are just as beautiful as you were then, and you have transmitted a deal of your comeliness to this fine boy. There,—if that speech moves you any, let's fly the flag of truce, with the understanding that I am conquered and confess it."

All of which was agreed to and accomplished, on the spot. When I went back to Harris, I said,—

"Now you see what a person with talent and address can do."

"Excuse me, I see what a person of colossal ignorance and simplicity can do. The idea of your going and intruding on a party of strangers, that way, and talking for half an hour; why I never heard of a man in his right mind doing such a thing before. What did you say to them?"

"I never said any harm. I merely asked the girl what her name was."

"I don't doubt it. Upon my word I don't. I think you were capable of it. It was stupid in me to let you go over there and make such an exhibition of yourself. But you know I couldn't really believe you would do such an inexcusable thing. What will those people think of us? But how did you say it?—I mean the manner of it. I hope you were not abrupt."

"No, I was careful about that. I said 'My friend and I would like to know what your name is, if you don't mind.'"

"No, that was not abrupt. There is a polish about it that does you infinite credit. And I am glad you put me in; that was a delicate attention which I appreciate at its full value. What did she do?"

"She didn't do anything in particular. She told me her name."

"Simply told you her name. Do you mean to say she did not show any surprise?"

"Well, now I come to think, she did show something; may be it was surprise; I hadn't thought of that,—I took it for gratification."

"O, undoubtedly you were right; it must have been gratification; it could not be otherwise than gratifying to be assaulted by a stranger with such a question as that. Then what did you do?"

"I offered my hand and the party gave me a shake."

"I saw it! I did not believe my own eyes, at the time. Did the gentleman say anything about cutting your throat?"

"No, they all seemed glad to see me, as far as I could judge."

"And do you know, I believe they were. I think they said to themselves, 'Doubtless this curiosity has got away from his keeper—let us amuse ourselves with him.' There is no other way of accounting for their facile docility. You sat down. Did they *ask* you to sit down?"

"No, they did not ask me, but I suppose they did not think of it."

"You have an unerring instinct. What else did you do? What did you talk about?"

"Well, I asked the girl how old she was."

"*Un*doubtedly. Your delicacy is beyond praise. Go on, go on,—don't mind my apparent misery,—I always look so when I am steeped in a profound and reverent joy. Go on,—she told you her age?"

"Yes, she told me her age, and all about her mother, and her grandmother, and her other relations, and all about herself."

"Did she volunteer these statistics?"

"No, not exactly that. I asked the questions and she answered them."

"This is divine. Go on,—it is not possible that you forgot to inquire into her politics?"

"No, I thought of that. She is a democrat, her husband is a republican, and both of them are Baptists."

"Her husband? Is that child married?"

"She is not a child. She is married, and that is her husband who is there with her."

"Has she any children?"

"Yes,—seven and a half."

"That is impossible."

"No, she has them. She told me herself."

"Well, but seven and a *half*? How do you make out the half? Where does the half come in?"

"That is a child which she had by another husband,—not this one but another one,—so it is a step-child, and they do not count it full measure."

"Another husband? Has she had another husband?"

"Yes, four. This one is number four."

"I do not believe a word of it. It is impossible, upon its face. Is that boy there her brother?"

"No, that is her son. He is her youngest. He is not as old as he looks; he is only eleven and a half."

"These things are all manifestly impossible. This is a wretched business. It is a plain case: they simply took your measure, and concluded to fill you up. They seem to have succeeded. I am glad I am not in the mess; they may at least be charitable enough to think there ain't a pair of us. Are they going to stay here long?"

"No, they leave before noon."

"There is one man who is deeply grateful for that. How did you find out? You asked, I suppose?"

"No, along at first I inquired into their plans, in a general way, and they said they were going to be here a week, and make trips round about; but toward the end of the interview, when I said you and I would tour around with them with pleasure, and offered to bring you over and introduce you, they hesitated a little, and asked if you were from the same establishment that I was. I said you were, and then they said they had changed their mind and considered it necessary to start at once and visit a sick relative in Siberia."

"Ah me, you struck the summit! You struck the loftiest altitude of stupidity that human effort has ever reached. You shall have a monument of jackass's skulls as high as the Strasburg spire if you die before I do. They wanted to know if I was from the same 'establishment' that you hail from, did they? What did they mean by 'establishment?' "

"I don't know; it never occurred to me to ask."

"Well *I* know. They meant an asylum—an *idiot* asylum, do you understand? So they *do* think there's a pair of us, after all. Now what do you think of yourself?"

"Well I don't know. I didn't know I was doing any harm; I didn't *mean* to do any harm. They were very nice people, and they seemed to like me."

Harris made some rude remarks and left for his bedroom—to break some furniture, he said. He was a singularly irascible man; any little thing would disturb his temper.

I had been well scorched by the young woman, but no matter, I took it out of Harris. One should always "get even" in some way, else the sore place will go on hurting.

From *A Tramp Abroad,* 1880

American in Europe

For some days we were content to enjoy looking at the blue lake Lucerne and at the piled-up masses of snow mountains that border it all around,—an enticing spectacle, this last, for there is a strange and fascinating beauty and charm about a majestic snow-peak with the sun blazing upon it or the moonlight softly enriching it,—but finally we concluded to try a bit of excursioning around on a steamboat, and a dash on foot at the Rigi. Very well, we had a delightful trip to Fluelen, on a breezy, sunny day. Everybody sat on the upper deck, on benches, under an awning; everybody talked, laughed, and exclaimed at the wonderful scenery; in truth, a trip on that lake is almost the perfection of pleasuring. The mountains were a never ceasing marvel. Sometimes they rose straight up out of the lake, and towered aloft and overshadowed our pigmy steamer with their prodigious bulk in the most impressive way. Not snow-clad mountains, these, yet they climbed high enough toward the sky to meet the clouds and veil their foreheads in them. They were not barren and repulsive, but clothed in green, and restful and pleasant to the eye. And they were so almost straight-up-and-down, sometimes, that one could not imagine a man being able to keep his footing upon such a surface, yet there are paths, and the Swiss people go up and down them every day.

Sometimes one of these monster precipices had the slight inclination of the huge ship-houses in dock yards,—then high aloft, toward the sky, it took a little stronger inclination, like that of a mansard roof,—and perched on this dizzy mansard one's eye detected little things like martin boxes, and presently perceived that these were the dwellings of peasants,—an airy place for a home, truly. And suppose a peasant should walk in his sleep, or his child should fall out of the front yard?—the friends would have a tedious long journey down out of those cloud-heights before they found the remains. And yet those far-away homes looked ever so seductive, they were so remote from the troubled world, they dozed in such an atmosphere of peace and dreams,—surely no one who had learned to live up there would ever want to live on a meaner level.

We swept through the prettiest little curving arms of the lake, among these colossal green walls, enjoying new delights, always, as the stately panorama unfolded itself before us and re-rolled and hid itself behind us; and now and then we had the thrilling surprise of bursting suddenly upon a tremendous white mass like the distant and dominating Jungfrau, or some kindred giant, looming head and shoulders above a tumbled waste of lesser Alps.

Once, while I was hungrily taking in one of these surprises, and doing my best to get all I possibly could of it while it should last, I was interrupted by a young and care-free voice,

"You're an American, I think,—so'm I."

He was about eighteen, or possibly nineteen; slender and of medium height; open, frank, happy face; a restless but independent eye; a snub nose, which had the air of drawing back with a decent reserve from the silky new-born moustache below it until it should be introduced; a loosely hung jaw, calculated to work easily in the sockets. He wore a low-crowned, narrow-brimmed straw hat, with a broad blue ribbon around it which had a white anchor embroidered on it in front; nobby short-tailed coat, pantaloons, vest, all trim and neat and up with the fashion; red-striped stockings, very low-quarter patent leather shoes, tied with black ribbon; blue ribbon around his neck, wide-open collar; tiny diamond studs; wrinkleless kids; projecting cuffs, fastened with large oxydized silver sleeve-buttons, bearing the device of a dog's face,—English pug. He carried a slim cane, surmounted with an English pug's head with red glass eyes. Under his arm he carried a German Grammar,—Otto's. His hair was short, straight and smooth, and presently when he turned his head a moment, I saw that it was nicely parted behind. He took a cigarette out of a dainty box, stuck it into a meerschaum holder which he carried in a morocco case, and reached for my cigar. While he was lighting, I said,—

"Yes,—I am an American."

"I knew it,—I can always tell them. What ship did you come over in?"

"Holsatia."

"We came in the Batavia,—Cunard, you know. What kind of a passage did you have?"

"Tolerably rough."

"So did we. Captain said he'd hardly ever seen it rougher. Where are you from?"

"New England."

"So'm I. I'm from New Bloomfield. Anybody with you?"

"Yes,—a friend."

"Our whole family's along. It's awful slow, going around alone,—don't you think so?"

"Rather slow."

"Ever been over here before?"

"Yes."

"I haven't. My first trip. But we've been all around,—Paris and everywhere. I'm to enter Harvard next year. Studying German all the time, now. Can't enter till I know German. I know considerable French,—I get along pretty well in Paris, or anywhere where they speak French. What hotel are you stopping at?"

"Schweitzerhof."

"No! is that so? I never see you in the reception room. I go to the reception room a good deal of the time, because there's so many Americans there. I make lots of acquaintances. I know an American as soon as I see him,—and so I speak to him and make his acquaintance. I like to be always making acquaintances,—don't you?"

"Lord, yes!"

"You see it breaks up a trip like this, first rate. I never get bored on a trip like this, if I can make acquaintances and have somebody to talk to. But I think a trip like this would be an awful bore, if a body couldn't find anybody to get acquainted with and talk to on a trip like this. I'm fond of talking, ain't you?"

"Passionately."

"Have you felt bored, on this trip?"

"Not all the time, part of it."

"That's it!—you see you ought to go around and get acquainted, and talk. That's my way. That's the way I always do,—I just go 'round, 'round, 'round, and talk, talk, talk,—I never get bored. You been up the Rigi yet?"

"No."

"Going?"

"I think so."

"What hotel you going to stop at?"

"I don't know. Is there more than one?"

"Three. You stop at the Schreiber—you'll find it full of Americans. What ship did you say you came over in?"

"City of Antwerp."

"German, I guess. You going to Geneva?"

"Yes."

"What hotel you going to stop at?"

"Hotel de l' Ecu de Genève."

"Don't you do it! No Americans there. You stop at one of those big hotels over the bridge,—they're packed full of Americans."

"But I want to practice my Arabic."

"Good gracious, do you speak Arabic?"

"Yes,—well enough to get along."

"Why, hang it, you won't get along in Geneva,—*they* don't speak Arabic, they speak French. What hotel are you stopping at here?"

"Hotel Pension-Beaurivage."

"Sho, you ought to stop at the Schweitzerhof. Didn't you know the Schweitzerhof was the best hotel in Switzerland?—look at your Baedecker."

"Yes, I know,—but I had an idea there warn't any Americans there."

"No Americans! Why bless your soul it's just alive with them! I'm in the great reception room most all the time. I make lots of acquaintances there. Not as many as I did at first, because now only the new ones stop in there,—the others go right along through. Where are you from?"

"Arkansaw."

"Is that so? I'm from New England,—New Bloomfield's my town when I'm at home. I'm having a mighty good time to-day, ain't you?"

"Divine."

"That's what I call it. I like this knocking around, loose and easy, and making acquaintances and talking. I know an American, soon as I see him; so I go and speak to him and make his acquaintance. I ain't ever bored, on a trip like this, if I can make new acquaintances and talk. I'm awful fond of talking when I can get hold of the right kind of a person, ain't you?"

"I prefer it to any other dissipation."

"That's my notion, too. Now some people like to take a book and sit down and read, and read, and read, or moon around yawping at the lake or these mountains and things, but that ain't my way; no, sir, if they like it, let 'em do it, I don't object; but as for me, talking's what *I* like. You been up the Rigi?"

"Yes."

"What hotel did you stop at?"

"Schreiber."

"That's the place!—I stopped there too. *Full* of Americans, *wasn't* it? It always is,—always is. That's what they say. Everybody says that. What ship did you come over in?"

"Ville de Paris."

"French, I reckon. What kind of a passage did .... excuse me a minute, there's some Americans I haven't seen before."

And away he went. He went uninjured, too,—I had the murderous impulse to harpoon him in the back with my alpenstock, but as I raised the weapon the disposition left me; I found I hadn't the heart to kill him, he was such a joyous, innocent, good-natured numscull.

Half an hour later I was sitting on a bench inspecting, with strong interest, a noble monolith which we were skimming by,—a monolith not shaped by man, but by Nature's free great hand,—a massy pyramidal rock eighty feet high, devised by Nature ten million years ago against the day when a man worthy of it should need it for his monument. The time came at last, and now this grand remembrancer bears Schiller's name in huge letters upon its face. Curiously enough, this rock was not degraded or defiled in any way. It is said that two years ago a stranger let himself down from the top of it with ropes and pulleys, and painted all over it, in blue letters bigger than those in Schiller's name, these words:

"TRY SOZODONT;"
"BUY SUN STOVE POLISH;"
"HELMBOLD'S BUCHU;"
"TRY BENZALINE FOR THE BLOOD."

He was captured, and it turned out that he was an American. Upon his trial the judge said to him,—

"You are from a land where any insolent that wants to, is privileged to profane and insult Nature, and through her, Nature's God, if by so doing he can put a sordid penny in his pocket. But here the case is different. Because you are a foreigner and ignorant, I will make your sentence light; if you were a native I would deal strenuously with you.—Hear and obey: You will immediately remove every trace of your offensive work from the Schiller monument; you will pay a fine of ten thousand francs; you will suffer two years' imprisonment at hard labor; you will then be horsewhipped, tarred and feathered, deprived of your ears, ridden on a rail to the confines of the canton, and banished forever. The severer penalties are omitted in your case,—not as a grace to you, but to that great republic which had the misfortune to give you birth."

The steamer's benches were ranged back to back across the deck. My back hair was mingling innocently with the back hair of a couple of ladies. Presently they were addressed by some one and I overheard this conversation:

"You are Americans, I think? So'm I."

"Yes,—we are Americans."

"I knew it,—I can always tell them. What ship did you come over in?"

"City of Chester."

"O yes,—Inman line. We came in the Batavia,—Cunard, you know. What kind of a passage did you have?"

"Pretty fair."

"That was luck. We had it awful rough. Captain said he'd hardly ever seen it rougher. Where are you from?"

"New Jersey."

"So'm I. No—I didn't mean that; I'm from New England. New Bloomfield's my place. These your children?—belong to both of you?"

"Only to one of us; they are mine; my friend is not married."

"Single, I reckon? So'm I. Are you two ladies traveling alone?"

"No,—my husband is with us."

"Our whole family's along. It's awful slow, going around alone,—don't you think so?"

"I suppose it must be."

"Hi, there's Mount Pilatus coming in sight again. Named after Pontius Pilate, you know, that shot the apple off of William Tell's head. Guide-book tells all about it, they say. I didn't read it—an American told me. I don't read when I'm knocking around like this, having a good time. Did you ever see the chapel where William Tell used to preach?"

"I did not know he ever preached there."

"O, yes he did. That American told me so. He don't ever shut up his guide-book. He knows more about this lake than the fishes in it.

Besides, they *call* it 'Tell's Chapel'—you know that yourself. You ever been over here before?"

"Yes."

"I haven't. It's my first trip. But we've been all around,—Paris and everywhere. I'm to enter Harvard next year.—Studying German all the time now. Can't enter till I know German. This book's Otto's Grammar. It's a mighty good book to get the *ich habe gehabt haben's* out of. But I don't really study when I'm knocking around this way. If the notion takes me, I just run over my little old *ich habe gehabt, du hast gehabt, er hat gehabt, wir haben gehabt, ihr habet gehabt, sie haben gehabt,*—kind of 'Now-I-lay-me-down-to-sleep' fashion, you know, and after that, maybe I don't buckle to it again for three days. It's awful undermining to the intellect, German is; you want to take it in small doses, or first you know your brains all run together, and you feel them sloshing around in your head same as so much drawn butter. But French is different; *French* ain't anything. I ain't any more afraid of French than a tramp's afraid of pie; I can rattle off my little *j'ai, tu as, il a,* and the rest of it, just as easy as a-b-c. I get along pretty well in Paris, or anywhere where they speak French. What hotel you stopping at?"

"The Schweitzerhof."

"No! is that so? I never see you in the big reception room. I go in there a good deal of the time, because there's so many Americans there. I make lots of acquaintances. You been up the Rigi yet?"

"No."

"Going?"

"We think of it."

"What hotel you going to stop at?"

"I don't know."

"Well, then, you stop at the Schreiber,—it's full of Americans. What ship did you come over in?"

"City of Chester."

"O, yes, I remember I asked you that before. But I always ask everybody what ship they came over in, and so sometimes I forget and ask again. You going to Geneva?"

"Yes."

"What hotel you going to stop at?"

"We expect to stop in a pension."

"I don't hardly believe you'll like that: there's very few Americans in the pensions. What hotel are you stopping at here?"

"The Schweitzerhof."

"O, yes, I asked you that before, too. But I always ask everybody what hotel they're stopping at, and so I've got my head all mixed up with hotels. But it makes talk, and I love to talk. It refreshes me up so,—don't it you—on a trip like this?"

"Yes,—sometimes."

"Well, it does me, too. As long as I'm talking I never feel bored,—ain't that the way with you?"

"Yes—generally. But there are exceptions to the rule."

"O, of course. *I* don't care to talk to everybody, *myself*. If a person starts in to jabber-jabber-jabber about scenery, and history, and pictures, and all sorts of tiresome things, I get the fan-tods mighty soon. I say 'Well, I must be going now,—hope I'll see you again'—and then I take a walk. Where you from?"

"New Jersey."

"Why, bother it all, I asked you *that* before, too. Have you seen the Lion of Lucerne?"

"Not yet."

"Nor I, either. But the man who told me about Mount Pilatus says it's one of the things to see. It's twenty-eight feet long. It don't seem reasonable, but he said so, anyway. He saw it yesterday; said it was dying, then, so I reckon it's dead by this time. But that ain't any matter, of course they'll stuff it. Did you say the children are yours,—or *hers*?"

"Mine."

"O, so you did. Are you going up the ...... no, I asked you that. What ship .... no, I asked you that, too. What hotel are you ...... no, you told me that. Let me see ...... um ...... O, what kind of a voy .... no, we've been over that ground, too. Um ...... um ...... well, I believe that is all. *Bonjour*—I am very glad to have made your acquaintance, ladies. *Guten Tag*."

From *A Tramp Abroad*, 1880

Ascending the Riffelberg

After I had finished my readings, I was no longer myself; I was tranced, uplifted, intoxicated, by the almost incredible perils and adventures I had been following my authors through, and the triumphs I had been sharing with them. I sat silent some time, then turned to Harris and said,–

"My mind is made up."

Something in my tone struck him; and when he glanced at my eye and read what was written there, his face paled perceptibly. He hesitated a moment, then said,–

"Speak."

I answered, with perfect calmness,–

"I WILL ASCEND THE RIFFELBERG."

If I had shot my poor friend he could not have fallen from his chair more suddenly. If I had been his father he could not have pleaded harder to get me to give up my purpose. But I turned a deaf ear to all he said. When he perceived at last that nothing could alter my determination, he ceased to urge, and for a while the deep silence was broken only by his sobs. I sat in marble resolution, with my eyes fixed upon vacancy, for in spirit I was already wrestling with the perils of the mountains, and my friend sat gazing at me in adoring admiration through his tears. At last he threw himself upon me in a loving embrace and exclaimed in broken tones:

"Your Harris will never desert you. We will die together!"

I cheered the noble fellow with praises, and soon his fears were forgotten and he was eager for the adventure. He wanted to summon the guides at once and leave at 2 in the morning, as he supposed the custom was; but I explained that nobody was looking, at that hour; and that the start in the dark was not usually made from the village but from the first night's resting place on the mountain side. I said we would leave the village at 3 or 4 p. m. on the morrow; meantime he could notify the guides, and also let the public know of the attempt which we proposed to make.

I went to bed, but not to sleep. No man can sleep when he is about to undertake one of these Alpine exploits. I tossed feverishly all night long, and was glad enough when I heard the clock strike half past eleven and knew it was time to get up for dinner. I rose jaded and rusty, and went to the noon meal, where I found myself the centre of interest and curiosity; for the news was already abroad. It is not easy to eat calmly when you are a lion, but it is very pleasant, nevertheless.

As usual, at Zermatt, when a great ascent is about to be undertaken, everybody, native and foreign, laid aside his own projects and took up a good position to observe the start. The expedition consisted of 198 persons, including the mules; or 205, including the cows. As follows:

CHIEFS OF SERVICE.		SUBORDINATES.	
	Myself.	1	Veterinary Surgeon.
	Mr. Harris.	1	Butler.
17	Guides.	12	Waiters.
4	Surgeons.	1	Footman.
1	Geologist.	1	Barber.
1	Botanist.	1	Head Cook.
3	Chaplains.	9	Assistants.
2	Draftsmen.	4	Pastry Cooks.
15	Barkeepers.	1	Confectionery Artist.
1	Latinist.		

TRANSPORTATION, etc.

27	Porters.	3	Coarse Washers and Ironers.
44	Mules.	1	Fine ditto.
44	Muleteers.	7	Cows.
		2	Milkers.

Total, 154 men, 51 animals. Grand Total, 205.

RATIONS, etc.		APPARATUS.	
16	Cases Hams.	25	Spring Mattresses.
2	Barrels Flour.	2	Hair ditto.
22	Barrels Whiskey.		Bedding for same.

RATIONS, etc.		APPARATUS.	
1	Barrel Sugar.	2	Mosquito Nets.
1	Keg Lemons.	29	Tents.
2,000	Cigars.		Scientific Instruments.
1	Barrel Pies.	97	Ice-axes.
1	Ton of Pemmican.	5	Cases Dynamite.
143	Pair Crutches.	7	Cans Nitro-glycerine.
2	Barrels Arnica.	22	40-foot Ladders.
1	Bale of Lint.	2	Miles of Rope.
27	Kegs Paregoric.	154	Umbrellas.

It was full four o'clock in the afternoon before my cavalcade was entirely ready. At that hour it began to move. In point of numbers and spectacular effect, it was the most imposing expedition that had ever marched from Zermatt.

I commanded the chief guide to arrange the men and animals in single file, twelve feet apart, and lash them all together on a strong rope. He objected that the first two miles was a dead level, with plenty of room, and that the rope was never used except in very dangerous places. But I would not listen to that. My reading had taught me that many serious accidents had happened in the Alps simply from not having the people tied up soon enough; I was not going to add one to the list. The guide then obeyed my order.

When the procession stood at ease, roped together, and ready to move, I never saw a finer sight. It was 3,122 feet long—over half a mile; every man but Harris and me was on foot, and had on his green veil and his blue goggles, and his white rag around his hat, and his coil of rope over one shoulder and under the other, and his ice-axe in his belt, and carried his alpenstock in his left hand, his umbrella (closed,) in his right, and his crutches slung at his back. The burdens of the pack mules, and the horns of the cows, were decked with the Edelweiss and the Alpine rose.

I and my agent were the only persons mounted. We were in the post of danger in the extreme rear, and tied securely to five guides apiece. Our armor-bearers carried our ice-axes, alpenstocks and other implements for us. We were mounted upon very small donkeys, as a measure of safety; in time of peril we could straighten our legs and stand up, and let the donkey walk from under. Still, I cannot recommend this sort of animal,—at least for excursions of mere pleasure, —because his ears interrupt the view. I and my agent possessed the regulation mountaineering costumes, but concluded to leave them behind. Out of respect for the great numbers of tourists of both sexes who would be assembled in front of the hotels to see us pass, and also out of respect for the many tourists, whom we expected to encounter on our expedition, we decided to make the ascent in evening dress.

At 15 minutes past 4 I gave the command to move, and my subordinates passed it along the line. The great crowd in front of the Monte Rosa hotel parted in twain, with a cheer, as the procession approached; and as the head of it was filing by I gave the order,—
"Unlimber—make ready—HOIST!"

—and with one impulse up went my half mile of umbrellas. It was a beautiful sight, and a total surprise to the spectators. Nothing like that had ever been seen in the Alps before. The applause it brought forth was deeply gratifying to me, and I rode by with my plug hat in my hand to testify my appreciation of it. It was the only testimony I could offer, for I was too full to speak.

We watered the caravan at the cold stream which rushes down a trough near the end of the village, and soon afterward left the haunts of civilization behind us. About half past 5 o'clock we arrived at a bridge which spans the Visp, and after throwing over a detachment to see if it was safe, the caravan crossed without accident. The way now led, by a gentle ascent, carpeted with fresh green grass, to the church of Winkelmatten. Without stopping to examine this edifice, I executed a flank movement to the right and crossed the bridge over the Findelenbach, after first testing its strength. Here I deployed to the right again, and presently entered an inviting stretch of meadow land which was unoccupied save by a couple of deserted huts toward its furthest extremity. These meadows offered an excellent camping place. We pitched our tents, supped, established a proper guard, recorded the events of the day, and then went to bed.

We rose at 2 in the morning and dressed by candle light. It was a dismal and chilly business. A few stars were shining, but the general heavens were overcast, and the great shaft of the Matterhorn was draped in a sable pall of clouds. The chief guide advised a delay; he said he feared it was going to rain. We waited until nine o'clock, and then got away in tolerably clear weather.

Our course led up some terrific steeps, densely wooded with larches and cedars, and traversed by paths which the rains had guttered and which were obstructed by loose stones. To add to the danger and inconvenience, we were constantly meeting returning tourists on foot or horseback, and as constantly being crowded and battered by ascending tourists who were in a hurry and wanted to get by.

Our troubles thickened. About the middle of the afternoon the seventeen guides called a halt and held a consultation. After consulting an hour they said their first suspicion remained intact,—that is to say, they believed they were lost. I asked if they did not *know* it? No, they said, they *couldn't* absolutely know whether they were lost or not, because none of them had ever been in that part of the country before. They had a strong instinct that they were lost, but they had no proofs,—except that they did not know where they were. They had met no tourists for some time, and they considered that a suspicious sign.

Plainly we were in an ugly fix. The guides were naturally unwilling to go alone and seek a way out of the difficulty; so we all went together. For better security we moved slow and cautiously, for the forest was very dense. We did not move up the mountain, but around it, hoping to strike across the old trail. Toward nightfall, when we were about tired out, we came up against a rock as big as a cottage. This barrier took all the remaining spirit out of the men, and a panic of fear and despair ensued. They moaned and wept, and said they should never see their homes and their dear ones again. Then they began to upbraid me for bringing them upon this fatal expedition. Some even muttered threats against me.

Clearly it was no time to show weakness. So I made a speech in which I said that other Alp-climbers had been in as perilous a position as this, and yet by courage and perseverance had escaped. I promised to stand by them, I promised to rescue them. I closed by saying we had plenty of provisions to maintain us for quite a siege,—and did they suppose Zermatt would allow half a mile of men and mules to mysteriously disappear during any considerable time, right above their noses, and make no inquiries? No, Zermatt would send out searching-expeditions and we should be saved.

This speech had a great effect. The men pitched the tents with some little show of cheerfulness, and we were snugly under cover when the night shut down. I now reaped the reward of my wisdom in providing one article which is not mentioned in any book of Alpine adventure but this. I refer to the paregoric. But for that beneficent drug, not one of those men would have slept a moment during that fearful night. But for that gentle persuader they must have tossed, unsoothed, the night through; for the whiskey was for me. Yes, they would have risen in the morning unfitted for their heavy task. As it was, everybody slept but my agent and me,—only we two and the barkeepers. I would not permit myself to sleep at such a time. I considered myself responsible for all those lives. I meant to be on hand and ready, in case of avalanches. I am aware now, that there were no avalanches up there, but I did not know it then.

We watched the weather all through that awful night, and kept an eye on the barometer, to be prepared for the least change. There was not the slightest change recorded by the instrument, during the whole time. Words cannot describe the comfort that that friendly, hopeful, steadfast thing was to me in that season of trouble. It was a defective barometer, and had no hand but the stationary brass pointer, but I did not know that until afterward. If I should be in such a situation again, I should not wish for any barometer but that one.

All hands rose at 2 in the morning and took breakfast, and as soon as it was light we roped ourselves together and went at that rock. For some time we tried the hook-rope and other means of scaling it, but without success. That is without perfect success. The hook caught once, and Harris started up it hand over hand, but the hold broke and if there had not happened to be a chaplain sitting underneath at the time, Harris would certainly have been crippled. As it was, it was the chaplain. He took to his crutches, and I ordered the hook-rope to be laid aside. It was too dangerous an implement where so many people were standing around.

We were puzzled for a while; then somebody thought of the ladders. One of these was leaned against the rock, and the men went up it tied together in couples. Another ladder was sent up for use in descending. At the end of half an hour everybody was over, and that rock was conquered. We gave our first grand shout of triumph. But the joy was short-lived, for somebody asked how we were going to get the animals over.

This was a serious difficulty; in fact it was an impossibility. The courage of the men began to waver immediately; once more we were threatened with a panic. But when the danger was most imminent, we were saved in a mysterious way. A mule which had attracted attention from the beginning by its disposition to experiment, tried to eat a five-pound can of nitro-glycerine. This happened right along-side the rock. The explosion threw us all to the ground, and covered us with dirt and débris; it frightened us extremely, too, for the crash it made was deafening, and the violence of the shock made the ground tremble. However, we were grateful, for the rock was gone. Its place was occupied by a new cellar, about thirty feet across, by fifteen feet deep. The explosion was heard as far as Zermatt; and an hour and a half afterward, many citizens of that town were knocked down and quite seriously injured by descending portions of mule meat, frozen solid. This shows, better than any estimate in figures how high the experimenter went.

We had nothing to do, now, but bridge the cellar and proceed on our way. With a cheer the men went at their work. I attended to the engineering, myself. I appointed a strong detail to cut down trees with ice-axes and trim them for piers to support the bridge. This was a slow business, for ice-axes are not good to cut wood with. I caused my piers to be firmly set up in ranks in the cellar, and upon them I laid six of my forty-foot ladders, side by side, and laid six more on top of them. Upon this bridge I caused a bed of boughs to be spread, and on top of the boughs a bed of earth six inches deep. I stretched ropes upon either side to serve as railings, and then my bridge was complete. A train of elephants could have crossed it in safety and comfort. By nightfall the caravan was on the other side and the ladders taken up.

Next morning we went on in good spirits for a while, though our way was slow and difficult, by reason of the steep and rocky nature of the ground and the thickness of the forest; but at last a dull despondency crept into the men's faces and it was apparent that not only they, but even the guides, were now convinced that we were lost. The fact that we still met no tourists was a circumstance that was but too significant. Another thing seemed to suggest that we were not only lost, but very badly lost: for there must surely be searching-parties on the road before this time, yet we had seen no sign of them.

Demoralization was spreading; something must be done, and done quickly, too. Fortunately, I am not unfertile in expedients. I contrived one now which commended itself to all, for it promised well. I took three-quarters of a mile of rope and fastened one end of it around the waist of a guide, and told him to go and find the road, whilst the caravan waited. I instructed him to guide himself back by the rope, in case of failure; in case of success, he was to give the rope a series of violent jerks, whereupon the Expedition would go to him at once. He departed, and in two minutes had disappeared among the trees. I payed out the rope myself, while everybody watched the crawling thing with eager eyes. The rope crept away quite slowly, at times, at other times with some briskness. Twice or thrice we seemed to get the signal, and a shout was just ready to break from the men's lips when they perceived it was a false alarm. But at last, when over half a mile of rope had slidden away it stopped gliding and stood absolutely still,—one minute,—two minutes,—three,—while we held our breath and watched.

Was the guide resting? Was he scanning the country from some high point? Was he inquiring of a chance mountaineer? Stop,—had he fainted from excess of fatigue and anxiety?

This thought gave us a shock. I was in the very act of detailing an expedition to succor him, when the cord was assailed with a series of such frantic jerks that I could hardly keep hold of it. The huzza that went up, then, was good to hear. "Saved! saved!" was the word that rang out, all down the long rank of the caravan.

We rose up and started at once. We found the route to be good enough for a while, but it began to grow difficult, by and by, and this feature steadily increased. When we judged we had gone half a mile, we momently expected to see the guide; but no, he was not visible anywhere; neither was he waiting, for the rope was still moving, consequently he was doing the same. This argued that he had not found the road, yet, but was marching to it with some peasant. There was nothing for us to do but plod along,—and this we did. At the end of three hours we were still plodding. This was not only mysterious, but exasperating. And very fatiguing, too; for we had tried hard, along at first, to catch up with the guide, but had only fagged ourselves, in vain; for although he was traveling slowly he was yet able to go faster than the hampered caravan over such ground.

At three in the afternoon we were nearly dead with exhaustion,—and still the rope was slowly gliding out. The murmurs against the guide had been growing, steadily, and at last they were become loud and savage. A mutiny ensued. The men refused to proceed. They declared that we had been traveling over and over the same ground all day, in a kind of circle. They demanded that our end of the rope be made fast to a tree, so as to halt the guide until we could overtake him and kill him. This was not an unreasonable requirement, so I gave the order.

As soon as the rope was tied, the Expedition moved forward with that alacrity which the thirst for vengeance usually inspires. But after a tiresome march of almost half a mile, we came to a hill covered thick with a crumbly rubbish of stones, and so steep that no man of us all was now in a condition to climb it. Every attempt failed, and ended in crippling somebody. Within twenty minutes I had five men on crutches. Whenever a climber tried to assist himself by the rope, it yielded and let him tumble backwards. The frequency of this result suggested an idea to me. I ordered the caravan to 'bout face and form in marching order; I then made the tow-rope fast to the rear mule, and gave the command,—

"Mark time—by the right flank—forward—march!"

The procession began to move, to the impressive strains of a battle-chant, and I said to myself, "Now, if the rope don't break I judge *this* will fetch that guide into the camp." I watched the rope gliding down the hill, and presently when I was all fixed for triumph I was confronted by a bitter disappointment: there was no guide tied to the rope, it was only a very indignant old black ram. The fury of the baffled Expedition exceeded all bounds. They even wanted to wreak their unreasoning vengeance on this innocent dumb brute. But I stood between them and their prey, menaced by a bristling wall of ice-axes and alpenstocks, and proclaimed that there was but one road to this murder, and it was directly over my corpse. Even as I spoke I saw that my doom was sealed, except a miracle supervened to divert these madmen from their fell purpose. I see that sickening wall of weapons now; I see that advancing host as I saw it then, I see the hate in those cruel eyes; I remember how I drooped my head upon my breast, I feel again the sudden earthquake shock in my rear, administered by the very ram I was sacrificing myself to save, I hear once more the typhoon of laughter that burst from the assaulting column as I clove it from van to rear like a Sepoy shot from a Rodman gun.

I was saved. Yes, I was saved, and by the merciful instinct of ingratitude which nature had planted in the breast of that treacherous beast. The grace which eloquence had failed to work in those men's hearts, had been wrought by a laugh. The ram was set free and my life was spared.

We lived to find out that that guide had deserted us as soon as he had placed a half mile between himself and us. To avert suspicion, he had judged it best that the line should continue to move; so he caught that ram, and at the time that he was sitting on it making the rope fast to it, we were imagining that he was lying in a swoon, overcome by fatigue and distress. When he allowed the ram to get up it fell to plunging around, trying to rid itself of the rope, and this was the signal which we had risen up with glad shouts to obey. We had followed this ram round and round in a circle all day—a thing which was proven by the discovery that we had watered the Expedition seven times at one and the same spring in seven hours. As expert a woodman as I am, I had somehow failed to notice this until my attention was called to it by a hog. This hog was always wallowing there, and as he was the only hog we saw, his frequent repetition, together with his unvarying similarity to himself, finally caused me to reflect that he must be the same hog, and this led me to the deduction that this must be the same spring, also,—which indeed it was.

I made a note of this curious thing, as showing in a striking manner the relative difference between glacial action and the action of the hog. It is now a well established fact, that glaciers move; I consider that my observations go to show, with equal conclusiveness, that a hog in a spring does not move. I shall be glad to receive the opinions of other observers upon this point.

To return, for an explanatory moment, to that guide, and then I shall be done with him. After leaving the ram tied to the rope, he had wandered at large a while, and then happened to run across a cow. Judging that a cow would naturally know more than a guide, he took her by the tail, and the result justified his judgment. She nibbled her leisurely way down hill till it was near milking time, then she struck for home and towed him into Zermatt.

We went into camp on that wild spot to which that ram had brought us. The men were greatly fatigued. Their conviction that we were lost was forgotten in the cheer of a good supper, and before the reaction had a chance to set in, I loaded them up with paregoric and put them to bed.

Next morning I was considering in my mind our desperate situation and trying to think of a remedy, when Harris came to me with a Baedeker map which showed conclusively that the mountain we were on was still in Switzerland,—yes, every part of it was in Switzerland. So we were not lost, after all. This was an immense relief; it lifted the weight of two such mountains from my breast. I immediately had the news disseminated and the map exhibited. The effect was wonderful. As soon as the men saw with their own eyes that they knew where they were, and that it was only the summit that was lost and not themselves, they cheered up instantly and said with one accord, let the summit take care of itself, they were not interested in its troubles.

Our distresses being at an end, I now determined to rest the men in camp and give the scientific department of the Expedition a chance. First, I made a barometric observation, to get our altitude, but I could not perceive that there was any result. I knew, by my scientific reading, that either thermometers or barometers ought to be boiled, to make them accurate; I did not know which it was, so I boiled both. There was still no result; so I examined these instruments and discovered that they possessed radical blemishes: the barometer had no hand but the brass pointer and the ball of the thermometer was stuffed with tin foil. I might have boiled those things to rags, and never found out anything.

I hunted up another barometer; it was new and perfect. I boiled it half an hour in a pot of bean soup which the cooks were making. The result was unexpected: the instrument was not affected at all, but there was such a strong barometer taste to the soup that the head cook, who was a most conscientious person, changed its name in the bill of fare. The dish was so greatly liked by all, that I ordered the cook to have barometer soup every day. It was believed that the barometer might eventually be injured, but I did not care for that. I had demonstrated to my satisfaction that it could not tell how high a mountain was, therefore I had no real use for it. Changes of the weather I could take care of without it; I did not wish to know when the weather was going to be good, what I wanted to know was when it was going to be bad, and this I could find out from Harris's corns. Harris had had his corns tested and regulated at the government observatory in Heidelberg, and one could depend upon them with confidence. So I transferred the new barometer to the cooking department, to be used for the official mess. It was found that even a pretty fair article of soup could be made with the defective barometer; so I allowed that one to be transferred to the subordinate messes.

I next boiled the thermometer, and got a most excellent result; the mercury went up to about 200° Fahrenheit. In the opinion of the other scientists of the Expedition, this seemed to indicate that we had attained the extraordinary altitude of 200,000 feet above sea level. Science places the line of eternal snow at about 10,000 feet above sea level. There was no snow where we were, consequently it was proven that the eternal snow line ceases somewhere above the 10,000 foot level and does not begin any more. This was an interesting fact, and one which had not been observed by any observer before. It was as valuable as interesting, too, since it would open up the deserted summits of the highest Alps to population and agriculture. It was a proud thing to be where we were, yet it caused us a pang to reflect that but for that ram we might just as well have been 200,000 feet higher.

The success of my last experiment induced me to try an experiment with my photographic apparatus. I got it out, and boiled one of my cameras, but the thing was a failure: it made the wood swell up and burst, and I could not see that the lenses were any better than they were before.

I now concluded to boil a guide. It might improve him, it could not impair his usefulness. But I was not allowed to proceed. Guides have no feeling for science, and this one would not consent to be made uncomfortable in its interest.

In the midst of my scientific work, one of those needless accidents happened which are always occurring among the ignorant and thoughtless. A porter shot at a chamois and missed it and crippled the Latinist. This was not a serious matter to me, for a Latinist's duties are as well performed on crutches as otherwise,—but the fact remained that if the Latinist had not happened to be in the way a mule would have got that load. That would have been quite another matter, for when it comes down to a question of value there is a palpable difference between a Latinist and a mule. I could not depend on having a Latinist in the right place every time; so, to make things safe, I ordered that in future the chamois must not be hunted within the limits of the camp with any other weapon than the forefinger.

My nerves had hardly grown quiet after this affair when they got another shake-up,—one which utterly unmanned me for a moment: a rumor swept suddenly through the camp that one of the barkeepers had fallen over a precipice!

However, it turned out that it was only a chaplain. I had laid in an extra force of chaplains, purposely to be prepared for emergencies like this, but by some unaccountable oversight had come away rather short-handed in the matter of barkeepers.

On the following morning we moved on, well refreshed and in good spirits. I remember this day with peculiar pleasure, because it saw our road restored to us. Yes, we found our road again, and in quite an extraordinary way. We had plodded along some two hours and a half, when we came up against a solid mass of rock about twenty feet high. I did not need to be instructed by a mule this time. —I was already beginning to know more than any mule in the Expedition.—I at once put in a blast of dynamite, and lifted that rock out of the way. But to my surprise and mortification, I found that there had been a chalet on top of it.

I picked up such members of the family as fell in my vicinity, and subordinates of my corps collected the rest. None of these poor people were injured, happily, but they were much annoyed. I explained to the head chaleteer just how the thing happened, and that I was only searching for the road, and would certainly have given him timely notice if I had known he was up there. I said I had meant no harm, and hoped I had not lowered myself in his estimation by raising him a few rods in the air. I said many other judicious things, and finally when I offered to rebuild his chalet, and pay for breakages, and throw in the cellar, he was mollified and satisfied. He hadn't any cellar at all, before; he would not have as good a view, now, as formerly, but what he had lost in view he had gained in cellar, by exact measurement. He said there wasn't another hole like that in the mountains,—and he would have been right if the late mule had not tried to eat up the nitro-glycerine.

I put a hundred and sixteen men at work, and they rebuilt the chalet from its own débris in fifteen minutes. It was a good deal more picturesque than it was before, too. The man said we were now on the Feli-Stutz, above the Schwegmatt,—information which I was glad to get, since it gave us our position to a degree of particularity which we had not been accustomed to for a day or so. We also learned that we were standing at the foot of the Riffelberg proper, and that the initial chapter of our work was completed.

We had a fine view, from here, of the energetic Visp, as it makes its first plunge into the world from under a huge arch of solid ice, worn through the foot-wall of the great Gorner Glacier; and we could also see the Furggenbach, which is the outlet of the Furggen Glacier.

The mule-road to the summit of the Riffelberg passed right in front of the chalet, a circumstance which we almost immediately noticed, because a procession of tourists was filing along it pretty much all the time.* The chaleteer's business consisted in furnishing refreshments to tourists. My blast had interrupted this trade for a few minutes, by breaking all the bottles on the place; but I gave the man a lot of whiskey to sell for Alpine champagne, and a lot of vinegar which would answer for Rhine wine, consequently trade was soon as brisk as ever.

* "Pretty much" may not be elegant English, but it is high time it was. There is no elegant word or phrase which means just what it means.—M. T.

Leaving the Expedition outside to rest, I quartered myself in the chalet, with Harris, purposing to correct my journals and scientific observations before continuing the ascent. I had hardly begun my work when a tall, slender, vigorous American youth of about twenty-three, who was on his way down the mountain, entered and came toward me with that breezy self-complacency which is the adolescent's idea of the well bred ease of the man of the world. His hair was short and parted accurately in the middle, and he had all the look of an American person who would be likely to begin his signature with an initial, and spell his middle name out. He introduced himself, smiling a smirky smile borrowed from the courtiers of the stage, extended a fair-skinned talon, and whilst he gripped my hand in it he bent his body forward three times at the hips, as the stage-courtier does, and said in the airiest and most condescending and patronizing way,—I quote his exact language,—

"Very glad to make your acquaintance, 'm sure; very glad indeed, assure you. I've read all your little efforts and greatly admired them, and when I heard you were here, I . . . . ."

I indicated a chair, and he sat down. This grandee was the grandson of an American of considerable note in his day, and not wholly forgotten yet,—a man who came so near being a great man that he was quite generally accounted one while he lived.

I slowly paced the floor, pondering scientific problems, and heard this conversation:

Grandson. First visit to Europe?

Harris. Mine? Yes.

G. S. (With a soft reminiscent sigh suggestive of by-gone joys that may be tasted in their freshness but once.) Ah, I know what it is to you. A first visit!—ah, the romance of it! I wish I could feel it again.

H. Yes, I find it exceeds all my dreams. It is enchantment. I go . . . .

G. S. (With a dainty gesture of the hand signifying, "Spare me your callow enthusiasms, good friend.") Yes, *I* know, I know; you go to cathedrals, and exclaim; and you drag through league-long picture galleries and exclaim; and you stand here, and there, and yonder, upon historic ground, and continue to exclaim; and you are permeated with your first crude conceptions of Art, and are proud and happy. Ah, yes, proud and happy—that expresses it. Yes-yes, enjoy it—it is right,—it is an innocent revel.

H. And you? Don't you do these things now?

G. S. I! O, that is *very* good! My dear sir, when you are as old a traveler as I am, you will not ask such a question as that. *I* visit the regulation gallery, moon around the regulation cathedral, do the worn round of the regulation sights, *yet*?—Excuse me!

H. Well what *do* you do, then?

G. S. Do? I flit,—and flit,—for I am ever on the wing,—but I avoid the herd. To-day I am in Paris, to-morrow in Berlin, anon in Rome; but you would look for me in vain in the galleries of the Louvre or the common resorts of the gazers in those other capitals. If you would find me, you must look in the unvisited nooks and corners where others never think of going. One day you will find me making myself at home in some obscure peasant's cabin, another day you will find me in some forgotten castle worshiping some little gem of art which the careless eye has overlooked and which the unexperienced would despise; again you will find me a guest in the inner sanctuaries of palaces while the herd is content to get a hurried glimpse of the unused chambers by feeing a servant.

H. You are a *guest* in such places?

G. S. And a welcome one.

H. It is surprising. How does it come?

G. S. My grandfather's name is a passport to all the courts in Europe. I have only to utter that name and every door is open to me. I flit from court to court at my own free will and pleasure, and am always welcome. I am as much at home in the palaces of Europe as you are among your relatives. I know every titled person in Europe, I think. I have my pockets full of invitations all the time. I am under promise now, to go to Italy, where I am to be the guest of a succession of the noblest houses in the land. In Berlin my life is a continued round of gayety in the imperial palace. It is the same, wherever I go.

H. It must be very pleasant. But it must make Boston seem a little slow when you are at home.

G. S. Yes, of course it does. But I don't go home much. There's no life there—little to feed a man's higher nature. Boston's very narrow, you know. She doesn't know it, and you couldn't convince her of it—so I say nothing when I'm there: where's the use? Yes, Boston is very narrow, but she has such a good opinion of herself that she can't see it. A man who has traveled as much as I have, and seen as much of the world, sees it plain enough, but he can't cure it, you know, so the best way is to leave it and seek a sphere which is more in harmony with his tastes and culture. I run across there, once a year, perhaps, when I have nothing important on hand, but I'm very soon back again. I spend my time in Europe.

H. I see. You map out your plans and .....

G. S. No, excuse me. I don't map out any plans. I simply follow the inclination of the day. I am limited by no ties, no requirements, I am not bound in any way. I am too old a traveler to hamper myself with deliberate purposes. I am simply a traveler—an inveterate traveler—a man of the world, in a word,—I can call myself by no other name. I do not say, "I am going here, or I am going there"—I say nothing at all, I only act. For instance, next week you may find me the guest of a grandee of Spain, or you may find me off for Venice, or flitting toward Dresden. I shall probably go to Egypt presently; friends will say to friends, "He is at the Nile cataracts"—and at that very moment they will be surprised to learn that I'm away off yonder in India somewhere. I am a constant surprise to people. They are always saying, "Yes, he was in Jerusalem when we heard of him last, but goodness knows where he is now."

Presently the Grandson rose to leave—discovered he had an appointment with some Emperor, perhaps. He did his graces over again: gripped me with one talon, at arm's length, pressed his hat against his stomach with the other, bent his body in the middle three times, murmuring,—

"Pleasure, 'm sure; great pleasure, 'm sure. Wish you much success."

Then he removed his gracious presence. It is a great and solemn thing to have a grandfather.

I have not purposed to misrepresent this boy in any way, for what little indignation he excited in me soon passed and left nothing behind it but compassion. One cannot keep up a grudge against a vacuum. I have tried to repeat the lad's very words; if I have failed anywhere I have at least not failed to reproduce the marrow and meaning of what he said. He and the innocent chatterbox whom I met on the Swiss lake are the most unique and interesting specimens of Young America I came across during my foreign tramping. I have made honest portraits of them, not caricatures. The Grandson of twenty-three referred to himself five or six times as an "old traveler," and as many as three times, (with a serene complacency which was maddening,) as a "man of the world." There was something very delicious about his leaving Boston to her "narrowness," unreproved and uninstructed.

I formed the caravan in marching order, presently, and after riding down the line to see that it was properly roped together, gave the command to proceed. In a little while the road carried us to open, grassy land. We were above the troublesome forest, now, and had an uninterrupted view, straight before us, of our summit,—the summit of the Riffelberg.

We followed the mule road, a zigzag course, now to the right, now to the left, but always up, and always crowded and incommoded by going and coming files of reckless tourists who were never, in a single instance, tied together. I was obliged to exert the utmost care and caution, for in many places the road was not two yards wide, and often the lower side of it sloped away in slanting precipices eight and even nine feet deep. I had to encourage the men constantly, to keep them from giving way to their unmanly fears.

We might have made the summit before night, but for a delay caused by the loss of an umbrella. I was for allowing the umbrella to remain lost, but the men murmured, and with reason, for in this exposed region we stood in peculiar need of protection against avalanches; so I went into camp and detached a strong party to go after the missing article.

The difficulties of the next morning were severe, but our courage was high, for our goal was near. At noon we conquered the last impediment—we stood at last upon the summit, and without the loss of a single man except the mule that ate the glycerine. Our great achievement was achieved—the possibility of the impossible was demonstrated, and Harris and I walked proudly into the great dining room of the Riffelberg Hotel and stood our alpenstocks up in the corner.

Yes, I had made the grand ascent; but it was a mistake to do it in evening dress. The plug hats were battered, the swallow-tails were fluttering rags, mud added no grace, the general effect was unpleasant and even disreputable.

There were about seventy-five tourists at the hotel,—mainly ladies and little children,—and they gave us an admiring welcome which paid us for all our privations and sufferings. The ascent had been made, and the names and dates now stand recorded on a stone monument there to prove it to all future tourists.

I boiled a thermometer and took an altitude, with a most curious result: ***the summit was not as high as the point on the mountain side where I had taken the first altitude.*** Suspecting that I had made an important discovery, I prepared to verify it. There happened to be a still higher summit (called the Gorner Grat,) above the hotel, and notwithstanding the fact that it overlooks a glacier from a dizzy height, and that the ascent is difficult and dangerous, I resolved to venture up there and boil a thermometer. So I sent a strong party, with some borrowed hoes, in charge of two chiefs of service, to dig a stairway in the soil all the way, and this I ascended, roped to the guides. This breezy height was the summit proper—so I accomplished even more than I had originally purposed to do. This fool-hardy exploit is recorded on another stone monument.

I boiled my thermometer, and sure enough, this spot, which purported to be 2,000 feet higher than the locality of the hotel, turned out to be 9,000 feet *lower.* Thus the fact was clearly demonstrated, that, ***above a certain point, the higher a point seems to be, the lower it actually is.*** Our ascent itself was a great achievement, but this contribution to science was an inconceivably greater matter.

Cavilers object that water boils at a lower and lower temperature the higher and higher you go, and hence the apparent anomaly. I answer that I do not base my theory upon what the boiling water does, but upon what a boiled thermometer says. You can't go behind the thermometer.

I had a magnificent view of Monte Rosa, and apparently all the rest of the Alpine world, from that high place. All the circling horizon was piled high with a mighty tumult of snowy crests. One might have imagined he saw before him the tented camps of a beleaguering host of Brobdignagians.

But lonely, conspicuous, and superb, rose that wonderful upright wedge, the Matterhorn. Its precipitous sides were powdered over with snow, and the upper half hidden in thick clouds which now and then dissolved to cobweb films and gave brief glimpses of the imposing tower as through a veil. A little later the Matterhorn took to himself the semblance of a volcano; he was stripped naked to his

NOTE—I had the very unusual luck to catch one little momentary glimpse of the Matterhorn wholly unencumbered by clouds. I leveled my photographic apparatus at it without the loss of an instant, and should have got an elegant picture if my donkey had not interfered. It was my purpose to draw this photograph all by myself for my book, but was obliged to put the mountain part of it into the hands of the professional artist because I found I could not do landscape well.—M. T.

apex—around this circled vast wreaths of white cloud which strung slowly out and streamed away slantwise toward the sun, a twenty-mile stretch of rolling and tumbling vapor, and looking just as if it were pouring out of a crater. Later again, one of the mountain's sides was clean and clear, and another side densely clothed from base to summit in thick smoke-like cloud which feathered off and blew around the shaft's sharp edge like the smoke around the corners of a burning building. The Matterhorn is always experimenting, and always gets up fine effects, too. In the sunset, when all the lower world is palled in gloom, it points toward heaven out of the pervading blackness like a finger of fire. In the sunrise—well, they say it is very fine in the sunrise.

Authorities agree that there is no such tremendous "layout" of snowy Alpine magnitude, grandeur and sublimity to be seen from any other accessible point as the tourist may see from the summit of the Riffelberg. Therefore, let the tourist rope himself up and go there; for I have shown that with nerve, caution, and judgment, the thing can be done.

I wish to add one remark, here,—in parentheses, so to speak,—suggested by the word "snowy," which I have just used. We have all seen hills and mountains and levels with snow on them, and so we think we know all the aspects and effects produced by snow. But indeed we do not, until we have seen the Alps. Possibly mass and distance add something,—at any rate something *is* added. Among other noticeable things, there is a dazzling, intense whiteness about the distant Alpine snow, when the sun is on it, which one recognizes as peculiar, and not familiar to the eye. The snow which one is accustomed to, has a tint to it,—painters usually give it a bluish cast,—but there is no perceptible tint to the distant Alpine snow when it is trying to look its whitest. As to the unimaginable splendor of it when the sun is blazing down on it,—well, it simply *is* unimaginable.

A guide book is a queer thing. The reader has just seen what a man who undertakes the great ascent from Zermatt to the Riffelberg hotel must experience. Yet Baedeker makes these strange statements concerning this matter:

1. Distance,—3 hours.
2. The road cannot be mistaken.
3. Guide unnecessary.
4. Distance from Riffelberg hotel to the Gorner Grat, one hour and a half.

5. Ascent simple and easy. Guide unnecessary.
6. Elevation of Zermatt above sea level, 5,315 feet.
7. Elevation of Riffelberg hotel above sea level, 8,429 feet.
8. Elevation of the Gorner Grat above sea level, 10,289 feet.

I have pretty effectually throttled these errors by sending him the following demonstrated facts:

1. Distance from Zermatt to Riffelberg hotel, 7 days.
2. The road *can* be mistaken. If I am the first that did it, I want the credit of it, too.
3. Guides *are* necessary, for none but a native can read those finger-boards.
4. The estimate of the elevation of the several localities above sea level is pretty correct—for Baedeker. He only misses it about a hundred and eighty or ninety thousand feet.

I found my arnica invaluable. My men were suffering excruciatingly, from the friction of sitting down so much. During two or three days, not one of them was able to do more than lie down or walk about; yet so effective was the arnica, that on the fourth all were able to sit up. I consider, that, more than to anything else, I owe the success of our great undertaking to arnica and paregoric.

My men being restored to health and strength, my main perplexity, now, was how to get them down the mountain again. I was not willing to expose the brave fellows to the perils, fatigues, and hardships of that fearful route again if it could be helped. First I thought of balloons; but of course I had to give that idea up, for balloons were not procurable. I thought of several other expedients, but upon consideration discarded them, for cause. But at last I hit it. I was aware that the movement of glaciers is an established fact, for I had read it in Baedeker; so I resolved to take passage for Zermatt on the great Gorner Glacier.

Very good. The next thing was, how to get down to the glacier comfortably,—for the mule-road to it was long, and winding, and wearisome. I set my mind at work, and soon thought out a plan. One looks straight down upon the vast frozen river called the Gorner Glacier, from the Gorner Grat, a sheer precipice 1200 feet high. We had 154 umbrellas,—and what is an umbrella but a parachute?

I mentioned this noble idea to Harris, with enthusiasm, and was about to order the Expedition to form on the Gorner Grat, with their umbrellas, and prepare for flight by platoons, each platoon in command of a guide, when Harris stopped me and urged me not to be too hasty. He asked me if this method of descending the Alps had ever been tried before. I said no, I had not heard of an instance. Then, in his opinion, it was a matter of considerable gravity; in his opinion it would not be well to send the whole command over the cliff at once: a better way would be to send down a single individual, first, and see how he fared.

I saw the wisdom of this idea instantly. I said as much, and thanked my agent cordially, and told him to take his umbrella and try the thing right away, and wave his hat when he got down, if he struck in a soft place, and then I would ship the rest right along.

Harris was greatly touched with this mark of confidence, and said so, in a voice that had a perceptible tremble in it; but at the same time he said he did not feel himself worthy of so conspicuous a favor; that it might cause jealousy in the command, for there were plenty who would not hesitate to say he had used underhand means to get the appointment, whereas his conscience would bear him witness that he had not sought it at all, nor even, in his secret heart, desired it.

I said these words did him extreme credit, but that he must not throw away the imperishable distinction of being the first man to descend an Alp per parachute, simply to save the feelings of some envious underlings. No, I said, he *must* accept the appointment,—it was no longer an invitation, it was a command.

He thanked me with effusion, and said that putting the thing in this form removed every objection. He retired, and soon returned with his umbrella, his eyes flaming with gratitude and his cheeks pallid with joy. Just then the head guide passed along. Harris's expression changed to one of infinite tenderness, and he said,—

"That man did me a cruel injury four days ago, and I said in my heart he should live to perceive and confess that the only noble revenge a man can take upon his enemy is to return good for evil. I resign in his favor. Appoint him."—

I threw my arms around the generous fellow and said,—

"Harris, you are the noblest soul that lives. You shall not regret this sublime act, neither shall the world fail to know of it. You shall have opportunities far transcending this one, too, if I live,—remember that."

I called the head guide to me and appointed him on the spot. But the thing aroused no enthusiasm in him. He did not take to the idea at all. He said,—

"Tie myself to an umbrella and jump over the Gorner Grat! Excuse me, there are a great many pleasanter roads to the devil than that."

Upon a discussion of the subject with him, it appeared that he considered the project distinctly and decidedly dangerous. I was not convinced, yet I was not willing to try the experiment in any risky way—that is, in a way that might cripple the strength and efficiency of the Expedition. I was about at my wits' end when it occurred to me to try it on the Latinist.

He was called in. But he declined, on the plea of inexperience, diffidence in public, lack of curiosity, and I don't know what all. Another man declined on account of a cold in the head; thought he ought to avoid exposure. Another could not jump well—never *could* jump well—did not believe he could jump so far without long and patient practice. Another was afraid it was going to rain, and his umbrella had a hole in it. Everybody had an excuse. The result was what the reader has by this time guessed: the most magnificent idea that was ever conceived had to be abandoned, from sheer lack of a person with enterprise enough to carry it out. Yes, I actually had to give that thing up,—whilst doubtless I should live to see somebody use it and take all the credit from me.

Well, I had to go overland—there was no other way. I marched the Expedition down the steep and tedious mule-path and took up as good a position as I could upon the middle of the Glacier—because Baedeker said the middle part travels the fastest. As a measure of economy, however, I put some of the heavier baggage on the shoreward parts, to go as slow freight.

I waited and waited, but the Glacier did not move. Night was coming on, the darkness began to gather—still we did not budge. It occurred to me then, that there might be a time-table in Baedeker: it would be well to find out the hours of starting. I called for the book—it could not be found. Bradshaw would certainly contain a time-table: but no Bradshaw could be found.

Very well, I must make the best of the situation. So I pitched the tents, picketed the animals, milked the cows, had supper, paregoricked the men, established the watch, and went to bed—with orders to call me as soon as we came in sight of Zermatt.

I awoke about half past ten, next morning, and looked around. We hadn't budged a peg! At first I could not understand it: then it occurred to me that the old thing must be aground. So I cut down some trees and rigged a spar on the starboard and another on the port side, and fooled away upwards of three hours trying to spar her off. But it was no use. She was half a mile wide and fifteen or twenty miles long, and there was no telling just whereabouts she *was* aground. The men began to show uneasiness, too, and presently they came flying to me with ashy faces, saying she had sprung a leak.

Nothing but my cool behavior at this critical time saved us from another panic. I ordered them to show me the place. They led me to a spot where a huge boulder lay in a deep pool of clear and brilliant water. It did look like a pretty bad leak, but I kept that to myself. I made a pump and set the men to work to pump out the glacier. We made a success of it. I perceived, then, that it was not a leak at all. This boulder had descended from a precipice and stopped on the ice in the middle of the glacier, and the sun had warmed it up, every day, and consequently it had melted its way deeper and deeper into the ice, until at last it reposed, as we had found it, in a deep pool of the clearest and coldest water.

Presently Baedeker was found again, and I hunted eagerly for the time-table. There was none. The book simply said the glacier was moving all the time. This was satisfactory, so I shut up the book and chose a good position to view the scenery as we passed along. I stood there some time enjoying the trip, but at last it occurred to me that we did not seem to be gaining any on the scenery. I said to myself, "This confounded old thing's aground again, sure,"—and opened Baedeker to see if I could run across any remedy for these annoying interruptions. I soon found a sentence which threw a dazzling light upon the matter. It said, "The Gorner Glacier travels at an average rate of a little less than an inch a day." I have seldom felt so outraged. I have seldom had my confidence so wantonly betrayed. I made a small calculation: 1 inch a day, say 30 feet a year; estimated distance to Zermatt, 3 1-18 miles. Time required to go by glacier, *a little over five hundred years!* I said to myself, "I can *walk* it quicker —and before I will patronize such a fraud as this, I will do it."

When I revealed to Harris the fact that the passenger-part of this glacier,—the central part,—the lighting-express part, so to speak,—was not due in Zermatt till the summer of 2378, and that the baggage, coming along the slow edge, would not arrive until some generations later, he burst out with,—

"That is European management, all over! An inch a day—think of that! Five hundred years to go a trifle over three miles! But I am not a bit surprised. It's a Catholic glacier. You can tell by the look of it. And the management."

I said, no, I believed nothing but the extreme end of it was in a Catholic canton.

"Well, then, it's a government glacier," said Harris. "It's all the same. Over here the government runs everything,—so everything's slow; slow, and ill managed. But with us, everything's done by private enterprise—and then there ain't much lolling around, you can depend on it. I wish Tom Scott could get his hands on this torpid old slab once,—you'd see it take a different gait from this."

I said I was sure he would increase the speed, if there was trade enough to justify it.

"He'd *make* trade," said Harris. "That's the difference between governments and individuals. Governments don't care, individuals do. Tom Scott would take all the trade; in two years Gorner stock would go to 200, and inside of two more you would see all the other glaciers under the hammer for taxes." After a reflective pause, Harris added, "A little less than an inch a day; a little less than an *inch,* mind you. Well, I'm losing my reverence for glaciers."

I was feeling much the same way myself. I have traveled by canal boat, ox-wagon, raft, and by the Ephesus and Smyrna railway; but when it comes down to good solid honest slow motion, I bet my money on the glacier. As a means of passenger transportation, I consider the glacier a failure; but as a vehicle for slow freight, I think she fills the bill. In the matter of putting the fine shades on that line of business, I judge she could teach the Germans something.

I ordered the men to break camp and prepare for the land journey to Zermatt. At this moment a most interesting find was made; a dark object, bedded in the glacial ice, was cut out with the ice-axes, and it proved to be a piece of the undressed skin of some animal,—a hair trunk, perhaps; but a close inspection disabled the hair trunk theory, and further discussion and examination exploded it entirely,—that is, in the opinion of all the scientists except the one who had advanced it. This one clung to his theory with the affectionate fidelity characteristic of originators of scientific theories, and afterwards won many of the first scientists of the age to his view, by a very able pamphlet which he wrote, entitled, "Evidences going to show that the hair trunk, in a wild state, belonged to the early glacial period, and roamed the wastes of chaos in company with the cave bear, primeval man, and the other Oolitics of the Old Silurian family."

Each of our scientists had a theory of his own, and put forward an animal of his own as a candidate for the skin. I sided with the geologist of the Expedition in the belief that this patch of skin had once helped to cover a Siberian elephant, in some old forgotten age—but we divided there, the geologist believing that this discovery proved that Siberia had formerly been located where Switzerland is now, whereas I held the opinion that it merely proved that the primeval Swiss was not the dull savage he is represented to have been, but was a being of high intellectual development, who liked to go to the menagerie.

We arrived that evening, after many hardships and adventures, in some fields close to the great ice-arch where the mad Visp boils and surges out from under the foot of the great Gorner Glacier, and here we camped, our perils over and our magnificent undertaking successfully completed. We marched into Zermatt the next day, and were received with the most lavish honors and applause. A document, signed and sealed by all the authorities, was given to me which established and endorsed the fact that I had made the ascent of the Riffelberg. This I wear around my neck, and it will be buried with me when I am no more.

From *A Tramp Abroad,* 1880

The Awful German Language

A little learning makes the whole world kin.—Proverbs xxxii, 7.

I went often to look at the collection of curiosities in Heidelberg Castle, and one day I surprised the keeper of it with my German. I spoke entirely in that language. He was greatly interested; and after I had talked awhile he said my German was very rare, possibly a "unique;" and wanted to add it to his museum.

If he had known what it had cost me to acquire my art, he would also have known that it would break any collector to buy it. Harris and I had been hard at work on our German during several weeks at that time, and although we had made good progress, it had been accomplished under great difficulty and annoyance, for three of our teachers had died in the meantime. A person who has not studied German can form no idea of what a perplexing language it is.

Surely there is not another language that is so slip-shod and systemless, and so slippery and elusive to the grasp. One is washed about in it, hither and hither, in the most helpless way; and when at last he thinks he has captured a rule which offers firm ground to take a rest on amid the general rage and turmoil of the ten parts of speech, he turns over the page and reads, "Let the pupil make careful note of the following *exceptions*." He runs his eye down and finds that there are more exceptions to the rule than instances of it. So overboard he goes again, to hunt for another Ararat and find another quicksand. Such has been, and continues to be, my experience. Every time I think I have got one of these four confusing "cases" where I am master of it, a seemingly insignificant preposition intrudes itself into my sentence, clothed with an awful and unsuspected power, and crumbles the ground from under me. For instance, my book inquires after a certain bird—(it is always inquiring after things which are of no sort of consequence to anybody): "Where is the bird?" Now the answer to this question,—according to the book,—is that the bird is waiting in the blacksmith shop on account of the rain. Of course no bird would do that, but then you must stick to the book. Very well, I begin to ciper out the German for that answer. I begin at the wrong end, necessarily, for that is the German idea. I say to myself, "*Regen*, (rain,) is masculine—or maybe it is feminine—or possibly neuter—it is too much trouble to look, now. Therefore, it is either *der* (the) Regen, or *die* (the) Regen, or *das* (the) Regen, according to which gender it may turn out to be when I look. In the interest of science, I will cipher it out on the hypothesis that it is masculine. Very well—then *the* rain is *der* Regen, if it is simply in the quiescent state of being *mentioned,* without enlargement or discussion—Nominative case; but if this rain is lying around, in a kind of a general way on the ground, it is then definitely located, it is *doing something*—that is, *resting,* (which is one of the German grammar's ideas of doing something,) and this throws the rain into the Dative case, and makes it *dem* Regen. However, this rain is not resting, but is doing something *actively,*—it is falling,—to interfere with the bird, likely,—and this indicates *movement,* which has the effect of sliding it into the Accusative case and changing *dem* Regen into *den* Regen." Having completed the grammatical horoscope of this matter, I answer up confidently and state in German that the bird is staying in the blacksmith shop "wegen (on account of) *den* Regen." Then the teacher lets me softly down with the remark that whenever the word "wegen" drops into a sentence, it *always* throws that subject into the *Genitive* case, regardless of consequences—and that therefore this bird staid in the blacksmith shop "wegen *des* Regens."

N. B. I was informed, later, by a higher authority, that there was an "exception" which permits one to say "wegen *den* Regen" in certain peculiar and complex circumstances, but that this exception is not extended to anything *but* rain.

There are ten parts of speech, and they are all troublesome. An average sentence, in a German newspaper, is a sublime and impressive curiosity; it occupies a quarter of a column; it contains all the ten parts of speech—not in regular order, but mixed; it is built mainly of compound words constructed by the writer on the spot, and not to be found in any dictionary—six or seven words compacted into one, without joint or seam—that is, without hyphens; it treats of fourteen or fifteen different subjects, each enclosed in a parenthesis of its own, with here and there extra parentheses which re-enclose three or four of the minor parentheses, making pens within pens; finally, all the parentheses and re-parentheses are massed together between a couple of king-parentheses, one of which is placed in the first line of the majestic sentence and the other in the middle of the last line of it—*after which comes the* VERB, and you find out for the first time what the man has been talking about; and after the verb—merely by way of ornament, as far as I can make out,—the writer shovels in "*haben sind gewesen gehabt haben geworden sein,*" or words to that effect, and the monument is finished. I suppose that this closing hurrah is in the nature of the flourish to a man's signature—not necessary, but pretty. German books are easy enough to read when you hold them before the looking-glass or stand on your head,—so as to reverse the construction,—but I think that to learn to read and understand a German newspaper is a thing which must always remain an impossibility to a foreigner.

Yet even the German books are not entirely free from attacks of the Parenthesis distemper—though they are usually so mild as to cover only a few lines, and therefore when you at last get down to the verb it carries some meaning to your mind because you are able to remember a good deal of what has gone before.

Now here is a sentence from a popular and excellent German novel,—with a slight parenthesis in it. I will make a perfectly literal translation, and throw in the parenthesis-marks and some hyphens for the assistance of the reader,—though in the original there are no parenthesis-marks or hyphens, and the reader is left to flounder through to the remote verb the best way he can:

"But when he, upon the street, the (in-satin-and-silk-covered-now-very-unconstrainedly-after-the-newest-fashion-dressed) government counsellor's wife *met,*" etc., etc.*

That is from "The Old Mamselle's Secret," by Mrs. Marlitt. And that sentence is constructed upon the most approved German model. You observe how far that verb is from the reader's base of operations; well, in a German newspaper they put their verb away over on the next page; and I have heard that sometimes after stringing along on exciting preliminaries and parentheses for a column or two, they get in a hurry and have to go to press without getting to the verb at all. Of course, then, the reader is left in a very exhausted and ignorant state.

* Wenn er aber auf der Strasse der in Sammt und Seide gehüllten jetz sehr ungenirt nach der neusten mode gekleideten Regierungsräthin begegnet."—M. T.

We have the Parenthesis disease in our literature, too; and one may see cases of it every day in our books and newspapers: but with us it is the mark and sign of an unpractised writer or a cloudy intellect, whereas with the Germans it is doubtless the mark and sign of a practised pen and of the presence of that sort of luminous intellectual fog which stands for clearness among these people. For surely it is *not* clearness,—it necessarily can't be clearness. Even a jury would have penetration enough to discover that. A writer's ideas must be a good deal confused, a good deal out of line and sequence, when he starts out to say that a man met a counsellor's wife in the street, and then right in the midst of this so simple undertaking halts these approaching people and makes them stand still until he jots down an inventory of the woman's dress. That is manifestly absurd. It reminds a person of those dentists who secure your instant and breathless interest in a tooth by taking a grip on it with the forceps, and then stand there and drawl through a tedious anecdote before they give the dreaded jerk. Parentheses in literature and dentistry are in bad taste.

The Germans have another kind of parenthesis, which they make by splitting a verb in two and putting half of it at the beginning of an exciting chapter and the *other half* at the end of it. Can any one conceive of anything more confusing than that? These things are called "separable verbs." The German grammar is blistered all over with separable verbs; and the wider the two portions of one of them are spread apart, the better the author of the crime is pleased with his performance. A favorite one is *reiste ab,*—which means, *departed.* Here is an example which I culled from a novel and reduced to English:

"The trunks being now ready, he DE- after kissing his mother and sisters, and once more pressing to his bosom his adored Gretchen, who, dressed in simple white muslin, with a single tuberose in the ample folds of her rich brown hair, had tottered feebly down the stairs, still pale from the terror and excitement of the past evening, but longing to lay her poor aching head yet once again upon the breast of him whom she loved more dearly than life itself, PARTED."

However, it is not well to dwell too much on the separable verbs. One is sure to lose his temper early; and if he sticks to the subject, and will not be warned, it will at last either soften his brain or petrify it. Personal pronouns and adjectives are a fruitful nuisance in this language, and should have been left out. For instance, the same sound, *sie,* means *you,* and it means *she,* and it means *her,* and it means *it,* and it means *they,* and it means *them.* Think of the ragged poverty of a language which has to make one word do the work of six,—and a poor little weak thing of only three letters at that. But mainly, think of the exasperation of never knowing which of these meanings the speaker is trying to convey. This explains why, whenever a person says *sie* to me, I generally try to kill him, if a stranger.

Now observe the Adjective. Here was a case where simplicity would have been an advantage; therefore, for no other reason, the inventor of this language complicated it all he could. When we wish to speak of our "good friend or friends," in our enlightened tongue, we stick to the one form and have no trouble or hard feeling about it; but with the German tongue it is different. When a German gets his hands on an adjective, he declines it, and keeps on declining it until the common sense is all declined out of it. It is as bad as Latin. He says, for instance:

SINGULAR

Nominative—Mein gut*er* Freund, my good friend.
Genitive—Mein*es* gut*en* Freund*es,* of my good friend.
Dative—Mein*em* gut*en* Freund, to my good friend.
Accusative—Mein*en* gut*en* Freund, my good friend.

PLURAL

N.—Mein*e* gut*en* Freund*e,* my good friends.
G.—Mein*er* gut*en* Freund*e,* of my good friends.
D.—Mein*en* gut*en* Freund*en,* to my good friends.
A.—Mein*e* gut*en* Freund*e,* my good friends.

Now let the candidate for the asylum try to memorize those variations, and see how soon he will be elected. One might better go without friends in Germany than take all this trouble about them. I have shown what a bother it is to decline a good (male) friend; well, this is only a third of the work, for there is a variety of new distortions of the adjective to be learned when the object is feminine, and still another when the object is neuter. Now there are more adjectives in this language than there are black cats in Switzerland, and they must all be as elaborately declined as the examples above suggested. Difficult?—troublesome?—these words cannot describe it. I heard a Californian student in Heidelberg, say, in one of his calmest moods, that he would rather decline two drinks than one German adjective.

The inventor of the language seems to have taken pleasure in complicating it in every way he could think of. For instance, if one is casually referring to a house, *Haus,* or a horse, *Pferd,* or a dog, *Hund,* he spells these words as I have indicated; but if he is referring to them in the Dative case, he sticks on a foolish and unnecessary *e* and spells them Hause, Pferde, Hunde. So, as an added *e* often signifies the plural, as the *s* does with us, the new student is likely to go on for a month making twins out of a Dative dog before he discovers his mistake; and on the other hand, many a new student who could ill afford loss, has bought and paid for two dogs and only got one of them, because he ignorantly bought that dog in the Dative singular when he really supposed he was talking plural,—which left the law on the seller's side, of course, by the strict rules of grammar, and therefore a suit for recovery could not lie.

In German, all the Nouns begin with a capital letter. Now that is a good idea; and a good idea, in this language, is necessarily conspicuous from its lonesomeness. I consider this capitalizing of nouns a good idea, because by reason of it you are almost always able to tell a noun the minute you see it. You fall into error occasionally, because you mistake the name of a person for the name of a thing, and waste a good deal of time trying to dig a meaning out of it. German names almost always do mean something, and this helps to deceive the student. I translated a passage one day, which said that "the infuriated tigress broke loose and utterly ate up the unfortunate fir-forest," (*Tannenwald.*) When I was girding up my loins to doubt this, I found out that Tannenwald, in this instance, was a man's name.

Every noun has a gender, and there is no sense or system in the distribution; so the gender of each must be learned separately and by heart. There is no other way. To do this, one has to have a memory like a memorandum book. In German, a young lady has no sex, while a turnip has. Think what overwrought reverence that shows for the turnip, and what callous disrespect for the girl. See how it looks in print—I translate this from a conversation in one of the best of the German Sunday-school books:

"*Gretchen.* Wilhelm, where is the turnip?

"*Wilhelm.* She has gone to the kitchen.

"*Gretchen.* Where is the accomplished and beautiful English maiden?

"*Wilhelm.* It has gone to the opera."

To continue with the German genders: a tree is male, its buds are female, its leaves are neuter; horses are sexless, dogs are male, cats are female,—Tomcats included, of course; a person's mouth, neck, bosom, elbows, fingers, nails, feet, and body, are of the male sex, and his head is male or neuter according to the word selected to signify it, and *not* according to the sex of the individual who wears it,—for in Germany all the women wear either male heads or sexless ones; a person's nose, lips, shoulders, breast, hands, hips, and toes are of the female sex; and his hair, ears, eyes, chin, legs, knees, heart, and conscience, haven't any sex at all. The inventor of the language probably got what he knew about a conscience from hearsay.

Now, by the above dissection, the reader will see that in Germany a man may *think* he is a man, but when he comes to look into the matter closely, he is bound to have his doubts; he finds that in sober truth he is a most ridiculous mixture; and if he ends by trying to comfort himself with the thought that he can at least depend on a third of this mess as being manly and masculine, the humiliating second thought will quickly remind him that in this respect he is no better off than any woman or cow in the land.

In the German it is true that by some oversight of the inventor of the language, a Woman is a female; but a Wife, (*Weib,*) is not,—which is unfortunate. A wife, here, has no sex; she is neuter; so, according to the grammar, a fish is *he,* his scales are *she,* but a fishwife is neither. To describe a wife as sexless, may be called under-description; that is bad enough, but over-description is surely worse. A German speaks of an Englishman as the *Engländer;* to change the sex, he adds *inn,* and that stands for Englishwoman,—*Engländerinn.* That seems descriptive enough, but still it is not exact enough for a German; so he precedes the word with that article which indicates that the creature to follow is feminine, and writes it down thus: "*die* Engländer*inn,*"—which means "the *she-Englishwoman.*" I consider that that person is over-described.

Well, after the student has learned the sex of a great number of nouns, he is still in a difficulty, because he finds it impossible to persuade his tongue to refer to things as "*he*" and "*she,*" and "*him*" and "*her,*" which it has been always accustomed to refer to as "*it.*" When he even frames a German sentence in his mind, with the hims and hers in the right places, and then works up his courage to the utterance-point, it is no use,—the moment he begins to speak his tongue flies the track and all those labored males and females come out as "*its*." And even when he is reading German to himself, he always calls those things "*it;*" whereas he ought to read in this way:

*TALE OF THE FISHWIFE AND ITS SAD FATE.**

It is a bleak Day. Hear the Rain, how he pours, and the Hail, how he rattles; and see the Snow, how he drifts along, and oh the Mud, how deep he is! Ah the poor Fishwife, it is stuck fast in the Mire; it has dropped its Basket of Fishes; and its Hands have been cut by the Scales as it seized some of the falling Creatures; and one Scale has even got into its Eye, and it cannot get her out. It opens its Mouth to cry for Help; but if any Sound comes out of him, alas he is drowned by the raging of the Storm. And now a Tomcat has got one of the Fishes and she will surely escape with him. No, she bites off a Fin, she holds her in her Mouth—will she swallow her? No, the Fishwife's brave Mother-Dog deserts his Puppies and rescues the Fin,—which he eats, himself, as his Reward. O, horror, the Lightning has struck the Fish-basket; he sets him on Fire; see the Flame, how she licks the doomed Utensil with her red and angry Tongue; now she attacks the helpless Fishwife's Foot,—she burns him up, all but the big Toe, and even *she* is partly consumed; and still she spreads, still she waves her fiery Tongues; she attacks the Fishwife's Leg and destroys *it;* she attacks its Hand and destroys *her;* she attacks its poor worn Garment and destroys *her* also; she attacks its Body and consumes *him;* she wreathes herself about its Heart and *it* is consumed; next about its Breast, and in a Moment *she* is a Cinder; now she reaches its Neck,—*he* goes; now its Chin,—*it* goes; now its Nose,—*she* goes. In another Moment, except Help come, the Fishwife will be no more. Time presses,—is there none to succor and save? Yes! Joy, joy, with flying Feet the she-Englishwoman comes! But alas, the generous she-Female is too late: where now is the fated Fishwife? It has ceased from its Sufferings, it has gone to a better Land; all that is left of it for its loved Ones to lament over, is this poor smouldering Ash-heap. Ah, woful, woful Ash-heap! Let us take him up tenderly, reverently,

* I capitalize the nouns in the German (and ancient English) fashion.—M. T.

upon the lowly Shovel, and bear him to his long Rest, with the Prayer that when he rises again it will be in a Realm where he will have one good square responsible Sex, and have it all to himself, instead of having a mangy lot of assorted Sexes scattered all over him in Spots.

There, now, the reader can see for himself that this pronoun-business is a very awkward thing for the unaccustomed tongue.

I suppose that in all languages the similarities of look and sound between words which have no similarity in meaning are a fruitful source of perplexity to the foreigner. It is so in our tongue, and it is notably the case in the German. Now there is that troublesome word *vermählt:* to me it has so close a resemblance,—either real or fancied,—to three or four other words, that I never know whether it means despised, painted, suspected, or married; until I look in the dictionary, and then I find it means the latter. There are lots of such words, and they are a great torment. To increase the difficulty there are words which *seem* to resemble each other, and yet do not; but they make just as much trouble as if they did. For instance, there is the word *vermiethen,* (to let, to lease, to hire); and the word *verheirathen,* (another way of saying to *marry.*) I heard of an Englishman who knocked at a man's door in Heidelberg and proposed, in the best German he could command, to "verheirathen" that house. Then there are some words which mean one thing when you emphasize the first syllable, but mean something very different if you throw the emphasis on the last syllable. For instance, there is a word which means a runaway, or the act of glancing through a book, according to the placing of the emphasis; and another word which signifies to *associate* with a man, or to *avoid* him, according to where you put the emphasis,—and you can generally depend on putting it in the wrong place and getting into trouble.

There are some exceedingly useful words in this language. *Schlag,* for example; and *Zug.* There are three-quarters of a column of Schlags in the dictionary, and a column and a half of Zugs. The word Schlag means Blow, Stroke, Dash, Hit, Shock, Clap, Slap, Time, Bar, Coin, Stamp, Kind, Sort, Manner, Way, Apoplexy, Wood-Cutting, Enclosure, Field, Forest-Clearing. This is its simple and *exact* meaning,—that is to say, its restricted, its fettered meaning; but there are ways by which you can set it free, so that it can soar away, as on the wings of the morning, and never be at rest. You can hang any word you please to its tail, and make it mean anything you want to. You can begin with *Schlag-ader,* which means artery, and you can hang on the whole dictionary, word by word, clear through the alphabet to *Schlag-wasser,* which means bilge-water,—and including *Schlag-mutter,* which means mother-in-law.

Just the same with *Zug.* Strictly speaking, Zug means Pull, Tug, Draught, Procession, March, Progress, Flight, Direction, Expedition, Train, Caravan, Passage, Stroke, Touch, Line, Flourish, Trait of Character, Feature, Lineament, Chess-move, Organ-stop, Team, Whiff, Bias, Drawer, Propensity, Inhalation, Disposition: but that thing which it does *not* mean,—when all its legitimate pendants have been hung on, has not been discovered yet.

One cannot over-estimate the usefulness of Schlag and Zug. Armed just with these two, and the word *Also,* what cannot the foreigner on German soil accomplish? The German word *Also* is the equivalent of the English phrase "You know," and does not mean anything at all,—in *talk,* though it sometimes does in print. Every time a German opens his mouth an *Also* falls out; and every time he shuts it he bites one in two that was trying to *get* out.

Now, the foreigner, equipped with these three noble words, is master of the situation. Let him talk right along, fearlessly; let him pour his indifferent German forth, and when he lacks for a word, let him heave a *Schlag* into the vacuum; all the chances are, that it fits it like a plug; but if it doesn't, let him promptly heave a *Zug* after it; the two together can hardly fail to bung the hole; but if, by a miracle, they *should* fail, let him simply say *Also!* and this will give him a moment's chance to think of the needful word. In Germany, when you load your conversational gun it is always best to throw in a *Schlag* or two and a *Zug* or two; because it doesn't make any difference how much the rest of the charge may scatter, you are bound to bag something with *them.* Then you blandly say *Also,* and load up again. Nothing gives such an air of grace and elegance and unconstraint to a German or an English conversation as to scatter it full of "Also's" or "You-knows."

In my note-book I find this entry:

July 1.—In the hospital, yesterday, a word of thirteen syllables was successfully removed from a patient,—a North-German from near Hamburg; but as most unfortunately the surgeons had opened him in the wrong place, under the impression that he contained a panorama, he died. The sad event has cast a gloom over the whole community.

That paragraph furnishes a text for a few remarks about one of the most curious and notable features of my subject,—the length of German words. Some German words are so long that they have a perspective. Observe these examples:

Freundschaftsbezeigungen.
Dilletantenaufdringlichkeiten.
Stadtverordnetenversammlungen.

These things are not words, they are alphabetical processions. And they are not rare; one can open a German newspaper any time and see them marching majestically across the page,—and if he has any imagination he can see the banners and hear the music, too. They impart a martial thrill to the meekest subject. I take a great interest in these curiosities. Whenever I come across a good one, I stuff it and put it in my museum. In this way I have made quite a valuable collection. When I get duplicates, I exchange with other collectors, and thus increase the variety of my stock. Here are some specimens which I lately bought at an auction sale of the effects of a bankrupt bric-a-brac hunter:

GENERALSTAATSVERORDNETENVERSAMMLUNGEN.
ALTERTHUMSWISSENSCHAFTEN.
KINDERBEWAHRUNGSANSTALTEN.
UNABHAENGIGKEITSERKLAERUNGEN.
WIEDERHERSTELLUNGSBESTREBUNGEN.
WAFFENSTILLSTANDSUNTERHANDLUNGEN.

Of course when one of these grand mountain ranges goes stretching across the printed page, it adorns and ennobles that literary landscape,—but at the same time it is a great distress to the new student, for it blocks up his way; he cannot crawl under it, or climb over it or tunnel through it. So he resorts to the dictionary for help; but there is no help there. The dictionary must draw the line somewhere,—so it leaves this sort of words out. And it is right, because these long things are hardly legitimate words, but are rather combinations of words, and the inventor of them ought to have been killed. They are compound words, with the hyphens left out. The various words used in building them are in the dictionary, but in a very scattered condition; so you can hunt the materials out, one by one, and get at the meaning at last, but it is a tedious and harassing business. I have tried this process upon some of the above examples. "Freundschaftsbezeigungen" seems to be "Friendship demonstrations," which is only a foolish and clumsy way of saying "demonstrations of friendship." "Unabhaengigkeitserklaerungen" seems to be "Independencedeclarations," which is no improvement upon "Declarations of Independence," as far as I can see. "Generalstaatsverordnetenversammlungen" seems to be "Generalstatesrepresentativesmeetings," as nearly as I can get at it,—a mere rhythmical, gushy euphuism for "meetings of the legislature," I judge. We used to have a good deal of this sort of crime in our literature, but it has gone out, now. We used to speak of a thing as a "never-to-be-forgotten" circumstance, instead of cramping it into the simple and sufficient word "memorable" and then going calmly about our business as if nothing had happened. In those days we were not content to embalm the thing and bury it decently, we wanted to build a monument over it.

But in our newspapers the compounding-disease lingers a little to the present day, but with the hyphens left out, in the German fashion. This is the shape it takes: instead of saying "Mr. Simmons, clerk of the county and district courts, was in town yesterday," the new form puts it thus: "Clerk of the County and District Court Simmons was in town yesterday." This saves neither time nor ink, and has an awkward sound besides. One often sees a remark like this in our papers: "*Mrs.* Assistant District Attorney Johnson returned to her city residence yesterday for the season." That is a case of really unjustifiable compounding; because it not only saves no time or trouble, but confers a title on Mrs. Johnson which she has no right to. But these little instances are trifles indeed, contrasted with the ponderous and dismal German system of piling jumbled compounds together. I wish to submit the following local item, from a Mannheim journal, by way of illustration:

"In the daybeforeyesterdayshortlyaftereleveno'clock Night, the inthistownstandingtavern called "The Wagoner" was downburnt. When the fire to the onthedownburninghouseresting Stork's Nest reached, flew the parent Storks away. But when the bytheraging, firesurrounded Nest *itself* caught Fire, straightway plunged the quickreturning Mother-Stork into the Flames and died, her Wings over her young ones outspread."

Even the cumbersome German construction is not able to take the pathos out of that picture,—indeed it somehow seems to strengthen it. This item is dated away back yonder months ago. I could have used it sooner, but I was waiting to hear from the Father-Stork. I am still waiting.

"*Also!*" If I have not shown that the German is a difficult language, I have at least intended to do it. I have heard of an American student who was asked how he was getting along with his German, and who answered promptly: "I am not getting along at all. I have worked at it hard for three level months, and all I have got to show for it is one solitary German phrase,—'*Zwei glas,*'" (two glasses of beer.) He paused a moment, reflectively, then added with feeling. "But I've got that *solid!*"

And if I have not also shown that German is a harassing and infuriating study, my execution has been at fault, and not my intent. I heard lately of a worn and sorely tried American student who used to fly to a certain German word for relief when he could bear up under his aggravations no longer,—the only word in the whole language whose sound was sweet and precious to his ear and healing to his lacerated spirit. This was the word *Damit.* It was only the *sound* that helped him, not the meaning*; and so, at last, when he learned that the emphasis was not on the first syllable, his only stay and support was gone, and he faded away and died.

I think that a description of any loud, stirring, tumultuous episode must be tamer in German than in English. Our descriptive words of this character have such a deep, strong, resonant sound, while their German equivalents do seem so thin and mild and energyless. Boom, burst, crash, roar, storm, bellow, blow, thunder, explosion; howl, cry, shout, yell, groan; battle, hell. These are magnificent words; they have a force and magnitude of sound befitting the things which they describe. But their German equivalents would be ever so nice to sing the children to sleep with, or else my awe-inspiring ears were made for display and not for superior usefulness in analyzing sounds. Would any man want to die in a battle which was called by so tame a term as a *Schlacht?* Or would not a consumptive feel too much bundled up, who was about to go out, in a shirt collar and a seal ring, into a storm which the bird-song word *Gewitter* was employed to describe? And observe the strongest of the several German equivalents for explosion,—*Ausbruch.* Our word Toothbrush is more powerful than that. It seems to me that the Germans could do worse than import it into their language to describe particularly tremendous ex-

* It merely means, in its general sense, "*herewith.*"—M. T.

plosions with. The German word for hell,—Hölle,—sounds more like *helly* than anything else; therefore, how necessarily chipper, frivolous and unimpressive it is. If a man were told in German to go there, could he really rise to the dignity of feeling insulted?

Having pointed out, in detail, the several vices of this language, I now come to the brief and pleasant task of pointing out its virtues. The capitalizing of the nouns, I have already mentioned. But far before this virtue stands another,—that of spelling a word according to the sound of it. After one short lesson in the alphabet, the student can tell how any German word is pronounced, without having to ask; whereas in our language if a student should inquire of us "What does B, O, W, spell?" we should be obliged to reply, "Nobody can tell what it spells, when you set it off by itself,—you can only tell by referring to the context and finding out what it signifies,—whether it is a thing to shoot arrows with, or a nod of one's head, or the forward end of a boat."

There are some German words which are singularly and powerfully effective. For instance, those which describe lowly, peaceful and affectionate home life; those which deal with love, in any and all forms, from mere kindly feeling and honest good will toward the passing stranger, clear up to courtship; those which deal with outdoor Nature, in its softest and loveliest aspects,—with meadows, and forests, and birds and flowers, the fragrance and sunshine of summer, and the moonlight of peaceful winter nights; in a word, those which deal with any and all forms of rest, repose, and peace; those also which deal with the creatures and marvels of fairyland; and lastly and chiefly, in those words which express pathos, is the language surpassingly rich and effective. There are German songs which can make a stranger to the language cry. That shows that the *sound* of the words is correct,—it interprets the meanings with truth and with exactness; and so the ear is informed, and through the ear, the heart.

The Germans do not seem to be afraid to repeat a word when it is the right one. They repeat it several times, if they choose. That is wise. But in English when we have used a word a couple of times in a paragraph, we imagine we are growing tautological, and so we are weak enough to exchange it for some other word which only approximates exactness, to escape what we wrongly fancy is a greater blemish. Repetition may be bad, but surely inexactness is worse.

There are people in the world who will take a great deal of trouble to point out the faults in a religion or a language, and then go blandly about their business without suggesting any remedy. I am not that kind of a person. I have shown that the German language needs reforming. Very well, I am ready to reform it. At least I am ready to make the proper suggestions. Such a course as this might be immodest in another; but I have devoted upwards of nine full weeks, first and last, to a careful and critical study of this tongue, and thus have acquired a confidence in my ability to reform it which no mere superficial culture could have conferred upon me.

In the first place, I would leave out the Dative Case. It confuses the plurals; and besides, nobody ever knows when he is in the Dative Case, except he discover it by accident,—and then he does not know when or where it was that he got into it, or how long he has been in it, or how he is ever going to get out of it again. The Dative Case is but an ornamental folly,—it is better to discard it.

In the next place, I would move the Verb further up to the front. You may load up with ever so good a Verb, but I notice that you never really bring down a subject with it at the present German range,—you only cripple it. So I insist that this important part of speech should be brought forward to a position where it may be easily seen with the naked eye.

Thirdly, I would import some strong words from the English tongue,—to swear with, and also to use in describing all sorts of vigorous things in a vigorous way.*

Fourthly, I would reorganize the sexes, and distribute them according to the will of the Creator. This as a tribute of respect, if nothing else.

Fifthly, I would do away with those great long compounded words; or require the speaker to deliver them in sections, with intermissions for refreshments. To wholly do away with them would be best, for ideas are more easily received and digested when they come one at a time than when they come in bulk. Intellectual food

* *"Verdammt,"* and its variations and enlargements, are words which have plenty of meaning, but the *sounds* are so mild and ineffectual that German ladies can use them without sin. German ladies who could not be induced to commit a sin by any persuasion or compulsion, promptly rip out one of these harmless little words when they tear their dresses or don't like the soup. It sounds about as wicked as our "My gracious." German ladies are constantly saying, "Ach! Gott!" "Mein Gott!" "Gott im Himmel!" "Herr Gott!" "Der Herr Jesus!" etc. They think our ladies have the same custom, perhaps, for I once heard a gentle and lovely old German lady say to a sweet young American girl, "The two languages are so alike—how pleasant that is; we say 'Ach! Gott!' you say *'Goddam.'* "—M. T.

is like any other; it is pleasanter and more beneficial to take it with a spoon than with a shovel.

Sixthly, I would require a speaker to stop when he is done, and not hang a string of those useless "haben sind gewesen gehabt haben geworden seins" to the end of his oration. This sort of gew-gaws undignify a speech, instead of adding a grace. They are therefore an offense, and should be discarded.

Seventhly, I would discard the Parenthesis. Also the re-Parenthesis, the re-re-parenthesis, and the re-re-re-re-re-re-parenthesis, and likewise the final wide-reaching all-enclosing King-parenthesis. I would require every individual, be he high or low, to unfold a plain straightforward tale, or else coil it and sit on it and hold his peace. Infractions of this law should be punishable with death.

And eighthly and lastly, I would retain *Zug* and *Schlag*, with their pendants, and discard the rest of the vocabulary. This would simplify the language.

I have now named what I regard as the most necessary and important changes. These are perhaps all I could be expected to name for nothing; but there are other suggestions which I can and will make in case my proposed application shall result in my being formally employed by the government in the work of reforming the language.

My philological studies have satisfied me that a gifted person ought to learn English (barring spelling and pronouncing), in 30 hours, French in 30 days, and German in 30 years. It seems manifest, then, that the latter tongue ought to be trimmed down and repaired. If it is to remain as it is, it ought to be gently and reverently set aside among the dead languages, for only the dead have time to learn it.

A FOURTH OF JULY ORATION IN THE GERMAN TONGUE, DELIVERED AT A BANQUET OF THE ANGLO-AMERICAN CLUB OF STUDENTS BY THE AUTHOR OF THIS BOOK.

Gentlemen: Since I arrived, a month ago, in this old wonderland, this vast garden of Germany, my English tongue has so often proved a useless piece of baggage to me, and so troublesome to carry around, in a country where they haven't the checking system for luggage, that I finally set to work, last week, and learned the German language. Also! Es freüt mich dass dies so ist, denn es muss, in ein hauptsächlich degree, höflich sein, dass man aüf ein occasion like this, sein Rede in die Sprache des Landes worin he boards, aüssprechen soll. Dafür habe ich, aüs reinische Verlegenheit,—no Vergangenheit,—no, I mean Höflichkeit,—aüs reinische Höflichkeit habe ich resolved to tackle this business in the German language, üm Gottes willen! Also! Sie müssen so freündlich sein, ünd verzeih mich die interlarding von ein oder zwei Englischer Worte, hie ünd da, denn ich finde dass die deütsche is not a very copious language, and so when you've really got anything to say, you've got to draw on a language that can stand the strain.

Wenn aber man kann nicht meinem Rede verstehen, so werde ich ihm später dasselbe übersetz, wenn er solche Dienst verlangen wollen haben werden sollen sein hätte. (I don't know what wollen haben werden sollen sein hätte means, but I notice they always put it at the end of a German sentence—merely for general literary gorgeousness, I suppose.)

This is a great and justly honored day,—a day which is worthy of the veneration in which it is held by the true patriots of all climes and nationalities,—a day which offers a fruitful theme for thought and speech; ünd meinem Freünde,—no, mein*en* Freünd*en*,—mein*es* Freünd*es*,—well, take your choice, they're all the same price; I don't know which one is right,—also! ich habe gehabt haben worden gewesen sein, as Goethe says, in his Paradise Lost,—ich,—ich,—that is to say,—ich,—but let us change cars.

Also! Die Anblick so viele Grossbrittanischer ünd Amerikanischer hier zusammengetroffen in Bruderliche concord, ist zwar a welcome and inspiriting spectacle. And what has moved you to it? Can the terse German tongue rise to the expression of this impulse? Is it Freündschaftsbezeigüngenstadtverordnetenversammlungenfamilieneigenthümlichkeiten? Nein, o nein! This is a crisp and noble word, but it fails to pierce the marrow of the impulse which has gathered this friendly meeting and produced diese Anblick,—eine Anblick welche ist güt zu sehen,—güt für die Aügen in a foreign land and a far country,—eine Anblick solche als in die gewönliche Heidelberger phrase nennt man ein "schönes Aussicht!" Ja, freilich natürlich wahrscheinlich ebensowohl! Also! Die Aussicht aüf dem Königstuhl mehr grösserer ist, aber geistlische sprechend nicht so schön, lob' Gott! Because sie sind hier zusammengetroffen, in Bruderlichem concord, ein grossen Tag zu feiern, whose high benefits were not for one land and one locality only, but have conferred a measure of good upon all lands that know liberty today, and love it. Hŭndert Jahre vorüber, waren die Engländer ŭnd die Amerikaner Feinde; aber heŭte sind sie herzlichen Freŭnde, Gott sei Dank! May this good fellowship endure; may these banners here blended in amity, so remain; may they never any more wave over opposing hosts, or be stained with blood which was kindred, is kindred, and always will be kindred, until a line drawn upon a map shall be able to say, "*This* bars the ancestral blood from flowing in the veins of the descendant!"

From *A Tramp Abroad*, 1880

Keelboat Talk and Manners

By way of illustrating keelboat talk and manners, and that now-departed and hardly-remembered raft-life, I will throw in, in this place, a chapter from a book which I have been working at, by fits and starts, during the past five or six years, and may possibly finish in the course of five or six more. The book is a story which details some passages in the life of an ignorant village boy, Huck Finn, son of the town drunkard of my time out west, there. He has run away from his persecuting father, and from a persecuting good widow who wishes to make a nice, truth-telling, respectable boy of him; and with him a slave of the widow's has also escaped. They have found a fragment of a lumber raft (it is high water and dead summer time), and are floating down the river by night, and hiding in the willows by day,—bound for Cairo,—whence the negro will seek freedom in the heart of the free States. But in a fog, they pass Cairo without knowing it. By and by they begin to suspect the truth, and Huck Finn is persuaded to end the dismal suspense by swimming down to a huge raft which they have seen in the distance ahead of them, creeping aboard under cover of the darkness, and gathering the needed information by eavesdropping:—

But you know a young person can't wait very well when he is impatient to find a thing out. We talked it over, and by and by Jim said it was such a black night, now, that it wouldn't be no risk to swim down to the big raft and crawl aboard and listen,—they would talk about Cairo, because they would be calculating to go ashore there for a spree, maybe, or anyway they would send boats ashore to buy whiskey or fresh meat or something. Jim had a wonderful level head, for a nigger: he could most always start a good plan when you wanted one.

I stood up and shook my rags off and jumped into the river, and struck out for the raft's light. By and by, when I got down nearly to her, I eased up and went slow and cautious. But everything was all right—nobody at the sweeps. So I swum down along the raft till I was most abreast the camp fire in the middle, then I crawled aboard and inched along and got in amongst some bundles of shingles on the weather side of the fire. There was thirteen men there—they was the watch on deck of course. And a mighty rough-looking lot, too. They had a jug, and tin cups, and they kept the jug moving. One man was singing—roaring, you may say; and it wasn't a nice song—for a parlor anyway. He roared through his nose, and strung out the last word of every line very long. When he was done they all fetched a kind of Injun war-whoop, and then another was sung. It begun:—

"There was a woman in our towdn,
  In our towdn did dwed'l (dwell,)
She loved her husband dear-i-lee,
  But another man twyste as wed'l.

Singing too, riloo, riloo, riloo,
  Ri-too, riloo, rilay - - - e,
She loved her husband dear-i-lee,
  But another man twyste as wed'l."

And so on—fourteen verses. It was kind of poor, and when he was going to start on the next verse one of them said it was the tune the old cow died on; and another one said, "Oh, give us a rest." And another one told him to take a walk. They made fun of him till he got mad and jumped up and begun to cuss the crowd, and said he could lam any thief in the lot.

They was all about to make a break for him, but the biggest man there jumped up and says:—

"Set whar you are, gentlemen. Leave him to me; he's my meat."

Then he jumped up in the air three times and cracked his heels together every time. He flung off a buckskin coat that was all hung with fringes, and says, "You lay thar tell the chawin-up's done;" and flung his hat down, which was all over ribbons, and says, "You lay thar tell his sufferins is over."

Then he jumped up in the air and cracked his heels together again and shouted out:—

"Whoo-oop! I'm the old original iron-jawed, brass-mounted, copper-bellied corpse-maker from the wilds of Arkansaw!—Look at me! I'm the man they call Sudden Death and General Desolation! Sired by a hurricane, dam'd by an earthquake, half-brother to the cholera, nearly related to the small-pox on the mother's side! Look at me! I take nineteen alligators and a bar'l of whiskey for breakfast when I'm in robust health, and a bushel of rattlesnakes and a dead body when I'm ailing! I split the everlasting rocks with my glance, and I squench the thunder when I speak! Whoo-oop! Stand back and give me room according to my strength! Blood's my natural drink, and the wails of the dying is music to my ear! Cast your eye on me, gentlemen!—and lay low and hold your breath, for I'm bout to turn myself loose!"

All the time he was getting this off, he was shaking his head and looking fierce, and kind of swelling around in a little circle, tucking up his wristbands, and now and then straightening up and beating his breast with his fist, saying, "Look at me, gentlemen!" When he got through, he jumped up and cracked his heels together three times, and let off a roaring "whoo-oop! I'm the bloodiest son of a wildcat that lives!"

Then the man that had started the row tilted his old slouch hat down over his right eye; then he bent stooping forward, with his back sagged and his south end sticking out far, and his fists a-shoving out and drawing in in front of him, and so went around in a little circle about three times, swelling himself up and breathing hard. Then he straightened, and jumped up and cracked his heels together three times before he lit again (that made them cheer), and he begun to shout like this:—

"Whoo-oop! bow your neck and spread, for the kingdom of sorrow's a-coming! Hold me down to the earth, for I feel my powers a-working! whoo-oop! I'm a child of sin, *don't* let me get a start! Smoked glass, here, for all! Don't attempt to look at me with the naked eye, gentlemen! When I'm playful I use the meridians of longitude and parallels of latitude for a seine, and drag the Atlantic Ocean for whales! I scratch my head with the lightning and purr myself to sleep with the thunder! When I'm cold, I bile the Gulf of Mexico and bathe in it; when I'm hot I fan myself with an equinoctial storm; when I'm thirsty I reach up and suck a cloud dry like a sponge; when I range the earth hungry, famine follows in my tracks! Whoo-oop! Bow your neck and spread! I put my hand on the sun's face and make it night in the earth; I bite a piece out of the moon and hurry the seasons; I shake myself and crumble the mountains! Contemplate me through leather—*don't* use the naked eye! I'm the man with a petrified heart and biler-iron bowels! The massacre of isolated communities is the pastime of my idle moments, the destruction of nationalities the serious business of my life! The boundless vastness of the great American desert is my enclosed property, and I bury my dead on my own premises!" He jumped up and cracked his heels together three times before he lit (they cheered him again), and as he come down he shouted out: "Whoo-oop! bow your neck and spread, for the pet child of calamity's a-coming!"

Then the other one went to swelling around and blowing again—the first one—the one they called Bob; next, the Child of Calamity chipped in again, bigger than ever; then they both got at it at the same time, swelling round and round each other and punching their fists most into each other's faces, and whooping and jawing like Injuns; then Bob called the Child names, and the Child called him names back again: next, Bob called him a heap rougher names and the Child come back at him with the very worst kind of language; next, Bob knocked the Child's hat off, and the Child picked it up and kicked Bob's ribbony hat about six foot; Bob went and got it and said never mind, this warn't going to be the last of this thing, because he was a man that never forgot and never forgive, and so the Child better look out, for there was a time a-coming, just as sure as he was a living man, that he would have to answer to him with the best blood in his body. The Child said no man was willinger than he was for that time to come, and he would give Bob fair warning, *now,* never to cross his path again, for he could never rest till he had waded in his blood, for such was his nature, though he was sparing him now on account of his family, if he had one.

Both of them was edging away in different directions, growling and shaking their heads and going on about what they was going to do; but a little black-whiskered chap skipped up and says:—

"Come back here, you couple of chicken-livered cowards, and I'll thrash the two of ye!"

And he done it, too. He snatched them, he jerked them this way and that, he booted them around, he knocked them sprawling faster than they could get up. Why, it warn't two minutes till they begged like dogs—and how the other lot did yell and laugh and clap their hands all the way through, and shout "Sail in, Corpse-Maker!" "Hi! at him again, Child of Calamity!" "Bully for you, little Davy!" Well, it was a perfect pow-wow for a while. Bob and the Child had red noses and black eyes when they got through. Little Davy made them own up that they was sneaks and cowards and not fit to eat with a dog or drink with a nigger; then Bob and the Child shook hands with each other, very solemn, and said they had always respected each other and was willing to let bygones be bygones. So then they washed their faces in the river; and just then there was a loud order to stand by for a crossing, and some of them went forward to man the sweeps there, and the rest went aft to handle the aftersweeps.

I laid still and waited for fifteen minutes, and had a smoke out of a pipe that one of them left in reach; then the crossing was finished, and they stumped back and had a drink around and went to talking and singing again. Next they got out an old fiddle, and one played, and another patted juba, and the rest turned themselves loose on a regular old-fashioned keel-boat break-down. They couldn't keep that up very long without getting winded, so by and by they settled around the jug again.

They sung "jolly, jolly raftsman's the life for me," with a rousing chorus, and then they got to talking about differences betwixt hogs, and their different kind of habits; and next about women and their different ways; and next about the best ways to put out houses that was afire; and next about what ought to be done with the Injuns; and next about what a king had to do, and how much he got; and next about how to make cats fight; and next about what to do when a man has fits; and next about differences betwixt clear-water rivers and muddy-water ones. The man they called Ed said the muddy Mississippi water was wholesomer to drink than the clear water of the Ohio; he said if you let a pint of this yaller Mississippi water settle, you would have about a half to three quarters of an inch of mud in the bottom, according to the stage of the river, and then it warn't no better then Ohio water—what you wanted to do was to keep it stirred up—and when the river was low, keep mud on hand to put in and thicken the water up the way it ought to be.

The Child of Calamity said that was so; he said there was nutritiousness in the mud, and a man that drunk Mississippi water could grow corn in his stomach if he wanted to. He says:—

"You look at the graveyards; that tells the tale. Trees won't grow worth shucks in a Cincinnati graveyard, but in a Sent Louis graveyard they grow upwards of eight hundred foot high. It's all on account of the water the people drunk before they laid up. A Cincinnati corpse don't richen a soil any."

And they talked about how Ohio water didn't like to mix with Mississippi water. Ed said if you take the Mississippi on a rise when the Ohio is low, you'll find a wide band of clear water all the way down the east side of the Mississippi for a hundred mile or more, and the minute you get out a quarter of a mile from shore and pass the line, it is all thick and yaller the rest of the way across. Then they talked about how to keep tobacco from getting mouldy, and from that they went into ghosts and told about a lot that other folks had seen; but Ed says:—

"Why don't you tell something that you've seen yourselves? Now let me have a say. Five years ago I was on a raft as big as this, and right along here it was a bright moonshiny night, and I was on watch and boss of the stabboard oar forrard, and one of my pards was a man named Dick Allbright, and he come along to where I was sitting, forrard—gaping and stretching, he was—and stooped down on the edge of the raft and washed his face in the river, and come and set down by me and got out his pipe, and had just got it filled, when he looks up and says,—

"'Why looky-here,' he says, 'ain't that Buck Miller's place, over yander in the bend?'

"'Yes,' says I, 'it is—why?' He laid his pipe down and leant his head on his hand, and says,—

"'I thought we'd be furder down.' I says,—

"'I thought it too, when I went off watch'—we was standing six hours on and six off—'but the boys told me,' I says, 'that the raft didn't seem to hardly move, for the last hour,'—says I, 'though she's a slipping along all right, now,' says I. He give a kind of a groan, and says,—

"'I've seed a raft act so before, along here,' he says, ''pears to me the current has most quit above the head of this bend durin' the last two years,' he says.

"Well, he raised up two or three times, and looked away off and around on the water. That started me at it, too. A body is always doing what he sees somebody else doing, though there mayn't be no sense in it. Pretty soon I see a black something floating on the water away off to stabboard and quartering behind us. I see he was looking at it, too. I says,—

"'What's that?' He says, sort of pettish,—

"'Tain't nothing but an old empty bar'l.'

"'An empty bar'l!' says I, 'why,' says I, 'a spy-glass is a fool to *your* eyes. How can you tell it's an empty bar'l?' He says,—

"'I don't know; I reckon it ain't a bar'l, but I thought it might be,' says he.

"'Yes,' I says, 'so it might be, and it might be anything else, too; a body can't tell nothing about it, such a distance as that,' I says.

"We hadn't nothing else to do, so we kept on watching it. By and by I says,—

"'Why looky-here, Dick Allbright, that thing's a-gaining on us, I believe.'

"He never said nothing. The thing gained and gained, and I judged it must be a dog that was about tired out. Well, we swung down into the crossing, and the thing floated across the bright streak of the moonshine, and, by George, it *was* a bar'l. Says I,—

"'Dick Allbright, what made you think that thing was a bar'l, when it was a half a mile off,' says I. Says he,—

"'I don't know.' Says I,—

"'You tell me, Dick Allbright.' He says,—

"'Well, I knowed it was a bar'l; I've seen it before; lots has seen it; they says it's a hanted bar'l.'

"I called the rest of the watch, and they come and stood there, and I told them what Dick said. It floated right along abreast, now, and didn't gain any more. It was about twenty foot off. Some was for having it aboard, but the rest didn't want to. Dick Allbright said rafts that had fooled with it had got bad luck by it. The captain of the watch said he didn't believe in it. He said he reckoned the bar'l gained on us because it was in a little better current than what we was. He said it would leave by and by.

"So then we went to talking about other things, and we had a song, and then a breakdown; and after that the captain of the watch called for another song; but it was clouding up, now, and the bar'l stuck right thar in the same place, and the song didn't seem to have much warm-up to it, somehow, and so they didn't finish it, and there warn't any cheers, but it sort of dropped flat, and nobody said anything for a minute. Then everybody tried to talk at once, and one chap got off a joke, but it warn't no use, they didn't laugh, and even the chap that made the joke didn't laugh at it, which ain't usual. We all just settled down glum, and watched the bar'l, and was oneasy and oncomfortable. Well, sir, it shut down black and still, and then the wind begin to moan around, and next the lightning begin to play and the thunder to grumble. And pretty soon there was a regular storm, and in the middle of it a man that was running aft stumbled and fell and sprained his ankle so that he had to lay up. This made the boys shake their heads. And every time the lightning come, there was that bar'l with the blue lights winking around it. We was always on the look-out for it. But by and by, towards dawn, she was gone. When the day come we couldn't see her anywhere, and we warn't sorry, neither.

"But next night about half-past nine, when there was songs and high jinks going on, here she comes again, and took her old roost on the stabboard side. There warn't no more high jinks. Everybody got solemn; nobody talked; you couldn't get anybody to do anything but set around moody and look at the bar'l. It begun to cloud up again. When the watch changed, the off watch stayed up, 'stead of turning in. The storm ripped and roared around all night, and in the middle of it another man tripped and sprained his ankle, and had to knock off. The bar'l left towards day, and nobody see it go.

"Everybody was sober and down in the mouth all day. I don't mean the kind of sober that comes of leaving liquor alone,—not that. They was quiet, but they all drunk more than usual,—not together,— but each man sidled off and took it private, by himself.

"After dark the off watch didn't turn in; nobody sung, nobody talked; the boys didn't scatter around, neither; they sort of huddled together, forrard; and for two hours they set there, perfectly still, looking steady in the one direction, and heaving a sigh once in a while. And then, here comes the bar'l again. She took up her old place. She staid there all night; nobody turned in. The storm come on again, after midnight. It got awful dark; the rain poured down; hail, too; the thunder boomed and roared and bellowed; the wind blowed a hurricane; and the lightning spread over everything in big sheets of glare, and showed the whole raft as plain as day; and the river lashed up white as milk as far as you could see for miles, and there was that bar'l jiggering along, same as ever. The captain ordered the watch to man the after sweeps for a crossing, and nobody would go,—no more sprained ankles for them, they said. They wouldn't even *walk* aft. Well then, just then the sky split wide open, with a crash, and the lightning killed two men of the after watch, and crippled two more. Crippled them how, says you? Why, *sprained their ankles!*

"The bar'l left in the dark betwixt lightnings, towards dawn. Well, not a body eat a bite at breakfast that morning. After that the men loafed around, in twos and threes, and talked low together. But none of them herded with Dick Allbright. They all give him the cold shake. If he come around where any of the men was, they split up and sidled away. They wouldn't man the sweeps with him. The captain had all the skiffs hauled up on the raft, alongside of his wigwam, and wouldn't let the dead men be took ashore to be planted; he didn't believe a man that got ashore would come back; and he was right.

"After night come, you could see pretty plain that there was going to be trouble if that bar'l come again; there was such a muttering going on. A good many wanted to kill Dick Allbright, because he'd seen the bar'l on other trips, and that had an ugly look. Some wanted to put him ashore. Some said, let's all go ashore in a pile, if the bar'l comes again.

"This kind of whispers was still going on, the men being bunched together forrard watching for the bar'l, when, lo and behold you, here she comes again. Down she comes, slow and steady, and settles into her old tracks. You could a heard a pin drop. Then up comes the captain, and says:—

"'Boys, don't be a pack of children and fools; I don't want this bar'l to be dogging us all the way to Orleans, and *you* don't; well, then, how's the best way to stop it? Burn it up,—that's the way. I'm going to fetch it aboard,' he says. And before anybody could say a word, in he went.

"He swum to it, and as he come pushing it to the raft, the men spread to one side. But the old man got it aboard and busted in the head, and there was a baby in it! Yes sir, a stark naked baby. It was Dick Allbright's baby; he owned up and said so.

"'Yes,' he says, a-leaning over it, 'yes, it is my own lamented darling, my poor lost Charles William Allbright deceased,' says he,—for he could curl his tongue around the bulliest words in the language when he was a mind to, and lay them before you without a jint started, anywheres. Yes, he said he used to live up at the head of this bend, and one night he choked his child, which was crying, not intending to kill it,—which was prob'ly a lie,—and then he was scared, and buried it in a bar'l, before his wife got home, and off he went, and struck the northern trail and went to rafting; and this was the third year that the bar'l had chased him. He said the bad luck always begun light, and lasted till four men was killed, and then the bar'l didn't come any more after that. He said if the men would stand it one more night,—and was a-going on like that,—but the men had got enough. They started to get out a boat to take him ashore and lynch him, but he grabbed the little child all of a sudden and jumped overboard with it hugged up to his breast and shedding tears, and we never see him again in this life, poor old suffering soul, nor Charles William neither."

"*Who* was shedding tears?" says Bob; "was it Allbright or the baby?"

"Why, Allbright, of course; didn't I tell you the baby was dead? Been dead three years—how could it cry?"

"Well, never mind how it could cry—how could it *keep* all that time?" says Davy. "You answer me that."

"I don't know how it done it," says Ed. "It done it though—that's all I know about it."

"Say—what did they do with the bar'l?" says the Child of Calamity.

"Why, they hove it overboard, and it sunk like a chunk of lead."

"Edward, did the child look like it was choked?" says one.

"Did it have its hair parted?" says another.

"What was the brand on that bar'l, Eddy?" says a fellow they called Bill.

"Have you got the papers for them statistics, Edmund?" says Jimmy.

"Say, Edwin, was you one of the men that was killed by the lightning?" says Davy.

"Him? O, no, he was both of 'em," says Bob. Then they all haw-hawed.

"Say, Edward, don't you reckon you'd better take a pill? You look bad—don't you feel pale?" says the Child of Calamity.

"O, come, now, Eddy," says Jimmy, "show up; you must a kept part of that bar'l to prove the thing by. Show us the bunghole—*do*—and we'll all believe you."

"Say, boys," says Bill, "less divide it up. Thar's thirteen of us. I can swaller a thirteenth of the yarn, if you can worry down the rest."

Ed got up mad and said they could all go to some place which he ripped out pretty savage, and then walked off aft cussing to himself, and they yelling and jeering at him, and roaring and laughing so you could hear them a mile.

"Boys, we'll split a watermelon on that," says the Child of Calamity; and he come rummaging around in the dark amongst the shingle bundles where I was, and put his hand on me. I was warm and soft and naked; so he says "Ouch!" and jumped back.

"Fetch a lantern or a chunk of fire here, boys—there's a snake here as big as a cow!"

So they run there with a lantern and crowded up and looked in on me.

"Come out of that, you beggar!" says one.

"Who are you?" says another.

"What are you after here? Speak up prompt, or overboard you go."

"Snake him out, boys. Snatch him out by the heels."

I began to beg, and crept out amongst them trembling. They looked me over, wondering, and the Child of Calamity says:—

"A cussed thief! Lend a hand and less heave him overboard!"

"No," says Big Bob, "less get out the paint-pot and paint him a sky blue all over from head to heel, and *then* heave him over!"

"Good! that's it. Go for the paint, Jimmy."

When the paint come, and Bob took the brush and was just going to begin, the others laughing and rubbing their hands, I begun to cry, and that sort of worked on Davy, and he says:—

"'Vast there! He's nothing but a cub. I'll paint the man that tetches him!"

So I looked around on them, and some of them grumbled and growled, and Bob put down the paint, and the others didn't take it up.

"Come here to the fire, and less see what you're up to here," says Davy. "Now set down there and give an account of yourself. How long have you been aboard here?"

"Not over a quarter of a minute, sir," says I.

"How did you get dry so quick?"

"I don't know, sir. I'm always that way, mostly."

"Oh, you are, are you? What's your name?"

I warn't going to tell my name. I didn't know what to say, so I just says:

"Charles William Allbright, sir."

Then they roared—the whole crowd; and I was mighty glad I said that, because maybe laughing would get them in a better humor.

When they got done laughing, Davy says:—

"It won't hardly do, Charles William. You couldn't have growed this much in five year, and you was a baby when you come out of the bar'l, you know, and dead at that. Come, now, tell a straight story, and nobody'll hurt you, if you ain't up to anything wrong. What *is* your name?"

"Aleck Hopkins, sir. Aleck James Hopkins."

"Well, Aleck, where did you come from, here?"

"From a trading scow. She lays up the bend yonder. I was born on her. Pap has traded up and down here all his life; and he told me to swim off here, because when you went by he said he would like to get some of you to speak to a Mr. Jonas Turner, in Cairo, and tell him—"

"Oh, come!"

"Yes, sir, it's as true as the world; Pap he says—"

"Oh, your grandmother!"

They all laughed, and I tried again to talk, but they broke in on me and stopped me.

"Now, looky-here," says Davy; "you're scared, and so you talk wild. Honest, now, do you live in a scow, or is it a lie?"

"Yes, sir, in a trading scow. She lays up at the head of the bend. But I warn't born in her. It's our first trip."

"Now you're talking! What did you come aboard here, for? To steal?"

"No, sir, I didn't.—It was only to get a ride on the raft. All boys does that."

"Well, I know that. But what did you hide for?"

"Sometimes they drive the boys off."

"So they do. They might steal. Looky-here; if we let you off this time, will you keep out of these kind of scrapes hereafter?"

"'Deed I will, boss. You try me."

"All right, then. You ain't but little ways from shore. Overboard with you, and don't you make a fool of yourself another time this way.—Blast it, boy, some raftsmen would rawhide you till you were black and blue!"

I didn't wait to kiss good-bye, but went overboard and broke for shore. When Jim come along by and by, the big raft was away out of sight around the point. I swum out and got aboard, and was mighty glad to see home again.

The boy did not get the information he was after, but his adventure has furnished the glimpse of the departed raftsman and keelboatman which I desire to offer in this place.

From *Life on the Mississippi*, 1883

An Incognito Exploded

After a close study of the face of the pilot on watch, I was satisfied that I had never seen him before; so I went up there. The pilot inspected me; I re-inspected the pilot. These customary preliminaries over, I sat down on the high bench, and he faced about and went on with his work. Every detail of the pilot-house was familiar to me, with one exception,—a large-mouthed tube under the breast-board. I puzzled over that thing a considerable time; then gave up and asked what it was for.

"To hear the engine-bells through."

It was another good contrivance which ought to have been invented half a century sooner. So I was thinking, when the pilot asked,—

"Do you know what this rope is for?"

I managed to get around this question, without committing myself.

"Is this the first time you were ever in a pilot-house?"

I crept under that one.

"Where are you from?"

"New England."

"First time you have ever been West?"

I climbed over this one.

"If you take an interest in such things, I can tell you what all these things are for."

I said I should like it.

"This," putting his hand on a backing-bell rope, "is to sound the fire-alarm; this," putting his hand on a go-a-head bell, "is to call the texas-tender; this one," indicating the whistle-lever, "is to call the captain"—and so he went on, touching one object after another, and reeling off his tranquil spool of lies.

I had never felt so like a passenger before. I thanked him, with emotion, for each new fact, and wrote it down in my note-book. The pilot warmed to his opportunity, and proceeded to load me up in the good old-fashioned way. At times I was afraid he was going to rupture his invention; but it always stood the strain, and he pulled through all right. He drifted, by easy stages, into revealments of the river's marvellous eccentricities of one sort and another, and backed them up with some pretty gigantic illustrations. For instance,—

"Do you see that little bowlder sticking out of the water yonder? well, when I first came on the river, that was a solid ridge of rock, over sixty feet high and two miles long. All washed away but that." [This with a sigh.]

I had a mighty impulse to destroy him, but it seemed to me that killing, in any ordinary way, would be too good for him.

Once, when an odd-looking craft, with a vast coal-scuttle slanting aloft on the end of a beam, was steaming by in the distance, he indifferently drew attention to it, as one might to an object grown wearisome through familiarity, and observed that it was an "alligator boat."

"An alligator boat? What's it for?"

"To dredge out alligators with."

"Are they so thick as to be troublesome?"

"Well, not now, because the government keeps them down. But they used to be. Not everywhere; but in favorite places, here and there, where the river is wide and shoal—like Plum Point, and Stack Island, and so on—places they call alligator beds."

"Did they actually impede navigation?"

"Years ago, yes, in very low water; there was hardly a trip, then, that we didn't get aground on alligators."

It seemed to me that I should certainly have to get out my tomahawk. However, I restrained myself and said,—

"It must have been dreadful."

"Yes, it was one of the main difficulties about piloting. It was so hard to tell anything about the water; the damned things shift around so—never lie still five minutes at a time. You can tell a wind-reef, straight off, by the look of it; you can tell a break; you can tell a sand-reef—that's all easy; but an alligator reef doesn't show up, worth anything. Nine times in ten you can't tell where the water is; and when you *do* see where it is, like as not it ain't there when *you* get there, the devils have swapped around so, meantime. Of course there were some few pilots that could judge of alligator water nearly as well as they could of any other kind, but they had to have natural talent for it; it wasn't a thing a body could *learn,* you had to be born with it. Let me see: there was Ben Thornburg, and Beck Jolly, and Squire Bell, and Horace Bixby, and Major Downing, and John Stevenson, and Billy Gordon, and Jim Brady, and George Ealer, and Billy Youngblood—all A 1 alligator pilots. *They* could tell alligator water as far as another Christian could tell whiskey. Read it?—Ah, *couldn't* they, though! I only wish I had as many dollars as they could read alligator water a mile and a half off. Yes, and it paid them to do it, too. A good alligator pilot could always get fifteen hundred dollars a month. Nights, other people had to lay up for alligators, but those fellows never laid up for alligators; they never laid up for anything but fog. They could *smell* the best alligator water—so it was said; I don't know whether it was so or not, and I think a body's got his hands full enough if he sticks to just what he knows himself, without going around backing up other people's say-so's, though there's a plenty that ain't backward about doing it, as long as they can roust out something wonderful to tell. Which is not the style of Robert Styles, by as much as three fathom—maybe quarter-*less.*"

[My! Was this Rob Styles?—This moustached and stately figure?—A slim enough cub, in my time. How he has improved in comeliness in five and twenty years—and in the noble art of inflating his facts.] After these musings, I said aloud,—

"I should think that dredging out the alligators wouldn't have done much good, because they could come back again right away."

"If you had had as much experience of alligators as I have, you wouldn't talk like that. You dredge an alligator once and he's *convinced.* It's the last you hear of *him.* He wouldn't come back for pie. If there's one thing that an alligator is more down on than another, it's being dredged. Besides, they were not simply shoved out of the way, the most of the scoopful were scooped aboard; they emptied them into the hold; and when they had got a trip, they took them to Orleans to the Government works."

"What for?"

"Why, to make soldier-shoes out of their hides. All the Government shoes are made of alligator hide. It makes the best shoes in the world. They last five years and they won't absorb water. The alligator fishery is a Government monopoly. All the alligators are Government property—just like the live-oaks. You cut down a live-oak, and Government fines you fifty dollars; you kill an alligator, and up you go for misprision of treason—lucky duck if they don't hang you, too.

And they will, if you're a Democrat. The buzzard is the sacred bird of the South, and you can't touch him; the alligator is the sacred bird of the Government, and you've got to let him alone."

"Do you ever get aground on the alligators now?"

"Oh, no! it hasn't happened for years."

"Well, then, why do they still keep the alligator boats in service?"

"Just for police duty—nothing more. They merely go up and down now and then. The present generation of alligators know them as easy as a burglar knows a rounds-man; when they see one coming, they break camp and go for the woods."

After rounding-out and finishing-up and polishing-off the alligator business, he dropped easily and comfortably into the historical vein, and told of some tremendous feats of half a dozen old-time steamboats of his acquaintance, dwelling at special length upon a certain extraordinary performance of his chief favorite among this distinguished fleet—and then adding:—

"That boat was the 'Cyclone,'—last trip she ever made—she sunk, that very trip—captain was Tom Ballou, the most immortal liar that ever I struck. He couldn't ever seem to tell the truth, in *any* kind of weather. Why, he would make you fairly shudder. He *was* the most scandalous liar! I left him, finally; I couldn't stand it. The proverb says, 'like master, like man;' and if you stay with that kind of a man, you'll come under suspicion by and by, just as sure as you live. He paid first-class wages; but said I, What's wages when your reputation's in danger? So I let the wages go, and froze to my reputation. And I've never regretted it. Reputation's worth everything, ain't it? That's the way I look at it. He had more selfish organs than any seven men in the world—all packed in the stern-sheets of his skull, of course, where they belonged. They weighed down the back of his head so that it made his nose tilt up in the air. People thought it was vanity, but it wasn't, it was malice. If you only saw his foot, you'd take him to be nineteen feet high, but he wasn't; it was because his foot was out of drawing. He was intended to be nineteen feet high, no doubt, if his foot was made first, but he didn't get there; he was only five feet ten. That's what he was, and that's what he is. You take the lies out of him, and he'll shrink to the size of your hat; you take the malice out of him, and he'll disappear. That 'Cyclone' was a rattler to go, and the sweetest thing to steer that ever walked the waters. Set her amidships, in a big river, and just let her go; it was all you had to do. She would hold herself on a star all night, if you let her alone.

You couldn't ever feel her rudder. It wasn't any more labor to steer her than it is to count the Republican vote in a South Carolina election. One morning, just at daybreak, the last trip she ever made, they took her rudder aboard to mend it; I didn't know anything about it; I backed her out from the wood-yard and went a-weaving down the river all serene. When I had gone about twenty-three miles, and made four horribly crooked crossings—"

"Without any rudder?"

"Yes—old Capt. Tom appeared on the roof and began to find fault with me for running such a dark night—"

"Such a *dark night?*—Why, you said—"

"Never mind what I said,—'twas as dark as Egypt *now,* though pretty soon the moon began to rise, and—"

"You mean the *sun*—because you started out just at break of—look here! Was this *before* you quitted the captain on account of his lying, or—"

"It was before—oh, a long time before. And as I was saying, he—"

"But was this the trip she sunk, or was—"

"Oh, no!—months afterward. And so the old man, he—"

"Then she made *two* last trips, because you said—"

He stepped back from the wheel, swabbing away his perspiration, and said—

"Here!" (calling me by name), "*you* take her and lie a while—you're handier at it than I am. Trying to play yourself for a stranger and an innocent!—why, I knew you before you had spoken seven words; and I made up my mind to find out what was your little game. It was to *draw me out.* Well, I let you, didn't I? Now take the wheel and finish the watch; and next time play fair, and you won't have to work your passage."

Thus ended the fictitious-name business. And not six hours out from St. Louis! but I had gained a privilege, anyway, for I had been itching to get my hands on the wheel, from the beginning. I seemed to have forgotten the river, but I hadn't forgotten how to steer a steamboat, nor how to enjoy it, either.

From *Life on the Mississippi,* 1883

The House Beautiful

We took passage in a Cincinnati boat for New Orleans; or on a Cincinnati boat—either is correct; the former is the eastern form of putting it, the latter the western.

Mr. Dickens declined to agree that the Mississippi steamboats were "magnificent," or that they were "floating palaces,"—terms which had always been applied to them; terms which did not over-express the admiration with which the people viewed them.

Mr. Dickens's position was unassailable, possibly; the people's position was certainly unassailable. If Mr. Dickens was comparing these boats with the crown jewels; or with the Taj, or with the Matterhorn; or with some other priceless or wonderful thing which he had seen, they were not magnificent—he was right. The people compared them with what *they* had seen; and, thus measured, thus judged, the boats were magnificent—the term was the correct one, it was not at all too strong. The people were as right as was Mr. Dickens. The steamboats were finer than anything on shore. Compared with superior dwelling-houses and first class hotels in the Valley, they were indubitably magnificent, they were "palaces." To a few people living in New Orleans and St. Louis, they were not magnificent, perhaps; not palaces; but to the great majority of those populations, and to the entire populations spread over both banks between Baton Rouge and St. Louis, they were palaces; they tallied with the citizen's dream of what magnificence was, and satisfied it.

Every town and village along that vast stretch of double river-frontage had a best dwelling, finest dwelling, mansion,—the home of its wealthiest and most conspicuous citizen. It is easy to describe it: large grassy yard, with paling fence painted white—in fair repair; brick walk from gate to door; big, square, two-story "frame" house, painted white and porticoed like a Grecian temple—with this difference, that the imposing fluted columns and Corinthian capitals were a pathetic sham, being made of white pine, and painted; iron knocker; brass door knob—discolored, for lack of polishing. Within, an uncarpeted hall, of planed boards; opening out of it, a parlor, fifteen feet by fifteen—in some instances five or ten feet larger; ingrain carpet; mahogany centre-table; lamp on it, with green-paper shade—standing on a gridiron, so to speak, made of high-colored yarns, by the young ladies of the house, and called a lamp-mat; several books, piled and disposed, with cast-iron exactness, according to an inherited and unchangeable plan; among them, Tupper, much pencilled; also, "Friendship's Offering," and "Affection's Wreath," with their sappy inanities illustrated in die-away mezzotints; also, Ossian; "Alonzo and Melissa;" maybe "Ivanhoe;" also "Album," full of original "poetry" of the Thou-hast-wounded-the-spirit-that-loved-thee breed; two or three goody-goody works—"Shepherd of Salisbury Plain," etc.; current number of the chaste and innocuous Godey's "Lady's Book," with painted fashion-plate of wax-figure women with mouths all alike—lips and eyelids the same size—each five-foot woman with a two-inch wedge sticking from under her dress and letting-on to be half of her foot. Polished air-tight stove (new and deadly invention), with pipe passing through a board which closes up the discarded good old fireplace. On each end of the wooden mantel, over the fireplace, a large basket of peaches and other fruits, natural size, all done in plaster, rudely, or in wax, and painted to resemble the originals—which they don't. Over middle of mantel, engraving—Washington Crossing the Delaware; on the wall by the door, copy of it done in thunder-and-lightning crewels by one of the young ladies—work of art which would have made Washington hesitate about crossing, if he could have foreseen what advantage was going to be taken of it. Piano—kettle in disguise—with music, bound and unbound, piled on it, and on a stand near by: Battle of Prague; Bird Waltz; Arkansas Traveller; Rosin the Bow; Marseilles Hymn; On a Lone Barren Isle (St. Helena); The Last Link is Broken; She wore a Wreath of Roses the Night when last we met; Go, forget me, Why should Sorrow o'er that Brow a Shadow fling; Hours there were to Memory Dearer; Long, Long Ago; Days of Absence; A Life on the Ocean Wave, a Home on the Rolling Deep; Bird at Sea; and spread open on the rack, where the plaintive singer has left it, *Ro*-holl on, silver *moo*-hoon, guide the *trav*-el-lerr his *way*, etc. Tilted pensively against the piano, a guitar—guitar capable of playing the Spanish Fandango by itself, if you give it a start.

Frantic work of art on the wall—pious motto, done on the premises, sometimes in colored yarns, sometimes in faded grasses: progenitor of the "God Bless Our Home" of modern commerce. Framed in black mouldings on the wall, other works of art, conceived and committed on the premises, by the young ladies; being grim black-and-white crayons; landscapes, mostly: lake, solitary sail-boat, petrified clouds, pre-geological trees on shore, anthracite precipice; name of criminal conspicuous in the corner. Lithograph, Napoleon Crossing the Alps. Lithograph, the Grave at St. Helena. Steel-plates, Trumbull's Battle of Bunker Hill, and the Sally from Gibraltar. Copper-plates, Moses Smiting the Rock, and Return of the Prodigal Son. In big gilt frame, slander of the family in oil: papa holding a book ("Constitution of the United States"); guitar leaning against mamma, blue ribbons fluttering from its neck; the young ladies, as children, in slippers and scalloped pantelettes, one embracing toy horse, the other beguiling kitten with ball of yarn, and both simpering up at mamma, who simpers back. These persons all fresh, raw, and red—apparently skinned. Opposite, in gilt frame, grandpa and grandma, at thirty and twenty-two, stiff, old-fashioned, high-collared, puff-sleeved, glaring pallidly out from a background of solid Egyptian night. Under a glass French clock dome, large bouquet of stiff flowers done in corpsy white wax. Pyramidal what-not in the corner, the shelves occupied chiefly with bric-a-brac of the period, disposed with an eye to best effect: shell, with the Lord's Prayer carved on it; another shell—of the long-oval sort, narrow, straight orifice, three inches long, running from end to end—portrait of Washington carved on it; not well done; the shell had Washington's mouth, originally—artist should have built to that. These two are memorials of the long-ago bridal trip to New Orleans and the French Market. Other bric-a-brac: Californian "specimens"—quartz, with gold wart adhering; old Guinea-gold locket, with circlet of ancestral hair in it; Indian arrow-heads, of flint; pair of bead moccasins, from uncle who crossed the Plains; three "alum" baskets of various colors—being skeleton-frame of wire, clothed-on with cubes of crystallized alum in the rock-candy style—works of art which were achieved by the young ladies; their doubles and duplicates to be found upon all what-nots in the land; convention of desiccated bugs and butterflies pinned to a card; painted toy-dog, seated upon bellows-attachment—drops its under jaw and squeaks when pressed upon; sugar-candy rabbit—limbs and features merged together, not strongly defined;

pewter presidential-campaign medal; miniature card-board wood-sawyer, to be attached to the stove-pipe and operated by the heat; small Napoleon, done in wax; spread-open daguerreotypes of dim children, parents, cousins, aunts, and friends, in all attitudes but customary ones; no templed portico at back, and manufactured landscape stretching away in the distance—that came in later, with the photograph; all these vague figures lavishly chained and ringed—metal indicated and secured from doubt by stripes and splashes of vivid gold bronze; all of them too much combed, too much fixed up; and all of them uncomfortable in inflexible Sunday-clothes of a pattern which the spectator cannot realize could ever have been in fashion; husband and wife generally grouped together—husband sitting, wife standing, with hand on his shoulder—and both preserving, all these fading years, some traceable effect of the daguerreotypist's brisk "Now smile, if you please!" Bracketed over what-not—place of special sacredness—an outrage in water-color, done by the young niece that came on a visit long ago, and died. Pity, too; for she might have repented of this in time. Horse-hair chairs, horse-hair sofa which keeps sliding from under you. Window shades, of oil stuff, with milk-maids and ruined castles stencilled on them in fierce colors. Lambrequins dependent from gaudy boxings of beaten tin, gilded. Bedrooms with rag carpets; bedsteads of the "corded" sort, with a sag in the middle, the cords needing tightening; snuffy feather-bed—not aired often enough; cane-seat chairs, splint-bottomed rocker; looking-glass on wall, school-slate size, veneered frame; inherited bureau; wash-bowl and pitcher, possibly—but not certainly; brass candlestick, tallow candle, snuffers. Nothing else in the room. Not a bathroom in the house; and no visitor likely to come along who has ever seen one.

That was the residence of the principal citizen, all the way from the suburbs of New Orleans to the edge of St. Louis. When he stepped aboard a big fine steamboat, he entered a new and marvellous world: chimney-tops cut to counterfeit a spraying crown of plumes—and maybe painted red; pilot-house, hurricane deck, boiler-deck guards, all garnished with white wooden filagree work of fanciful patterns; gilt acorns topping the derricks; gilt deer-horns over the big bell; gaudy symbolical picture on the paddle-box, possibly; big roomy boiler-deck, painted blue, and furnished with Windsor armchairs; inside, a far receding snow-white "cabin;" porcelain knob and oil-picture on every state-room door; curving patterns of filagree-work touched up with gilding, stretching overhead all down the converging vista; big chandeliers every little way, each an April shower of glittering glass-drops; lovely rainbow-light falling everywhere from the colored glazing of the skylights; the whole a long-drawn, resplendent tunnel, a bewildering and soul-satisfying spectacle! in the ladies' cabin a pink and white Wilton carpet, as soft as mush, and glorified with a ravishing pattern of gigantic flowers. Then the Bridal Chamber—the animal that invented that idea was still alive and unhanged, at that day—Bridal Chamber whose pretentious flummery was necessarily overawing to the now tottering intellect of that hosannahing citizen. Every state-room had its couple of cosy clean bunks, and perhaps a looking-glass and a snug closet; and sometimes there was even a wash-bowl and pitcher, and part of a towel which could be told from mosquito netting by an expert—though generally these things were absent, and the shirt-sleeved passengers cleansed themselves at a long row of stationary bowls in the barber shop, where were also public towels, public combs, and public soap.

Take the steamboat which I have just described, and you have her in her highest and finest, and most pleasing, and comfortable, and satisfactory estate. Now cake her over with a layer of ancient and obdurate dirt, and you have the Cincinnati steamer awhile ago referred to. Not all over—only inside; for she was ably officered in all departments except the steward's.

But wash that boat and repaint her, and she would be about the counterpart of the most complimented boat of the old flush times: for the steamboat architecture of the West has undergone no change; neither has steamboat furniture and ornamentation undergone any.

From *Life on the Mississippi*, 1883

Manufactures

Speaking of manufactures reminds me of a talk upon that topic which I heard—which I overheard—on board the Cincinnati boat. I awoke out of a fretted sleep, with a dull confusion of voices in my ears. I listened—two men were talking; subject, apparently, the great inundation. I looked out through the open transom. The two men were eating a late breakfast; sitting opposite each other; nobody else around. They closed up the inundation with a few words—having used it, evidently, as a mere ice-breaker and acquaintanceship-breeder—then they dropped into business. It soon transpired that they were drummers—one belonging in Cincinnati, the other in New Orleans. Brisk men, energetic of movement and speech; the dollar their god, how to get it their religion.

"Now as to this article," said Cincinnati, slashing into the ostensible butter and holding forward a slab of it on his knife-blade, "it's from our house; look at it—smell of it—taste it. Put any test on it you want to. Take your own time—no hurry—make it thorough. There now—what do you say? butter, ain't it? Not by a thundering sight—it's oleomargarine! Yes, sir, that's what it is—oleomargarine. You can't tell it from butter; by George, an *expert* can't. It's from our house. We supply most of the boats in the West; there's hardly a pound of butter on one of them. We are crawling right along—*jumping* right along is the word. We are going to have that entire trade. Yes, and the hotel trade, too. You are going to see the day, pretty soon, when you can't find an ounce of butter to bless yourself with, in any hotel in the Mississippi and Ohio Valleys, outside of the biggest cities. Why, we are turning out oleomargarine *now* by the thousands of tons. And we can sell it so dirt-cheap that the whole country has *got* to take it—can't get around it you see. Butter don't stand any show—there ain't any chance for competition. Butter's had its *day*—and from this out, butter goes to the wall. There's more money in oleomargarine than—why, you can't imagine the business we do. I've stopped in every town, from Cincinnati to Natchez; and I've sent home big orders from every one of them."

And so-forth and so-on, for ten minutes longer, in the same fervid strain. Then New Orleans piped up and said:—

"Yes, it's a first-rate imitation, that's a certainty; but it ain't the only one around that's first-rate. For instance, they make olive-oil out of cotton-seed oil, now-a-days, so that you can't tell them apart."

"Yes, that's so," responded Cincinnati, "and it was a tip-top business for a while. They sent it over and brought it back from France and Italy, with the United States custom-house mark on it to indorse it for genuine, and there was no end of cash in it; but France and Italy broke up the game—of course they naturally would. Cracked on such a rattling impost that cotton-seed olive-oil couldn't stand the raise; had to hang up and quit."

"Oh, it *did*, did it? You wait here a minute."

Goes to his state-room, brings back a couple of long bottles, and takes out the corks—says:—

"There now, smell them, taste them, examine the bottles, inspect the labels. One of 'm's from Europe, the other's never been out of this country. One's European olive-oil, the other's American cotton-seed olive-oil. Tell 'm apart? 'Course you can't. Nobody can. People that want to, can go to the expense and trouble of shipping their oils to Europe and back—it's their privilege; but our firm knows a trick worth six of that. We turn out the whole thing—clean from the word go—in our factory in New Orleans: labels, bottles, oil, everything. Well, no, not labels: been buying *them* abroad—get them dirt-cheap there. You see, there's just one little wee speck, essence, or whatever it is, in a gallon of cotton-seed oil, that gives it a smell, or a flavor, or something—get that out, and you're all right—perfectly easy then to turn the oil into any kind of oil you want to, and there ain't anybody that can detect the true from the false. Well, we know how to get that one little particle out—and we're the only firm that does. And we turn out an olive-oil that is just simply perfect—undetectable! We are doing a ripping trade, too—as I could easily show you by my order-book for this trip. Maybe you'll butter everybody's bread pretty soon, but we'll cotton-seed his salad for him from the Gulf to Canada, and that's a dead-certain thing."

Cincinnati glowed and flashed with admiration. The two scoundrels exchanged business-cards, and rose. As they left the table, Cincinnati said,—

"But you have to have custom-house marks, don't you? How do you manage that?"

I did not catch the answer.

From *Life on the Mississippi,* 1883

The Art of Inhumation

About the same time, I encountered a man in the street, whom I had not seen for six or seven years, and something like this talk followed. I said,—

"But you used to look sad and oldish; you don't now. Where did you get all this youth and bubbling cheerfulness? Give me the address."

He chuckled blithely, took off his shining tile, pointed to a notched pink circlet of paper pasted into its crown, with something lettered on it, and went on chuckling while I read, "J. B—, UNDERTAKER." Then he clapped his hat on, gave it an irreverent tilt to leeward, and cried out,—

"That's what's the matter! It used to be rough times with me when you knew me—insurance-agency business, you know; mighty irregular. Big fire, all right—brisk trade for ten days while people scared; after that, dull policy-business till next fire. Town like this don't have fires often enough—a fellow strikes so many dull weeks in a row that he gets discouraged. But you bet you, *this* is the business! People don't wait for examples to *die*. No, sir, they drop off right along—there ain't any dull spots in the undertaker line. I just started in with two or three little old coffins and a hired hearse, and *now* look at the thing! I've worked up a business here that would satisfy any man, don't care who he is. Five years ago, lodged in an attic; live in a swell house now, with a mansard roof, and all the modern inconveniences."

"Does a coffin pay so well? Is there much profit on a coffin?"

"*Go*-way! How you talk!" Then, with a confidential wink, a dropping of the voice, and an impressive laying of his hand on my arm; "Look here; there's one thing in this world which isn't ever cheap. That's a coffin. There's one thing in this world which a person don't ever try to jew you down on. That's a coffin. There's one thing in this world which a person don't say,—'I'll look around a little, and if I find I can't do better I'll come back and take it.' That's a coffin. There's one thing in this world which a person won't take in pine if he can go walnut; and won't take in walnut if he can go mahogany; and won't take in mahogany if he can go an iron casket with silver door-plate and bronze handles. That's a coffin. And there's one thing in this world which you don't have to worry around after a person to get him to pay for. And *that's* a coffin. Undertaking?—why it's the dead-surest business in Christendom, and the nobbiest.

"Why, just look at it. A rich man won't have anything but your very best; and you can just pile it on, too—pile it on and sock it to him—he won't ever holler. And you take in a poor man, and if you work him right he'll bust himself on a single lay-out. Or especially a woman. F'r instance: Mrs. O'Flaherty comes in—widow—wiping her eyes and kind of moaning. Unhandkerchiefs one eye, bats it around tearfully over the stock; says,—

"'And fhat might ye ask for that wan?'

"'Thirty-nine dollars, madam,' says I.

"'It's a foine big price, sure, but Pat shall be buried like a gintleman, as he was, if I have to work me fingers off for it. I'll have that wan, sor.'

"'Yes, madam,' says I, 'and it is a very good one, too; not costly, to be sure, but in this life we must cut our garment to our clothes, as the saying is.' And as she starts out, I heave in, kind of casually, 'This one with the white satin lining is a beauty, but I am afraid—well, sixty-five dollars *is* a rather—rather—but no matter, I felt obliged to say to Mrs. O'Shaughnessy,—'

"'D'ye mane to soy that Bridget O'Shaughnessy bought the mate to that joo-ul box to ship that dhrunken divil to Purgatory in?'

"'Yes, madam.'

"'Then Pat shall go to heaven in the twin to it, if it takes the last rap the O'Flaherties can raise; and moind you, stick on some extras, too, and I'll give ye another dollar.'

"And as I lay-in with the livery stables, of course I don't forget to mention that Mrs. O'Shaughnessy hired fifty-four dollars' worth of hacks and flung as much style into Dennis's funeral as if he had been a duke or an assassin. And of course she sails in and goes the O'Shaughnessy about four hacks and an omnibus better. That *used* to be, but that's all played now; that is, in this particular town. The Irish got to piling up hacks so, on their funerals, that a funeral left them ragged and hungry for two years afterward; so the priest pitched in and broke it all up. He don't allow them to have but two hacks now, and sometimes only one."

"Well," said I, "if you are so light-hearted and jolly in ordinary times, what *must* you be in an epidemic?"

He shook his head.

"No, you're off, there. We don't like to see an epidemic. An epidemic don't pay. Well, of course I don't mean that, exactly; but it don't pay in proportion to the regular thing. Don't it occur to you, why?"

"No."

"Think."

"I can't imagine. What is it?"

"It's just two things."

"Well, what *are* they?"

"One's Embamming."

"And what's the other?"

"Ice."

"How is that?"

"Well, in ordinary times, a person dies, and we lay him up in ice; one day, two days, maybe three, to wait for friends to come. Takes a lot of it—melts fast. We charge jewelry rates for that ice, and war-prices for attendance. Well, don't you know, when there's an epidemic, they rush 'em to the cemetery the minute the breath's out. No market for ice in an epidemic. Same with Embamming. You take a family that's able to embam, and you've got a soft thing. You can mention sixteen different ways to do it—though there *ain't* only one or two ways, when you come down to the bottom facts of it—and they'll take the highest-priced way, every time. It's human nature—human nature in grief. It don't reason, you see. 'Time being, it don't care a dam. All it wants is physical immortality for deceased, and they're willing to pay for it. All you've got to do is to just be ca'm and stack it up—they'll stand the racket. Why, man, you can take a defunct that you couldn't *give* away; and get your embamming traps around you and go to work; and in a couple of hours he is worth a cool six hundred—that's what *he's* worth. There ain't anything equal to it but trading rats for di'monds in time of famine. Well, don't you see, when there's an epidemic, people don't wait to embam. No, indeed they don't; and it hurts the business like hellth, as we say—hurts it like hell-th, *health,* see?—Our little joke in the trade. Well, I must be going. Give me a call whenever you need any—I mean, when you're going by, sometime."

In his joyful high spirits, he did the exaggerating himself, if any has been done. I have not enlarged on him.

With the above brief references to inhumation, let us leave the subject. As for me, I hope to be cremated. I made that remark to my pastor once, who said, with what he seemed to think was an impressive manner,—

"I wouldn't worry about that, if I had your chances."

Much he knew about it—the family all so opposed to it.

From *Life on the Mississippi,* 1883

Pap, His Own Self

Miss Watson's nigger, Jim, had a hair-ball as big as your fist, which had been took out of the fourth stomach of an ox, and he used to do magic with it. He said there was a spirit inside of it, and it knowed everything. So I went to him that night and told him pap was here again, for I found his tracks in the snow. What I wanted to know, was, what he was going to do, and was he going to stay? Jim got out his hair-ball, and said something over it, and then he held it up and dropped it on the floor. It fell pretty solid, and only rolled about an inch. Jim tried it again, and then another time, and it acted just the same. Jim got down on his knees and put his ear against it and listened. But it warn't no use; he said it wouldn't talk. He said sometimes it wouldn't talk without money. I told him I had an old slick counterfeit quarter that warn't no good because the brass showed through the silver a little, and it wouldn't pass nohow, even if the brass didn't show, because it was so slick it felt greasy, and so that would tell on it every time. (I reckoned I wouldn't say nothing about the dollar I got from the judge.) I said it was pretty bad money, but maybe the hair-ball would take it, because maybe it wouldn't know the difference. Jim smelt it, and bit it, and rubbed it, and said he would manage so the hair-ball would think it was good. He said he would split open a raw Irish potato and stick the quarter in between and keep it there all night, and next morning you couldn't see no brass, and it wouldn't feel greasy no more, and so anybody in town would take it in a minute, let alone a hair-ball. Well, I knowed a potato would do that, before, but I had forgot it.

Jim put the quarter under the hair-ball and got down and listened again. This time he said the hair-ball was all right. He said it would tell my whole fortune if I wanted it to. I says, go on. So the hair-ball talked to Jim, and Jim told it to me. He says:

"Yo' ole father doan' know, yit, what he's a-gwyne to do. Sometimes he spec he'll go 'way, en den agin he spec he'll stay. De bes' way is to res' easy en let de ole man take his own way. Dey's two angels hoverin' roun' 'bout him. One uv 'em is white en shiny, en 'tother one is black. De white one gits him to go right, a little while, den de black one sail in en bust it all up. A body can't tell, yit, which one gwyne to fetch him at de las'. But you is all right. You gwyne to have considable trouble in yo' life, en considable joy. Sometimes you gwyne to git hurt, en sometimes you gwyne to git sick; but every time you's gwyne to git well agin. Dey's two gals flyin' 'bout you in yo' life. One uv 'em's light en 'tother one is dark. One is rich en 'tother is po'. You's gwyne to marry de po' one fust en de rich one by-en-by. You wants to keep 'way fum de water as much as you kin, en don't run no resk, 'kase it's down in de bills dat you's gwyne to git hung."

When I lit my candle and went up to my room that night, there sat pap, his own self!

I had shut the door to. Then I turned around, and there he was. I used to be scared of him all the time, he tanned me so much. I reckoned I was scared now, too; but in a minute I see I was mistaken. That is, after the first jolt, as you may say, when my breath sort of hitched—he being so unexpected; but right away after, I see I warn't scared of him worth bothering about.

He was most fifty, and he looked it. His hair was long and tangled and greasy, and hung down, and you could see his eyes shining through like he was behind vines. It was all black, no gray; so was his long, mixed-up whiskers. There warn't no color in his face, where his face showed; it was white; not like another man's white, but a white to make a body sick, a white to make a body's flesh crawl—a tree-toad white, a fish-belly white. As for his clothes—just rags, that was all. He had one ankle resting on 'tother knee; the boot on that foot was busted, and two of his toes stuck through, and he worked them now and then. His hat was laying on the floor; an old black slouch with the top caved in, like a lid.

I stood a-looking at him; he set there a-looking at me, with his chair tilted back a little. I set the candle down. I noticed the window was up; so he had clumb in by the shed. He kept a-looking me all over. By-and-by he says:

"Starchy clothes—very. You think you're a good deal of a big-bug, *don't* you?"

"Maybe I am, maybe I ain't," I says.

"Don't you give me none o' your lip," says he. "You've put on considerable many frills since I been away. I'll take you down a peg before I get done with you. You're educated, too, they say; can read and write. You think you're better'n your father, now, don't you, because he can't? *I*'ll take it out of you. Who told you you might meddle with such hifalut'n foolishness, hey?—who told you you could?"

"The widow. She told me."

"The widow, hey?—and who told the widow she could put in her shovel about a thing that ain't none of her business?"

"Nobody never told her."

"Well, I'll learn her how to meddle. And looky here—you drop that school, you hear? I'll learn people to bring up a boy to put on airs over his own father and let on to be better'n what *he* is. You lemme catch you fooling around that school again, you hear? Your mother couldn't read, and she couldn't write, nuther, before she died. None of the family couldn't, before *they* died. *I* can't; and here you're a-swelling yourself up like this. I ain't the man to stand it—you hear? Say—lemme hear you read."

I took up a book and begun something about General Washington and the wars. When I'd read about a half a minute, he fetched the book a whack with his hand and knocked it across the house. He says:

"It's so. You can do it. I had my doubts when you told me. Now looky here; you stop that putting on frills. I won't have it. I'll lay for you, my smarty; and if I catch you about that school I'll tan you good. First you know you'll get religion, too. I never see such a son."

He took up a little blue and yaller picture of some cows and a boy, and says:

"What's this?"

"It's something they give me for learning my lessons good."

He tore it up, and says—

"I'll give you something better—I'll give you a cowhide."

He set there a-mumbling and a-growling a minute, and then he says—

"*Ain't* you a sweet-scented dandy, though? A bed; and bedclothes; and a look'n-glass; and a piece of carpet on the floor—and your own father got to sleep with the hogs in the tanyard. I never see such a son. I bet I'll take some o' these frills out o' you before I'm done with you. Why there ain't no end to your airs—they say you're rich. Hey?—how's that?"

"They lie—that's how."

"Looky here—mind how you talk to me; I'm a-standing about all I can stand, now—so don't gimme no sass. I've been in town two days, and I hain't heard nothing but about you bein' rich. I heard about it away down the river, too. That's why I come. You git me that money to-morrow—I want it."

"I hain't got no money."

"It's a lie. Judge Thatcher's got it. You git it. I want it."

"I hain't got no money, I tell you. You ask Judge Thatcher; he'll tell you the same."

"All right. I'll ask him; and I'll make him pungle, too, or I'll know the reason why. Say—how much you got in your pocket? I want it."

"I hain't got only a dollar, and I want that to——"

"It don't make no difference what you want it for—you just shell it out."

He took it and bit it to see if it was good, and then he said he was going down town to get some whisky; said he hadn't had a drink all day. When he had got out on the shed, he put his head in again, and cussed me for putting on frills and trying to be better than him; and when I reckoned he was gone, he come back and put his head in again, and told me to mind about that school, because he was going to lay for me and lick me if I didn't drop that.

Next day he was drunk, and he went to Judge Thatcher's and bully-ragged him and tried to make him give up the money, but he couldn't, and then he swore he'd make the law force him.

The judge and the widow went to law to get the court to take me away from him and let one of them be my guardian; but it was a new judge that had just come, and he didn't know the old man; so he said courts mustn't interfere and separate families if they could help it; said he'd druther not take a child away from its father. So Judge Thatcher and the widow had to quit on the business.

That pleased the old man till he couldn't rest. He said he'd cowhide me till I was black and blue if I didn't raise some money for him. I borrowed three dollars from Judge Thatcher, and pap took it and got drunk and went a-blowing around and cussing and whooping and carrying on; and he kept it up all over town, with a tin pan, till most midnight; then they jailed him, and next day they had him before court, and jailed him again for a week. But he said *he* was satisfied; said he was boss of his son, and he'd make it warm for *him.*

When he got out the new judge said he was agoing to make a man of him. So he took him to his own house, and dressed him up clean and nice, and had him to breakfast and dinner and supper with the family, and was just old pie to him, so to speak. And after supper he talked to him about temperance and such things till the old man cried, and said he'd been a fool, and fooled away his life; but now he was agoing to turn over a new leaf and be a man nobody wouldn't be ashamed of, and he hoped the judge would help him and not look down on him. The judge said he could hug him for them words; so *he* cried, and his wife she cried again; pap said he'd been a man that had always been misunderstood before, and the judge said he believed it. The old man said that what a man wanted that was down, was sympathy; and the judge said it was so; so they cried again. And when it was bedtime, the old man rose up and held out his hand, and says:

"Look at it gentlemen, and ladies all; take ahold of it; shake it. There's a hand that was the hand of a hog; but it ain't so no more; it's the hand of a man that's started in on a new life, and 'll die before he'll go back. You mark them words—don't forget I said them. It's a clean hand now; shake it—don't be afeard."

So they shook it, one after the other, all around, and cried. The judge's wife she kissed it. Then the old man he signed a pledge—made his mark. The judge said it was the holiest time on record, or something like that. Then they tucked the old man into a beautiful room, which was the spare room, and in the night sometime he got powerful thirsty and clumb out onto the porch-roof and slid down a stanchion and traded his new coat for a jug of forty-rod, and clumb back again and had a good old time; and towards daylight he crawled out again, drunk as a fiddler, and rolled off the porch and broke his left arm in two places and was most froze to death when somebody found him after sun-up. And when they come to look at that spare room, they had to take soundings before they could navigate it.

The judge he felt kind of sore. He said he reckoned a body could reform the ole man with a shot-gun, maybe, but he didn't know no other way.

Well, pretty soon the old man was up and around again, and then he went for Judge Thatcher in the courts to make him give up that money, and he went for me, too, for not stopping school. He catched me a couple of times and thrashed me, but I went to school just the same, and dodged him or out-run him most of the time. I didn't want to go to school much, before, but I reckoned I'd go now to spite pap. That law trial was a slow business; appeared like they warn't ever going to get started on it; so every now and then I'd borrow two or three dollars off of the judge for him, to keep from getting a cowhiding. Every time he got money he got drunk; and every time he got drunk he raised Cain around town; and every time he raised Cain he got jailed. He was just suited—this kind of thing was right in his line.

He got to hanging around the widow's too much, and so she told him at last, that if he didn't quit using around there she would make trouble for him. Well, *wasn't* he mad? He said he would show who was Huck Finn's boss. So he watched out for me one day in the spring, and catched me, and took me up the river about three mile, in a skiff, and crossed over to the Illinois shore where it was woody and there warn't no houses but an old log hut in a place where the timber was so thick you couldn't find it if you didn't know where it was.

He kept me with him all the time, and I never got a chance to run off. We lived in that old cabin, and he always locked the door and put the key under his head, nights. He had a gun which he had stole, I reckon, and we fished and hunted, and that was what we lived on. Every little while he locked me in and went down to the store, three miles, to the ferry, and traded fish and game for whisky and fetched it home and got drunk and had a good time, and licked me. The widow she found out where I was, by-and-by, and she sent a man over to try to get hold of me, but pap drove him off with the gun, and it warn't long after that till I was used to being where I was, and liked it, all but the cowhide part.

It was kind of lazy and jolly, laying off comfortable all day, smoking and fishing, and no books nor study. Two months or more run along, and my clothes got to be all rags and dirt, and I didn't see how I'd ever got to like it so well at the widow's, where you had to wash, and eat on a plate, and comb up, and go to bed and get up regular, and be forever bothering over a book and have old Miss Watson pecking at you all the time. I didn't want to go back no more. I had stopped cussing, because the widow didn't like it; but now I took to it again because pap hadn't no objections. It was pretty good times up in the woods there, take it all around.

But by-and-by pap got too handy with his hick'ry, and I couldn't stand it. I was all over welts. He got to going away so much, too, and locking me in. Once he locked me in and was gone three days. It was dreadful lonesome. I judged he had got drowned and I wasn't ever going to get out any more. I was scared. I made up my mind I would fix up some way to leave there. I had tried to get out of that cabin many a time, but I couldn't find no way. There warn't a window to it big enough for a dog to get through. I couldn't get up the chimbly, it was too narrow. The door was thick solid oak slabs. Pap was pretty careful not to leave a knife or anything in the cabin when he was away; I reckon I had hunted the place over as much as a hundred times; well, I was 'most all the time at it, because it was about the only way to put in the time. But this time I found something at last; I found an old rusty wood-saw without any handle; it was laid in between a rafter and the clapboards of the roof. I greased it up and went to work. There was an old horse-blanket nailed against the logs at the far end of the cabin behind the table, to keep the wind from blowing through the chinks and putting the candle out. I got under the table and raised the blanket and went to work to saw a section of the big bottom log out, big enough to let me through. Well, it was a good long job, but I was getting towards the end of it when I heard pap's gun in the woods. I got rid of the signs of my work, and dropped the blanket and hid my saw, and pretty soon pap come in.

Pap warn't in a good humor—so he was his natural self. He said he was down to town, and everything was going wrong. His lawyer said he reckoned he would win his lawsuit and get the money, if they ever got started on the trial; but then there was ways to put it off a long time, and Judge Thatcher knowed how to do it. And he said people allowed there'd be another trial to get me away from him and give me to the widow for my guardian, and they guessed it would win, this time. This shook me up considerable, because I didn't want to go back to the widow's any more and be so cramped up and sivilized, as they called it. Then the old man got to cussing, and cussed everything and everybody he could think of, and then cussed them all over again to make sure he hadn't skipped any, and after that he polished off with a kind of a general cuss all round, including a considerable parcel of people which he didn't know the names of, and so called them what's-his-name, when he got to them, and went right along with his cussing.

He said he would like to see the widow get me. He said he would watch out, and if they tried to come any such game on him he knowed of a place six or seven mile off, to stow me in, where they might hunt till they dropped and they couldn't find me. That made me pretty uneasy again, but only for a minute; I reckoned I wouldn't stay on hand till he got that chance.

The old man made me go to the skiff and fetch the things he had got. There was a fifty-pound sack of corn meal, and a side of bacon, ammunition, and a four-gallon jug of whisky, and an old book and two newspapers for wadding, besides some tow. I toted up a load, and went back and set down on the bow of the skiff to rest. I thought it all over, and I reckoned I would walk off with the gun and some lines, and take to the woods when I run away. I guessed I wouldn't stay in one place, but just tramp right across the country, mostly night times, and hunt and fish to keep alive, and so get so far away that the old man nor the widow couldn't ever find me any more. I judged I would saw out and leave that night if pap got drunk enough, and I reckoned he would. I got so full of it I didn't notice how long I was staying, till the old man hollered and asked me whether I was asleep or drownded.

I got the things all up to the cabin, and then it was about dark. While I was cooking supper the old man took a swig or two and got sort of warmed up, and went to ripping again. He had been drunk over in town, and laid in the gutter all night, and he was a sight to look at. A body would a thought he was Adam, he was just all mud. Whenever his liquor begun to work, he most always went for the govment. This time he says:

"Call this a govment! why, just look at it and see what it's like. Here's the law a-standing ready to take a man's son away from him—a man's own son, which he has had all the trouble and all the anxiety and all the expense of raising. Yes, just as that man has got that son raised at last, and ready to go to work and begin to do suthin' for *him* and give him a rest, the law up and goes for him. And they call *that* govment! That ain't all, nuther. The law backs that old Judge Thatcher up and helps him to keep me out o' my property. Here's what the law does. The law takes a man worth six thousand dollars and upards, and jams him into an old trap of a cabin like this, and lets him go round in clothes that ain't fitten for a hog. They call that govment! A man can't get his rights in a govment like this. Sometimes I've a mighty notion to just leave the country for good and all. Yes, and I *told* 'em so; I told old Thatcher so to his face. Lots of 'em heard me, and can tell what I said. Says I, for two cents I'd leave the blamed country and never come anear it agin. Them's the very words. I says, look at my hat—if you call it a hat—but the lid raises up and the rest of it goes down till it's below my chin, and then it ain't rightly a hat at all, but more like my head was shoved up through a jint o' stove-pipe. Look at it, says I—such a hat for me to wear—one of the wealthiest men in this town, if I could git my rights.

"Oh, yes, this is a wonderful govment, wonderful. Why, looky here. There was a free nigger there, from Ohio; a mulatter, most as white as a white man. He had the whitest shirt on you ever see, too, and the shiniest hat; and there ain't a man in that town that's got as fine clothes as what he had; and he had a gold watch and chain, and a silver-headed cane—the awfulest old gray-headed nabob in the State. And what do you think? they said he was a p'fessor in a college, and could talk all kinds of languages, and knowed everything. And that ain't the wust. They said he could *vote,* when he was at home. Well, that let me out. Thinks I, what is the country a-coming to? It was 'lection day, and I was just about to go and vote, myself, if I warn't too drunk to get there; but when they told me there was a State in this country where they'd let that nigger vote, I drawed out. I says I'll never vote agin. Them's the very words I said; they all heard me; and the country may rot for all me—I'll never vote agin as long as I live. And to see the cool way of that nigger—why, he wouldn't a give me the road if I hadn't shoved him out o' the way. I says to the people, why ain't this nigger put up at auction and sold?—that's what I want to know. And what do you reckon they said? Why, they said he couldn't be sold till he'd been in the State six months, and he hadn't been there that long yet. There, now—that's a specimen. They call that a govment that can't sell a free nigger till he's been in the State six months. Here's a govment that calls itself a govment, and lets on to be a govment, and thinks it is a govment, and yet's got to set stock-still for six whole months before it can take ahold of a prowling, thieving, infernal, white-shirted free nigger, and——"

Pap was agoing on so, he never noticed where his old limber legs was taking him to, so he went head over heels over the tub of salt pork, and barked both shins, and the rest of his speech was all the hottest kind of language—mostly hove at the nigger and the govment, though he give the tub some, too, all along, here and there. He hopped around the cabin considerable, first on one leg and then on the other, holding first one shin and then the other one, and at last he let out with his left foot all of a sudden and fetched the tub a rattling kick. But it warn't good judgment, because that was the boot that had a couple of his toes leaking out of the front end of it; so now he raised a howl that fairly made a body's hair raise, and down he went in the dirt, and rolled there, and held his toes; and the cussing he done then laid over anything he had ever done previous. He said so his own self, afterwards. He had heard old Sowberry Hagan in his best days, and he said it laid over him, too; but I reckon that was sort of piling it on, maybe.

After supper pap took the jug, and said he had enough whisky there for two drunks and one delirium tremens. That was always his word. I judged he would be blind drunk in about an hour, and then I would steal the key, or saw myself out, one or 'tother. He drank, and drank, and tumbled down on his blankets, by-and-by; but luck didn't run my way. He didn't go sound asleep, but was uneasy. He groaned, and moaned, and thrashed around this way and that, for a long time. At last I got so sleepy I couldn't keep my eyes open all I could do, and so before I knowed what I was about I was sound asleep, and the candle burning.

I don't know how long I was asleep, but all of a sudden there was an awful scream and I was up. There was pap, looking wild and skipping around every which way and yelling about snakes. He said they was crawling up his legs; and then he would give a jump and scream, and say one had bit him on the cheek—but I couldn't see no snakes. He started and run round and round the cabin, hollering "take him off! take him off! he's biting me on the neck!" I never see a man look so wild in the eyes. Pretty soon he was all fagged out, and fell down panting; then he rolled over and over, wonderful fast, kicking things every which way, and striking and grabbing at the air with his hands, and screaming, and saying there was devils ahold of him. He wore out, by-and-by, and laid still a while, moaning. Then he laid stiller, and didn't make a sound. I could hear the owls and the wolves, away off in the woods, and it seemed terrible still. He was laying over by the corner. By-and-by he raised up, part way, and listened, with his head to one side. He says very low:

"Tramp—tramp—tramp; that's the dead; tramp—tramp—tramp; they're coming after me; but I won't go— Oh, they're here! don't touch me—don't! hands off—they're cold; let go— Oh, let a poor devil alone!"

Then he went down on all fours and crawled off begging them to let him alone, and he rolled himself up in his blanket and wallowed in under the old pine table, still a-begging; and then he went to crying. I could hear him through the blanket.

By-and-by he rolled out and jumped up on his feet looking wild, and he see me and went for me. He chased me round and round the place, with a clasp-knife, calling me the Angel of Death and saying he would kill me and then I couldn't come for him no more. I begged, and told him I was only Huck, but he laughed *such* a screechy laugh, and roared and cussed, and kept on chasing me up. Once when I turned short and dodged under his arm he made a grab and got me by the jacket between my shoulders, and I thought I was gone; but I slid out of the jacket quick as lightning, and saved myself. Pretty soon he was all tired out, and dropped down with his back against the door, and said he would rest a minute and then kill me. He put his knife under him, and said he would sleep and get strong, and then he would see who was who.

So he dozed off, pretty soon. By-and-by I got the old split-bottom chair and clumb up, as easy as I could, not to make any noise, and got down the gun. I slipped the ramrod down it to make sure it was loaded, and then I laid it across the turnip barrel, pointing towards pap, and set down behind it to wait for him to stir. And how slow and still the time did drag along.

From *Adventures of Huckleberry Finn,* 1884

The Duke and the Dauphin

One morning about day-break, I found a canoe and crossed over a chute to the main shore—it was only two hundred yards—and paddled about a mile up a crick amongst the cypress woods, to see if I couldn't get some berries. Just as I was passing a place where a kind of a cowpath crossed the crick, here comes a couple of men tearing up the path as tight as they could foot it. I thought I was a goner, for whenever anybody was after anybody I judged it was *me*—or maybe Jim. I was about to dig out from there in a hurry, but they was pretty close to me then, and sung out and begged me to save their lives—said they hadn't been doing nothing, and was being chased for it—said there was men and dogs a-coming. They wanted to jump right in, but I says—

"Don't you do it. I don't hear the dogs and horses yet; you've got time to crowd through the brush and get up the crick a little ways; then you take to the water and wade down to me and get in—that'll throw the dogs off the scent."

They done it, and soon as they was aboard I lit out for our tow-head, and in about five or ten minutes we heard the dogs and the men away off, shouting. We heard them come along towards the crick, but couldn't see them; they seemed to stop and fool around a while; then, as we got further and further away all the time, we couldn't hardly hear them at all; by the time we had left a mile of woods behind us and struck the river, everything was quiet, and we paddled over to the tow-head and hid in the cottonwoods and was safe.

One of these fellows was about seventy, or upwards, and had a bald head and very gray whiskers. He had an old battered-up slouch hat on, and a greasy blue woolen shirt, and ragged old blue jeans britches stuffed into his boot tops, and home-knit galluses—no, he only had one. He had an old long-tailed blue jeans coat with slick brass buttons, flung over his arm, and both of them had big fat ratty-looking carpet-bags.

The other fellow was about thirty and dressed about as ornery. After breakfast we all laid off and talked, and the first thing that come out was that these chaps didn't know one another.

"What got you into trouble?" says the baldhead to t'other chap.

"Well, I'd been selling an article to take the tartar off the teeth—and it does take it off, too, and generly the enamel along with it—but I staid about one night longer than I ought to, and was just in the act of sliding out when I ran across you on the trail this side of town, and you told me they were coming, and begged me to help you to get off. So I told you I was expecting trouble myself and would scatter out *with* you. That's the whole yarn—what's yourn?"

"Well, I'd ben a-runnin' a little temperance revival thar, 'bout a week, and was the pet of the women-folks, big and little, for I was makin' it mighty warm for the rummies, I *tell* you, and takin' as much as five or six dollars a night—ten cents a head, children and niggers free—and business a growin' all the time; when somehow or another a little report got around, last night, that I had a way of puttin' in my time with a private jug, on the sly. A nigger rousted me out this mornin', and told me the people was getherin' on the quiet, with their dogs and horses, and they'd be along pretty soon and give me 'bout half an hour's start, and then run me down, if they could; and if they got me they'd tar and feather me and ride me on a rail, sure. I didn't wait for no breakfast—I warn't hungry."

"Old man," says the young one, "I reckon we might double-team it together; what do you think?"

"I ain't undisposed. What's your line—mainly?"

"Jour printer, by trade; do a little in patent medicines; theatre-actor—tragedy, you know; take a turn at mesmerism and phrenology when there's a chance; teach singing-geography school for a change; sling a lecture, sometimes—oh, I do lots of things—most anything that comes handy, so it ain't work. What's your lay?"

"I've done considerable in the doctoring way in my time. Layin' on o' hands is my best holt—for cancer, and paralysis, and sich things; and I k'n tell a fortune pretty good, when I've got somebody along to find out the facts for me. Preachin's my line, too; and workin' camp-meetin's; and missionaryin' around."

Nobody never said anything for a while; then the young man hove a sigh and says—

"Alas!"

"What 're you alassin' about?" says the baldhead.

"To think I should have lived to be leading such a life, and be degraded down into such company." And he begun to wipe the corner of his eye with a rag.

"Dern your skin, ain't the company good enough for you?" says the baldhead, pretty pert and uppish.

"Yes, it *is* good enough for me; it's as good as I deserve; for who fetched me so low, when I was so high? *I* did myself. I don't blame *you*, gentlemen—far from it; I don't blame anybody. I deserve it all. Let the cold world do its worst; one thing I know—there's a grave somewhere for me. The world may go on just as it's always done, and take everything from me—loved ones, property, everything—but it can't take that. Some day I'll lie down in it and forget it all, and my poor broken heart will be at rest." He went on a-wiping.

"Drot your pore broken heart," says the baldhead; "what are you heaving your pore broken heart at *us* f'r? *We* hain't done nothing."

"No, I know you haven't. I ain't blaming you, gentlemen. I brought myself down—yes, I did it myself. It's right I should suffer—perfectly right—I don't make any moan."

"Brought you down from whar? Whar was you brought down from?"

"Ah, you would not believe me; the world never believes—let it pass—'tis no matter. The secret of my birth——"

"The secret of your birth? Do you mean to say——"

"Gentlemen," says the young man, very solemn, "I will reveal it to you, for I feel I may have confidence in you. By rights I am a duke!"

Jim's eyes bugged out when he heard that; and I reckon mine did, too. Then the baldhead says: "No! you can't mean it?"

"Yes. My great-grandfather, eldest son of the Duke of Bridgewater, fled to this country about the end of the last century, to breathe the pure air of freedom; married here, and died, leaving a son, his own father dying about the same time. The second son of the late duke seized the title and estates—the infant real duke was ignored. I am the lineal descendant of that infant—I am the rightful Duke of Bridgewater; and here am I, forlorn, torn from my high estate, hunted of men, despised by the cold world, ragged, worn, heart-broken, and degraded to the companionship of felons on a raft!"

Jim pitied him ever so much, and so did I. We tried to comfort him, but he said it warn't much use, he couldn't be much comforted;

said if we was a mind to acknowledge him, that would do him more good than most anything else; so we said we would, if he would tell us how. He said we ought to bow, when we spoke to him, and say "Your Grace," or "My Lord," or "Your Lordship"—and he wouldn't mind it if we called him plain "Bridgewater," which he said was a title, anyway, and not a name; and one of us ought to wait on him at dinner, and do any little thing for him he wanted done.

Well, that was all easy, so we done it. All through dinner Jim stood around and waited on him, and says, "Will yo' Grace have some o' dis, or some o' dat?" and so on, and a body could see it was mighty pleasing to him.

But the old man got pretty silent, by-and-by—didn't have much to say, and didn't look pretty comfortable over all that petting that was going on around that duke. He seemed to have something on his mind. So, along in the afternoon, he says:

"Looky here, Bilgewater," he says, "I'm nation sorry for you, but you ain't the only person that's had troubles like that."

"No?"

"No, you ain't. You ain't the only person that's ben snaked down wrongfully out'n a high place."

"Alas!"

"No, you ain't the only person that's had a secret of his birth." And by jings, *he* begins to cry.

"Hold! What do you mean?"

"Bilgewater, kin I trust you?" says the old man, still sort of sobbing.

"To the bitter death!" He took the old man by the hand and squeezed it, and says, "The secret of your being: speak!"

"Bilgewater, I am the late Dauphin!"

You bet you Jim and me stared, this time. Then the duke says:

"You are what?"

"Yes, my friend, it is too true—your eyes is lookin' at this very moment on the pore disappeared Dauphin, Looy the Seventeen, son of Looy the Sixteen and Marry Antonette."

"You! At your age! No! You mean you're the late Charlemagne; you must be six or seven hundred years old, at the very least."

"Trouble has done it, Bilgewater, trouble has done it; trouble has brung these gray hairs and this premature balditude. Yes, gentlemen, you see before you, in blue jeans and misery, the wanderin', exiled, trampled-on and sufferin' rightful King of France."

Well, he cried and took on so, that me and Jim didn't know hardly what to do, we was so sorry—and so glad and proud we'd got him with us, too. So we set in, like we done before with the duke, and tried to comfort *him*. But he said it warn't no use, nothing but to be dead and done with it all could do him any good; though he said it often made him feel easier and better for a while if people treated him according to his rights, and got down on one knee to speak to him, and always called him "Your Majesty," and waited on him first at meals, and didn't set down in his presence till he asked them. So Jim and me set to majestying him, and doing this and that and t'other for him, and standing up till he told us we might set down. This done him heaps of good, and so he got cheerful and comfortable. But the duke kind of soured on him, and didn't look a bit satisfied with the way things was going; still, the king acted real friendly towards him, and said the duke's great-grandfather and all the other Dukes of Bilgewater was a good deal thought of by *his* father and was allowed to come to the palace considerable; but the duke staid huffy a good while, till by-and-by the king says:

"Like as not we got to be together a blamed long time, on this h-yer raft, Bilgewater, and so what's the use o' your bein' sour? It'll only make things oncomfortable. It ain't my fault I warn't born a duke, it ain't your fault you warn't born a king—so what's the use to worry? Make the best o' things the way you find 'em, says I—that's my motto. This ain't no bad thing that we've struck here—plenty grub and an easy life—come, give us your hand, Duke, and less all be friends."

The duke done it, and Jim and me was pretty glad to see it. It took away all the uncomfortableness, and we felt mighty good over it, because it would a been a miserable business to have any unfriendliness on the raft; for what you want, above all things, on a raft, is for everybody to be satisfied, and feel right and kind towards the others.

It didn't take me long to make up my mind that these liars warn't no kings nor dukes, at all, but just low-down humbugs and frauds. But I never said nothing, never let on; kept it to myself; it's the best way; then you don't have no quarrels, and don't get into no trouble. If they wanted us to call them kings and dukes, I hadn't no objections, 'long as it would keep peace in the family; and it warn't no use to tell Jim, so I didn't tell him. If I never learnt nothing else out of pap, I learnt that the best way to get along with his kind of people is to let them have their own way.

From *Adventures of Huckleberry Finn,* 1884

Curing a Cold

It is a good thing, perhaps, to write for the amusement of the public, but it is a far higher and nobler thing to write for their instruction, their profit, their actual and tangible benefit. The latter is the sole object of this article. If it prove the means of restoring to health one solitary sufferer among my race, of lighting up once more the fire of hope and joy in his faded eyes, or bringing back to his dead heart again the quick, generous impulses of other days, I shall be amply rewarded for my labor; my soul will be permeated with the sacred delight a Christian feels when he has done a good, unselfish deed.

Having led a pure and blameless life, I am justified in believing that no man who knows me will reject the suggestions I am about to make, out of fear that I am trying to deceive him. Let the public do itself the honor to read my experience in doctoring a cold, as herein set forth, and then follow in my footsteps.

When the White House was burned in Virginia City, I lost my home, my happiness, my constitution, and my trunk. The loss of the two first-named articles was a matter of no great consequence, since a home without a mother, or a sister, or a distant young female relative in it, to remind you, by putting your soiled linen out of sight and taking your boots down off the mantelpiece, that there are those who think about you and care for you, is easily obtained. And I cared nothing for the loss of my happiness, because, not being a poet, it could not be possible that melancholy would abide with me long. But to lose a good constitution and a better trunk were serious misfortunes. On the day of the fire my constitution succumbed to a severe cold, caused by undue exertion in getting ready to do something. I suffered to no purpose, too, because the plan I was figuring at for the extinguishing of the fire was so elaborate that I never got it completed until the middle of the following week.

The first time I began to sneeze, a friend told me to go and bathe my feet in hot water and go to bed. I did so. Shortly afterward, another friend advised me to get up and take a cold shower-bath. I did that also. Within the hour, another friend assured me that it was policy to "feed a cold and starve a fever." I had both. So I thought it best to fill myself up for the cold, and then keep dark and let the fever starve awhile.

In a case of this kind, I seldom do things by halves; I ate pretty heartily; I conferred my custom upon a stranger who had just opened his restaurant that morning; he waited near me in respectful silence until I had finished feeding my cold, when he inquired if the people about Virginia City were much afflicted with colds? I told him I thought they were. He then went out and took in his sign.

I started down toward the office, and on the way encountered another bosom friend, who told me that a quart of salt-water, taken warm, would come as near curing a cold as anything in the world. I hardly thought I had room for it, but I tried it anyhow. The result was surprising. I believed I had thrown up my immortal soul.

Now, as I am giving my experience only for the benefit of those who are troubled with the distemper I am writing about, I feel that they will see the propriety of my cautioning them against following such portions of it as proved inefficient with me, and acting upon this conviction, I warn them against warm salt-water. It may be a good enough remedy, but I think it is too severe. If I had another cold in the head, and there were no course left me but to take either an earthquake or a quart of warm salt-water, I would take my chances on the earthquake.

After the storm which had been raging in my stomach had subsided, and no more good Samaritans happening along, I went on borrowing handkerchiefs again and blowing them to atoms, as had been my custom in the early stages of my cold, until I came across a lady who had just arrived from over the plains, and who said she had lived in a part of the country where doctors were scarce, and had from necessity acquired considerable skill in the treatment of simple "family complaints." I knew she must have had much experience, for she appeared to be a hundred and fifty years old.

She mixed a decoction composed of molasses, aquafortis, turpentine, and various other drugs, and instructed me to take a wineglass full of it every fifteen minutes. I never took but one dose; that was enough, it robbed me of all moral principle, and awoke every unworthy impulse of my nature. Under its malign influence my brain conceived miracles of meanness, but my hands were too feeble to execute them; at that time, had it not been that my strength had surrendered to a succession of assaults from infallible remedies for my cold, I am satisfied that I would have tried to rob the graveyard. Like most other people, I often feel mean, and act accordingly; but until I took that medicine I had never reveled in such supernatural depravity, and felt proud of it. At the end of two days I was ready to go to doctoring again. I took a few more unfailing remedies, and finally drove my cold from my head to my lungs.

I got to coughing incessantly, and my voice fell below zero; I conversed in a thundering bass, two octaves below my natural tone; I could only compass my regular nightly repose by coughing myself down to a state of utter exhaustion, and then the moment I began to talk in my sleep, my discordant voice woke me up again.

My case grew more and more serious every day. Plain gin was recommended; I took it. Then gin and molasses; I took that also. Then gin and onions; I added the onions, and took all three. I detected no particular result, however, except that I had acquired a breath like a buzzard's.

I found I had to travel for my health. I went to Lake Bigler with my reportorial comrade, Wilson. It is gratifying to me to reflect that we traveled in considerable style; we went in the Pioneer coach, and my friend took all his baggage with him, consisting of two excellent silk handkerchiefs and a daguerreotype of his grandmother. We sailed and hunted and fished and danced all day, and I doctored my cough all night. By managing in this way, I made out to improve every hour in the twenty-four. But my disease continued to grow worse.

A sheet-bath was recommended. I had never refused a remedy yet, and it seemed poor policy to commence then; therefore I determined to take a sheet-bath, notwithstanding I had no idea what sort of arrangement it was. It was administered at midnight, and the weather was very frosty. My breast and back were bared, and a sheet (there appeared to be a thousand yards of it) soaked in ice-water, was wound around me until I resembled a swab for a Columbiad.

It is a cruel expedient. When the chilly rag touches one's warm flesh, it makes him start with sudden violence, and gasp for breath just as men do in the death-agony. It froze the marrow in my bones and stopped the beating of my heart. I thought my time had come.

Young Wilson said the circumstance reminded him of an anecdote about a negro who was being baptized, and who slipped from the parson's grasp, and came near being drowned. He floundered around, though, and finally rose up out of the water considerably strangled and furiously angry, and started ashore at once, spouting water like a whale, and remarking, with great asperity, that "one o' dese days some gen'l'man's nigger gwyne to get killed wid jis' such damn foolishness as dis!"

Never take a sheet-bath—never. Next to meeting a lady acquaintance who, for reasons best known to herself, don't see you when she looks at you, and don't know you when she does see you, it is the most uncomfortable thing in the world.

But, as I was saying, when the sheet-bath failed to cure my cough, a lady friend recommended the application of a mustard plaster to my breast. I believe that would have cured me effectually, if it had not been for young Wilson. When I went to bed, I put my mustard plaster—which was a very gorgeous one, eighteen inches square—where I could reach it when I was ready for it. But young Wilson got hungry in the night, and—here is food for the imagination.

After sojourning a week at Lake Bigler, I went to Steamboat Springs, and, besides the steam-baths, I took a lot of the vilest medicines that were ever concocted. They would have cured me, but I had to go back to Virginia City, where, notwithstanding the variety of new remedies I absorbed every day, I managed to aggravate my disease by carelessness and undue exposure.

I finally concluded to visit San Francisco, and the first day I got there a lady at the hotel told me to drink a quart of whisky every twenty-four hours, and a friend up-town recommended precisely the same course. Each advised me to take a quart; that made half a gallon. I did it, and still live.

Now, with the kindest motives in the world, I offer for the consideration of consumptive patients the variegated course of treatment I have lately gone through. Let them try it; if it don't cure, it can't more than kill them.

1863

Aurelia's Unfortunate Young Man

The facts in the following case came to me by letter from a young lady who lives in the beautiful city of San José; she is perfectly unknown to me, and simply signs herself "Aurelia Maria," which may possibly be a fictitious name. But no matter, the poor girl is almost heartbroken by the misfortunes she has undergone, and so confused by the conflicting counsels of misguided friends and insidious enemies that she does not know what course to pursue in order to extricate herself from the web of difficulties in which she seems almost hopelessly involved. In this dilemma she turns to me for help, and supplicates for my guidance and instruction with a moving eloquence that would touch the heart of a statue. Hear her sad story:

She says that when she was sixteen years old she met and loved, with all the devotion of a passionate nature, a young man from New Jersey, named Williamson Breckinridge Caruthers, who was some six years her senior. They were engaged, with the free consent of their friends and relatives, and for a time it seemed as if their career was destined to be characterized by an immunity from sorrow beyond the usual lot of humanity. But at last the tide of fortune turned; young Caruthers became infected with smallpox of the most virulent type, and when he recovered from his illness his face was pitted like a waffle-mold, and his comeliness gone forever. Aurelia thought to break off the engagement at first, but pity for her unfortunate lover caused her to postpone the marriage-day for a season, and give him another trial.

The very day before the wedding was to have taken place, Breckinridge, while absorbed in watching the flight of a balloon, walked into a well and fractured one of his legs, and it had to be taken off above the knee. Again Aurelia was moved to break the engagement, but again love triumphed, and she set the day forward and gave him another chance to reform.

And again misfortune overtook the unhappy youth. He lost one arm by the premature discharge of a Fourth of July cannon, and within three months he got the other pulled out by a carding-machine. Aurelia's heart was almost crushed by these latter calamities. She could not but be deeply grieved to see her lover passing from her by piecemeal, feeling, as she did, that he could not last forever under this disastrous process of reduction, yet knowing of no way to stop its dreadful career, and in her tearful despair she almost regretted, like brokers who hold on and lose, that she had not taken him at first, before he had suffered such an alarming depreciation. Still, her brave soul bore her up, and she resolved to bear with her friend's unnatural disposition yet a little longer.

Again the wedding-day approached, and again disappointment overshadowed it; Caruthers fell ill with the erysipelas, and lost the use of one of his eyes entirely. The friends and relatives of the bride, considering that she had already put up with more than could reasonably be expected of her, now came forward and insisted that the match should be broken off; but after wavering awhile, Aurelia, with a generous spirit which did her credit, said she had reflected calmly upon the matter, and could not discover that Breckinridge was to blame.

So she extended the time once more, and he broke his other leg.

It was a sad day for the poor girl when she saw the surgeons reverently bearing away the sack whose uses she had learned by previous experience, and her heart told her the bitter truth that some more of her lover was gone. She felt that the field of her affections was growing more and more circumscribed every day, but once more she frowned down her relatives and renewed her betrothal.

Shortly before the time set for the nuptials another disaster occurred. There was but one man scalped by the Owens River Indians last year. That man was Williamson Breckinridge Caruthers of New Jersey. He was hurrying home with happiness in his heart, when he lost his hair forever, and in that hour of bitterness he almost cursed the mistaken mercy that had spared his head.

At last Aurelia is in serious perplexity as to what she ought to do. She still loves her Breckinridge, she writes, with truly womanly feeling—she still loves what is left of him—but her parents are bitterly opposed to the match, because he has no property and is disabled from working, and she has not sufficient means to support both comfortably. "Now, what should she do?" she asked with painful and anxious solicitude.

It is a delicate question; it is one which involves the lifelong happiness of a woman, and that of nearly two-thirds of a man, and I feel that it would be assuming too great a responsibility to do more than make a mere suggestion in the case. How would it do to build to him? If Aurelia can afford the expense, let her furnish her mutilated lover with wooden arms and wooden legs, and a glass eye and a wig, and give him another show; give him ninety days, without grace, and if he does not break his neck in the mean time, marry him and take the chances. It does not seem to me that there is much risk, anyway, Aurelia, because if he sticks to his singular propensity for damaging himself every time he sees a good opportunity, his next experiment is bound to finish him, and then you are safe, married or single. If married, the wooden legs and such other valuables as he may possess revert to the widow, and you see you sustain no actual loss save the cherished fragment of a noble but most unfortunate husband, who honestly strove to do right, but whose extraordinary instincts were against him. Try it, Maria. I have thought the matter over carefully and well, and it is the only chance I see for you. It would have been a happy conceit on the part of Caruthers if he had started with his neck and broken that first; but since he has seen fit to choose a different policy and string himself out as long as possible, I do not think we ought to upbraid him for it if he has enjoyed it. We must do the best we can under the circumstances, and try not to feel exasperated at him.

1864

The Facts in the Case of the Senate Doorkeeper

Since this case has excited so much attention in diplomatic circles, and has provoked so much comment in the newspapers, both of this country and Europe, I will make a plain, simple statement of the facts in the matter, and leave the public to judge between myself and the Administration. When I resigned the office of Page of the House of Representatives, the best men of the nation were alarmed for the welfare of the Republic. That this alarm was well founded, I cannot undertake to say. It would be indelicate in me to do more than call passing attention to the fact, that while I was connected with the Government in the capacity already named, the affairs of the Government prospered, and no cloud darkened the political horizon. I had no sooner resigned my office than the negotiations with England for the settlement of the Alabama claims came to an abrupt and unsatisfactory termination. This may have been a result of my resignation; it may not have been. I shall express no opinion in the premises.

However, as before stated, the best men of the nation were alarmed. They visited me in my self-imposed exile and begged me to come to the rescue, and take again the helm of the ship of state. They urged that the foreign complications likely to grow out of the new order of things, rendered my re-entry into the Cabinet imperatively necessary; that to me the country turned for succor in this season of peril; that if I would live in the hearts of the people, I must not desert them at a time like this. Thus importuned, I consigned to oblivion my grievous wrongs, my bitterness of spirit, and rejoined Mr. Johnson's Administration as Doorkeeper of the Senate.

I surely thought that by this time persecution had tired of hunting its victim. Was I right? The facts will show. On the first morning of my occupation of my new post, I locked all the entrances to the Senate Chamber but one, and took my station there. Presently a gentleman approached, and tried to pass in. I stopped him, and said:

"Well, sir, what do *you* want?"

"I want to go in, of course."

"You want to go in. That is all right, no doubt, but we will consider on it a moment, if you have the time to spare. Who are you?"

"You are insolent, sir! I am the President of the Senate."

"President of the Senate. Ah—what might your name be?"

"I will just see, out of curiosity, how far you will venture to carry this thing. My name is Wade—Benjamin F. Wade."

"Wade—Wade. I don't remember hearing of you before. Is that your regular name, or is it a *nom de plume?*"

"It is my regular name, as you call it, of course."

"Where are you from, Mr. Wade?"

"From Ohio."

"About how old might you be, friend?"

"Fifty-two in January."

"Fifty-two. You look—you look rather older than that, Wade. I should say—well, I should say you look as much as a hundred and thirty, or a hundred and forty, or along there. But age isn't anything—it is blood that tells. Give me blood, above everything. That is my sentiment. But about this business of President of the Senate. Have you got your little credentials along with you?"

He had them. Considering that he was the ring-master of the circus, I let him in free. But I had trouble with the others. Some of them had no credentials, and had to stay out. I taxed the balance fifty cents admission, and as soon as they got a quorum they passed a resolution of instruction to the Sergeant-at-arms, and I was arrested and compelled to disgorge. This high-handed usurpation of power came near making another split between myself and the Government, but I submitted, and resolved to bide my time.

During the afternoon one of the Senators addressed the Chair, and said he wished to offer a resolution recognizing his Majesty King Theodorus as a belligerent.

I said: "Your Highness, I rise to a point of order. This old gentleman that has just taken his seat—"

"Silence! The Doorkeeper will resume his station by the door."

This from the man—and the only man—that I had passed in free!

My heart was too full for utterance. From this time forward, for three days, I could never get the floor. I was snubbed every time I attempted to speak; whenever a *viva voce* vote was taken, my voice did not affect the result; when there was a division, I was not counted, either when I stood up or sat down; when there was a call of the house, my name was studiously omitted by the secretary and his minions. I frequently voted on both sides of the same question, purposely to catch the secretary, and I succeeded. During all this time the galleries were filled with people from all parts of the country, who were anxious to hear me speak. No matter—their feelings were not respected—the venomous persecution went on.

On the fourth day, at one o'clock, the ring-master announced the special order of the day—the Senate bill for the recognition of General Garibaldi as a Roman General, an Italian Deputy, and an American citizen. Here was my opportunity. I had been waiting, just waiting, to catch the house on a special order. I arose and said:

"Your Imperial Highness, I hold in my hand an Act entitled an Act supplementary to an Act entitled an Act amendatory of an Act to Confer Universal Suffrage upon Women. Woman! your Royal Highness—Oh, woman! in our hours of ease, uncertain, coy, and hard to please—"

"Silence!" It is not worth while to repeat more of the tirade uttered by the individual whom the fortuitous accident of a majority vote has elevated to the position of President of the Senate. I was subjugated. That is sufficient.

I waited one hour. A Senator from some obscure Indian reservation was tiring everybody to death with a stupid harangue about Garibaldi and several other incendiary Frenchmen, and it was plain that the crowd in the galleries was growing impatient. I arose and said:

"Your Royal Highness, woman! Oh, woman, in our hours of ease, uncertain—"

It was as far as I could get. A storm of malignant outcries assailed me, and for a time it seemed that I was going to be subjected to personal violence. The Sergeant-at-arms was ordered to put me in my seat and keep me there. In this humiliating position I remained for full two hours. I leave my countrymen to imagine what my feelings were. A spectacle was here presented to the nation such as has no parallel in history—the spectacle of a Senate degrading and trampling upon one of its own members. I could not long bear this. Every fibre of my being, every emotion of my nature, revolted at it. In the midst of some solemn, sentimental bosh by the Chair, concerning one of the new Senators from Walrussia, who had lost his way in the wilds of his native land, and had had nothing to eat for eighteen days but an iceberg, I emerged from the impressive silence, and thundered forth:

"Woman! Oh, woman! in—"

The door was in the way, and that is how it got broken down. The Senatorial mob did it. I fell in the hall, and in a single instant the aggregated wisdom of the nation was piled above me. Let us drop the curtain upon the disgraceful scene.

I approach the last chapter in the sad record of my official career. Its events transpired the next day. They culminated in a report of the Judiciary Committee—or rather two reports. Five members of it—a majority—brought in a wild document, which they styled "Articles of Impeachment Against the Doorkeeper of the United States Senate." The minority, of four members, reported against impeachment. The curious document first mentioned set forth that I had rendered my impeachment a just and righteous measure for the following specific reasons—viz:

In that I had transcended the powers vested in me by the Constitution of the United States by charging divers and sundry Senators fifty cents admission to their own department of the Capitol.

In that I had voted, during a regular session of the United States Senate, by word of mouth, and upon a division, and also upon the yeas and nays, in direct violation of a clause of the Constitution of the United States, which expressly forbids the Doorkeeper of the Senate to vote upon any question whatever which that body may have under consideration.

In that I had frequently risen to points of order, questions of privilege, etc., and had at divers and sundry times interrupted the Senate with attempts to deliver a speech upon a subject which was not before the house at the time, and always commencing with the same tiresome formula of "Woman! Oh, woman," etc.—all of which was in direct violation of that clause in the Constitution of the United States which expressly decrees that the Doorkeeper of the Senate shall at no time take part in the deliberations of that body.

In that I had attempted to introduce Female Suffrage at a time when the Hero of Italy was the special order of the day—which was in direct violation of that article of the Constitution of the United

States which expressly stipulates that special orders of the day shall at all times take precedence of other matters.

In that, after disrupting and disorganizing the Senate time and again by repetitions of the beforementioned speech, commencing "Woman! Oh, woman!" I incited the said Senate to rebellion and insurrection by still another attempt to inflict that speech upon them, and thus materially retarded the reconstruction of the aforesaid Senate at the period of its most promising progress—all of which, when taken in connection with the aforementioned charge of fifty cents admission to the Senate, is in flagrant violation of that article of the Constitution of the United States which decrees that for the Doorkeeper of the Senate to levy war or collect taxes on his individual responsibility is high treason and punishable with death.

The infamy of the Senate is complete. Their work is done, and I stand before my country to-day a Doorkeeper on Sufferance! But firm as a rock I stand at my post and await the verdict.

MARK TWAIN, Doorkeeper *ad interim*

1867

Female Suffrage

Editors Missouri Democrat:

I have read the long list of lady petitioners in favor of female suffrage, and as a husband and a father I want to protest against the whole business. It will never do to allow women to vote. It will never do to allow them to hold office. You know, and I know, that if they were granted these privileges there would be no more peace on earth. They would swamp the country with debt. They like to hold office too well. They like to be Mrs. President Smith of the Dorcas society, or Mrs. Secretary Jones of the Hindoo aid association, or Mrs. Treasurer of something or other. They are fond of the distinction of the thing, you know; they revel in the sweet jingle of the title. They are always setting up sanctified confederations of all kinds, and then running for president of them. They are even so fond of office that they are willing to serve without pay. But you allow them to vote and to go to the Legislature once, and then see how it will be. They will go to work and start a thousand more societies, and cram them full of salaried offices. You will see a state of things then that will stir your feelings to the bottom of your pockets. The first fee bill would exasperate you some. Instead of the usual schedule for judges, State printer, Supreme court clerks, &c., the list would read something like this:

OFFICES AND SALARIES.

President Dorcas society	$4,000
Subordinate officers of same, each	2,000
President Ladies' Union prayer meeting	3,000
President Pawnee Educational society	4,000
President of Ladies' society for Dissemination of Belles Lettres among the Shoshones	5,000

State Crinoline Directress	10,000
State Superintendent of waterfalls	10,000
State Hair Oil inspectress	10,000
State milliner	50,000

You know what a state of anarchy and social chaos that fee bill would create. Every woman in the commonwealth of Missouri would let go everything and run for State Milliner. And instead of ventilating each other's political antecedents, as men do, they would go straight after each other's private moral character. (I know them—they are all like my wife.) Before the canvass was three days old it would be an established proposition that every woman in the State was "no better than she ought to be." Only think how it would lacerate me to have an opposition candidate say that about my wife. That is the idea, you know—having other people say these hard things. Now, I know that my wife isn't any better than she ought to be, poor devil—in fact, in matters of orthodox doctrine, she is particularly shaky—but still I would not like these things aired in a political contest. I don't really suppose that that woman will stand any more show hereafter than—however, she may improve—she may even become a beacon light for the saving of others—but if she does, she will burn rather dim, and she will flicker a good deal, too. But, as I was saying, a female political canvass would be an outrageous thing.

Think of the torch-light processions that would distress our eyes. Think of the curious legends on the transparencies:

"Robbins forever! Vote for Sallie Robbins, the only virtuous candidate in the field!"

And this:

"Chastity, modesty, patriotism! Let the great people stand by Maria Sanders, the champion of morality and progress, and the only candidate with a stainless reputation!"

And this: "Vote for Judy McGinniss, the incorruptible! Nine children—one at the breast!"

In that day a man shall say to his servant, "What is the matter with the baby?" And the servant shall reply, "It has been sick for hours." "And where is its mother?" "She is out electioneering for Sallie Robbins." And such conversations as these shall transpire between ladies and servants applying for situations: "Can you cook?" "Yes." "Wash?" "Yes." "Do general housework?" "Yes." "All right;

who is your choice for State milliner?" "Judy McGinniss." "Well, you can tramp." And women shall talk politics instead of discussing the fashions; and they shall neglect the duties of the household to go out and take a drink with candidates; and men shall nurse the baby while their wives travel to the polls to vote. And also in that day the man who hath beautiful whiskers shall beat the homely man of wisdom for Governor, and the youth who waltzes with exquisite grace shall be Chief of Police, in preference to the man of practiced sagacity and determined energy.

Every man, I take it, has a selfish end in view when he pours out eloquence in behalf of the public good in the newspapers, and such is the case with me. I do not want the privileges of women extended, because my wife already holds office in nineteen different infernal female associations and I have to do all her clerking. If you give the women full sweep with the men in political affairs, she will proceed to run for every confounded office under the new dispensation. That will finish me. It is bound to finish me. She would not have time to do anything at all then, and the one solitary thing I have shirked up to the present time would fall on me and my family would go to destruction; for I am *not* qualified for a wet nurse.

MARK TWAIN

A VOLLEY FROM THE DOWN-TRODDEN

DEFENSE

Editors Missouri Democrat:

I should think you would be ashamed of yourselves. I would, anyway—to publish the vile, witless drivelings of that poor creature who degrades me with his name. I say you ought to be ashamed of yourselves. Two hundred noble, Spartan women cast themselves into the breach to free their sex from bondage, and instead of standing with bowed heads before the majesty of such a spectacle, you permit this flippant ass, my husband, to print a weak satire upon it. The wretch! I combed him with a piano stool for it. And I mean to comb every newspaper villain I can lay my hands on. They are nothing but villains anyhow. They published our names when nobody asked them to, and therefore they are low, mean and depraved, and fit for any crime however black and infamous.

Mr. Editor, I have not been appointed the champion of my sex in this matter; still, if I could know that any argument of mine in favor of female suffrage which has been presented in the above communication will win over any enemy to our cause, it would soften and soothe my dying hour; ah, yes, it would soothe it as never another soother could soothe it.

MRS. MARK TWAIN
President Afghanistan Aid Association,
Secretary of the Society
for introducing the Gospel into New Jersey, etc., etc., etc.

[The old woman states a case well, don't she? She states a case mighty well, for a woman of her years? She even soars into moving eloquence in that place where she says: "two hundred noble Spartan women cast themselves into the breeches," etc. And those "arguments" of hers afford her a prodigious satisfaction, don't they? She may possibly die easy on account of them, but she won't if I am around to stir her up in her last moments. That woman has made my life a burthen to me, and I mean to have a hand in soothing her myself when her time is up.—MARK TWAIN]

MORE DEFENSE

Editors Missouri Democrat:

I have read the article in your paper on female suffrage, by the atrocious scoundrel Mark Twain. But do not imagine that such a thing as that will deter us from demanding and enforcing our rights. Sir, we will have our rights, though the heavens fall. And as for this wretch, he had better find something else to do than meddling with matters he is incapable of understanding. I suppose he votes—such is law!—such is justice!—he is allowed to vote, but women a thousand times his superiors in intelligence are ruled out! —he!—a creature who don't know enough to follow the wires and find the telegraph office. Comment is unnecessary. If I get my hands on that whelp I will snatch hair out of his head till he is as bald as a phrenological bust.

Mr. Editor, I may not have done as much good for my species as I ought, in my time, but if any of the arguments I have presented in this article in favor of female suffrage shall aid in extending the privileges of woman, I shall die happy and content.

MRS. ZEB. LEAVENWORTH
Originator and President of the Association for the Establishment of a Female College in Kamschatka.

[I perceive that I have drawn the fire of another heavy gun. I feel as anxious as any man could to answer this old Kamschatkan, but I do not know where to take hold. Her "arguments" are too subtle for me. If she can die happy and content on that mild sort of gruel, though, let her slide.—MARK TWAIN]

MORE YET

Editors Missouri Democrat:

The depths of my heart of hearts are stirred. Gentle chiding from those that love me has ever fallen upon my wounded spirit like soothing moonlight upon a troubled sea, but harsh words from wretches is more than I can bear. I am not formed like others of my sex. All with me is ideal—is romance. I live in a world of my own that is peopled with the fairy creatures of fancy. When that is rudely invaded, my ethereal soul recoils in horror. For long years I have collected buttons, and door-plates and dictionaries, and all such things as I thought would make the poor savages of the South seas contented with their lot and lift them out of their ignorance and degradation—and no longer than a month ago I sent them Horace Greeley's speeches and some other cheerful literature, and the pure delight I felt was only marred by the reflection that the poor creatures could not read them—and yet I may not vote! Our petition for our rights is humanly attacked by one who has no heart, no soul, no gentle emotions, no poesy! In tuneful numbers I will bid this cold world adieu, and perchance when I am gone, Legislatures will drop a tear over one whose budding life they blighted, and be torn with vain regrets when it is all too late:

In sorrow I sorrow, O sorrowful day!
In grief-stricken tears O joy speed away!

I weep and I wail, and I waft broken sighs,
And I cry in my anguish, O Woman arise!

But I shout it in vain! for Demons have come,
Who drown my appeal with foul blasphemous tongue;
Yes, in sorrow I fade, and flicker and die!
Lo! a martyr to Suffrage in the tomb let me lie!

If I dared to hope that any argument I have here presented may be the means of securing justice to my down-trodden sex, I could lay me down and pass away as peacefully as the sighing of a breeze in summer forests.

MISS AUGUSTA JOSEPHINE MAITLAND,
Secretary of the Society for the Dissemination of Poetry among the Pawnees.

[Now, this old maid is a little spooney, of course, but she does not abuse me as much as the others, and it really touches me to know that she is going to fade, and flicker out. Her "arguments" are a little vague, but that is of no consequence. I haven't anything in the world against her, except that inspired atrocity of inflicting Horace Greeley's speeches on the poor heathen of the South Seas. What harm have they ever done her, that she should want to * * * * ?

You must excuse me. I see a procession of ladies filing in at my street door with tar-buckets and feather-beds, and other arrangements. I do not wish to crowd them. I will go out the back way. But I will singe that pestilent old wild-cat, my wife, for leading them.—MARK TWAIN]

"MARK TWAIN" GETS AN OVERHAULING FROM "COUSIN JENNIE"

"A. L." PITCHES IN, TOO

DEAR MARK:

I have just read the article in the Democrat wherein your views on "Female Suffrage" are so *characteristically* set forth. I am sorry you did not apprise me of your intentions previous to placing yourself before the public in such a light, for, as your cousin, I would, and as a woman I could have told you just how such an article would be received, and thus your good name might have been allowed to preserve untarnished its *sparkling* lustre. As you did not take me into your confidence, I have no right to respect your feelings by scolding you through the postoffice—you shall hear me through your own chosen medium.

And, in the first place, I venture the assertion that you yourself do not believe a word you say. Doubtless you are anxious it should be received as veritable truth. There are many who, when truth and justice give them the challenge, in their heart of hearts are with woman in her endeavors to do all and to be all, that she can do and be, still preserving her womanly dignity and integrity; yet through a selfish, unmanly fear—a fear that certain honors, and pleasant emoluments would be worthily worn and enjoyed by her, are loud and bitter in their denunciations against such endeavors.

As for voting, they are confident that for every stupid, thick brained man who is *sent* to the polls, a dozen clear thinking, unbiased women might *go*. As for offices, they know there is many a one that could as well, *fully as well,* be filled by even a weak woman as by a strong man. And as for the "jingle," Mark, they dare not say it is less sweet to their ears than to ours. Many a page of history will have to be obliterated, and many a memory clouded, before that will be received for truth. Then be honest, cousin Mark—confess that all light is not concealed in man's brain—admit that there is a ray or two in woman's, and after a while you will be prepared to see that mother nature has been as kind to her as to you, to say the least.

Of course, man's natural vanity and I-am-ism will suffer some in the contest. He has been taught that, although the other part of humanity is very beautiful and very lovely, it is every way unquestionably *weak;* and it is his enviable prerogative to fashion the laws and rules which shall regulate the life of that weak part. No wonder then his fancied superiority, and no wonder now, when the light that has been struggling for years to be admitted is seen and believed in, that many of the *strong* party are somewhat crestfallen. We are strong enough to see *that,* cousin Mark, and we see, too, a very good thing that may spring out of your disappointment—for we take it you *are* disappointed—since you see we are just as smart as you, you will bestir yourselves lest we outstrip you; for the opportunity given us, we will soar as high as we can. In this way, many a talent which is now folded away in a napkin, will be brought to light and polished. There is the "sweet" in the "bitter" for you, Mark Twain.

COUSIN JENNIE,
(*not one of the "signers"*)

THE DUTY OF MAN

Editors Missouri Democrat:

I am exceedingly curious to know why no one ever sees fit to write anything about the duty of man, when every issue of the press contains some lengthy article on woman's duty. Is it because man is so superior to the other sex, and created so perfect that his duties are always promptly and perfectly performed, leaving no room for advice or comment? or, is it because he is so inferior and insignificant that neither Creator nor creature ever saw fit to assign any duties for his performance? The press would have us believe the latter case, for how frequently it gives us illustrations of his weakness, in publishing the alarming numbers of drunkard's and suicide's graves, caused by some dereliction of woman's duty—say, for instance, a "missing button"; and then again it speaks of the drinking saloons, gambling halls, and worse places, being filled by men driven from their homes through woman's neglect. To give another instance, say an overdone joint, or a cup of weak coffee; and how many of the lords of creation are annually driven to insanity by the cruel treatment of their wives in having failed (perhaps but once) to meet their husbands with a smile; but no one seems to write anything about the cause of that smile's absence. Perhaps that very missing button might have had something to do with it. Might she not have been for many weary hours busy with her needle, not only for her husband but for their six or dozen children, and satisfied at last that she has all their garments in apple pie order; but when her "lord" comes to don a clean shirt preparatory to his club meeting, and draws from the very bottom of two dozen or more in *perfect* order one minus a button, with what heartache must that wife listen to cruel taunts and harsh fault-finding—harsher than even the most flagrant fault would justify. I don't wonder that "Mark Twain" and the male sex in general *should tremble in their shoes* at the *very idea* of having female influence extended, for if they wield such a mighty and almost miraculous influence *now* within the small sphere granted to them by the lords of creation, limited to the supervision of pots, kettles, buttons and babies, permitted to occupy the position of housekeeper and "wet nurse" for their victuals and clothes, what imagination could depict the unbounded influence she would exert if allowed to "*swing 'round the whole circle.*" We are truly grateful to man for condescending to admit that woman possesses such mighty power, but we don't altogether thank him for the impression he would convey that that same power is exerted *entirely for evil.* At the same time we pity him sincerely from the very bottom of our hearts for being so contemptibly weak as to allow his evil nature to yield to temptation; and what a miserable existence would be his but for his many comforts—*cards, liquor, tobacco, etc.* Alas for man's *strength of mind* and superiority. "*I don't see it.*"

A.L.

THE INIQUITOUS CRUSADE AGAINST MAN'S REGAL BIRTHRIGHT MUST BE CRUSHED

ANOTHER LETTER FROM MARK TWAIN

Dear Cousin Jennie:

I did not know I had a cousin named Jennie, but I am proud to claim such a relationship with you. I have no idea who you are, but you talk well—you talk exceedingly well. You seem inclined to treat the question of female suffrage seriously, and for once I will drop foolishness, and speak with the gravity the occasion demands. You fully understand the difference between justice and expediency? I am satisfied you do. You know very well that it would have been a just and righteous act if we had rescued struggling Poland four or five years ago, but you know also that it would not have been good policy to do it. No one will say that it is not just and right that women should vote; no one will say that an educated American woman would not vote with fifty times the judgment and independence exercised by stupid, illiterate newcomers from foreign lands; I will even go so far myself as to say that in my experience only third-rate intelligence is sent to Legislatures to make laws, because the first-rate article will not leave important private interests go unwatched to go and serve the public for a beggarly four or five dollars a day, and a miserably trivial distinction, while it is possible that a talented matron, unincumbered with children, might go with no great detriment to the affairs of her household. We know also that between constable and United States Senator, the one thousand offices of mere honor (though burdened with high responsibilities) are held by third-rate ability because first-rate ability can only afford to hold offices of great emolument—and we know that first-rate female talent *could* afford to hold those offices of mere honor without making business sacrifices. You see I have made a very strong argument for your side; and I repeat that no one will deny the truth of any of the above propositions; but behold that matter of expediency comes in here—policy!

Now, you think I am going to string out a long argument on my own side, but I am not. I only say this: The ignorant foreign women would vote with the ignorant foreign men—the bad women would vote with the bad men—the good women would vote with the good men. The same candidate who would be elected now would be elected then, the only difference being that there might be twice as many votes polled then as now. Then in what respect is the condition of things improved? I cannot see.

So, I conceive that if nothing is to be gained by it, it is inexpedient to extend the suffrage to women. That must be a benefit beyond the power of figures to estimate, which can make us consent to take the High Priestess we reverence at the sacred fireside and send her forth to electioneer for votes among a mangy mob who are unworthy to touch the hem of her garment. A lady of my acquaintance came very near putting my feeling in this matter into words the other day, Jennie, when she said she was opposed to female suffrage, because she was not willing to see her sex reduced to a level with negroes and men!

Female suffrage would do harm, my dear—it would actually do harm. A very large proportion of our best and wisest women would still cling to the holy ground of the home circle, and refuse to either vote or hold office—but every grand rascal among your sex would work, bribe and vote with all her might; and, behold, mediocrity and dishonesty would be appointed to conduct the affairs of government more surely than ever before. You see the policy of the thing is bad, very bad. It would augment the strength of the bad vote. I consider it a very strong point on our side of the question.

I think I could write a pretty strong argument in favor of female suffrage, but I do not want to do it. I never want to see women voting, and gabbling about politics, and electioneering. There is something revolting in the thought. It would shock me inexpressibly for an angel to come down from above and ask me to take a drink with him (though I should doubtless consent); but it would shock me still more to see one of our blessed earthly angels peddling election tickets among a mob of shabby scoundrels she never saw before.

There is one insuperable obstacle in the way of female suffrage, Jennie; I approach the subject with fear and trembling, but it must out: A woman would never vote, because she would have to tell her age at the polls. And even if she did dare to vote once or twice when she was just of age, you know what dire results would flow from "putting this and that together" in after times. For instance, in an unguarded moment, Miss A. says she voted for Mr. Smith. Her auditor, who knows it has been seven years since Smith ran for anything, easily ciphers out that she is at least seven years over age, instead of the tender young pullet she has been making herself out to be. No, Jennie, this new fashion of registering the name, age, residence and occupation of every voter, is a fatal bar to female suffrage.

Women will never be permitted to vote or hold office, Jennie, and it is a lucky thing for me, and for many other men, that such is the decree of fate. Because, you see, there are some few measures they would all unite on—there are one or two measures that would bring out their entire voting strength, in spite of their antipathy to making themselves conspicuous; and there being vastly more women than men in this State, they would trot those measures through the Legislature with a velocity that would be appalling. For instance, they would enact:

1. That all men should be at home by ten P.M., without fail.

2. That married men should bestow considerable attention on their own wives.

3. That it should be a hanging offense to sell whisky in saloons, and that fine and disfranchisement should follow the drinking of it in such places.

4. That the smoking of cigars to excess should be forbidden, and the smoking of pipes utterly abolished.

5. That the wife should have a little of her own property when she married a man who hadn't any.

Jennie, such tyranny as this, we could never stand. Our free souls could never endure such degrading thraldom. Women, go your ways! Seek not to beguile us of our imperial privileges. Content yourself with your little feminine trifles—your babies, your benevolent societies and your knitting—and let your natural bosses do the voting. Stand back—you will be wanting to go to war next. We will let you teach school as much as you want to, and we will pay you half wages for it, too, but beware! we don't want you to crowd us too much.

If I get time, Cousin Jennie, I will furnish you a picture of a female legislature that will distress you—I know it will, because you cannot disguise from me the fact that you are no more in favor of female suffrage, really, than I am.

In conclusion, honesty compels me to tell you that I have been highly complimented a dozen times on *my* articles signed "Cousin Jennie" and "A.L." The same honesty, though, compelled me to confess that I did not write either of those articles.

MARK TWAIN

P.S. That tiresome old goose, my wife, is prancing around like a lunatic, up stairs, rehearsing a speech in favor of female suffrage which she is going to deliver before a mass meeting of seditious old maids in my back parlor to-night. (She is a vigorous speaker, but you can smell her eloquence further than you can hear it; it is on account of gin, I think.) It is a pity those old skeletons have chosen my back parlor, because I have concluded to touch off a keg of powder under there to-night, and I am afraid the noise may disturb their deliberations some.

M.T.

ANOTHER FROM A.L.

Editors Missouri Democrat:

I think Cousin Jennie has handled the late popular subject pretty cleverly; but I think she has perpetrated somewhat of an "Irish bull," in calling upon "Mark Twain" to "confess that all light was not concealed in man's brain"; or, perhaps she was only cunningly contriving to have Mark commit himself and his sex irretrievably by strenuously maintaining that such was really the case. For so far as the light of man's brain *exists*—"that's just what's the matter"—it is always so *completely concealed*, that it never by any chance emits a single ray. Man runs away with the *fact* that by actual measurement the weight of his brain exceeds that of woman's, and he immediately builds up his everlasting reputation for intellect on that flimsy foundation, forgetting that quantity cannot make up for quality: when his very love for the "jingle" should have taught him that an ounce of gold is worth more than a pound of lead.

A.L.

1867

The Facts Concerning the Recent Resignation

Washington, December 2, 1867

I have resigned. The government appears to go on much the same, but there is a spoke out of its wheel, nevertheless. I was clerk of the Senate Committee on Conchology, and I have thrown up the position. I could see the plainest disposition on the part of the other members of the government to debar me from having any voice in the counsels of the nation, and so I could no longer hold office and retain my self-respect. If I were to detail all the outrages that were heaped upon me during the six days that I was connected with the government in an official capacity, the narrative would fill a volume. They appointed me clerk of that Committee on Conchology, and then allowed me no amanuensis to play billiards with. I would have borne that, lonesome as it was, if I had met with that courtesy from the other members of the Cabinet which was my due. But I did not. Whenever I observed that the head of a department was pursuing a wrong course, I laid down everything and went and tried to set him right, as it was my duty to do; and I never was thanked for it in a single instance. I went, with the best intentions in the world, to the Secretary of the Navy, and said:

"Sir, I cannot see that Admiral Farragut is doing anything but skirmishing around there in Europe, having a sort of picnic. Now, that may be all very well, but it does not exhibit itself to me in that light. If there is no fighting for him to do, let him come home. There is no use in a man having a whole fleet for a pleasure excursion. It is too expensive. Mind, I do not object to pleasure excursions for the naval officers—pleasure excursions that are in reason—pleasure excursions that are economical. Now, they might go down the Mississippi on a raft—"

You ought to have heard him storm! One would have supposed I had committed a crime of some kind. But I didn't mind. I said it was cheap, and full of republican simplicity, and perfectly safe. I said that, for a tranquil pleasure excursion, there was nothing equal to a raft.

Then the Secretary of the Navy asked me who I was; and when I told him I was connected with the government, he wanted to know in what capacity. I said that, without remarking upon the singularity of such a question, coming, as it did, from a member of that same government, I would inform him that I was clerk of the Senate Committee on Conchology. Then there was a fine storm! He finished by ordering me to leave the premises, and give my attention strictly to my own business in future. My first impulse was to get him removed. However, that would harm others besides himself, and do me no real good, and so I let him stay.

I went next to the Secretary of War, who was not inclined to see me at all until he learned that I was connected with the government. If I had not been on important business, I suppose I could not have got in. I asked him for a light (he was smoking at the time), and then I told him I had no fault to find with his defending the parole stipulations of General Lee and his comrades in arms, but that I could not approve of his method of fighting the Indians on the Plains. I said he fought too scattering. He ought to get the Indians more together—get them together in some convenient place, where he could have provisions enough for both parties, and then have a general massacre. I said there was nothing so convincing to an Indian as a general massacre. If he could not approve of the massacre, I said the next surest thing for an Indian was soap and education. Soap and education are not as sudden as a massacre, but they are more deadly in the long run; because a half-massacred Indian may recover, but if you educate him and wash him, it is found to finish him some time or other. It undermines his constitution; it strikes at the foundation of his being. "Sir," I said, "the time has come when blood-curdling cruelty has become necessary. Inflict soap and a spelling-book on every Indian that ravages the Plains, and let them die!"

The Secretary of War asked me if I was a member of the Cabinet, and I said I was. He inquired what position I held, and I said I was clerk of the Senate Committee on Conchology. I was then ordered under arrest for contempt of court, and restrained of my liberty for the best part of the day.

I almost resolved to be silent thenceforward, and let the Government get along the best way it could. But duty called, and I obeyed. I called on the Secretary of the Treasury. He said:

"What will *you* have?"

The question threw me off my guard. I said, "Rum punch."

He said: "If you have got any business here, sir, state it—and in as few words as possible."

I then said that I was sorry he had seen fit to change the subject so abruptly, because such conduct was very offensive to me; but under the circumstances I would overlook the matter and come to the point. I now went into an earnest expostulation with him upon the extravagant length of his report. I said it was expensive, unnecessary, and awkwardly constructed; there were no descriptive passages in it, no poetry, no sentiment—no heroes, no plot, no pictures —not even woodcuts. Nobody would read it, that was a clear case. I urged him not to ruin his reputation by getting out a thing like that. If he ever hoped to succeed in literature he must throw more variety into his writings. He must beware of dry detail. I said that the main popularity of the almanac was derived from its poetry and conundrums, and that a few conundrums distributed around through his Treasury report would help the sale of it more than all the internal revenue he could put into it. I said these things in the kindest spirit, and yet the Secretary of the Treasury fell into a violent passion. He even said I was an ass. He abused me in the most vindictive manner, and said that if I came there again meddling with his business he would throw me out of the window. I said I would take my hat and go, if I could not be treated with the respect due to my office, and I did go. It was just like a new author. They always think they know more than anybody else when they are getting out their first book. Nobody can tell *them* anything.

During the whole time that I was connected with the government it seemed as if I could not do anything in an official capacity without getting myself into trouble. And yet I did nothing, attempted nothing, but what I conceived to be for the good of my country. The sting of my wrongs may have driven me to unjust and harmful conclusions, but it surely seemed to me that the Secretary of State, the Secretary of War, the Secretary of the Treasury, and others of my *confrères* had conspired from the very beginning to drive me from the Administration. I never attended but one Cabinet meeting while I was connected with the government. That was sufficient for me. The servant at the White House door did not seem disposed to make way for me until I asked if the other members of the Cabinet had arrived. He said they had, and I entered. They were all there; but nobody offered me a seat. They stared at me as if I had been an intruder. The President said:

"Well, sir, who are *you*?"

I handed him my card, and he read: "The HON. MARK TWAIN, Clerk of the Senate Committee on Conchology." Then he looked at me from head to foot, as if he had never heard of me before. The Secretary of the Treasury said:

"This is the meddlesome ass that came to recommend me to put poetry and conundrums in my report, as if it were an almanac."

The Secretary of War said: "It is the same visionary that came to me yesterday with a scheme to educate a portion of the Indians to death, and massacre the balance."

The Secretary of the Navy said: "I recognize this youth as the person who has been interfering with my business time and again during the week. He is distressed about Admiral Farragut's using a whole fleet for a pleasure excursion, as he terms it. His proposition about some insane pleasure excursion on a raft is too absurd to repeat."

I said: "Gentlemen, I perceive here a disposition to throw discredit upon every act of my official career; I perceive, also, a disposition to debar me from all voice in the counsels of the nation. No notice whatever was sent to me to-day. It was only by the merest chance that I learned that there was going to be a Cabinet meeting. But let these things pass. All I wish to know is, is this a Cabinet meeting or is it not?"

The President said it was.

"Then," I said, "let us proceed to business at once, and not fritter away valuable time in unbecoming fault-findings with each other's official conduct."

The Secretary of State now spoke up, in his benignant way, and said, "Young man, you are laboring under a mistake. The clerks of the Congressional committees are not members of the Cabinet. Neither are the doorkeepers of the Capitol, strange as it may seem. Therefore, much as we could desire your more than human wisdom in our deliberations, we cannot lawfully avail ourselves of it. The counsels of the nation must proceed without you; if disaster follows, as follow full well it may, be it balm to your sorrowing spirit that by deed and voice you did what in you lay to avert it. You have my blessing. Farewell."

These gentle words soothed my troubled breast, and I went away. But the servants of a nation can know no peace. I had hardly reached my den in the Capitol, and disposed my feet on the table like a representative, when one of the Senators on the Conchological Committee came in in a passion and said:

"Where have you been all day?"

I observed that, if that was anybody's affair but my own, I had been to a Cabinet meeting.

"To a Cabinet meeting? I would like to know what business you had at a Cabinet meeting?"

I said I went there to consult—allowing for the sake of argument that he was in any wise concerned in the matter. He grew insolent then, and ended by saying he had wanted me for three days past to copy a report on bomb-shells, egg-shells, clam-shells, and I don't know what all, connected with conchology, and nobody had been able to find me.

This was too much. This was the feather that broke the clerical camel's back. I said, "Sir, do you suppose that I am going to *work* for six dollars a day? If that is the idea, let me recommend the Senate Committee on Conchology to hire somebody else. I am the slave of *no* faction! Take back your degrading commission. Give me liberty, or give me death!"

From that hour I was no longer connected with the government. Snubbed by the department, snubbed by the Cabinet, snubbed at last by the chairman of a committee I was endeavoring to adorn, I yielded to persecution, cast far from me the perils and seductions of my great office, and forsook my bleeding country in the hour of her peril.

But I had done the state some service, and I sent in my bill:

The United States of America in account with
the Hon. Clerk of the Senate Committee on Conchology, Dr.

To consultation with Secretary of War	$50
To consultation with Secretary of Navy	50
To consultation with Secretary of the Treasury	50
Cabinet consultation	No charge.

To mileage to and from Jerusalem,* *via* Egypt, Algiers, Gibraltar, and Cadiz, 14,000 miles, at 20c. a mile	2,800
To salary as Clerk of Senate Committee on Conchology, six days, at $6 per day	36
Total	$2,986

Not an item of this bill has been paid, except that trifle of thirty-six dollars for clerkship salary. The Secretary of the Treasury, pursuing me to the last, drew his pen through all the other items, and simply marked in the margin "Not allowed." So, the dread alternative is embraced at last. Repudiation had begun! The nation is lost.

I am done with official life for the present. Let those clerks who are willing to be imposed on remain. I know numbers of them in the departments who are never informed when there is to be a Cabinet meeting, whose advice is never asked about war, or finance, or commerce, by the heads of the nation, any more than if they were not connected with the government, and who actually stay in their offices day after day and work! They know their importance to the nation, and they unconsciously show it in their bearing, and the way they order their sustenance at the restaurant—but they work. I know one who has to paste all sorts of little scraps from the newspapers into a scrapbook—sometimes as many as eight or ten scraps a day. He doesn't do it well, but he does it as well as he can. It is very fatiguing. It is exhausting to the intellect. Yet he only gets eighteen hundred dollars a year. With a brain like his, that young man could amass thousands and thousands of dollars in some other pursuit, if he chose to do it. But no—his heart is with his country, and he will serve her as long as she has got a scrapbook left. And I know clerks that don't know how to write very well, but such knowledge as they possess they nobly lay at the feet of their country, and toil on and suffer for twenty-five hundred dollars a year. What they write has to be written over again by other clerks sometimes; but when a man has done his best for his country, should his country complain? Then there are clerks that have no clerkships, and are waiting, and waiting, and waiting for a vacancy—waiting patiently for a chance to help their country out—and while they are waiting, they only get barely two thousand dollars a year for it. It is

* Territorial delegates charge mileage both ways, although they never go back when they get here once. Why my mileage is denied me is more than I can understand.

sad—it is very, very sad. When a member of Congress has a friend who is gifted, but has no employment wherein his great powers may be brought to bear, he confers him upon his country, and gives him a clerkship in a department. And there that man has to slave his life out, fighting documents for the benefit of a nation that never thinks of him, never sympathizes with him—and all for two thousand or three thousand dollars a year. When I shall have completed my list of all the clerks in the several departments, with my statement of what they have to do, and what they get for it, you will see that there are not half enough clerks, and that what there are do not get half enough pay.

1868

My Late Senatorial Secretaryship

I am not a private secretary to a senator any more now. I held the berth two months in security and in great cheerfulness of spirit, but my bread began to return from over the waters then—that is to say, my works came back and revealed themselves. I judged it best to resign. The way of it was this. My employer sent for me one morning tolerably early, and, as soon as I had finished inserting some conundrums clandestinely into his last great speech upon finance, I entered the presence. There was something portentous in his appearance. His cravat was untied, his hair was in a state of disorder, and his countenance bore about it the signs of a suppressed storm. He held a package of letters in his tense grasp, and I knew that the dreaded Pacific mail was in. He said:

"I thought you were worthy of confidence."

I said, "Yes, sir."

He said, "I gave you a letter from certain of my constituents in the State of Nevada, asking the establishment of a post-office at Baldwin's Ranch, and told you to answer it, as ingeniously as you could, with arguments which should persuade them that there was no real necessity for an office at that place."

I felt easier. "Oh, if that is all, sir, I *did* do that."

"Yes, you *did*. I will read your answer for your own humiliation:

"'*Washington, Nov. 24*

"'*Messrs. Smith, Jones, and others.*

"'Gentlemen: What the mischief do you suppose you want with a post-office at Baldwin's Ranch? It would not do you any good. If any letters came there, you couldn't read them, you know; and, besides, such letters as ought to pass through, with money in them, for other localities, would not be likely to *get* through, you must perceive at once; and that would make trouble for us all. No, don't bother about a post-office in your camp. I have your best interests at heart, and feel that it would only be an ornamental folly. What you want is a nice jail, you know—a nice, substantial jail and a free school. These will be a lasting benefit to you. These will make you really contented and happy. I will move in the matter at once.

"'Very truly, etc.,
"'MARK TWAIN,
"'For James W. N——, U. S. Senator.'

"That is the way you answered that letter. Those people say they will hang me, if I ever enter that district again; and I am perfectly satisfied they *will*, too."

"Well, sir, I did not know I was doing any harm. I only wanted to convince them."

"Ah. Well, you *did* convince them, I make no manner of doubt. Now, here is another specimen. I gave you a petition from certain gentlemen of Nevada, praying that I would get a bill through Congress incorporating the Methodist Episcopal Church of the State of Nevada. I told you to say, in reply, that the creation of such a law came more properly within the province of the state legislature; and to endeavor to show them that, in the present feebleness of the religious element in that new commonwealth, the expediency of incorporating the church was questionable. What did you write?

"'*Washington, Nov. 24*

"'*Rev. John Halifax and others.*

"'GENTLEMEN: You will have to go to the state legislature about the speculation of yours—Congress don't know anything about religion. But don't you hurry to go there, either; because this thing you propose to do out in that new country isn't expedient—in fact, it is ridiculous. Your religious people there are too feeble, in intellect, in morality, in piety—in everything, pretty much. You had better drop this—you can't make it work. You can't issue stock on an incorporation like that—or if you could, it would only keep you in trouble all the time. The other denominations would abuse it, and "bear" it, and "sell it short," and break it down. They would do with it just as they would with one of your silver-mines out there—they would try to make all the world believe it was "wildcat." You ought not to do anything that is calculated to bring a sacred thing into disrepute. You ought to be ashamed of yourselves—that is what *I* think about it. You close your petition with the words: "And we will ever pray." I think you had better—you need to do it.

"'Very truly, etc.,
"'MARK TWAIN,
"'For James W. N——, U. S. Senator.'

"*That* luminous epistle finishes me with the religious element among my constitutents. But that my political murder might be made sure, some evil instinct prompted me to hand you this memorial from the grave company of elders composing the board of aldermen of the city of San Francisco, to try your hand upon—a memorial praying that the city's right to the water-lots upon the city front might be established by law of Congress. I told you this was a dangerous matter to move in. I told you to write a non-committal letter to the aldermen—an ambiguous letter—a letter that should avoid, as far as possible, all real consideration and discussion of the water-lot question. If there is any feeling left in you—any shame—surely this letter you wrote, in obedience to that order, ought to evoke it, when its words fall upon your ears:

"'*Washington, Nov. 27*

"'*The Honorable Board of Aldermen, etc.*

"'GENTLEMEN: George Washington, the revered Father of his Country, is dead. His long and brilliant career is closed, alas! forever. He was greatly respected in this section of the country, and his untimely decease cast a gloom over the whole community. He died on the 14th day of December, 1799. He passed peacefully away from the scene of his honors and his great achievements, the most lamented hero and the best beloved that ever earth hath yielded unto Death. At such a time as this, *you* speak of water-lots! —what a lot was his!

"'What is fame! Fame is an accident. Sir Isaac Newton discovered an apple falling to the ground—a trivial discovery, truly, and one which a million men had made before him—but his parents were influential, and so they tortured that small circumstance into something wonderful, and, lo! the simple world took up the shout and, in almost the twinkling of an eye, that man was famous. Treasure these thoughts.

"'Poesy, sweet poesy, who shall estimate what the world owes to thee!'

"Mary had a little lamb, its fleece was white as snow—
And everywhere that Mary went, the lamb was sure to go."

"Jack and Gill went up the hill
To draw a pail of water;
Jack fell down and broke his crown,
And Gill came tumbling after."

"'For simplicity, elegance of diction, and freedom from immoral tendencies, I regard those two poems in the light of gems. They are suited to all grades of intelligence, to every sphere of life—to the field, to the nursery, to the guild. Especially should no Board of Aldermen be without them.

"'Venerable fossils! write again. Nothing improves one so much as friendly correspondence. Write again—and if there is anything in this memorial of yours that refers to anything in particular, do not be backward about explaining it. We shall always be happy to hear you chirp.

"'Very truly, etc.,
"'MARK TWAIN,
"'For James W. N——, U. S. Senator.'

"That is an atrocious, a ruinous epistle! Distraction!"

"Well, sir, I am really sorry if there is anything wrong about it—but—but it appears to me to dodge the water-lot question."

"Dodge the mischief! Oh!—but never mind. As long as destruction must come now, let it be complete. Let it be complete—let this last of your performances, which I am about to read, make a finality of it. I am a ruined man. I *had* my misgivings when I gave you the letter from Humboldt, asking that the post route from Indian Gulch to Shakespeare Gap and intermediate points be changed partly to the old Mormon trail. But I told you it was a delicate question, and warned you to deal with it deftly—to answer it dubiously, and leave them a little in the dark. And your fatal imbecility impelled you to make *this* disastrous reply. I should think you would stop your ears, if you are not dead to all shame:

"'*Washington, Nov. 30*

"'*Messrs. Perkins, Wagner, et al.*

"'GENTLEMEN: It is a delicate question about this Indian trail, but, handled with proper deftness and dubiousness, I doubt not we shall succeed in some measure or otherwise, because the place where the route leaves the Lassen Meadows, over beyond where those two Shawnee chiefs, Dilapidated-Vengeance and Biter-of-the-Clouds, were scalped last winter, this being the favorite direction to some, but others preferring something else in consequence of things, the Mormon trail leaving Mosby's at three in the morning, and passing through Jawbone Flat to Blucher, and then down by Jug-Handle, the road passing to the right of it, and naturally leaving it on the right, too, and Dawson's on the left of the trail where it passes to the left of said Dawson's and onward thence to Tomahawk, thus making the route cheaper, easier of access to all who can get at it, and compassing all the desirable objects so considered by others, and, therefore, conferring the most good upon the greatest number, and, consequently, I am encouraged to hope we shall. However, I shall be ready, and happy, to afford you still further information upon the subject, from time to time, as you may desire it and the Post-office Department be enabled to furnish it to me.

"'Very truly, etc.,
"'MARK TWAIN,
"'For James W. N——, U. S. Senator.'

"There—now *what* do you think of that?"

"Well, I don't know, sir. It—well, it appears to me—to be dubious enough."

"Du—leave the house! I am a ruined man. Those Humboldt savages never will forgive me for tangling their brains up with this inhuman letter. I have lost the respect of the Methodist Church, the board of aldermen—"

"Well, I haven't anything to say about that, because I may have missed it a little in their cases, but I *was* too many for the Baldwin's Ranch people, General!"

"Leave the house! Leave it forever and forever, too."

I regarded that as a sort of covert intimation that my service could be dispensed with, and so I resigned. I never will be a private secretary to a senator again. You can't please that kind of people. They don't know anything. They can't appreciate a party's efforts.

1868

Private Habits of Horace Greeley

An intimate acquaintance with a distant relative of the editor of the *Tribune* puts it in my power to furnish the public with the last—positively the very last—link necessary to perfect the chain of knowledge already in its possession concerning Mr. Greeley: I mean his private habits. We know *all* about him as regards every other department of his life and service. Because, whenever a magazinist or a bookmaker is employed to write, and cannot think of a subject, he writes about Horace Greeley. Even the boys in the schools have quit building inspired "compositions" on "The Horse," and have gone to doing Horace Greeley instead; and when declamation-day comes around, their voices are no longer "still for war" and Patrick Henry, but for peace and Horace Greeley. Now, the natural result of all this is that the public have come at last to think that this man has no life but public life, no nature but a public nature, no habits but public habits. This is all wrong. Mr. Greeley *has* a private life. Mr. Greeley *has* private habits.

Mr. Greeley gets up at three o'clock in the morning; for it is one of his favorite maxims that only early rising can keep the health unimpaired and the brain vigorous. He then wakes up all the household and assembles them in the library, by candle-light: and, after quoting the beautiful lines,

> "Early to bed and early to rise
> Make a man healthy, wealthy, and wise,"

he appoints each individual's task for the day, sets him at it with encouraging words, and goes back to bed again. I mention here, in no fault-finding spirit, but with the deference justly due a man who is older and wiser and worthier than I, that he snores awfully. In a moment of irritation, once, I was rash enough to say I never would sleep with him until he broke himself of the unfortunate habit. I have kept my word with bigoted and unwavering determination.

At half-past eleven o'clock Mr. Greeley rises again. He shaves himself. He considers that there is great virtue and economy in shaving himself. He does it with a dull razor, sometimes humming a part of a tune (he knows part of a tune and takes an innocent delight in regarding it as the first half of Old Hundred; but parties familiar with that hymn have felt obliged to confess that they could not recognize it, and, therefore, the noise he makes is doubtless an unconscious original composition of Mr. Greeley's) and sometimes, when the razor is especially dull, he accompanies himself with a formula like this: "Damn the damned razor, and the damned outcast who made it."—H.G.

He then goes out into his model garden, and applies his vast store of agricultural knowledge to the amelioration of his cabbage: after which he writes an able agricultural article for the instruction of American farmers, his soul cheered the while with the reflection that if cabbages were worth eleven dollars apiece his model farm would pay.

He next goes to breakfast, which is a frugal, abstemious meal with him, and consists of nothing but just such things as the market affords, nothing more. He drinks nothing but water—nothing whatever but water and coffee, and tea, and Scotch ale, and lager beer and lemonade with a fly in it—sometimes a house fly, and sometimes a horse fly, according to the amount of inspiration required to warm him up to his daily duties. During breakfast he reads the *Tribune* all through, and enjoys the satisfaction of knowing that all the brilliant things in it, written by Young and Cooke and Hazard, and myself, are attributed to *him* by a confiding and infernal public.

After breakfast he writes a short editorial, and puts a large dash at the beginning of it, thus (——), which is the same as if he put H.G. after it, and takes a savage pleasure in reflecting that none of us understrappers can use that dash, except in profane conversation when chaffing over the outrage. He writes this editorial in his own handwriting. He does it because he is so vain of his penmanship. He always did take an inordinate pride in his penmanship. He hired out once, in his young days, as a writing master, but the enterprise failed. The pupils could not translate his marks with any certainty. His first copy was "Virtue is its own reward," and they got it "Washing with soap is wholly absurd," and so the trustees discharged him for attempting to convey bad morals, through the medium of worse penmanship. But, as I was saying, he writes his morning editorial. Then he tries to read it over, and can't do it, and so sends it to the printers, and *they* try to read it, and can't do it; and so they set it up at random, as you may say, putting in what words they can make out, and when they get aground on a long word they put in "reconstruction" or "universal suffrage," and spar off the paddle ahead, and next morning, if the degraded public can tell what it is all about, they say H.G. wrote it, and if they can't, they say it is one of those imbecile understrappers, and that is the end of it.

On Sundays Mr. Greeley sits in a prominent pew in Mr. Chaplin's church and lets on that he is asleep, and the congregation regard it as an eccentricity of genius.

When he is going to appear in public, Mr. Greeley spends two hours on his toilet. He is the most painstaking and elaborate man about getting up his dress that lives in America. This is his chiefest and his pleasantest foible. He puts on a soiled shirt, saved from the wash, and leaves one end of the collar unbuttoned. He puts on his most dilapidated hat, turns it wrong side before, cants it onto the back of his head, and jams an extra dent in the side of it. He puts on his most atrocious boots, and spends fifteen minutes tucking the left leg of his pants into his boottop in what shall seem the most careless and unstudied way. But his cravat—it is into the arrangement of his cravat that he throws all his soul, all the powers of his great mind. After fixing at it for forty minutes before the glass it is perfect—it is askew in every way—it overflows his coat-collar on one side and sinks into oblivion on the other—it climbs and it delves around about his neck—the knot is conspicuously displayed under his left ear, and it stretches one of its long ends straight out horizontally, and the other goes after his eye, in the good old Toodles fashion—and then, completely and marvelously apparelled, Mr. Greeley strides forth, rolling like a sailor, a miracle of astounding costumery, the awe and wonder of the nations!

But I haven't time to tell the rest of his private habits. Suffice it that he is an upright and an honest man—a practical, great-brained man—a useful man to his nation and his generation—a famous man who has justly earned his celebrity—and withal the worst-dressed man in this or any other country, even though he *does* take so thundering much pains and put on so many frills about it.

1868

Last Words of Great Men

Marshal Neil's last words were: "L'armée francaise!" (The French army.)—*Exchange.*

What a sad thing it is to see a man close a grand career with a plagiarism in his mouth. Napoleon's last words were: "Tête d'armée." (Head of the army.) Neither of those remarks amounts to anything as "last words," and reflects little credit upon the utterer. A distinguished man should be as particular about his last words as he is about his last breath. He should write them out on a slip of paper and take the judgment of his friends on them. He should never leave such a thing to the last hour of his life, and trust to an intellectual spirit at the last moment to enable him to say something smart with his latest gasp and launch into eternity with grandeur. No—a man is apt to be too much fagged and exhausted, both in body and mind, at such a time, to be reliable; and maybe the very thing he wants to say, he cannot think of to save him; and besides there are his weeping friends bothering around; and worse than all as likely as not he may have to deliver his last gasp before he is expecting to. A man cannot always expect to think of a natty thing to say under such circumstances, and so it is pure egotistic ostentation to put it off. There is hardly a case on record where a man came to his last moment unprepared and said a good thing—hardly a case where a man trusted to that last moment and did not make a solemn botch of it and go out of the world feeling absurd.

Now there was Daniel Webster. Nobody could tell him anything. *He* was not afraid. *He* could do something neat when the time came. And how did it turn out? Why, his will had to be fixed over; and then all the relations came; and first one thing and then another interfered, till at last he only had a chance to say, "I still live," and up he went. Of course he didn't still live, because he died—and so he might as well have kept his last words to himself as to have gone and made such a failure of it as that. A week before that fifteen minutes of calm reflection would have enabled that man to contrive some last words that would have been a credit to himself and a comfort to his family for generations to come.

And there was John Quincy Adams. Relying on his splendid abilities and his coolness in emergencies, *he* trusted to a happy hit at the last moment to carry him through, and what was the result? Death smote him in the House of Representatives, and he observed, casually, "This is the last of earth." The last of earth! Why "the last of earth" when there was so much more left? If he had said it was the last rose of summer or the last run of shad, it would have had as much point in it. What he meant to say was, "Adam was the first and Adams is the last of earth," but he put it off a trifle too long, and so he had to go with that unmeaning observation on his lips.

And there we have Napoleon's "Tête d'armée." That don't mean anything. Taken by itself, "Head of the army," is no more important than "Head of the police." And yet that was a man who could have said a good thing if he had barred out the doctor and studied over it a while. Marshal Neil, with half a century at his disposal, could not dash off anything better in his last moments than a poor plagiarism of another man's words, which were not worth plagiarizing in the first place. "The French army." Perfectly irrelevant—perfectly flat—utterly pointless. But if he had closed one eye significantly, and said, "The subscriber has made it lively for the French army," and then thrown a little of the comic into his last gasp, it would have been a thing to remember with satisfaction all the rest of his life. I do wish our great men would quit saying these flat things just at the moment they die. Let us have their next-to-the-last words for a while, and see if we cannot patch up from them something that will be more satisfactory. The public does not wish to be outraged in this way all the time.

But when we come to call to mind the last words of parties who took the trouble to make the proper preparation for the occasion, we immediately notice a happy difference in the result.

There was Chesterfield. Lord Chesterfield had labored all his life to build up the most shining reputation for affability and elegance of speech and manners the world has ever seen. And could you suppose he failed to appreciate the efficiency of characteristic "last words," in the matter of seizing the successfully driven nail of such a reputation and clinching on the other side for ever? Not he. He prepared himself. He kept his eye on the clock and his finger on his pulse. He awaited his chance. And at last, when he knew his time was come, he pretended to think a new visitor had entered, and so, with the rattle in his throat emphasised for dramatic effect, he said to the servant, "Shin around, John, and get the gentleman a chair." And so he died, amid thunders of applause.

Next we have Benjamin Franklin. Franklin, the author of Poor Richard's quaint sayings; Franklin the immortal axiom-builder, who used to sit up at nights reducing the rankest old threadbare platitudes to crisp and snappy maxims that had a nice, varnished, original look in their regimentals; who said, "Virtue is its own reward"; who said, "Procrastination is the thief of time"; who said, "Time and tide wait for no man" and "Necessity is the mother of invention"; good old Franklin, the Josh Billings of the eighteenth century—though, sooth to say, the latter transcends him in proverbial originality as much as he falls short of him in correctness of orthography. What sort of tactics did Franklin pursue? He pondered over his last words for as much as two weeks, and then when the time came, he said, "None but the brave deserve the fair," and died happy. He could not have said a sweeter thing if he had lived till he was an idiot.

Byron made a poor business of it, and could not think of anything to say, at the last moment but, "Augusta-sister-Lady Byron—tell Harriet Beecher Stowe"—etc., etc.,—but Shakespeare was ready and said, "England expects every man to do his duty!" and went off with splendid eclat.

And there are other instances of sagacious preparation for a felicitous closing remark. For instance:

Joan of Arc said, "Tramp, tramp, tramp the boys are marching."

Alexander the Great said, "Another of those Santa Cruz punches, if you please."

The Empress Josephine said, "Not for Jo—" and could get no further.

Cleopatra said, "The Old Guard dies, but never surrenders."

Sir Walter Raleigh said, "Executioner, can I take your whetstone a moment, please?" though what for is not clear.

John Smith said, "Alas, I am the last of my race."

Queen Elizabeth said, "Oh, I would give my kingdom for one moment more—I have forgotten my last words."

And Red Jacket, the noblest Indian brave that ever wielded a tomahawk in defence of a friendless and persecuted race, expired with these touching words upon his lips, "*Wawkawampanoosuc, winnebagowallawsagamoresaskatchewan.*" There was not a dry eye in the wigwam.

Let not this lesson be lost upon our public men. Let them take a healthy moment for preparation, and contrive some last words that shall be neat and to the point. Let Louis Napoleon say,

"I am content to follow my uncle—still, I do not wish to improve upon his last word. Put me down for 'Tête d'armée.'"

And Garret Davis, "Let me recite the unabridged dictionary."

And H.G., "I desire, now, to say a few words on political economy."

And Mr. Bergh, "Only take part of me at a time, if the load will be fatiguing to the hearse horses."

And Andrew Johnson, "I have been an Alderman, Member of Congress, Governor, Senator, Pres—adieu, you know the rest."

And Seward, "Alas!-ka."

And Grant, "O."

All of which is respectfully submitted, with the most honorable intentions.

M.T.

P.S.—I am obliged to leave out the illustrations. The artist finds it impossible to make a picture of people's last words.

1869

A Mystery Cleared Up

Ex-Secretary Stanton had an interview with Secretary Fish, yesterday.—

Sensation Telegram of Associated Press.

I was present at that interview. The subject of it was Warts.

Ex-Secretary Stanton said that when he was a boy, he had sixteen on his left hand, one or two on his right thumb, and one on his elbow. He said he used to always hunt for old hollow stumps, with rain-water standing in them, to soak his warts in.

Secretary Fish said he had a million of warts when he was a boy, and sometimes he split a bean and tied it over his wart, and then took that bean and buried it in the cross roads at midnight in the dark of the moon.

Ex-Secretary Stanton said he had tried that, but it never worked.

Secretary Fish said he could not remember that it worked—he only remembered trying it a good many times, and in the most unquestioning good faith.

Ex-Secretary Stanton said his usual plan was to run a needle through the wart, and then hold the end of the needle in the candle till it warmed the wart to that degree that it would never take an interest in this world's follies and vanities any more forever.

Secretary Fish said he thought likely he was the wartiest boy that ever——

At this opportune moment ex-Secretary Stanton's carriage was announced, and he arose and took his leave. The next Associated Press dispatch that distressed the people through the columns of every single newspaper in America read as follows:

"The subject of the interview between ex-Secretary Stanton and Secretary Fish has not transpired. There are various flying rumors.

It is generally believed that it referred to the Alabama question, and was very important."

And yet they were only talking about Warts.

Hereafter, when I see vague, dreadful Associated Press dispatches, stating that Jones called on the Secretary of the Interior last night, or Smith had an interview with the Attorney General, or Brown was closeted with the President until a late hour yesterday evening, I shall feel certain that they were only talking about Warts, or something like that. They can never fire my interest again with one of those dispatches, unless they state *what* the interview was about.

1869

The Late Benjamin Franklin

["Never put off till to-morrow what you can do day after to-morrow just as well."—B. F.]

This party was one of those persons whom they call Philosophers. He was twins, being born simultaneously in two different houses in the city of Boston. These houses remain unto this day, and have signs upon them worded in accordance with the facts. The signs are considered well enough to have, though not necessary, because the inhabitants point out the two birthplaces to the stranger anyhow, and sometimes as often as several times in the same day. The subject of this memoir was of a vicious disposition, and early prostituted his talents to the invention of maxims and aphorisms calculated to inflict suffering upon the rising generation of all subsequent ages. His simplest acts, also, were contrived with a view to their being held up for the emulation of boys forever—boys who might otherwise have been happy. It was in this spirit that he became the son of a soap-boiler, and probably for no other reason than that the efforts of all future boys who tried to be anything might be looked upon with suspicion unless they were the sons of soap-boilers. With a malevolence which is without parallel in history, he would work all day, and then sit up nights, and let on to be studying algebra by the light of a smoldering fire, so that all other boys might have to do that also, or else have Benjamin Franklin thrown up to them. Not satisfied with these proceedings, he had a fashion of living wholly on bread and water, and studying astronomy at meal-time—a thing which has brought affliction to millions of boys since, whose fathers had read Franklin's pernicious biography.

His maxims were full of animosity toward boys. Nowadays a boy cannot follow out a single natural instinct without tumbling over some of those everlasting aphorisms and hearing from Franklin on the spot. If he buys two cents' worth of peanuts, his father says, "Remember what Franklin has said, my son—'A groat a day's a penny a year' "; and the comfort is all gone out of those peanuts. If he wants to spin his top when he has done work, his father quotes, "Procrastination is the thief of time." If he does a virtuous action, he never gets anything for it, because "Virtue is its own reward." And that boy is hounded to death and robbed of his natural rest, because Franklin said once, in one of his inspired flights of malignity:

> Early to bed and early to rise
> Makes a man healthy and wealthy and wise.

As if it were any object to a boy to be healthy and wealthy and wise on such terms. The sorrow that that maxim has cost me, through my parents, experimenting on me with it, tongue cannot tell. The legitimate result is my present state of general debility, indigence, and mental aberration. My parents used to have me up before nine o'clock in the morning sometimes when I was a boy. If they had let me take my natural rest where would I have been now? Keeping store, no doubt, and respected by all.

And what an adroit old adventurer the subject of this memoir was! In order to get a chance to fly his kite on Sunday he used to hang a key on the string and let on to be fishing for lightning. And a guileless public would go home chirping about the "wisdom" and the "genius" of the hoary Sabbath-breaker. If anybody caught him playing "mumble-peg" by himself, after the age of sixty, he would immediately appear to be ciphering out how the grass grew—as if it was any of his business. My grandfather knew him well, and he says Franklin was always fixed—always ready. If a body, during his old age, happened on him unexpectedly when he was catching flies, or making mud-pies, or sliding on a cellar door, he would immediately look wise, and rip out a maxim, and walk off with his nose in the air and his cap turned wrong side before, trying to appear absent-minded and eccentric. He was a hard lot.

He invented a stove that would smoke your head off in four hours by the clock. One can see the almost devilish satisfaction he took in it by his giving it his name.

He was always proud of telling how he entered Philadelphia for the first time, with nothing in the world but two shillings in his pocket and four rolls of bread under his arm. But really, when you come to examine it critically, it was nothing. Anybody could have done it.

To the subject of this memoir belongs the honor of recommending the army to go back to bows and arrows in place of bayonets and muskets. He observed, with his customary force, that the bayonet was very well under some circumstances, but that he doubted whether it could be used with accuracy at a long range.

Benjamin Franklin did a great many notable things for his country, and made her young name to be honored in many lands as the mother of such a son. It is not the idea of this memoir to ignore that or cover it up. No; the simple idea of it is to snub those pretentious maxims of his, which he worked up with a great show of originality out of truisms that had become wearisome platitudes as early as the dispersion from Babel; and also to snub his stove, and his military inspirations, his unseemly endeavor to make himself conspicuous when he entered Philadelphia, and his flying his kite and fooling away his time in all sorts of such ways when he ought to have been foraging for soap-fat, or constructing candles. I merely desired to do away with somewhat of the prevalent calamitous idea among heads of families that Franklin *acquired* his great genius by working for nothing, studying by moonlight, and getting up in the night instead of waiting till morning like a Christian; and that this program, rigidly inflicted, will make a Franklin of every father's fool. It is time these gentlemen were finding out that these execrable eccentricities of instinct and conduct are only the *evidences* of genius, not the *creators* of it. I wish I had been the father of my parents long enough to make them comprehend this truth, and thus prepare them to let their son have an easier time of it. When I was a child I had to boil soap, notwithstanding my father was wealthy, and I had to get up early and study geometry at breakfast, and peddle my own poetry, and do everything just as Franklin did, in the solemn hope that I would be a Franklin some day. And here I am.

1870

The Reception at the President's

After I had drifted into the White House with the flood tide of humanity that had been washing steadily up the street for an hour, I obeyed the orders of the soldier at the door and the policeman within, and banked my hat and umbrella with a colored man, who gave me a piece of brass with a number on it and said that that thing would reproduce the property at any time of the night. I doubted it, but I was on unknown ground now, and must be content to take a good many chances.

Another person told me to drop in with the crowd and I would come to the President presently. I joined, and we drifted along till we passed a certain point, and then we thinned out to double and single file. It was a right gay scene, and a right stirring and lively one; for the whole place was brightly lighted, and all down the great hall, as far as one could see, was a restless and writhing multitude of people, the women powdered, painted, jewelled, and splendidly upholstered, and many of the men gilded with the insignia of great naval, military, and ambassadorial rank. It was bewildering.

Our long line kept drifting along, and by and by we came in sight of the President and Mrs. Grant. They were standing up shaking hands and trading civilities with our procession. I grew somewhat at home little by little, and then I began to feel satisfied and contented. I was getting to be perfectly alive with interest by the time it came my turn to talk with the President. I took him by the hand and looked him in the eye, and said:

"Well, I reckon I see you at last, General. I have said as much as a thousand times, out in Nevada, that if ever I went home to the States I would just have the private satisfaction of going and saying to you by word of mouth that *I* thought you was considerable of a soldier, anyway. Now, you know, out there we—"

I turned round and said to the fellow behind me:

"Now, look here, my good friend, how the nation do you suppose I can talk with any sort of satisfaction, with you crowding me this way? I am surprised at your manners."

He was a modest-looking creature. He said:

"But you see the whole procession's stopped, and they're crowding up on me."

I said:

"Some people have got more cheek. Just suggest to the parties behind you to have some respect for the place they are in and not try to shove in on a private conversation. What the General and me are talking about ain't of the least interest to them."

Then I resumed with the President:

"Well, well, well. Now this is fine. This is what I call something *like*. Gay? Well, I should say so. And so *this* is what you call a Presidential reception. I'm free to say that it just lays over anything that ever *I* saw out in the sage-brush. I have been to Governor Nye's Injun receptions at Honey Lake and Carson City, many and many a time—he that's Senator Nye now—*you* know him, of course. I never saw a man in all my life that Jim Nye didn't know—and not only that, but he could tell him *where* he knew him, and all about him, family included, even if it was forty years ago. Most remarkable man, Jim Nye—remarkable. He can tell a lie with that purity of accent, and that grace of utterance, and that convincing emotion——"

I turned again, and said:

"My friend, your conduct surprises me. I have come three thousand miles to have a word with the President of the United States upon subjects with which you are not even remotely connected, and by the living geewhillikins I can't proceed with any sort of satisfaction on account of your cussed crowding. Will you just please to go a little slow, now, and not attract so much attention by your strange conduct? If you had any eyes you could see how the bystanders are staring."

He said:

"But I tell you, sir, it's the people behind. They are just growling and surging and shoving, and I wish I was in Jericho, I do."

I said:

"I wish you was, myself. You might learn some delicacy of feeling in that ancient seat of civilization, maybe. Drat if you don't need it."

And then I resumed with the President:

"Yes, sir, I've been at receptions before, plenty of them—old Nye's Injun receptions. But they warn't as starchy as this by considerable. No great long strings of high-fliers like these galoots here, you know, but old high-flavored Washoes and Pi-Utes, each one of them as powerful as a rag-factory on fire. Phew! Those were halcyon days. Yes, indeed, General; and madam, many and many's the time, out in the wilds of Nevada, I've been——"

"Perhaps you had better discontinue your remarks till another time, sir, as the crowd behind you are growing somewhat impatient," the President said.

"Do you hear that?" I said to the fellow behind me. "I suppose you will take *that* hint, anyhow. I tell you he is milder than *I* would be. If I was President, I would waltz you people out at the back door if you came crowding a gentleman this way, that *I* was holding a private conversation with."

And then I resumed with the President:

"I think that hint of yours will start them. I never saw people act so. It is really about all I can do to hold my ground with that mob shoving up behind. But don't you worry on my account, General—don't give yourself any uneasiness about me—I can stand it as long as they can. I've been through this kind of a mill before. Why, as I was just saying to you, many and many a time, out in the wilds of Nevada, I have been at Governor Nye's Injun receptions—and between you and me that old man was a good deal of a Governor, take him all round. I don't know what for Senator he makes, though I think you'll admit that him and Bill Steward and Tom Fitch take a bigger average of brains into that Capitol up yonder, by a hundred and fifty fold, than any other State in America, according to population. Now that is so. Those three men represent only twenty or twenty-five thousand people—bless you, the least little bit of a trifling ward in the city of New York casts two votes to Nevada's one—and yet those three men haven't their superiors in Congress for straight-out, simon pure brains and ability. And if you could just have been at one of old Nye's Injun receptions and seen those savages—not high-fliers like these, you know, but frowsy old bummers with nothing in the world on, in the summer time, but an old battered plug hat and a pair of spectacles—I tell you it was a swell affair, was one of Governor Nye's early-day receptions. Many and many's the time I have been to them, and seen him stand up and beam and smile on his children, as he called them in his motherly way—beam on them by the hour out of his splendid eyes, and fascinate them with his handsome face, and comfort them with his persuasive tongue—seen him stand up there and tell them anecdotes and lies, and quote Watts's hymns to them, until he just took the war spirit all out of them—and grim chiefs that came two hundred miles to tax the whites for whole wagon-loads of blankets and things or make eternal war if they didn't get them, he has sent away bewildered with his inspired mendacity and perfectly satisfied and enriched with an old hoop skirt or two, a lot of Patent Office reports, and a few sides of condemned army bacon that they would have to chain up to a tree when they camped, or the skippers would walk off with them. I tell you he is a rattling talker. Talk! It's no name for it. He—well, he is bound to launch straight into close quarters and a heap of trouble hereafter, of course—we all know that—but you can rest satisfied that he will take off his hat and put out his hand and introduce himself to the King of Darkness perfectly easy and comfortable, and let on that he has seen him somewhere before; and he will remind him of parties he used to know, and things that's slipped out of his memory—and he'll tell him a thousand things that he can't *help* taking an interest in, and every now and then he will just gently mix in an anecdote that will fetch him if there's any laugh in him—he will, indeed—and Jim Nye will chip in and help cross-question the candidates, and he will just hang around and hang around and hang around, getting more and more sociable all the time, and doing this, that, and the other thing in the handiest sort of way, till he has made himself perfectly indispensable—and then, the very first thing you know——"

I wheeled and said:

"My friend, your conduct grieves me to the heart. A dozen times at least your unseemly crowding has seriously interfered with the conversation I am holding with the President, and if the thing occurs again I shall take my hat and leave the premises."

"I wish to the mischief you would! Where did you come from anyway, that you've got the unutterable cheek to spread yourself here and keep fifteen hundred people standing waiting half an hour to shake hands with the President?"

An officer touched me on the shoulder and said:

"Move along, please; you're annoying the President beyond all patience. You have blocked the procession, and the people behind you are getting furious. Come, move along, please."

Rather than have trouble, I moved along. So I had no time to do more than look back over my shoulder and say: "Yes, sir, and the first thing they would know, Jim Nye would have that place, and the salary doubled! I do reckon he is the handiest creature about making the most of his chances that ever found an all-sufficient substitute for mother's milk in politics and sin. Now that is the kind of man old Nye is—and in less than two months he would talk every—— But I can't make you hear the rest, General, without hollering too loud."

1870

The Widow's Protest

One of the saddest things that ever came under my notice (said the banker's clerk) was there in Corning during the war. Dan Murphy enlisted as a private, and fought very bravely. The boys all liked him, and when a wound by and by weakened him down till carrying a musket was too heavy work for him, they clubbed together and fixed him up as a sutler. He made money then, and sent it always to his wife to bank for him. She was a washer and ironer, and knew enough by hard experience to keep money when she got it. She didn't waste a penny. On the contrary, she began to get miserly as her bank-account grew. She grieved to part with a cent, poor creature, for twice in her hard-working life she had known what it was to be hungry, cold, friendless, sick, and without a dollar in the world, and she had a haunting dread of suffering so again. Well, at last Dan died; and the boys, in testimony of their esteem and respect for him, telegraphed to Mrs. Murphy to know if she would like to have him embalmed and sent home; when you know the usual custom was to dump a poor devil like him into a shallow hole, and *then* inform his friends what had become of him. Mrs. Murphy jumped to the conclusion that it would only cost two or three dollars to embalm her dead husband, and so she telegraphed "Yes." It was at the "wake" that the bill for embalming arrived and was presented to the widow.

She uttered a wild, sad wail that pierced every heart, and said, "Sivinty-foive dollars for stooffin' Dan, blister their sowls! Did thim divils suppose I was goin' to start a Museim, that I'd be dalin' in such expinsive curiassities!"

The banker's clerk said there was not a dry eye in the house.

1870

About Barbers

All things change except barbers, the ways of barbers, and the surroundings of barbers. These never change. What one experiences in a barber's shop the first time he enters one is what he always experiences in barbers' shops afterward till the end of his days. I got shaved this morning as usual. A man approached the door from Jones Street as I approached it from Main—a thing that always happens. I hurried up, but it was of no use; he entered the door one little step ahead of me, and I followed in on his heels and saw him take the only vacant chair, the one presided over by the best barber. It always happens so. I sat down, hoping that I might fall heir to the chair belonging to the better of the remaining two barbers, for he had already begun combing his man's hair, while his comrade was not yet quite done rubbing up and oiling his customer's locks. I watched the probabilities with strong interest. When I saw that No. 2 was gaining on No. 1 my interest grew to solicitude. When No. 1 stopped a moment to make change on a bath ticket for a new-comer, and lost ground in the race, my solicitude rose to anxiety. When No. 1 caught up again, and both he and his comrade were pulling the towels away and brushing the powder from their customers' cheeks, and it was about an even thing which one would say "Next!" first, my very breath stood still with the suspense. But when at the culminating moment No. 1 stopped to pass a comb a couple of times through his customer's eyebrows, I saw that he had lost the race by a single instant, and I rose indignant and quitted the shop, to keep from falling into the hands of No. 2; for I have none of that enviable firmness that enables a man to look calmly into the eyes of a waiting barber and tell him he will wait for his fellow-barber's chair.

I stayed out fifteen minutes, and then went back, hoping for better luck. Of course all the chairs were occupied now, and four men sat waiting, silent, unsociable, distraught, and looking bored, as men always do who are waiting their turn in a barber's shop. I sat down in one of the iron-armed compartments of an old sofa, and put in the time for a while reading the framed advertisements of all sorts of quack nostrums for dyeing and coloring the hair. Then I read the greasy names on the private bay-rum bottles; read the names and noted the numbers on the private shaving-cups in the pigeonholes; studied the stained and damaged cheap prints on the walls, of battles, early Presidents, and voluptuous recumbent sultanas, and the tiresome and everlasting young girl putting her grandfather's spectacles on; execrated in my heart the cheerful canary and the distracting parrot that few barbers' shops are without. Finally, I searched out the least dilapidated of last year's illustrated papers that littered the foul center-table, and conned their unjustifiable misrepresentations of old forgotten events.

At last my turn came. A voice said "Next!" and I surrendered to—No. 2, of course. It always happens so. I said meekly that I was in a hurry, and it affected him as strongly as if he had never heard it. He shoved up my head, and put a napkin under it. He plowed his fingers into my collar and fixed a towel there. He explored my hair with his claws and suggested that it needed trimming. I said I did not want it trimmed. He explored again and said it was pretty long for the present style—better have a little taken off; it needed it behind especially. I said I had had it cut only a week before. He yearned over it reflectively a moment, and then asked with a disparaging manner, who cut it? I came back at him promptly with a "You did!" I had him there. Then he fell to stirring up his lather and regarding himself in the glass, stopping now and then to get close and examine his chin critically or inspect a pimple. Then he lathered one side of my face thoroughly, and was about to lather the other, when a dog-fight attracted his attention, and he ran to the window and stayed and saw it out, losing two shillings on the result in bets with the other barbers, a thing which gave me great satisfaction. He finished lathering, and then began to rub in the suds with his hand.

He now began to sharpen his razor on an old suspender, and was delayed a good deal on account of a controversy about a cheap masquerade ball he had figured at the night before, in red cambric and bogus ermine, as some kind of a king. He was so gratified with being chaffed about some damsel whom he had smitten with his charms that he used every means to continue the controversy by pretending to be annoyed at the chaffings of his fellows. This matter begot more surveyings of himself in the glass, and he put down his razor and brushed his hair with elaborate care, plastering an inverted arch of it down on his forehead, accomplishing an accurate "part" behind, and brushing the two wings forward over his ears with nice exactness. In the mean time the lather was drying on my face, and apparently eating into my vitals.

Now he began to shave, digging his fingers into my countenance to stretch the skin and bundling and tumbling my head this way and that as convenience in shaving demanded. As long as he was on the tough sides of my face I did not suffer; but when he began to rake, and rip, and tug at my chin, the tears came. He now made a handle of my nose, to assist him shaving the corners of my upper lip, and it was by this bit of circumstantial evidence that I discovered that a part of his duties in the shop was to clean the kerosene-lamps. I had often wondered in an indolent way whether the barbers did that, or whether it was the boss.

About this time I was amusing myself trying to guess where he would be most likely to cut me this time, but he got ahead of me, and sliced me on the end of the chin before I had got my mind made up. He immediately sharpened his razor—he might have done it before. I do not like a close shave, and would not let him go over me a second time. I tried to get him to put up his razor, dreading that he would make for the side of my chin, my pet tender spot, a place which a razor cannot touch twice without making trouble; but he said he only wanted to just smooth off one little roughness, and in the same moment he slipped his razor along the forbidden ground, and the dreaded pimple-signs of a close shave rose up smarting and answered to the call. Now he soaked his towel in bay rum, and slapped it all over my face nastily; slapped it over as if a human being ever yet washed his face in that way. Then he dried it by slapping with the dry part of the towel, as if a human being ever dried his face in such a fashion; but a barber seldom rubs you like a Christian. Next he poked bay rum into the cut place with his towel, then choked the wound with powdered starch, then soaked it with bay rum again, and would have gone on soaking and powdering it forevermore, no doubt, if I had not rebelled and begged off. He powdered my whole face now, straightened me up, and began to plow my hair thoughtfully with his hands. Then he suggested a shampoo, and said my hair needed it badly, very badly. I observed that I shampooed it myself very thoroughly in the bath yesterday. I "had him" again. He next recommended some of "Smith's Hair Glorifier," and offered to sell me a bottle. I declined. He praised the new perfume, "Jones's Delight of the Toilet," and proposed to sell me some of that. I declined again. He tendered me a tooth-wash atrocity of his own invention, and when I declined offered to trade knives with me.

He returned to business after the miscarriage of this last enterprise, sprinkled me all over, legs and all, greased my hair in defiance of my protest against it, rubbed and scrubbed a good deal of it out by the roots, and combed and brushed the rest, parting it behind, and plastering the eternal inverted arch of hair down on my forehead, and then, while combing my scant eyebrows and defiling them with pomade, strung out an account of the achievements of a six-ounce black-and-tan terrier of his till I heard the whistles blow for noon, and knew I was five minutes too late for the train. Then he snatched away the towel, brushed it lightly about my face, passed his comb through my eyebrows once more, and gaily sang out "Next!"

This barber fell down and died of apoplexy two hours later. I am waiting over a day for my revenge—I am going to attend his funeral.

1871

A Burlesque Biography

Two or three persons having at different times intimated that if I would write an autobiography they would read it when they got leisure, I yield at last to this frenzied public demand and herewith tender my history.

Ours is a noble old house, and stretches a long way back into antiquity. The earliest ancestor the Twains have any record of was a friend of the family by the name of Higgins. This was in the eleventh century, when our people were living in Aberdeen, county of Cork, England. Why it is that our long line has ever since borne the maternal name (except when one of them now and then took a playful refuge in an alias to avert foolishness), instead of Higgins, is a mystery which none of us has ever felt much desire to stir. It is a kind of vague, pretty romance, and we leave it alone. All the old families do that way.

Arthour Twain was a man of considerable note—a solicitor on the highway in William Rufus's time. At about the age of thirty he went to one of those fine old English places of resort called Newgate, to see about something, and never returned again. While there he died suddenly.

Augustus Twain seems to have made something of a stir about the year 1160. He was as full of fun as he could be, and used to take his old saber and sharpen it up, and get in a convenient place on a dark night, and stick it through people as they went by, to see them jump. He was a born humorist. But he got to going too far with it; and the first time he was found stripping one of these parties, the authorities removed one end of him, and put it up on a nice high place on Temple Bar, where it could contemplate the people and have a good time. He never liked any situation so much or stuck to it so long.

Then for the next two hundred years the family tree shows a succession of soldiers—noble, high-spirited fellows, who always went into battle singing, right behind the army, and always went out a-whooping, right ahead of it.

This is a scathing rebuke to old dead Froissart's poor witticism that our family tree never had but one limb to it, and that that one stuck out at right angles, and bore fruit winter and summer.

Early in the fifteenth century we have Beau Twain, called "the Scholar." He wrote a beautiful, beautiful hand. And he could imitate anybody's hand so closely that it was enough to make a person laugh his head off to see it. He had infinite sport with his talent. But by and by he took a contract to break stone for a road, and the roughness of the work spoiled his hand. Still, he enjoyed life all the time he was in the stone business, which, with inconsiderable intervals, was some forty-two years. In fact, he died in harness. During all those long years he gave such satisfaction that he never was through with one contract a week till the government gave him another. He was a perfect pet. And he was always a favorite with his fellow-artists, and was a conspicuous member of their benevolent secret society, called the Chain Gang. He always wore his hair short, had a preference for striped clothes, and died lamented by the government. He was a sore loss to his country. For he was so regular.

Some years later we have the illustrious John Morgan Twain. He came over to this country with Columbus in 1492 as a passenger. He appears to have been of a crusty, uncomfortable disposition. He complained of the food all the way over, and was always threatening to go ashore unless there was a change. He wanted fresh shad. Hardly a day passed over his head that he did not go idling about the ship with his nose in the air, sneering about the commander, and saying he did not believe Columbus knew where he was going to or had ever been there before. The memorable cry of "Land ho!" thrilled every heart in the ship but his. He gazed awhile through a piece of smoked glass at the penciled line lying on the distant water, and then said: "Land be hanged—it's a raft!"

When this questionable passenger came on board the ship, he brought nothing with him but an old newspaper containing a handkerchief marked "B. G.," one cotton sock marked "L. W. C.," one woollen one marked "D. F.," and a night-shirt marked "O. M. R." And yet during the voyage he worried more about his "trunk," and gave himself more airs about it, than all the rest of the passengers put together. If the ship was "down by the head," and would not steer, he would go and move his "trunk" farther aft, and then watch the effect. If the ship was "by the stern," he would suggest to Columbus to detail some men to "shift that baggage." In storms he had to be gagged, because his wailings about his "trunk" made it impossible for the men to hear the orders. The man does not appear to have been openly charged with any gravely unbecoming thing, but it is noted in the ship's log as a "curious circumstance" that albeit he brought his baggage on board the ship in a newspaper, he took it ashore in four trunks, a queensware crate, and a couple of champagne baskets. But when he came back insinuating, in an insolent, swaggering way, that some of his things were missing, and was going to search the other passengers' baggage, it was too much, and they threw him overboard. They watched long and wonderingly for him to come up, but not even a bubble rose on the quietly ebbing tide. But while every one was most absorbed in gazing over the side, and the interest was momentarily increasing, it was observed with consternation that the vessel was adrift and the anchor-cable hanging limp from the bow. Then in the ship's dimmed and ancient log we find this quaint note:

"In time it was discouvered yt ye troblesome passenger hadde gonne downe and got ye anchor, and toke ye same and solde it to ye dam sauvages from ye interior, saying yt he hadde founde it, ye sonne of a ghun!"

Yet this ancestor had good and noble instincts, and it is with pride that we call to mind the fact that he was the first white person who ever interested himself in the work of elevating and civilizing our Indians. He built a commodious jail and put up a gallows, and to his dying day he claimed with satisfaction that he had had a more restraining and elevating influence on the Indians than any other reformer that ever labored among them. At this point the chronicle becomes less frank and chatty, and closes abruptly by saying that the old voyager went to see his gallows perform on the first white man ever hanged in America, and while there received injuries which terminated in his death.

The great-grandson of the "Reformer" flourished in sixteen hundred and something, and was known in our annals as "the old Admiral," though in history he had other titles. He was long in command of fleets of swift vessels, well armed and manned, and did great service in hurrying up merchantmen. Vessels which he followed and kept his eagle eye on, always made good fair time across the ocean. But if a ship still loitered in spite of all he could do, his indignation would grow till he could contain himself no longer—and then he would take that ship home where he lived and keep it there carefully, expecting the owners to come for it, but they never did. And he would try to get the idleness and sloth out of the sailors of that ship by compelling them to take invigorating exercise and a bath. He called it "walking a plank." All the pupils liked it. At any rate, they never found any fault with it after trying it. When the owners were late coming for their ships, the Admiral always burned them, so that the insurance money should not be lost. At last this fine old tar was cut down in the fullness of his years and honors. And to her dying day, his poor heartbroken widow believed that if he had been cut down fifteen minutes sooner he might have been resuscitated.

Charles Henry Twain lived during the latter part of the seventeenth century, and was a zealous and distinguished missionary. He converted sixteen thousand South Sea islanders, and taught them that a dog-tooth necklace and a pair of spectacles was not enough clothing to come to divine service in. His poor flock loved him very, very dearly; and when his funeral was over, they got up in a body (and came out of the restaurant) with tears in their eyes, and saying, one to another, that he was a good tender missionary, and they wished they had some more of him.

Pah-go-to-wah-wah-pukketekeewis (Mighty-Hunter-with-a-Hog-Eye-Twain) adorned the middle of the eighteenth century, and aided General Braddock with all his heart to resist the oppressor Washington. It was this ancestor who fired seventeen times at our Washington from behind a tree. So far the beautiful romantic narrative in the moral story-books is correct; but when that narrative goes on to say that at the seventeenth round the awe-stricken savage said solemnly that that man was being reserved by the Great Spirit for some mighty mission, and he dared not lift his sacrilegious rifle against him again, the narrative seriously impairs the integrity of history. What he did say was:

"It ain't no (hic) no use. 'At man's so drunk he can't stan' still long enough for a man to hit him. I (hic) I can't 'ford to fool away any more am'nition on him."

That was why he stopped at the seventeenth round, and it was a good, plain, matter-of-fact reason, too, and one that easily commends itself to us by the eloquent, persuasive flavor of probability there is about it.

I always enjoyed the story-book narrative, but I felt a marring misgiving that every Indian at Braddock's Defeat who fired at a soldier a couple of times (two easily grows to seventeen in a century), and missed him, jumped to the conclusion that the Great Spirit was reserving that soldier for some grand mission; and so I somehow feared that the only reason why Washington's case is remembered and the others forgotten is, that in his the prophecy came true, and in that of the others it didn't. There are not books enough on earth to contain the record of the prophecies Indians and other unauthorized parties have made; but one may carry in his overcoat pockets the record of all the prophecies that have been fulfilled.

I will remark here, in passing, that certain ancestors of mine are so thoroughly well-known in history by their aliases, that I have not felt it to be worth while to dwell upon them, or even mention them in the order of their birth. Among these may be mentioned Richard Brinsley Twain, alias Guy Fawkes; John Wentworth Twain, alias Sixteen-String Jack; William Hogarth Twain, alias Jack Sheppard; Ananias Twain, alias Baron Munchausen; John George Twain, alias Captain Kydd; and then there are George Francis Train, Tom Pepper, Nebuchadnezzar, and Baalam's Ass—they all belong to our family, but to a branch of it somewhat distinctly removed from the honorable direct line—in fact, a collateral branch, whose members chiefly differ from the ancient stock in that, in order to acquire the notoriety we have always yearned and hungered for, they have got into a low way of going to jail instead of getting hanged.

It is not well, when writing an autobiography, to follow your ancestry down too close to your own time—it is safest to speak only vaguely of your great-grandfather, and then skip from there to yourself, which I now do.

I was born without teeth—and there Richard III had the advantage of me; but I was born without a humpback, likewise, and there I had the advantage of him. My parents were neither very poor nor conspicuously honest.

But now a thought occurs to me. My own history would really seem so tame contrasted with that of my ancestors, that it is simply wisdom to leave it unwritten until I am hanged. If some other biographies I have read had stopped with the ancestry until a like event occurred, it would have been a felicitous thing for the reading public. How does it strike you?

1871

An Encounter with an Interviewer

The nervous, dapper, "peart" young man took the chair I offered him, and said he was connected with the *Daily Thunderstorm,* and added:

"Hoping it's no harm, I've come to interview you."

"Come to what?"

"*Interview* you."

"Ah! I see. Yes—yes. Um! Yes—yes."

I was not feeling bright that morning. Indeed, my powers seemed a bit under a cloud. However, I went to the bookcase, and when I had been looking six or seven minutes I found I was obliged to refer to the young man. I said:

"How do you spell it?"

"Spell what?"

"Interview."

"Oh, my goodness! what do you want to spell it for?"

"I don't want to spell it; I want to see what it means."

"Well, this is astonishing, I must say. *I* can tell you what it means, if you—if you—"

"Oh, all right! That will answer, and much obliged to you, too."

"In, *in*, ter, *ter*, *in*ter—"

"Then you spell it with an *I*?"

"Why, certainly!"

"Oh, that is what took me so long."

"Why, my *dear* sir, what did *you* propose to spell it with?"

"Well, I—I—hardly know. I had the Unabridged, and I was ciphering around in the back end, hoping I might tree her among the pictures. But it's a very old edition."

"Why, my friend, they wouldn't have a *picture* of it in even the latest e— My dear sir, I beg your pardon, I mean no harm in the world, but you do not look as—as—intelligent as I had expected you would. No harm—I mean no harm at all."

"Oh, don't mention it! It has often been said, and by people who would not flatter and who could have no inducement to flatter, that I am quite remarkable in that way. Yes—yes; they always speak of it with rapture."

"I can easily imagine it. But about this interview. You know it is the custom, now, to interview any man who has become notorious."

"Indeed, I had not heard of it before. It must be very interesting. What do you do it with?"

"Ah, well—well—well—this is disheartening. It *ought* to be done with a club in some cases; but customarily it consists in the interviewer asking questions and the interviewed answering them. It is all the rage now. Will you let me ask you certain questions calculated to bring out the salient points of your public and private history?"

"Oh, with pleasure—with pleasure. I have a very bad memory, but I hope you will not mind that. That is to say, it is an irregular memory—singularly irregular. Sometimes it goes in a gallop, and then again it will be as much as a fortnight passing a given point. This is a great grief to me."

"Oh, it is no matter, so you will try to do the best you can."

"I will. I will put my whole mind on it."

"Thanks. Are you ready to begin?"

"Ready."

Q. How old are you?

A. Nineteen, in June.

Q. Indeed. I would have taken you to be thirty-five or six. Where were you born?

A. In Missouri.

Q. When did you begin to write?

A. In 1836.

Q. Why, how could that be, if you are only nineteen now?

A. I don't know. It does seem curious, somehow.

Q. It does, indeed. Whom do you consider the most remarkable man you ever met?

A. Aaron Burr.

Q. But you never could have met Aaron Burr, if you are only nineteen years—

A. Now, if you know more about me than I do, what do you ask me for?

Q. Well, it was only a suggestion; nothing more. How did you happen to meet Burr?

A. Well, I happened to be at his funeral one day, and he asked me to make less noise, and—

Q. But, good heavens! if you were at his funeral, he must have been dead, and if he was dead how could he care whether you made a noise or not?

A. I don't know. He was always a particular kind of a man that way.

Q. Still, I don't understand it at all. You say he spoke to you, and that he was dead.

A. I didn't say he was dead.

Q. But wasn't he dead?

A. Well, some said he was, some said he wasn't.

Q. What did you think?

A. Oh, it was none of my business! It wasn't any of my funeral.

Q. Did you— However, we can never get this matter straight. Let me ask about something else. What was the date of your birth?

A. Monday, October 31, 1693.

Q. What! Impossible! That would make you a hundred and eighty years old. How do you account for that?

A. I don't account for it at all.

Q. But you said at first you were only nineteen, and now you make yourself out to be one hundred and eighty. It is an awful discrepancy.

A. Why, have you noticed that? (Shaking hands.) Many a time it has seemed to me like a discrepancy, but somehow I couldn't make up my mind. How quick you notice a thing!

Q. Thank you for the compliment, as far as it goes. Had you, or have you, any brothers or sisters?

A. Eh! I—I—I think so—yes—but I don't remember.

Q. Well, that is the most extraordinary statement I ever heard!

A. Why, what makes you think that?

Q. How could I think otherwise? Why, look here! Who is this a picture of on the wall? Isn't that a brother of yours?

A. Oh, yes, yes, yes! Now you remind me of it; that *was* a brother of mine. That's William—*Bill* we called him. Poor old Bill!

Q. Why? Is he dead, then?

A. Ah! Well, I suppose so. We never could tell. There was a great mystery about it.

Q. That is sad, very sad. He disappeared, then?

A. Well, yes, in a sort of general way. We buried him.

Q. *Buried* him! *Buried* him, without knowing whether he was dead or not?

A. Oh, no! Not that. He was dead enough.

Q. Well, I confess that I can't understand this. If you buried him, and you knew he was dead—

A. No! no! We only thought he was.

Q. Oh, I see! He came to life again?

A. I bet he didn't.

Q. Well, I never heard anything like this. *Somebody* was dead. *Somebody* was buried. Now, where was the mystery?

A. Ah! that's just it! That's it exactly. You see, we were twins—defunct and I—and we got mixed in the bathtub when we were only two weeks old, and one of us was drowned. But we didn't know which. Some think it was Bill. Some think it was me.

Q. Well, that *is* remarkable. What do *you* think?

A. Goodness knows! I would give whole worlds to know. This solemn, this awful mystery has cast a gloom over my whole life. But I will tell you a secret now, which I never have revealed to any creature before. One of us had a peculiar mark—a large mole on the back of his left hand; that was *me. That child was the one that was drowned!*

Q. Very well, then, I don't see that there is any mystery about it, after all.

A. You don't? Well, *I* do. Anyway, I don't see how they could ever have been such a blundering lot as to go and bury the wrong child. But, 'sh!—don't mention it where the family can hear of it. Heaven knows they have heartbreaking troubles enough without adding this.

Q. Well, I believe I have got material enough for the present, and I am very much obliged to you for the pains you have taken. But I was a good deal interested in that account of Aaron Burr's funeral. Would you mind telling me what particular circumstance it was that made you think Burr was such a remarkable man?

A. Oh! it was a mere trifle! Not one man in fifty would have noticed it at all. When the sermon was over, and the procession all ready to start for the cemetery, and the body all arranged nice in the hearse, he said he wanted to take a last look at the scenery, and so he *got up and rode with the driver.*

Then the young man reverently withdrew. He was very pleasant company, and I was sorry to see him go.

1875

The Frog Jumping of the County of Calaveras

Even a criminal is entitled to fair play; and certainly when a man who has done no harm has been unjustly treated, he is privileged to do his best to right himself. My attention has just been called to an article some three years old in a French Magazine entitled, *Revue des Deux Mondes* (Review of Some Two Worlds), wherein the writer treats of "Les Humoristes Americaines" (These Humorists Americans). I am one of these humorists Americans dissected by him, and hence the complaint I am making.

This gentleman's article is an able one (as articles go, in the French, where they always tangle up everything to that degree that when you start into a sentence you never know whether you are going to come out alive or not). It is a very good article, and the writer says all manner of kind and complimentary things about me—for which I am sure I thank him with all my heart; but then why should he go and spoil all his praise by one unlucky experiment? What I refer to is this: he says my Jumping Frog is a funny story, but still he can't see why it should ever really convulse any one with laughter—and straightway proceeds to translate it into French in order to prove to his nation that there is nothing so very extravagantly funny about it. Just there is where my complaint originates. He has not translated it at all; he has simply mixed it all up; it is no more like the Jumping Frog when he gets through with it than I am like a meridian of longitude. . . . In order that even the unlettered may know my injury and give me their compassion, I have been at infinite pains and trouble to retranslate this French version back into English; and to tell the truth I have well-nigh worn myself out at it, having scarcely rested from my work during five days and nights. I cannot speak the French language, but I can translate very well, though not fast, I being self-educated.

It there was one time here an individual known under the name of Jim Smiley; it was in the winter of '49, possibly well at the spring of '50, I no me recollect not exactly. This which me makes to believe that it was the one or the other, it is that I shall remember that the grand flume is not achieved when he arrives at the camp for the first time, but of all sides he was the man the most fond of to bet which one have seen, betting upon all that which is presented, when he could find an adversary; and when he not of it could not, he passed to the side opposed. All that which convenienced to the other, to him convenienced also; seeing that he had a bet, Smiley was satisfied. And he had a chance! a chance even worthless; nearly always he gained. It must to say that he was always near to himself expose, but one no could mention the least thing without that this gaillard offered to bet the bottom, no matter what, and to take the side that one him would, as I you it said all at the hour (tout à l'heure). If it there was of races, you him find rich or ruined at the end; if it there is a combat of dogs, he bring his bet; he himself laid always for a combat of cats, for a combat of cocks;—by-blue! If you have see two birds upon a fence, he you should have offered of to bet which of those birds shall fly the first; and if there is *meeting* at the camp (*meeting* au camp) he comes to bet regularly for the curé Walker, which he judged to be the best predicator of the neighborhood (prédicateur des environs) and which he was in effect, and a brave man. He would encounter a bug of wood in the road, whom he will bet upon the time which he shall take to go where she would go—and if you him have take at the word, he will follow the bug as far as Mexique, without himself caring to go so far; neither of the time which he there lost. One time the woman of the curé Walker is very sick during long time, it seemed that one not her saved not; but one morning the curé arrives, and Smiley him demanded how she goes, and he said that she is well better, grace to the infinite misery (lui demande comment elle va, et il dit qu'elle est bien mieux, grâce à l'infinie miséricorde) so much better that with the benediction of the Providence she herself of it would pull out (elle s'en tirerait); and behold that without there thinking Smiley responds: "Well, I gage two-and-half that she will die all of same."

This Smiley had an animal which the boys called the nag of the quarter of hour, but solely for pleasantry, you comprehend, because, well understand, she was more fast as that! [Now why that exclamation?—M. T.] And it was custom of to gain of the silver with this beast, notwithstanding she was poussive, cornarde, always taken of asthma, of colics or of consumption, or something of approaching. One him would give two or three hundred yards at the departure, then one him passed without pain; but never at the last she not fail of herself échauffer, of herself exasperate, and she arrives herself écartant, se défendant, her legs grêles in the air before the obstacles, sometimes them elevating and making with this more of dust than any horse, more of noise above with his éternumens and reniflemens—crac! she arrives then always first by one head, as just as one can it measure. An he had a small bulldog (bouledogue!) who, to him see, no value, not a cent; one would believe that to bet against him it was to steal, so much he was ordinary; but as soon as the game made, she becomes another dog. Her jaw inferior commence to project like a deck of before, his teeth themselves discover brilliant like some furnaces, and a dog could him tackle (le taquiner), him excite, him murder (le mordre), him throw two or three times over his shoulder, André Jackson—this was the name of the dog—André Jackson takes that tranquilly, as if he not himself was never expecting other thing, and when the bets were doubled and redoubled against him, he you seize the other dog just at the articulation of the leg of behind, and he not it leave more, not that he it masticate, you conceive, but he himself there shall be holding during until that one throws the sponge in the air, must he wait a year. Smiley gained always with this beast-là; unhappily they have finished by elevating a dog who no had not of feet of behind, because one them had sawed; and when things were at the point that he would, and that he came to himself throw upon his morsel favorite, the poor dog comprehended in an instant that he himself was deceived in him, and that the other dog him had. You no have never seen person having the air more penaud and more discouraged; he not made no effort to gain the combat, and was rudely shucked.

Eh bien! this Smiley nourished some terriers à rats, and some cocks of combat, and some cats, and all sorts of things; and with his rage of betting one no had more of repose. He trapped one day a frog and him imported with him (et l'emporta chez lui) saying that he pretended to make his education. You me believe if you will, but during three months he not has nothing done but to him apprehend to jump (apprendre à sauter) in a court retired of her mansion (de sa maison). And I you respond that he have succeeded. He him gives a small blow by behind, and the instant after you shall see the frog turn in the air like a grease-biscuit, make one summersault, sometimes two, when she was well started, and refall upon his feet like a cat. He him had accomplished in the art of to gobble the flies (gober des mouches), and him there exercised continually—so well that a fly at the most far that she appeared was a fly lost. Smiley had custom to say that all which lacked to a frog it was the education, but with the education she could do nearly all—and I him believe. Tenez, I him have seen pose Daniel Webster there upon this plank—Daniel Webster was the name of the frog—and to him sing, "Some flies, Daniel, some flies!"—in a flash of the eye Daniel had bounded and seized a fly here upon the counter, then jumped anew at the earth, where he rested truly to himself scratch the head with his behind foot, as if he no had not the least idea of his superiority. Never you not have seen frog as modest, as natural, sweet as she was. And when he himself agitated to jump purely and simply upon plain earth, she does more ground in one jump than any beast of his species than you can know. To jump plain—this was his strong. When he himself agitated for that, Smiley multiplied the bets upon her as long as there to him remained a red. It must to know, Smiley was monstrously proud of his frog, and he of it was right, for some men who were traveled, who had all seen, said that they to him would be injurious to him compare to another frog. Smiley guarded Daniel in a little box latticed which he carried bytimes to the village for some bet.

One day an individual stranger at the camp him arrested with his box and him said:

"What is this that you have them shut up there within?"

Smiley said, with an air indifferent:

"That could be a paroquet, or a syringe (ou un serin), but this no is nothing of such, it not is but a frog."

The individual it took, it regarded with care, it turned from one side and from the other, then he said:

"Tiens! in effect!—At what is she good?"

"My God!" respond Smiley, always with an air disengaged, "she is good for one thing, to my notice (à mon avis), she can batter in jumping (elle peut battre en sautant) all frogs of the county of Calaveras."

The individual retook the box, it examined of new longly, and it rendered to Smiley in saying with an air deliberate:

"Eh bien! I no saw not that that frog had nothing of better than each frog." (Je ne vois pas que cette grenouille ait rien de mieux qu'aucune grenouille.) [If that isn't grammar gone to seed, then I count myself no judge.—M. T.]

"Possible that you not it saw not," said Smiley, "possible that you—you comprehend frogs; possible that you not you there comprehend nothing; possible that you had of the experience, and possible that you not be but an amateur. Of all manner (De toute manière) I bet forty dollars that she batter in jumping no matter which frog of the county of Calaveras."

The individual reflected a second, and said like sad:

"I not am but a stranger here, I no have not a frog; but if I of it had one, I would embrace the bet."

"Strong well!" respond Smiley; "nothing of more facility. If you will hold my box a minute, I go you to search a frog (j'irai vous chercher)."

Behold, then, the individual, who guards the box, who puts his forty dollars upon those of Smiley, and who attends (et qui attend). He attended enough longtimes, reflecting all solely. And figure you that he takes Daniel, him opens the mouth by force and with a teaspoon him fills with shot of the hunt, even him fills just to the chin, then he him puts by the earth. Smiley during these times was at slopping in a swamp. Finally he trapped (attrape) a frog, him carried to that individual, and said:

"Now if you be ready, put him all against Daniel, with their before feet upon the same line, and I give the signal"—then he added: "One, two, three—advance!"

Him and the individual touched their frogs by behind, and the frog new put to jump smartly, but Daniel himself lifted ponderously, exalted the shoulders thus, like a Frenchman—to what good? he not could budge, he is planted solid like a church, he not advance no more than if one him had put at the anchor.

Smiley was surprised and disgusted, but he not himself doubted not of the turn being intended (mais il ne se doutait pas du tour, bien entendu). The individual empocketed the silver, himself with it went, and of it himself in going is it that he no gives not a jerk of thumb over the shoulder—like that—at the poor Daniel, in saying with his air deliberate—(L'individu empoche l'argent, s'en va et en s'en allant est-ce qu'il ne donne pas un coup de pouce par-dessus l'épaule, comme ça au pauvre Daniel, en disant de son air délibéré):

"Eh bien! *I no see not that that frog has nothing of better than another.*"

Smiley himself scratched longtimes the head, the eyes fixed upon Daniel, until that which at last he said:

"I me demand how the devil it makes itself that this beast has refused. Is it that she had something? One would believe that she is stuffed."

He grasped Daniel by the skin of the neck, him lifted and said:

"The wolf me bite if he no weigh not five pounds."

He him reversed and the unhappy belched two handfuls of shot (et le malheureux, etc.). When Smiley recognized how it was, he was like mad. He deposited his frog by the earth and ran after that individual, but he not him caught never.

Such is the Jumping Frog, to the distorted French eye. I claim that I never put together such an odious mixture of bad grammar and delirium tremens in my life. And what has a poor foreigner like me done, to be abused and misrepresented like this? When I say, "Well, I don't see no p'ints about that frog that's any better'n any other frog," is it kind, is it just, for this Frenchman to try to make it appear that I said, "Eh bien! I no saw not that that frog had nothing of better than each frog"? I have no heart to write more. I never felt so about anything before.

1875

Punch, Brothers, Punch

Will the reader please to cast his eye over the following lines, and see if he can discover anything harmful in them?

Conductor, when you receive a fare,
Punch in the presence of the passenjare!
A blue trip slip for an eight-cent fare,
A buff trip slip for a six-cent fare,
A pink trip slip for a three-cent fare,
Punch in the presence of the passenjare!

CHORUS

Punch, brothers! punch with care!
Punch in the presence of the passenjare!

I came across these jingling rhymes in a newspaper, a little while ago, and read them a couple of times. They took instant and entire possession of me. All through breakfast they went waltzing through my brain; and when, at last, I rolled up my napkin, I could not tell whether I had eaten anything or not. I had carefully laid out my day's work the day before—a thrilling tragedy in the novel which I am writing. I went to my den to begin my deed of blood. I took up my pen, but all I could get it to say was, "Punch in the presence of the passenjare." I fought hard for an hour, but it was useless. My head kept humming, "A blue trip slip for an eight-cent fare, a buff trip slip for a six-cent fare," and so on and so on, without peace or respite. The day's work was ruined—I could see that plainly enough. I gave up and drifted down-town, and presently discovered that my feet were keeping time to that relentless jingle. When I could stand it no longer I altered my step. But it did no good; those rhymes accommodated themselves to the new step and went on harassing me just as before. I returned home, and suffered all the afternoon; suffered all through an unconscious and unrefreshing dinner; suffered, and cried, and jingled all through the evening; went to bed and rolled, tossed, and jingled right along, the same as ever; got up at midnight frantic, and tried to read; but there was nothing visible upon the whirling page except "Punch! punch in the presence of the passenjare." By sunrise I was out of my mind, and everybody marveled and was distressed at the idiotic burden of my ravings—"Punch! oh, punch! punch in the presence of the passenjare!"

Two days later, on Saturday morning, I arose, a tottering wreck, and went forth to fulfil an engagement with a valued friend, the Rev. Mr. ——, to walk to the Talcott Tower, ten miles distant. He stared at me, but asked no questions. We started. Mr. —— talked, talked, talked—as is he wont. I said nothing; I heard nothing. At the end of a mile, Mr. —— said:

"Mark, are you sick? I never saw a man look so haggard and worn and absent-minded. Say something, do!"

Drearily, without enthusiasm, I said: "Punch, brothers, punch with care! Punch in the presence of the passenjare!"

My friend eyed me blankly, looked perplexed, then said:

"I do not think I get your drift, Mark. There does not seem to be any relevancy in what you have said, certainly nothing sad; and yet —maybe it was the way you *said* the words—I never heard anything that sounded so pathetic. What is—"

But I heard no more. I was already far away with my pitiless, heart-breaking "blue trip slip for an eight-cent fare, buff trip slip for a six-cent fare, pink trip slip for a three-cent fare; punch in the presence of the passenjare." I do not know what occurred during the other nine miles. However, all of a sudden Mr. —— laid his hand on my shoulder and shouted:

"Oh, wake up! wake up! wake up! Don't sleep all day! Here we are at the Tower, man! I have talked myself deaf and dumb and blind, and never got a response. Just look at this magnificent autumn landscape! Look at it! look at it! Feast your eyes on it! You have traveled; you have seen boasted landscapes elsewhere. Come, now, deliver an honest opinion. What do you say to this?"

I sighed wearily, and murmured:

"A buff trip slip for a six-cent fare, a pink trip slip for a three-cent fare, punch in the presence of the passenjare."

Rev. Mr. —— stood there, very grave, full of concern, apparently, and looked long at me; then he said:

"Mark, there is something about this that I cannot understand. Those are about the same words you said before; there does not seem to be anything in them, and yet they nearly break my heart when you say them. Punch in the—how is it they go?"

I began at the beginning and repeated all the lines.

My friend's face lighted with interest. He said:

"Why, what a captivating jingle it is! It is almost music. It flows along so nicely. I have nearly caught the rhymes myself. Say them over just once more, and then I'll have them, sure."

I said them over. Then Mr. —— said them. He made one little mistake, which I corrected. The next time and the next he got them right. Now a great burden seemed to tumble from my shoulders. That torturing jingle departed out of my brain, and a grateful sense of rest and peace descended upon me. I was light-hearted enough to sing; and I did sing for half an hour, straight along, as we went jogging homeward. Then my freed tongue found blessed speech again, and the pent talk of many a weary hour began to gush and flow. It flowed on and on, joyously, jubilantly, until the fountain was empty and dry. As I wrung my friend's hand at parting, I said:

"Haven't we had a royal good time! But now I remember, you haven't said a word for two hours. Come, come, out with something!"

The Rev. Mr. —— turned a lack-luster eye upon me, drew a deep sigh, and said, without animation, without apparent consciousness:

"Punch, brothers, punch with care! Punch in the presence of the passenjare!"

A pang shot through me as I said to myself, "Poor fellow, poor fellow! *he* has got it, now."

I did not see Mr. —— for two or three days after that. Then, on Tuesday evening, he staggered into my presence and sank dejectedly into a seat. He was pale, worn; he was a wreck. He lifted his faded eyes to my face and said:

"Ah, Mark, it was a ruinous investment that I made in those heartless rhymes. They have ridden me like a nightmare, day and night, hour after hour, to this very moment. Since I saw you I have suffered the torments of the lost. Saturday evening I had a sudden call, by telegraph, and took the night train for Boston. The occasion was the death of a valued old friend who had requested that I should preach his funeral sermon. I took my seat in the cars and set myself to framing the discourse. But I never got beyond the opening paragraph; for then the train started and the car-wheels began their 'clack, clack—clack-clack-clack! clack-clack—clack-clack-clack!' and right away those odious rhymes fitted themselves to that accompaniment. For an hour I sat there and set a syllable of those rhymes to every separate and distinct clack the car-wheels made. Why, I was as fagged out, then, as if I had been chopping wood all day. My skull was splitting with headache. It seemed to me that I must go mad if I sat there any longer; so I undressed and went to bed. I stretched myself out in my berth, and—well, you know what the result was. The thing went right along, just the same. 'Clack-clack-clack, a blue trip slip, clack-clack-clack, for an eight-cent fare; clack-clack-clack, a buff trip slip, clack-clack-clack, for a six cent fare, and so on, and so on, and so on—*punch* in the presence of the passenjare!' Sleep? Not a single wink! I was almost a lunatic when I got to Boston. Don't ask me about the funeral. I did the best I could, but every solemn individual sentence was meshed and tangled and woven in and out with 'Punch, brothers, punch with care, punch in the presence of the passenjare.' And the most distressing thing was that my *delivery* dropped into the undulating rhythm of those pulsing rhymes, and I could actually catch absent-minded people nodding *time* to the swing of it with their stupid heads. And, Mark, you may believe it or not, but before I got through the entire assemblage were placidly bobbing their heads in solemn unison, mourners, undertaker, and all. The moment I had finished, I fled to the anteroom in a state bordering on frenzy. Of course it would be my luck to find a sorrowing and aged maiden aunt of the deceased there, who had arrived from Springfield too late to get into the church. She began to sob, and said:

"'Oh, oh, he is gone, he is gone, and I didn't see him before he died!'

"'Yes!' I said, 'he *is* gone, he *is* gone, he *is* gone—oh, *will* this suffering never cease!'

"'You loved him, then! Oh, you too loved him!'

"'Loved him! Loved *who?*'

"'Why, my poor George! my poor nephew!'

"'Oh—*him!* Yes—oh, yes, yes. Certainly—certainly. Punch—punch—oh, this misery will kill me!'

"'Bless you! bless you, sir, for these sweet words! *I*, too, suffer in this dear loss. Were you present during his last moments?'

"'Yes. I—*whose* last moments?'

"'*His.* The dear departed's.'

"'Yes! Oh, yes—yes—*yes!* I suppose so, I think so, *I* don't know! Oh, certainly—I was there—*I* was there!'

"'Oh, what a privilege! what a precious privilege! And his last words—oh, tell me, tell me his last words! What did he say?'

"'He said—he said—oh, my head, my head, my head! He said—he said—he never said *any*thing but Punch, punch, *punch* in the presence of the passenjare! Oh, leave me, madam! In the name of all that is generous, leave me to my madness, my misery, my despair!—a buff trip slip for a six-cent fare, a pink trip slip for a three-cent fare—endu-rance *can* no fur-ther go!—PUNCH in the presence of the passenjare!'"

My friend's hopeless eyes rested upon mine a pregnant minute, and then he said impressively:

"Mark, you do not say anything. You do not offer me any hope. But, ah me, it is just as well—it is just as well. You could not do me any good. The time has long gone by when words could comfort me. Something tells me that my tongue is doomed to wag forever to the jigger of that remorseless jingle. There—there it is coming on me again: a blue trip slip for an eight-cent fare, a buff trip slip for a—"

Thus murmuring faint and fainter, my friend sank into a peaceful trance and forgot his sufferings in a blessed respite.

How did I finally save him from an asylum? I took him to a neighboring university and made him discharge the burden of his persecuting rhymes into the eager ears of the poor, unthinking students. How is it with *them,* now? The result is too sad to tell. Why did I write this article? It was for a worthy, even a noble, purpose. It was to warn you, reader, if you should come across those merciless rhymes, to avoid them—avoid them as you would a pestilence!

1876

Remarkable Gold Mines

I have just seen your dispatch from San Francisco in Saturday's *Evening Post* about gold in solution in Calistoga Springs, and about the proprietor having extracted $1600 in gold of the utmost fineness from ten barrels of water, during the past fortnight, by a process known only to himself.

This will surprise many of your readers, but it does not surprise me, for I once owned these springs myself. What does surprise me, however, is the falling off in richness of the water. In my time, the yield was a dollar a dipperful. I am not saying this to injure the property in case a sale is contemplated. I am saying it in the interest of history. It may be that this hotel proprietor's process may be an inferior one. Yes, that may be the fault. Mine was to take my uncle (I had an extra at that time, on account of his parents dying and leaving him on my hands) and fill him up and let him stand fifteen minutes, to give the water a chance to settle. Well, then I insert him in an exhausted receiver, which had the effect of sucking gold out through his pores. I have taken more than $11,000 out of that old man in a day and a half.

I should have held on to those springs but for the badness of the roads and the difficulty of getting the gold to market. I consider that the gold-yielding water is in many respects remarkable, and yet no more remarkable than the gold-bearing air of Catgut Canon, up there toward the head of the auriferous range. This air or this wind, for it is a kind of trade wind which blows steadily down through 600 miles of the richest quartz croppings during an hour and a quarter every day, except Sundays, is heavily charged with exquisitely fine, impalpable gold.

Nothing precipitates and solidifies this gold so readily as contact with human flesh heated by passion. The time that William Abrahams was disappointed in love he used to step out doors when that wind was blowing, and come in again and begin to sigh, and I would extract over a dollar and a half out of every sigh. He sighed right along, and the time that John Harbison and Aleck Norton quarreled about Harbison's dog they stood there swearing at each other; and they knew how, and what they did not know about swearing they couldn't learn from you and me, not by a good deal, and at the end of every three or four minutes they had to stop and make a dividend. If they didn't their jaws would clog up so that they couldn't get big nine-syllabled ones out at all, and when the wind was done blowing they cleared up just a little over $1600 apiece. I know these facts to be absolutely true, because I got them from a man whose mother I knew personally.

I did not suppose a person could buy the water-privilege at Calistoga now at any price, but several good locations along the course of the Catgut Canon gold-bearing trade-wind are for sale. They are going to be stocked for the New York market. They will sell, too; people will swarm for them as thick as Hancock veterans in the South.

1885

A Petition to the Queen of England

Hartford, Nov. 6, 1887

MADAM: You will remember that last May Mr. Edward Bright, the clerk of the Inland Revenue Office, wrote me about a tax which he said was due from me to the government on books of mine published in London—that is to say, an income tax on the royalties. I do not know Mr. Bright, and it is embarrassing to me to correspond with strangers; for I was raised in the country and have always lived there, the early part in Marion County, Missouri, before the war, and this part in Hartford County, Connecticut, near Bloomfield and about eight miles this side of Farmington, though some call it nine, which it is impossible to be, for I have walked it many and many a time in considerably under three hours, and General Hawley says he has done it in two and a quarter, which is not likely; so it has seemed best that I write your Majesty. It is true that I do not know your Majesty personally, but I have met the Lord Mayor, and if the rest of the family are like him, it is but just that it should be named royal; and likewise plain that in a family matter like this, I cannot better forward my case than to frankly carry it to the head of the family itself. I have also met the Prince of Wales once in the fall of 1873, but it was not in any familiar way, but in a quite informal way, being casual, and was, of course, a surprise to us both. It was in Oxford Street, just where you come out of Oxford into Regent Circus, and just as he turned up one side of the circle at the head of a procession, I went down the other side on the top of an omnibus. He will remember me on account of a gray coat with flap pockets that I wore, as I was the only person on the omnibus that had on that kind of a coat; I remember him of course as easy as I would a comet. He looked quite proud and satisfied, but that is not to be wondered at, he has a good situation. And once I called on your Majesty, but you were out.

But this is no matter, it happens with everybody. However, I have wandered a little away from what I started about. It was this way. Young Bright wrote my London publishers, Chatto and Windus—their place is the one on the left as you come down Piccadilly, about a block and a half above where the minstrel show is—he wrote them that he wanted them to pay income tax on the royalties of some foreign authors, namely, "Miss De La Ramé (Ouida), Dr. Oliver Wendell Holmes, Mr. Francis Bret Harte, and Mr. Mark Twain." Well, Mr. Chatto diverted him from the others, and tried to divert him from me, but in this case he failed. So then young Bright wrote me. And not only that, but he sent me a printed document the size of a newspaper, for me to sign all over in different places. Well, it was that kind of a document that the more you study it the more it undermines you and makes everything seem uncertain to you; and so, while in that condition, and really not responsible for my acts, I wrote Mr. Chatto to pay the tax and charge to me. Of course my idea was that it was for only one year, and that the tax would be only about one per cent, or along there somewhere, but last night I met Professor Sloane of Princeton—you may not know him, but you have probably seen him every now and then, for he goes to England a good deal, a large man and very handsome and absorbed in thought, and if you have noticed such a man on platforms after the train is gone, that is the one, he generally gets left, like all those specialists and other scholars who know everything but how to apply it—and he said it was a back tax for *three* years, and not one per cent., but two and a half!

That gave what had seemed a little matter a new aspect. I then began to study the printed document again, to see if I could find anything in it that might modify my case, and I had what seems to be a quite promising success. For instance, it opens thus—polite and courteous, the way those English government documents always are—I do not say that to hear myself talk, it is just the fact, and it is a credit:

"To Mr. Mark Twain: IN PURSUANCE of the Acts of Parliament for granting to Her Majesty Duties and Profits," etc.

I had not noticed that before. My idea had been that it was for the government, and so I wrote *to* the government; but now I saw that it was a private matter, a family matter, and that the proceeds went to yourself, not the government. I would always rather treat with principals, and I am glad I noticed that clause. With a principal, one can always get at a fair and right understanding, whether it is about potatoes, or continents, or any of those things, or something entirely different; for the size or nature of the thing does not affect the fact; whereas, as a rule, a subordinate is more or less troublesome to satisfy. And yet this is not against them, but the other way. They have their duties to do, and must be harnessed to rules, and not allowed any discretion. Why, if your Majesty should equip young Bright with discretion—I mean his own discretion—it is an even guess that he would discretion you out of house and home in two or three years. He would not *mean* to get the family into straits, but that would be the upshot, just the same. Now then, with Bright out of the way, this is not going to be any Irish question; it is going to be settled pleasantly and satisfactorily for all of us, and when it is finished your Majesty is going to stand with the American people just as you have stood for fifty years, and surely no monarch can require better than that of an alien nation. They do not all pay a British income tax, but the most of them will in time, for we have shoals of new authors coming along every year; and of the population of your Canada, upward of four-fifths are wealthy Americans, and more going there all the time.

Well, another thing which I noticed in the Document was an item about "Deductions." I will come to that presently, your Majesty. And another thing was this: that Authors are not mentioned in the Document at all. No, we have "Quarries, Mines, Iron-works, Salt-springs, Alum-mines, Water-works, Canals, Docks, Drains, Levels, Fishings, Fairs, Tolls, Bridges, Ferries," and so forth and so forth and so on—well, as much as a yard or a yard and a half of them, I should think—anyway a very large quantity or number. I read along—down, and down, and down the list, further, and further, and further, and as I approached the bottom my hopes began to rise higher and higher, because I saw that everything in England *that* far was taxed by name and in detail, except perhaps the family, and maybe Parliament, and yet still no mention of Authors. Apparently they were going to be overlooked. And sure enough, they were! My heart gave a great bound. But I was too soon. There was a footnote, in Mr. Bright's hand, which said: "You are taxed under Schedule D, section 14." I turned to that place, and found these three things: "Trades, Offices, Gas-works."

Of course, after a moment's reflection, hope came up again, and then certainty: Mr. Bright was in error, and clear off the track; for Authorship is not a Trade, it is an inspiration; Authorship does not keep an Office, its habitation is all out under the sky, and everywhere where the winds are blowing and the sun is shining and the creatures of God are free. Now then, since I have no Trade and keep no Office, I am not taxable under Schedule D, section 14, your Majesty sees that; so I will go on to that other thing that I spoke of, the "deductions"—deductions from my tax which I may get allowed, under conditions. Mr. Bright says all deductions to be claimed by me must be restricted to the provisions made in Paragraph No. 8, entitled "Wear and Tear of Machinery, or Plant." This is curious, and shows how far he has gotten away on his wrong course after once he has got started wrong: for Offices and Trades do not have Plant, they do not have Machinery, such a thing was never heard of; and, moreover, they do not wear and tear. You see that, your Majesty, and that it is true. Here is the Paragraph No. 8:

Amount claimed as a deduction for diminished value by reason of Wear and Tear, where the Machinery or Plant belongs to the Person or Company carrying on the Concern, or is let to such Person or Company so that the Lessee is bound to maintain and deliver over the same in good condition:—

Amount £————

There it is—the very words.

I could answer Mr. Bright thus:

It is my pride to say that my Brain is my Plant; and I do not claim any deduction for diminished value by reason of Wear and Tear, for the reason that it does not wear and tear, but stays sound and whole all the time. Yes, I could say to him, my Brain is my Plant, my Skull is my Workshop, my Hand is my Machinery, and I am the Person carrying on the Concern; it is not leased to anybody, and so there is no Lessee bound to maintain and deliver over the same in good condition. There. I do not wish to any way overrate this argument and answer, dashed off just so, and not a word of it altered from the way I first wrote it, your Majesty, but indeed it does seem to pulverize that young fellow, you can see that yourself. But that is all I say; I stop there; I never pursue a person after I have got him down.

Having thus shown your Majesty that I am not taxable, but am the victim of the error of a clerk who mistakes the nature of my commerce, it only remains for me to beg that you will of your justice annul my letter that I spoke of, so that my publisher can keep back that tax money which, in the confusion and aberration caused by the Document, I ordered him to pay. You will not miss the sum, but this is a hard year for authors; and as for lectures, I do not suppose your Majesty ever saw such a dull season.

With always great and ever-increasing respect, I beg to sign myself your Majesty's servant to command,

MARK TWAIN

HER MAJESTY THE QUEEN, LONDON

1887

A Cure for the Blues

By courtesy of Mr. Cable I came into possession of a singular book eight or ten years ago. It is likely that mine is now the only copy in existence. Its title-page, unabbreviated, reads as follows:

"The Enemy Conquered; or, Love Triumphant. By G. Ragsdale McClintock,* author of 'An Address,' etc., delivered at Sunflower Hill, South Carolina, and member of the Yale Law School. New Haven: published by T. H. Pease, 83 Chapel Street, 1845."

No one can take up this book and lay it down again unread. Whoever reads one line of it is caught, is chained; he has become the contented slave of its fascinations; and he will read and read, devour and devour, and will not let it go out of his hand till it is finished to the last line, though the house be on fire over his head. And after a first reading he will not throw it aside, but will keep it by him, with his Shakespeare and his Homer, and will take it up many and many a time, when the world is dark and his spirits are low, and be straightway cheered and refreshed. Yet this work has been allowed to lie wholly neglected, unmentioned, and apparently unregretted, for nearly half a century.

The reader must not imagine that he is to find in it wisdom, brilliancy, fertility of invention, ingenuity of construction, excellence of form, purity of style, perfection of imagery, truth to nature, clearness of statement, humanly possible situations, humanly possible people, fluent narrative, connected sequence of events—or philosophy, or logic, or sense. No; the rich, deep, beguiling charm of the book lies in the total and miraculous *absence* from it of all these qualities—a charm which is completed and perfected by the evident fact that the author, whose naïve innocence easily and surely wins our regard, and almost our worship, does not know that they are

* The name here given is a substitute for the one actually attached to the pamphlet.

absent, does not even suspect that they are absent. When read by the light of these helps to an understanding of the situation, the book is delicious—profoundly and satisfyingly delicious.

I call it a book because the author calls it a book, I call it a work because he calls it a work; but, in truth, it is merely a duodecimo pamphlet of thirty-one pages. It was written for fame and money, as the author very frankly—yes, and very hopefully, too, poor fellow—says in his preface. The money never came—no penny of it ever came; and how long, how pathetically long, the fame has been deferred—forty-seven years! He was young then, it would have been so much to him then; but will he care for it now?

As time is measured in America, McClintock's epoch is antiquity. In his long-vanished day the Southern author had a passion for "eloquence"; it was his pet, his darling. He would be eloquent, or perish. And he recognized only one kind of eloquence—the lurid, the tempestuous, the volcanic. He liked words—big words, fine words, grand words, rumbling, thundering, reverberating words; with sense attaching if it could be got in without marring the sound, but not otherwise. He loved to stand up before a dazed world, and pour forth flame and smoke and lava and pumice-stone into the skies, and work his sub-terranean thunders, and shake himself with earthquakes, and stench himself with sulphur fumes. If he consumed his own fields and vineyards, that was a pity, yes; but he would have his eruption at any cost. Mr. McClintock's eloquence—and he is always eloquent, his crater is always spouting—is of the pattern common to his day, but he departs from the custom of the time in one respect: his brethren allowed sense to intrude when it did not mar the sound, but he does not allow it to intrude at all. For example, consider this figure, which he uses in the village "Address" referred to with such candid complacency in the title-page above quoted—"like the topmost topaz of an ancient tower." Please read it again; contemplate it; measure it; walk around it; climb up it; try to get at an approximate realization of the size of it. Is the fellow to that to be found in literature, ancient or modern, foreign or domestic, living or dead, drunk or sober? One notices how fine and grand it sounds. We know that if it was loftily uttered, it got a noble burst of applause from the villagers; yet there isn't a ray of sense in it, or meaning to it.

McClintock finished his education at Yale in 1843, and came to Hartford on a visit that same year. I have talked with men who at that time talked with him, and felt of him, and knew he was real. One needs to remember that fact and to keep fast hold of it; it is the only way to keep McClintock's book from undermining one's faith in McClintock's actuality.

As to the book. The first four pages are devoted to an inflamed eulogy of Woman—simply Woman in general, or perhaps as an Institution—wherein, among other compliments to her details, he pays a unique one to her voice. He says it "fills the breast with fond alarms, echoed by every rill." It sounds well enough, but it is not true. After the eulogy he takes up his real work and the novel begins. It begins in the woods, near the village of Sunflower Hill.

Brightening clouds seemed to rise from the mist of the fair Chattahoochee, to spread their beauty over the thick forest, to guide the hero whose bosom beats with aspirations to conquer the enemy that would tarnish his name, and to win back the admiration of his long-tried friend.

It seems a general remark, but it is not general; the hero mentioned is the to-be hero of the book; and in this abrupt fashion, and without name or description, he is shoveled into the tale. "With aspirations to conquer the enemy that would tarnish his name" is merely a phrase flung in for the sake of the sound—let it not mislead the reader. No one is trying to tarnish this person; no one has thought of it. The rest of the sentence is also merely a phrase; the man has no friend as yet, and of course has had no chance to try him, or win back his admiration, or disturb him in any other way.

The hero climbs up over "Sawney's Mountain," and down the other side, making for an old Indian "castle"—which becomes "the red man's hut" in the next sentence; and when he gets there at last, he "surveys with wonder and astonishment" the invisible structure, "which time had buried in the dust, and thought to himself his happiness was not yet complete." One doesn't know why it wasn't, nor how near it came to being complete, nor what was still wanting to round it up and make it so. Maybe it was the Indian; but the book does not say. At this point we have an episode:

Beside the shore of the brook sat a young man, about eighteen or twenty, who seemed to be reading some favorite book, and who had a remarkably noble countenance—eyes which betrayed more than a common mind. This of course made the youth a welcome guest, and gained him friends in whatever condition of life he might be placed. The traveler observed that he was a well-built figure which showed strength and grace in every movement. He accordingly addressed him in quite a gentlemanly manner, and inquired of him the way to the village. After he had received the desired information, and was about taking his leave, the youth said, "Are you not Major Elfonzo, the great musician†—the champion of a noble cause—the modern Achilles, who gained so many victories in the Florida War?" "I bear that name," said the Major, "and those titles, trusting at the same time that the ministers of grace will carry me triumphantly through all my laudable undertakings, and if," continued the Major, "you, sir, are the patronizer of noble deeds, I should like to make you my confidant and learn your address." The youth looked somewhat amazed, bowed low, mused for a moment, and began: "My name is Roswell. I have been recently admitted to the bar, and can only give a faint outline of my future success in that honorable profession; but I trust, sir, like the Eagle, I shall look down from lofty rocks upon the dwellings of man, and shall ever be ready to give you any assistance in my official capacity, and whatever this muscular arm of mine can do, whenever it shall be called from its buried *greatness.*" The Major grasped him by the hand, and exclaimed: "O! thou exalted spirit of inspiration—thou flame of burning prosperity, may the Heaven-directed blaze be the glare of thy soul, and battle down every rampart that seems to impede your progress!"

There is a strange sort of originality about McClintock; he imitates other people's styles, but nobody can imitate his, not even an idiot. Other people can be windy, but McClintock blows a gale; other people can blubber sentiment, but McClintock spews it; other people can mishandle metaphors, but only McClintock knows how to make a business of it. McClintock is always McClintock, he is always consistent, his style is always his own style. He does not make the mistake of being relevant on one page and irrelevant on another; he is irrelevant on all of them. He does not make the mistake of being lucid in one place and obscure in another; he is obscure all the time. He does not make the mistake of slipping in a name here and there that is out of character with his work; he always uses names that exactly and fantastically fit his lunatics. In the matter of undeviating consistency he stands alone in authorship. It is this that makes his style unique, and entitles it to a name of its own—McClintockian. It is this that protects it from being mistaken for anybody else's. Uncredited quotations from other writers often

† Further on it will be seen that he is a country expert on the fiddle, and has a three-township fame.

leave a reader in doubt as to their authorship, but McClintock is safe from that accident; an uncredited quotation from him would always be recognizable. When a boy nineteen years old, who had just been admitted to the bar, says, "I trust, sir, like the Eagle, I shall look down from lofty rocks upon the dwellings of man," we know who is speaking through that boy; we should recognize that note anywhere. There be myriads of instruments in this world's literary orchestra, and a multitudinous confusion of sounds that they make, wherein fiddles are drowned, and guitars smothered, and one sort of drum mistaken for another sort; but whensoever the brazen note of the McClintockian trombone breaks through that fog of music, that note is recognizable, and about it there can be no blur of doubt.

The novel now arrives at the point where the Major goes home to see his father. When McClintock wrote this interview he probably believed it was pathetic.

The road which led to the town presented many attractions. Elfonzo had bid farewell to the youth of deep feeling, and was now wending his way to the dreaming spot of his fondness. The south winds whistled through the woods, as the waters dashed against the banks, as rapid fire in the pent furnace roars. This brought him to remember while alone, that he quietly left behind the hospitality of a father's house, and gladly entered the world, with higher hopes than are often realized. But as he journeyed onward, he was mindful of the advice of his father, who had often looked sadly on the ground, when tears of cruelly deceived hope moistened his eyes. Elfonzo had been somewhat of a dutiful son; yet fond of the amusements of life—had been in distant lands—had enjoyed the pleasure of the world, and had frequently returned to the scenes of his boyhood, almost destitute of many of the comforts of life. In this condition, he would frequently say to his father, "Have I offended you, that you look upon me as a stranger, and frown upon me with stinging looks? Will you not favor me with the sound of your voice? If I have trampled upon your veneration, or have spread a humid veil of darkness around your expectations, send me back into the world, where no heart beats for me—where the foot of man has never yet trod; but give me at least one kind word—allow me to come into the presence sometimes of thy winter-worn locks." "Forbid it, Heaven, that I should be angry with thee," answered the father, "my son, and yet I send thee back to the children of the world—to the cold charity of the combat, and to a land of victory. I read another destiny in thy countenance—I learn thy inclinations from the flame that has already kindled in my soul a strange sensation. It will seek thee, my dear *Elfonzo,* it will find thee—thou canst not escape that lighted torch, which shall blot out from the remembrance of men a long train of prophecies which they have foretold against thee. I once thought not so. Once, I was blind; but now the path of life is plain before me, and my sight is clear; yet, Elfonzo, return to thy worldly occupation—take again in thy hand that chord of sweet sounds—struggle with the civilized world and with your own heart; fly swiftly to the enchanted ground—let the night-*Owl* send forth its screams from the stubborn oak—let the sea sport upon the beach, and the stars sing together; but learn of these, Elfonzo, thy doom, and thy hiding-place. Our most innocent as well as our most lawful *desires* must often be denied us, that we may learn to sacrifice them to a Higher will."

Remembering such admonitions with gratitude, Elfonzo was immediately urged by the recollection of his father's family to keep moving.

McClintock has a fine gift in the matter of surprises; but as a rule they are not pleasant ones, they jar upon the feelings. His closing sentence in the last quotation is of that sort. It brings one down out of the tinted clouds in too sudden and collapsed a fashion. It incenses one against the author for a moment. It makes the reader want to take him by his winter-worn locks, and trample on his veneration, and deliver him over to the cold charity of combat, and blot him out with his own lighted torch. But the feeling does not last. The master takes again in his hand that concord of sweet sounds of his, and one is reconciled, pacified.

His steps became quicker and quicker—he hastened through the *piny* woods, dark as the forest was, and with joy he very soon reached the little village of repose, in whose bosom rested the boldest chivalry. His close attention to every important object—his modest questions about whatever was new to him—his reverence for wise old age, and his ardent desire to learn many of the fine arts, soon brought him into respectable notice.

One mild winter day, as he walked along the streets toward the Academy, which stood upon a small eminence, surrounded by native growth—some venerable in its appearance, others young and prosperous—all seemed inviting, and seemed to be the very place for learning as well as for genius to spend its research beneath its spreading shade. He entered its classic walls in the usual mode of southern manners.

The artfulness of this man! None knows so well as he how to pique the curiosity of the reader—and how to disappoint it. He raises the hope, here, that he is going to tell all about how one enters a classic wall in the usual mode of Southern manners; but does he? No; he smiles in his sleeve, and turns aside to other matters.

The principal of the Institution begged him to be seated and listen to the recitations that were going on. He accordingly obeyed the request, and seemed to be much pleased. After the school was dismissed, and the young hearts regained their freedom, with the songs of the evening, laughing at the anticipated pleasures of a happy home, while others tittered at the actions of the past day, he addressed the teacher in a tone that indicated a resolution—with an undaunted mind. He said he had determined to become a student, if he could meet with his approbation. "Sir," said he, "I have spent much time in the world. I have traveled among the uncivilized inhabitants of America. I have met with friends, and combated with foes; but none of these gratify my ambition, or decide what is to be my destiny. I see the learned world have an influence with the voice of the people themselves. The despoilers of the remotest kingdoms of the earth refer their differences to this class of persons. This the illiterate and inexperienced little dream of; and now if you will receive me as I am, with these deficiencies—with all my misguided opinions, I will give you my honor, sir, that I will never disgrace the Institution, or those who have placed you in this honorable station." The instructor, who had met with many disappointments, knew how to feel for a stranger who had been thus turned upon the charities of an unfeeling community. He looked at him earnestly, and said: "Be of good cheer—look forward, sir, to the high destination you may attain. Remember, the more elevated the mark at which you aim, the more sure, the more glorious, the more magnificent the prize." From wonder to wonder, his encouragement led the impatient listener. A strange nature bloomed before him—giant streams promised him success—gardens of hidden treasures opened to his view. All this, so vividly described, seemed to gain a new witchery from his glowing fancy.

It seems to me that this situation is new in romance. I feel sure it has not been attempted before. Military celebrities have been disguised and set at lowly occupations for dramatic effect, but I think McClintock is the first to send one of them to school. Thus, in this book, you pass from wonder to wonder, through gardens of hidden treasure, where giant streams bloom before you, and behind you, and all around, and you feel as happy, and groggy, and satisfied with your quart of mixed metaphor aboard as you would if it had been mixed in a sample-room and delivered from a jug.

Now we come upon some more McClintockian surprises—a

sweetheart who is sprung upon us without any preparation, along with a name for her which is even a little more of a surprise than she herself is.

In 1842 he entered the class, and made rapid progress in the English and Latin departments. Indeed, he continued advancing with such rapidity that he was like to become the first in his class, and made such unexpected progress, and was so studious, that he had almost forgotten the pictured saint of his affections. The fresh wreaths of the pine and cypress had waited anxiously to drop once more the dews of Heaven upon the heads of those who had so often poured forth the tender emotions of their souls under its boughs. He was aware of the pleasure that he had seen there. So one evening, as he was returning from his reading, he concluded he would pay a visit to this enchanting spot. Little did he think of witnessing a shadow of his former happiness, though no doubt he wished it might be so. He continued sauntering by the roadside, meditating on the past. The nearer he approached the spot, the more anxious he became. At that moment a tall female figure flitted across his path, with a bunch of roses in her hand; her countenance showed uncommon vivacity, with a resolute spirit; her ivory teeth already appeared as she smiled beautifully, promenading—while her ringlets of hair dangled unconsciously around her snowy neck. Nothing was wanting to complete her beauty. The tinge of the rose was in full bloom upon her cheek; the charms of sensibility and tenderness were always her associates. In Ambulinia's bosom dwelt a noble soul—one that never faded—one that never was conquered.

Ambulinia! It can hardly be matched in fiction. The full name is Ambulinia Valeer. Marriage will presently round it out and perfect it. Then it will be Mrs. Ambulinia Valeer Elfonzo. It takes the chromo.

Her heart yielded to no feeling but the love of Elfonzo, on whom she gazed with intense delight, and to whom she felt herself more closely bound, because he sought the hand of no other. Elfonzo was roused from his apparent reverie. His books no longer were his inseparable companions—his thoughts arrayed themselves to encourage him to the field of victory. He endeavored to speak to his supposed Ambulinia, but his speech appeared not in words. No, his effort was a stream of fire, that kindled his soul into a flame of admiration, and carried his senses away captive. Ambulinia had disappeared, to make him more mindful of his duty. As she walked speedily away through the piny woods, she calmly echoed: "O! Elfonzo, thou wilt now look from thy sunbeams. Thou shalt now walk in a new path—perhaps thy way leads through darkness; but fear not, the stars foretell happiness."

To McClintock that jingling jumble of fine words meant something, no doubt, or seemed to mean something; but it is useless for us to try to divine what it was. Ambulinia comes—we don't know whence nor why; she mysteriously intimates—we don't know what; and then she goes echoing away—we don't know whither; and down comes the curtain. McClintock's art is subtle; McClintock's art is deep.

Not many days afterward, as surrounded by fragrant flowers she sat one evening at twilight, to enjoy the cool breeze that whispered notes of melody along the distant groves, the little birds perched on every side, as if to watch the movements of their new visitor. The bells were tolling, when Elfonzo silently stole along by the wild wood flowers, holding in his hand his favorite instrument of music—his eye continually searching for Ambulinia, who hardly seemed to perceive him, as she played carelessly with the songsters that hopped from branch to branch. Nothing could be more striking than the difference between the two. Nature seemed to have given the more tender soul to Elfonzo, and the stronger and more courageous to Ambulinia. A deep feeling spoke from the eyes of Elfonzo—such a feeling as can only be expressed by those who are blessed as admirers, and by those who are able to return the same with sincerity of heart. He was a few years older than Ambulinia: she had turned a little into her seventeenth. He had almost grown up in the Cherokee country, with the same equal proportions as one of the natives. But little intimacy had existed between them until the year forty-one—because the youth felt that the character of such a lovely girl was too exalted to inspire any other feeling than that of quiet reverence. But as lovers will not always be insulted, at all times and under all circumstances, by the frowns and cold looks of crabbed old age, which should continually reflect dignity upon those around, and treat the unfortunate as well as the fortunate with a graceful mien, he continued to use diligence and perseverance. All this lighted a spark in his heart that changed his whole character, and like the unyielding Deity that follows the storm to check its rage in the forest, he resolves for the first time to shake off his embarrassment and return where he had before only worshiped.

At last we begin to get the Major's measure. We are able to put this and that casual fact together, and build the man up before our eyes, and look at him. And after we have got him built, we find him worth the trouble. By the above comparison between his age and Ambulinia's, we guess the war-worn veteran to be twenty-two; and the other facts stand thus: he had grown up in the Cherokee country with the same equal proportions as one of the natives—how flowing and graceful the language, and yet how tantalizing as to meaning!—he had been turned adrift by his father, to whom he had been "somewhat of a dutiful son"; he wandered in distant lands; came back frequently "to the scenes of his boyhood, almost destitute of many of the comforts of life," in order to get into the presence of his father's winterworn locks, and spread a humid veil of darkness around his expectations; but he was always promptly sent back to the cold charity of the combat again; he learned to play the fiddle, and made a name for himself in that line; he had dwelt among the wild tribes; he had philosophized about the despoilers of the kingdoms of the earth, and found out—the cunning creature—that they refer their differences to the learned for settlement; he had achieved a vast fame as a military chieftain, the Achilles of the Florida campaigns, and then had got him a spelling-book and started to school; he had fallen in love with Ambulinia Valeer while she was teething, but had kept it to himself awhile, out of the reverential awe which he felt for the child; but now at last, like the unyielding Deity who follows the storm to check its rage in the forest, he resolves to shake off his embarrassment, and to return where before he had only worshiped. The Major, indeed, has made up his mind to rise up and shake his faculties together, and to see if *he* can't do that thing himself. This is not clear. But no matter about that: there stands the hero, compact and visible; and he is no mean structure, considering that his creator had never created anything before, and hadn't anything but rags and wind to build with this time. It seems to me that no one can contemplate this odd creature, this quaint and curious blatherskite, without admiring McClintock, or, at any rate, loving him and feeling grateful to him; for McClintock made him, he gave him to us; without McClintock we could not have had him, and would now be poor.

But we must come to the feast again. Here is a courtship scene, down there in the romantic glades among the raccoons, alligators, and things, that has merit, peculiar literary merit. See how Achilles woos. Dwell upon the second sentence (particularly the close of it) and the beginning of the third. Never mind the new personage, Leos, who is intruded upon us unheralded and unexplained. That is McClintock's way; it is his habit; it is part of his genius; he cannot help it; he never interrupts the rush of his narrative to make introductions.

It could not escape Ambulinia's penetrating eye that he sought an interview with her, which she as anxiously avoided, and assumed a more distant calmness than before, seemingly to destroy all hope. After many efforts and struggles with his own person, with timid steps the Major approached the damsel, with the same caution as he would have done in a field of battle. "Lady Ambulinia," said he, trembling, "I have long desired a moment like this. I dare not let it escape. I fear the consequences; yet I hope your indulgence will at least hear my petition. Can you not anticipate what I would say, and what I am about to express? Will not you, like Minerva, who sprung from the brain of Jupiter, release me from thy winding chains or cure me—" "Say no more, Elfonzo," answered Ambulinia, with a serious look, raising her hand as if she intended to swear eternal hatred against the whole world; "another lady in my place would have perhaps answered your question in bitter coldness. I know not the little arts of my sex. I care but little for the vanity of those who would chide me, and am unwilling as well as ashamed to be guilty of anything that would lead you to think 'all is not gold that glitters'; so be not rash in your resolution. It is better to repent now, than to do it in a more solemn hour. Yes, I know what you would say. I know you have a costly gift for me—the noblest that man can make—*your heart!* You should not offer it to one so unworthy. Heaven, you know, has allowed my father's house to be made a house of solitude, a home of silent obedience, which my parents say is more to be admired than big names and high-sounding titles. Notwithstanding all this, let me speak the emotions of an honest heart—allow me to say in the fullness of my hopes that I anticipate better days. The bird may stretch its wings toward the sun, which it can never reach; and flowers of the field appear to ascend in the same direction, because they cannot do otherwise; but man confides his complaints to the saints in whom he believes; for in their abodes of light they know no more sorrow. From your confession and indicative looks, I must be that person; if so deceive not yourself."

Elfonzo replied, "Pardon me, my dear madam, for my frankness. I have loved you from my earliest days—everything grand and beautiful hath borne the image of Ambulinia; while precipices on every hand surrounded me, your *guardian angel* stood and beckoned me away from the deep abyss. In every trial, in every misfortune, I have met with your helping hand; yet I never dreamed or dared to cherish thy love, till a voice impaired with age encouraged the cause, and declared they who acquired thy favor should win a victory. I saw how Leos worshiped thee. I felt my own unworthiness. I began to *know jealousy,* a strong guest—indeed, in my bosom,—yet I could see if I gained your admiration Leos was to be my rival. I was aware that he had the influence of your parents, and the wealth of a deceased relative, which is too often mistaken for permanent and regular tranquillity; yet I have determined by your permission to beg an interest in your prayers—to ask you to animate my drooping spirits by your smiles and your winning looks; for if you but speak I shall be conqueror, my enemies shall stagger like Olympus shakes. And though earth and sea may tremble, and the charioteer of the sun may forget his dashing steed, yet I am assured that it is only to arm me with divine weapons which will enable me to complete my long-tried intention."

"Return to yourself, Elfonzo," said Ambulinia, pleasantly: "a dream of vision has disturbed your intellect; you are above the atmosphere, dwelling in the celestial regions; nothing is there that urges or hinders, nothing that brings discord into our present litigation. I entreat you to condescend a little, and be a man, and forget it all. When Homer describes the battle of the gods and noble men fighting with giants and dragons, they represent under this image our struggles with the delusions of our passions. You have exalted me, an unhappy girl, to the skies; you have called me a saint, and portrayed in your imagination an angel in human form. Let her remain such to you, let her continue to be as you have supposed, and be assured that she will consider a share in your esteem as her highest treasure. Think not that I would allure you from the path in which your conscience leads you; for you know I respect the conscience of others, as I would die for my own. Elfonzo, if I am worthy of thy love, let such conversation never again pass between us. Go, seek a nobler theme! we will seek it in the stream of time, as the sun set in the Tigris." As she spake these words she grasped the hand of Elfonzo, saying at the same time—"Peace and prosperity attend you, my hero; be up and doing!" Closing her remarks with this expression, she walked slowly away, leaving Elfonzo astonished and amazed. He ventured not to follow or detain her. Here he stood alone, gazing at the stars; confounded as he was, here he stood.

Yes; there he stood. There seems to be no doubt about that. Nearly half of this delirious story has now been delivered to the reader. It seems a pity to reduce the other half to a cold synopsis. Pity! it is more than a pity, it is a crime; for to synopsize McClintock is to reduce a sky-flushing conflagration to dull embers, it is to reduce barbaric splendor to ragged poverty. McClintock never wrote a line that was not precious; he never wrote one that could be spared; he never framed one from which a word could be removed without damage. Every sentence that this master has produced may be likened to a perfect set of teeth, white, uniform, beautiful. If you pull one, the charm is gone.

Still, it is now necessary to begin to pull, and to keep it up; for lack of space requires us to synopsize.

We left Elfonzo standing there amazed. At what, we do not know. Not at the girl's speech. No; we ourselves should have been amazed at it, of course, for none of us has ever heard anything resembling it; but Elfonzo was used to speeches made up of noise and vacancy, and could listen to them with undaunted mind like the "topmost topaz of an ancient tower"; he was used to making them himself; he—but let it go, it cannot be guessed out; we shall never know what it was that astonished him. He stood there awhile; then he said, "Alas! am I now Grief's disappointed son at last?" He did not stop to examine his mind, and to try to find out what he probably meant by that, because, for one reason, "a mixture of ambition and greatness of soul moved upon his young heart," and started him for the village. He resumed his bench in school, "and reasonably progressed in his education." His heart was heavy, but he went into society, and sought surcease of sorrow in its light distractions. He made himself popular with his violin, "which seemed to have a thousand chords—more symphonious than the Muses of Apollo, and more enchanting than the ghost of the Hills." This is obscure, but let it go.

During this interval Leos did some unencouraged courting, but at last, "choked by his undertaking," he desisted.

Presently "Elfonzo again wends his way to the stately walls and new-built village." He goes to the house of his beloved; she opens the door herself. To my surprise—for Ambulinia's heart had still seemed free at the time of their last interview—love beamed from the girl's eyes. One sees that Elfonzo was surprised, too; for when he caught that light, "a halloo of smothered shouts ran through every vein." A neat figure—a very neat figure, indeed! Then he kissed her. "The scene was overwhelming." They went into the parlor. The girl said it was safe, for her parents were abed, and would never know. Then we have this fine picture—flung upon the canvas with hardly an effort, as you will notice.

> Advancing toward him, she gave a bright display of her rosy neck, and from her head the ambrosial locks breathed divine fragrance; her robe hung waving to his view, while she stood like a goddess confessed before him.

There is nothing of interest in the couple's interview. Now at this point the girl invites Elfonzo to a village show, where jealousy is the motive of the play, for she wants to teach him a wholesome lesson, if he is a jealous person. But this is a sham, and pretty shallow. McClintock merely wants a pretext to drag in a plagiarism of his upon a scene or two in "Othello."

The lovers went to the play. Elfonzo was one of the fiddlers. He and Ambulinia must not be seen together, lest trouble follow with the girl's malignant father; we are made to understand that clearly. So the two sit together in the orchestra, in the midst of the musicians. This does not seem to be good art. In the first place, the girl would be in the way, for orchestras are always packed closely together, and there is no room to spare for people's girls; in the next place, one cannot conceal a girl in an orchestra without everybody taking notice of it. There can be no doubt, it seems to me, that this is bad art.

Leos is present. Of course, one of the first things that catches his eye is the maddening spectacle of Ambulinia "leaning upon Elfonzo's chair." This poor girl does not seem to understand even the rudiments of concealment. But she is "in her seventeenth," as the author phrases it, and that is her justification.

Leos meditates, constructs a plan—with personal violence as a basis, of course. It was their way down there. It is a good plain plan, without any imagination in it. He will go out and stand at the front door, and when these two come out he will "arrest Ambulinia from the hands of the insolent Elfonzo," and thus make for himself a "more prosperous field of immortality than ever was decreed by Omnipotence, or ever pencil drew or artist imagined." But, dear me, while he is waiting there the couple climb out at the back window and scurry home! This is romantic enough, but there is a lack of dignity in the situation.

At this point McClintock puts in the whole of his curious play—which we skip.

Some correspondence follows now. The bitter father and the distressed lovers write the letters. Elopements are attempted. They are idiotically planned, and they fail. Then we have several pages of romantic powwow and confusion signifying nothing. Another elopement is planned; it is to take place on Sunday, when everybody is at church. But the "hero" cannot keep the secret; he tells everybody. Another author would have found another instrument when he decided to defeat this elopement; but that is not McClintock's way. He uses the person that is nearest at hand.

The evasion failed, of course. Ambulinia, in her flight, takes refuge in a neighbor's house. Her father drags her home. The villagers gather, attracted by the racket.

Elfonzo was moved at this sight. The people followed on to see what was going to become of Ambulinia, while he, with downcast looks, kept at a distance, until he saw them enter the abode of the father, thrusting her, that was the sight of his soul, out of his presence into a solitary apartment, when she exclaimed, "Elfonzo! Elfonzo! oh, Elfonzo! where art thou, with all thy heroes? haste, oh! haste, come thou to my relief. Ride on the wings of the wind! Turn thy force loose like a tempest, and roll on thy army like a whirlwind, over this mountain of trouble and confusion. Oh, friends! if any pity me, let your last efforts throng upon the green hills, and come to the relief of Ambulinia, who is guilty of nothing but innocent love." Elfonzo called out with a loud voice, "My God, can I stand this! arouse up, I beseech you, and put an end to this tyranny. Come, my brave boys," said he, "are you ready to go forth to your duty?" They stood around him. "Who," said he, "will call us to arms? Where are my thunderbolts of war? Speak ye, the first who will meet the foe! Who will go forward with me in this ocean of grievous temptation? If there is one who desires to go, let him come and shake hands upon the altar of devotion, and swear that he will be a hero; yes, a Hector in a cause like this, which calls aloud for a speedy remedy." "Mine be the deed," said a young lawyer, "and mine alone; Venus alone shall quit her station before I will forsake one jot or tittle of my promise to you; what is death to me? what is all this warlike army, if it is not to win a victory? I love the sleep of the lover and the mighty; nor would I give it over till the blood of my enemies should wreak with that of my own. But God forbid that our fame should soar on the blood of the slumberer." Mr. Valeer stands at his door with the frown of a demon upon his brow, with his dangerous weapon‡ ready to strike the first man who should enter his door. "Who will arise and go forward through blood and carnage to the rescue of my Ambulinia?" said Elfonzo. "All," exclaimed the multitude; and onward they went, with their implements of battle. Others, of a more timid nature, stood among the distant hills to see the result of the contest.

It will hardly be believed that after all this thunder and lightning not a drop of rain fell; but such is the fact. Elfonzo and his gang stood up and blackguarded Mr. Valeer with vigor all night, getting their outlay back with interest; then in the early morning the army and its general retired from the field, leaving the victory with their solitary adversary and his crowbar. This is the first time this has happened in romantic literature. The invention is original. Every-

‡ It is a crowbar.—M.T.

thing in this book is original; there is nothing hackneyed about it anywhere. Always, in other romances, when you find the author leading up to a climax, you know what is going to happen. But in this book it is different; the thing which seems inevitable and unavoidable never happens; it is circumvented by the art of the author every time.

Another elopement was attempted. It failed.

We have now arrived at the end. But it is not exciting. McClintock thinks it is; but it isn't. One day Elfonzo sent Ambulinia another note—a note proposing elopement No. 16. This time the plan is admirable; admirable, sagacious, ingenious, imaginative, deep—oh, everything, and perfectly easy. One wonders why it was never thought of before. This is the scheme. Ambulinia is to leave the breakfast-table, ostensibly to "attend to the placing of those flowers, which should have been done a week ago"—artificial ones, of course; the others wouldn't keep so long—and then, instead of fixing the flowers, she is to walk out to the grove, and go off with Elfonzo. The invention of this plan overstrained the author, that is plain, for he straightway shows failing powers. The details of the plan are not many or elaborate. The author shall state them himself—this good soul, whose intentions are always better than his English:

"You walk carelessly toward the academy grove, where you will find me with a lightning steed, elegantly equipped to bear you off where we shall be joined in wedlock with the first connubial rights."

Last scene of all, which the author, now much enfeebled, tries to smarten up and make acceptable to his spectacular heart by introducing some new properties—silver bow, golden harp, olive branch—things that can all come good in an elopement, no doubt, yet are not to be compared to an umbrella for real handiness and reliability in an excursion of that kind.

And away she ran to the sacred grove, surrounded with glittering pearls, that indicated her coming. Elfonzo hails her with his silver bow and his golden harp. They meet—Ambulinia's countenance brightens—Elfonzo leads up the winged steed. "Mount," said he, "ye true-hearted, ye fearless soul—the day is ours." She sprang upon the back of the young thunderbolt, a brilliant star sparkles upon her head, with one hand she grasps the reins, and with the other she holds an olive branch. "Lend thy aid, ye strong winds," they exclaimed, "ye moon, ye sun, and all ye fair heaven, witness the enemy conquered." "Hold," said Elfonzo, "thy ng steed." "Ride on," said Ambulinia, "the voice of thunder is be- us." And onward they went, with such rapidity that they very soon arrived at Rural Retreat, where they dismounted, and were united with all the solemnities that usually attend such divine operations.

There is but one Homer, there is but one Shakespeare, there is but one McClintock—and his immortal book is before you. Homer could not have written this book, Shakespeare could not have written it, I could not have done it myself. There is nothing just like it in the literature of any country or of any epoch. It stands alone; it is monumental. It adds G. Ragsdale McClintock's to the sum of the republic's imperishable names.

1893

Traveling with a Reformer

Last spring I went out to Chicago to see the Fair, and although I did not see it my trip was not wholly lost—there were compensations. In New York I was introduced to a major in the regular army who said he was going to the Fair, and we agreed to go together. I had to go to Boston first, but that did not interfere; he said he would go along, and put in the time. He was a handsome man, and built like a gladiator. But his ways were gentle, and his speech was soft and persuasive. He was companionable, but exceedingly reposeful. Yes, and wholly destitute of the sense of humor. He was full of interest in everything that went on around him, but his serenity was indestructible; nothing disturbed him, nothing excited him.

But before the day was done I found that deep down in him somewhere he had a passion, quiet as he was—a passion for reforming petty public abuses. He stood for citizenship—it was his hobby. His idea was that every citizen of the republic ought to consider himself an unofficial policeman, and keep unsalaried watch and ward over the laws and their execution. He thought that the only effective way of preserving and protecting public rights was for each citizen to do his share in preventing or punishing such infringements of them as came under his personal notice.

It was a good scheme, but I thought it would keep a body in trouble all the time; it seemed to me that one would be always trying to get offending little officials discharged, and perhaps getting laughed at for all reward. But he said no, I had the wrong idea; that there was no occasion to get anybody discharged; that in fact you *mustn't* get anybody discharged; that that would itself be a failure; no, one must reform the man—reform him and make him useful where he was.

"Must one report the offender and then beg his superior not to discharge him, but reprimand him and keep him?"

"No, that is not the idea; you don't report him at all, for then you risk his bread and butter. You can act as if you are *going* to report him—when nothing else will answer. But that's an extreme case. That is a sort of *force,* and force is bad. Diplomacy is the effective thing. Now if a man has tact—if a man will exercise diplomacy—"

For two minutes we had been standing at a telegraph wicket, and during all this time the Major had been trying to get the attention of one of the young operators, but they were all busy skylarking. The Major spoke now, and asked one of them to take his telegram. He got for reply:

"I reckon you can wait a minute, can't you?" and the skylarking went on.

The Major said yes, he was not in a hurry. Then he wrote another telegram:

President Western Union Tel. Co.:

Come and dine with me this evening. I can tell you how business is conducted in one of your branches.

Presently the young fellow who had spoken so pertly a little before reached out and took the telegram, and when he read it he lost color and began to apologize and explain. He said he would lose his place if this deadly telegram was sent, and he might never get another. If he could be let off this time he would give no cause of complaint again. The compromise was accepted.

As we walked away, the Major said:

"Now, you see, that was diplomacy—and you see how it worked. It wouldn't do any good to bluster, the way people are always doing—that boy can always give you as good as you send, and you'll come out defeated and ashamed of yourself pretty nearly always. But you see he stands no chance against diplomacy. Gentle words and diplomacy—those are the tools to work with."

"Yes, I see; but everybody wouldn't have had your opportunity. It isn't everybody that is on those familiar terms with the president of the Western Union."

"Oh, you misunderstand. I don't know the president—I only used him diplomatically. It is for his good and for the public good. There's no harm in it."

I said, with hesitation and diffidence:

"But is it ever right or noble to tell a lie?"

He took no note of the delicate self-righteousness of the question, but answered, with undisturbed gravity and simplicity:

"Yes, sometimes. Lies told to injure a person, and lies told to profit yourself are not justifiable, but lies told to help another person, and lies told in the public interest—oh, well, that is quite another matter. Anybody knows that. But never mind about the methods: you see the result. That youth is going to be useful now, and well behaved. He had a good face. He was worth saving. Why, he was worth saving on his mother's account if not his own. Of course, he has a mother—sisters, too. Damn those people who are always forgetting that! Do you know, I've never fought a duel in my life—never once—and yet have been challenged, like other people. I could always see the other man's unoffending women folks or his little children standing between him and me. *They* hadn't done anything—I couldn't break *their* hearts, you know."

He corrected a good many little abuses in the course of the day, and always without friction—always with a fine and dainty "diplomacy" which left no sting behind; and he got such happiness and such contentment out of these performances that I was obliged to envy him his trade—and perhaps would have adopted it if I could have managed the necessary deflections from fact as confidently with my mouth as I believe I could with a pen, behind the shelter of print, after a little practice.

Away late that night we were coming up-town in a horse-car when three boisterous roughs got aboard, and began to fling hilarious obscenities and profanities right and left among the timid passengers, some of whom were women and children. Nobody resisted or retorted; the conductor tried soothing words and moral suasion, but the roughs only called him names and laughed at him. Very soon I saw that the Major realized that this was a matter which was in his line; evidently he was turning over his stock of diplomacy in his mind and getting ready. I felt that the first diplomatic remark he made in this place would bring down a landslide of ridicule upon him and maybe something worse; but before I could whisper to him and check him he had begun, and it was too late. He said, in a level and dispassionate tone:

"Conductor, you must put these swine out. I will help you."

I was not looking for that. In a flash the three roughs plunged at him. But none of them arrived. He delivered three such blows as one could not expect to encounter outside the prize-ring, and neither of the men had life enough left in him to get up from where he fell. The Major dragged them out and threw them off the car, and we got under way again.

I was astonished; astonished to see a lamb act so; astonished at the strength displayed, and the clean and comprehensive result; astonished at the brisk and business-like style of the whole thing. The situation had a humorous side to it, considering how much I had been hearing about mild persuasion and gentle diplomacy all day from this pile-driver, and I would have liked to call his attention to that feature and do some sarcasms about it; but when I looked at him I saw that it would be of no use—his placid and contented face had no ray of humor in it; he would not have understood. When we left the car, I said:

"That was a good stroke of diplomacy—three good strokes of diplomacy, in fact."

"*That*? That wasn't diplomacy. You are quite in the wrong. Diplomacy is a wholly different thing. One cannot apply it to that sort; they would not understand it. No, that was not diplomacy; it was force."

"Now that you mention it, I—yes, I think perhaps you are right."

"Right? Of course I am right. It was just force."

"I think, myself, it had the outside aspect of it. Do you often have to reform people in that way?"

"Far from it. It hardly ever happens. Not oftener than once in half a year, at the outside."

"Those men will get well?"

"Get well? Why, certainly they will. They are not in any danger. I know how to hit and where to hit. You noticed that I did not hit them under the jaw. That would have killed them."

I believed that. I remarked—rather wittily, as I thought—that he had been a lamb all day, but now had all of a sudden developed into a ram—battering-ram; but with dulcet frankness and simplicity he said no, a battering-ram was quite a different thing and not in use now. This was maddening, and I came near bursting out and saying he had no more appreciation of wit than a jackass—in fact, I had it right on my tongue, but did not say it, knowing there was no hurry and I could say it just as well some other time over the telephone.

We started to Boston the next afternoon. The smoking-compartment in the parlor-car was full, and we went into the regular smoker. Across the aisle in the front seat sat a meek, farmer-looking old man with a sickly pallor in his face, and he was holding the door open with his foot to get the air. Presently a big brakeman came rushing through, and when he got to the door he stopped, gave the farmer an ugly scowl, then wrenched the door to with such energy as to almost snatch the old man's boot off. Then on he plunged about his business. Several passengers laughed, and the old gentleman looked pathetically shamed and grieved.

After a little the conductor passed along, and the Major stopped him and asked him a question in his habitually courteous way:

"Conductor, where does one report the misconduct of a brakeman? Does one report to you?"

"You can report him at New Haven if you want to. What has he been doing?"

The Major told the story. The conductor seemed amused. He said, with just a touch of sarcasm in his bland tones:

"As I understand you, the brakeman didn't *say* anything."

"No, he didn't say anything."

"But he scowled, you say."

"Yes."

"And snatched the door loose in a rough way."

"Yes."

"That's the whole business, is it?"

"Yes, that is the whole of it."

The conductor smiled pleasantly, and said:

"Well, if you want to report him, all right, but I don't quite make out what it's going to amount to. You'll say—as I understand you—that the brakeman insulted this old gentleman. They'll ask you what he *said*. You'll say he didn't say anything at all. I reckon they'll say, how are you going to make out an insult when you acknowledge yourself that he didn't say a word."

There was a murmur of applause at the conductor's compact reasoning, and it gave him pleasure—you could see it in his face. But the Major was not disturbed. He said:

"There—now you have touched upon a crying defect in the complaint system. The railway officials—as the public think and as you also seem to think—are not aware that there are any kind of insults except *spoken* ones. So nobody goes to headquarters and reports insults of manner, insults of gesture, look, and so forth; and yet these are sometimes harder to bear than any words. They are bitter hard to bear because there is nothing tangible to take hold of; and the insulter can always say, if called before the railway officials, that he never dreamed of intending any offense. It seems to me that the officials ought to specially and urgently request the public to report *unworded* affronts and incivilities."

The conductor laughed, and said:

"Well, that *would* be trimming it pretty fine, sure!"

"But not too fine, I think. I will report this matter at New Haven, and I have an idea that I'll be thanked for it."

The conductor's face lost something of its complacency; in fact, it settled to a quite sober cast as the owner of it moved away. I said:

"You are not really going to bother with that trifle, are you?"

"It isn't a trifle. Such things ought always to be reported. It is a public duty, and no citizen has a right to shirk it. But I sha'n't have to report this case."

"Why?"

"It won't be necessary. Diplomacy will do the business. You'll see."

Presently the conductor came on his rounds again, and when he reached the Major he leaned over and said:

"That's all right. You needn't report him. He's responsible to me, and if he does it again I'll give him a talking to."

The Major's response was cordial:

"Now that is what I like! You mustn't think that I was moved by any vengeful spirit, for that wasn't the case. It was duty—just a sense of duty, that was all. My brother-in-law is one of the directors of the road, and when he learns that you are going to reason with your brakeman the very next time he brutally insults an unoffending old man it will please him, you may be sure of that."

The conductor did not look as joyous as one might have thought he would, but on the contrary looked sickly and uncomfortable. He stood around a little; then said:

"I think something ought to be done to him *now*. I'll discharge him."

"Discharge him? What good would that do? Don't you think it would be better wisdom to teach him better ways and keep him?"

"Well, there's something in that. What would you suggest?"

"He insulted the old gentleman in presence of all these people.

How would it do to have him come and apologize in their presence?"

"I'll have him here right off. And I want to say this: If people would do as you've done, and report such things to me instead of keeping mum and going off and blackguarding the road, you'd see a different state of things pretty soon. I'm much obliged to you."

The brakeman came and apologized. After he was gone the Major said:

"Now, you see how simple and easy that was. The ordinary citizen would have accomplished nothing—the brother-in-law of a director can accomplish anything he wants to."

"But are you really the brother-in-law of a director?"

"Always. Always when the public interests require it. I have a brother-in-law on all the boards—everywhere. It saves me a world of trouble."

"It is a good wide relationship."

"Yes. I have over three hundred of them."

"Is the relationship never doubted by a conductor?"

"I have never met with a case. It is the honest truth—I never have."

"Why didn't you let him go ahead and discharge the brakeman, in spite of your favorite policy? You know he deserved it."

The Major answered with something which really had a sort of distant resemblance to impatience:

"If you would stop and think a moment you wouldn't ask such a question as that. Is a brakeman a dog, that nothing but dog's methods will do for him? He is a man, and has a man's fight for life. And he always has a sister, or a mother, or wife and children to support. Always—there are no exceptions. When you take his living away from him you take theirs away too—and what have they done to you? Nothing. And where is the profit in discharging an uncourteous brakeman and hiring another just like him? It's unwisdom. Don't you see that the rational thing to do is to *reform* the brakeman and keep him? Of course it is."

Then he quoted with admiration the conduct of a certain division superintendent of the Consolidated road, in a case where a switchman of two years' experience was negligent once and threw a train off the track and killed several people. Citizens came in a passion to urge the man's dismissal, but the superintendent said:

"No, you are wrong. He has learned his lesson, he will throw no more trains off the track. He is twice as valuable as he was before. I shall keep him."

We had only one more adventure on the trip. Between Hartford and Springfield the train-boy came shouting in with an armful of literature and dropped a sample into a slumbering gentleman's lap, and the man woke up with a start. He was very angry, and he and a couple of friends discussed the outrage with much heat. They sent for the parlor-car conductor and described the matter, and were determined to have the boy expelled from his situation. The three complainants were wealthy Holyoke merchants, and it was evident that the conductor stood in some awe of them. He tried to pacify them, and explained that the boy was not under his authority, but under that of one of the news companies; but he accomplished nothing.

Then the Major volunteered some testimony for the defense. He said:

"I saw it all. You gentlemen have not meant to exaggerate the circumstances, but still that is what you have done. The boy has done nothing more than all train-boys do. If you want to get his ways softened down and his manners reformed, I am with you and ready to help, but it isn't fair to get him discharged without giving him a chance."

But they were angry, and would hear of no compromise. They were well acquainted with the president of the Boston & Albany, they said, and would put everything aside next day and go up to Boston and fix that boy.

The Major said he would be on hand too, and would do what he could to save the boy. One of the gentlemen looked him over, and said:

"Apparently it is going to be a matter of who can wield the most influence with the president. Do you know Mr. Bliss personally?"

The Major said, with composure:

"Yes; he is my uncle."

The effect was satisfactory. There was an awkward silence for a minute or more; then the hedging and the half-confessions of overhaste and exaggerated resentment began, and soon everything was smooth and friendly and sociable, and it was resolved to drop the matter and leave the boy's bread-and-butter unmolested.

It turned out as I had expected: the president of the road was not the Major's uncle at all—except by adoption, and for this day and train only.

We got into no episodes on the return journey. Probably it was because we took a night train and slept all the way.

We left New York Saturday night by the Pennsylvania road. After breakfast the next morning we went into the parlor-car, but found it a dull place and dreary. There were but few people in it and nothing going on. Then we went into the little smoking-compartment of the same car and found three gentlemen in there. Two of them were grumpling over one of the rules of the road—a rule which forbade card-playing on the trains on Sunday. They had started an innocent game of high-low-jack and been stopped. The Major was interested. He said to the third gentleman:

"Did you object to the game?"

"Not at all. I am a Yale professor and a religious man, but my prejudices are not extensive."

Then the Major said to the others:

"You are at perfect liberty to resume your game, gentlemen; no one here objects."

One of them declined the risk, but the other one said he would like to begin again if the Major would join him. So they spread an overcoat over their knees and the game proceeded. Pretty soon the parlor-car conductor arrived, and said brusquely:

"There, there, gentlemen, that won't do. Put up the cards—it's not allowed."

The Major was shuffling. He continued to shuffle, and said:

"By whose order is it forbidden?"

"It's my order. I forbid it."

The dealing began. The Major asked:

"Did you invent the idea?"

"What idea?"

"The idea of forbidding card-playing on Sunday."

"No—of course not."

"Who did?"

"The company."

"Then it isn't your order, after all, but the company's. Is that it?"

"Yes. But you don't stop playing; I have to require you to stop playing immediately."

"Nothing is gained by hurry, and often much is lost. Who authorized the company to issue such an order?"

"My dear sir, that is a matter of no consequence to me, and—"

"But you forget that you are not the only person concerned. It may be a matter of consequence to me. It is indeed a matter of very great importance to me. I cannot violate a legal requirement of my country without dishonoring myself; I cannot allow any man or corporation to hamper my liberties with illegal rules—a thing which railway companies are always trying to do—without dishonoring my citizenship. So I come back to that question: By whose authority has the company issued this order?"

"I don't *know*. That's *their* affair."

"Mine, too. I doubt if the company has any right to issue such a rule. This road runs through several states. Do you know what state we are in now, and what its laws are in matters of this kind?"

"Its laws do not concern me, but the company's orders do. It is my duty to stop this game, gentlemen, and it *must* be stopped."

"Possibly; but still there is no hurry. In hotels they post certain rules in the rooms, but they always quote passages from the state laws as authority for these requirements. I see nothing posted here of this sort. Please produce your authority and let us arrive at a decision, for you see yourself that you are marring the game."

"I have nothing of the kind, but I have my orders, and that is sufficient. They must be obeyed."

"Let us not jump to conclusions. It will be better all around to examine into the matter without heat or haste, and see just where we stand before either of us makes a mistake—for the curtailing of the liberties of a citizen of the United States is a much more serious matter than you and the railroads seem to think, and it cannot be done in my person until the curtailer proves his right to do so. Now—"

"My dear sir, *will* you put down those cards?"

"All in good time, perhaps. It depends. You say this order must be obeyed. *Must*. It is a strong word. You see yourself how strong it is. A wise company would not arm you with so drastic an order as this, of *course*, without appointing a penalty for its infringement. Otherwise it runs the risk of being a dead letter and a thing to laugh at. What is the appointed penalty for an infringement of this law?"

"Penalty? I never heard of any."

"Unquestionably you must be mistaken. Your company orders you to come here and rudely break up an innocent amusement, and furnishes you no way to enforce the order? Don't you see that that is nonsense? What do you *do* when people refuse to obey this order? Do you take the cards away from them?"

"No."

"Do you put the offender off at the next station?"

"Well, no—of course we couldn't if he had a ticket."

"Do you have him up before a court?"

The conductor was silent and apparently troubled. The Major started a new deal, and said:

"You see that you are helpless, and that the company has placed you in a foolish position. You are furnished with an arrogant order, and you deliver it in a blustering way, and when you come to look into the matter you find you haven't any way of enforcing obedience."

The conductor said, with chill dignity:

"Gentlemen, you have heard the order, and my duty is ended. As to obeying it or not, you will do as you think fit." And he turned to leave.

"But wait. The matter is not yet finished. I think you are mistaken about your duty being ended; but if it really is, I myself have a duty to perform yet."

"How do you mean?"

"Are you going to report my disobedience at headquarters in Pittsburgh?"

"No. What good would that do?"

"You must report me, or I will report you."

"Report me for what?"

"For disobeying the company's orders in not stopping this game. As a citizen it is my duty to help the railway companies keep their servants to their work."

"Are you in earnest?"

"Yes, I am in earnest. I have nothing against you as a man, but I have this against you as an officer—that you have not carried out that order, and if you do not report me I must report you. And I will."

The conductor looked puzzled, and was thoughtful a moment; then he burst out with:

"I seem to be getting *myself* into a scrape! It's all a muddle; I can't make head or tail of it; it's never happened before; they always knocked under and never said a word, and so *I* never saw how ridiculous that stupid order with no penalty is. *I* don't want to report anybody, and I don't want to *be* reported—why, it might do me no end of harm! Now *do* go on with the game—play the whole day if you want to—and don't let's have any more trouble about it!"

"No, I only sat down here to establish this gentleman's rights—he can have his place now. But before you go won't you tell me what you think the company made this rule for? Can you imagine an excuse for it? I mean a rational one—an excuse that is not on its face silly, and the invention of an idiot?"

"Why, surely I can. The reason it was made is plain enough. It is to save the feelings of the other passengers—the religious ones among them, I mean. They would not like it, to have the Sabbath desecrated by card-playing on the train."

"I just thought as much. They are willing to desecrate it themselves by traveling on Sunday, but they are not willing that other people—"

"By gracious, you've hit it! I never thought of that before. The fact is, it *is* a silly rule when you come to look into it."

At this point the train-conductor arrived, and was going to shut down the game in a very high-handed fashion, but the parlor-car conductor stopped him and took him aside to explain. Nothing more was heard of the matter.

I was ill in bed eleven days in Chicago and got no glimpse of the Fair, for I was obliged to return east as soon as I was able to travel. The Major secured and paid for a stateroom in a sleeper the day before we left, so that I could have plenty of room and be comfortable; but when we arrived at the station a mistake had been made and our car had not been put on. The conductor had reserved a section for us—it was the best he could do, he said. But the Major said we were not in a hurry, and would wait for the car to be put on. The conductor responded, with pleasant irony:

"It may be that *you* are not in a hurry, just as you say, but we *are*. Come, get aboard, gentlemen, get aboard—don't keep us waiting."

But the Major would not get aboard himself nor allow me to do it. He wanted his car, and said he must have it. This made the hurried and perspiring conductor impatient, and he said:

"It's the best we can *do*—we can't do impossibilities. You will take the section or go without. A mistake has been made and can't be rectified at this late hour. It's a thing that happens now and then, and there is nothing for it but to put up with it and make the best of it. Other people do."

"Ah, that is just it, you see. If they had stuck to their rights and enforced them you wouldn't be trying to trample mine underfoot in this bland way now. I haven't any disposition to give you unnecessary trouble, but it is my duty to protect the next man from this kind of imposition. So I must have my car. Otherwise I will wait in Chicago and sue the company for violating its contract."

"Sue the company?—for a thing like that!"

"Certainly."

"Do you really mean that?"

"Indeed, I do."

The conductor looked the Major over wonderingly, and then said:

"It beats me—it's bran-new—I've never struck the mate to it before. But I swear I think you'd do it. Look here, I'll send for the station-master."

When the station-master came he was a good deal annoyed—at the Major, not at the person who had made the mistake. He was rather brusque, and took the same position which the conductor had taken in the beginning; but he failed to move the soft-spoken artilleryman, who still insisted that he must have his car. However, it was plain that there was only one strong side in this case, and that that side was the Major's. The station-master banished his annoyed manner, and became pleasant and even half apologetic. This made a good opening for a compromise, and the Major made a concession. He said he would give up the engaged stateroom, but he must have *a* stateroom. After a deal of ransacking, one was found whose owner was persuadable; he exchanged it for our section, and we got away at last. The conductor called on us in the evening, and was kind and courteous and obliging, and we had a long talk and got to be good friends. He said he wished the public would make trouble oftener—it would have a good effect. He said that the railroads could not be expected to do their whole duty by the traveler unless the traveler would take some interest in the matter himself.

I hoped that we were done reforming for the trip now, but it was not so. In the hotel-car, in the morning, the Major called for broiled chicken. The waiter said:

"It's not in the bill of fare, sir; we do not serve anything but what is in the bill."

"That gentleman yonder is eating a broiled chicken."

"Yes, but that is different. He is one of the superintendents of the road."

"Then all the more must I have broiled chicken. I do not like these discriminations. Please hurry—bring me a broiled chicken."

The waiter brought the steward, who explained in a low and polite voice that the thing was impossible—it was against the rule, and the rule was rigid.

"Very well, then, you must either apply it impartially or break it impartially. You must take that gentleman's chicken away from him or bring me one."

The steward was puzzled, and did not quite know what to do. He began an incoherent argument, but the conductor came along just then, and asked what the difficulty was. The steward explained that here was a gentleman who was insisting on having a chicken when it was dead against the rule and not in the bill. The conductor said:

"Stick by your rules—you haven't any option. Wait a moment—is this the gentleman?" Then he laughed and said: "Never mind your rules—it's my advice, and sound; give him anything he wants—don't get him started on his rights. Give him whatever he asks for; and if you haven't got it, stop the train and get it."

The Major ate the chicken, but said he did it from a sense of duty and to establish a principle, for he did not like chicken.

I missed the Fair, it is true, but I picked up some diplomatic tricks which I and the reader may find handy and useful as we go along.

1893

Fenimore Cooper's Literary Offenses

The Pathfinder and *The Deerslayer* stand at the head of Cooper's novels as artistic creations. There are others of his works which contain parts as perfect as are to be found in these, and scenes even more thrilling. Not one can be compared with either of them as a finished whole.

The defects in both of these tales are comparatively slight. They were pure works of art.—*Prof. Lounsbury.*

The five tales reveal an extraordinary fullness of invention.

. . . One of the very greatest characters in fiction, Natty Bumppo. . . .

The craft of the woodsman, the tricks of the trapper, all the delicate art of the forest, were familiar to Cooper from his youth up.—*Prof. Brander Matthews.*

Cooper is the greatest artist in the domain of romantic fiction yet produced by America.—*Wilkie Collins.*

It seems to me that it was far from right for the Professor of English Literature in Yale, the Professor of English Literature in Columbia, and Wilkie Collins to deliver opinions on Cooper's literature without having read some of it. It would have been much more decorous to keep silent and let persons talk who have read Cooper.

Cooper's art has some defects. In one place in *Deerslayer,* and in the restricted space of two-thirds of a page, Cooper has scored 114 offenses against literary art out of a possible 115. It breaks the record.

There are nineteen rules governing literary art in the domain of romantic fiction—some say twenty-two. In *Deerslayer* Cooper violated eighteen of them. These eighteen require:

1. That a tale shall accomplish something and arrive somewhere. But the *Deerslayer* tale accomplishes nothing and arrives in the air.

2. They require that the episodes of a tale shall be necessary parts of the tale, and shall help to develop it. But as the *Deerslayer* tale is not a tale, and accomplishes nothing and arrives nowhere, the episodes have no rightful place in the work, since there was nothing for them to develop.

3. They require that the personages in a tale shall be alive, except in the case of corpses, and that always the reader shall be able to tell the corpses from the others. But this detail has often been overlooked in the *Deerslayer* tale.

4. They require that the personages in a tale, both dead and alive, shall exhibit a sufficient excuse for being there. But this detail also has been overlooked in the *Deerslayer* tale.

5. They require that when the personages of a tale deal in conversation, the talk shall sound like human talk, and be talk such as human beings would be likely to talk in the given circumstances, and have a discoverable meaning, also a discoverable purpose, and a show of relevancy, and remain in the neighborhood of the subject in hand, and be interesting to the reader, and help out the tale, and stop when the people cannot think of anything more to say. But this requirement has been ignored from the beginning of the *Deerslayer* tale to the end of it.

6. They require that when the author describes the character of a personage in his tale, the conduct and conversation of that personage shall justify said description. But this law gets little or no attention in the *Deerslayer* tale, as Natty Bumppo's case will amply prove.

7. They require that when a personage talks like an illustrated, gilt-edged, tree-calf, hand-tooled, seven-dollar Friendship's Offering in the beginning of a paragraph, he shall not talk like a négro minstrel in the end of it. But this rule is flung down and danced upon in the *Deerslayer* tale.

8. They require that crass stupidities shall not be played upon the reader as "the craft of the woodsman, the delicate art of the forest," by either the author or the people in the tale. But this rule is persistently violated in the *Deerslayer* tale.

9. They require that the personages of a tale shall confine themselves to possibilities and let miracles alone; or, if they venture a miracle, the author must so plausibly set it forth as to make it look

possible and reasonable. But these rules are not respected in the *Deerslayer* tale.

10. They require that the author shall make the reader feel a deep interest in the personages of his tale and in their fate; and that he shall make the reader love the good people in the tale and hate the bad ones. But the reader of the *Deerslayer* tale dislikes the good people in it, is indifferent to the others, and wishes they would all get drowned together.

11. They require that the characters in a tale shall be so clearly defined that the reader can tell beforehand what each will do in a given emergency. But in the *Deerslayer* tale this rule is vacated.

In addition to these large rules there are some little ones. These require that the author shall

12. *Say* what he is proposing to say, not merely come near it.
13. Use the right word, not its second cousin.
14. Eschew surplusage.
15. Not omit necessary details.
16. Avoid slovenliness of form.
17. Use good grammar.
18. Employ a simple and straightforward style.

Even these seven are coldly and persistently violated in the *Deerslayer* tale.

Cooper's gift in the way of invention was not a rich endowment; but such as it was he liked to work it, he was pleased with the effects, and indeed he did some quite sweet things with it. In his little box of stage-properties he kept six or eight cunning devices, tricks, artifices for his savages and woodsmen to deceive and circumvent each other with, and he was never so happy as when he was working these innocent things and seeing them go. A favorite one was to make a moccasined person tread in the tracks of the moccasined enemy, and thus hide his own trail. Cooper wore out barrels and barrels of moccasins in working that trick. Another stage-property that he pulled out of his box pretty frequently was his broken twig. He prized his broken twig above all the rest of his effects, and worked it the hardest. It is a restful chapter in any book of his when somebody doesn't step on a dry twig and alarm all the reds and whites for two hundred yards around. Every time a Cooper person is in peril, and absolute silence is worth four dollars a minute, he is sure to step on a dry twig. There may be a hundred handier things to step on, but that wouldn't satisfy Cooper. Cooper requires him to turn out and find a dry twig; and if he can't do it, go and borrow one. In fact, the Leatherstocking Series ought to have been called the Broken Twig Series.

I am sorry there is not room to put in a few dozen instances of the delicate art of the forest, as practised by Natty Bumppo and some of the other Cooperian experts. Perhaps we may venture two or three samples. Cooper was a sailor—a naval officer; yet he gravely tells us how a vessel, driving toward a lee shore in a gale, is steered to a particular spot by her skipper because he knows of an *undertow* there which will hold her back against the gale and save her. For just pure woodcraft, or sailorcraft, or whatever it is, isn't that neat? For several years Cooper was daily in the society of artillery, and he ought to have noticed that when a cannon-ball strikes the ground it either buries itself or skips a hundred feet or so; skips again a hundred feet or so—and so on, till finally it gets tired and rolls. Now in one place he loses some "females"—as he always calls women—in the edge of a wood near a plain at night in a fog, on purpose to give Bumppo a chance to show off the delicate art of the forest before the reader. These mislaid people are hunting for a fort. They hear a cannon-blast, and a cannon-ball presently comes rolling into the wood and stops at their feet. To the females this suggests nothing. The case is very different with the admirable Bumppo. I wish I may never know peace again if he doesn't strike out promptly and *follow the track* of that cannon-ball across the plain through the dense fog and find the fort. Isn't it a daisy? If Cooper had any real knowledge of Nature's ways of doing things, he had a most delicate art in concealing the fact. For instance: one of his acute Indian experts, Chingachgook (pronounced Chicago, I think), has lost the trail of a person he is tracking through the forest. Apparently that trail is hopelessly lost. Neither you nor I could ever have guessed out the way to find it. It was very different with Chicago. Chicago was not stumped for long. He turned a running stream out of its course, and there, in the slush in its old bed, were that person's moccasin tracks. The current did not wash them away, as it would have done in all other like cases—no, even the eternal laws of Nature have to vacate when Cooper wants to put up a delicate job of woodcraft on the reader.

We must be a little wary when Brander Matthews tell us that Cooper's books "reveal an extraordinary fullness of invention." As a rule, I am quite willing to accept Brander Matthews's literary judgments and applaud his lucid and graceful phrasing of them; but that particular statement needs to be taken with a few tons of salt. Bless your heart, Cooper hadn't any more invention than a horse; and I don't mean a high-class horse, either; I mean a clothes-horse. It would be very difficult to find a really clever "situation" in Cooper's books, and still more difficult to find one of any kind which he has failed to render absurd by his handling of it. Look at the episodes of "the caves"; and at the celebrated scuffle between Maqua and those others on the table-land a few days later; and at Hurry Harry's queer water-transit from the castle to the ark; and at Deerslayer's half-hour with his first corpse; and at the quarrel between Hurry Harry and Deerslayer later; and at—but choose for yourself; you can't go amiss.

If Cooper had been an observer his inventive faculty would have worked better; not more interestingly, but more rationally, more plausibly. Cooper's proudest creations in the way of "situations" suffer noticeably from the absence of the observer's protecting gift. Cooper's eye was splendidly inaccurate. Cooper seldom saw anything correctly. He saw nearly all things as through a glass eye, darkly. Of course a man who cannot see the commonest little every-day matters accurately is working at a disadvantage when he is constructing a "situation." In the *Deerslayer* tale Cooper has a stream which is fifty feet wide where it flows out of a lake; it presently narrows to twenty as it meanders along for no given reason, and yet when a stream acts like that it ought to be required to explain itself. Fourteen pages later the width of the brook's outlet from the lake has suddenly shrunk thirty feet, and become "the narrowest part of the stream." This shrinkage is not accounted for. The stream has bends in it, a sure indication that it has alluvial banks and cuts them; yet these bends are only thirty and fifty feet long. If Cooper had been a nice and punctilious observer he would have noticed that the bends were oftener nine hundred feet long than short of it.

Cooper made the exit of that stream fifty feet wide, in the first place, for no particular reason; in the second place, he narrowed it to less than twenty to accommodate some Indians. He bends a "sapling" to the form of an arch over this narrow passage, and conceals six Indians in its foliage. They are "laying" for a settler's scow or ark which is coming up the stream on its way to the lake; it is being hauled against the stiff current by a rope whose stationary end is anchored in the lake; its rate of progress cannot be more than a mile an hour. Cooper describes the ark, but pretty obscurely. In the matter of dimensions "it was little more than a modern canal-boat." Let us guess, then, that it was about one hundred and forty feet long. It was of "greater breadth than common." Let us guess, then, that it was about sixteen feet wide. This leviathan had been prowling down bends which were but a third as long as itself, and scraping between banks where it had only two feet of space to spare on each side. We cannot too much admire this miracle. A low-roofed log dwelling occupies "two-thirds of the ark's length"—a dwelling ninety feet long and sixteen feet wide, let us say—a kind of vestibule train. The dwelling has two rooms—each forty-five feet long and sixteen feet wide, let us guess. One of them is the bedroom of the Hutter girls, Judith and Hetty; the other is the parlor in the daytime, at night it is papa's bedchamber. The ark is arriving at the stream's exit now, whose width has been reduced to less than twenty feet to accommodate the Indians—say to eighteen. There is a foot to spare on each side of the boat. Did the Indians notice that there was going to be a tight squeeze there? Did they notice that they could make money by climbing down out of that arched sapling and just stepping aboard when the ark scraped by? No, other Indians would have noticed these things, but Cooper's Indians never notice anything. Cooper thinks they are marvelous creatures for noticing, but he was almost always in error about his Indians. There was seldom a sane one among them.

The ark is one hundred and forty feet long; the dwelling is ninety feet long. The idea of the Indians is to drop softly and secretly from the arched sapling to the dwelling as the ark creeps along under it at the rate of a mile an hour, and butcher the family. It will take the ark a minute and a half to pass under. It will take the ninety-foot dwelling a minute to pass under. Now, then, what did the six Indians do? It would take you thirty years to guess, and even then you would have to give it up, I believe. Therefore, I will tell you what the Indians did. Their chief, a person of quite extraordinary intellect for a Cooper Indian, warily watched the canal-boat as it squeezed along under him, and when he had got his calculations fined down to exactly the right shade, as he judged, he let go and dropped. And *missed the house!* That is actually what he did. He missed the house, and landed in the stern of the scow. It was not much of a fall, yet it knocked him silly. He lay there unconscious. If the house had been ninety-seven feet long he would have made the trip. The fault was Cooper's, not his. The error lay in the construction of the house. Cooper was no architect.

There still remained in the roost five Indians. The boat has passed under and is now out of their reach. Let me explain what the five did—you would not be able to reason it out for yourself. No. 1 jumped for the boat, but fell in the water astern of it. Then No. 2 jumped for the boat, but fell in the water still farther astern of it. Then No. 3 jumped for the boat, and fell a good way astern of it. Then No. 4 jumped for the boat, and fell in the water *away* astern. Then even No. 5 made a jump for the boat—for he was a Cooper Indian. In the matter of intellect, the difference between a Cooper Indian and the Indian that stands in front of the cigar-shop is not spacious. The scow episode is really a sublime burst of invention; but it does not thrill, because the inaccuracy of the details throws a sort of air of fictitiousness and general improbability over it. This comes of Cooper's inadequacy as an observer.

The reader will find some examples of Cooper's high talent for inaccurate observation in the account of the shooting-match in *The Pathfinder*.

> A common wrought nail was driven lightly into the target, its head having been first touched with paint.

The color of the paint is not stated—an important omission, but Cooper deals freely in important omissions. No, after all, it was not an important omission; for this nail-head is *a hundred yards from* the marksmen, and could not be seen by them at that distance, no matter what its color might be. How far can the best eyes see a common house-fly? A hundred yards? It is quite impossible. Very well; eyes that cannot see a house-fly that is a hundred yards away cannot see an ordinary nail-head at that distance, for the size of the two objects is the same. It takes a keen eye to see a fly or a nail-head at fifty yards—one hundred and fifty feet. Can the reader do it?

The nail was lightly driven, its head painted, and game called. Then the Cooper miracles began. The bullet of the first marksman chipped an edge of the nail-head; the next man's bullet drove the nail a little way into the target—and removed all the paint. Haven't the miracles gone far enough now? Not to suit Cooper; for the purpose of this whole scheme is to show off his prodigy, Deerslayer-

Hawkeye-Long-Rifle-Leatherstocking-Pathfinder-Bumppo before the ladies.

"Be all ready to clench it, boys!" cried out Pathfinder, stepping into his friend's tracks the instant they were vacant. "Never mind a new nail; I can see that, though the paint is gone, and what I can see I can hit at a hundred yards, though it were only a mosquito's eye. Be ready to clench!"

The rifle cracked, the bullet sped its way, and the head of the nail was buried in the wood, covered by the piece of flattened lead.

There, you see, is a man who could hunt flies with a rifle, and command a ducal salary in a Wild West show to-day if we had him back with us.

The recorded feat is certainly surprising just as it stands; but it is not surprising enough for Cooper. Cooper adds a touch. He has made Pathfinder do this miracle with another man's rifle; and not only that, but Pathfinder did not have even the advantage of loading it himself. He had everything against him, and yet he made that impossible shot; and not only made it, but did it with absolute confidence, saying, "Be ready to clench." Now a person like that would have undertaken that same feat with a brickbat, and with Cooper to help he would have achieved it, too.

Pathfinder showed off handsomely that day before the ladies. His very first feat a thing which no Wild West show can touch. He was standing with the group of marksmen, observing—a hundred yards from the target, mind; one Jasper raised his rifle and drove the center of the bull's-eye. Then the Quartermaster fired. The target exhibited no result this time. There was a laugh. "It's a dead miss," said Major Lundie. Pathfinder waited an impressive moment or two; then said, in that calm, indifferent, know-it-all way of his, "No, Major, he has covered Jasper's bullet, as will be seen if any one will take the trouble to examine the target."

Wasn't it remarkable! How *could* he see that little pellet fly through the air and enter that distant bullet-hole? Yet that is what he did; for nothing is impossible to a Cooper person. Did any of those people have any deep-seated doubts about this thing? No; for that would imply sanity, and these were all Cooper people.

The respect for Pathfinder's skill and for his *quickness and accuracy of sight* [the italics are mine] was so profound and general, that the instant he made this declaration the spectators began to distrust their own opinions, and a dozen rushed to the target in order to ascertain the fact.

There, sure enough, it was found that the Quartermaster's bullet had gone through the hole made by Jasper's, and that, too, so accurately as to require a minute examination to be certain of the circumstance, which, however, was soon clearly established by discovering one bullet over the other in the stump against which the target was placed.

They made a "minute" examination; but never mind, how could they know that there were two bullets in that hole without digging the latest one out? for neither probe nor eyesight could prove the presence of any more than one bullet. Did they dig? No; as we shall see. It is the Pathfinder's turn now; he steps out before the ladies, takes aim, and fires.

But, alas! here is a disappointment; an incredible, an unimaginable disappointment—for the target's aspect is unchanged; there is nothing there but that same old bullet-hole!

"If one dared to hint at such a thing," cried Major Duncan, "I should say that the Pathfinder has also missed the target!"

As nobody had missed it yet, the "also" was not necessary; but never mind about that, for the Pathfinder is going to speak.

"No, no, Major," said he, confidently, "that *would* be a risky declaration. I didn't load the piece, and can't say what was in it; but if it was lead, you will find the bullet driving down those of the Quartermaster and Jasper, else is not my name Pathfinder."

A shout from the target announced the truth of this assertion.

Is the miracle sufficient as it stands? Not for Cooper. The Pathfinder speaks again, as he "now slowly advances toward the stage occupied by the females":

"That's not all, boys, that's not all; if you find the target touched at all, I'll own to a miss. The Quartermaster cut the wood, but you'll find no wood cut by that last messenger."

The miracle is at last complete. He knew—doubtless *saw*—at the distance of a hundred yards—that his bullet had passed into the hole *without fraying the edges.* There were now three bullets in that one hole—three bullets embedded processionally in the body of the stump back of the target. Everybody knew this—somehow or other—and yet nobody had dug any of them out to make sure. Cooper is not a close observer, but he is interesting. He is certainly always that, no matter what happens. And he is more interesting when he is not noticing what he is about than when he is. This is a considerable merit.

The conversations in the Cooper books have a curious sound in our modern ears. To believe that such talk really ever came out of people's mouths would be to believe that there was a time when time was of no value to a person who thought he had something to say; when it was the custom to spread a two-minute remark out to ten; when a man's mouth was a rolling-mill, and busied itself all day long in turning four-foot pigs of thought into thirty-foot bars of conversational railroad iron by attenuation; when subjects were seldom faithfully stuck to, but the talk wandered all around and arrived nowhere; when conversations consisted mainly of irrelevancies, with here and there a relevancy, a relevancy with an embarrassed look, as not being able to explain how it got there.

Cooper was certainly not a master in the construction of dialogue. Inaccurate observation defeated him here as it defeated him in so many other enterprises of his. He even failed to notice that the man who talks corrupt English six days in the week must and will talk it on the seventh, and can't help himself. In the *Deerslayer* story he lets Deerslayer talk the showiest kind of book-talk sometimes, and at other times the basest of base dialects. For instance, when some one asks him if he has a sweetheart, and if so, where she abides, this is his majestic answer:

"She's in the forest—hanging from the boughs of the trees, in a soft rain—in the dew on the open grass—the clouds that float about in the blue heavens—the birds that sing in the woods—the sweet springs where I slake my thirst—and in all the other glorious gifts that come from God's Providence!"

And he preceeded that, a little before, with this:

"It consarns me as all things that touches a fri'nd consarns a fri'nd."

And this is another of his remarks:

"If I was Injin born, now, I might tell of this, or carry in the scalp and boast of the expl'ite afore the whole tribe; or if my inimy had only been a bear"—[and so on].

We cannot imagine such a thing as a veteran Scotch Commander-in-Chief comporting himself in the field like a windy melodramatic actor, but Cooper could. On one occasion Alice and Cora were being chased by the French through a fog in the neighborhood of their father's fort:

"*Point de quartier aux coquins!*" cried an eager pursuer, who seemed to direct the operations of the enemy.

"Stand firm and be ready, my gallant 60ths!" suddenly exclaimed a voice above them; "wait to see the enemy; fire low, and sweep the glacis."

"Father! father" exclaimed a piercing cry from out the mist. "It is I! Alice! thy own Elsie! spare, O! save your daughters!"

"Hold!" shouted the former speaker, in the awful tones of parental agony, the sound reaching even to the woods, and rolling back in solemn echo. "'Tis she! God has restored me my children! Throw open the sally-port; to the field, 60ths, to the field! pull not a trigger, lest ye kill my lambs! Drive off these dogs of France with your steel!"

Cooper's word-sense was singularly dull. When a person has a poor ear for music he will flat and sharp right along without knowing it. He keeps near the tune, but it is *not* the tune. When a person has a poor ear for words, the result is a literary flatting and sharping; you perceive what he is intending to say, but you also perceive that he doesn't *say* it. This is Cooper. He was not a word-musician. His ear was satisfied with the *approximate* word. I will furnish some circumstantial evidence in support of this charge. My instances are gathered from half a dozen pages of the tale called *Deerslayer*. He uses "Verbal" for "oral"; "precision" for "facility"; "phenomena" for "marvels"; "necessary" for "predetermined"; "unsophisticated" for "primitive"; "preparation" for "expectancy"; "rebuked" for "subdued"; "dependent on" for "resulting from"; "fact" for "condition"; "fact" for "conjecture"; "precaution" for "caution"; "explain" for "determine"; "mortified" for "disappointed"; "meretricious" for "factitious"; "materially" for "considerably"; "decreasing" for "deepening"; "increasing" for "disappearing"; "embedded" for "inclosed"; "treacherous" for "hostile"; "stood" for "stooped"; "softened" for "replaced"; "rejoined" for "remarked"; "situation" for "condition"; "different" for "differing"; "insensible" for "unsentient"; "brevity" for "celerity"; "distrusted" for "suspicious"; "mental imbecility" for "imbecility"; "eyes" for "sight"; "counteracting" for "opposing"; "funeral obsequies" for "obsequies."

There have been daring people in the world who claimed that Cooper could write English, but they are all dead now—all dead but Lounsbury. I don't remember that Lounsbury makes the claim in so many words, still he makes it, for he says that *Deerslayer* is a "pure work of art." Pure, in that connection, means faultless—faultless in all details—and language is a detail. If Mr. Lounsbury had only compared Cooper's English with the English which he writes himself—but it is plain that he didn't; and so it is likely that he imagines until this day that Cooper's is as clean and compact as his own. Now I feel sure, deep down in my heart, that Cooper wrote about the poorest English that exists in our language, and that the English of *Deerslayer* is the very worst that even Cooper ever wrote.

I may be mistaken, but it does seem to me that *Deerslayer* is not a work of art in any sense; it does seem to me that it is destitute of every detail that goes to the making of a work of art; in truth, it seems to me that *Deerslayer* is just simply a literary *delirium tremens.*

A work of art? It has no invention; it has no order, system, sequence, or result; it has no lifelikeness, no thrill, no stir, no seeming of reality; its characters are confusedly drawn, and by their acts and words they prove that they are not the sort of people the author claims that they are; its humor is pathetic; its pathos is funny; its conversations are—oh! indescribable; its love-scenes odious; its English a crime against the language.

Counting these out, what is left is Art. I think we must all admit that.

1895

My First Lie, and How I Got Out of It

As I understand it, what you desire is information about "my first lie, and how I got out of it." I was born in 1835; I am well along, and my memory is not as good as it was. If you had asked about my first truth it would have been easier for me and kinder of you, for I remember that fairly well; I remember it as if it were last week. The family think it was week before, but that is flattery and probably has a selfish project back of it. When a person has become seasoned by experience and has reached the age of sixty-four, which is the age of discretion, he likes a family compliment as well as ever, but he does not lose his head over it as in the old innocent days.

I do not remember my first lie, it is too far back; but I remember my second one very well. I was nine days old at the time, and had noticed that if a pin was sticking in me and I advertised it in the usual fashion, I was lovingly petted and coddled and pitied in a most agreeable way and got a ration between meals besides. It was human nature to want to get these riches, and I fell. I lied about the pin—advertising one when there wasn't any. You would have done it; George Washington did it; anybody would have done it. During the first half of my life I never knew a child that was able to rise above that temptation and keep from telling that lie. Up to 1867 all the civilized children that were ever born into the world were liars—including George. Then the safety-pin came in and blocked the game. But is that reform worth anything? No; for it is reform by force and has no virtue in it; it merely stops that form of lying; it doesn't impair the disposition to lie, by a shade. It is the cradle application of conversion by fire and sword, or of the temperance principle through prohibition.

To return to that early lie. They found no pin, and they realized that another liar had been added to the world's supply. For by grace of a rare inspiration, a quite commonplace but seldom noticed fact was borne in upon their understandings—that almost all lies are acts, and speech has no part in them. Then, if they examined a little further they recognized that all people are liars from the cradle onward, without exception, and that they begin to lie as soon as they wake in the morning, and keep it up, without rest or refreshment, until they go to sleep at night. If they arrived at that truth it probably grieved them—did, if they had been heedlessly and ignorantly educated by their books and teachers; for why should a person grieve over a thing which by the eternal law of his make he cannot help? He didn't invent the law; it is merely his business to obey it and keep still; join the universal conspiracy and keep so still that he shall deceive his fellow-conspirators into imagining that he doesn't know that the law exists. It is what we all do—we that know. I am speaking of the lie of silent assertion; we can tell it without saying a word, and we all do it—we that know. In the magnitude of its territorial spread it is one of the most majestic lies that the civilizations make it their sacred and anxious care to guard and watch and propagate.

For instance: It would not be possible for a humane and intelligent person to invent a rational excuse for slavery; yet you will remember that in the early days of the emancipation agitation in the North, the agitators got but small help or countenance from any one. Argue and plead and pray as they might, they could not break the universal stillness that reigned, from pulpit and press all the way down to the bottom of society—the clammy stillness created and maintained by the lie of silent assertion—the silent assertion that there wasn't anything going on in which humane and intelligent people were interested.

From the beginning of the Dreyfus case to the end of it, all France, except a couple of dozen moral paladins, lay under the smother of the silent-assertion lie that no wrong was being done to a persecuted and unoffending man. The like smother was over England lately, a good half of the population silently letting on that they were not aware that Mr. Chamberlain was trying to manufacture a war in South Africa and was willing to pay fancy prices for the materials.

Now there we have instances of three prominent ostensible civilizations working the silent-assertion lie. Could one find other instances in the three countries? I think so. Not so very many, perhaps, but say a billion—just so as to keep within bounds. Are those countries working that kind of lie, day in and day out, in thousands and thousands of varieties, without ever resting? Yes, we know that to be true. The universal conspiracy of the silent-assertion lie is hard at work always and everywhere, and always in the interest of a stupidity or a sham, never in the interest of a thing fine or respectable. Is it the most timid and shabby of all lies? It seems to have the look of it. For ages and ages it has mutely labored in the interest of despotisms and aristocracies and chattel slaveries, and military slaveries, and religious slaveries, and has kept them alive; keeps them alive yet, here and there and yonder, all about the globe; and will go on keeping them alive until the silent-assertion lie retires from business—the silent assertion that nothing is going on which fair and intelligent men are aware of and are engaged by their duty to try to stop.

What I am arriving at is this: When whole races and peoples conspire to propagate gigantic mute lies in the interest of tyrannies and shams, why should we care anything about the trifling lies told by individuals? Why should we try to make it appear that abstention from lying is a virtue? Why should we want to beguile ourselves in that way? Why should we without shame help the nation lie, and then be ashamed to do a little lying on our own account? Why shouldn't we be honest and honorable, and lie every time we get a chance? That is to say, why shouldn't we be consistent, and either lie all the time or not at all? Why should we help the nation lie the whole day long and then object to telling one little individual private lie in our own interest to go to bed on? Just for the refreshment of it, I mean, and to take the rancid taste out of our mouth.

Here in England they have the oddest ways. They won't tell a spoken lie—nothing can persuade them. Except in a large moral interest, like politics or religion, I mean. To tell a spoken lie to get even the poorest little personal advantage out of it is a thing which is impossible to them. They make me ashamed of myself sometimes, they are so bigoted. They will not even tell a lie for the fun of it; they will not tell it when it hasn't even a suggestion of damage or advantage in it for any one. This has a restraining influence upon me in spite of reason, and I am always getting out of practice.

Of course, they tell all sorts of little unspoken lies, just like anybody; but they don't notice it until their attention is called to it. They have got me so that sometimes I never tell a verbal lie now except in a modified form; and even in the modified form they don't approve of it. Still, that is as far as I can go in the interest of the growing friendly relations between the two countries; I must keep some of my self-respect—and my health. I can live on a low diet, but I can't get along on no sustenance at all.

Of course, there are times when these people have to come out with a spoken lie, for that is a thing which happens to everybody once in a while, and would happen to the angels if they came down here much. Particularly to the angels, in fact, for the lies I speak of are self-sacrificing ones told for a generous object, not a mean one; but even when these people tell a lie of that sort it seems to scare them and unsettle their minds. It is a wonderful thing to see, and shows that they are all insane. In fact, it is a country full of the most interesting superstitions.

I have an English friend of twenty-five years' standing, and yesterday when we were coming downtown on top of the bus I happened to tell him a lie—a modified one, of course; a half-breed, a mulatto: I can't seem to tell any other kind now, the market is so flat. I was explaining to him how I got out of an embarrassment in Austria last year. I do not know what might have become of me if I hadn't happened to remember to tell the police that I belonged to the same family as the Prince of Wales. That made everything pleasant, and they let me go; and apologized, too, and were ever so kind and obliging and polite, and couldn't do too much for me, and explained how the mistake came to be made, and promised to hang the officer that did it, and hoped I would let bygones be bygones and not say anything about it; and I said they could depend on me. My friend said, austerely:

"You call it a modified lie? Where is the modification?"

I explained that it lay in the form of my statement to the police.

"I didn't say I belonged to the royal family: I only said I belonged to the same family as the Prince—meaning the human family, of course; and if those people had had any penetration they would have known it. I can't go around furnishing brains to the police; it is not to be expected."

"How did you feel after that performance?"

"Well, of course I was distressed to find that the police had misunderstood me, but as long as I had not told any lie I knew there was no occasion to sit up nights and worry about it."

My friend struggled with the case several minutes, turning it over and examining it in his mind; then he said that so far as he could see the modification was itself a lie, being a misleading reservation of an explanatory fact; so I had told two lies instead of one.

"I wouldn't have done it," said he: "I have never told a lie, and I should be very sorry to do such a thing."

Just then he lifted his hat and smiled a basketful of surprised and delighted smiles down at a gentleman who was passing in a hansom.

"Who was that, G——?"

"I don't know."

"Then why did you do that?"

"Because I saw he thought he knew me and was expecting it of me. If I hadn't done it he would have been hurt. I didn't want to embarrass him before the whole street."

"Well, your heart was right, G——, and your act was right. What you did was kindly and courteous and beautiful; I would have done it myself: but it was a lie."

"A lie? I didn't say a word. How do you make it out?"

"I know you didn't speak, still you said to him very plainly and enthusiastically in dumb show, 'Hello! you in town? Awful glad to see you, old fellow; when did you get back?' Concealed in your actions was what you have called 'a misleading reservation of an explanatory fact'—the fact that you had never seen him before. You expressed joy in encountering him—a lie; and you made that reservation—another lie. It was my pair over again. But don't be troubled—we all do it."

Two hours later, at dinner, when quite other matters were being discussed, he told how he happened along once just in the nick of time to do a great service for a family who were old friends of his. The head of it had suddenly died in circumstances and surroundings of a ruinously disgraceful character. If known, the facts would break the hearts of the innocent family and put upon them a load of unendurable shame. There was no help but in a giant lie, and he girded up his loins and told it.

"The family never found out, G——?"

"Never. In all these years they have never suspected. They were proud of him, and always had reason to be; they are proud of him yet, and to them his memory is sacred and stainless and beautiful."

"They had a narrow escape, G——."

"Indeed they had."

"For the very next man that came along might have been one of these heartless and shameless truth-mongers. You have told the truth a million times in your life, G——, but that one golden lie atones for it all. Persevere."

Some may think me not strict enough in my morals, but that position is hardly tenable. There are many kinds of lying which I do not approve. I do not like an injurious lie, except when it injures somebody else; and I do not like the lie of bravado, nor the lie of virtuous ecstasy: the latter was affected by Bryant, the former by Carlyle.

Mr. Bryant said, "Truth crushed to earth will rise again."

I have taken medals at thirteen world's fairs, and may claim to be not without capacity, but I never told as big a one as that which Mr. Bryant was playing to the gallery; we all do it. Carlyle said, in substance, this—I do not remember the exact words: "This gospel is eternal—that a lie shall not live."

I have a reverent affection for Carlyle's books, and have read his *Revolution* eight times; and so I prefer to think he was not entirely at himself when he told that one. To me it is plain that he said it in a moment of excitement, when chasing Americans out of his back yard with brickbats. They used to go there and worship. At bottom he was probably fond of them, but he was always able to conceal it. He kept bricks for them, but he was not a good shot, and it is matter of history that when he fired they dodged, and carried off the brick; for as a nation we like relics, and so long as we get them we do not much care what the reliquary thinks about it. I am quite sure that when he told that large one about a lie not being able to live, he had just missed an American and was over-excited. He told it above thirty years ago, but it is alive yet; alive, and very healthy and hearty, and likely to outlive any fact in history. Carlyle was truthful when calm, but give him Americans enough and bricks enough and he could have taken medals himself.

As regards that time that George Washington told the truth, a word must be said, of course. It is the principal jewel in the crown of America, and it is but natural that we should work it for all it is worth, as Milton says in his "Lay of the Last Minstrel." It was a timely and judicious truth, and I should have told it myself in the circumstances. But I should have stopped there. It was a stately truth, a lofty truth—a Tower; and I think it was a mistake to go on and distract attention from its sublimity by building another Tower alongside of it fourteen times as high. I refer to his remark that he "could not lie." I should have fed that to the marines: or left it to Carlyle; it is just in his style. It would have taken a medal at any European fair, and would have got an Honorable Mention even at Chicago if it had been saved up. But let it pass: the Father of his Country was excited. I have been in those circumstances, and I recollect.

With the truth he told I have no objection to offer, as already indicated. I think it was not premeditated, but an inspiration. With his fine military mind, he had probably arranged to let his brother Edward in for the cherry-tree results, but by an inspiration he saw his opportunity in time and took advantage of it. By telling the truth he could astonish his father; his father would tell the neighbors; the neighbors would spread it; it would travel to all firesides; in the end it would make him President, and not only that, but First President. He was a far-seeing boy and would be likely to think of these things. Therefore, to my mind, he stands justified for what he did. But not for the other Tower: it was a mistake. Still, I don't know about that; upon reflection I think perhaps it wasn't. For indeed it is that Tower that makes the other one live. If he hadn't said "I cannot tell a lie," there would have been no convulsion. That was the earthquake that rocked the planet. That is the kind of statement that lives forever, and a fact barnacled to it has a good chance to share its immortality.

To sum up, on the whole I am satisfied with things the way they are. There is a prejudice against the spoken lie, but none against any other, and by examination and mathematical computation I find that the proportion of the spoken lie to the other varieties is as 1 to 22,894. Therefore the spoken lie is of no consequence, and it is not worth while to go around fussing about it and trying to make believe that it is an important matter. The silent colossal National Lie that is the support and confederate of all the tyrannies and shams and inequalities and unfairnesses that afflict the peoples—that is the one to throw bricks and sermons at. But let us be judicious and let somebody else begin.

And then— But I have wandered from my text. How did I get out of my second lie? I think I got out with honor, but I cannot be sure, for it was a long time ago and some of the details have faded out of my memory. I recollect that I was reversed and stretched across some one's knee, and that something happened, but I cannot now remember what it was. I think there was music; but it is all dim now and blurred by the lapse of time, and this may be only a senile fancy.

1899

Amended Obituaries

To the Editor:

SIR,—I am approaching seventy; it is in sight; it is only three years away. Necessarily, I must go soon. It is but matter-of-course wisdom, then, that I should begin to set my worldly house in order now, so that it may be done calmly and with thoroughness, in place of waiting until the last day, when, as we have often seen, the attempt to set both houses in order at the same time has been marred by the necessity for haste and by the confusion and waste of time arising from the inability of the notary and the ecclesiastic to work together harmoniously, taking turn about and giving each other friendly assistance—not perhaps in fielding, which could hardly be expected, but at least in the minor offices of keeping game and umpiring; by consequence of which conflict of interests and absence of harmonious action a draw has frequently resulted where this ill-fortune could not have happened if the houses had been set in order one at a time and hurry avoided by beginning in season, and giving to each the amount of time fairly and justly proper to it.

In setting my earthly house in order I find it of moment that I should attend in person to one or two matters which men in my position have long had the habit of leaving wholly to others, with consequences often most regrettable. I wish to speak of only one of these matters at this time: Obituaries. Of necessity, an Obituary is a thing which cannot be so judiciously edited by any hand as by that of the subject of it. In such a work it is not the Facts that are of chief importance, but the light which the obituarist shall throw upon them, the meanings which he shall dress them in, the conclusions which he shall draw from them, and the judgments which he shall deliver upon them. The Verdicts, you understand: that is the danger-line.

In considering this matter, in view of my approaching change, it has seemed to me wise to take such measures as may be feasible, to acquire, by courtesy of the press, access to my standing obituaries, with the privilege—if this is not asking too much—of editing, not their Facts, but their Verdicts. This, not for present profit, further than as concerns my family, but as a favorable influence usable on the Other Side, where there are some who are not friendly to me.

With this explanation of my motives, I will now ask you of your courtesy to make an appeal for me to the public press. It is my desire that such journals and periodicals as have obituaries of me lying in their pigeonholes, with a view to sudden use some day, will not wait longer, but will publish them now, and kindly send me a marked copy. My address is simply New York City—I have no other that is permanent and not transient.

I will correct them—not the Facts, but the Verdicts—striking out such clauses as could have a deleterious influence on the Other Side, and replacing them with clauses of a more judicious character. I should, of course, expect to pay double rates for both the omissions and the substitutions; and I should also expect to pay quadruple rates for all obituaries which proved to be rightly and wisely worded in the originals, thus requiring no emendations at all.

It is my desire to leave these Amended Obituaries neatly bound behind me as a perennial consolation and entertainment to my family, and as an heirloom which shall have a mournful but definite commercial value for my remote posterity.

I beg, sir, that you will insert this Advertisement (1t-eow, agate, inside), and send the bill to

Yours very respectfully.
MARK TWAIN

P.S.—For the best Obituary—one suitable for me to read in public, and calculated to inspire regret—I desire to offer a Prize, consisting of a Portrait of me done entirely by myself in pen and ink without previous instructions. The ink warranted to be the kind used by the very best artists.

1902

Sources

The stories were selected from *The Complete Short Stories of Mark Twain,* edited by me. "The Notorious Jumping Frog of Calaveras County": 1–6. "Journalism in Tennessee": 27–32. "The Facts in the Great Beef Contract": 40–45. "How I Edited an Agricultural Paper": 46–50. "Experience of the McWilliamses with Membranous Croup": 99–104. "The Invalid's Story": 187–92. "The McWilliamses and the Burglar Alarm": 193–99. "Playing Courier": 253–65.

Two of the speeches, "The Fourth of July" and "Plymouth Rock and the Pilgrims," were selected from *The Complete Humorous Sketches and Tales of Mark Twain,* edited by me. Pages 253–55 and 491–95. The third, "Woman, God Bless Her!" was selected from *Mark Twain: Life As I Find It,* edited by me. Pages 204–6.

The pieces from *The Innocents Abroad* were selected from Volume I of *The Complete Travel Books of Mark Twain,* edited by me. "Glove Purchase in Gibraltar": 52–54. "Parisian Shave": 78–80. "Billfinger": 81–85. "Guide-English": 120–22. "Shortage of Soap": 124–26. "A Sort of People": 154–55. "A Skinning": 156–60. "An Ancient Playbill": 184–88. "Guying the Guides": 190–95. "Turkish Bath": 248–51. "That Girl in Yalta": 270–71. "'Jericho'": 289–90. "A Party of Eight": 306–8. "King Solomon-in-all-his-glory": 340–42. "A Fearless Man": 351–54, 357. "The Benton House": 409–11. "The Great Pyramid of Cheops": 413–17. "Cookery Complaints": 425. "A Newspaper Valedictory": 427–32.

The pieces from *Roughing It* were selected from Volume I of *The Complete Travel Books.* "The Cayote": 468–70. "When the Buffalo Climbed a Tree": 474–78. "A Hundred and Ten Tin Whistles": 509–13. "A Genuine Mexican Plug": 547–51. "Mr. Arkansas": 572–75. "The Great Landslide Case": 583–87. "Buck Fanshaw's Funeral": 636–43. "The Story of the Old Ram": 671–75. "Fetch Her Out!": 691–93. "Tom Quartz": 705–8. "'Blanketing' the Admiral": 709–15. "The Greeley Correspondence with Erickson": 748–53. "Markiss, King of Liars": 776–80. "A Practical Joke": 784–87.

The pieces from *A Tramp Abroad* were selected from Volume II of *The Complete Travel Books.* "Jim Baker's Bluejay Yarn": 21–25. "The Great

French Duel": 41–48. "Cholley Adams": 111–14. "The Laborious Ant": 124–27. "Nicodemus Dodge": 130–33. "An American Party": 141–48. "American in Europe": 156–64. "Ascending the Riffelberg": 227–51. "The Awful German Language": 326–38.

The pieces from *Life on the Mississippi* were selected from Volume II of *The Complete Travel Books*. "Keelboat Talk and Manners": 367–77. "An Incognito Exploded": 474–78. "The House Beautiful": 542–46. "Manufactures": 548–50. "The Art of Inhumation": 560–63.

The pieces from *Adventures of Huckleberry Finn* were selected from *The Complete Novels of Mark Twain,* edited by me. "Pap, His Own Self": 751–61. "The Duke and the Dauphin": 832–37.

With seven exceptions the sketches and tales were selected from *The Complete Humorous Sketches and Tales of Mark Twain,* edited by me. "Curing a Cold": 25–28. "Aurelia's Unfortunate Young Man": 28–31. "The Facts Concerning the Recent Resignation": 83–88. "My Late Senatorial Secretaryship": 94–98. "The Late Benjamin Franklin": 137–39. "The Widow's Protest": 170. "About Barbers": 174–77. "A Burlesque Biography": 177–82. "An Encounter with an Interviewer": 256–60. "The Frog Jumping of the County of Calaveras": 261–62, 271–76. "Punch, Brothers, Punch": 303–7. "A Petition to the Queen of England": 528–31. "A Cure for the Blues": 558–73. "Traveling with a Reformer": 610–22. "Fenimore Cooper's Literary Offenses": 631–42. "My First Lie, and How I Got Out of It": 671–78. "Amended Obituaries": 684–86. The seven exceptions were selected from *Mark Twain: Life As I Find It,* edited by me. "The Facts in the Case of the Senate Doorkeeper": 5–9. "Female Suffrage": 10–21. "Private Habits of Horace Greeley": 22–24. "Last Words of Great Men": 29–32. "A Mystery Cleared Up": 36–37. "The Reception at the President's": 115–19. "Remarkable Gold Mines": 212–13.

Index of Titles